FROM THE PAGES OF
LES MISÉRABLES

What is said about men often has as much influence upon their lives, and especially upon their destinies, as what they do. (page 11)

Great grief is a divine and terrible radiance which transfigures the wretched. (page 122)

"In the winter, it is so cold that you thresh your arms to warm them; but the bosses won't allow that; they say it is a waste of time. It is tough work to handle iron when there is ice on the pavements. It wears a man out quick. You get old when you are young at this trade. A man is used up by forty. I was fifty-three." (page 175)

No one ever keeps a secret so well as a child. (page 329)

The jostlings of young minds against each other have this wonderful attribute, that one can never foresee the spark, nor predict the flash. What may spring up in a moment? Nobody knows. (page 379)

All the problems which the socialists propounded, aside from the cosmogonic visions, dreams, and mysticism, may be reduced to two principal problems. First problem: To produce wealth. Second problem: To distribute it. (page 505)

Social prosperity means, man happy, the citizen free, the nation great. (page 505)

He did not even know at night what he had done in the morning, nor where he had breakfasted, nor who had spoken to him; he had songs in his ear which rendered him deaf to every other thought; he existed only during the hours in which he saw Cosette. Then, as he was in Heaven, it was quite natural that he should forget the earth. (page 581)

Marius felt Cosette living within him. To have Cosette, to possess Cosette, this to him was not separable from breathing. (page 590)

The book which the reader has now before his eyes is, from one end to the other, in its whole and in its details, whatever may be the intermissions, the exceptions, or the defaults, the march from evil to good, from injustice to justice, from the false to the true, from night to day, from appetite to conscience, from rottenness to life, from brutality to duty, from Hell to Heaven, from nothingness to God. Starting point: matter; goal: the soul. Hydra at the beginning, angel at the end. (page 698)

Without cartridges, without a sword, he had now in his hand only the barrel of his carbine, the stock of which he had broken over the heads of those who were entering. He had put the billiard table between the assailants and himself; he had retreated to the corner of the room, and there, with proud eye, haughty head, and that stump of a weapon in his grasp, he was still so formidable that a large space was left about him. (page 703)

LES MISÉRABLES

(ABRIDGED)

Victor Hugo

*Edited and Abridged,
with an Introduction and Notes
by Laurence M. Porter*

George Stade
Consulting Editorial Director

BARNES & NOBLE CLASSICS
NEW YORK

𝓑

BARNES & NOBLE CLASSICS

NEW YORK

Published by Barnes & Noble Books
122 Fifth Avenue
New York, NY 10011

www.barnesandnoble.com/classics

Les Misérables was published in French in 1862. Charles E. Wilbour's English
translation was revised and edited by Frederick Mynon Cooper
and published later that same year.

Published in 2003 by Barnes & Noble Classics with new
Introduction, Notes, Biography, Chronology, Inspired By,
Comments & Questions, and For Further Reading.

Les Misérables
ISBN-13: 978-1-59308-066-2
ISBN-10: 1-59308-066-2
LC Control Number 2003108030

Produced and published in conjunction with:
Fine Creative Media, Inc.
322 Eighth Avenue
New York, NY 10001

Michael J. Fine, President and Publisher

Printed in the United States of America

QM

12   14   16   18   20   19   17   15   13

VICTOR HUGO

Novelist, poet, dramatist, essayist, idealist politician, and leader of the French Romantic movement from 1830 on, Victor-Marie Hugo was born the youngest of three sons in Besançon, France, on February 26, 1802. Victor's early childhood was turbulent: His father, Joseph-Léopold, traveled frequently as a general in Napoléon Bonaparte's army, forcing the family to move throughout France, Italy, and Spain. Weary of this upheaval, Hugo's wife, Sophie, separated from her husband and settled with her three sons in Paris. Victor's brilliance declared itself early in the form of illustrations, plays, and nationally recognized verse. Against his mother's wishes, the passionate young man fell in love and secretly became engaged to his neighbor, Adèle Foucher. Following the death of Sophie Hogo, and self-supporting thanks to a royal pension granted for his first book of odes, Hugo wed Adèle in 1822.

In the 1820s and 30s, Hugo came into his own as a writer and figurehead of the new Romanticism, a movement that sought to liberate literature from its stultifying classical influences. His preface to the play *Cromwell,* in 1827, proclaimed a new aesthetics inspired by Shakespeare and Velázquez, based on the shock effects of juxtaposing the grotesque with the sublime (for example, the deformed hunchback inhabiting the magnificent cathedral of Notre-Dame). The play *Hernani* incited violent public disturbances among scandalized audiences in 1830. The next year, the great success of *Notre Dame de Paris (The Hunchback of Notre Dame)* confirmed Hugo's primacy among the Romantics.

By 1830 the Hugos had four children. Exhausted from her pregnancies and Hugo's insatiable sexual demands, Adèle began to sleep alone, and soon fell in love with Hugo's best friend, the critic Charles-Augustin Sainte-Beuve. They began an affair. The Hugos stayed together as friends, and in 1833 Hugo met the actress Juliette Drouet, who would remain his primary mistress until her death fifty years later.

Personal tragedy pursued Hugo relentlessly. His jealous brother Eugène went permanently insane at Victor's wedding to Adèle. Three of Victor's children died before him. His favorite, Léopoldine, together with her unborn child and her devoted husband, died at nineteen in a boating accident on the Seine. The one survivor, Adèle (named after her mother), would be institutionalized for more than thirty years.

Hugo's early royalist sympathies shifted toward liberalism during the late 1820s under the influences of the fiery liberal priest Félicité de Lamennais; of his close friend Charles Nodier, an ardent opponent of capital punishment; and of his father, a general under Napoléon I. He first held political office in 1843, and as he became more engaged in France's social troubles, he was elected to the Constitutional Assembly following the Revolution of 1848. A lifetime advocate of freedom and justice, often at his own peril, Hugo spearheaded the Romantic movement that linked artists to the political realm. After Napoléon III's coup d'état in 1851, Hugo's open opposition created hostilities that ended in his flight abroad from the new government.

Hugo's exile took him first to Belgium, and then to the Channel Islands of Jersey and Guernsey. Declining at least two offers of amnesty—which would have meant curtailing his opposition to the Empire—Hugo remained abroad for nineteen years, until Napoléon's fall in 1870. Meanwhile, the seclusion of the islands enabled Hugo to write some of his most famous verse and his masterpiece, the novel *Les Misérables*. When he returned to Paris, the country hailed him as a hero. Hugo then weathered, within a brief period, the siege of Paris, the institutionalization of his daughter for insanity, and the death of his two sons. Despite this personal anguish, the aging author remained committed to political change. He became an internationally revered figure who helped to preserve and shape the Third Republic and democracy in France. Hugo's death on May 22, 1885, generated intense national mourning; more than two million people joined his funeral procession in Paris from the Arc de Triomphe to the Panthéon where he was buried.

TABLE OF CONTENTS

The World of Victor Hugo and *Les Misérables*
ix

Introduction by Laurence M. Porter
xvii

LES MISÉRABLES
1

Endnotes
831

Inspired by *Les Misérables*
839

Comments & Questions
841

For Further Reading
845

THE WORLD OF VICTOR HUGO AND
LES MISÉRABLES

1797	Hugo's parents, Joseph-Léopold Hugo and Sophie Trébuchet, marry. They will have three sons: Abel (1798), Eugène (1800), and Victor-Marie (1802), who is born in Besançon on February 26. An officer in the army of Napoléon Bonaparte (Napoléon I), Léopold must travel constantly during Victor's youth.
1803–1812	Marital problems occur as Sophie cannot tolerate the transience of army life; finally, she settles in Paris with her three children. Both parents start extramarital affairs. The family travels to Corsica and Elba, where Léopold is stationed. He later commands the troops that will suppress freedom fighters in occupied Italy and Spain, sometimes nailing their severed heads above church doors.
1804	Napoléon proclaims himself Emperor of the French. Literary critic Charles-Augustin Sainte-Beuve is born.
1807	Léopold Hugo receives a post in Naples, where his family soon joins him.
1808	Léopold Hugo follows a cortege of Napoléon's brother, Joseph, to Spain. Weary of travel, Sophie returns with her young sons to Paris, where she begins an affair with General Victor Lahorie, a conspirator against Napoléon.
1809	Napoléon promotes Major Hugo to general, and honors him with the title of count.
1810	The police arrest Lahorie in Mme Hugo's house on December 30.
1811	Sophie journeys to Spain to save her marriage, but problems in the relationship persist. Léopold, knowing of his wife's infidelity, asks for a divorce. Sophie and her sons return to Paris.
1812	General Lahorie is executed for plotting against Napoléon.
1814	Napoléon abdicates and is banished to the island of Elba.
1815	Napoléon is defeated at Waterloo, after "The Hundred Days" of his renewed reign following his secret return from exile. Louis XVIII returns to power, reinstating France's monarchy.
1816	A marvelously gifted and precocious writer, Victor Hugo proclaims his ambition to rival François-René de Chateaubriand, the most famous Romantic author of his generation. Estranged from his father and influenced by his mother, a

royalist by expediency, he skillfully curries favor with the conservative literary establishment and the King, whom he praises in odes.

1817   Hugo wins honorable mention in the national poetry contest sponsored by the l'Académie française (the French Academy).

1818   Sophie and Léopold are legally separated (divorce was illegal in France between 1814 and 1886). Victor composes a first, brief version of his novel *Bug-Jargal,* an account of a slave revolt in the Caribbean after the French Revolution; this version will appear in 1820.

1819   Despite his mother's wishes for a more ambitious union, Victor falls in love with—and secretly asks the hand of—his neighbor, Adèle Foucher. But as a minor, he cannot marry her without his mother's consent, which is denied. The three Hugo brothers found a literary journal called *Le Conservateur littéraire.*

1820–   Hugo writes over one hundred essays and more than twenty
1821   poems for *Le Conservateur.*

1821   Victor becomes friends with the famous priest Félicité de Lamennais, who preaches a socially committed Christianity. Victor's mother dies on June 27. In July his father marries his mistress, Catherine Thomas. Victor becomes reconciled with his father, who does not oppose Victor's marriage to Adèle.

1822   Granted a small pension by Louis XVIII for his first volume of *Odes* praising the monarchy, Victor marries Adèle Foucher on October 12. Eugène Hugo, who also loves her, has a psychotic breakdown at the wedding; he will never recover.

1823   Hugo publishes a pioneering historical novel, *Han d'Islande* (sometimes translated as *The Demon Dwarf*), a bloodthirsty melodrama. He helps found the periodical *La Muse française* and attends weekly gatherings hosted by the then leader of the French Romantic movement, Charles Nodier (1780–1844).

1824   Hugo publishes the *Nouvelles Odes.* His first child, a daughter Léopoldine is born. Charles X assumes the throne, and Victor serves as the historian of the coronation.

1826   *Odes et Ballades* is published, as is the full version of *Bug-Jargal,* noteworthy for its altruistic black hero. Adèle gives birth to Hugo's second child, Charles-Victor.

1827   Hugo becomes best friends with the critic Sainte-Beuve. The play *Cromwell* is published: its famous preface proposes a Romantic aesthetic that contrasts the sublime with the grotesque, in emulation of Shakespeare. Hugo declares his independence from the conservative, divine-right royalists.

1828   General Léopold Hugo dies unexpectedly on January 29. Hugo's third child, François-Victor, is born.

1829	Hugo's prodigious literary output includes the picturesque verse collection *Les Orientales*, the tale *Le Dernier Jour d'un condamné à mort* (*The Last Day of a Condemned Man*), opposing capital punishment, and the historical play *Marion de Lorme*, censored by the French monarchy because it portrays the sixteenth-century ruler François I as a degenerate.
1830	Hugo's fourth child, a daughter named Adèle, named after her mother, is born. Mme Hugo wants no more children, and from then on sleeps alone. Sainte-Beuve betrays his best friend, Victor, by telling Adèle he loves her. Hugo's play *Hernani,* defiantly Romantic in its use of informal language and its violation of the classical "three unities" of time, place, and action, causes riots in the theater where it is performed.
1831	*Notre-Dame de Paris: 1482* (*The Hunchback of Notre Dame*), a tale of the era of the cruel, crafty Charles XI, is published and becomes a bestseller. The visionary poetry collection *Les Feuilles d'automne* is published. In it Hugo displays a profundity and a mastery of the art of verse that rival the greatest European poets of the era, Goethe and Shelley.
1832	Hugo's play *Le Roi s'amuse* (*The King's Fool*), which will inspire Giuseppi Verdi's great opera *Rigoletto* (1851), is banned after opening night owing to its disrespectful portrayal of a king. Hugo occupies an apartment in what is today called la place des Vosges, where he will remain until 1848.
1833	The minor actress Juliette Drouet enters Hugo's life. He provides her with an apartment near him, forbids her to go out alone, and occupies her with making fair copies of his manuscripts. The couple will continue their liaison until her death fifty years later. The first version of George Sand's feminist novel *Lelia* is published.
1834	Hugo ends his friendship with Sainte-Beuve.
1835	Hugo's great verse collection *Les Chants du crépuscule* (*Songs of Twilight*) appears.
1837	Hugo is made an officer of the Légion d'honneur. *Les Voix intérieures,* the third of four collections of visionary poetry during Hugo's middle lyric period (1831–1840), appears. Eugène Hugo dies confined in the Charenton madhouse.
1838	*Ruy Blas,* Hugo's best play, outrages the monarchists by depicting a queen and a valet in love.
1840	*Les Rayons et les Ombres* (*Sunlight and Shadows*), the last great poetic collection before Hugo's exile, is published.
1841	After several failed attempts, Hugo is elected to the French Academy, the body of "Forty Immortals"—the greatest honor a French writer can receive.
1843	A tragic year is punctuated by the failure of Hugo's *Les Burgraves* and the drowning of his beloved elder daughter, Léopoldine, her unborn child, and her husband, a strong

swimmer who tried to save her after a boating accident. Hugo will dedicate his poetic masterpiece, *Les Contemplations,* to her. Alexandre Dumas's *The Count of Monte Cristo* appears.

1845   Hugo is made a *pair de France,* an appointive position in a body roughly equivalent to the British House of Lords. Ten weeks later, his affair with Mme Léonie Biard (from 1844 to 1851) comes to light when they are arrested in their love nest and charged with adultery. She goes to prison. Hugo's rank saves him from prosecution.

1847   Balzac publishes *La Cousine Bette.*

1848   The monarchy is overthrown, and the Second Republic proclaimed. Hugo is elected to its Constitutional Assembly, with the support of the conservatives. With his son Charles, he founds and edits *L'Événement,* a liberal paper that unwisely campaigns to have Louis-Napoléon Bonaparte, the nephew of the former Emperor, elected President.

1849   Hugo presides over the International Peace Conference in Paris, and delivers the first public speech that proposes the creation of a United States of Europe. Eugène Delacroix paints the ceiling of the Louvre's Salon d'Apollon.

1849–   Hugo increasingly criticizes the government's policies, making
1851   fiery speeches on poverty, liberty, and the church. His positions provoke the ire of the government.

1851   The government briefly imprisons Hugo's two sons in June for having published disloyal articles in *L'Événement.* Soon after Louis-Napoléon's coup d'état (actually, a legal election that creates the Second Empire) in early December, Hugo learns that the imperial police have issued a warrant for his arrest. He flees with his family and mistress to Belgium, and then to the Isle of Jersey, a British possession in the English Channel.

1852–   In 1852 Louis-Napoléon declares himself emperor as
1853   Napoléon III. Hugo writes a scathing satire, *Napoléon le petit.* From 1853 to 1855 he attends séances at which the spirits of both the living and the dead (including Shakespeare, Jesus, and a cowering Napoléon III) seem to communicate by tapping on the table. They explain that all living beings must expiate their sins through a cycle of punitive reincarnations, but that all, even Satan, will finally be pardoned and merge with the Godhead. These ideas figure prominently in Hugo's visionary poetry for the remainder of his life. Georges Haussmann (1809–1891) begins the urban renewal of Paris.

1853   Hugo publishes *Les Châtiments (The Punishments),* powerful anti-Napoleonic satire.

1855   Hugo moves to the Channel island of Guernsey.

1856   Hugo's *Les Contemplations,* his poetic masterpiece, appears. Profits from its sales allow him to purchase Hauteville House on Guernsey—today a museum.

1857	Gustave Flaubert's novel of adultery, *Madame Bovary*—the work most influential on Western novelists until after World War II—is published in book form, as is the first edition of Charles Baudelaire's poetry, *Les Fleurs du mal*. Both men and their publishers are placed on trial for offenses to public morals. Baudelaire's publisher is fined and must remove seven poems treating lesbianism and sadism.
1859	The first volume of Hugo's poetic history of the world, *La Légende des siècles (The Legend of the Centuries),* appears.
1861	The danger of arrest having subsided, Hugo's wife, Adèle, and her sons begin leaving him to stay in Paris during the winter months. She secretly meets with Sainte-Beuve there.
1862	*Les Misérables,* a 1,200-page epic completed in fourteen months, is published on the heels of a fertile period during which Hugo wrote many political speeches and creative works. Hugo's famous novel gains an enormous popular audience, although the book is panned by critics and banned by the government. He begins hosting a weekly banquet for fifty poor children.
1866	Guernsey provides the setting for Hugo's regional novel *Les Travailleurs de la mer (The Toilers of the Sea)*. Edgar Degas commences his series of ballet paintings. Works of Cézanne, Renoir, Monet, and other Impressionists appear. The next year Emile Zola's novel *Thérèse Raquin* is published.
1868	Hugo's wife, Adèle, dies unexpectedly in Brussels. She had been living apart from Victor for several years, but the two had remained friends.
1869	Hugo publishes the historical novel *L'Homme qui rit* (sometimes translated *By Order of the King*). He declines a second offer of amnesty from Napoléon III. Sainte-Beuve dies.
1870	Defeated by the Prussians at Sedan, Napoléon III surrenders to them and is deposed. France's Third Republic is proclaimed. Hugo returns to Paris in triumph after nineteen years in exile.
1871	Hugo is elected to the National Assembly, but resigns due to the opposition of right-wing members. His son Charles dies.
1872	Consumed by madness, Hugo's daughter Adèle is institutionalized until her death in 1915. Jules Verne's *Around the World in Eighty Days* is published.
1873	Hugo's younger son, François-Victor, dies. Arthur Rimbaud's *A Season in Hell* is published.
1874	Hugo publishes *Quatrevingt-treize (Ninety-three)*, a historical novel about the counter-revolutionary rebellion in la Vendée, and events leading to the Reign of Terror in 1793. He provides nuanced portraits of both sides.
1876	Hugo is elected to the Senate.

1877   As senator, Hugo plays a leading role in preventing Marshal Marie Edmé MacMahon from becoming dictator of France. Because the monarchists have split their support among various claimants to the throne, the republicans achieve a working majority. The second volume of Hugo's poetic history of the world, *La Légende des siècles,* appears.

1878   A stroke leaves Hugo incapable of composing additional literary works.

1880   After years of efforts, Hugo arranges amnesty for the Communards, popular-front rebels in the Paris of 1871 opposed to surrender to the Prussians. Some 20,000 of them, including women and children, had been slaughtered by French government troops—more than the total of those guillotined during the Reign of Terror in 1793. Guy de Maupassant's collected *Contes (Stories)* are published.

1881   On February 26, Hugo's birthday, a national holiday is proclaimed, and 600,000 marchers pass his windows. The street where he lives is renamed L'avenue Victor-Hugo.

1882   Hugo is reelected to the Senate. His play *Torquemada* (1869) is performed.

1883   Juliette Drouet, Hugo's mistress since 1833, dies after a prolonged struggle with cancer. The final volume of Hugo's poetic history of the world, *La Légende des siècles,* appears.

1885   Victor Hugo dies May 22. Two million mourners pass his coffin underneath the Arc de Triomphe. Hugo is entombed in the Panthéon, the first of a series of culture heroes and great leaders to be placed there. June 1 is declared a day of national mourning. Posthumous publications will enhance his reputation for decades—notably, the verse collections *La Fin de Satan* (*The End of Satan,* 1886), *Toute la lyre* (1888, 1893), and *Dieu* (1891). His experimental plays, eventually published in a Pléïade edition as "Le Théâtre en liberté," brilliantly anticipate the Theater of the Absurd in the 1950s.

1902   On the centenary of his birth, the French government opens the Maison de Victor Hugo museum in the apartment where he once lived on la place des Vosges.

1912–   In collaboration with André Antoine, the director of the
1918   naturalistic Théatre-Libre, the filmmaker Albert Capellani, with the Pathé firm, produces a series of movies based on Hugo's works: *Les Misérables* (1912), *Marie Tudor* (1912), *Quatrevingt-treize* (1914), and *Les Travailleurs de la mer* (1918).

1926   The Buddhist sect, Cao Dai, originates in Vietnam. It now has about 2,000 temples and several million followers worldwide. The worshipers venerate Hugo and his two sons, whom they believe, return to earth, reincarnated.

1975   François Truffaut's film *Adèle H.*, retelling the tragedy of Hugo's second daughter, wins Le Grand Prix du Cinéma Français.

1980   Alain Boublil and Claude-Michel Schoenberg create a rock-opera version of *Les Misérables*. Translated into English, the musical has been produced internationally more times than any other—*Cats* being the previous record holder.

1996   Walt Disney issues an animated, freely altered film version of *The Hunchback of Notre Dame*, distinctive in its politically correct treatment of gypsies, women, and persons with disabilities.

INTRODUCTION

Background

Victor Hugo (1802–1885) was a child prodigy with a precocious vocation as a creative writer. He would excel in the novel, the essay, drama, and poetry. He became an instant celebrity when he received honorable mention in a poetry contest sponsored by the Académie Française in 1817. Concerning the construction of varied versification and stanzaic form, he would soon demonstrate a virtuosity that only Goethe and Shelley could rival in Europe. In 1819 and 1820 he received two annual prizes for odes submitted to the prestigious national contest, the Jeux Floraux in Toulouse. In the latter year he and his two older brothers founded a literary magazine, for which he wrote 112 articles and twenty-two poems in sixteen months. In 1821 he met the priest Félicité de Lamennais, who greatly influenced Hugo's views on the importance of the social utility of Christianity, a perspective that was to dominate *Les Misérables* forty years later. He became the leader of the French Romantic movement in 1827. Inspired by Shakespeare, he formulated a romantic esthetic based on the shocking, incongruous juxtaposition of the sublime and the grotesque, which exemplified most of his novels, including *Les Misérables,* in which the Thénardier couple embody the grotesque.

The visionary bent that is so pronounced in *Les Misérables* emerges in *Les Feuilles d'automne,* one of Hugo's greatest collections of verse, in 1831. In the early 1830s, Hugo began to elaborate a visionary system of theodicy influenced by the Jewish Kabala that claimed God had had to conceal his grandeur from humans (the sun and stars are his masks), so that they could act independently and earn salvation without being overwhelmed by the unmediated spectacle of God's glory. Only thus was free will possible. Regarding Creation itself, Hugo held the organic worldview widespread in European romanticism: as the DNA in a single cell allows modern geneticists to identify the creature from which it came, so the spark of spirituality inherent in every part of Creation allowed the visionary romantic writers to intuit its divine source. Thus the physical world can guide humans—more accurately, it allows poet-priests to guide their fellows—toward God. Hugo believed that all creation was ordered by hierarchy as well as affinity; it consisted in an endless gradated array of all conceivable creatures, separated by infinitesimal degrees of spiritual excellence. Humans, he thought, would be rewarded or punished by being reincarnated in "higher" (angels) or "lower" (animals, plants, and objects) forms after death, depending on how meritorious their lives had been. Once reincarnated in lower forms, they could see God directly, but could only suffer passively from memories of their sins and from their remoteness from the Creator, as they gradually expiated those sins. As for the angels, none fell after the fall of Satan and his legions, and the remaining angels plus new angels evolving from the ranks of saintly humans would gradually evolve toward a closer affinity with the Godhead—always separated from it, however, by an infinite spiritual distance. At the end of time, all living things, even Satan, would be saved, and reabsorbed into the bosom of God, from which they had emerged at the Creation. This theological system is close to the Pelagian heresy of early Christianity. As Hugo put it in the final lines of his collection of visionary poetry, *Les Contemplations,* at the end of time Jesus will lead his brother Satan by the hand up the stairs of heaven, and God will no longer be able to tell them apart. *Les Misérables* explicitly states this view: "The book which the reader has now before his eyes is, from one end to the other, in its whole and in its details, whatever may be the intermissions, the exceptions, or the defaults, the march from evil to good, . . . from nothingness to God. Starting point: matter; goal: the soul. Hydra at the beginning, angel at the end (p. 698)." Not only did Hugo sketch and expound this vision throughout the last half-century of his career, but also he reserved many visionary poems that he planned to have published at five-year intervals after his death—and thanks to his faithful executors, they were. The posterity of his religious ideas, although unexpected, would have gratified him. The cult of Cao Dai Buddhism, which numbers several million adherents and several thousand temples throughout the world, believes that several of its priests are reincarnations of Hugo and his sons.

Hugo's election to the Académie Française in 1841 consecrated the militant romantic movement. In 1845 he was appointed as a *pair de France,* equivalent to a member of the British House of Lords. Becoming increasingly liberal in politics, he became a member of the Constitutional Convention (Assemblée Constituante) of the Second French Republic in 1848. He presided over the International Peace Conference in Paris in 1849, and there gave the first known speech advocating the creation of a "United States of Europe," a vision partially anticipated by Immanuel Kant, Thomas Jefferson, and Madame de Staël, but fully realized only recently with the formation of the European Union, followed by the adoption of a common currency, the Euro.

Starting in 1848, Hugo and his son Charles founded and coedited the liberal newspaper *L'Événement,* which strongly supported the return from exile, and the candidacy for President of the Republic, of Louis Napoléon, Emperor Napoléon I's nephew, who had established his credentials as a liberal with a term in prison. Hugo proved to have been "a useful idiot," for Louis Napoléon craved absolute power, and eventually managed a combination of elections and a coup d'état to become Emperor for Life on December 2, 1851. Hugo had already broken with the Right and formally declared himself a Republican on July 18, 1851. Hunted by the police, with his sons already jailed, he fled France to take refuge on the English Channel Islands of Jersey (1852–1855) and Guernsey (1855–1870). Unlike all his prominent contemporaries, he refused amnesty, and published vehement satires of the new regime, *Napoléon le petit* (1852) and *Les Châtiments* (1853). When he had vented his rage against the ruler who betrayed him, he turned inward to meditate on Providence and human spiritual destiny in the great poem cycles *Les Contemplations* (1856, mainly composed 1853–1855), *La Légende des Siècles* (1859, with sequels published in 1877 and 1883), *La Fin de Satan* (composed 1854, published 1886), and *Dieu* (composed 1855, published 1891). Only then, after nearly a decade in exile, did he synthesize the individual, the historical, and the cosmic in *Les Misérables*.

Motivated is not determined: many people have experienced family situations similar to Hugo's, but there is only one author of *Les Misérables*. Nevertheless, numerous factors in Hugo's life converged to reinforce his proclivity to become a savior, particularly by advocating compromise. His parents became estranged, lived apart, and each took a lover when he was only one year old. In response, he later elaborated the myth that his mother was a monarchist and his father a republican; the compromise of a constitutional monarchy such as Louis Philippe's (1830–1848) was therefore attractive to him, and under it he began his political career, symbolically finding a middle ground between his two parents' supposed positions. In fact, however, his mother's family was closely associated with the Jacobins (rabid egalitarians), who massacred rebellious monarchists in the Vendée region. She later became a monarchist of convenience, while her lover was conspiring against the Emperor Napoléon.

Hugo opposed the death penalty (the uncompromising solution *par excellence* for crime), not only because of the influence of his older friend Charles Nodier, but also because, as a small child, he had seen the severed heads of freedom fighters in Spain and Italy nailed to church doors by the troops commanded by his father, General Hugo, charged with suppressing independence movements in those countries. The violent insanity of his older brother, Eugène, which first became obvious at Victor's wedding with Adèle, the woman Eugène also loved, inflicted survivor guilt on Hugo, as did the premature death of his beloved younger daughter Léopoldine, who drowned with her husband and her unborn child in a boating accident shortly after her marriage, and the insanity of his older daughter Adèle, to say nothing of the early death of his two sons before him. Under the circumstances, the possibility of finding Léopoldine again after death was a comforting thought, and *Les Contemplations* is framed with hopes for their reunion.

His enforced sojourn on an island left a strong imprint on that work. First of all, it reflects a powerful nostalgia for Paris, where he had lived—all the more so because Napoléon III's assistant for urban renewal, Baron Haussmann, tore up many old neighborhoods to open wide avenues down which it was easy to fire grapeshot from cannons to disperse rebellious crowds. The constant presence of the sea makes itself felt continually in the visionary poetry, but it probably also inspired several scenes in *Les Misérables,* such as the galleys at Toulon, and metaphors such as the depiction of Jean Valjean, released from prison but abandoned and cursed by society, as a man overboard who slowly, agonizingly despairs and drowns. Unable to exercise his keen visual sensitivity on medieval monuments, as he had done in Paris (in several poems and essays as well as in *Notre-Dame de Paris*), Hugo turned to botany, gardening, and agriculture. Signs of this new interest pervade *Les Misérables,* but it culminates only in the rich, lovingly detailed descriptions of the flora in the introductory section of the great regional novel *Les Travailleurs de la mer* (1866). Surrounded by the poor, who had to make their living from the sea, Hugo found many occasions—like Monseigneur Myriel and Jean Valjean in his novel—to exercise charity. For a time, he hosted and paid for a weekly meal for fifty people. Finally, Parisian nightlife was replaced, between 1853 and 1855, by evening séances during which Hugo believed that he and his family and friends could communicate with the spirits of both the living and the dead. He summoned the soul of the sleeping Napoléon III, to harangue and intimidate him; he advised Shakespeare on how to correct errors in his prosody; and he dialogued with Jesus Christ as well as dozens of other notables.

The Story

Hugo already had composed a version of his masterpiece, first entitled *Les Misères,* between 1845 and 1848, during the height of his activity in the House of Peers. During fourteen months of intense activity between 1860 and 1862, Hugo expanded this original version by 60 percent. *Les Misérables* embeds the story of a poor workman in a vast mythic-historical context. It tells of the fall and redemption of Jean Valjean, a young tree pruner in the region of Paris, the sole support of his widowed sister and her seven children. One winter, unemployed and desperate to feed his dependents, he breaks a bakery window at night to steal a loaf of bread. He is arrested and sentenced to five years' hard labor in the galleys of Toulon. Four escapes, attempted instinctively and unreasoningly, lead only to additional sentences, which finally total nineteen years. The harsh punishment embitters him against society, and after his release this attitude is reinforced by the scorn and rejection he experiences whenever he must show his convict's yellow passport. But a saintly Catholic Bishop, Monseigneur Myriel, treats Jean Valjean respectfully, feeds him, and gives him lodging for the night. Despite this kindness, Valjean cannot resist stealing the bishop's last remaining luxuries—for the cleric has given everything else to the poor—his silver place settings. When the gendarmes bring Valjean back, the bishop saves him from further imprisonment by saying he had given the place settings to Valjean. And the bishop adds the two silver candlesticks that his guest had "forgotten." As Valjean sets off again, the bishop whispers that he has purchased the ex-convict's soul with his gifts, that Valjean has promised him to live a virtuous life henceforth.

On the road north, a last flicker of brute instinct takes over: the convict cannot resist the temptation to steal a coin dropped by a little itinerant chimney sweep. Then he repents and resolves to lead a virtuous life, guided by an inner voice inspired by the bishop's kindness to him. (Hugo identifies our conscience with God.) He manages to conceal his identity, educate himself, and transform himself into the benevolent "Monsieur Madeleine" (an allusion to the penitent prostitute Mary Magdalene in the Gospels). By inventing a superior method for making glassware, he ensures the prosperity of an entire village enriched through the "trickle-down" theory of economics. The grateful townspeople elect him mayor in a town where the rigid, self-righteous Javert, overcompensating for having been born in prison as the illegitimate son of a fortune-teller, serves as chief of police.

Meanwhile, Fantine, a young working woman in Paris, has been seduced, impregnated, and cynically abandoned by her lover. Once her baby, Cosette, is born, she innocently leaves her in the care of the evil Thénardier couple, dishonest innkeepers, and goes to her native village, where Jean Valjean has settled. She finds work there in the glassware factory, but is fired by a self-righteous female foreman who discovers that she has an illegitimate child. The Thénardiers have been starving Cosette, dressing her in rags, and forcing her to do hard labor, while sending Fantine exorbitant, fraudulent medical bills. She must turn to prostitution to support her daughter. At the same time, the Thénardier daughters Eponine and Azelma are pampered, creating a Cinderella-like situation.

"Monsieur Madeleine" finally learns of this situation when Fantine has been unjustly accused of assault against a wealthy idler who had assaulted her first. He overrules Javert, who is blinded by social prejudice, and orders her release. He promises to care for her and to reunite her with her baby. But his defense of a social outcast alienates Javert and intensifies his suspicions, which derive from his preconscious memories of having seen Jean Valjean as a galley slave at Toulon twenty years earlier, when he served as assistant warden there. His suspicions intensify when the mayor demonstrates enormous strength by lifting a heavily loaded cart to free a man being crushed beneath it. Only the former convict Jean Valjean, nicknamed "Jean le Cric" (Jack the jack), still sought for having robbed the chimney sweep, would have been capable of this feat, Javert believes. Events soon confirm the policeman's intuition. An innocent, inarticulate vagrant, Champmathieu, has been falsely accused of stealing apples (a third offense, leading to life imprisonment). Former convicts have identified him as Jean Valjean. After intense struggles with his conscience, M. Madeleine feels morally obligated to step forward and denounce himself. He has had time to bury in the woods the fortune he made legally from glassware, but the rigid Javert will not allow him to take Cosette to visit Fantine before Fantine dies. Then Jean Valjean is sent back to the galleys.

He escapes by feigning a drowning accident, rescues Cosette from the Thénardiers, and takes refuge with her in Paris. Javert, however, has been reassigned there, and recognizes him in the street. Fleeing the police, Valjean climbs a high wall with Cosette and finds himself in a convent garden tended by the grateful man he had saved from underneath the cart. A false burial in an empty coffin allows him to reenter the convent from the outside as an assistant gardener. In this shelter, he raises Cosette as his beloved daughter, and the nuns educate her. Comparing the voluntary austerities and self-sacrifice of the nuns for the good of humanity with his own past sufferings as a convict, Jean Valjean overcomes his resentment toward society and learns humility. Cosette's dependency gives him reasons to live; her weakness keeps him strong.

After seven years, however, he leaves the convent with her to prevent her from pursuing a religious vocation by default. They live in seclusion. Nevertheless, Cosette's growing beauty attracts the attention of a poor young man, Marius, who has been alienated from his royalist grandfather, his only living relative, because of his loyalty to his deceased father, who was a heroic colonel under Napoléon. Fearful of losing the only person who gives meaning to his life, and fearing detection, Valjean evades Marius by moving across Paris. But there his generous almsgiving attracts the attention of the Thénardiers and their criminal gang, although the innkeeper does not recognize him. Failures in business, Thénardier and his monstrous wife have come to join the Parisian underworld.

Thénardier's moral decline criss-crosses Jean Valjean's progressive moral redemption. Potentially law-abiding in prosperity, in poverty Thénardier becomes increasingly vicious. He plans to kidnap and torture Jean Valjean, force him to reveal where Cosette is staying, and then kidnap her to force Valjean to pay a huge ransom. Meanwhile, he becomes increasingly indifferent toward his own children. He uses Eponine as a spy and lookout for his burglaries and callously risks her life. He makes no effort to find his son Gavroche when the little boy becomes separated from his family, and he deliberately abandons Gavroche's two younger brothers.

By yet another coincidence of many in the novel, Marius has moved into a cheap room next door to the Thénardiers. Listening and watching through a hole in the wall, he learns of their plans to kidnap Cosette. Marius denounces them to Javert, but then learns that Thénardier had "saved his father's life" (had inadvertently revived him by rifling though his clothes after he had fallen at the Battle of Waterloo). His father's dying wish had been that his son find and reward Thénardier.

Eponine has fallen in love with Marius. Now her former relationship with Cosette is reversed. Cosette is wealthy, privileged, and beloved, while Eponine, formerly coddled, must choose between her father's beatings and sleeping in ditches. The two girls do not recognize each other. Hopelessly devoted, Eponine helps Marius find Cosette again: Marius and Cosette fall in love, meeting in Cosette's garden at night for a chaste but passionate romance. When Thénardier's gang has staked out Valjean's isolated new residence for a burglary, without realizing that it belongs to their former intended extortion victim, Eponine drives them away with false warnings about the police, and anonymously advises Valjean to move. He plans to flee to England. By accident, Cosette is prevented from communicating with Marius.

Knowing that Marius cares only for Cosette, Eponine despairs and writes an anonymous note summoning him to join his friends fighting on the barricades of the worker-student insurrection of 1832. She hopes he will die there; but she wants to die first, by his side. In despair at not finding Cosette at home, Marius seeks death on the barricades. There, a sudden political illumination makes his commitment to his friends' republican cause authentic. Eponine, disguised as a young worker, saves Marius by throwing herself in front of a bullet aimed at him.

Meanwhile, Valjean has discovered the imprint of Cosette's desperate note to Marius on her blotter. Her adoptive father is taking her away; she does not know where. Valjean hates Marius for threatening to deprive him of the only person he has ever loved. He struggles to overcome his possessiveness, and despite his rage, he goes to the barricades to protect Marius. Behind the barricade, Javert has been unmasked as a police spy. Valjean asks permission to execute him, but secretly sets him free. As the barricade falls to the government troops, Marius collapses, wounded and unconscious. Valjean escapes through the sewers, carrying the young man through the foul muck on his shoulders for four miles.

At the locked exit by the Seine, Valjean meets Thénardier, who has hidden there from Javert. Thénardier does not recognize Valjean. He thinks Valjean has killed Marius for his money, and demands all Valjean's cash in exchange for opening the gate with his skeleton key so that Valjean can escape. He hopes to divert the waiting Javert by offering him a substitute fugitive. Javert does indeed arrest Valjean, but feels morally obligated to release him, because he owes the convict his life. Then, torn by an insoluble conflict between religious and legal duty, Javert drowns himself. Marius's repentant grandfather nurses Marius back to health and marries him to Cosette. Valjean has given her all his fortune. The novel reaches its moral climax on the wedding night. Should Valjean confess that he is an escaped convict, and renounce all contact with Cosette to spare the young couple the shame of his possible denunciation and arrest? "He had reached the last crossing of good and evil. . . . two roads opened before him; the one tempting, the other terrible. Which should he take? The one which terrified him was advised by the mysterious indicating finger which we all perceive whenever we fix our eyes upon the shadow. . . . We are never done with conscience. . . . It is bottomless, being God" (pp. 769–770). Human love alone cannot bring us closer to God. Sacrifice is required.

The next day, Valjean secretly confesses to Marius that he is an escaped convict, and not Cosette's father. Marius, believing that Valjean's fortune was stolen, does not touch it. Thinking that Valjean killed Javert at the barricade, Marius only reluctantly allows him to see Cosette in the anteroom to his grandfather's house. Persona non grata to Marius, Valjean stops coming, stops eating, and wastes away. But Thénardier unwittingly serves as the instrument of Providence. He comes to extort money from Marius by threatening to reveal the "secret" that his father-in-law is an escaped convict who has recently killed a man (he unwittingly refers to Marius himself). As he speaks, he accidentally reveals that Valjean made his fortune legally, that he did not kill Javert, and that he saved Marius. The latter pays his debt of honor to Thénardier by giving him enough money to travel to America, where he becomes a slave owner (an even further degradation, in Hugo's eyes). Marius and Cosette, repentant, rush to Valjean's bedside. They arrive too late to save him, but he dies happy in one of the most pathetic scenes in literature. In the shadows, an enormous, invisible angel awaits his soul.

The Plot

Traditional analyses of fiction distinguish between "story," meaning what happens, and "plot," meaning how the things that happen are arranged (straight-line temporal sequence or flashbacks and flash-forwards, a single story line or several story lines, parallel or embedded stories, and so forth). Parallel stories (while A is doing X, B is doing Y, etc.) characterize television situation comedies and melodramas, or epistolary novels; embedded stories (A tells B a story about C, who in turn tells D a story about E, etc.) characterize the fantastic tale, memoirs and autobiography, and many other long novels.

Plot also explains *why* things happen: are they "events" ("acts of God," to which the characters must react) or "acts" (initiated by the characters)? In either case, is the agent unconscious (a floor or a fire), blind (a mistaken or compulsive act), or lucid? Is the act premeditated or impulsive?

At first glance, chance encounters among the characters seem to motivate most of the action. Javert happens to be assigned to the galleys, then to the town of M—— sur M——, and finally to Paris when Jean Valjean arrives at each of those places. In Paris their paths cross decisively several times. At M—— sur M——, Valjean happens by just when Fantine and then Fauchelevant need to be rescued. Thénardier's wife happens to be sitting on her doorstep as Fantine is passing, in need of a place to board her child; after Thénardier releases Cosette to Jean Valjean for extortionate sums, he moves to Paris and encounters Valjean in three different places there, at critical moments, without recognizing him. Thénardier just happens to loot Marius's unconscious father's body on the battlefield, incurring a mistaken debt of honor for Marius, who then happens to rent a room next to Thénardier's in Paris. Thénardier's elder daughter, Eponine, and Cosette, both fall in love with Marius after the happenstance of running into him. The coincidental resemblance between the vagrant Champmathieu and Valjean moves the plot by forcing the latter to denounce himself and leave M—— sur M—— for a second trip to the galleys. Only because the former enemy whom Valjean saved from being crushed beneath his cart has become the gardener in the convent into whose garden Valjean and Cosette escape when fleeing from Javert, do they find a safe refuge and does Cosette receive a good education. Only because Thénardier tries to blackmail Marius by threatening to reveal that his father-in-law is an escaped convict, does Marius accidentally learn that Jean

Valjean has committed no crimes, and has saved his life, all of which prepares the final, climactic reconciliation between the son-in-law and Cosette's former guardian. These many coincidences attempt indirectly to persuade us that God intervenes in human affairs, while preserving the imperatives of human commitment and responsibility in the overt rhetoric of the narrator.

As in Stendhal's *Le Rouge et le Noir,* but in both upward and downward directions, a departure from the horizontal sometimes symbolizes independent choice: Jean Valjean plunging off the prison ship into the sea to feign drowning, so that he can escape to rescue Cosette; his climbing over the wall of the convent with her; and his descent into the depths of the sewers to save Marius. Hugo, moreover, refuses to let us hold God, rather than ourselves, responsible for political events. Suffering, violence, and injustice will be eliminated by *philia,* by a community of active mutual concern. Hugo, nevertheless, offers a realistic image of political change: one finds only a few fully committed militants on either side; others are drawn in through love, despair, affection, anxiety, greed, or hatred.

The Major Subjects of the Novel

How can we make sense of this sprawling, complex story? To a superficial reader, the numerous coincidences that bind the characters' lives together seem like mere melodramatic contrivances. But for Hugo, multiple coincidences reflect his belief in an unseen, overarching Providence that interrelates and governs human destiny. The preface to *Les Travailleurs de la mer* (*The Toilers of the Sea*) identifies three "fatalities" in the fallen, material order: nature, religious dogma, and social inequities. By "fatalities" Hugo means obstacles to progress, which tempt us to despair and to renounce effort. How can we exercise our free will when we are caught between a spiritual Providence and a material/institutional fatality?

Considered in isolation, the generalizations and aphorisms with which Hugo characterizes the moral dynamics of his story might seem to rule out the possibility of enlightened choice: "Be it true or false, what is said about men often has as much influence upon their lives, and especially upon their destinies, as what they do" (p. 11); "it seems as if it were necessary that a woman should be a mother to be venerable [instead of merely respectable]" (p. 12); "there is always more misery among the lower classes than there is humanity in the higher" (p. 15). Such generalizations appear to reflect a traditional belief in a "human nature" that remains invariable. But this impression is misleading. First, Hugo always grounds his maxims solidly in a social context, and in the social, financial, and biological contingencies of one's individual existence. He is not La Rochefoucauld, the classicist whose aphorisms describe unvarying relationships among abstract nouns, as if wealth, health, gender, or ethnicity made no difference: "Hypocrisy is a form of respect that vice pays to virtue." Second, throughout the novel he dramatizes the titanic inner struggles of Jean Valjean with his conscience; and he richly analyzes the moral evolution of many other characters such as Bishop Myriel, Fantine, Thénardier, Marius, Gillenormand, Eponine, and Javert.

Throughout most of *Les Misérables,* cosmic motifs are muted and implicit. They often appear subtly in descriptions of looming darkness and unexpected radiance. Nature seems hostile to the outcast Jean Valjean; as he contemplates the sleeping bishop, that man's face seems to glow with an inner light; Eponine, hating her life as an outlaw and pursued by a larval form of conscience, describes the hallucinations of starvation to Marius by saying that the stars seem like floodlights, and the trees like gallows—her crimes are known to God, and she is doomed to hang, she feels. Hugo adopts the motif of the Transfiguration from the Bible: filled with the Holy Spirit, the faces of Moses or of Jesus shine.

Characters

Hugo integrates this worldview with his character depiction and plot development through the implied religious doctrine of supererogation (in French, *réversibilité*): exceptional individuals may accrue sufficient merit, through their loyal faith and virtuous acts, not only to ensure their own salvation but also to aid in the salvation of others, to whom some of their extra merit may be transferred. Supererogation is the dynamic and positive mode of the archetype of Inversion: what seemed bad (Christ's betrayal by his friends, humiliation, torture, and agonizing death on the cross) proves good (mankind will be redeemed). It allows the concept of free will to be synthesized with the concept of Providence. Hugo represents this force not mystically, but quite realistically, through the influence of conversation and example, which often occurs partially, gradually, and belatedly. Good influences, in his view, are not compulsions, but invitations to which their objects must choose to respond. But they can create a chain reaction.

The first example appears in the figure of the conventionist G—— (a representative of the assembly that dissolved the monarchy, and of which a majority excluding G—— condemned Louis XVI to death). He humbles the initially scornful Bishop Myriel, who comes to recognize the moral excellence of his devotion to humanity and kneels before him to ask his blessing. "No one could say that the passage of that soul before [Myriel's] own, and the reflection of that grand conscience upon his own had not had its effect upon [the Bishop's] approach to perfection" (p. 34). This blessing is later transferred, so to speak, from Myriel to Valjean, thus saving the ex-convict from further hatred and crime: "Jean Valjean, my brother: you belong no longer to evil, but to good. It is your soul that I am buying for you. I am withdrawing it from dark thoughts and from the spirit of perdition, and I am giving it to God!" (p. 63). In turn, Valjean later symbolically transfers his own superabundance of merit to the dying Fantine, assuring her that since her motivation for prostituting herself was her pure wish to provide for her daughter, she remained innocent in the eyes of God. And in the final scene the repentant Marius, kneeling at the dying

Valjean's bedside to ask his blessing, recalls the initial scene between the conventionist and Myriel.

Hugo broadly signals the presence of supererogatory merit in his characters. He compares the parables of Bishop Myriel to Christ's (p. 17). He suggests that the origin of Jean Valjean's name is "Voila Jean"—there's John (p. 48). That phrase recalls Pontius Pilate's *ecce homo* (there is the man), spoken when he shows Christ, wearing the crown of thorns, to the Jewish priests who have accused him; see the Bible, John 19:5). A person condemned according to one law, and destined for suffering, will be vindicated according to a higher law. Years later in the plot, Hugo associates Valjean clearly with Christ in the Garden of Gethsemane, when the mayor hesitates over whether to denounce himself in order to exculpate the pruner Champmathieu (pp. 148–149). Hugo reintroduces the image of the bitter chalice in the title of part V, book seven, "The Last Drop in the Chalice." Marius's point of view affirms Valjean's absolute, self-sacrificial goodness and his total transformation unequivocally: "The convict was transfigured into Christ" (p. 821).

But although Bishop Myriel demonstrates for Jean Valjean the power of absolute trust in God, and active benevolence, this influence cannot be definitive. Through practicing virtue, he risks succumbing to pride. His "accidental" discovery of a refuge in the convent helps save him from pride: he must compare his involuntary suffering from social inequities and vindictiveness to the voluntary, altruistic suffering of the nuns (pp. 334–335). Their example foreshadows his voluntary self-sacrifice at the end. Through Cosette, he has learned of human love; but this love remains selfish (pp. 267–270). Cosette becomes indispensable to him. The illusion that she will grow up ugly, and thus stay with him always, consoles him. The narrator speculates that Jean Valjean might have needed Cosette's filial love to persevere in the virtue that Myriel first inspired in him. As mayor, he had learned much more than before about social injustice; he had been sent back to prison for doing good; he needed the support of Cosette's dependency to keep him morally strong (p. 70; see also pp. 523–524). And finally, he must accept his need to let her become independent of him as she matures. His desire to kill his "rival" Marius, or at least to let him die on the insurrectionists' barricade, is so powerful that Hugo does not describe Jean Valjean's next-to-last struggle with his conscience. The final struggle, ending in his decision to confess to Marius that he is an escaped convict, finally kills him.

Hugo does not consider redemption automatic. Some characters deteriorate morally: the criminal anti-father Thénardier becomes indifferent to not only the sufferings of his victims, but even to the survival of his own children. When his two youngest boys disappear, he makes no effort to locate them. And he does not care whether his older daughter Eponine will be killed by other members of their gang for interfering in a burglary. Others such as the police detective Javert, born to a prostitute in prison and lacking any family himself, react toward the accused with merciless moral brutality.

Gavroche, Eponine, Javert, Jean Valjean—the first two risk their lives and perish to save others, Javert commits suicide so that he will not have to denounce the man who saved him, and Jean Valjean wastes away to consummate his renunciation of Cosette. The motif of self-sacrifice shades into melancholy (anger against others turned back against the self) and even masochism. Virtuous suicide associated with renunciation recurs throughout Hugo's career, from *Bug-Jargal* (1818 and 1826) to *Notre-Dame de Paris* (1831), *Les Travailleurs de la mer* (1866), and *Quatrevingt-treize* (1874), not to mention the hero's suicide in order to join his beloved in the afterlife, in *L'Homme qui rit* (1869). One could interpret this obsessive plot element variously: as a symptom of the weakness of the idealistic romantic hero who cannot bear to live in an imperfect world; as inspiring examples of the temporal sublime, of the choice to sacrifice one's life to a transcendent value; or as a means by which the historical Hugo purged himself of any lingering traces of a desire to sacrifice himself for others—as opposed to treating them with benevolence. But his texts provide no clear answers.

When wisely used in critical discourse, all categories represent not ways of establishing Truth, but of raising questions. On the borderline between the conventional critical categories of literary Character and Theme we find what could be called "moral themes": generalizations about human nature that are illustrated by the characters' discourse (by representations of their thoughts, writings, and words) and dramatized by their actions. Hugo's central "moral theme" is that even the best of us is tempted—if not by rebellion against human laws, then by pride and complacency—and that such temptations are spiritual ordeals that test and strengthen us in the way of virtue. Unlike Milton, Goethe, Flaubert, or Thomas Mann, Hugo does not create personified seductive devils, but depicts characters at risk of being seduced by their own selfish desires and hypocrisy. Mistaken for Jean Valjean, alias the venerated mayor M. Madeleine, the obscure old tree pruner Champmathieu seems to Valjean expendable, whereas M. Madeleine's arrest and imprisonment would end the prosperity of the village that depends on him, and doom Cosette to the streets. The accidental delays Valjean encounters while rushing to Champmathieu's trial at Arras further tempt the ex-convict to abandon the attempt to exonerate his unfortunate substitute. (To heighten the urgency of this melodramatic situation, Hugo never raises the possibility that Valjean could still denounce himself *after* Champmathieu had been sentenced. Even idealistic love can deteriorate into possessiveness. Eventually, it must be refined into altruistic self-sacrifice—a theme also prominent in the novels of Hugo's contemporaries Charles Dickens and Fyodor Dostoevsky.

Themes

So far we have discussed the prominent topics of self-sacrifice and supererogation in *Les Misérables* and throughout Hugo's career, but we have not identified any themes. As the pun in Hugo's title suggests, the theme he foregrounds in this novel is that we should not judge a book by its cover, or a person by appearances and social condition. *Les Misérables* can refer either to the underclass, people who are wretchedly poor, or to people who are morally depraved, or both. At one point, Jean Valjean calls himself *un misérable* in the second, moral sense. Hugo not only distinguishes between wealth and virtue, but also between premeditation and impulse (Jean Valjean acts impulsively when he steals the loaf of bread, or the chimneysweep's coin), and between acts (Fantine's prostitution) and their motives (her altruistic desire to support her daughter).

The initial inspiration for the creation of Jean Valjean, the protagonist of *Les Misérables,* probably came from Hugo's work on *Le Dernier Jour d'un condamné à mort* (*The Last Day of a Condemned Man*, 1829). He was a lifelong opponent of the death penalty, much in the spirit of the recent American films *The Green Mile* and *Dead Man Walking*. He dramatized the plight of prisoners in the galleys at Toulon, especially one who, like Jean Valjean, had initially been sentenced to five years at hard labor for stealing a loaf of bread. "There but for the grace of God go I" is his message. He emphasizes the brutalization of the poor by society. Like his contemporary Charles Dickens in *Oliver Twist* or *Our Mutual Friend,* he deconstructs the simplistic opposition of innocence and crime that allows us to evade social responsibility. Jean Valjean's only actual crimes are two acts of petty larceny, plus a third of which he is falsely accused (stealing a loaf of bread, a coin, and some apples). Hugo's attribution of near-Satanic resentment to him seems overblown, but Hugo is making the point he had made in *Claude Gueux* (Claude the Beggar): harsh law enforcement breeds the monsters it claims to want to eliminate (Grant, *The Perilous Quest,* pp. 157–158; see "For Further Reading").

But Hugo's dominant theme, which pervades his novels, poems, and essays (less so his plays) on every level, and which guided his life for decades, is that individuals, the world, and the cosmos all need rescuers. In his personal life, from 1833 until her death decades later, Hugo felt that he was "redeeming" the "fallen woman" Juliette Drouet, his mistress, through his love—although he never seemed to worry about the moral import of his own extraordinary promiscuity. In society, through paternalistic charitable acts and strategies of enlightened self-interest that allow wealth to trickle down to the poor, the wealthy and privileged must act to alleviate suffering and improve the material conditions of humanity, increasing productivity and eliminating crime.

Critics have often spoken of Hugo's keen visual sensitivity, manifested in the dramatic opposition of light and darkness in many scenes and in his striking visionary drawings, but they have not paid much attention to his use of color. It is important to recognize it, in order to understand the full profundity of his vision. In *Les Misérables,* bright colors and light accompany scenes of oblivious, shallow happiness. See, for instance, the color notations starting in paragraph five of "Four to Four," chapter 3 of part I, book three: "long white strings," "thick blond tresses," "rosy lips," "a dress of mauve barege, little reddish-brown buskins," "sea-green eyes." The sensuous iridescence of the material world gives way elsewhere to stark contrasts of good and evil, rendered in black and white; but the duality of these two non-colors is itself an illusion, as Hugo underlines in the chapter "Black and White," in which Javert cannot endure the breakdown of his simplistic, polarized moral vision. Like colors, black and white are mere deceptive manifestations of a world based on a single ground of reality: God. The chapter explaining Napoléon's defeat at Waterloo (and anticipating General Kutusov's Providentialist meditations in Tolstoy's *War and Peace*) explains this vision clearly in another way, through causality rather than through color.

As this discussion of the symbolism of color versus black and white just above suggests, Hugo often implies themes rather than stating them, by relating two passages of which the second nevertheless invites a new interpretation of the pair through its manifest contrasts with the first: he achieves a dialectical movement of thesis—antithesis—synthesis. In this way he particularly exploits the archetype of Inversion, and pairs of digressions. Inversion refers to a transvaluation of values, whereby that which had seemed bad proves good, or vice versa. Hugo invokes negative inversion to characterize the police agent Javert when the latter learns that M. Madeleine, who had humiliated him earlier, is really the convict Jean Valjean: "A monstrous Saint Michael," Javert seems both imposing and hideous. "The pitiless, sincere joy of a fanatic in an act of atrocity preserves an indescribably mournful radiance. . . . Nothing could be more poignant and terrible than this face, which revealed what we may call all the evil of good" (p. 194). The sinister, deformed grandeur of Thénardier's visionary engraving of Napoléon may also exemplify this archetype, like a spider's ambition to rival the sun (p. 437; compare the poem in *Les Contemplations,* "Puissance égale bonté"). Thénardier, by trying to capture the emperor's image, seems to aspire to appropriate for himself the soul of Napoléon's genius.

The positive form of Inversion reveals that what seemed bad, proves good. Outstanding examples are the Beatitudes in Christ's Sermon on the Mount (Matthew 5:2–12), and the Passion and Resurrection (Matthew 27–28, Mark 15–16, Luke 23–24, John 19–20). Appropriately expressing his tidy sense of structure, Hugo frames his epic novel with nesting layers of inversions. At the beginning and the end, we learn that humility can exalt the soul (in Bishop Myriel, whose last name is a near-anagram of "lumière" or light, and in Jean Valjean). In the middle, Javert's bad excess of goodness yields to his shocked awareness of the possible goodness of badness, as he learns of Jean Valjean's moral sublimity.

Near the end, Jean Valjean thematizes Inversion as he wins his final spiritual battle by confessing his past to Marius. Speaking for the author, who unlike all his contemporaries accepted two decades of exile rather than make any compromise with Napoléon III, he explains, "In order that I may respect myself, I must be despised. Then I hold myself erect. I am a galley slave who obeys his conscience. I know well that is improbable [*ressemblant*]. But what would you have me do? it is so" (p. 779). The word *ressem-*

blant echoes Hugo's pirouette at the beginning of the novel, as he concludes his idealized moral portrait of Bishop Myriel—"We do not claim that the portrait which we present here is plausible [*ressemblant*]; we say only that it resembles him" (p. 15). This subtle, nearly subliminal association of the two men reminds us of Myriel's enduring moral influence on Valjean. Switching from the narrator's voice to the hero's voice in the second of these mirroring scenes makes the novel's moral impact more immediate at the climax.

Hugo's historical and cultural digressions set the stage for the characters, explain the limits of their possibilities, and often hint at, foreshadow, or symbolize what he sees as an overarching spiritual odyssey of Fall and Redemption. Unless we sin in thought or deed, we cannot benefit from grace and ascend nearer God. William Blake's scandalous slogan "Damn braces; bless relaxes," like Johann Wolfgang von Goethe's concept of Faustian striving with its inevitable errors as essential to spiritual progress, are earlier, condensed versions of Hugo's theme that godliness requires us to reject society's image of a God who demands self-righteousness and conformity.

Hugo's five main pairs of digressions are:

1) "The Year 1817" (p. 73) and "The Story of an Improvement in Jet-Work" (p. 99), which contrast social irresponsibility and responsibility; 2) "Waterloo" (p. 205) and the Convent of the Perpetual Adoration (described in part II, books six and seven, which do not appear in this unabridged edition), which contrast self-aggrandizement and material pomp with self-effacing service and spiritual grandeur; 3) the street urchin (p. 341) and the underworld (part III, book seven, chapters 1 and 2), contrasting social dysfunction in the idealistic child and the corrupt adult; 4) King Louis Philippe (part IV, book one) and slang (part IV, book six, chapter 3), contrasting the summit and the underside of society; and 5) the origins of the insurrection of June 5–6, 1832, (see the unabridged edition) and the sewers of Paris (part V, book two), offering political and metaphorical analyses of social corruption. The brutal treatment of the workers who provide the foundations of prosperity causes rebellion; similarly, unless the sewers are studied, rebuilt, and cleaned out, he argues, they will overflow onto the streets above as they have done before. Flushing fecal matter into rivers poisons our environment and wastes a precious potential resource, Hugo argues, as does locking the poor into prisons. Hugo skewers the euphemistic pseudo-progress that claims to be making humanitarian advances while merely changing the words or their order, which refer to our instruments of control. "Formerly these grim cells, in which prison discipline delivers the condemned to himself, were composed of four stone walls, a stone ceiling, a floor of paving stones, a camp bed, a grated air-hole, a door reinforced with iron, and were called *dungeons;* but the dungeon came to be thought too horrible: today it is composed of an iron door, a grated air-hole, a camp bed, a floor of paving stones, a stone ceiling, four stone walls, and it is called a *punitive detention cell*" (p. 566).

The Writer's Role

Hugo believed that the culture hero must also enter politics to ensure social justice, as he did before and after his exile, during the 1840s and 1870s. There he preached international understanding, imagining (like Thomas Paine, Immanuel Kant, and Madame de Staël before him) a united Europe led by France together with the German states. The genius must reveal God's purposes to humans. When unable to act directly—Hugo's situation during his two decades of exile on the Channel Islands of Jersey and Guernsey—he can write; and writing always supplements personal contacts. Thus, *Les Misérables*.

Les Misérables focuses on the work of class reconciliation. The title, a syllepsis (a supersegmental pun, a word used with two different meanings depending on its context), seems to confuse material poverty (*la misère*; *les misérables* are the impoverished underclass) with moral degradation (*un misérable* can mean a wretch or morally reprehensible person), but Hugo's plot of fall and redemption works precisely to dissociate the two notions through the protagonist Jean Valjean's progressive regeneration. Poverty dehumanizes the poor, Hugo demonstrates, leading to prostitution, child abuse, and other crimes that subject the underclass to a purely punitive prison system that offers no hope of rehabilitation. Hugo wants us not to prejudge the poor, but to separate their unsavory reputation from their varying reality and its extenuating circumstances.

Historical and Political Dimensions

In part I, the chapter entitled "The Year 1817," Hugo characterizes the immoral frivolity of the early Restoration period (1814–1830). In so doing, he dissociates himself from the Royalism of his early career: at twenty-two, he had even managed to wangle an appointment as the Poet Laureate to commemorate the coronation of the arch-conservative Comte d'Artois, who became Charles X. The remainder of the first part details the horrific consequences of such immorality for the unwed, abandoned single mother Fantine. Hugo shows as much as he tells his opposition to the sexual double standard that treats prostitutes as criminals while their clients go free. The wealthy young men of 1817 who abandon their impoverished mistresses are respected; their victims are blamed. Fantine, as a streetwalker working to pay for her baby's room and board after having been fired from her factory job for being an unwed mother, is despised; M. Batambois, who assaults her by shoving snow down her dress, seems exempt from the law; later, indeed, we find him serving on a jury. Jean Valjean, as a convict evading a warrant for robbery, is considered a menace to society; but, disguised as M. Madeleine (whose name, evoking Mary Magdalene, evokes repentance), he alone can ensure the prosperity of his entire community through his responsible, enlightened capitalism in establishing the manufacture of glassware in the town where he has come to serve as mayor.

Hugo wants to excite our compassion. But his benevolence remains paternalistic, and his modest proposals for the partial, voluntary redistribution of wealth—as in Charles Dickens's *A Christmas Carol*—could not threaten wealthy readers. Regarding social progress in general, Hugo was optimistic. He shows Jean Valjean, alias M. Madeleine, reading at every meal. Hugo once declared that twenty years of good free mandatory education for all would be the last word and bring the dawn. Having become a utopian socialist, as was his creation M. Madeleine, Hugo believed that salaries would increase naturally along with profits, and that the dynamism of capital expansion would naturally resolve the problems of working conditions for the better. In fairness to Hugo, one must recognize that in 1862 an organized proletariat had not yet formed, although it was foreshadowed by a workers' uprising in Lyons in 1832 and by the medieval guilds, an institution to which he pays his respects in the novel *Notre-Dame de Paris* (see Porter, *Victor Hugo*, pp. 20–23). Labor union movements as such had not yet developed. Hugo still thinks that guidance and enlightenment must descend on the people from "above," from intellectuals. Nevertheless, at times his trenchant political analyses reveal the irresolvable contradictions one encounters by adopting either of two opposing positions—which, as it happens, are those of liberal Democrats and conservative Republicans in the United States today:

> All the problems which the socialists propounded, aside from the cosmogonic visions, dreams, and mysticism, may be reduced to two principal problems.
> First problem:
> To produce wealth.
> Second problem:
> To distribute it. . . .
> England solves the first of these two problems. She creates wealth wonderfully; she distributes it badly. . . . [she has] a grandeur ill constituted, in which all the material elements are combined, and into which no moral element enters.
> Communism and agarian law think they have solved the second problem. They are mistaken. Their distribution kills production. Equal division abolishes emulation. And consequently labour. It is a distribution made by the butcher, who kills what he divides (pp. 505–506).

Hugo suggests a balance of these two extreme solutions, egalitarian socialism and mercantilism.

Thus he characteristically deconstructs naively categorical views that risk blocking compromise and solution. He contests the dichotomies of middle class and lower class, of police and criminals. He argues that the bourgeoisie is simply the materially satisfied portion of "the people," and that on the other hand the mob can betray the best interest of "the people" through unthinking violence.

Aside from his steadfast opposition to capital punishment, Hugo offered no practical solutions for reforming the police, the courts, or the prisons. He merely tries to stimulate our moral sensibilities, as Fantine's misadventures and her selfless love for her child stimulated the moral sensibilities of Jean Valjean. Hugo intends the reformed convict to provide a model for us as Valjean comes to know God, whom Hugo equates with conscience. His message comes from the Gospels: "Inasmuch as you have done unto the least of these my brethren, so you have done unto me" (Matthew 25:40). At length, Hugo explicitly compares the redeemed Valjean to Christ (Grant, pp. 158–176, and Brombert, pp. 86–139).

As a symbolic representative of the working class enslaved by the former monarchy, Jean Valjean had been too debased and brutalized, Hugo believed, to promote historical progress through militant political action. But his destiny prefigures the eventual reconciliation of social classes: the ex-convict presides over the marriage of Cosette—the proletarian daughter of a prostitute—and Marius, the aristocrat adopted and cherished by the bourgeois Gillenormand. Cosette herself does not participate in or even become clearly aware of the insurrection. We must await the next generation that includes Cosette's and Marius's children to witness the full embodiment of the spirit of the new France. The courageous street urchin Gavroche, killed fighting on the barricades, foreshadowed the flowering of this spirit.

Hugo chose the now-forgotten uprising of 1832 rather than the glorious revolution of 1830 as the historical crux of the novel because he had been struck by the great historian Louis Blanc's account of the 1832 worker-student insurrection. Hugo was less concerned with creating a practical manual for revolutionaries, or with celebrating any particular liberal, historical triumph than with providing a symbolic illustration of the French people struggling toward the light. Hugo thought that minor events as well as major ones could reveal the intentions of Providence. The self-sacrifice of Enjolras and his friends would serve to inspire and mobilize others. Like Bertolt Brecht a century later, Hugo does not want to serve up a cathartic vision of history: he prefers to imply that much work remains to be done.

Critics have generally been relatively unaware of how thoroughly realism and idealism in Hugo's fictions are interconnected. He is not vapidly optimistic; his concept of Providence always represents a dimension of human responsibility that can alter outcomes. Hugo's moral complexity appears when he describes how Jean Valjean learns how to read and write while in prison. Although Hugo associates education with the light that dispels darkness, he acknowledges that education can empower the evildoer. Jean Valjean "felt that to increase his knowledge was to strengthen his hatred. Under certain circumstances, instruction and enlightenment may serve as rallying-points for evil" (p. 53). But Thénardier, on the contrary,

was one of those double natures who sometimes appear among us without our knowledge, and disappear without ever being known, because destiny has shown us but one side of them. It is the fate of many men to live thus half submerged. In a quiet ordinary situation,

Thénardier had all that is necessary to make—we do not say to be—what passes for an honest tradesman, a good citizen. At the same time, under certain circumstances, under the operation of certain occurrences exciting his baser nature, he had in him all that was necessary to be a villain. He was a shopkeeper in which lay hidden a monster (p. 257).

Even the arch-villain of the novel might not have had to become irremediably evil, but, as Jean Valjean had within himself the potential for redemption and saintliness, Thénardier's soul contained seeds of the demonic.

[He and his wife] were of those dwarfish natures, which, if perchance heated by some sullen fire, easily become monstrous. The woman was at heart a brute; the man a blackguard: both in the highest degree capable of that hideous species of progress which can be made towards evil. There are souls which, crablike, crawl continually towards darkness, going back in life rather than advancing in it; using what experience they have to increase their deformity; growing worse without ceasing, and becoming steeped more and more thoroughly in an intensifying wickedness. Such souls were this man and this woman (p. 93).

Although many characters in *Les Misérables,* including Tholomyès (part I, book three) and Monsieur Batambois, who is explicitly characterized as a provincial version of Tholomyès (part I, book five, chapter 12), seem to damn themselves through their fatuous complacency, which as they age hardens into indifferent cruelty, they illustrate a mainly passive or heedless evil, the banality of evil. Hugo demonstrates in his depiction of the Thénardier couple a dramatic evolution toward a calculated evil. By creating such characters, Hugo counteracts whatever tendencies toward vapid optimism one may find in a moral universe where even Satan might be saved (the Pelagian Heresy: in addition to *Les Contemplations,* see *La Fin de Satan*).

The Great French Novel

Why do we still read *Les Misérables*? Not too many years ago, it was added to the required reading list for the *agrégation* in French literature, the competitive state examination that qualifies teachers at advanced levels. Its moral, social, and political messages remain pertinent to many of the situations we confront. But above all, *Les Misérables* is the unrecognized "Great French Novel," analogous to Herman Melville's *Moby Dick*, Alessandro Manzoni's *The Betrothed,* Leo Tolstoy's *War and Peace,* or Thomas Mann's *The Magic Mountain*. I do not mean that it is necessarily *the greatest* French novel: one might prefer Proust's *À la recherche du temps perdu,* just as in the literature of other languages, one might prefer Faulkner's *The Sound and the Fury,* James Joyce's *Ulysses,* Fyodor Dostoevsky's *The Brothers*

Karamazov, Kafka's *The Trial,* or Gunther Grass's *The Tin Drum.* The social, moral, and intellectual range of Hugo's characters far exceeds what we find in all these other great authors, whose social density is nonetheless noteworthy. Beyond that impressive achievement, *Les Misérables* in many respects conforms to an ideal type, an influential theoretical entity whose traits are realized only in part by any concrete example.

The Great National Novel is capacious: it covers substantial amounts of time and space. It contains many vivid characters belonging to varied social conditions: it is not intimist in its setting, not a drawing-room adventure limited to family, friends, and courtship. It tells its sprawling story in a traditional mode, dominated by the controlling perspective of an omniscient author who, despite flashbacks and digressions, generally proceeds steadily forward, following the protagonists as they age. It usually deploys *la grande histoire* ("big" history, revolutions and wars) in the background, although the main characters, affected as they are by political dramas, usually are not leading players in them. It implies some connection between individual and national destinies. By the time he wrote *Les Misérables,* Hugo had had more direct political experience at the highest levels of government than had many other writers of his time. Very often the Great National Novel suggests the looming presence of the supernatural, hidden but at times glimpsed behind the scenes, or during "second states" of consciousness such as dreams, drug experiences, visions, hallucinations, illness, passion, or prayer. Hugo began writing *Les Misérables* shortly after spending several years of evenings at mystical séances, and after elaborating the religious system, based on punitive and redemptive reincarnation, that he finally made explicit in his visionary poem *La Fin de Satan.* The Great National Novel usually relegates artistic self-consciousness to the background: it does not become a *Künstlerroman*—the portrait of the artist as a young man—nor does it foreground the cleverness of the writer's craft by radical experiments in point of view, plot structure, stylistic innovations, or characterization. Instead, the Great National Novel quietly insinuates the mature author's hard-won wisdom through a series of aphorisms, or pithy, penetrating generalizations about human nature. These maxims demonstrate the author's ability to synthesize many experiences. The digressions are miniature essays on varied subjects—authors of the Great National Novel are born essayists and amateur philosophers—that aim to instruct the audience. In contrast to the Self-Conscious Novel (Cervantes, Sterne, Diderot), digressions do not serve to tease the expectant reader by delaying the forward progress of the story, but to establish the writer's authority as a portraitist of a wide world by giving glimpses into his or her encyclopedic knowledge.

The Influence of Les Misérables

In the late nineteenth century, *Les Misérables* anticipated both the naturalistic movement and its opposite pole, the Catholic Renaissance. Whereas the realistic novel typically deals with the middle class, Naturalism deals with the working class and with the underworld. Repetitious, menial labor is difficult to dramatize in a novel; but Hugo devotes ample space to describing members of the working class at play (Fantine and her friends), and the criminal class at work or trying to escape from the police. In the Paris scenes, he depicts the *grisettes* (young proletarian women who wore gray smocks at their jobs, and who were stereotypically easy targets for seduction). Notably in the chapter "L'Année 1817," he emphasizes the inequities of their sexual exploitation by middle-class men in a direct way that Zola, with his sexual insecurities, could not (compare Zola's *Nana,* 1880, depicting female sexuality as a monstrous source of social corruption). Hugo has not yet received due credit for anticipating the naturalist movement in the chapters devoted to Fantine's life both in Paris and in her hometown..

The Catholic Renaissance, which deplored Hugo's bombastic prophetic rhetoric and his pretensions to revealing a new religion, also derived considerable indirect inspiration from Hugo. Like Claudel, who detested him and made a point of saying so, like Mauriac, or like Bernanos, from thirty to ninety years after him, Hugo in 1862 dramatizes his heroes' relentless pursuit by conscience, meaning our instinctive awareness of God.

Hugo's appeal to posterity depends not only on the awe-inspiring range and depth of his masterpiece, *Les Misérables,* not only on his inspiring, idealistic visions of political and social progress, but also on the acute visual sense that put him well ahead of his time, but that can be captured and reinforced by modern media such as film and television. His extraordinary visual imagination is both impressionistic—sensitive to colors, including colored shadows, and to changes in light—and cinematic, aware of varying angles of vision and shifting vantage points. It involves an exceptional responsiveness to both light and motion. One can find striking proof of this in Hugo's correspondence. He does not write interesting letters; he wrote letters while resting from his continuous periods of creative work on most days, on his feet in front of his writing stand from 5 A.M. to noon, with a cup of hot chocolate nearby. In letters, he cares more about making contact with others than about thinking of precisely what he has to say. But the one interesting letter in the first volume of his correspondence describes his first ride on a train, and his fascination with how the landscape blurs and flickers as he passes it at speeds far greater than he had ever experienced before. Compare the description of what Jean Valjean sees on his carriage ride to denounce himself at the court in Arras (pp. 157–161). *Notre-Dame de Paris* provides even better examples. Hugo anticipates Claude Monet's famous series of paintings of the same subject when he evokes the changing light on the façade of the Cathedral of Notre Dame. Following this passage, he executes the verbal equivalent of a zoom-in shot to approach a balcony on which an engagement party has gathered. Earlier, the description circling Paris from the top of the cathedral towers ("A Bird's-Eye View of Paris") anticipates the cinematic technique of the traveling shot. At the beginning of the twentieth century, polls rated Hugo as the greatest nineteenth-century French poet, but his gifts as a storyteller in his plays and novels were fully acknowledged on an international scale only when

Les Misérables was produced as the first full-length feature film in France in 1909; within a few years Albert Capellani of Pathé and André Antoine of Le Théâtre-Libre produced a noteworthy series of silent films of Hugo's works: *Les Misérables* (1912), the play *Marie Tudor* (1912), and the novels *Quatrevingt-treize* (1914) and *Les Travailleurs de la mer* (1918). Lon Chaney's celebrated performance as Quasimodo in W. Worsley's film *The Hunchback of Notre-Dame de Paris* (1924) consolidated these triumphs. More recently, television versions of the plays *Les Burgraves* (1968) and *Torquemada* (1976) were triumphs. Today (November 2002), Alain Boublil and Claude-Michel Schoenberg's stage version of *Les Misérables* (1980), inspired by the rock opera *Jesus-Christ Superstar*, is still running in New York and on tour in the United States. It eclipsed the record number of international productions of a musical, previously held by *Cats* (see Porter, *Victor Hugo,* pp. 152–156).

We cannot fully understand the novel *Les Misérables* by watching film, television, or staged versions. The flawed humanity that makes Valjean's ambiguous rehabilitation and Javert's anguished forgiveness of him possible is lacking from the "event theater" stage, where two forces must contend in stark opposition. And the successive political and moral awakenings of the young hero Marius cannot be represented in a musical. The same leveling affects lesser characters. Thénardier onstage is merely comic, a grotesque counterpart to the sublimity of self-sacrifice and young love, whereas in the novel he degenerates morally, while more than once unwittingly serving the designs of Providence. Hugo's moments of blatant sentimentality and melodramatic contrasts of pure good with pure evil appeal to some readers and repel others, but tempt both camps to overlook his true complexity. Whereas *Les Miz* rushes to judgment, *Les Misérables* urges us to suspend judgment, to ponder the profundity of character, history, and Providence.

Chronology

Part I ("Fantine"), book two ("The Fall"), chapter 6 mentions that Jean Valjean was 25 when, at some indeterminate date, he began supporting his widowed sister and her seven children. During the hard winter of 1795, when he had no work, he stole a loaf of bread for them, and was immediately arrested. He was imprisoned in 1796, and released after 19 years, in 1815. Cosette is born around 1817. Hugo says Jean Valjean is 50 and Cosette is 8 when he rescues her. The insurrection described at the end of part IV and the beginning of part V occurs in 1832. Cosette is 16 or 17. She and Marius marry a year or two later, and Jean Valjean probably dies within the year—no later than 1835. Hugo says he is 80 then, which would mean he had been born in 1755, but it sounds as if he had managed to support his sister and her children only for two or three years, which would make him in his late 60s in 1835. Hugo has aged him artificially, as a melodramatic way of emphasizing his emotional suffering when he loses Cosette to Marius.

Money

Hugo's novel has many realistic elements, notably the importance of money. Precise sums are frequently mentioned, and nearly all the characters must earn, beg, or steal money in order to live. Here are the units of currency referred to in the text:

3 *deniers* ("the widow's mite") made a *liard*. 240 of them made a *franc*.
5 *centimes* or 4 *liards* made a *sou*.
20 *sous* made a *franc* (also referred to as a *livre*).
3 *francs* made an *écu*.
20 *francs* made a gold *Napoléon* or *Louis* (both were in circulation).

Because the relative cost of items differed greatly from their cost today, 1 franc—the most common unit of currency—equaled between 5 and 30 U.S. dollars in today's purchasing power. Rent was cheap; clothing, transportation, and food were expensive (farms had no tractors or combines; flour was ground in mills by water power; each loaf of bread was made by hand). A worker who earned less than 1 *franc* a day was being severely exploited. The Thénardiers' rent in the Gorbeau tenement is 20 francs a quarter (7 a month), the equivalent of $200 a month. Bishop Myriel makes 15,000 francs a year (say, $150,000) with free lodging, but gives all but 1,500 to the poor. Jean Valjean accumulates a fortune of 600,000 francs in manufacturing, making Cosette a multimillionaire. The formidable Patron-Minette gang is happy to risk six to ten years' imprisonment in a double kidnapping-torture-ransom scheme, in exchange for a chance at 500 francs apiece.

Napoléon's Name

Napoléon's last name becomes highly significant in this novel. As First Consul and then as Emperor, he ruled from 1799 till 1814, with another three months (*Les Cent Jours*) after his escape from exile in 1815 until he was defeated at Waterloo. Louis XVIII took over as King in 1814, and was succeeded by Charles X from 1824 to 1830. After Charles X was ousted by a revolution, he was replaced by the constitutional monarch Louis Philippe from 1830 to 1848. Those who supported the institution of the monarchy, and particularly those who believed in the divine right of kings to rule, always said *Buonaparte* (pronouncing the final *e* as an extra syllable) to emphasize the Emperor's foreign origins (he was born in Corsica before that island became French) and therefore to imply his illegitimacy. Those who say *Bonaparte* in the French manner, without pronouncing the final *e*, are already suspect to the legitimists; and those who say *L'Empéreur,* betraying lingering admiration and nostalgia for his grandeur, label themselves as enemies of the throne and the church. Thus the presiding judge (under a monarchist regime) at the Champmathieu trial, although he admires Monsieur Madeleine, issues an order for his arrest because the mayor said "Bonaparte," showing that his political convictions are left of center. And Fauchelevant, speaking with the Mother Superior in the convent, catches himself just in time as he is about to refer to Napoléon as *"L'Empéreur."* Fortunately for him and Jean Valjean, his slip "L'Emp-" goes unnoticed.

Even more serious, in the relationship between Marius and his grandfather M. Gillmormand, is Marius's admiration for his father, le Baron (the title reveals a person ennobled by Napoléon) de Pontmercy, who fought in Napoléon's armies as a colonel. The Revolution brought Napoléon to power, and Pontmercy is therefore associated in the monarchist Gillenormand's mind with the revolutionary excesses of the Reign of Terror in 1793, which began with the execution of the King and Queen in January, and eventually killed 20,000 people (fewer than the right-wing repression of the Paris Commune in 1871).

Transportation

Railroads were beginning to be constructed in France in the 1830s, but they are not mentioned in *Les Misérables.* All transportation is in horse-drawn carriages, on muleback (Bishop Myriel), or on foot. *Fiacres* are enclosed public cabs in Paris, holding up to six passengers, and drawn by a single horse. *Diligences* are stagecoaches, drawn by two to four horses; they provide transportation between towns, and transport packages (like UPS) and mail. Outside of cities, nearly all roads were unpaved and unlighted. Fresh horses and drivers are maintained at relay stations along the stage routes, including some that can be rented by individual travelers. These vehicles would travel at a slow trot, about 6 miles an hour on good roads, and could go up to 50 miles a day—even farther if the teams were changed. The major unit of distance, the league, was 4 kilometers (2.5 miles). Some other types of vehicles were the *calèche* (with four wheels, a raised front bench, and a hood sheltering the back seats), the *carosse* (a luxurious enclosed vehicle with four wheels, used by noble and wealthy families), the *cabriolet* (a light, two-wheeled vehicle), and a *tilbury* (a *cabriolet* with just two seats). The *cacolet* was a basket containing two seats with backs, placed over the back of a beast of burden such as a donkey, as opposed to the saddle, which had no back and held only one person.

A Note on Untranslated Words

The original translator left a number of words in French, without italics, to capture shades of meaning and to add a foreign flavor. We have left the following in French as well:

Argot: Slang, or thieves' cant, used for secrecy. Opposed to professional jargon, the language of the professions.

Émeute: Insurrection (considered a violent but legitimate protest) or riot (undiscriminating mob violence).
Fiacre: Cab; see above.
Francs, livres: Units of money; see above.

Laurence M. Porter has published twelve books and a hundred articles and book chapters on Francophone studies, comparative literature, critical theory, French culture, and every period of French literature. These include a comprehensive book, *Victor Hugo* (1999), and several other articles and chapters on Hugo, including one on Hugo's novels published by Legenda, the Humanities Research Institute at Oxford University, England. He was an NEH Senior Research Fellow in 1998, and has held other grants from the Ford Foundation, NEH, and USIS. He teaches French at Michigan State University; he won the Distinguished Faculty Award in 1995. He serves on the Editorial or Advisory Boards of *Nineteenth-Century French Studies, Studies in Twentieth Century Literature,* and *Women in French Studies*.

Acknowledgments

I gratefully acknowledge the permission from the Gale Research Company of Detroit, Michigan, to reproduce elements of Chapter Eight, "The Masterpiece," from my book *Victor Hugo* (New York: Twayne/Macmillan, 1999), which form a portion of the preface to this edition of *Les Misérables*. Marjorie Porter helped substantially to clarify my writing, and John Rauk, the current Chair of Romance and Classical Languages at Michigan State University, kindly allowed me to defer one course from spring 2003 to next year, which made it possible to complete this edition— as well as tracking down an allusion from Horace.

A NOTE ON THE ABRIDGMENT

In the complex structure of *Les Misérables*, each of five long parts is divided into several books, and each book into several chapters. Hugo wrote simultaneously as an idealist who used a classical dramatic progression and as a realist who digressed into sociological essays. The idealist composed a vast drama of redemption in five acts, which correspond with the five parts of the novel. Part I presents the initial situation: society scornfully rejects two potentially virtuous, self-sacrificial characters, the former convict Jean Valjean and the prostitute Fantine. Part II introduces the complication that initiates the main action: Jean Valjean tries to protect Fantine's orphaned daughter, Cosette, while fleeing the police. Part III, the moment of resolve, depicts the young Marius, who will learn to work for the political liberation of society through collective effort, after Valjean has been shown trying to achieve economic progress to be shared by all. Part IV, the climax, shows Marius risking his life behind the revolutionaries' barricade, while Valjean knowingly sacrifices his happiness to save Marius's life, allowing the youth to marry Cosette. Part V, the denouement, traces Valjean's spiritual apotheosis, which will inspire Marius and Cosette. As a realist, Hugo shows how the glorious spiritual motivations mentioned above become entangled with selfish impulses, and he grounds his depiction of character in serious historical and sociological research.

In this abridged edition, the following long sections have been cut: the history of a religious order (part II, books six and seven); a linguistic examination of the secret languages of thieves (part IV, book seven); and the historical background of the 1832 insurrection in Paris (part IV, book ten). The titles of omitted books are enclosed in square brackets in the table of contents on pages 5–6 below.

Some entire chapters and opening sections of chapters have been cut. Chapter names come from the unabridged version, but chapters have been numbered to preserve an uninterrupted sequence. Above a chapter title, a larger number in parentheses, following a smaller number, is the chapter number in the unabridged version: for example, 5 (7).

Within the text, plain prose summaries *in italics* for chapters or other pieces of text that have been cut allow the reader to follow the action without reading all of Hugo's subplots and side remarks.

LES MISÉRABLES

PREFACE

So long as civilisation shall permit law and custom to impose a social condemnation that creates artificial hells on earth, complicating our divine destiny with a fatality driven by humans; so long as the three problems of the age—man degraded by poverty, woman demoralised by starvation, childhood stunted by physical and spiritual night—remain unsolved; as long as people may be suffocated, in certain regions, by society; in other words, taking a longer view, so long as ignorance and misery endure on earth, books such as this cannot but be useful.

CONTENTS

Part I: Fantine

Book		**Page**
One	An Upright Man	9
Two	The Fall	35
Three	In the Year 1817	71
Four	To Entrust Is Sometimes to Abandon	85
Five	The Descent	97
Six	Javert	129
Seven	The Champmathieu Case	141
Eight	Counter-stroke	185

Part II: Cosette

One	Waterloo	205
Two	The Convict Ship *Orion*	211
Three	Keeping the Promise to the Dead Woman	219
Four	The Old Gorbeau House	263
Five	A Sinister Hunt Requires a Silent Pack	275
[Six	Petit Picpus]	297
[Seven	A Parenthesis]	297
Eight	Cemeteries Take What Is Given Them	299

Part III: Marius

One	Paris Studied through Its Microcosm	339
[Two	The Grand Bourgeois]	346
Three	The Grandfather and the Grandson	347
Four	The Friends of the A B C	365
Five	The Excellence of Misfortune	385
Six	The Conjunction of Two Stars	395
Seven	Patron-Minette	413
Eight	The Criminal Poor	421

Part IV: The Epic on the Rue Saint-Denis
and the Idyll of the Rue Plumet

One	A Few Pages of History	495
Two	Eponine	507
Three	The House in the Rue Plumet	517
Four	Aid from Below May Be Aid from Above	531
Five	The End of Which Is Unlike the Beginning	535
Six	Little Gavroche	549
[Seven	Argot (On Slang)]	576
Eight	Enchantment and Despair	577
Nine	Where Are They Going?	605
[Ten	June 5th, 1832]	610
Eleven	The Atom Fraternises with the Hurricane	611
Twelve	Corinth	615
Thirteen	Marius Enters the Shadow	629
Fourteen	The Grandeur of Despair	635
Fifteen	The Rue de L'Homme Armé	649

Part V: Jean Valjean

One	War between Four Walls	663
[Two	The Leviathan's Bowels]	707
Three	Mire, but Soul	709
Four	Javert Derailed	739
Five	The Grandson and the Grandfather	745
Six	The Sleepless Night	763
Seven	The Last Drop in the Chalice	771
Eight	The Final Twilight	791
Nine	The Last Night Yields to the Last Dawn	803

FANTINE

BOOK ONE
AN UPRIGHT MAN

1

M. MYRIEL

In 1815, M. Charles François-Bienvenu Myriel was Bishop of D——. He was a man of about seventy-five, and had occupied the bishopric of D—— since 1806. Although it in no manner concerns, even in the remotest degree, what we have to relate, it may not be useless, were it only for the sake of exactness in all things, to indicate here the reports and gossip which had arisen on his account from the time of his arrival in the diocese.

Be it true or false, what is said about men often has as much influence upon their lives, and especially upon their destinies, as what they do.

M. Myriel was the son of a counsellor of the Parlement of Aix who had acquired noble rank by belonging to the legal profession. His father, intending him to inherit his place, had contracted a marriage for him at the early age of eighteen or twenty, according to a widespread custom among parliamentary families. Charles Myriel, notwithstanding this marriage, had, it was said, been an object of much attention. He was well built, although rather short, he was elegant, witty, and graceful; all the earlier part of his life had been devoted to the world and to its pleasures. The revolution came, events crowded upon each other; the parliamentary families, decimated and hunted down, were soon dispersed. M. Charles Myriel, on the first outbreak of the revolution, emigrated to Italy. His wife died there of a lung complaint with which she had been long threatened. They had no children. What followed in the fate of M. Myriel? The decay of the old French society, the fall of his own family, the tragic sights of '93, still more fearful, perhaps, to the exiles who beheld them from afar, magnified by fright—did these arouse in him ideas of renunciation and of solitude? Was he, in the midst of one of the reveries or attachments which then consumed his life, suddenly struck by one of those mysterious, terrible blows which sometimes overwhelm, by smiting to the heart, the man whom public disasters could not shake, by affecting his private life? No one could have answered; all that was known was that when he returned from Italy he was a priest.

In 1804, M. Myriel was curé of B—— (Brignolles). He was then an old man, and lived in the deepest seclusion.

Near the time of the coronation,* a trifling matter of business belonging

---

*Napoléon was crowned Emperor on December 2, 1804, in the Cathedral of Notre-Dame.

to his curacy—what it was, is not now known precisely—took him to Paris.

Among other personages of authority he went to Cardinal Fesch on behalf of his parishioners.

One day, when the emperor had come to visit his uncle, he happened to pass by the worthy priest, who was waiting in the anteroom. Napoleon noticing that the old man looked at him with a certain curiousness, turned around and said brusquely:

"Who is this goodman who is looking at me?"

"Sire," said M. Myriel, "you behold a good man, and I a great man. Each of us may profit by it."

That evening the emperor asked the cardinal the name of the curé and some time afterwards M. Myriel was overwhelmed with surprise on learning that he had been appointed Bishop of D——.

When M. Myriel came to D—— he was accompanied by an old lady, Mademoiselle Baptistine, who was his sister, ten years younger than himself.

Their only domestic was a woman of about the same age as Mademoiselle Baptistine, who was called Madame Magloire, and who after having been the servant of M. le curé, now took the double title of femme de chambre of Mademoiselle and housekeeper of Monseigneur.

Mademoiselle Baptistine was a tall, pale, thin, sweet person. She fully realised the idea which is expressed by the word "respectable;" for it seems as if it were necessary that a woman should be a mother to be venerable. She had never been pretty; her whole life, which had been but a succession of pious works, had produced upon her a kind of transparent whiteness, and in growing old she had acquired what may be called the beauty of goodness. What had been thinness in her youth had become in maturity transparency, and this etherialness permitted the angel within to shine through. She was more a spirit than a virgin mortal. Her form was shadow-like, hardly enough body to convey the thought of sex—a little earth containing a spark—large eyes, always cast down; a pretext for a soul to remain on earth.

Madame Magloire was a little, white, fat, jolly, bustling old woman, always out of breath, caused first by her activity, and then by the asthma.[*]

M. Myriel, upon his arrival, was installed in his episcopal palace with the honours ordained by the imperial decrees, which class the bishop next in rank to the field-marshal. The mayor and the president made him the first visit, and he, for his part, paid like honour to the general and the prefect.

The installation being completed, the town was curious to see its bishop at work.

---

[*]Madame Baptistine and Madame Magloire serve to contrast the contemplative with the active life; their names, respectively, suggest the spiritual and the material.

2

M. MYRIEL BECOMES MONSEIGNEUR BIENVENU

THE BISHOP'S PALACE at D—— was contiguous to the hospital: the palace was a spacious and beautiful edifice, built of stone near the beginning of the last century by Monseigneur Henri Pujet, a doctor of theology of the Faculty of Paris, abbé of Simore, who was bishop of D—— in 1712. The palace was in truth a lordly dwelling: there was an air of grandeur about everything, the apartments of the bishop, the parlors, the chambers, the court of honour, which was very wide, with arched walks after the antique Florentine style; and a garden planted with magnificent trees.

The hospital was a low, narrow, one-story building with a small garden.

Three days after the bishop's advent he visited the hospital; when the visit was ended, he invited the director to oblige him by coming to the palace.

"Monsieur," he said to the director of the hospital, "how many patients have you?"

"Twenty-six, monseigneur."

"That is as I counted them," said the bishop.

"The beds," continued the director, "are very crowded."

"I noticed it."

"The wards are only small rooms, and are not easily ventilated."

"It seems so to me."

"And then, when the sun does shine, the garden is very small for the convalescents."

"That was what I was thinking."

"Of epidemics we have had typhus fever this year; two years ago we had military fever, sometimes one hundred patients, and we did not know what to do."

"That occurred to me."

"What can we do, monseigneur?" said the director; "we must be resigned."

This conversation took place in the dining gallery on the ground floor.

The bishop was silent a few moments: then he turned suddenly towards the director.

"Monsieur," he said, "how many beds do you think this hall alone would contain?"

"The dining hall of monseigneur!" exclaimed the director, stupefied.

The bishop ran his eyes over the hall, seemingly taking measure and making calculations.

"It will hold at least twenty beds," said he to himself; then raising his voice, he said:

"Listen, Monsieur Director, to what I have to say. There is evidently a mistake here. There are twenty-six of you in five or six small rooms: there are only three of us here, and space for sixty. There is a mistake, I tell you. You have my house and I have yours. Give me back my house; the palace is your home now."

Next day the twenty-six poor invalids were installed in the bishop's palace, and the bishop was in the hospital.

M. Myriel had no property, his family having been impoverished by the revolution. His sister had a life income of five hundred francs which in the vicarage sufficed for her personal needs. M. Myriel received from the government as bishop a salary of fifteen thousand francs.

Bishop Myriel receives a salary of 15,000 francs a year. Instead of tithing—giving 10 percent of his income to the poor—he gives them 90 percent, carefully accounted for in his household budget.

Mademoiselle Baptistine accepted this arrangement with entire submission; for that saintly woman, M. Myriel was at once her brother and her bishop, her companion by ties of blood and her superior by ecclesiastical authority. She loved and venerated him unaffectedly; when he spoke, she obeyed; when he acted, she gave him her co-operation. Madame Magloire, however, their servant, grumbled a little. The bishop, as will be seen, had reserved but a thousand francs for himself; this, added to the income of Mademoiselle Baptistine, gave them a yearly independence of fifteen hundred francs, upon which the three old people subsisted.

Thanks, however, to the rigid economy of Madame Magloire, and the excellent management of Mademoiselle Baptistine, whenever a curate came to D——, the bishop found means to extend to him his hospitality.

About three months after the installation, the bishop said one day, "With all this money I have to scrimp a good deal." "I think so too," said Madame Magloire: "Monseigneur has not even asked for the sum due him by the department for his carriage expenses in town, and in his circuits in the diocese. It was formerly the custom with all bishops."

"Yes!" said the bishop; "you are right, Madame Magloire."

He made his application.

Some time afterwards the conseil-général took his claim into consideration and voted him an annual stipend of three thousand francs under this head: "Allowance to the bishop for carriage expenses, and travelling expenses for pastoral visits."

The bourgeoisie of the town complained vociferously and a senator of the empire, formerly a member of the Council of Five Hundred, formerly in favor of the Eighteenth Brumaire and now provided with a rich senatorial seat near D——, wrote to M. Bigot de Préameneu, Minister of Public Worship, a fault-finding confidential epistle,[1] from which we make the following extract:—

"Carriage expenses! What can he want it for in a town of fewer than 4000 inhabitants? Expenses of pastoral visits! And what good do they do, in the first place; and then, how is it possible to travel by post in this mountain region? There are no roads; he can go only on horseback. Even the bridge over the Durance at Château-Arnoux is scarcely passable for oxcarts. These priests are always so; greedy and miserly. This one played the good apostle at the outset: now he acts like the rest; he must have a carriage and post-chaise. He must have luxury like the former bishops. Bah! this whole priesthood! Monsieur le Comte, things will never be better till the emperor delivers us from these macaroni priests. Down with the pope! (Relations with Rome were becoming tense.) As for me, I am for Cæsar alone," etc., etc., etc.

This application, on the other hand, pleased Madame Magloire exceedingly. "Good," said she to Mademoiselle Baptistine; "Monseigneur began with others, but he has found at last that he must end by taking care of himself. He has arranged all his charities, and so now here are three thousand francs for us."

Bishop Myriel drafts and gives to his sister, who had hoped for a little more comfort, a budget for his "carriage expenses": all of this extra money will be given to the poor.

Such was the budget of M. Myriel.

In regard to the official perquisites, payments for marriage licenses, dispensations, private baptisms, and preaching, consecrations of churches or chapels, marriages, etc., the bishop collected them from the wealthy with all the more determination because he dispensed them to the poor.

In a short time donations of money began to come in; those who had and those who had not, knocked at the bishop's door; some came to receive alms and others to bestow them, and in less than a year he had become the treasurer of all the benevolent, and the dispenser to all the needy. Large sums passed through his hands; but nothing could make him change his simple way of life, nor indulge in any luxuries.

On the contrary, as there is always more misery among the lower classes than there is humanity in the higher, everything was given away, so to speak, before it was received, like water on thirsty soil; it was well that money came to him, for he never kept any; and besides he robbed himself. It being the custom that all bishops should put their baptismal names at the head of their orders and pastoral letters, the poor people of the district had chosen by a sort of affectionate instinct, from among the names of the bishop, that which was expressive to them, and they always called him Monseigneur Bienvenu. We shall follow their example and shall call him thus; besides, this pleased him. "I like this name," said he; "Bienvenu counterbalances Monseigneur."

We do not claim that the portrait which we present here is plausible; we say only that it resembles him.

3

A DIFFICULT DIOCESE
FOR A GOOD BISHOP

THE BISHOP, after converting his carriage into alms, none the less regularly made his round of visits, and in the diocese of D—— this was a wearisome task. There was very little plain, a good deal of mountain; and hardly any roads, as a matter of course; thirty-two curacies, forty-one vicarages, and two hundred and eighty-five sub-curacies. To visit all these is a great labour, but the bishop went through with it. He travelled on foot in his own neighbourhood, in a cart when he was in the plains, and in a *cacolet,* a basket strapped on the back of a mule, when in the mountains. The two women usually accompanied him, but when the journey was too difficult for them he went alone.

One day he arrived at Senez, formerly the seat of a bishopric, mounted on an ass. His purse was very empty at the time, and would not permit any better conveyance. The mayor of the city came to receive him at the gate of the episcopal residence, and saw him dismount from his ass with astonishment and mortification. Several of the citizens stood near by, laughing. "Monsieur Mayor," said the bishop, "and Messieurs citizens, I see what astonishes you; you think that it shows a good deal of pride for a poor priest to use the same conveyance which was used by Jesus Christ. I have done it from necessity, I assure you, and not from vanity."

In his visits he was indulgent and gentle, and preached less than he talked. He never used far-fetched reasons or examples. To the inhabitants of one region he would cite the example of a neighbouring region. In the cantons* where the necessitous were treated with severity he would say, "Look at the people of Briançon. They have given to the poor, and to widows and orphans, the right to mow their meadows three days before any one else. When their houses are in ruins they rebuild them without cost. And so it is a country blessed of God. For a whole century they have not had a single murderer."

In villages where the people were greedy for gain at harvest time he would say, "Look at Embrun. If a father of a family, at harvest time, has his sons in the army, and his daughters at service in the city, and he is sick, the priest recommends him in his sermons, and on Sunday, after mass,

---

*Created as an administrative unit in 1789, a *canton* (roughly equivalent to a township) is larger than a *commune* (municipality) and smaller than an *arrondissement* (roughly equivalent to a county, and a subdivision of a *département*).

the whole population of the village, men, women, and children, go into the poor man's field and harvest his crop, and put the straw and the grain into his granary." To families divided by questions of property and inheritance, he would say, "See the mountaineers of Devolny, a country so wild that the nightingale is not heard there once in fifty years. Well now, when the father dies, in a family, the boys go away to seek their fortunes, and leave the property to the girls, so that they may get husbands." In those cantons where people liked to sue each other, and where the farmers were ruining themselves paying for notarized documents, he would say, "Look at those good peasants of the valley of Queyras. There are three thousand souls there. Why, it is like a little republic! Neither judge nor constable is known there. The mayor does everything. He taxes each one according to his judgment, resolves their disputes without charge, distributes their patrimony without fees, gives judgment without expense; and he is obeyed, because he is a just man among simple-hearted men." In the villages which he found without a schoolmaster, he would again refer to the valley of Queyras. "Do you know how they do?" he would say. "As a little district of twelve or fifteen houses cannot always support a teacher, they have schoolmasters that are paid by the whole valley, who go around from village to village, passing a week in this place, and ten days in that, and give instruction. These masters attend the fairs, where I have seen them. They are known by quills which they wear in their hatband. Those who teach only how to read have one quill; those who teach reading and arithmetic have two; and those who teach reading, arithmetic, and Latin, have three; the latter are esteemed great scholars. But what a shame to be ignorant! Do like the people of Queyras."

In such fashion would he talk, gravely and paternally, in default of examples he would invent parables, going straight to his object, with few phrases and many images, which was the very eloquence of Jesus Christ, convincing and persuasive.

4

GOOD WORKS THAT MATCH THE WORDS

His conversation was affable and pleasant. He adapted himself to the capacity of the two old women who lived with him, but when he laughed, it was the laugh of a schoolboy.

Madame Magloire usually called him *Your Greatness*. One day he rose from his armchair, and went to his library for a book. It was upon one of the upper shelves, and as the bishop was rather short, he could not reach it.

"Madame Magloire," said he, "bring me a chair. My greatness does not extend to this shelf."

When soliciting aid for any charity, he was not silenced by a refusal; he was at no loss for words that would set the hearers thinking. One day, he was receiving alms for the poor in a parlour in the city, where the Marquis of Champtercier, who was old, rich, and miserly, was present. The marquis managed to be, at the same time, an ultra-royalist and an ultra-Voltairean, a species of which he was not the only representative.* The bishop coming to him in turn, touched his arm and said, "Monsieur le Marquis, you must give me something." The marquis turned and answered drily, "Monseigneur, I have my own poor." "Give them to me," said the bishop.

One day he preached this sermon in the cathedral:——

"My very dear brethren, my good friends, there are in France thirteen hundred and twenty thousand peasants' cottages that have but three openings; eighteen hundred and seventeen thousand that have two, the door and one window; and finally, three hundred and forty-six thousand cabins, with only one opening—the door. And this is in consequence of what is called the excise upon doors and windows. In these poor families, among the aged women and the little children, dwelling in these huts, how abundant is fever and disease? Alas! God gives light to men; the law sells it. I do not blame the law, but I bless God. In Isère, in Var, and in the Upper and the Lower Alps, the peasants have not even wheelbarrows, they carry the manure on their backs; they have no candles, but burn pine knots, and bits of rope soaked in pitch. And the same is the case all through the upper part of Dauphiné. They make bread once in six months, and bake it by burning dried cow patties. In the winter it becomes so hard that they cut it up with an axe, and soak it for twenty-four hours, before they can eat it. My brethren, be compassionate; behold how much suffering there is around you."

Moreover, his manners with the rich were the same as with the poor.

He condemned nothing hastily, or without taking account of circumstances. He would say, "Let us see the way in which the fault came to pass."

Being, as he smilingly described himself, a recovering sinner, he had none of the inaccessibility of a rigorist, and boldly professed, even under the frowning eyes of the ferociously virtuous, a doctrine that may be summed up more or less as follows:—

"Man has a body which is at once his burden and his temptation. He drags it along, and yields to it.

"He ought to watch over it, to keep it in bounds; to repress it, and to obey it only at the last extremity. It may be wrong to obey even then, but if so, the fault is venial. It is a fall, but a fall upon the knees, which may end in prayer.

"To be a saint is the exception; to be upright is the rule. Err, falter, sin, but be upright.

---

*An ultra-royalist believes that kings rule by God's will; a Voltairean is a Deist, who believes that God does not intervene in human affairs.

"To commit the least possible sin is the law for man. To live without sin is the dream of an angel. Everything terrestrial is subject to sin. Sin is like gravitational force."

When he heard many exclaiming, and expressing great indignation against anything, "Oh! oh!" he would say, smiling. "It would seem that this is a great crime, of which they are all guilty. How frightened hypocrisy hastens to defend itself, and to get under cover."

He was indulgent towards women, and towards the poor, upon whom the weight of society falls most heavily; and said: "The faults of women, children, and servants, of the feeble, the indigent and the ignorant, are the faults of their husbands, fathers, and masters, of the strong, the rich, and the wise." At other times, he said, "Teach the ignorant as much as you can; society is culpable in not providing a free education for all and it must answer for the night which it produces.* If the soul is left in darkness, sins will be committed. The guilty one is not he who commits the sin, but he who causes the darkness."

As we see, he had a strange and peculiar way of judging things. I suspect that he acquired it from the Gospel.

In company one day he heard an account of a criminal case that was about to be tried. A miserable man, through love for a woman and for the child she had borne him, had been making false coin, his means being exhausted. At that time counterfeiting was still punished with death. The woman was arrested for passing the first coin that he had made. She was held a prisoner, but there was no evidence against her lover. She alone could testify against him, and convict him by her confession. She denied his guilt. They insisted, but she was obstinate in her denial. In this state of the case, the *procureur du roi* devised a shrewd plan.† He represented to her that her lover was unfaithful, and by means of fragments of letters skilfully put together, succeeded in persuading the unfortunate woman that she had a rival, and that this man had deceived her. At once exasperated by jealousy, she denounced her lover, confessed all, and proved his guilt. He was to be tried in a few days, at Aix, with his accomplice, and his conviction was certain. The story was told, and everybody was in ecstasy at the adroitness of the officer. In bringing jealousy into play he had brought truth to light by means of anger, and justice had sprung from revenge. The bishop listened to all this in silence. When it was finished he asked:

"Where are this man and woman to be tried?"

"At the Circuit Court."

"And where is the *procureur du roi* to be tried?"

---

*Myriel believes in universal, free primary education; until the Guizot Law of 1833, some 38 percent of French communes had no primary schools at all. In 1870, about 30 percent of peasants were still illiterate.

†The prosecuting attorney uses libel, slander, and forgery to persuade a woman to denounce her lover; he is more criminal than the man he condemns.

A tragic event occurred at D——. A man had been condemned to death for murder. The unfortunate prisoner was a poorly educated, but not entirely ignorant man, who had been a performer at fairs, and a public letterwriter. The people were greatly interested in the trial. The evening before the day fixed for the execution of the condemned, the almoner of the prison fell ill. A priest was needed to attend the prisoner in his last moments. The curé was sent for, but he refused to go, saying, "That does not concern me. I have nothing to do with such drudgery, or with that mountebank; besides, I am sick myself; and moreover it is not my place." When this reply was reported to the bishop, he said, "The curé is right. It is not his place, it is mine."

He went, on the instant, to the prison, went down into the dungeon of the "mountebank," called him by his name, took him by the hand, and talked with him. He passed the whole day with him forgetful of food and sleep, praying to God for the soul of the condemned, and exhorting the condemned to join with him. He spoke to him the best truths, which are the simplest. He was father, brother, friend; bishop for blessing only. He taught him everything by encouraging and consoling him. This man would have died in despair. Death, for him, was like an abyss. Standing shivering upon the dreadful brink, he recoiled with horror. He was not ignorant enough to be indifferent. The terrible shock of his condemnation had in some sort broken here and there that partition which separates us from the mystery of things beyond, and which we call life. Through these fatal breaches, he was constantly looking beyond this world, and he could see nothing but darkness; the bishop showed him the light.

On the morrow when they came for the poor man, the bishop was with him. He followed him, and showed himself to the eyes of the crowd in his violet camail,* with his bishop's cross about his neck, side by side with the miserable being, who was bound with cords.

He mounted the cart with him, he ascended the scaffold with him. The sufferer, so gloomy and so horror-stricken in the evening, was now radiant with hope. He felt that his soul was reconciled, and he trusted in God. The bishop embraced him, and at the moment when the axe was about to fall, he said to him, "whom man kills, him God restoreth to life, whom his brethren put away, he findeth the Father. Pray, believe, enter into life! The Father is there." When he descended from the scaffold, something in his look made the people fall back. It would be hard to say which was the most wonderful, his paleness or his serenity. As he entered the humble dwelling which he smilingly called his *palace,* he said to his sister, "I have been officiating pontifically."†

As the most sublime things are often least comprehended, there were those in the city who said, in commenting upon the bishop's conduct that it was affectation, but such ideas were confined to the upper classes. The

---

*A *camail* is a blue or purple ornament worn by a bishop over his vestments.
†By "pontifically," Myriel means "as a bishop should: humbling himself to exalt God."

people, who do not look for unworthy motives in holy works, admired and were softened.

As to the bishop, the sight of the guillotine was a shock to him, from which it was long before he recovered.

The scaffold, indeed, when it is prepared and set up, has the effect of a hallucination. We may be indifferent to the death penalty, and may not declare ourselves, yes or no, so long as we have not seen a guillotine with our own eyes. But when we see one, the shock is violent, and we are compelled to decide and take part, for or against. Some admire it, like Le Maistre; others execrate it, like Beccaria.[2] The guillotine is the embodiment of the law; it is called the Avenger; it is not neutral and does not permit you to remain neutral. He who sees it quakes with the most mysterious of tremblings. All social questions set up their points of interrogation about this axe. The scaffold is vision. The scaffold is not a mere frame, the scaffold is not a machine, the scaffold is not an inert piece of mechanism made of wood, of iron, and of ropes. It seems to have an indefinable, sinister life of its own, of whose origin we can have no idea; one would say that this frame can see, that this machine can hear, that this mechanism can understand; that this wood, this iron, and these ropes, have a will. In the fearful reverie into which its presence casts the soul, the awe-inspiring apparition of the scaffold blends with its horrid work. The scaffold becomes the accomplice of the executioner; it devours, it eats flesh, and it drinks blood. The scaffold is a sort of monster created by the judge and the workman, a spectre which seems to live with a kind of unspeakable life, drawn from all the death which it has wrought.

Thus the impression was horrible and deep, on the morrow of the execution, and for many days, the bishop appeared to be overwhelmed. The almost violent calm of the fatal moment had disappeared; the phantom of social justice took possession of him. He, who ordinarily looked back upon all his actions with a satisfaction so radiant, now seemed to be a subject of self-reproach. At times he would talk to himself, and in an undertone mutter dismal monologues. One evening his sister overheard and wrote down the following: "I did not believe that it could be so monstrous. It is wrong to be so absorbed in the divine law as not to perceive the human law. Death belongs to God alone. By what right do men touch that unknown thing?"

With the lapse of time these impressions faded away, and were probably effaced. Nevertheless it was remarked that the bishop ever after avoided passing by the public square where executions were carried out.

M. Myriel could be called at all hours to the bedside of the sick and the dying. He well knew that there was his highest duty and his greatest work. Widowed or orphan families had no need to send for him; he came by himself. He would sit silent for long hours by the side of a man who had lost the wife whom he loved, or of a mother who had lost her child. As he knew the time for silence, he knew also the time for speech. Oh, admirable consoler! he did not seek to drown grief in oblivion, but to exalt and to dignify it by hope. He would say, "Be careful of the way in which you think of the dead. Think not of what might have been. Look steadfastly and you shall see the living glory of your well-beloved dead in the depths of heaven." He believed that faith is healthful. He sought to counsel and to calm the despairing man by pointing out to him the man of resignation, and to transform the grief which looks down into the grave by showing it the grief which looks up to the stars.

His room was large, and rather difficult to warm in bad weather. As wood is very dear at D——, he conceived the idea of having a room partitioned off from the cow-stable with a tight plank ceiling. In the coldest weather he passed his evenings there, and called it his *winter parlour.*

In this winter parlour, as in the dining-room, the only furniture was a square white wooden table, and four straw chairs. The dining-room, however, was furnished with an old sideboard stained pink. A similar sideboard, suitably draped with white linen and imitation lace, served for the altar which decorated the oratory.

His rich penitents and the pious women of D—— had often contributed the money for a beautiful new altar for monseigneur's oratory; he had always taken the money and given it to the poor. "The most beautiful of altars," said he, "is the soul of an unfortunate man who is comforted and thanks God."

In his oratory he had two straw prayer-stools, and an armchair, also of straw, in the bedroom. When he happened to have seven or eight visitors at once, the prefect, or the general, or the general staff of the regiment in the garrison, or some of the pupils of the little seminary, he was obliged to go to the stable for the chairs that were in the winter parlour, to the oratory for the prie-dieu, and to the bedroom for the armchair; in this way he could get together as many as eleven seats for his visitors. As each new visitor arrived, a room was stripped.

It happened sometimes that there were twelve; then the bishop concealed the embarrassment of the situation by standing before the fire if it were winter, or by walking in the garden if it were summer.

We must confess that he still retained of what he had formerly, six silver dishes and a silver soup ladle, which Madame Magloire contemplated every day with new joy as they shone on the coarse, white, linen table-cloth. And as we are drawing the portrait of the Bishop of D—— just as he was, we must add that he had said, more than once, "It would be difficult for me to give up eating from silver."

With this silver ware should be counted two large, massive silver candlesticks which he inherited from a great-aunt. These candlesticks held two wax-candles, and their place was upon the bishop's mantel. When he had any one to dinner, Madame Magloire lighted the two candles and placed the two candlesticks upon the table.

There was in the bishop's chamber, at the head of his bed, a small cupboard in which Madame Magloire placed the six silver dishes and the great ladle every evening. But the key was never taken out of it.

Not a door in the house had a lock. The door of the dining-room which, we have mentioned, opened into the cathedral grounds, was formerly loaded with bars and bolts like the door of a prison. The bishop had had all this iron-work taken off, and the door, by night as well as by day, was closed only with a latch. The passer-by, whatever might be the hour, could open it with a simple push. At first the two women had been very much troubled at the door being never locked; but Monseigneur de D—— said to them: "Have bolts on your own doors, if you like." They shared his confidence at last, or at least acted as if they shared it. Madame Magloire alone had occasional attacks of fear. As to the bishop, the reason for this is explained, or at least pointed at in these three lines written by him in the margin of a Bible: "This is the shade of meaning; the door of a physician should never be closed; the door of a priest should always be open."

In another book, entitled *Philosophie de la Science Medicale,* he wrote this further note: "Am I not a physician as well as they? I also have my patients; first I have theirs, whom they call the sick; and then I have my own, whom I call the unfortunate."

Yet again he had written: "Ask not the name of him who asks you for a bed. It is especially he whose name is a burden to him, who has need of an asylum."

It occurred to a worthy curé, I am not sure whether it was the curé of Couloubroux or the curé of Pomprierry, to ask him one day probably at the instigation of Madame Magloire, if monseigneur were quite sure that there was not a degree of imprudence in leaving his door, day and night, at the mercy of whoever might wish to enter, and if he did not fear that some evil would befall a house so poorly defended. The bishop touched him gently on the shoulder, and said: *"Nisi Dominus custodierit domum, in vanum vigilant qui custodiunt eam."**

And then he changed the subject.

He very often said: "There is a bravery for the priest as well as a bravery for the colonel of dragoons." "Only," added he, "ours should be quiet."

5 (7)

CRAVATTE

THIS IS THE PROPER PLACE for an incident which we must not omit, for it is one of those which most clearly shows what manner of man the Bishop of D—— was.

After the destruction of the band of Gaspard Bès, which had infested the gorges of Ollivolles, one of his lieutenants, Cravatte, took refuge in the

---

*Unless God protects a house, they who guard it watch in vain.

mountains. He concealed himself for some time with his bandits, the remnant of the troop of Gaspard Bès, in the county of Nice, then made his way to Piedmont, and suddenly reappeared in France in the neighbourhood of Barcelonnette. He was first seen at Jauziers, then at Tuiles. He concealed himself in the caverns of the Joug de l'Aigle, from which he made descents upon the hamlets and villages by the ravines of Ubaye and Ubayette.

He even pushed as far as Embrun, and one night broke into the cathedral and stripped the sacristy. His robberies devastated the country. The gendarmes were put upon his trail, but in vain. He always escaped; sometimes by forcible resistance. He was a bold wretch. In the midst of all this terror, the bishop arrived. He was making his visit to Chastelar. The mayor came to see him and urged him to turn back. Cravatte held the mountains as far as Arche and beyond; it would be dangerous even with an escort. It would expose three or four poor gendarmes to useless danger.

"And so," said the bishop, "I intend to go without an escort."

"Do not think of such a thing," exclaimed the mayor.

"I think so much of it, that I absolutely refuse the gendarmes, and I am going to start in an hour."

"But, monseigneur, the brigands?"

"True," said the bishop, "I am thinking of that. You are right. I may meet them. They too must need some one to tell them of the goodness of God."

"Monseigneur, but it is a band! A pack of wolves!"

"Monsieur Mayor, perhaps Jesus has made me the keeper of that very flock. Who knows the ways of providence?"

"Monseigneur, they will rob you."

"I have nothing."

"They will kill you."

"A simple old priest who passes along muttering his prayer? No, no; what good would it do them?"

"Oh, my good sir, suppose you should meet them!"

"I should ask them for alms for my poor."

"Monseigneur, do not go. In the name of heaven! You are risking your life."

"Monsieur Mayor," said the bishop, "that is just it. I am not in the world to care for my life, but for souls."

He would not be dissuaded. He set out, accompanied only by a child, who offered to go as his guide. His obstinacy was the talk of the country, and all dreaded the result.

He would not take along his sister, or Madame Magloire. He crossed the mountain on a mule, met no one, and arrived safe and sound among his "good friends" the shepherds. He remained there a fortnight, preaching, administering the holy rites, teaching and exhorting. When he was about to leave, he resolved to chant a Te Deum with pontifical ceremonies. He talked with the curé about it. But what could be done? There was no episcopal furniture. They could only place at his disposal a paltry village sacristy with a few old robes of worn-out damask, trimmed with imitation braids.

"No matter," said the bishop. "Monsieur le curé, at the sermon announce our Te Deum. That will take care of itself."

All the neighbouring churches were ransacked, but the assembled magnificence of these humble parishes could not have suitably clothed a single cathedral singer.

While they were in this embarrassment, a large chest was brought to the parsonage, and left for the bishop by two unknown horsemen, who immediately rode away. The chest was opened; it contained a cope of cloth of gold, a mitre ornamented with diamonds, an archbishop's cross, a magnificent crosier, all the pontifical raiment stolen a month before from the treasures of Our Lady of Embrun. In the chest was a paper on which were written these words: "Cravatte to Monseigneur Bienvenu."

"I said that it would take care of itself," said the bishop. Then he added with a smile: "To him who is contented with a curé's surplice, God sends an archbishop's cope."

"Monseigneur," murmured the curé, with a shake of the head and a smile, "God—or the devil."

The bishop looked steadily upon the curé, and replied with authority: "God!"

When he returned to Chastelar, all along the road, the people came with curiosity to see him. At the parsonage in Chastelar he found Mademoiselle Baptistine and Madame Magloire waiting for him, and he said to his sister, "Well, was I not right? the poor priest went among those poor mountaineers with empty hands; he comes back with hands filled. I went forth placing my trust in God alone; I bring back the treasures of a cathedral."

In the evening before going to bed he said further: "Have no fear of robbers or murderers. Such dangers are without, and are but petty. We should fear ourselves. Prejudices are the real robbers; vices the real murderers. The great dangers are within us. What matters it what threatens our heads or our purses? Let us think only of what threatens our souls."

Then turning to his sister: "My sister, a priest should never take any precaution against a neighbour. What his neighbour does, God permits. Let us confine ourselves to prayer to God when we think that danger hangs over us. Let us beseech him, not for ourselves, but that our brother may not fall into crime on our account."

To sum up, events were rare in his life. We relate those we know of; but usually he spent his life in always doing the same things at the same hours. A month of his year was like an hour of his day.

As to what became of the "treasures" of the Cathedral of Embrun, it would embarrass us to be questioned on that point. There were among them very fine things, and very tempting, and very good to steal for the benefit of the unfortunate. Stolen they had already been by others. Half the work was done; it only remained to change the course of the theft, and to make it turn to the side of the poor. We can say nothing more on the subject. Except that, there was found among the bishop's papers a rather obscure note, which is possibly connected with this affair, that reads as follows: *The question is, whether this ought to be returned to the cathedral or to the hospital.*

6 (10)

THE BISHOP IN THE PRESENCE
OF AN UNKNOWN LIGHT

A LITTLE WHILE later, the bishop performed an act, which the whole town thought far more perilous than his excursion across the mountains infested by the bandits.

In the country near D——, there was a man who lived alone. This man, to state the startling fact without preface, had been a member of the National Convention.[3] His name was G——.

The little circle of D—— spoke of the conventionist with a certain sort of horror. A conventionist, think of it; that was in the time when folks thee-and-thoued one another, and said "citizen." This man came very near being a monster; he had not exactly voted for the execution of the king, but almost; he was half a regicide, and had been a terrible creature altogether. How was it, then, on the return of the legitimate princes, that they had not arraigned this man before the provost court?* He would not have been beheaded, perhaps, but even if clemency were necessary he might have been banished for life; in fact, an example, etc., etc. Besides, he was an atheist, as all those people are. Babblings of geese against a vulture!

But was this G—— a vulture? Yes, if one should judge him by the savageness of his solitude. As he had not voted for the king's execution, he was not included in the sentence of exile, and could remain in France.

He lived about an hour's walk from the town, far from any hamlet or road, in a secluded ravine of a very wild valley. It was said he had a sort of resting-place there, a hole, a den. He had no neighbours or even passers-by. Since he had lived there the path which led to the place had become overgrown, and people spoke of it as of the house of a hangman.

From time to time, however, the bishop reflectingly gazed upon the horizon at the spot where a clump of trees indicated the ravine of the aged conventionist, and he would say: "There lives a soul which is alone." And in the depths of his thought he would add "I owe him a visit."

But this idea, we must confess, though it appeared natural at first, yet, after a few moments' reflection, seemed strange, impracticable, and almost repulsive. For at heart he shared the general impression and the

---

*The Provost's Court was a tribunal that passed judgment on the accused without giving them the right of appeal; it served Royalist vengeance after Napoléon's fall in 1815.

conventionist inspired him, he knew not how, with that sentiment which is the fringe of hatred, and which the word "aversion" so well expresses.

However, the shepherd should not recoil from the diseased sheep. Ah! but what a sheep!

The good bishop was perplexed: sometimes he walked in that direction, but he returned.

At last, one day the news was circulated in the town that the young herdsboy who served the conventionist G—— in his retreat, had come for a doctor; that the old wretch was dying, that he was becoming paralyzed, and could not live through the night. "Thank God!" added many.

The bishop took his cane, put on his overcoat, because his cassock was badly worn, as we have said, and besides the night wind was evidently rising, and set out.

The sun was setting; it had nearly touched the horizon when the bishop reached the accursed spot. He felt a certain quickening of the pulse as he drew near the den. He strode over a ditch, crossed through a hedge, lifted a pole out of his way, found himself in a dilapidated garden, and after a bold advance across the open ground, suddenly, behind some high brushwood, he discovered the retreat.

It was a low, poverty-stricken hut, small and clean, with a little vine nailed up in front.

Before the door in an old chair on rollers, a peasant's armchair, there sat a man with white hair, looking with smiling gaze upon the setting sun.

The young herdsboy stood near him, handing him a bowl of milk.

While the bishop was looking, the old man raised his voice.

"Thank you," he said, "I shall need nothing more;" and his smile changed from the sun to rest upon the boy.

The bishop stepped forward. At the sound of his footsteps the old man turned his head, and his face expressed as much surprise as one can feel after a long life.

"This is the first time since I have lived here," said he, "that I have had a visitor. Who are you, monsieur?"

"My name is Bienvenu-Myriel," the bishop replied.

"Bienvenu-Myriel? I have heard that name before. Are you he whom the people call Monseigneur Bienvenu?"

"I am."

The old man continued half-smiling. "Then you are my bishop?"

"A bit."

"Come in, monsieur."

The conventionist extended his hand to the bishop, who did not take it. He only said:

"I am glad to find that I have been misinformed. You do not appear to me very ill."

"Monsieur," replied the old man, "I shall soon be better."

He paused and said:

"I shall be dead in three hours."

Then he continued:

"I am something of a physician; I know the steps by which death approaches; yesterday my feet only were cold; to-day the cold has crept to my knees, now it has reached the waist; when it touches the heart all will be over. The sunset is lovely, is it not? I had myself wheeled out to get a final look at nature. You can speak to me; that will not tire me. You do well to come to see a man who is dying. It is good that these moments should have witnesses. Every one has his fancy; I should like to live until the dawn, but I know I have scarcely life for three hours. It will be night, but no matter: to end is a very simple thing. One does not need morning for that. So be it; I shall die in the starlight."

The old man turned towards the herdsboy:

"Little one, go to bed: thou didst watch the other night: thou art weary."

The child went into the hut.

The old man followed him with his eyes and added, as if speaking to himself: "While he is sleeping, I shall lie: the two slumbers keep fit company."

The bishop was not as much affected as he might have been: it was not his idea of a godly death; we must tell all for the little inconsistencies of great souls should be mentioned; he who had laughed so heartily at "His Highness," was still slightly shocked at not being called monseigneur, and was almost tempted to answer "citizen." He felt a desire to use the brusque familiarity common enough with doctors and priests, but which was not customary with him.

This conventionist after all, this representative of the people, had been a power on the earth; and perhaps for the first time in his life the bishop felt himself in a mood to be severe. The conventionist, however, watched him with a modest cordiality, in which perhaps might have been discerned that humility which is befitting to one so nearly dust unto dust.

The bishop, on his side, although he generally kept himself free from curiosity, which he thought was almost offensive, could not avoid examining the conventionist with an attention for which, as it had not its source in sympathy, his conscience would have condemned him as to any other man; but a conventionist he looked upon as an outlaw, even beyond the law of charity.

G——, with his self-possessed manner, erect figure, and resonant voice, was one of those noble octogenarians who are the marvel of the physiologist. The revolution produced many of these men equal to the epoch: one felt that here was a man who had endured ordeals. Though so near death, he preserved all the appearance of health. His bright glances, his firm accent, and the muscular movements of his shoulders seemed almost sufficient to disconcert death. Azrael, the Mahometan angel of the sepulchre, would have turned back, thinking he had mistaken the door. G—— appeared to be dying because he wished to die. There was freedom in his agony; his legs only were paralysed; his feet were cold and dead, but his head lived in full power of life and light. At this solemn moment G—— seemed like the king in the oriental tale, flesh above and marble below.

The bishop seated himself upon a stone near by. The beginning of their conversation was *ex abrupto*:

"I congratulate you," he said, in a tone of reprimand. "At least you did not vote for the execution of the king."

The conventionist did not seem to notice the bitter emphasis placed upon the words "at least." The smiles vanished from his face and he replied:

"Do not congratulate me too much, monsieur; I did vote for the destruction of the tyrant."

And the tone of austerity confronted the tone of severity.

"What do you mean?" asked the bishop.

"I mean that man has a tyrant, Ignorance. I voted for the abolition of that tyrant. That tyrant has begotten royalty, which is authority springing from the False, while science is authority springing from the True. Man should be governed by science."

"And conscience," added the bishop.

"The same thing: conscience is innate knowledge that we have."

Monsieur Bienvenu listened with some amazement to this language, novel as it was to him.

The conventionist went on:

"As to Louis XVI: I said no. I do not believe that I have the right to kill a man, but I feel it a duty to exterminate evil. I voted for the downfall of the tyrant; that is to say, for the abolition of prostitution for woman, of slavery for man, of night for the child. In voting for the republic I voted for that: I voted for fraternity, for harmony, for light. I assisted in casting down prejudices and errors: their downfall brings light! We caused the old world to fall; the old world, a vase of misery, overturned, becomes an urn of joy to the human race."

"Joy alloyed," said the bishop.

"You might say joy troubled, and, at present, after this fatal return of the past which we call 1814, joy disappeared.* Alas! the work was imperfect I admit; we demolished the ancient order of things physically, but not entirely in the idea. To destroy abuses is not enough; habits must be changed. The windmill has gone, but the Wind is there yet."

"You have demolished. To demolish may be useful, but I distrust a demolition effected in anger!"

"Justice has its anger, Monsieur Bishop, and the wrath of justice is an element of progress. Whatever may be said matters not, the French revolution is the greatest step forward taken by mankind since the advent of Christ; incomplete it may be, but it is sublime. It loosened all the secret bonds of society, it softened all hearts, it calmed, appeased, enlightened; it made the waves of civilisation flow over the earth; it was good. The French revolution is the consecration of humanity."

---

*Myriel feels the joy of political progress was tainted by revolutionary atrocities; the conventionist feels this joy was blasted by the Restoration of the monarchy in 1814.

The bishop could not help murmuring: "Yes, '93!"*

The conventionist raised himself in his chair with a solemnity well nigh mournful, and as nearly as a dying person could exclaim, he exclaimed:

"Ah! you are there! '93! I was expecting that. A cloud had been forming for fifteen hundred years; at the end of fifteen centuries it burst. You condemn the thunderbolt."

Without perhaps acknowledging it to himself, the bishop felt that something in him had been struck; however, he made the best of it, and replied:

"The judge speaks in the name of justice, the priest in the name of pity, which is only a more exalted justice. A thunderbolt should not be mistaken."

And he added, looking fixedly at the conventionist; "Louis XVII?"

The conventionist stretched out his hand and seized the bishop's arm.

"Louis XVII. Let us see! For whom do you weep?—for the innocent child? It is well; I weep with you. For the royal child? I ask time to reflect. To my view the brother of Cartouche, an innocent child, hung by a rope under his arms in the Place de Grève till he died, for the sole crime of being the brother of Cartouche, is no less sad sight than the grandson of Louis XV; an innocent child, murdered in the tower of the Temple for the sole crime of being the grandson of Louis XV."

"Monsieur," said the bishop, "I dislike this coupling of names."

"Cartouche or Louis XV; for which are you concerned?"

There was a moment of silence; the bishop regretted almost that he had come, and yet he felt strangely and inexplicably moved.

The conventionist resumed: "Oh, Monsieur Priest! you do not love the harshness of the truth, but Christ loved it. He took a scourge and purged the temple; his flashing whip was a harsh speaker of truths; when he said, *'Sinite parvulos,'* he made no distinctions among the little ones.† He was not pained at coupling the dauphin of Barabbas with the dauphin of Herod. Monsieur, innocence is its own crown! Innocence has only to act to be noble! She is as august in rags as in the fleur de lys."

"That is true," said the bishop, in a low tone.

"I repeat," continued the old man; "you have mentioned Louis XVII. Let us weep together for all the innocent, for all the martyrs, for all the children, for the low as well as for the high. I am one of them, but then, as I have told you, we must go further back than '93, and our tears must begin before Louis XVII. I will weep for the children of kings with you, if you will weep with me for the little ones of the people."

"I weep for all," said the bishop.

"Equally," exclaimed G———, "and if the balance inclines, let it be on the side of the people; they have suffered longer."

---

*Myriel counters the claim that the Revolution was "the consecration of humanity" by alluding to the Reign of Terror in 1793, when the King and Queen, and 20,000 others, were guillotined.

†The conventionist quotes Christ's "let the little children come unto Me," and implies that the class system under the monarchy invalidates the monarchy's claims to be truly Christian.

There was silence again, broken at last by the old man. He raised himself upon one elbow, took a pinch of his cheek between his thumb and his bent forefinger, as one does mechanically in questioning and forming an opinion, and addressed the bishop with a look full of all the energies of agony. It was almost an anathema.

"Yes, Monsieur, it is for a long time that the people have been suffering, and then, sir, that is not all; why do you come to question me and to speak to me of Louis XVII? I do not know you. Since I have been in this region I have lived within this plot alone, never passing beyond it, seeing none but this child who helps me. Your name, has, it is true, reached me faintly, and I must say with rather favorable reports, but that matters not. Adroit men have so many ways of imposing upon this good simple people. For instance I did not hear the sound of your carriage. You left it doubtless behind the thicket, down there at the branching of the road. You have told me that you were the bishop, but that tells me nothing about your moral personality. Now, then, I repeat my question—Who are you? You are a bishop, a prince of the church, one of those men who are covered with gold, with a coat of arms, and wealth, who have fat livings—the see of D——, fifteen thousand francs regular, ten thousand francs contingent, total twenty-five thousand francs—who have kitchens, who have retinues, who give good dinners, who eat moor-hens on Friday, who strut about in your gaudy coach, like peacocks, with lackeys before and lackeys behind, and who have palaces, and who roll in your carriages in the name of Jesus Christ who went bare-footed. You are a prelate; rents, palaces, horses, valets, a good table, all the pleasures of life, you have these like all the rest, and you enjoy them like all the rest; very well, but that says too much or not enough; that does not enlighten me as to your intrinsic worth, that which is peculiar to yourself, you who come probably with the claim of bringing me wisdom. To whom am I speaking? Who are you?"

The bishop bowed his head and replied, *"Vermis sum."*

"A worm of the earth in a carriage!" grumbled the old man.

It was the turn of the conventionist to be haughty, and of the bishop to be humble.

The bishop replied with mildness:

"Monsieur, be it so. But explain to me how my carriage, which is there a few steps behind the trees, how my good table and the moor-fowl that I eat on Friday, how my twenty-five thousand livres of income, how my palace and my lackeys prove that pity is not a virtue, that kindness is not a duty, and that '93 was not inexorable?"

The old man passed his hand across his forehead as if to dispel a cloud.

"Before answering you," said he, "I beg your pardon. I have done wrong, monsieur; you are in my house, you are my guest. I owe you courtesy. You are discussing my ideas; it is fitting that I confine myself to combating your reasoning. Your riches and your enjoyments are advantages that I have over you in the debate, but it is not in good taste to avail myself of them. I promise you to use them no more."

"I thank you," said the bishop.

G—— went on:

"Let us get back to the explanation that you asked of me. Where were we? What were you saying to me? that '93 was inexorable?"

"Inexorable, yes," said the bishop. "What do you think of Marat clapping his hands at the guillotine?"

"What do you think of Bossuet chanting the Te Deum over the dragonnades?"[4]

The answer was severe, but it reached its aim with the keenness of a dagger. The bishop was staggered, no reply presented itself; but it shocked him to hear Bossuet spoken of in that manner. The best men have their fetishes, and sometimes they feel vaguely wounded at the little respect that logic shows them.

The conventionist began to gasp; the agonising asthma, which mingles with the latest breath, made his voice broken; nevertheless, his soul yet appeared perfectly lucid in his eyes. He continued:

"Let us have a few more words here and there—I would like it. Outside of the revolution which, taken as a whole, is an immense human affirmation, '93, alas! is a reply. You think it inexorable, but the whole monarchy, monsieur? Carrier is a bandit; but what name do you give to Montrevel? Fouquier-Tainville is a wretch; but what is your opinion of Lamoignon Bâville? Maillard is frightful, but Saulx Tavannes, if you please? Le père Duchêne is ferocious, but what epithet will you furnish me for le père Letellier? Jourdan-Coupe-Tête is a monster, but less than the Marquis of Louvois. Monsieur, monsieur, I lament Marie Antoinette, arch-duchess and queen, but I lament also that poor Huguenot woman who, in 1685, under Louis le Grand, monsieur, while nursing her child, was stripped to the waist and tied to a post, while her child was held before her; her breast swelled with milk, and her heart with anguish; the little one, weak and famished, seeing the breast, cried with agony; and the executioner said to the woman, to the nursing mother, 'Recant!' giving her the choice between the death of her child and the death of her conscience. What say you to this Tantalus torture adapted to a mother? Monsieur, forget not this; the French revolution had its reasons. Its wrath will be pardoned by the future; its result is a better world. From its most terrible blows comes a caress for the human race. I must be brief. I must stop. I have too good a cause; and I am dying."

And, ceasing to look at the bishop, the old man completed his idea in these few tranquil words:

"Yes, the brutalities of progress are called revolutions. When they are over, this is recognised: that the human race has been harshly treated, but that it has advanced."

The conventionist thought that he had borne down successively one after the other all the inner defenses of the bishop. There was one left, however, and from this, the last resource of Monseigneur Bienvenu's resistance, came forth these words, in which nearly all the rudeness of the exordium reappeared.

"Progress must believe in God. The good cannot have an impious servitor. An atheist is an evil leader of the human race."

The old representative of the people did not answer. He was trembling. He looked up into the sky, and a tear gathered slowly in his eye. When the lid was full, the tear rolled down his livid cheek, and he said, almost stammering, low, and talking to himself, his eye lost in the depths:

"O thou! O ideal! thou alone dost exist!"

The bishop felt a kind of inexpressible emotion.

After brief silence, the old man raised his finger towards heaven, and said:

"The infinite exists. It is there. If the infinite had no *selfhood,* the *self* would be its limit; it would not be the infinite; in other words it would not be. But it is. Therefore it has a self. This *selfhood* of the infinite is God."

The dying man pronounced these last words in a loud voice, and with a shudder of ecstasy, as if he saw some one. When he ceased, his eyes closed. The effort had exhausted him. It was evident that he had lived through in one minute the few hours that remained to him. What he had said had brought him near to him who is in death. The last moment was at hand.

The bishop perceived it, time was pressing. He had come as a priest; from extreme coldness he had passed by degrees to extreme emotion; he looked upon those closed eyes, he took that old, wrinkled and icy hand, and drew closer to the dying man.

"This hour is the hour of God. Do you not think it would be a source of regret, if we should have met in vain?"

The conventionist re-opened his eyes. Seriousness mingled with shadow imprinted itself upon his face.

"Monsieur Bishop," said he with a deliberation which perhaps came still more from the dignity of his soul than from the ebb of his strength, "I have passed my life in meditation, study, and contemplation. I was sixty years old when my country called me, and ordered me to take part in her affairs. I obeyed. There were abuses, I fought them; there were tyrannies, I destroyed them; there were rights and principles, I proclaimed and confessed them. The soil was invaded, I defended it; France was threatened, I offered her my breast. I was not rich; I am poor. I was one of the masters of the state, the vaults of the bank were piled with specie, so that we had to strengthen the walls or they would have fallen under the weight of gold and of silver; I dined in the Rue de l'Arbre-Sec at twenty-two sous for the meal. I succoured the oppressed, I solaced the suffering. True, I tore the drapery from the altar; but it was to staunch the wounds of the country. I have always supported the forward march of the human race towards the light, and I have sometimes resisted a progress which was without pity. I have, on occasion, protected my own adversaries, your friends. There is at Peteghem in Flanders, at the very place where the Merovingian kings had their summer palace, a monastery of Urbanists, the Abbey of Sainte Claire in Beaulieu, which I saved in 1793, I have done my duty according to my strength, and the good that I could. After which I was hunted, hounded, pursued, persecuted, slandered, railed at, spit upon, cursed, proscribed. For many years now, with my white hairs, I have perceived that many people believed they had a right to despise me; to the poor, ignorant crowd I have the face of the damned, and I accept, hating no man myself, the isolation of hatred. Now I am eighty-six years old; I am about to die. What have you come to ask of me?"

"Your blessing," said the bishop. And he fell upon his knees.

When the bishop raised his head, the face of the old man had become august. He had expired.

The bishop went home deeply absorbed in ineffable thoughts. He spent the whole night in prayer. The next day, some persons, emboldened by curiosity, tried to talk with him of the conventionist G——; he merely pointed to Heaven.

From that moment he redoubled his tenderness and brotherly love for the weak and the suffering.

Every allusion to "that old scoundrel G——," threw him into a strange reverie. No one could say that the passage of that soul before his own, and the reflection of that grand conscience upon his own had not had its effect upon his approach to perfection.

BOOK TWO
THE FALL

1

THE EVENING AFTER A LONG DAY'S WALK

AN HOUR BEFORE SUNSET, on the evening of a day in the beginning of October, 1815, a man travelling afoot entered the little town of D——. The few persons who at this time were at their windows or their doors, regarded this traveller with apprehension. It would have been hard to find a passer-by more wretched in appearance. He was a man of middle height, burly and hardy, in the prime of life; he might have been forty-six or seven. A leather slouch cap half hid his face, bronzed by the sun and wind, and dripping with sweat. His hairy chest could be seen through the coarse yellow shirt which at the neck was fastened by a small silver anchor; he wore a cravat twisted like a rope; coarse blue trousers, worn and shabby, white on one knee, and with holes in the other; an old ragged grey smock, patched on one side with a piece of green cloth sewed with twine: upon his back was a well-filled knapsack, strongly buckled and quite new. In his hand he carried an enormous knotted stick: his stockingless feet were in hobnailed shoes; his hair was cropped and his beard long.

The sweat, the heat, his long walk, and the dust, added an indescribable squalor to his tattered appearance.

His hair was shorn, but bristly, for it had begun to grow a little and seemingly had not been cut for some time. Nobody knew him, he was evidently a traveller. Whence had he come? From the south—perhaps from the sea; for he was making his entrance into D—— by the same road by which, seven months before, the Emperor Napoleon went from Cannes to Paris.* This man must have walked all day long; for he appeared very weary. Some women of the old city which is at the lower part of the town, had seen him stop under the trees of the boulevard Gassendi, and drink at the fountain which is at the end of the promenade. He must have been very thirsty, for some children who followed him, saw him stop not two hundred steps further on and drink again at the fountain in the market-place.

When he reached the corner of the Rue Poichevert he turned to the left and went towards the mayor's office. He went in, and a quarter of an hour afterwards he came out.

The man raised his cap humbly and saluted a gendarme who was seated near the door, upon the stone bench which General Drouot mounted on

---

*Hugo makes Jean Valjean's life parallel the history of France: he is imprisoned during Napoléon's dictatorship, and hides in the convent during the rule of the reactionary Charles X; when he is free, France also is freer.

the fourth of March, to read to the terrified inhabitants of D—— the proclamation of the *Golfe Juan*.[5]

Without returning his salutation, the gendarme looked at him attentively, watched him for some distance, and then went into the city hall.

There was then in D——, a good inn called *La Croix de Colbas*. The traveller turned his steps towards this inn, which was the best in the place, and went at once into the kitchen, which opened out of the street. All the ranges were fuming, and a great fire was burning briskly in the chimney-place. Mine host, who was at the same time head cook, was going from the fireplace to the saucepans, very busy superintending an excellent dinner for some wagoners who were laughing and talking noisily in the next room. Whoever has travelled knows that nobody lives better than wagoners. A fat marmot, flanked by white partridges and gamecocks, was turning on a long spit before the fire; upon the ranges were cooking two large carps from Lake Lauzet, and a trout from Lake Alloz.

The host, hearing the door open, and a new-comer enter, said, without raising his eyes from his ovens——

"What will monsieur have?"

"Something to eat and lodging."

"Nothing more easy," said mine host, but on turning his head and taking an observation of the traveller, he added, "for pay."

The man drew from his pocket a large leather purse, and answered,

"I have money."

"Then," said mine host, "I am at your service."

The man put his purse back into his pocket, took off his knapsack and put it down hard by the door, and holding his stick in his hand, sat down on a low stool by the fire. D—— being in the mountains, the evenings of October are cold there.

However, as the host passed backwards and forwards, he kept a careful eye on the traveller.

"Is dinner almost ready?" said the man.

"Directly," said mine host.

While the new-comer was warming himself with his back turned, the worthy innkeeper, Jacquin Labarre, took a pencil from his pocket, and then tore off the corner of an old paper which he pulled from a little table near the window. On the margin he wrote a line or two, folded it, and handed the scrap of paper to a child, who appeared to serve him as lackey and scullion at the same time. The innkeeper whispered a word to the boy and he ran off in the direction of the mayor's office.

The traveller saw nothing of this.

He asked a second time: "Is dinner ready?"

"Yes; in a few moments," said the host.

The boy came back with the paper. The host unfolded it hurriedly, as one who is expecting an answer. He seemed to read with attention, then throwing his head on one side, thought for a moment. Then he took a step towards the traveller, who seemed drowned in disturbing thoughts.

"Monsieur," said he, "I cannot receive you."

The traveller half rose from his seat.

"Why? Are you afraid I shall not pay you, or do you want me to pay in advance? I have money, I tell you."

"It is not that."

"What then?"

"You have money——"

"Yes," said the man.

"And I," said the host; "I have no room."

"Well, put me in the stable," quietly replied the man.

"I cannot."

"Why?"

"Because the horses take all the room."

"Well," responded the man, "a corner in the garret; a truss of straw: we will see about that after dinner."

"I cannot give you any dinner."

This declaration, made in a measured but firm tone, appeared serious to the traveller. He got up.

"Ah, bah! but I am dying with hunger. I have walked since sunrise; I have travelled twelve leagues. I will pay, and I want something to eat."

"I have nothing," said the host.

The man burst into a laugh, and turned towards the fireplace and the ranges.

"Nothing! and all that?"

"All that is reserved."

"By whom?"

"By those persons, the wagoners."

"How many are there of them?"

"Twelve."

"There is enough there for twenty."

"They have ordered and paid for it all in advance."

The man sat down again and said, without raising his voice: "I am at an inn. I am hungry, and I shall stay."

The host bent down his ear, and said in a voice which made him tremble: "Go away!"

At these words the traveller, who was bent over, poking some embers in the fire with the iron-shod end of his stick, turned suddenly around, and opened his mouth, as if to reply, when the host looking steadily at him, added in the same low tone: "Stop, no more of that. Shall I tell you your name? your name is Jean Valjean, now shall I tell you *who* you are? When I saw you enter, I suspected something. I sent to the mayor's office, and here is the reply. Can you read?" So saying, he held towards him the open paper, which had just come from the mayor. The man cast a look upon it; the innkeeper, after a short silence, said: "It is my custom to be polite to all: Go!"

The man bowed his head, picked up his knapsack, and went out.

He took the main street; he walked at random, slinking near the houses like a sad and humiliated man: he did not once turn around. If he had turned, he would have seen the innkeeper of the *Croix de Colbas*, standing in his doorway with all his guests, and the passers-by gathered about him, speaking excitedly, and pointing him out; and from the looks of fear and distrust which were exchanged, he would have guessed that before long his arrival would be the talk of the whole town.

He saw nothing of all this: people overwhelmed with trouble do not look behind; they know only too well that misfortune follows them.

Jean Valjean wanders until he finds another tavern, but word of his criminal history has spread, and he is turned away there too. He asks to sleep in the prison, but is refused; he is driven from a private home at gunpoint, and refused even a glass of water. As night falls, he takes refuge in a small hut, but it proves to be a dog kennel, and when the dog returns, it bites and scratches him. Finally he meets an old woman in front of the church, and she directs him to Bishop Myriel by saying simply, "Knock at that door there."

It was about eight o'clock in the evening: as he did not know the streets, he walked at random.

So he came to the prefecture, then to the seminary; on passing by the Cathedral square, he shook his fist at the church.

At the corner of this square stands a printing-office; there were first printed the proclamations of the emperor, and the Imperial Guard to the army, brought from the island of Elba, and dictated by Napoleon himself.

Exhausted with fatigue, and hoping for nothing better, he lay down on a stone bench in front of this printing-office.

Just then an old woman came out of the church. She saw the man lying there in the dark and said:

"What are you doing there, my friend?"

He replied harshly, and with anger in his tone:

"You see, my good woman, I am going to sleep."

The good woman, who really merited the name, was Madame la Marquise de R——.

"Upon the bench?" said she.

"For nineteen years I have had a wooden mattress," said the man; "tonight I have a stone one."

"You have been a soldier?"

"Yes, my good woman, a soldier."

"Why don't you go to the inn?"

"Because I have no money."

"Alas!" said Madame de R—, "I have only four sous in my purse."

"Give them then." The man took the four sous, and Madame de R—— continued:

"You cannot find lodging for so little in an inn. But have you tried? You cannot pass the night so. You must be cold and hungry. They should give you lodging for charity."

"I have knocked at every door."

"Well, what then?"

"Everybody has driven me away."

The good woman touched the man's arm and pointed out to him on the other side of the square, a little low house beside the bishop's palace.

"You have knocked at every door?" she asked.

"Yes."

"Have you knocked at that one there?"

"No."

"Knock there."

2

PRUDENCE COMMENDED TO WISDOM

THAT EVENING, after his walk in the town, the Bishop of D—— remained quite late in his room. He was busy with his great work on Duty, which unfortunately remains incomplete.

At eight o'clock he was still at work, writing with some inconvenience on little slips of paper, with a large book open on his knees, when Madame Magloire, as usual, came in to take the silver from the cupboard near the bed. A moment after, the bishop, knowing that the table was laid, and that his sister was perhaps waiting, closed his book and went into the dining-room.

This dining-room was an oblong apartment, with a fireplace, and with a door upon the street, as we have said, and a window opening into the garden.

Madame Magloire had just finished setting the table.

While she was arranging the table, she was talking with Mademoiselle Baptistine.

The lamp was on the table, which was near the fireplace, where a good fire was burning.

One can readily fancy these two women, both past their sixtieth year: Madame Magloire, small, fat, and quick in her movements; Mademoiselle Baptistine, sweet, thin, fragile, a little taller than her brother, wore a silk puce colour dress, in the style of 1806, which she had bought at that time in Paris, and which still lasted her. To borrow a common mode of expression, which has the merit of saying in a single word what a page would hardly express, Madame Magloire had the air of a peasant, and Mademoiselle Baptistine that of a lady. Madame Magloire had an intelligent, clever, and kindly air; the two corners of her mouth unequally raised, and the upper lip projecting beyond the under one, gave something morose and imperious to her expression. So long as monseigneur was silent, she talked to him without reserve, and with a mingled respect and freedom; but from the time that he opened his mouth as we have seen, she implicitly obeyed like mademoiselle. Mademoiselle Baptistine, however, did not speak. She confined herself to obeying, and endeavouring to please. Even when she was young, she was not pretty; she had large and very prominent blue eyes, and a long pinched nose, but her whole face and person, as we said in the outset, breathed an ineffable goodness. She had been fore-ordained to meekness, but faith, charity, hope, these three virtues which gently warm the heart, had gradually sublimated this meekness into sanctity. Nature had made her a lamb; religion had made her an angel. Poor, sainted woman! gentle, but lost memory.

Mademoiselle Baptistine has so often related what occurred at the bishop's house that evening, that many persons are still living who can recall the minutest details.

Just as the bishop entered, Madame Magloire was speaking with some warmth. She was talking to *Mademoiselle* upon a familiar subject, and one to which the bishop was quite accustomed. It was a discussion on the means of fastening the front door.

It seems that while Madame Magloire was out making provision for supper, she had heard the news in sundry places. There was talk that an ill-favoured runaway, a suspicious vagabond, had arrived and was lurking somewhere in the town, and that some unpleasant adventures might befall those who should come home late that night; besides, that the surveillance was very unreliable, as the prefect and the mayor did not like one another, and were hoping to injure each other by provoking untoward events; that it was the part of wise people to be their own police, and to protect their own persons; and that every one ought to be careful to shut up, bolt, and bar his house properly, and *secure his door thoroughly.*

Madame Magloire dwelt upon these last words; but the bishop having come from a cold room, seated himself before the fire and began to warm himself, and then, he was thinking of something else. He did not hear a word of what was let fall by Madame Magloire, and she repeated it. Then Mademoiselle Baptistine, endeavouring to satisfy Madame Magloire without displeasing her brother, ventured to say timidly:

"Brother, do you hear what Madame Magloire says?"

"I heard something of it indistinctly," said the bishop. Then turning his chair half round, putting his hands on his knees, and raising towards the old servant his cordial and good-humoured face which the firelight shone upon, he said: "Well, well! what is the matter? Are we in any great danger?"

Then Madame Magloire began her story again, unconsciously exaggerating it a little. It appeared that a gipsy tramp, a sort of dangerous beggar, was in the town. He had gone for lodging to Jacquin Labarre, who had refused to receive him; he had been seen to enter the town by the boulevard Gassendi, and to roam through the street at dusk. A man with a knapsack and a rope, and a terrible-looking face.

"Indeed!" said the bishop.

This readiness to question her encouraged Madame Magloire; it seemed to indicate that the bishop was really well-nigh alarmed. She continued triumphantly: "Yes, monseigneur; it is true. Something bad will happen to-night in the town: everybody says so. The surveillance is so badly organised (a convenient repetition). To live in this mountainous country, and not even to have street lamps! If one goes out, it is dark as an oven. And I say, monseigneur, and mademoiselle says also—"

"Me?" interrupted the sister; "I say nothing. Whatever my brother does is well done."

Madame Magloire went on as if she had not heard this protest:

"We say that this house is not safe at all; and if monseigneur will permit me, I will go and tell Paulin Musebois, the locksmith, to come and put the old bolts in the door again; they are there, and it will take but a minute. I say we must have bolts, were it only for to-night; for I say that a door which opens by a latch on the outside to the first comer, nothing could be more horrible: and then monseigneur has the habit of always saying 'Come in,' even at midnight. But, my goodness! there is no need even to ask leave—"

At this moment there was a violent knock on the door.

"Come in!" said the bishop.

3

THE HEROISM OF PASSIVE OBEDIENCE

THE DOOR OPENED.

It opened quickly, quite wide, as if pushed by some one boldly and with energy.

A man entered.

That man, we know already; it was the traveller we have seen wandering about in search of a lodging.

He came in, took one step, and paused, leaving the door open behind him. He had his knapsack on his back, his stick in his hand, and a rough, bold, tired, and fierce look in his eyes, as seen by the firelight. He was hideous. It was an apparition of ill omen.

Madame Magloire had not even the strength to scream. She stood trembling with her mouth open.

Mademoiselle Baptistine turned, saw the man enter, and started up half alarmed; then, slowly turning back again towards the fire, she looked at her brother, and her face resumed its usual calmness and serenity.

The bishop looked upon the man with a tranquil eye.

As he was opening his mouth to speak, doubtless to ask the stranger what he wanted, the man, leaning with both hands on his staff, glanced from one to another in turn, and without waiting for the bishop to speak, said in a loud voice:

"See here! My name is Jean Valjean. I am a convict; I have been nineteen years in the galleys. Four days ago I was set free, and started for Pontarlier, which is my destination; during those four days I have walked from Toulon. To-day I have walked thirty miles. When I reached this place this evening I went to an inn, and they sent me away on account of my yellow passport, which I had shown at the mayor's office, as was necessary. I went to another inn, they said: 'Get out!' It was the same with one as with another; nobody would have me. I went to the prison, and the turnkey would not let me in. I crept into a dog-kennel, the dog bit me, and drove me away as if he had been a man; you would have said that he knew who I was. I went into the fields to sleep beneath the stars: there were no stars; I thought it would rain, and there was no good God to stop the drops, so I came back to the town to get the shelter of some doorway. There in the square I lay down upon a stone, a good woman showed me your house, and said: 'Knock there!' I have knocked. What is this place? Are you an inn? I have money; my savings, one hundred and nine francs and fifteen sous which I have earned in the galleys by my work for nineteen years. I will pay. What do I care? I have money. I am very tired—thirty miles on foot, and I am so hungry. Can I stay?"

"Madame Magloire," said the bishop, "set another place."

The man took three steps, and came near the lamp which stood on the table. "Stop," he exclaimed; as if he had not been understood, "not that, did you understand me? I am a galley-slave—a convict—I am just from the galleys." He drew from his pocket a large sheet of yellow paper, which he unfolded. "There is my passport, yellow as you see. That is enough to have me kicked out wherever I go. Will you read it? I know how to read, I do. I learned in the galleys. There is a school there for those who care for it. See, here is what they have put in the passport: 'Jean Valjean, a liberated convict, native of'——, you don't care about that, 'has been nineteen years in the galleys; five years for burglary; fourteen years for having attempted four times to escape. This man is very dangerous.' There you have it! Everybody has thrust me out; will you take me in? Is this an inn? Can you give me something to eat, and a place to sleep? Have you a stable?"

"Madame Magloire," said the bishop, "put some sheets on the bed in the alcove."

We already described the kind of obedience yielded by these two women.

Madame Magloire went out to fulfil her orders.

The bishop turned to the man:

"Monsieur, sit down and warm yourself: we are going to take supper presently, and your bed will be made ready while you sup."

At last the man quite understood; his face, the expression of which till then had been gloomy and hard, now expressed stupefaction, doubt, and joy, and became absolutely wonderful. He began to stutter like a madman.

"True? What! You will keep me? You won't drive me away? A convict! You call me *Monsieur* and don't say 'Get out, dog!' as everybody else does. I thought that you would send me away, so I told first off who I am. Oh! The fine woman who sent me here! I shall have a supper! A bed like other people with mattress and sheets—a bed! It is nineteen years that I have not slept on a bed. You are really willing that I should stay? You are good people! Besides I have money: I will pay well. I beg your pardon, Monsieur Innkeeper, what is your name? I will pay all you say. You are a fine man. You are an innkeeper, an't you?"

"I am a priest who lives here," said the bishop.

"A priest," said the man. "Oh, noble priest! Then you do not ask any money? You are the curé, an't you? the curé of this big church? Yes, that's it. How stupid I am, I didn't notice your skull cap."

While he was talking, the bishop shut the door, which he had left wide open.

Madame Magloire brought in an extra place setting.

"Madame Magloire," said the bishop, "put this plate as near the fire as you can." Then turning towards his guest, he added: "The night wind is raw in the Alps; you must be cold, monsieur."

Every time he said this word monsieur, with his gently solemn, and heartily hospitable voice, the man's countenance lighted up. *Monsieur* to a convict, is a glass of water to a man dying of thirst at sea. Ignominy thirsts for respect.

"The lamp," said the bishop, "gives a very poor light."

Madame Magloire understood him, and going to his bedchamber, took from the mantel the two silver candlesticks, lighted the candles, and placed them on the table.

"Monsieur Curé," said the man, "you are good; you don't despise me. You take me into your house; you light your candles for me, and I hav'n't hid from you where I come from, and how unfortunate I am."

The bishop, who was sitting near him, touched his hand gently and said: "You need not tell me who you are. This is not my house; it is the house of Christ. It does not ask any comer whether he has a name, but whether he has an affliction. You are suffering; you are hungry and thirsty; be welcome. And do not thank me; do not tell me that I take you into my house. This is the home of no man, except him who needs an asylum. I tell you, who are a traveller, that you are more at home here than I; whatever is here is yours. What need have I to know your name? Besides, before you told me, I knew it."

The man opened his eyes in astonishment:

"Really? You knew my name?"

"Yes," answered the bishop, "your name is my brother."

"Stop, stop, Monsieur Curé," exclaimed the man. "I was famished when I came in, but you are so kind that now I don't know what I am; that is all gone."

The bishop looked at him again and said:

"You have seen much suffering?"

"Oh, the red smock, the ball and chain, the plank to sleep on, the heat, the cold, the work, the guards, the beatings, the double chain for nothing, solitary confinement for a word—even when sick in bed, the chain. Dogs,

dogs are better off! Nineteen years! And I am forty-six, and now a yellow passport. That is all."

"Yes," answered the bishop, "you have left a place of suffering. But listen, there will be more joy in heaven over the tears of a repentant sinner, than over the white robes of a hundred good men. If you are leaving that sorrowful place with hate and anger against men, you are worthy of compassion; if you leave it with goodwill, gentleness, and peace, you are better than any of us."

Meantime Madame Magloire had served up supper; it consisted of soup made of water, oil, bread, and salt, a little pork, a scrap of mutton, a few figs, a green cheese, and a large loaf of rye bread. She had, without asking, added to the usual dinner of the bishop a bottle of fine old Mauves wine.

The bishop's countenance was lighted up with this expression of pleasure, peculiar to hospitable natures. "To supper!" he said briskly, as was his habit when he had a guest. He seated the man at his right. Mademoiselle Baptistine, perfectly quiet and natural, took her place at his left.

The bishop said the blessing, and then served the soup himself, according to his usual custom. The man fell to, eating greedily.

Suddenly the bishop said: "It seems to me something is lacking on the table."

The fact was, that Madame Magloire had set out only the three plates which were necessary. Now it was the custom of the house when the bishop had any one to supper, to set all six of the silver plates on the table, an innocent display. This graceful appearance of luxury was a sort of child-likeness which was full of charm in this gentle but austere household, which elevated poverty to dignity.

Madame Magloire understood the remark; without a word she went out, and a moment afterwards the three plates for which the bishop had asked were shining on the cloth, symmetrically arranged before each of the three guests.

4 (5)

TRANQUILLITY

AFTER HAVING SAID good-night to his sister, Monseigneur Bienvenu took one of the silver candlesticks from the table, handed the other to his guest, and said to him:

"Monsieur, I will show you to your room."

The man followed him.

As may have been understood from what has been said before, the house was so arranged that one could reach the alcove in the oratory only by passing through the bishop's sleeping chamber. Just as they were passing through this room Madame Magloire was putting up the silver in the cupboard at the head of the bed. It was the last thing she did every night before going to bed.

The bishop left his guest in the alcove, before a clean white bed. The man set down the candlestick upon a small table.

"Come," said the bishop, "a good night's rest to you: to-morrow morning, before you go, you shall have a cup of warm milk from our cows."

"Thank you, Monsieur l'Abbé," said the man.

Scarcely had he pronounced these words of peace, when suddenly he made a singular motion which would have chilled the two good women of the house with horror, had they witnessed it. Even now it is hard for us to understand what impulse he obeyed at that moment. Did he intend to give a warning or a threat? or was he simply obeying a sort of instinctive impulse, obscure even to himself? He turned abruptly towards the old man, crossed his arms, and casting a wild look upon his host, exclaimed in a harsh voice:

"Ah, now, indeed! you lodge me in your house, as near you as that!"

He checked himself, and added, with a laugh, in which there was something horrible:

"Have you reflected upon it? Who tells you that I am not a murderer?"

The bishop responded:

"God will take care of that."

Then with gravity, moving his lips like one praying or talking to himself, he raised two fingers of his right hand and blessed the man, who, however, did not bow; and without turning his head or looking behind him, went back into his room.

When the alcove was occupied, a heavy serge curtain was drawn in the oratory, concealing the altar. Before this curtain the bishop knelt as he passed out, and offered a short prayer.

A moment afterwards he was walking in the garden, surrendering mind and soul to a dreamy contemplation of these grand and mysterious works of God, which night makes visible to the eye.

As to the man, he was so completely exhausted that he did not even avail himself of the clean white sheets; he blew out the candle with his nostril, after the manner of convicts, and fell on the bed, dressed as he was, into a sound sleep.

Midnight struck as the bishop came back to his room.

A few moments afterwards all in the little house slept.

5 (6)

JEAN VALJEAN

TOWARDS THE MIDDLE of the night, Jean Valjean awoke.

Jean Valjean was born of a poor peasant family of Brie. In his childhood he had not been taught to read: when he was grown up, he chose the occupation of a pruner at Faverolles. His mother's name was Jeanne Mathieu, his father's Jean Valjean or Vlajean, probably a nickname, a contraction of *Voilà Jean.*

Jean Valjean was of a thoughtful disposition, but not sad, which is characteristic of affectionate natures. Upon the whole, however, there was something torpid and insignificant, in the appearance at least, of Jean Valjean. He had lost his parents when very young. His mother died of malpractice in an undulant fever: his father, a pruner before him, was killed by a fall from a tree. Jean Valjean now had but one relative left, his sister, a widow with seven children, girls and boys. This sister had brought up Jean Valjean, and, as long as her husband lived, she had taken care of her younger brother. Her husband died, leaving the eldest of these children eight, the youngest one year old. Jean Valjean had just reached his twenty-fifth year: he took the father's place, and, in his turn, supported the sister who reared him. This he did naturally, as a duty, and even with a sort of moroseness on his part. His youth was spent in rough and ill-recompensed labour: he never was known to have a sweetheart; he had not time to be in love.

At night he came in weary and ate his soup without saying a word. While he was eating, his sister, *Mère Jeanne,* frequently took from his porringer the best of his meal, a bit of meat, a slice of pork, the heart of the cabbage, to give to one of her children. He went on eating, his head bent down nearly into the soup, his long hair falling over his dish, hiding his eyes, he did not seem to notice anything that was done. At Faverolles, not far from the house of the Valjeans, there was on the other side of the road a farmer's wife named Marie Claude; the Valjean children, who were always famished, sometimes went in their mother's name to borrow a pint of milk, which they would drink behind a hedge, or in some corner of the lane, snatching away the pitcher so greedily one from another, that the little girls would spill it upon their aprons and their neckpieces; if their mother had known of this exploit she would have punished the delinquents severely. Jean Valjean, rough and grumbler as he was, paid Marie Claude; their mother never knew it, and so the children escaped.

He earned in the pruning season eighteen sous a day: after that he hired out as a reaper, workman, teamster, or labourer. He did whatever he could find to do. His sister worked also, but what could she do with seven little children? It was a sad group, which misery was grasping and closing upon, little by little. There was a very severe winter; Jean had no work, the family had no bread; literally, no bread, and seven children.

One Sunday night, Maubert Isabeau, the baker on the Place de l'Eglise, in Faverolles, was just going to bed when he heard a violent blow against the barred window of his shop. He got down in time to see an arm thrust through the aperture made by the blow of a fist on the glass. The arm seized a loaf of bread and took it out. Isabeau rushed out; the thief used his legs valiantly; Isabeau pursued him and caught him. The thief had thrown away the bread, but his arm was still bleeding. It was Jean Valjean.

All that happened in 1795. Jean Valjean was brought before the tribunals of the time for "burglary at night, in an inhabited house." He had a gun which he used as well as any marksman in the world and was something of a poacher, which hurt him, there being a natural prejudice against poachers. The poacher, like the smuggler, approaches very nearly to the brigand. We must say, however, by the way, that there is yet a deep gulf between this race of men and the hideous assassin of the city. The poacher dwells in the forest, and the smuggler in the mountains or upon the sea; cities produce ferocious men, because they produce corrupt men; the mountains, the forest, and the sea, render men savage; they develop the fierce, but yet do not destroy the human.

Jean Valjean was found guilty: the terms of the code were explicit; in our civilisation there are fearful hours; such are those when the criminal law pronounces shipwreck upon a man. What a mournful moment is that in which society withdraws itself and gives up a thinking being for ever. Jean Valjean was sentenced to five years in the galleys.

On the 22nd of April, 1796, there was announced in Paris the victory of Montenotte, achieved by the commanding-general of the army of Italy, whom the message of the Directory, to the Five Hundred, of the 2nd Floréal, year IV, called Buonaparte; that same day a great chain was riveted at the Bicêtre. Jean Valjean was a part of this chain. An old turnkey of the prison, now nearly ninety, well remembers this miserable man, who was ironed at the end of the fourth plinth in the north angle of the court. Sitting on the ground like the rest, he seemed to comprehend nothing of his position, except its horror: probably there was also mingled with the vague ideas of a poor ignorant man a notion that there was something excessive in the penalty. While they were with heavy hammer-strokes behind his head riveting the bolt of his iron collar, he was weeping. The tears choked his words, and he only succeeded in saying from time to time: "I was a *pruner at Faverolles.*" Then sobbing as he was, he raised his right hand and lowered it seven times, as if he was touching seven heads of unequal height, and at this gesture one could guess that whatever he had done, had been to feed and clothe seven little children.

He was taken to Toulon, at which place he arrived after a journey of twenty-seven days, on a cart, the chain still about his neck. At Toulon he was dressed in a red smock, all his past life was effaced, even to his name. He was no longer Jean Valjean: he was Number 24,601. What became of the sister? What became of the seven children? Who troubled himself about that? What becomes of the handful of leaves of the young tree when it is sawn at the trunk?

It is the old story. These poor little lives, these creatures of God, henceforth without support, or guide, or asylum; they passed away wherever chance led, who knows even? Each took a different path, it may be, and sank little by little into the chilling dark which engulfs solitary destinies; that sullen gloom where are lost so many ill-fated souls in the sombre advance of the human race. They left that region; the church of what had been their village forgot them; the stile of what had been their field forgot them; after a few years in the galleys, even Jean Valjean forgot them. In that heart, in which there had been a wound, there was a scar; that was all. During the time he was at Toulon, he heard but once of his sister; that was, I think, at the end of the fourth year of his confinement. I do not know how the news reached him: some one who had known him at home had seen his sister. She was in Paris, living in a poor street near Saint Sulpice, the Rue du Geindre. She had with her but one child, the youngest, a little boy. Where were the other six? She did not know herself, perhaps. Every morning she went to a bindery, No. 3 Rue du Sabot, where she was employed as a folder and bookstitcher. She had to be there by six in the morning, long before the dawn in the winter. In the same building with the bindery, there was a school, where she sent her little boy, seven years old. As the school did not open until seven, and she must be at her work at six, her boy had to wait in the yard an hour, until the school opened—an hour of cold and darkness in the winter. They would not let the child wait in the bindery, because he was troublesome, they said. The workmen, as they passed in the morning, saw the poor little fellow sometimes sitting on the pavement nodding with weariness, and often sleeping in the dark, crouched and bent over his basket. When it rained, an old woman, the portress, took pity on him; she let him come into her lodge, the furniture of which was only a pallet bed, a spinning-wheel, and two wooden chairs; and the little one slept there in a corner, hugging the cat to keep himself warm. At seven o'clock the school opened and he went in. That is what was told Jean Valjean. It was as if a window had suddenly been opened looking upon the destiny of those he had loved, and then all was closed again, and he heard nothing more for ever. Nothing more came to him; he had not seen them, never will he see them again! and through the remainder of this sad history we shall not meet them again.

Near the end of this fourth year, his chance of liberty came to Jean Valjean. His comrades helped him as they always do in that dreary place, and he escaped. He wandered two days in freedom through the fields; if it is freedom to be hunted, to turn your head each moment, to tremble at the least noise, to be afraid of everything, of the smoke of a chimney, the passing of a man, the baying of a dog, the gallop of a horse, the striking of a clock, of the day because you see, and of the night because you do not; of the road, of the path, the bush, of sleep. During the evening of the second day he was retaken; he had neither eaten nor slept for thirty-six hours. The maritime tribunal extended his sentence three years for this attempt, which made eight.

In the sixth year his turn of escape came again; he tried it, but failed again. He did not answer at roll-call, and the alarm cannon was fired. At night the people of the vicinity discovered him hidden beneath the keel of a vessel on the stocks; he resisted the galley guard which seized him. Escape and resistance. This the provisions of the special code punished by an addition of five years, two with the double chain, thirteen years. The tenth year his turn came round again; he made another attempt with no better success. Three years for this new attempt. Sixteen years. And finally, I think it was in the thirteenth year, he made yet another, and was retaken after an absence of only four hours. Three years for these four hours. Nineteen years. In October, 1815, he was set at large: he had entered in 1796 for having broken a pane of glass, and taken a loaf of bread.

Claude Gueux stole a loaf of bread, Jean Valjean stole a loaf of bread; English statistics show that in London starvation is the immediate cause of four thefts out of five.

Jean Valjean entered the galleys sobbing and shuddering: he went out hardened; he entered in despair: he went out sullen.

What had happened within this soul?

6 (7)

THE DEPTHS OF DESPAIR

LET US endeavour to tell.

It is an imperative necessity that society should look into these things: they are its own work.

He was, as we have said, ignorant, but he was not an imbecile. The natural light of reason was enkindled in him. Misfortune, which has also its illumination, added to the few rays that he had in his mind. Under the club, under the chain, in the cell, in fatigue, under the burning sun of the galleys, upon the convict's bed of plank, he turned to his own conscience, and he reflected.

He constituted himself a tribunal.

He began by arraigning himself.

He recognised, that he was not an innocent man, unjustly punished. He acknowledged that he had committed an extreme and a blamable action; that the loaf perhaps would not have been refused him, had he asked for it; that at all events it would have been better to wait, either for pity, or for work; that it is not altogether an unanswerable reply to say: "could I wait when I was hungry?" that, in the first place, it is very rare that any one dies of actual hunger; and that, fortunately or unfortunately, man is so made that he can suffer long and much, morally and physically, without dying; that he should, therefore, have had patience; that that would have been better even for those poor little ones; that it was an act of folly in him, poor, worthless man, to seize society in all its strength, forcibly by the collar, and imagine that he could escape from misery by theft; that that was, at all events, a bad door for getting out of misery by which one entered into infamy; in short, that he had done wrong.

Then he asked himself:

If he were the only one who had done wrong in the course of his fatal history? If, in the first place, it were not a grievous thing that he, a workman, should have been in want of work; that he, an industrious man, should have lacked bread. If, moreover, the fault having been committed and avowed, the punishment had not been savage and excessive. If there were not a greater abuse, on the part of the law, in the penalty, than there had been, on the part of the guilty, in the crime. If there were not an excess of weight in one of the scales of the balance—on the side of the expiation. If the excessiveness of the penalty did not erase the crime; and if the result were not to reverse the situation, to replace the wrong of the delinquent by the wrong of the repression, to make a victim of the guilty, and a creditor of the debtor, and actually to put the right on the side of him who had violated it. If that penalty, taken in connection with its successive extensions for his attempts to escape, had not at last come to be a sort of outrage of the stronger on the weaker, a crime of society towards the individual, a crime which was committed afresh every day, a crime which had endured for nineteen years.

He asked whether human society could have the right alike to crush its members, in the one case by its unreasonable carelessness, and in the other by its pitiless care; and to keep a poor man for ever between a lack and an excess, a lack of work, an excess of punishment.

If it were not outrageous that society should treat with such rigid precision those of its members who were most poorly endowed in the distribution or wealth that chance had made, and who were, therefore, most worthy of indulgence.

These questions asked and decided, he condemned society and sentenced it.

He sentenced it to his hatred.

He made it responsible for the fate which he had undergone, and promised himself that he, perhaps, would not hesitate some day to call it to an account. He declared to himself that there was no proportion between the harm that he had caused and the injury that had been done to him; he concluded, in short, that his punishment was not, really, an injustice, but that beyond all doubt it was an iniquity.

Anger may be foolish and absurd, and one may be irritated when in the wrong; but a man never feels outraged unless in some respect he is at bottom right. Jean Valjean felt outraged.

And then, human society had done him nothing but injury; never had he seen anything of her, but this wrathful face which she calls justice, and which she shows to those whom she strikes down. No man had ever touched him but to bruise him. All his contact with men had been by blows. Never, since his infancy, since his mother, since his sister, never had he been greeted with a friendly word or a kind regard. Through suffering on suffering he came little by little to the conviction, that life was a war; and that in that war he was the vanquished. He had no weapon but his hate. He resolved to sharpen it in the galleys and to take it with him when he went out.

There was at Toulon a school for the prisoners conducted by some teaching friars, who offered an elementary education to such of these poor men as were willing. He was one of the willing ones. He went to school at forty and learned to read, write, and do arithmetic. He felt that to increase his knowledge was to strengthen his hatred. Under certain circumstances, instruction and enlightenment may serve as rallying-points for evil.

It is sad to tell; but after having judged society, which had caused his misfortunes, he judged the Providence which created society, and condemned it also.

Thus, during those nineteen years of torture and slavery, did this soul rise and fall at the same time. Light entered on the one side, and darkness on the other.

Jean Valjean was not, we have seen, of an evil nature. His heart was still right when he arrived at the galleys. While there he condemned society, and felt that he became wicked; he condemned Providence, and felt that he became impious.

The peculiarity of punishment of this kind, in which what is pitiless, that is to say, what is brutalising, predominates, is to transform little by little, by a slow stupefaction, a man into an animal, sometimes into a wild beast. Jean Valjean's repeated and obstinate attempts to escape are enough to prove that such is the strange effect of the law upon a human soul. Jean Valjean had renewed these attempts, so wholly useless and foolish, as often as an opportunity offered, without one moment's thought of the result, or of experience already undergone. He escaped wildly, like a wolf on seeing his cage-door open. Instinct said to him: "Away!" Reason would have said to him: "Stay!" But before a temptation so mighty, reason fled; instinct alone remained. The beast alone was in play. When he was retaken, the new severities that were inflicted upon him only made him still more fierce.

We must not omit one circumstance, which is, that in physical strength he far surpassed all the other inmates of the prison. At hard work, at twisting a cable, or turning a windlass, Jean Valjean was equal to four men. He would sometimes lift and hold enormous weights on his back, and would occasionally act the part of what is called a *jack,* or what was called in old French an *orgeuil,* whence came the name, we may say by the way, of the Rue Montorgeuil near the Halles of Paris. His comrades had nicknamed him Jean the Jack. At one time, while the balcony of the City Hall of Toulon was undergoing repairs, one of Puget's admirable caryatides, which support the balcony, slipped from its place, and was about to fall, when Jean Valjean, who happened to be there, held it up on his shoulder till the workmen came.

His suppleness surpassed his strength. Certain convicts, always planning escape, have developed a veritable science of strength and skill combined,— the science of the muscles. A mysterious system of statics is practised throughout daily by prisoners, who are eternally envying the birds and flies. To scale a wall, and to find a foothold where you could hardly see a projection, was child's play for Jean Valjean. Given an angle in a wall, with the tension of his back and his knees, with elbows and hands braced against the rough face of the stone, he would ascend, as if by magic, to a fourth story. Sometimes he climbed up in this manner to the roof of the galleys.

He talked but little, and never laughed. Some extreme emotion was required to draw from him, once or twice a year, that lugubrious sound of the convict, which is like the echo of a demon's laugh. To those who saw him, he seemed to be absorbed in continually looking upon something terrible.

He was absorbed, in fact.

Through the diseased perceptions of an incomplete nature and a smothered intelligence, he vaguely felt that a monstrous weight was over him. In that pallid and sullen shadow in which he crawled, whenever he turned his head and endeavoured to raise his eyes, he saw, with mingled rage and terror, forming, massing, and mounting up out of sight above him with horrid escarpments, a kind of frightful accumulation of things, of laws, of prejudices, of men, and of acts, the outlines of which escaped him, the weight of which appalled him, and which was no other than that prodigious pyramid that we call civilisation. Here and there in that shapeless and swarming mass, sometimes near at hand, sometimes afar off, and upon inaccessible heights, he distinguished some group, some detail vividly clear, here the jailer with his staff, here the gendarme with his sword, yonder the mitred archbishop; and on high, in a sort of blaze of glory, the emperor crowned and resplendent. It seemed to him that these distant splendours, far from dissipating his night, made it blacker and more deathly. All this, laws, prejudices, acts, men, things, went and came above him, according to the complicated and mysterious movement that God impresses upon civilisation, marching over him and crushing him with an indescribably tranquil cruelty and inexorable indifference. Souls sunk to the bottom of possible misfortune, and unfortunate men lost in the lowest depths, where they are no longer seen, the rejected of the law, feel upon their heads the whole weight of that human society, so formidable to him who is outside of it, so terrible to him who is beneath it.

To sum up, in conclusion, what can be summed up and reduced to positive results, of all that we have been showing, we will confine ourselves to declaring this, that in the course of nineteen years, Jean Valjean, the inoffensive pruner of Faverolles, the terrible galley-slave of Toulon, had become capable, thanks to the training he had received in the galleys, of two species of crime; first, a sudden, unpremeditated action, full of rashness, all instinct, a sort of reprisal for the wrong he had suffered; secondly, a serious, premeditated act, discussed by his conscience, and pondered over with the false ideas which such a fate will give. His premeditations passed through the three successive phases to which natures of a certain stamp are limited—reason, will, and obstinacy. He had as motives, habitual indignation, bitterness of soul, a deep sense of injuries suffered, a reaction even against the good, the innocent, and the upright, if any such there are. The beginning as well as the end of all his thoughts was hatred of human law; that hatred which, if it be not checked in its growth by some providential event, becomes, in a certain time, hatred of society, then hatred of the human race, and then hatred of creation, and reveals itself by a vague, brutal desire to injure some living being, it matters not who. So, the passport was right which described Jean Valjean as *a very dangerous man.*

From year to year this soul had withered more and more, slowly but fatally. With this withered heart, he had a dry eye. When he left the galleys, he had not shed a tear for nineteen years.

7 *(9)*

GRIEVANCES

WHEN THE TIME for leaving the galleys came, and when there sounded in the ear of Jean Valjean the strange words: You *are free!* the moment seemed improbable and unreal, a ray of living light, a ray of the true light of living men, suddenly penetrated his soul. But this ray quickly dimmed. Jean Valjean had been dazzled with the idea of liberty. He had believed in a new life. He soon saw what sort of liberty that is which has a yellow passport.

And along with that there were many bitter experiences. He had calculated that his savings, during his stay at the galleys, would amount to a hundred and seventy-one francs. It is proper to say that he had forgotten to take into account the compulsory rest on Sundays and holidays, which, in nineteen years, required deduction of about twenty-four francs. However that might be, his savings had been reduced, by various local charges, to the sum of a hundred and nine francs and fifteen sous, which was counted out to him on his departure.

He understood nothing of this, and thought himself wronged, or to speak plainly, robbed.

The day after his liberation, he saw before the door of an orange blossom distillery at Grasse, some men who were unloading bales. He offered his services. They were in need of help and accepted them. He set at work. He was intelligent, robust, and handy; he did his best; the foreman appeared to be satisfied. While he was at work, a gendarme passed, noticed him, and asked for his papers. He was compelled to show the yellow passport. That done, Jean Valjean resumed his work. A little while before, he had asked one of the labourers how much they were paid per day for this work and the reply was: thirty *sous*. At night, as he was obliged to leave the town next morning, he went to the foreman of the distillery, and asked for his pay. The foreman did not say a word, but handed him fifteen sous. He remonstrated. The man replied: *"That is good enough for you."* He insisted. The foreman looked him in the eyes and said: *"Watch it, or you'll be back inside!"*

There again he thought himself robbed.

Society, the state, in reducing his savings, had robbed him by wholesale. Now it was the turn of the individual, who was robbing him by retail.

Liberation is not deliverance. A convict may leave the galleys behind, but not his condemnation.

This was what befell him at Grasse. We have seen how he was received at D——.

8 *(10)*

THE MAN AWAKES

AS THE CATHEDRAL CLOCK struck two, Jean Valjean awoke.

What awakened him was, too good a bed. For nearly twenty years he had not slept in a bed, and, although he had not undressed, the sensation was too novel not to disturb his sleep.

He had slept something more than four hours. His fatigue had passed away. He was not accustomed to give many hours to repose.

He opened his eyes, and looked for a moment into the obscurity about him, then he closed them to go to sleep again.

When many diverse sensations have disturbed the day, when the mind is preoccupied, we can fall asleep once, but not a second time. Sleep comes at first much more readily than it comes again. Such was the case with Jean Valjean. He could not get to sleep again, and so he began to think.

He was in one of those moods in which the ideas we have in our minds are perturbed. There was a kind of vague ebb and flow in his brain. His oldest and his latest memories floated about pell mell, and intersected confusedly, losing their own shapes, swelling beyond measure, then disappearing all at once, as if in a muddy and troubled stream. Many thoughts came to him, but there was one which continually presented itself, and which drove away all others. What that thought was, we shall tell directly. He had noticed the six silver plates and the large ladle that Madame Magloire had put on the table.

Those six silver plates took possession of him. There they were, within a few steps. At the very moment that he passed through the middle room to reach the one he was now in, the old servant was placing them in a little cupboard at the head of the bed. He had marked that cupboard well: on the right, coming from the dining-room. They were solid; and old silver. With the big ladle, they would bring at least two hundred francs, double what he had got for nineteen years' labour. True; he would have got more if the *"government"* had not *"robbed"* him.

His mind wavered a whole hour, and a long one, in fluctuation and in struggle. The clock struck three. He opened his eyes, rose up hastily in bed, reached out his arm and felt his haversack, which he had put into the corner of the alcove, then he thrust out his legs and placed his feet on the ground, and found himself, he knew not how, seated on his bed.

He remained for some time lost in thought in that attitude, which would have had a rather ominous look, had any one seen him there in the dusk—he only awake in the slumbering house. All at once he stooped down, took off his shoes, and put them softly upon the mat in front of the bed, then he resumed his thinking posture, and was still again.

In that hideous meditation, the ideas which we have been pointing out, troubled his brain without ceasing, entered, departed, returned, and became a sort of weight upon him; and then he thought, too, he knew not why, and with that mechanical obstinacy that belongs to reverie, of a convict named Brevet, whom he had known in the galleys, and whose trousers were only held up by a single knit cotton suspender. The checked pattern of that suspender came continually before his mind.

He continued in this situation, and would perhaps have remained there until daybreak, if the clock had not struck the quarter or the half-hour. The clock seemed to say to him: "Let's go!"

He rose to his feet, hesitated for a moment longer and listened; all was still in the house; he walked straight and cautiously towards the window, which he could discern. The night was not very dark; there was a full moon, across which large clouds were driving before the wind. This produced alternations of light and shade, out-of-doors eclipses and illuminations, and in-doors a kind of twilight. This twilight, enough to enable him to find his way, changing with the passing clouds, resembled that sort of livid light which falls through the window of a dungeon before which men are passing. On reaching the window, Jean Valjean examined it. It had no bars, opened into the garden, and was fastened, according to the fashion of the country, with a little wedge only. He opened it; but as the cold, keen air rushed into the room, he closed it again immediately. He looked into the garden with that absorbed look which studies rather than sees. The garden was enclosed with a white wall quite low, and readily scaled. Beyond, against the sky, he distinguished the tops of trees at equal distances apart, which showed that this wall separated the garden from an avenue or a lane planted with trees.

When he had made this observation, he turned like a man whose mind is made up, went to his alcove, took his haversack, opened it, fumbled in it, took out something which he laid upon the bed, put his shoes into one of his pockets, tied up his bundle, swung it upon his shoulders, put on his cap, and pulled the vizor down over his eyes, felt for his stick, and went and put it in the corner of the window, then returned to the bed, and resolutely took up the object which he had laid on it. It looked like a short iron bar, pointed at one end like a spear.

It would have been hard to distinguish in the darkness for what use this piece of iron had been made. Could it be a lever? Could it be a club?

In the day-time, it would have been seen to be nothing but a miner's drill. At that time, the convicts were sometimes employed in quarrying stone on the high hills that surround Toulon, and they often had miners' tools in their possession. Miners' drills are of solid iron, terminating at the lower end in a point, by means of which they are sunk into the rock.

He took the drill in his right hand, and holding his breath, with stealthy steps, he moved towards the door of the next room, which was the bishop's, as we know. On reaching the door, he found it ajar. The bishop had not closed it.

9 (11)

WHAT HE DOES

JEAN VALJEAN listened. Not a sound.

He pushed the door.

He pushed it lightly with the end of his finger, with the stealthy and timorous carefulness of a cat. The door yielded to the pressure with a silent, imperceptible movement, which made the opening a little wider.

He waited a moment, and then pushed the door again more boldly.

It yielded gradually and silently. The opening was now wide enough for him to pass through; but there was a small table near the door which with it formed a troublesome angle, and which barred the entrance.

Jean Valjean saw the obstacle. At all hazards the opening must be made still wider.

He so determined, and pushed the door a third time, harder than before. This time a rusty hinge suddenly sent out into the darkness a harsh and prolonged creak.

Jean Valjean shivered. The noise of this hinge sounded in his ears as clear and terrible as the trumpet of the Judgment Day.

In the fantastic exaggeration of the first moment, he almost imagined that this hinge had become animate, and suddenly endowed with a terrible life; and that it was barking like a dog to warn everybody, and rouse the sleepers.

He stopped, shuddering and distracted, and dropped from his tiptoes to his feet. He felt the pulses of his temples beat like trip-hammers, and it appeared to him that his breath came from his chest with the roar of wind from a cavern. It seemed impossible that the horrible sound of this incensed hinge had not shaken the whole house with the shock of an earthquake: the door pushed by him had taken alarm, and had called out; the old man would arise, the two old women would scream; help would come; in a quarter of an hour the town would be alive with it, and the gendarmes in pursuit. For a moment he thought he was lost.

He stood still, petrified like the pillar of salt,* not daring to stir. Some minutes passed. The door was wide open; he ventured a look into the room. Nothing had moved. He listened. Nothing was stirring in the house. The noise of the rusty hinge had wakened nobody.

This first danger was over, but still he felt within him a frightful tumult. Nevertheless he did not flinch. Not even when he thought he was lost had he flinched. His only thought was to make an end of it quickly. He took one step and was inside.

A deep calm filled the chamber. Here and there indistinct, dim forms could be distinguished; which by day, were papers scattered over a table, open folios, books piled on a stool, an arm-chair with clothes on it, a prayer stool, but now were only dark corners and whitish spots. Jean Valjean advanced, carefully avoiding the furniture. At the further end of the room he could hear the regular, quiet breathing of the sleeping bishop.

Suddenly he stopped: he was near the bed, he had reached it sooner than he thought.

Nature sometimes joins her effects and her appearances to our acts with a sort of gloomy, intelligent appropriateness, as if she would compel us to reflect. For nearly a half hour a great cloud had darkened the sky. At the moment when Jean Valjean paused before the bed the cloud broke as if purposely, and a ray of moonlight crossing the high window, suddenly lighted up the bishop's pale face. He slept tranquilly. He was almost entirely dressed, though in bed, on account of the cold nights of the lower Alps, with a dark woollen garment which covered his arms to the wrists. His head had fallen on the pillow in the unstudied attitude of slumber; over the side of the bed hung his hand, ornamented with the pastoral ring, and which had done so many good deeds, so many pious acts. His entire countenance was lit up with a vague expression of content, hope, and happiness. It was more than a smile and almost a radiance. On his forehead rested the indescribable reflection of an unseen light.† The souls of the upright in sleep have vision of a mysterious heaven.

A reflection from this heaven shone upon the bishop.

But it was also a luminous transparency, for this heaven was within him; this heaven was his conscience.

At the instant when the moonbeam overlay, so to speak, this inward

---

*Lot's wife, spared by the angels who destroyed Sodom in a rain of fire, disobeyed them, looked back at the city, and was turned to salt.

†Hugo often described his most saintly characters with a glowing or gleaming countenance, transfigured by grace as was Moses descending from Sinai.

radiance, the sleeping bishop appeared as if in a halo. But it was very mild, and veiled in an ineffable twilight. The moon in the sky, nature drowsing, the garden without a quiver, the quiet house, the hour, the moment, the silence, added something strangely solemn and unutterable to the venerable repose of this man, and enveloped his white locks and his closed eyes with a serene and majestic glory, this face where all was hope and confidence—this old man's head and infant's slumber.

There was something of divinity almost in this man, thus unconsciously august.

Jean Valjean was in the shadow with the iron drill in his hand erect, motionless, terrified, at this radiant figure. He had never seen anything comparable to it. This confidence filled him with fear. The moral world has no greater spectacle than this; a troubled and restless conscience on the verge of committing an evil deed, contemplating the sleep of a righteous man.

This sleep in this solitude, with a neighbour such as he, contained a touch of the sublime, which he felt vaguely but powerfully.

None could have told what was happening within him, not even himself. To attempt to realise it, the utmost violence must be imagined in the presence of the most extreme mildness. In his face nothing could be distinguished with certainty. It was a sort of haggard astonishment. He saw it; that was all. But what were his thoughts; it would have been impossible to guess. It was clear that he was moved and agitated. But of what nature was this emotion?

He did not remove his eyes from the old man. The only thing which was plain from his attitude and his countenance was a strange indecision. You would have said he was hesitating between two realms, that of the doomed and that of the saved. He appeared ready either to cleave this skull, or to kiss this hand.

In a few moments he raised his left hand slowly to his forehead and took off his hat; then, letting his hand fall with the same slowness, Jean Valjean resumed his contemplations, his cap in his left hand, his club in his right, and his hair bristling on his fierce-looking head.

Under this frightful gaze the bishop still slept in profoundest peace.

The crucifix above the mantelpiece was dimly visible in the moonlight, apparently extending its arms towards both, with a blessing for the one and a pardon for the other.

Suddenly Jean Valjean put on his cap, then passed quickly, without looking at the bishop, along the bed, straight to the cupboard which he perceived near its head; he raised the drill to force the lock; the key was in it; he opened it; the first thing he saw was the basket of silver, he took it, crossed the room with hasty stride, careless of noise, reached the door, entered the oratory, took his stick, stepped out, put the silver in his knapsack, threw away the basket, ran across the garden, leaped over the wall like a tiger, and fled.*

---

*This description of fleeing a holy dwelling by climbing over a wall constitutes an advance mention, with the situation reversed, of Jean Valjean finding refuge for himself and Cosette in Paris by climbing over the wall of a convent.

10 (12)

THE BISHOP AT WORK

THE NEXT DAY AT SUNRISE, Monseigneur Bienvenu was walking in the garden. Madame Magloire ran towards him quite beside herself.

"Monseigneur, monseigneur," cried she, "does your greatness know where the silver basket is?"

"Yes," said the bishop.

"God be praised!" said she, "I did not know what had become of it."

The bishop had just found the basket on a flower-bed. He gave it to Madame Magloire and said: "There it is."

"Yes," said she, "but there is nothing in it. The silver?"

"Ah!" said the bishop, "it is the silver then that troubles you. I do not know where that is."

"Good heavens! it is stolen. That man who came last night stole it."

And in the twinkling of an eye, with all the agility of which her age was capable, Madame Magloire ran to the oratory, went into the alcove, and came back to the bishop. The bishop was bending with some sadness over a cochlearia des Guillons, which the basket had broken in falling. He looked up at Madame Magloire's cry:

"Monseigneur, the man has gone! the silver is stolen!"

While she was uttering this exclamation her eyes fell on an angle of the garden where she saw traces left by someone who had clambered over the wall. A capstone had been knocked down.

"See, there is where he got out; he jumped into Cochefilet lane. The abominable fellow! he has stolen our silver!"

The bishop was silent for a moment, then raising his serious eyes, he said mildly to Madame Magloire:

"Now first, did this silver belong to us?"

Madame Magloire did not answer; after a moment the bishop continued:

"Madame Magloire, I have for a long time wrongfully withheld this silver; it belonged to the poor. Who was this man? A poor man evidently."

"Alas! alas!" returned Madame Magloire. "It is not on my account or mademoiselle's; it is all the same to us. But it is on yours, monseigneur. What is monsieur going to eat from now?"

The bishop looked at her with amazement:

"How so! have we no pewter plates?"

Madame Magloire shrugged her shoulders.

"Pewter smells bad."

"Well, then, iron plates."

Madame Magloire grimaced.

"Iron leaves a taste."

"Well," said the bishop, "then, wooden plates."

In a few minutes he was breakfasting at the same table at which Jean Valjean sat the night before. While breakfasting, Monseigneur Bienvenu pleasantly remarked to his sister who said nothing, and Madame Magloire who was grumbling to herself, that there was really no need even of a wooden spoon or fork to dip a piece of bread into a cup of milk.

"Was there ever such an idea?" said Madame Magloire to herself, as she went backwards and forwards: "to take in a man like that, and to give him a bed beside him; and yet what a blessing it was that he did nothing but steal! Oh, my stars! it makes the chills run over me when I think of it!"

Just as the brother and sister were rising from the table, there was a knock at the door.

"Come in," said the bishop.

The door opened. A strange, violent group appeared on the threshold. Three men were holding a fourth by the collar. The three men were gendarmes; the fourth Jean Valjean.

A brigadier of gendarmes, who appeared to head the group, was near the door. He advanced towards the bishop, giving a military salute.

"Monseigneur," said he—

At this word Jean Valjean, who was sullen and seemed entirely cast down, raised his head with a stupefied air—

"Monseigneur!" he murmured, "then it is not the curé!"

"Silence!" said a gendarme, "it is monseigneur, the bishop."

In the meantime Monsieur Bienvenu had approached as quickly as his great age permitted:

"Ah, there you are!" said he, looking towards Jean Valjean. "I am glad to see you. But! I gave you the candlesticks also, which are silver like the rest, and would bring two hundred francs. Why did you not take them along with your plates?"

Jean Valjean opened his eyes and looked at the venerable bishop with an expression which no human tongue could describe.

"Monseigneur," said the brigadier, "then what this man said was true? We met him. He seemed to be running away, and we arrested him in order to see. He had this silver."

"And he told you," interrupted the bishop, with a smile, "that it had been given him by a good old priest with whom he had passed the night. I see it all. And you brought him back here? It is all a mistake."

"If that is so," said the brigadier, "we can let him go."

"Certainly," replied the bishop.

The gendarmes released Jean Valjean, who shrank back—

"Is it true that they let me go?" he said in a voice almost inarticulate, as if he were speaking in his sleep.

"Yes! you can go. Do you not understand?" said a gendarme.

"My friend," said the bishop, "before you go away, here are your candlesticks; take them."

He went to the mantelpiece, took the two candlesticks, and brought them to Jean Valjean. The two women beheld the action without a word, or gesture, or look, that might disturb the bishop.

Jean Valjean was trembling in every limb. He took the two candlesticks mechanically, and with a wild appearance.

"Now," said the bishop, "go in peace. By the way, my friend, when you come again, you need not come through the garden. You can always come in and go out by the front door. It is closed only with a latch, day or night."

Then turning to the gendarmes, he said:

"Messieurs, you can retire." The gendarmes withdrew.

Jean Valjean felt like a man who is just about to faint.

The bishop approached him, and said, in a low voice:

"Forget not, never forget that you have promised me to use this silver to become an honest man."

Jean Valjean, who had no recollection of this promise, stood confounded. The bishop had laid much stress upon these words as he uttered them. He continued, solemnly:

"Jean Valjean, my brother: you belong no longer to evil, but to good. It is your soul that I am buying for you. I am withdrawing it from dark thoughts and from the spirit of perdition, and I am giving it to God!"

11 (13)

PETIT GERVAIS

JEAN VALJEAN went out of the city as if he were escaping. He made all haste to get into the open country, taking the first lanes and bypaths that offered, without noticing that he was every moment retracing his steps. He wandered thus all the morning. He had eaten nothing, but he felt no hunger. He was the prey of a multitude of new sensations. He felt somewhat angry, he knew not against whom. He could not have told whether he were touched or humiliated. There came over him, at times, a strange relenting which he struggled with, and to which he opposed the hardening of his past twenty years. This condition wearied him. He saw, with disquietude, shaken within him that species of frightful calm which the injustice of his fate had given him. He asked himself what should replace it. At times he would really have liked better to be in prison with the gendarmes, and that things had not happened thus; that would have given him less agitation. Although the season was well advanced, there were yet here and there a few late flowers in the hedges, the odour of which, as it met him in his walk, recalled the memories of his childhood. These memories were almost unbearable, it was so long since they had occurred to him.

Inexpressible thoughts thus gathered in his mind the whole day.

As the sun was sinking towards the horizon, lengthening the shadow on the ground of the smallest pebble, Jean Valjean was seated behind a thicket in a large reddish plain, absolutely deserted. There was no horizon but the Alps. Not even the steeple of a village church. Jean Valjean might have been seven miles from D——. A by-path which crossed the plain passed a few steps from the thicket.

In the midst of this meditation, which would have heightened not a little the frightful effect of his rags to any one who might have met him, he heard a joyous sound.

He turned his head, and saw coming along the path a little Savoyard,* a dozen years old, singing, with his hurdygurdy at his side, and his cherry-wood box on his back.

One of those pleasant and gay youngsters who go from place to place, with their knees sticking through their trousers.

Always singing, the boy stopped from time to time, and played at tossing up some pieces of money that he had in his hand, probably his whole fortune. Among them there was one forty-sous coin.

The boy stopped by the side of the thicket without seeing Jean Valjean, and tossed up his handful of sous; until this time he had skilfully caught the whole of them upon the back of his hand.

This time the forty-sous coin got away from him, and rolled towards the thicket, near Jean Valjean.

Jean Valjean put his foot upon it.

The boy, however, had followed the coin with his eye, and had seen where it went.

He was not frightened, and walked straight to the man.

It was an entirely solitary place. Far as the eye could reach there was no one on the plain or in the path. Nothing could be heard, but the faint cries of a flock of birds of passage, that were flying across the sky at an immense height. The child turned his back to the sun, which made his hair like threads of gold, and flushed the savage face of Jean Valjean with a lurid glow.

"Monsieur," said the little Savoyard, with that childish confidence which is made up of ignorance and innocence, "my coin?"

"What is your name?" said Jean Valjean.

"Petit Gervais, monsieur."

"Go away," said Jean Valjean.

"Monsieur," continued the boy, "give me my coin."

Jean Valjean dropped his head and did not answer.

The child repeated:

---

*Chimneysweeps were called "little Savoyards," because only children were small enough to climb into chimneys to clean them, and because many such children came from Savoy in eastern France.

"My coin, monsieur!"

Jean Valjean's eye remained fixed on the ground.

"My coin!" exclaimed the boy, "my white coin! my silver!"

Jean Valjean did not appear to understand. The boy took him by the collar of his smock and shook him. And at the same time he made an effort to move the big, iron-soled shoe which was placed upon his treasure.

"I want my coin! my forty-sous coin!"

The child began to cry. Jean Valjean raised his head. He still kept his seat. His look was troubled. He looked upon the boy with an air of wonder, then reached out his hand towards his stick, and exclaimed in a terrible voice: "Who is there?"

"Me, monsieur," answered the boy. "Petit Gervais! me! me! give me back my forty sous, if you please! Take away your foot, monsieur, if you please!" Then becoming angry, small as he was, and almost threatening:

"Come, now, will you take away your foot? Why don't you take away your foot?"

"Ah! you here yet!" said Jean Valjean, and rising hastily to his feet, without releasing the coin, he added: "You'd better run!"

The boy looked at him in terror, then began to tremble from head to foot, and after a few seconds of stupor, took to flight and ran with all his might without daring to turn his head or to utter a cry.

At a little distance, however, he stopped for want of breath, and Jean Valjean in his reverie heard him sobbing.

In a few minutes the boy was gone.

The sun had gone down.

The shadows were deepening around Jean Valjean. He had not eaten during the day; probably he had some fever.

He had remained standing, and had not changed his position since the child fled. His breathing came at long and unequal intervals. His eyes were fixed on a spot ten or twelve steps before him, and seemed to be studying with profound attention the form of an old piece of blue crockery that was lying in the grass. All at once he shivered; he began to feel the cold night air.

He pulled his cap down over his forehead, sought mechanically to fold and button his smock around him, stepped forward and stooped to pick up his stick.

At that instant he perceived the forty-sous coin which his foot had half buried in the ground, and which glistened among the pebbles. It was like an electric shock. "What is that?" said he, between his teeth. He drew back a step or two, then stopped without the power to withdraw his gaze from this point which his foot had covered the instant before, as if the thing that glistened there in the obscurity had been an open eye fixed upon him.

After a few minutes, he sprang convulsively towards the coin, seized it, and, rising, looked away over the plain, straining his eyes towards all points of the horizon, standing and trembling like a wild beast which is seeking a place of refuge.

He saw nothing. Night was falling, the plain was cold and bare, thick purple mists were rising in the glimmering twilight.

He said: "Oh!" and began to walk rapidly in the direction in which the child had gone. After some thirty steps, he stopped, looked about, and saw nothing.

Then he called with all his might "Petit Gervais! Petit Gervais!"

And then he listened.

There was no answer.

The countryside was desolate and gloomy. On all sides was space. There was nothing about him but a shadow in which his gaze was lost, and a silence in which his voice was lost.

A biting norther was blowing, which gave a kind of dismal life to everything about him. The bushes shook their little thin arms with an incredible fury. One would have said that they were threatening and pursuing somebody.*

He began to walk again, then quickened his pace to a run, and from time to time stopped and called out in that solitude, in a most desolate and terrible voice:

"Petit Gervais! Petit Gervais!"

Surely, if the child had heard him, he would have been frightened, and would have hid himself. But doubtless the boy was already far away.

He met a priest on horseback. He went up to him and said:

"Monsieur curé, have you seen a child go by?"

"No," said the priest.

"Petit Gervais was his name?"

"I have seen nobody."

He took two five-franc coins from his bag, and gave them to the priest.

"Monsieur curé, this is for your poor. Monsieur curé, he is a little fellow, about ten years old, with a cherrywood box, I think, and a hurdygurdy. He went this way. One of these Savoyards, you know?"

"I have not seen him."

"Petit Gervais? is his village near here? can you tell me?"

"If it be as you say, my friend, the little fellow is a foreigner. They roam about this country. Nobody knows them."

Jean Valjean hastily took out two more five-franc coins, and gave them to the priest.

"For your poor," said he.

Then he added wildly:

"Monsieur abbé, have me arrested. I am a robber."

The priest put spurs to his horse, and fled in great fear.

Jean Valjean began to run again in the direction which he had first taken.

He went on in this wise for a considerable distance, looking around, calling and shouting, but met nobody else. Two or three times he left the path to look at what seemed to be somebody lying down or crouching; it was only low bushes or rocks. Finally, at a place where three paths met, he

---

*The hallucination of menacing bushes comes from Jean Valjean's guilty conscience, and anticipates Eponine's impression that the bare trees are gallows.

stopped. The moon had risen. He strained his eyes in the distance, and called out once more "Petit Gervais! Petit Gervais! Petit Gervais!" His cries died away into the mist, without even awakening an echo. Again he murmured: "Petit Gervais!" but with a feeble, and almost inarticulate voice. That was his last effort; his knees suddenly bent under him, as if an invisible power overwhelmed him at a blow, with the weight of his bad conscience; he fell exhausted upon a great stone, his hands clenched in his hair, and his face on his knees, and exclaimed: "What a wretch I am!"

Then his heart swelled, and he burst into tears. It was the first time he had wept for nineteen years.

When Jean Valjean left the bishop's house, as we have seen, his mood was one that he had never known before. He could understand nothing of what was going on within him. He set himself stubbornly in opposition to the angelic deeds and the gentle words of the old man, "you have promised me to become an honest man. I am purchasing your soul, I withdraw it from the spirit of perversity and I give it to God Almighty." This came back to him incessantly. To this celestial tenderness, he opposed pride, which is the fortress of evil in man. He felt dimly that the pardon of this priest was the hardest assault, and the most formidable attack which he had yet sustained; that his hardness of heart would be complete, if it resisted this kindness; that if he yielded, he must renounce that hatred with which the acts of other men had for so many years filled his soul, and in which he found satisfaction; that, this time, he must conquer or be conquered, and that the struggle, a gigantic and decisive struggle, had begun between his own wickedness, and the goodness of this man.

Confronted with all these revelations, he staggered like a drunken man. While thus walking on with haggard look, had he a distinct perception of what the result of his adventure at D—— might mean? Did he hear those mysterious murmurs which warn or entreat the spirit at certain moments of life? Did a voice whisper in his ear that he had just passed through the decisive hour of his destiny, that there was no longer a middle course for him, that if, thereafter, he should not be the best of men, he would be the worst, that he must now, so to speak, mount higher than the bishop, or fall lower than the galley slave; that, if he would become good, he must become an angel; that, if he would remain wicked, he must become a monster?

One thing was certain, nor did he himself doubt it, that he was no longer the same man, that all was changed in him, that it was no longer in his power to prevent the bishop from having talked to him and having moved him.

In this frame of mind, he had met Petit Gervais, and stolen his forty sous. Why? He could not have explained it, surely; was it the final effect, the final effort of the evil thoughts he had brought from the galleys, a remnant of impulse, a result of what is called in physics *momentum*? It was that, and it was also perhaps even less than that. We will say plainly, it was not he who had stolen, it was not the man, it was the beast which, from habit and instinct, had stupidly set its foot upon that money, while the intellect was struggling in the midst of so many new and unknown influences. When the intellect awoke and saw this act of the brute, Jean Valjean recoiled in anguish and uttered a cry of horror.

It was a strange phenomenon, possible only in the condition in which he then was, but the fact is, that in stealing this money from that child, he had done a thing of which he was no longer capable.

However that may be, this last misdeed had a decisive effect upon him; it rushed across the chaos of his intellect and dissipated it, set the light on one side and the dark clouds on the other, and acted upon his soul, in the condition it was in, as certain chemical reagents act upon a turbid mixture, by precipitating one element and producing a clear solution of the other.

At first, even before self-examination and reflection, distractedly, like one who seeks to escape, he endeavoured to find the boy to give him back his money; then, when he found that that was useless and impossible, he stopped in despair. At the very moment when he exclaimed: "What a wretch I am!" he saw himself as he was, and was already so far separated from himself that it seemed to him that he was only a phantom, and that he had there before him, in flesh and bone with his stick in his hand, his smock on his back, his knapsack filled with stolen articles on his shoulders, with his stern and gloomy face, and his thoughts full of abominable projects, the hideous galley slave, Jean Valjean.

Excess of misfortune, we have remarked, had made him, in some sort, a visionary. This then was like a vision. He veritably saw this Jean Valjean, this ominous face, before him. He was on the point of asking himself who that man was, and he was horror-stricken by it.

His brain was in one of those violent, and yet frightfully calm, conditions where reverie is so profound that it swallows up reality. We no longer see the objects that are before us, but we see, as if outside of ourselves, the forms that we have in our minds.

He beheld himself then, so to speak, face to face, and at the same time, through that hallucination, he saw, at a mysterious distance, a sort of light which he took at first to be a torch. Examining more attentively this light which dawned upon his conscience, he recognised that it had a human form, and that this torch was the bishop.

His conscience weighed in turn these two men thus placed before it, the bishop and Jean Valjean. Anything less than the first would have failed to soften the second. By one of those singular effects which are peculiar to this kind of ecstasy, as his reverie continued, the bishop grew grander and more resplendent in his eyes, Jean Valjean shrank and faded away. At one moment he was but a shadow. Suddenly he disappeared. The bishop alone remained.

He filled the whole soul of this wretched man with a magnificent radiance.

Jean Valjean wept long. He shed hot tears, he wept bitterly, with more weakness than a woman, with more terror than a child.

While he wept, the light grew brighter and brighter in his mind—an extraordinary light, a light at once ravishing and terrible. His past life, his first offence, his long expiation, his brutal exterior, his hardened interior, his release made glad by so many schemes of vengeance, what had happened to him at the bishop's, his last action, this theft of forty sous from a child, a crime meaner and the more monstrous that it came after the bishop's pardon, all this returned and appeared to him, clearly, but in a light that he had never seen before. He beheld his life, and it seemed to him horrible; his soul, and it seemed to him frightful. There was, however, a softened light upon that life and upon that soul. It seemed to him that he was looking upon Satan by the light of Paradise.*

How long did he weep thus? What did he do after weeping? Where did he go? Nobody ever knew. It is known simply that, on that very night, the stage-driver who drove at that time on the Grenoble route, and arrived at D—— about three o'clock in the morning, saw, as he passed through the bishop's street, a man in the attitude of prayer, kneeling upon the pavement in the shadow, before the door of Monseigneur Bienvenu.

---

*Comparisons between Jean Valjean and Satan or (later) Christ seem melodramatic, but they underline that damnation or salvation is at stake.

BOOK THREE
IN THE YEAR 1817

1

THE YEAR 1817

With dozens of examples from current events and popular culture, Hugo characterizes the mediocrity, frivolity, and superficiality of the early Restoration years. Exhausted by twenty-five years of war, France wishes only to relax. The dark side of these attitudes, a callous disregard for the poor and for social justice, will be exemplified by Tholomyès abandoning his lover Fantine without taking any responsibility for supporting their child.

2

DOUBLE FOURSOME

IN THIS YEAR, 1817, four young Parisians played "a good joke." These Parisians were, one from Toulouse, another from Limoges, the third from Cahors, and the fourth from Montauban; but they were students, and to say student is to say Parisian; to study in Paris is to be born in Paris.

These young men were unremarkable; everybody has seen such persons, the four first comers will serve as samples; neither good nor bad, neither learned nor ignorant, neither talented nor stupid; handsome in that charming April of life which we call twenty. They were four run-of-the-mill Oscars; for at this time, Arthurs were not yet in existence. *Burn the perfumes of Arabia in his honour,* exclaims the romance. *Oscar approaches! Oscar, I am about to see him!* Ossian was in fashion, elegance was Scandinavian and Caledonian; the pure English style did not prevail till later, and the first of the Arthurs, Wellington, had but just won the victory of Waterloo.

The first of these Oscars was called Félix Tholomyès, of Toulouse; the second, Listolier, of Cahors; the third, Fameuil, of Limoges; and the last, Blacheville, of Montauban. Of course each had his mistress. Blacheville loved Favourite, so called, because she had been in England; Listolier adored Dahlia, who had taken the name of a flower as her *nom de guerre,* Fameuil idolised Zéphine, the diminutive of Josephine, and Tholomyès had Fantine, called *the Blonde,* on account of her beautiful hair, the colour of the sun. Favourite, Dahlia, Zéphine, and Fantine were four enchanting girls, perfumed and sparkling, something of workwomen still, since they had not wholly given up the needle, agitated by love-affairs, yet preserving on their countenances a remnant of the serenity of labour, and in their souls that flower of purity, which in woman survives the first fall. One of the four was called the child, because she was the youngest; and another was called the old one—the Old One was twenty-three. To conceal nothing, the three first were more experienced, more heedless, and better versed in the ways of the world than Fantine, the Blonde, who was still in her first illusion.

The young men were comrades, the young girls were friends. Such loves are always accompanied by such friendships.

Wisdom and philosophy are two things; a proof of which is that, with all necessary reservations for these little, irregular households, Favourite, Zéphine, and Dahlia, were philosophical, and Fantine was wise.

"Wise!" you will say, and Tholomyès? Solomon would answer that love is a part of wisdom. We content ourselves with saying that the love of Fantine was a first, an only, a faithful love.

She was the only one of the four who had been addressed as "tu" by but one.[*]

Fantine was one of those beings which are brought forth from the heart of the people. Sprung from the most unfathomable depths of social darkness, she bore on her brow the mark of the anonymous and unknown. She was born at M—— on M——. Who were her parents? None could tell, she had never known either father or mother. She was called Fantine—why so? because she had never been known by any other name. At the time of her birth, the Directory was still in existence.[†] She could have no family name, for she had no family; she could have no baptismal name, for then there was no church. She was named at the pleasure of the first passer-by who found her, a mere infant, straying barefoot in the streets. She received a name as she received the water from the clouds on her head when it rained. She was called little Fantine. Nobody knew anything more of her. Such was the manner in which this human being had come into life. At the age of ten, Fantine left the city and went to work among the tenant farmers of the suburbs. At fifteen, she came to Paris, to "seek her fortune." Fantine was beautiful and remained pure as long as she could. She was a pretty blonde with fine teeth. She had gold and pearls for her dowry; but the gold was on her head and the pearls in her mouth.

She worked to live; then, also to live, for the heart too has its hunger, she loved.

She loved Tholomyès.

---

[*]French tradition distinguished sharply between the *femme sensible,* who has had only one love affair outside marriage, and the *femme galante,* who has had more.

[†]The Directory (1795–1799) was the transitional government between the Revolution and Napoléon's assumption of the supreme power.

To him, it was a fling; to her a passion. The streets of the Latin Quarter, which swarm with students and grisettes, saw the beginning of this dream.* Fantine, in those labyrinths of the hill of the Pantheon, where so many affairs are knotted and unloosed, long fled from Tholomyès, but in such a way as always to meet him again. There is a way of avoiding a person which resembles a search. In short, the eclogue took place.†

Blacheville, Listolier, and Fameuil formed a sort of group of which Tholomyès was the head. He was the wit of the company.

Tholomyès was an old student of the old style; he was rich, having an income of four thousand francs—a splendid scandal on the Montagne Sainte-Geneviève. He was a good liver, thirty years old and ill preserved. He was wrinkled, his teeth were broken, and he was beginning to show signs of baldness, of which he said, gaily: *"The head at thirty, the knees at forty."* His digestion was not good, and he had a weeping eye. But in proportion as his youth died out, his gaiety increased; he replaced his teeth by jests, his hair by joy, his health by irony, and his weeping eye was always laughing. He was dilapidated, but covered with flowers. His youth, decamping long before its time, was beating a retreat in good order, bursting with laughter and everyone was fooled. He had had a play refused by the Vaudeville; he wrote poems now and then on any subject; moreover, he expressed skepticism about everything with a superior air—a great strength in the eyes of the weak. So, being bald and ironical, he was the leader. Can the word *iron* be the root from which irony is derived?‡

One day, Tholomyès took the other three aside, and said to them with an oracular gesture:

"For nearly a year, Fantine, Dahlia, Zéphine, and Favourite have been asking us to give them a surprise; we have solemnly promised them one. They are constantly reminding us of it, me especially. Just as the old women at Naples cry to Saint January, '*Faccia gialluta, fa o miracolo,* yellow face, do your miracle,' our pretty ones are always saying: 'Tholomyès, when are you going to give birth to your surprise?' At the same time, our parents are asking us to come visit. It's a bore on both sides. It seems to me the time has come. Let us talk it over."

Upon this, Tholomyès lowered his voice, and mysteriously articulated something so ludicrous that a prolonged and enthusiastic sniggering arose from the four throats at once, and Blacheville exclaimed: "What an idea!"

An ale-house, filled with smoke, was before them; they entered and the rest of their conference was lost in its shadows.

The result of this mystery was a brilliant pleasure party, which took place on the following Sunday, the four young men inviting the four young girls.

---

*The *grisettes*, poor young working women who wore gray smocks, were traditional targets of seduction attempts by students and young male professionals.
†In ancient Greek and Roman literature, an eclogue was a poem about the idealized loves of imaginary shepherds and shepherdesses; Hugo's tone is sarcastic.
‡The sentence means "are people who jest always hard-hearted?"

3

FOUR TO FOUR

IT IS DIFFICULT to picture to oneself, today, a country outing of students and grisettes as it was forty-five years ago. Paris has no longer the same environs; the aspect of what we might call circum-Parisian life has completely changed in half a century; in place of the crude, one-horse chaise, we have now the railroad car; in place of the sloop, we have now the steamboat; we say Fécamp to-day, as we then said Saint Cloud. The Paris of 1862 is a city which has France for its suburbs.[6]

The four couples scrupulously accomplished all the country follies then possible. It was in the beginning of the holidays, and a hot, clear summer's day. The night before, Favourite, the only one who knew how to write, had written to Tholomyès in the name of the four: "It is lucky to go out early." For this reason, they rose at five in the morning. Then they went to Saint Cloud by the coach, looked at the dry waterfall and exclaimed: "How beautiful it must be when there is any water!" breakfasted at the *Tête Noire,* where Castaing had not yet passed by, amused themselves with a game of ringtoss at the quincunx of the great basin, ascended to Diogenes' lantern, wagered macaroons at the roulette game on the Sèvres bridge, gathered bouquets at Puteaux, bought reed pipes at Neuilly, ate apple puffs everywhere, and were perfectly happy.

The girls whispered and chattered like uncaged warblers. They were delirious with joy. Now and then they would playfully pat the young men. Intoxication of the morning of life! Adorable years!

As to Fantine, she was joy itself. Her splendid teeth had evidently been endowed by God with one function—that of laughing. She carried in her hand rather than on her head her little hat of sewed straw, with long, white strings. Her thick blond tresses, inclined to wave, and easily escaping from their confinement, obliging her to fasten them continually, seemed designed for the flight of Galatea under the willows. Her rosy lips babbled with enchantment. The corners of her mouth, turned up voluptuously like the antique masks of Erigone, seemed to encourage audacity; but her long, shadowy eyelashes were cast discreetly down towards the lower part of her face as if to check its festive tendencies. Her whole toilette was indescribably harmonious and enchanting. She wore a dress of mauve barege, little reddish-brown buskins, the strings of which were crossed over her fine, white, open-worked stockings, and that species of spencer, invented at Marseilles, the name of which, *canezou,* a corruption of the words *quinze août* in the Canebière dialect, signifies fine weather, warmth, and noon.

The three others, less timid as we have said, wore low-necked dresses, which in summer, beneath bonnets covered with flowers, are full of grace and allurement; but by the side of this daring toilette, the canezou of the blond Fantine, with its transparencies, indiscretions, and concealments, at once hiding and disclosing, seemed a provocative godsend of decency; and the famous court of love, presided over by the Viscountess de Cette, with the sea-green eyes, might have given the prize for coquetry to this canezou, which had entered the lists for that of modesty. The simplest is sometimes the wisest. So things go.

A brilliant face, delicate profile, eyes of a deep blue, heavy eyelashes, small, arching feet, the wrists and ankles neatly encased, the white skin showing here and there the azure aborescence of the veins; a cheek small and fresh, a neck robust as that of Egean Juno; the nape firm and supple, shoulders modelled as if by Coustou, with a voluptuous dimple in the centre, just visible through the muslin: a gaiety tempered with reverie, sculptured and exquisite—such was Fantine, and you divined beneath this dress and these ribbons a statue, and in this statue a soul.

Fantine was beautiful, without being too conscious of it. Those rare dreamers, the mysterious priests of the beautiful, who silently compare all things with perfection, would have had a dim vision in this little workwoman, through the transparency of Parisian grace, of the ancient sacred Euphony. This daughter of obscurity had race. She possessed both types of beauty—style and rhythm. Style is the force of the ideal, rhythm is its movement.

We have said that Fantine was joy; Fantine also was modesty.

For an observer who had studied her attentively would have found through all this intoxication of youth, of the season, and of love, an unconquerable expression of reserve and modesty. She still seemed surprised at having a lover. This chaste restraint is the shade which separates Psyche from Venus. Fantine had the long, white, slender fingers of the vestals that stir the ashes of the sacred fire with a golden rod.[*] Although she would have refused nothing to Tholomyès, as we shall see only too well, her face, in repose, was in the highest degree maidenly; a kind of serious and almost austere dignity suddenly possessed it at times, and nothing could be more strange or disquieting than to see gaiety vanish there so quickly, and reflection instantly succeed to delight. This sudden seriousness, sometimes strangely marked, resembled the disdain of a goddess. Her forehead, nose, and chin presented that equilibrium of line, quite distinct from the equilibrium of proportion, which produces harmony of features; in the characteristic interval which separates the base of the nose from the upper lip, she had that almost imperceptible but charming fold, the mysterious sign

---

*Vestals were virgin priestesses who served the temples of the gods in ancient Greece.

of chastity, which enamoured Barbarossa with a Diana, found in the excavations of Iconium.*

Love is a fault; be it so. Fantine was innocence floating upon the surface
of this fault.[7]

4

THOLOMYÈS IS SO MERRY THAT
HE SINGS A SPANISH SONG

THAT DAY was sunshine from one end to the other. All nature seemed to
be out on a holiday. The flowerbeds of Saint Cloud were balmy with perfumes; the breeze from the Seine gently waved the leaves; the boughs
were gesticulating in the wind; the bees were pillaging the jessamine, a
whole gypsy crew of butterflies had settled in the milfoil, clover, and wild
oats. The august park of the King of France was invaded by a swarm of
vagabonds, the birds.

The four joyous couples shone resplendently in concert with the sunshine, the flowers, the fields, and the trees.

And in this paradisaical community, speaking, singing, running, danc-
ing, chasing butterflies, gathering bindweed, wetting their pink open-
worked stockings in the high grass, fresh, wild, but not wicked, stealing
kisses from each other indiscriminately now and then, all except Fantine,
who was shut up in her vague, dreary, severe resistance, and who was in
love. "You always have the air of being out of sorts," said Favourite to her.

These are true pleasures. These passages in the lives of happy couples are a
profound appeal to life and nature, and call forth endearment and light from
everything. There was once upon a time a fairy, who created meadows and
trees expressly for lovers. Thence, among the groves, that everlasting school
for lovers, always in session. Thence the popularity of spring among thinkers.
The patrician and the plebeian, the duke and peer, and the magistrate, the
men of the court, and the men of the town, as was said in olden times, all play
a part in this festivity. They laugh, they look for each other, the air seems filled
with a new brightness; what a transfiguration is it to love! Law clerks are gods.
And the little shrieks, the pursuits among the grass, the waists encircled by

---

*Khair ed-Din Barbarossa (1466?–1546) was a notorious Turkish pirate who ruled
most of the Mediterranean near the end of his life; he greatly admired a Byzantine
statue of Diana, the ancient goddess of the hunt, the moon, and chastity.

stealth, that silly chatter which is melody, that adoration which breaks forth in the way one says a syllable, those cherries snatched from one pair of lips by another—all flame up, and become transformed into celestial glories. Beautiful girls lavish their charms with sweet prodigality. We fancy that it will never end. Philosophers, poets, painters behold these ecstasies and know not what to make of them. So dazzling are they. The departure for Cythera! exclaims Watteau; Lancret, the painter of the common man, contemplates his bourgeois soaring in the sky; Diderot stretches out his arms to all these loves, and d'Urfé associates them with the Druids.

After breakfast, the four couples went to see, in what was then called the king's garden plot, a plant newly arrived from the Indies, the name of which escapes us at present, and which at this time was attracting all Paris to Saint Cloud: it was a strange and beautiful shrub with a long stalk, the innumerable branches of which, fine as threads, tangled, and leafless, were covered with millions of little white blossoms, which gave it the appearance of flowing hair, powdered with flowers. There was always a crowd admiring it.

When they had viewed the shrub, Tholomyès exclaimed, "I propose donkeys," and making a bargain with a donkey-driver, they returned through Vanvres and Issy. At Issy, they had an adventure. The park, a National Preserve, owned at this time by the munitions manufacturer Bourguin, was by sheer good luck open. They passed through the grating, visited the statue of a hermit in his grotto, and tried the little, mysterious effects of the famous cabinet of mirrors—a wanton trap, worthy of a satyr become a millionaire, or Turcaret metamorphosed into Priapus.* They swung stoutly in the great swing, attached to the two chestnut trees, celebrated by the Abbé de Bernis. While swinging the girls, one after the other, and making folds of flying crinoline that Greuze would have found worth his study, the Toulousian Tholomyès, who was something of a Spaniard—Toulouse is cousin to Tolosa—sang in a melancholy key, the old *gallega* song, probably inspired by some beautiful damsel swinging in the air between two trees.

> *Soy de Badaioz.*
> *Amor me llama.*
> *Toda mi alma*
> *Es en mi ojos*
> *Porque enseñas*
> *A tus piernas.*

Fantine alone refused to swing.

"I do not like that kind of affectation," murmured Favourite, rather sharply.

They left the donkeys for a new pleasure, crossed the Seine in a boat, and walked from Passy to the Barrière de l'Etoile. They had been on their

---

*Alain-René Lesage's play *Turcaret* (1709) satirizes a lustful financier from the provinces. Priapus, son of Dionysus, was the Greek god of virility and procreation.

feet, it will be remembered, since five in the morning, but *bah! there is no weariness on Sunday,* said Favourite; on Sunday fatigue has a holiday. Towards three o'clock, the four couples, wild with happiness, were climbing down from the roller-coaster, a peculiar construction where sinuous contour you could see above the trees of the Champs-Elysées.

From time to time Favourite exclaimed:

"But the surprise? I want the surprise."

"Be patient," answered Tholomyès.

5

AT BOMBARDA'S

Having tired of the roller-coaster, they thought of dinner, and the happy eight a little weary at last, stranded on Bombarda's, a branch establishment, set up in the Champs-Elysées by the celebrated restaurateur, Bombarda, whose sign was then seen on the Rue de Rivoli, near the Delorme arcade.

6

A CHAPTER OF SELF-ADMIRATION

TABLE TALK and lovers' talk equally elude the grasp; lovers' talk is clouds, table talk is smoke.

Fameuil and Dahlia hummed airs; Tholomyès drank, Zéphine laughed, Fantine smiled. Listolier blew a wooden trumpet that he had bought at Saint Cloud. Favourite looked tenderly at Blacheville and said:

"Blacheville, I adore you."

This brought forth a question from Blacheville:

"What would you do, Favourite, if I should leave you?"

"Me!" cried Favourite. "Oh! do not say that, even in sport! If you should leave me, I would run after you, I would scratch you, I would pull your hair, I would throw water on you, I would have you arrested."

Blacheville smiled with the effeminate foppery of a man whose self-love is tickled. Favourite continued:

"Yes! I would call the police! I wouldn't hold back! I would scream, for example: scoundrel!"

Blacheville, in ecstasy, leaned back in his chair, and closed both eyes with a satisfied air.

Dahlia, still eating, whispered to Favourite in the hubbub:

"Are you really so fond of your Blacheville, then?"

"I detest him," whispered Favourite, taking up her fork. "He is stingy; I am in love with the little fellow over the way from where I live. He is a nice young man; do you know him? Anybody can see that he was born to be an actor! I love actors. As soon as he comes into the house, his mother cries out: 'Oh, dear! my peace is all gone. There, he is going to hallo! You will split my head;' just because he goes into the garret among the rats, into the dark corners, as high as he can go, and sings and declaims—something or other so loud that they can hear him below! He already makes twenty sous a day by copying documents for a lawyer. He is the son of an old chorister of Saint-Jacques du Haut-Pas! Oh, he is a nice young man! He is so fond of me that he said one day, when he saw me making dough for pancakes: 'Mamselle, make your gloves into fritters and I will eat them.' Nobody but artists can say things like these; I am on the high road to go crazy about this little fellow. It is all the same, I tell Blacheville that I adore him. How I lie! Oh, how I lie!"

Favourite paused, then continued:

"Dahlia, you see I am melancholy. It has done nothing but rain all summer; the wind irritates me, it is always in a bad mood. Blacheville is very stingy; there are hardly any green peas in the market yet, people care for nothing but eating; I have the spleen, as the English say; butter is so dear! and then, just think of it—it is horrible! We are dining in a room with a bed in it. I am disgusted with life."

7

THE WISDOM OF THOLOMYÈS

AT THIS MOMENT, Favourite, crossing her arms and turning round her head, looked fixedly at Tholomyès and said:

"Come! the surprise?"

"Precisely. The moment has come," replied Tholomyès. "Gentlemen, the hour has come for surprising these ladies. Ladies, wait for us a moment."

"It begins with a kiss," said Blacheville.

"On the forehead," added Tholomyès.

Each one gravely placed a kiss on the forehead of his mistress; after which they directed their steps towards the door, all four in file, laying their fingers on their lips.

Favourite clapped her hands as they went out.

"It is amusing already," said she.

"Do not be too long," murmured Fantine. "We are waiting for you."*

8 (9)

JOYOUS END OF JOY

THE GIRLS, left alone, leaned their elbows on the window sills in couples, and chattered together, bending their heads and speaking from one window to the other.

They saw the young men go out of Bombarda's, arm in arm; they turned round, made signals to them laughingly, then disappeared in the dusty Sunday crowd which takes possession of the Champs-Elysées once a week.

"Do not be long!" cried Fantine.

"What are they going to bring us?" said Zéphine.

"Surely something pretty," said Dahlia.

"I hope it will be gold," resumed Favourite.

Some time passed in this manner. Suddenly Favourite started as if from sleep.

"Well!" said she, "and the surprise?"

"Yes," returned Dahlia, "the famous surprise."

"They are taking a very long time!" said Fantine.

As Fantine finished the sigh, the boy who had waited at dinner entered. He had in his hand something that looked like a letter.

"What is that?" asked Favourite.

"It is a paper that the gentlemen left for these ladies," he replied.

"Why did you not bring it at once?"

"Because the gentlemen ordered me not to give it to the ladies before an hour," returned the boy.

Favourite snatched the paper from his hands. It was really a letter.

"Stop!" said she. "There is no address; but see what is written on it:

---

*Here, as elsewhere, Fantine's remark shows that only she among the four companions really cares for her lover. See the first half of the next chapter as well.

She hastily unsealed the letter, opened it, and read (she knew how to read):

"Oh, our lovers!

"Know that we have parents. Parents—you scarcely know the meaning of the word, they are what are called fathers and mothers in the civil code, simple but honest. Now these parents bemoan us, these old men claim us, these good men and women call us prodigal sons, desire our return and offer to kill for us the fatted calf. We obey them, being virtuous. At the moment when you read this, five mettlesome horses will be bearing us back to our papas and mammas. We are pitching our camps, as Bossuet says. We are going, we are gone. We fly in the arms of Laffitte, and on the wings of Caillard. The Toulouse stage snatches us from the abyss, and you are this abyss, our beautiful darlings! We are returning to society, to duty and order, on a full trot, at the rate of seven miles an hour. It is necessary to the country that we become, like everybody else, prefects, fathers of families, rural guards, and councillors of state. Venerate us. We sacrifice ourselves. Mourn for us rapidly, and replace us speedily. If this letter rends you, rend it in turn. Adieu.

"For nearly two years we have made you happy. Bear us no ill will for it."

SIGNED: BLACHEVILLE,
FAMEUIL,
LISTOLIER,
FÉLIX THOLOMYÈS.

"P. S. The dinner is paid for."

The four girls gazed at each other.

Favourite was the first to break silence.

"Well!" said she, "it is a good farce all the same."

"It is very droll," said Zéphine.

"It must have been Blacheville that had the idea," resumed Favourite. "This makes me in love with him. Soon loved, soon gone. That is the story."

"No," said Dahlia, "it is an idea of Tholomyès. This is clear."

"In that case," returned Favourite, "down with Blacheville, and long live Tholomyès!"

"Long live Tholomyès!" cried Dahlia and Zéphine.

And they burst into laughter.

Fantine laughed like the rest.

An hour afterwards, when she had returned to her bedroom, she wept. It was her first love, as we have said; she had given herself to this Tholomyès as to a husband, and the poor girl had a child.

BOOK FOUR
TO ENTRUST IS SOMETIMES TO ABANDON

1

ONE MOTHER MEETS ANOTHER

THERE WAS, during the first quarter of the present century, at Montfermeil, near Paris, a sort of tavern; it is not there now. It was kept by a man and his wife, named Thénardier and was situated in the Boulanger Alley. Above the door, nailed flat against the wall, was a board, upon which something was painted that looked like a man carrying on his back another man wearing the heavy epaulettes of a general, gilt and with large silver stars; red blotches typified blood; the remainder of the picture was smoke, and probably represented a battle. Beneath was this inscription: THE SERGEANT OF WATERLOO PLACE.

Nothing is commoner than a cart or wagon before the door of an inn; nevertheless the vehicle, or more properly speaking, the fragment of a vehicle which obstructed the street in front of the Sergeant of Waterloo one evening in the spring of 1818, certainly would have attracted by its bulk the attention of any painter who might have been passing.

It was the fore-carriage of one of those drays for carrying heavy articles, used in wooded countries for transporting beams and trunks of trees: it consisted of a massive iron axle-tree with a pivot to which a heavy pole was attached, and which was supported by two enormous wheels. As a whole, it was squat, crushing, and misshapen: it might have been fancied a gigantic gun-carriage.

The ruts in the roads had covered the wheels, rims, hubs, axle, and the pole with a coating of hideous yellow-hued mud, similar in tint to that with which cathedrals are sometimes decorated. The wood had disappeared beneath mud; and the iron beneath rust.

Under the axle-tree hung festooned a huge chain fit for a Goliath of the galleys.

The middle of the chain was hanging quite near the ground under the axle; and upon the bend, as on a swinging rope, two little girls were seated that evening in exquisite grouping, the smaller, eighteen months old, in the lap of the larger, who was two years and a half old.

A handkerchief carefully knotted kept them from falling. A mother, looking upon this frightful chain, had said: "Ah! there is a plaything for my children!"

The radiant children, picturesquely and tastefully decked, might be fancied two roses twining the rusty iron, with their triumphantly sparkling eyes, and their blooming, laughing faces. One was a rosy blonde, the other a brunette; their artless faces were two ravishing surprises; the perfume that was shed upon the air by a flowering shrub near by seemed to emanate from them; the smaller one was showing her pretty little body with the chaste indecency of babyhood. Above and around these delicate heads moulded in happiness and bathed in light, the gigantic carriage, black with rust and almost frightful with its entangled curves and abrupt angles, arched like the mouth of a cavern.

The mother, a woman whose appearance was rather forbidding, but touching at this moment, was seated a few steps away on the sill of the inn, swinging the two children by a long string, while she brooded them with her eyes for fear of accident with that animal but heavenly expression peculiar to maternity. At each vibration the hideous links uttered a creaking noise like an angry cry; the little ones were in ecstasies, the setting sun mingled in the joy, and nothing could be more charming than this caprice of chance which made of a Titan's chain a swing for cherubim.

While rocking the babes the mother sang with a voice out of tune a then popular song:

"Il le faut, disait un guerrier."

Her song and watching her children prevented her hearing and seeing what was passing in the street.

Some one, however, had approached her as she was beginning the first couplet of the song, and suddenly she heard a voice say quite near her ear:

"You have two pretty children there, madame."

"A la belle et tendre Imogine,"

answered the mother, continuing her song; then she turned her head.

A woman was before her at a little distance; she also had a child, which she bore in her arms.

She was carrying in addition a large carpet-bag, which seemed heavy.

This woman's child was one of the divinest beings that can be imagined: a little girl of two or three years. She might have entered the lists with the other little ones for coquetry of attire, she wore a head-dress of fine linen; ribbons at her shoulders and Valenciennes lace on her cap. The folds of her skirt were raised enough to show her plump fine white leg; she was charmingly rosy and healthful. The pretty little creature gave one a desire to bite her cherry cheeks. We can say nothing of her eyes except that they must have been very large, and were fringed with superb lashes. She was asleep.

She was sleeping in the absolutely confiding slumber peculiar to her age. Mothers' arms are made of tenderness, and sweet sleep blesses the child who lies therein.

As to the mother, she seemed poor and sad; she had the appearance of a working woman who is seeking to return to the life of a peasant. She was young,—and pretty? It was possible, but in that garb beauty could not be displayed. Her hair, one blonde mesh of which had fallen, seemed very thick, but it was severely fastened up beneath an ugly, close, narrow nun's head-dress, tied under the chin. Laughing shows fine teeth when one has them, but she did not laugh. Her eyes seemed not to have been tearless for a long time. She was pale, and looked very weary, and somewhat sick. She gazed upon her child, sleeping in her arms, with that peculiar look which only a mother possesses who nurses her own child. Her form was clumsily masked by a large blue handkerchief folded across her bosom. Her hands were tanned and spotted with freckles, the forefinger hardened and pricked with the needle; she wore a coarse brown delaine mantle, a calico dress, and large heavy shoes. It was Fantine.

Yes, Fantine. Hard to recognise, yet on looking attentively, you saw that she still retained her beauty. A sad line, such as is formed by irony, had marked her right cheek. As to her toilette—that airy toilette of muslin and ribbons which seemed as if made of gaiety, folly, and music, full of baubles and perfumed with lilacs—that had vanished like the beautiful sparkling hoarfrost, which we take for diamonds in the sun; they melt, and leave the branch dreary and black.

Ten months had slipped away since "the good farce."

What had happened during these ten months? We can guess.

After recklessness, trouble. Fantine had lost sight of Favourite, Zéphine, and Dahlia; the tie, broken on the part of the men, was unloosed on the part of the women; they would have been astonished if any one had said a fortnight afterwards they were friends; they had no longer cause to be so. Fantine was left alone. The father of her child gone—Alas! such partings are irrevocable—she found herself absolutely isolated, with the habit of labour lost, and the taste for pleasure acquired. Led by her liaison with Tholomyès to disdain the small business that she knew how to do, she had neglected her opportunities, they were all gone. No resource. Fantine could scarcely read, and did not know how to write. She had only been taught in childhood how to sign her name. She had a letter written by a public letter-writer to Tholomyès, then a second, then a third. Tholomyès had replied to none of them. One day, Fantine heard some old women saying as they saw her child: "Do people ever take such children to heart? They only shrug their shoulders at such children!" Then she thought of Tholomyès, who shrugged his shoulders at his child, and who did not take this innocent child to heart, and her heart became dark in the place that was his. What should she do? She had no one to ask. She had committed a fault; but, in the depths of her nature, we know dwelt modesty and virtue. She had a vague feeling that she was on the eve of falling into distress, of slipping into the street. She must have courage, she had it, and bore up bravely. The idea occurred to her of returning to her native village M—— sur M——, there perhaps some one would know her, and give her work. Yes, but she must hide her fault. And she had a confused glimpse of the possible necessity of a separation still more painful than the first. Her heart ached, but she took her resolution. It will be seen that Fantine possessed the stern courage of life. She had already valiantly renounced her finery, was draped in calico, and had put all her silks, her gew-gaws, her ribbons, and laces on her daughter—the only vanity that remained, and that a holy one. She sold all she had, which gave her two hundred francs; when her little debts were paid, she had but about eighty left. At twenty-two years of age, on a fine spring morning, she left Paris, carrying her child on her back. He who had seen the two passing, must have pitied them. The woman had nothing in the world but this child, and this child had nothing in the world but this woman. Fantine had nursed her child; that had weakened her chest somewhat, and she coughed slightly.

We shall have no further need to speak of M. Félix Tholomyès. We will only say here, that twenty years later, under King Louis Philippe, he was a fat provincial attorney, rich and influential, a wise elector and rigid jury-man; always, however, a man of pleasure.

Towards noon, after having, for the sake of rest, travelled from time to time at a cost of three or four cents a league, in what they called then the Petites Voitures of the environs of Paris, Fantine reached Montfermeil, and stood in Boulanger Alley.

As she was passing by the Thénardier tavern, the two little children, sitting in delight on their monstrous swing, had a sort of dazzling effect upon her, and she paused before this joyous vision.

There are charms. These two little girls were one for this mother.

She beheld them with emotion. The presence of angels is a herald of paradise. She thought she saw above this inn the mysterious "HERE" of Providence. These children were evidently happy; she gazed upon them, she admired them, so much affected that at the moment when the mother was taking breath between the verses of her song, she could not help saying what we have been reading.

"You have two pretty children there, madame."

The most ferocious animals are disarmed by caresses to their young.

The mother raised her head and thanked her and made the stranger sit down on the stone step, she herself being on the doorsill: the two women began to talk together.

"My name is Madame Thénardier," said the mother of the two girls: "we keep this inn."

Then going on with her song, she sang between her teeth:

"Il le faut, je suis chevalier
Et je pars pour la Palestine."

This Madame Thénardier was a red-haired, brawny, angular woman, of the soldier's slut type in all its horror, and, singularly enough, she had a lolling air which she had gained from novel-reading. She was a simpering, mannish woman. Old romances impressed on the imaginations of mistresses of taverns have such effects. She was still young, scarcely thirty years old. If this woman, who was seated stooping, had been upright, perhaps her towering form and her broad shoulders, those of a movable colossus, fit for a market-woman, would have dismayed the traveller, disturbed her confidence, and prevented what we have to relate. A person seated instead of standing; fate hangs on such a thread as that.

The traveller told her story, a little modified.

She said she was a working woman, and her husband was dead. Not being able to procure work in Paris she was going in search of it elsewhere; in her own province; that she had left Paris that morning on foot, that carrying her child she had become tired, and meeting the Ville-momble stage had got in; that from Villemomble she had come on foot to Montfermeil; that the child had walked a little but not much, she was so young, that she was compelled to carry her, and the jewel had fallen asleep.

And at these words she gave her daughter a passionate kiss which wakened her. The child opened its large blue eyes, like its mother's, and saw— what? Nothing, everything, with that serious and sometimes severe air of little children, which is one of the mysteries of their shining innocence before our shadowy virtues. One would say that they felt themselves to be angels, and knew us to be human. Then the child began to laugh, and, although the mother restrained her, slipped to the ground, with the indomitable energy of a little one that wants to run about. All at once she perceived the two others in their swing, stopped short, and put out her tongue in token of admiration.

Mother Thénardier untied the children and took them from the swing saying:

"Play together, all three of you."

At that age acquaintance is easy, and in a moment the little Thénardiers were playing with the new-comer, making holes in the ground to their intense delight.

This new-comer was very sprightly: the goodness of the mother is written in the gaiety of the child; she had taken a splinter of wood, which she used as a spade, and was stoutly digging a hole fit for a fly. The gravedigger's work is charming when done by a child.

The two women continued to chat.

"What do you call your brat?"

"Cosette."

"How old is she?"

"She is going on three years."

"The age of my oldest."

The three girls were grouped in an attitude of deep anxiety and bliss; a great event had occurred; a large worm had come out of the ground; they were afraid of it, and yet in ecstasies over it.

Their bright foreheads touched each other: three heads in one halo of glory.

"Children," exclaimed the Thénardier mother; "how soon they know one another. See them! one would swear they were three sisters."

These words were the spark which the other mother was probably awaiting. She seized the hand of Madame Thénardier and said:

"Will you keep my child for me?"

Madame Thénardier made a motion of surprise, which was neither consent nor refusal.

Cosette's mother continued:

"You see I cannot take my child into the country. Work forbids it. With a child I could not find a place there; they are so absurd in that district. It is God who has led me before your inn. The sight of your little ones, so pretty, and clean, and happy, has overwhelmed me. I said: there is a good mother; they will be like three sisters, and then it will not be long before I come back. Will you keep my child for me?"

"I must think over it," said Thénardier.

"I will give six francs a month."

Here a man's voice was heard from within:

"Not less than seven francs, and six months paid in advance."

"Six times seven are forty-two," said Thénardier.

"I will give it," said the mother.

"And fifteen francs extra for the first expenses," added the man.

"That's fifty-seven francs," said Madame Thénardier, and in the midst of her reckoning she sang indistinctly:

"Il le faut, disait un guerrier."

"I will give it," said the mother; "I have eighty francs. That will leave me enough to go into the country if I walk. I will earn some money there, and as soon as I have I will come for my little love."

The man's voice returned:

"Has the child a wardrobe?"

"That is my husband," said Thénardier.

"Certainly she has, the poor darling. I knew it was your husband. And a fine wardrobe it is too, an extravagant wardrobe, everything in dozens, and silk dresses like a lady. They are there in my carpet-bag."

"You must leave that here," put in the man's voice.

"Of course I shall give it to you," said the mother; "it would be strange if I should leave my child naked."

The face of the master appeared.

"It is all right," said he.

The bargain was concluded. The mother passed the night at the inn, gave her money and left her child, fastened again her carpet-bag, diminished by her child's wardrobe, and very light now, and set off next morning, expecting soon to return. These partings are arranged tranquilly, but they are full of despair.

A neighbour of the Thénardiers met this mother on her way, and came in, saying:

"I have just met a woman in the street, who was crying as if her heart would break."

When Cosette's mother had gone, the man said to his wife:

"That will do me for my note of 110 francs which falls due tomorrow; I was fifty francs short. Do you realize I would have received a summons? You have proved a good mousetrap with your little ones."

"Without knowing it," said the woman.

2

FIRST SKETCH OF TWO
SUSPICIOUS-LOOKING FACES

THE CAPTURED MOUSE was a very puny one, but the cat exulted even over a lean mouse.

What were the Thénardiers?

We will say but a word just here; by-and-by the sketch shall be completed.

They belonged to that bastard class formed of low people who have risen, and intelligent people who have fallen, which lies between the classes called middle and lower, and which unites some of the faults of the latter with nearly all the vices of the former, without possessing the generous impulses of the workman, or the respectability of the bourgeois.

They were of those dwarfish natures, which, if perchance heated by some sullen fire, easily become monstrous. The woman was at heart a brute; the man a blackguard: both in the highest degree capable of that hideous species of progress which can be made towards evil. There are souls which, crablike, crawl continually towards darkness, going back in life rather than advancing in it; using what experience they have to increase their deformity; growing worse without ceasing, and becoming steeped more and more thoroughly in an intensifying wickedness. Such souls were this man and this woman.

The man especially would have been a puzzle to a physiognomist. We have only to look at some men to distrust them, for we feel the darkness of their souls in two ways. They are uneasy as to what is behind them, and threatening as to what is before them. They are full of mystery. We can no more answer for what they have done, than for what they will do. The shadow in their looks denounces them. If we hear them utter a word, or see them make a gesture, we catch glimpses of guilty secrets in their past, and dark mysteries in their future.

This Thénardier, if we may believe him, had been a soldier, a sergeant he said; he probably had made the campaign of 1815, and had even borne himself bravely according to all that appeared. We shall see hereafter in what his bravery consisted. The sign of his inn was an allusion to one of his feats of arms. He had painted it himself, for he knew how to do a little of everything—badly.

3

THE LARK

To be wicked does not insure prosperity—for the inn did not turn a profit.

Thanks to Fantine's fifty-seven francs, Thénardier had been able to avoid a protest and to honour his signature. The next month they were still in need of money, and the woman carried Cosette's wardrobe to Paris and pawned it for sixty francs. When this sum was spent, the Thénardiers began to look upon the little girl as a child which they sheltered for charity, and treated her as such. Her clothes being gone, they dressed her in the cast-off garments of the little Thénardiers, that is in rags. They fed her on the leftovers, a little better than the dog, and a little worse than the cat. The dog and cat were her messmates. Cosette ate with them under the table in a wooden dish like theirs.

Her mother, as we shall see hereafter, who had found employment at M—— sur M——, wrote, or rather had some one write for her every month, inquiring news of her child. The Thénardiers replied invariably:

"Cosette is doing wonderfully well."

The six months passed away: the mother sent seven francs for the seventh month, and continued to send this sum regularly month after month. The year was not ended before Thénardier said: "A pretty price that is. What does she expect us to do for her seven francs?" And he wrote demanding twelve francs. The mother, whom he persuaded that her child was happy and doing well, assented, and forwarded the twelve francs.

There are certain natures which cannot have love on one side without hatred on the other. This Thénardier mother passionately loved her own little ones: this made her detest the young stranger. It is sad to think that a mother's love can have such a dark side. Little as was the place Cosette occupied in the house, it seemed to her that this little was taken from her children, and that the little one lessened the air hers breathed. This woman, like many women of her kind, had a certain amount of caresses, and blows, and hard words to dispense each day. If she had not had Cosette, it is certain that her daughters, idolised as they were, would have received all, but the little stranger did them the service to attract the blows to herself; her children had only the caresses. Cosette could not stir that she did not draw down upon herself a hailstorm of undeserved and severe chastisements. A weak, soft little one who knew nothing of this world, or of God, continually ill-treated, scolded, punished, beaten, she saw beside her two other young things like herself, who lived in a halo of glory!

The woman was unkind to Cosette, Eponine and Azelma were unkind also. Children at that age are only copies of the mother; the size is reduced, that is all.

A year passed and then another.

People used to say in the village:

"What good people these Thénardiers are! They are not rich, and yet they bring up a poor child, that has been left with them."

They thought Cosette was forgotten by her mother.

Meantime Thénardier, having learned in some obscure way that the child was probably illegitimate, and that its mother could not acknowledge it, demanded fifteen francs a month, saying "that the 'creature' was growing and eating," and threatening to send her away. "She won't humbug me," he exclaimed. "I will confound her with the brat in the midst of her concealment. I must have more money." The mother paid the fifteen francs.

From year to year the child grew, and her misery also.

So long as Cosette was very small, she was the scapegoat of the two other children; as soon as she began to grow a little, that is to say, before she was five years old, she became the servant of the house.

Five years old, it will be said, that is improbable. Alas! it is true, social suffering begins at all ages. Have we not seen lately the trial of Dumollard, an orphan become a bandit, who, from the age of five, say the homicidal documents, being alone in the world, "worked for his living and stole!"

Cosette was made to run errands, sweep the rooms, the yard, the street, wash the dishes, and even carry burdens. The Thénardiers felt doubly authorised to treat her thus, as the mother, who still remained at M—— sur M——, began to be remiss in her payments. Some months remained due.

Had this mother returned to Montfermeil, at the end of these three years, she would not have known her child, Cosette, so fresh and pretty when she came to that house, was now thin and wan. She had a peculiar restless air. Sly! said the Thénardiers.

Injustice had made her sullen, and misery had made her ugly. Her fine eyes only remained to her, and they were painful to look at, for, large as they were, they seemed to increase the sadness.

It was a harrowing sight to see in the winter time the poor child, not yet six years old, shivering under the tatters of what was once a calico dress, sweeping the street before daylight with an enormous broom in her little red hands and tears in her large eyes.

In the place she was called the Lark. People like figurative names and were pleased thus to name this little being, not larger than a bird, trembling, frightened, and shivering, awake every morning first of all in the house and the village, always in the street or in the fields before dawn.

Only the poor Lark never sang.

BOOK FIVE
THE DESCENT

1

THE STORY OF AN IMPROVEMENT IN JET-WORK

BUT THIS MOTHER, in the meanwhile, who, according to the people of Montfermeil, seemed to have abandoned her child? What had become of her? Where was she? What was she doing?

After leaving her little Cosette with the Thénardiers, she went on her way and reached M—— sur M——.

This, it will be remembered, was in 1818.

Fantine had left the province some twelve years before, and M—— sur M—— had changed in appearance. While Fantine had been slowly sinking deeper and deeper into misery, her native village had become prosperous.

About two years ago there had been accomplished there one of those industrial changes which are the great events of small communities.

This circumstance is important and we think it well to relate it, we might even say to italicise it.

From time immemorial the special occupation of the inhabitants of M—— sur M—— had been the imitation of English jets and German black glass trinkets. The business had always been sluggish because of the high price of the raw material, which reacted upon the manufacture. At the time of Fantine's return to M—— sur M—— an unheard-of transformation had been effected in the production of these 'black goods.' Towards the end of the year 1815, an unknown man had established himself in the city, and had conceived the idea of substituting gum-lac for resin in the manufacture; and for bracelets, in particular, he made the clasps by simply bending the ends of the metal together instead of soldering them.

This very slight change had in fact reduced the price of the raw material enormously, and this had rendered it possible, first, to raise the wages of the labourer—a benefit to the region—secondly, to improve the quality of the goods—an advantage for the consumer—and thirdly, to sell them at a lower price even while making three times the profit—a gain for the manufacturer.

Thus we have three results from one idea.

In less than three years the inventor of this process had become rich, which was well, and had made all around him rich, which was better. He was a stranger in the Department. Nothing was known of his birth, and but little of his early history: he had come to the city with very little money, a few hundred francs at most.

From this slender capital, under the inspiration of an ingenious idea, made fruitful by order and care, he had drawn a fortune for himself, and a fortune for the whole region.

On his arrival at M—— sur M—— he had the dress, the manners, and the language of a mere labourer.

It seems that the very day on which he thus obscurely entered the little city of M—— sur M——, just at dusk on a December evening, with his bundle on his back, and a thorn stick in his hand, a great fire had broken out in the Town Hall. This man rushed into the fire and saved, at the peril of his life, two children, who proved to be those of the captain of the gendarmerie, so no one thought to ask him for his passport. He was known from that time by the name of Old Madeleine.

2

MADELEINE

HE WAS A MAN of about fifty, who always appeared to be pre-occupied in mind, and who was good-natured; this was all that could be said about him.

Thanks to the rapid progress of this manufacture, which he had reshaped so admirably, M—— sur M—— had become a considerable centre of business. Immense purchases were made there every year for the Spanish markets, where there is a large demand for jet work, and M—— sur M——, in this branch of trade, almost competed with London and Berlin. The profits of Father Madeleine were so great that by the end of the second year he was able to build a large factory, in which there were two immense workshops, one for men and the other for women: whoever was needy could go there and be sure of finding work and wages. Father Madeleine required the men to be willing, the women to be of good morals, and all to be honest. He divided the workshops, and separated the sexes in order that the girls and the women might not lose their modesty. On this point he was inflexible, although it was the only one in which he was in any degree rigid. He was confirmed in this severity by the opportunities for corruption that abounded in M—— sur M——, it being a garrisoned city. Besides, his coming had been a benefit, and his presence was a providence. Before the arrival of Father Madeleine, the whole region was languishing; now it was all alive with the healthy strength of labour. An active circulation kindled everything and penetrated everywhere. Idleness and misery were unknown. There was no pocket so obscure that it did not contain some money and no dwelling so poor that it was not the abode of some joy.

Father Madeleine employed everybody; he had only one condition, "Be an honest man!" "Be an honest woman!"

As we have said, in the midst of this activity, of which he was the cause and the pivot, Father Madeleine had made his fortune, but, very strangely for a mere man of business, that did not appear to be his principal care. It seemed that he thought much for others and little for himself. In 1820, it was known that he had six hundred and thirty thousand francs standing to his credit in the banking-house of Laffitte; but before setting aside this six hundred and thirty thousand francs for himself, he had expended more than a million for the city and for the poor.

The hospital was poorly endowed, and he made provision for ten additional beds. M—— sur M—— is divided into the upper city and the lower city. The lower city, where he lived, had only one school-house, a miserable hovel which was fast going to ruin; he built two, one for girls, and the other for boys, and paid the two teachers, from his own pocket, double the amount of their meagre salary from the government; and one day, he said to a neighbour who expressed surprise at this: "The two highest functionaries of the state are the nurse and the schoolmaster." He built, at his own expense, a homeless shelter, an institution then almost unknown in France, and provided a fund for old and infirm labourers. About his factory, as a centre, a new neighbourhood had rapidly grown up, containing many indigent families, and he established a pharmacy that was free to all.

In 1820, five years after his arrival at M—— sur M——, the services that he had rendered to the region were so brilliant, and the wish of the whole population was so unanimous, that the king again appointed him mayor of the city. He refused again; but the prefect resisted his determination, the principal citizens came and urged him to accept, and the people in the streets begged him to do so; all insisted so strongly that at last he yielded. It was remarked that what appeared most of all to bring him to this determination, was the almost angry exclamation of an old woman belonging to the poorer class, who cried out to him irritably from her doorstep, with some temper:

"A good mayor is a good thing. Are you afraid of the good you can do?"

This was the third step in his ascent. Father Madeleine had become Monsieur Madeleine, and Monsieur Madeleine now became Monsieur the Mayor.

3

MONEYS DEPOSITED WITH LAFFITTE

NEVERTHELESS he remained as simple as at first. He had grey hair, a serious eye, the brown complexion of a labourer, and the thoughtful countenance of a philosopher. He usually wore a hat with a wide brim, and a long coat of coarse cloth, buttoned to the chin. He fulfilled his duties as mayor, but beyond that his life was isolated. He talked with very few persons. He shrank from compliments, and with a touch of the hat walked on rapidly; he smiled to avoid talking, and gave to avoid smiling. The women said of him: "What a good bear!" His pleasure was to walk in the fields.

He always took his meals alone with a book open before him in which he read. His library was small but well selected. He loved books; books are cold but sure friends. As his growing fortune gave him more leisure, it seemed that he profited by it to cultivate his mind. Since he had been at M—— sur M——, it was remarked from year to year that his language became more polished, choicer, and more gentle.

In his walks he liked to carry a gun, though he seldom used it. When he did so, however, his aim was frightfully certain. He never killed an inoffensive animal, and never fired at any of the small birds.

Although he was no longer young, it was reported that he was of prodigious strength. He would offer a helping hand to any one who needed it, help up a fallen horse, push at a stalled wheel, or seize by the horns a bull that had broken loose. He always had his pockets full of money when he went out, and empty when he returned. When he passed through a village the ragged little youngsters would run after him with joy, and surround him like a swarm of flies.

It was surmised that he must have lived formerly in the country, for he had all sorts of useful secrets which he taught the peasants. He showed them how to destroy the grain-moth by sprinkling the granary and washing the cracks of the floor with a solution of common salt, and how to drive away the weevil by hanging up all about the ceiling and walls, in the pastures, and in the houses, the flowers of the orviot. He had recipes for clearing a field of rust, of vetches, of moles, of doggrass, and all the parasitic herbs which live upon the grain. He defended a rabbit warren against rats, with nothing but the odour of a little Barbary pig that he placed there.

One day he saw some country people very busy pulling up nettles; he looked at the heap of plants, uprooted, and already wilted, and said: "This is dead; but it would be well if we knew how to put it to some use. When the nettle is young, the leaves make excellent greens; when it grows old it has filaments and fibres like hemp and flax. Cloth made from the nettle is as good as that made from hemp. Chopped up, the nettle is good for poultry; pounded, it is good for horned cattle. The seed of the nettle mixed with the fodder of animals gives a lustre to their skin; the root, mixed with salt, produces a beautiful yellow dye. It makes, however, excellent hay, as it can be cut twice in a season. And what does the nettle need? very little soil, no care, no culture; except that the seeds fall as fast as they ripen, and it is difficult to gather them; that is all. If we would take a little pains, the nettle would be useful; we neglect it, and it becomes harmful. Then we kill it. How much men are like the nettle!" After a short silence, he added: "My friends, remember this, that there are no weeds, and no worthless men, there are only bad farmers."*

The children loved him yet more, because he knew how to make charming little playthings out of straw and cocoanuts.

When he saw the door of a church shrouded with black, he entered: he sought out a funeral as others seek out a christening. The bereavement and the misfortune of others attracted him, because of his great gentleness; he mingled with friends who were in mourning, with families dressing in black, with the priests who were groaning around a corpse. He seemed glad to take as a text for his thoughts these funeral psalms, full of the vision of another world. With his eyes raised to heaven, he listened with a sort of aspiration towards all the mysteries of the infinite, to these sad voices, which sing upon the brink of the dark abyss of death.†

He did a multitude of good deeds as secretly as bad ones are usually done. He would steal into houses in the evening, and furtively mount the stairs. A poor devil, on returning to his garret, would find that his door had been opened, sometimes even forced, during his absence. The poor man would cry out: "Some thief has been here!" When he got in, the first thing that he would see would be a piece of gold lying on the table. "The thief" who had been there was Father Madeleine.

He was affable and sad. The people used to say: "There is a rich man who does not show pride. There is a fortunate man who does not appear contented."

Some pretended that he was a mysterious personage, and declared that no one ever went into his room, which was a true hermit's cell furnished with winged hour-glasses, and enlivened with death's heads and cross-bones. So much was said of this kind that some of the more mischievous of the elegant young ladies of M—— sur M—— called on him one day and said: "Monsieur Mayor, will you show us your room? We have heard that it is a grotto." He smiled, and introduced them on the spot to this "grotto." They

---

*M. Madeleine's assumed name, borrowed from Mary Magdalene in the New Testament of the Bible, connotes repentance; his attitudes here reflect wholehearted faith in Providence.

†Hugo believed in punitive reincarnation, and in universal salvation at the end of time (the Pelagian heresy). See "Ce que dit la Bouche d'Ombre" in his *Contemplations* (1856).

were well punished for their curiosity. It was a room very well fitted up with mahogany furniture, ugly as all furniture of that kind is, and the walls covered with cheap wallpaper. They could see nothing but two candlesticks in an outmoded style that stood on the mantel, and appeared to be silver, "for they were marked," a remark full of the spirit of these little towns.

But none the less did it continue to be said that nobody ever went into that chamber, and that it was a hermit's cave, a place of dreams, a hole, a tomb.

It was also whispered that he had "immense" sums deposited with Laffitte, with the special condition that they were always at his immediate command, in such a way, it was added, that Monsieur Madeleine might arrive in the morning at Laffitte's, sign a receipt and carry away his two or three millions in ten minutes. In reality these "two or three millions" dwindled down, as we have said, to six hundred and thirty or forty thousand francs.

4

MONSIEUR MADELEINE IN MOURNING

NEAR THE BEGINNING of the year 1821, the journals announced the decease of Monsieur Myriel, Bishop of D——, "surnamed *Monseigneur Bienvenu,*" who died in the odour of sanctity at the age of eighty-two years.

The announcement of his death was reproduced in the local paper of M—— sur M——. Monsieur Madeleine appeared next morning dressed in black with crape on his hat.

This mourning was noticed and talked about all over the town. It appeared to throw some light upon the origin of Monsieur Madeleine. The conclusion was that he was in some way related to the venerable bishop. *"He wears black for the Bishop of D——,"* was the talk of the drawing-rooms; it elevated Monsieur Madeleine very much, and gave him suddenly, and in a trice, marked consideration in the noble world of M—— sur M——. The microscopic Faubourg Saint Germain of the little place thought of raising the quarantine for Monsieur Madeleine, the probable relative of a bishop.* Monsieur Madeleine perceived the advancement

---

*The Faubourg Saint Germain refers to high society in Paris, and is applied to Montreuil-sur-Mer as a whimsical antonomasia (another example: "the champagne of bottled beers").

that he had obtained, by the greater reverence of the old ladies, and the more frequent smiles of the young ladies. One evening, one of the dowagers of that little high society, curious by right of age, ventured to ask him: "The mayor is doubtless a relative of the late Bishop of D——?"

He said: "No, madame."

"But," the dowager persisted, "you wear mourning for him?"

He answered: "In my youth I was a servant in his family."

It was also remarked that whenever there passed through the city a little chimneysweep who was tramping about the country in search of work, the mayor would send for him, ask his name and give him money. The little Savoyards told each other, and many of them passed that way.

5

FAINT LIGHTNING FLASHES
ON THE HORIZON

LITTLE BY LITTLE as time went by all opposition had ceased. At first there had been, as always happens with those who rise by their own efforts, slanders and calumnies against Monsieur Madeleine, soon this was reduced to satire, then it was only wit, then it vanished entirely; respect became complete, unanimous, cordial, and there came a moment, about 1821, when the words Monsieur the Mayor were pronounced at M—— sur M—— with almost the same accent as the words Monseigneur the Bishop at D—— in 1815. People came from thirty miles around to consult Monsieur Madeleine. He settled differences, he prevented lawsuits, he reconciled enemies. Everybody, of his own will, chose him for judge. He seemed to have the book of the natural law by heart. A contagion of veneration had, in the course of six or seven years, from person to person, spread over the whole country.

One man alone, in the city and its neighbourhood, held himself entirely clear from this contagion, and, whatever Father Madeleine did, he remained indifferent, as if a sort of instinct, unchangeable and imperturbable, kept him awake and on the watch. It would seem, indeed, that there is in certain men a veritable animal instinct, pure and uncorrupted like all instinct, which creates antipathies and sympathies, which inevitably separates one nature from another for ever; which never hesitates, never is perturbed, never keeps silent, and never proves mistaken; clear in its obscurity, infallible, imperious, refractory to all the counsels of intelligence, and all the solvents of reason, and which, whatever may be their destinies, secretly warns the dog-man of the presence of the cat-man, and the fox-man of the presence of the lion-man.

Often, when Monsieur Madeleine passed along the street, calm, affectionate, followed by the benedictions of all, it happened that a tall man, wearing a hat pulled down over his eyes and an iron-grey coat, and armed with a stout cane, would turn around abruptly behind him, and follow him with his eyes until he disappeared, crossing his arms, slowly shaking his head, and pushing his upper with his under lip up to his nose, a sort of significant grimace which might be rendered by: "But what is that man? I am sure I have seen him somewhere. At all events, I at least am not his dupe."

This personage, grave with an almost threatening gravity, was one of those who, even in a hurried interview, command the attention of the observer.

His name was Javert, and he was one of the police.

He exercised at M—— sur M—— the unpleasant, but useful, function of inspector. He was not there at the date of Madeleine's arrival. Javert owed his position to the protection of Monsieur Chabouillet, the secretary of the Minister of State, Count Anglès, then prefect of police at Paris. When Javert arrived at M—— sur M—— the fortune of the great manufacturer had been made already, and Father Madeleine had become Monsieur Madeleine.

Certain police officers have a peculiar physiognomy in which can be traced an air of baseness mingled with an air of authority. Javert had this physiognomy, without baseness.

Javert was born in a prison. His mother was a fortune-teller whose husband was in the galleys. He grew up to think himself without the pale of society, and despaired of ever entering it. He noticed that society closes its doors, without pity, on two classes of men, those who attack it and those who guard it; he could choose between these two classes only; at the same time he felt that he had an indescribable basis of rectitude, order, and honesty, associated with an irrepressible hatred for that gypsy race to which he belonged. He entered the police. He succeeded. At forty he was an inspector.[*]

In his youth he had been stationed in the galleys at the South.

Before going further, let us understand what we mean by the words human face, which we have just now applied to Javert.

The human face of Javert consisted of a snub nose, with two deep nostrils, which were bordered by large bushy sideburns that covered both his cheeks. One felt ill at ease the first time he saw those two forests and those two caverns. When Javert laughed, which was rarely and terribly, his thin lips parted, and showed, not only his teeth, but his gums; and around his nose there was a wrinkle as broad and wild as the muzzle of a wild beast. Javert, when serious, was a bull-dog; when he laughed, he was a tiger. For the rest, a small head, large jaws, hair hiding the forehead and falling over

---

[*]Reacting vehemently and blindly against his criminal family origins, Javert illustrates the psychological mechanism of overcompensation.

the eyebrows, between the eyes a permanent central frown like an angry star, a gloomy look, a mouth pinched and frightful, and an air of fierce command.

This man was a compound of two sentiments, very simple and very good in themselves, but he almost made them evil by his exaggeration of them, respect for authority and hatred of rebellion; and in his eyes, theft, murder, all crimes, were only forms of rebellion. In his strong and implicit faith he included all who held any function in the state, from the prime minister to the constable. He had nothing but disdain, aversion, and disgust for all who had once overstepped the bounds of the law. He was judgmental, and admitted no exceptions. On the one hand he said: "A public officer cannot be deceived; a magistrate never does wrong!" And on the other he said: "They are irremediably lost; no good can come out of them." He shared fully the opinion of those extremists who attribute to human laws an inde-scribable power of making, or, if you will, of determining, demons, and who place a Styx at the bottom of society.* He was stoical, serious, austere: a dreamer of stern dreams, humble and haughty, like all fanatics. His stare was cold and as piercing as a gimlet. His whole life was contained in these two words: waking and watching. He marked out a straight path through the most tortuous thing in the world; he was aware of his utility, conscien-tious in his duties, and he was a spy as others are priests. Woe to him who should fall into his hands! He would have arrested his father escaping from the galleys, and denounced his mother for violating her restraining order. And he would have done it with that sort of interior satisfaction that springs from virtue. His life was a life of privations, isolation, self-denial, and chastity: never any amusement. He was implacable duty incar-nate, the police understood as the Spartans understood Sparta, a pitiless detective, an intransigent honesty, a marble-hearted informer, Brutus united with Vidocq.†

The whole being of Javert expressed the spy and the informer. The mystic school of Joseph de Maistre, which at that time enlivened what were called the ultra journals with high-sounding cosmogonies, would have said that Javert was a symbol. You could not see his forehead which disappeared under his hat, you could not see his eyes which were lost under his brows, you could not see his chin which was buried in his cravat, you could not see his hands which were drawn up into his sleeves, you could not see his cane which he carried under his coat. But when the time came, you would see spring all at once out of this shadow, as from an

---

*The Styx, the river of Death, surrounded the ancient Greek and Roman Hades nine times; once you crossed, there was no return. Javert believes redemption is impossible.

†Lucius Junius Brutus, founder of the Roman Republic, condemned his son to death as a conspirator (509 B.C.); François-Eugène Vidocq (1775–1857), a famous criminal who became Chief of Police, inspired romantic writers with his badly written *Memoirs* (1828).

ambush, a steep and narrow forehead, an ominous look, a threatening chin, enormous hands, and a monstrous club.

In his leisure moments, which were rare, although he hated books he read; wherefore he was not entirely illiterate. This was perceptible from a certain pomposity in his speech.

He was free from vice, we have said. When he was satisfied with himself, he allowed himself a pinch of snuff. That was his link to humanity.

It will be easily understood that Javert was the terror of all that class which the annual statistics of the Minister of Justice include under the heading: *People without a fixed abode*. To speak the name of Javert would put all such to flight; the face of Javert petrified them.

Such was this formidable man.

Javert was like an eye always fixed on Monsieur Madeleine; an eye full of suspicion and conjecture. Monsieur Madeleine finally noticed it, but seemed to consider it of no consequence. He asked no question of Javert, he neither sought him nor shunned him, he endured this unpleasant and annoying stare without appearing to pay any attention to it. He treated Javert as he did everybody else, at ease and with kindness.

From some words that Javert had dropped, it was guessed that he had secretly hunted up, with that curiosity which belongs to his race, and which is more a matter of instinct than of will, all the traces of his previous life which Father Madeleine had left elsewhere. He appeared to know, and he said sometimes in a covert way, that somebody had gathered certain information in a certain region about a certain missing family. Once he happened to say, speaking to himself: "I think I have got him!" Then for three days he remained moody without speaking a word. It appeared that the clue which he thought he had was broken.

But, and this is the necessary corrective to what the meaning of certain words may have presented in too absolute a sense, there can be nothing really infallible in a human creature, and the very peculiarity of instinct is that it can be disturbed, detected, and thrown off the scent. Were this not so, it would be superior to intelligence, and the beast would be more enlightened than man.

Javert was evidently somewhat disconcerted by the completely natural air and the tranquillity of Monsieur Madeleine.

One day, however, his strange manner appeared to make an impression upon Monsieur Madeleine. The occasion was this:

6

OLD FAUCHELEVENT

MONSIEUR MADELEINE was walking one morning along one of the unpaved alleys of M—— sur M——; he heard a shouting and saw a crowd at a little distance. He went to the spot. An old man, named Father Fauchelevent, had fallen under his cart, his horse having collapsed.

This Fauchelevent was one of the few who were still enemies of Monsieur Madeleine at this time. When Madeleine arrived in the place, the business of Fauchelevent, who was a notary of long-standing, and very well-read for a rustic, was beginning to decline. Fauchelevent had seen this mere artisan grow rich, while he himself, a professional man, had been going to ruin. This had filled him with jealousy, and he had done what he could on all occasions to injure Madeleine. Then came bankruptcy, and the old man, having nothing but a horse and cart, as he was without family, and without children, was compelled to earn his living by hauling loads.

The horse had his thighs broken, and could not stir. The old man was caught between the wheels. Unluckily he had fallen so that the whole weight rested upon his breast. The cart was heavily loaded. Father Fauchelevent was uttering doleful groans. They had tried to pull him out, but in vain. An unlucky effort, inexpert help, a false push, might crush him. It was impossible to extricate him otherwise than by raising the waggon from beneath. Javert, who came up at the moment of the accident, had sent for a jack.

Monsieur Madeleine came. The crowd fell back with respect.

"Help," cried old Fauchelevent. "Who is a good fellow to save an old man?"

Monsieur Madeleine turned towards the bystanders:

"Has anybody a jack?"

"They have gone for one," replied a peasant.

"How soon will it be here?"

"We sent to the nearest place, to Flachot Place, where there is a blacksmith; but it will take a good quarter of an hour at least."

"A quarter of an hour!" exclaimed Madeleine.

It had rained the night before, the road was soft, the cart was sinking deeper every moment, and pressing more and more on the breast of the old carman. It was evident that in less than five minutes his ribs would be crushed.

"We cannot wait a quarter of an hour," said Madeleine to the peasants who were looking on.

"We must!"

"But it will be too late! Don't you see that the waggon is sinking all the while?"

"It can't be helped."

"Listen," resumed Madeleine, "there is room enough still under the waggon for a man to crawl in, and lift it with his back. In half a minute we will have the poor man out. Is there nobody here who has strength and courage? Five louis d'ors for him!"

Nobody stirred in the crowd.

"Ten louis," said Madeleine.

The bystanders dropped their eyes. One of them muttered: "He'd have to be devilish strong. And then he would risk getting crushed."

"Come," said Madeleine, "twenty louis."

The same silence.

"It is not willingness which they lack," said a voice.

Monsieur Madeleine turned and saw Javert. He had not noticed him when he came.

Javert continued:

"It is strength. You'd need a fearsome man to raise a waggon like that on his back."

Then, looking fixedly at Monsieur Madeleine, he went on emphasising every word that he uttered:

"Monsieur Madeleine, I have known but one man capable of doing what you call for."

Madeleine shuddered.

Javert added, with an air of indifference, but without taking his eyes from Madeleine:

"He was a convict."

"Ah!" said Madeleine.

"In the galleys at Toulon."

Madeleine became pale.

Meanwhile the cart was slowly settling down. Father Fauchelevent roared and screamed:

"I am dying! my ribs are breaking! a jack! anything! oh!"

Madeleine looked around him:

"Is there nobody, then, who wants to earn twenty louis and save this poor old man's life?"

None of the bystanders moved. Javert resumed:

"I have known but one man who could take the place of a jack; that was that convict."

"Oh! how it crushes me!" cried the old man.

Madeleine raised his head, met the falcon eye of Javert still fixed upon him, looked at the immovable peasants, and smiled sadly. Then, without saying a word, he fell on his knees, and even before the crowd had time to utter a cry, he was under the cart.

There was an awful moment of suspense and of silence.

Madeleine, lying almost flat under the fearful weight, was twice seen to try in vain to bring his elbows and knees nearer together. They cried out to him: "Father Madeleine! come out from there!" Old Fauchelevent himself said: "Monsieur Madeleine! go away! I must die, you see that; leave me! you will be crushed too." Madeleine made no answer.

The bystanders held their breath. The wheels were still sinking and it had already become almost impossible for Madeleine to extricate himself.

All at once the enormous mass budged, the cart rose slowly, the wheels came half out of the ruts. A smothered voice was heard crying: "Quick! help!" It was Madeleine, who had just made a final effort.

They all rushed to the work. The devotion of one man had given strength and courage to all. The cart was lifted by twenty arms. Old Fauchelevent was safe.

Madeleine arose. He was very pale, though dripping with sweat. His clothes were torn and covered with mud. All wept. The old man kissed his knees and called him the good Lord. He himself wore on his face an indescribable expression of joyous and celestial suffering, and he looked with tranquil eye upon Javert, who was still watching him.

7

FAUCHELEVENT BECOMES A GARDENER AT PARIS

FAUCHELEVENT had broken his knee-cap in his fall. Father Madeleine had him carried to an infirmary that he had established for his workmen in the same building with his factory, which was attended by two sisters of charity. The next morning the old man found a thousand franc bill upon the stand by the side of the bed, with this note in the handwriting of Father Madeleine: I have purchased your horse and cart. The cart was broken and the horse was dead. Fauchelevent got well, but he had a stiff knee. Monsieur Madeleine, through the recommendations of the sisters and the curé, got the old man a place as gardener at a convent in the Quartier Saint Antoine at Paris.

Some time afterwards Monsieur Madeleine was appointed mayor. The first time that Javert saw Monsieur Madeleine clothed with the scarf which gave him full authority over the city, he felt the same sort of shudder which a bull-dog would feel who should scent a wolf in his master's clothes. From that time he avoided him as much as he could. When the necessities of the service imperiously demanded it, and he could not do otherwise than come in contact with the mayor, he spoke to him with profound respect.

Such was the condition of the region when Fantine returned. No one remembered her. Luckily the door of M. Madeleine's factory was like the face of a friend. She presented herself there, and was admitted into the workshop for women. The business was entirely new to Fantine; she could not be very expert in it, and consequently did not receive much for her day's work; but that little was enough, the problem was solved; she was earning her living.

8

MADAME VICTURNIEN SPENDS THIRTY FRANCS ON MORALITY

WHEN FANTINE realised how she was living, she had a moment of joy. To live honestly by her own labour; what a heavenly boon! The taste for labour returned to her, in truth. She bought a mirror, delighted herself with the sight of her youth, her fine hair and her fine teeth, forgot many things, thought of nothing save Cosette and the possibilities of the future, and was almost happy. She hired a small room and furnished it on the credit of her future labour; a remnant of her habits of disorder.

Not being able to say that she was married, she took good care, as we have already intimated, not to speak of her little girl.

At first, as we have seen, she paid the Thénardiers punctually. As she only knew how to sign her name she was obliged to write through a public letter-writer.

She wrote often; that was noticed. They began to whisper in the women's workshop that Fantine "wrote letters," and that "she had airs."

Some people are malicious from the mere necessity of talking. Their conversation, tattling in the drawing-room, gossip in the ante-chamber, is like those fireplaces that use up wood rapidly; they need a great deal of fuel; the fuel is their neighbour.

So Fantine was watched.

Beyond this, more than one was jealous of her fair hair and of her white teeth.

It was reported that in the shop, with all the rest about her, she often turned aside to wipe away a tear. Those were moments when she thought of her child; perhaps also of the man whom she had loved.

It is a mournful task to break the sombre attachments of the past.[8]

It was ascertained that she wrote, at least twice a month, and always to the same address, and that she prepaid the postage. They succeeded in learning the address: *Monsieur, Monsieur Thénardier, inn-keeper Montfermeil.* The public letter-writer, a simple old fellow, who could not fill his stomach with red-wine without emptying his pocket of his secrets, was made to reveal this at a drinking-house. In short, it became known that Fantine had a child. "She must be that sort of a woman." And there was one old gossip who went to Montfermeil, talked with the Thénardiers, and said on her return: "For my thirty-five francs, I have found out all about it. I have seen the child!"

All this took time; Fantine had been more than a year at the factory, when one morning the overseer of the workshop handed her, on behalf of the mayor, fifty francs, saying that she was no longer wanted in the shop, and enjoining her, on behalf of the mayor, to leave the city.

This was the very same month in which the Thénardiers, after having asked twelve francs instead of six, had demanded fifteen francs instead of twelve.

Fantine was thunderstruck. She could not leave the city; she was in debt for her lodging and her furniture. Fifty francs were not enough to clear off that debt. She faltered out some suppliant words. The overseer gave her to understand that she must leave the shop instantly. Fantine was moreover only a moderate worker. Overwhelmed with shame even more than with despair, she left the shop, and returned to her room. Her fault then was now known to all!

She felt no strength to say a word. She was advised to see the mayor; she dared not. The mayor gave her fifty francs, because he was kind, and sent her away, because he was just. She bowed to that decree.

9

SUCCESS OF MADAME VICTURNIEN

THE MONK'S WIDOW was then good for something.

Moreover, Monsieur Madeleine had known nothing of all this. These are combinations of events of which life is full. It was Monsieur Madeleine's habit scarcely ever to enter the women's workshop.

He had placed at the head of this shop an old spinster whom the curé had recommended to him, and he had entire confidence in this overseer, a very respectable person, firm, just, upright, full of that charity which consists in giving, but not having to the same extent that charity which consists in understanding and pardoning. Monsieur Madeleine left everything to her. The best men are often compelled to delegate their authority. It was in the exercise of this full power, and with the conviction that she was doing right, that the overseer had framed the indictment, tried, condemned, and executed Fantine.

As to the fifty francs, she had given them from a fund that Monsieur Madeleine had entrusted her with for alms-giving and aid to work-women, and of which she rendered no account.

Fantine offered herself as a servant in the neighbourhood; she went from one house to another. Nobody wanted her. She could not leave the city. The second-hand dealer to whom she was in debt for her furniture, and such furniture! had said to her: "If you go away, I will have you arrested as a thief." The landlord, whom she owed for rent, had said to her: "You are young and pretty, you can pay." She divided the fifty francs between the landlord and the dealer, returned to the latter three-quarters of his goods, kept only what was necessary, and found herself without work, without position, having nothing but her bed, and owing still about a hundred francs.

She began to make coarse shirts for the soldiers of the garrison, and earned twelve sous a day. Her daughter cost her ten. It was at this time that she began to get behindhand with the Thénardiers.

However, an old woman, who lit her candle for her when she came home at night, taught her the art of living in misery. Behind living on a little, lies the art of living on nothing. They are two rooms; the first is obscure, the second is utterly dark.

Fantine learned how to do entirely without fire in winter, how to give up a bird that eats a farthing's worth of millet every other day, how to make a coverlet of her petticoat, and a petticoat of her coverlet, how to save her candle in taking her meals by the light of an opposite window. Few know how much certain feeble beings who have grown old in privation and honesty, can extract from a sou. This finally becomes a talent. Fantine acquired this sublime talent and took heart a little.

During these times, she said to a neighbour: "Bah! I say to myself: by sleeping but five hours and working all the rest at my sewing, I shall always succeed in nearly earning bread. And then, when one is sad, one eats less. Well! what with sufferings, troubles, a little bread on the one hand, anxiety on the other, all that will keep me alive."

In this distress, to have had her little daughter would have been a strange happiness. She thought of having her come. But what? to make her share her privation? and then, she owed the Thénardiers? How could she pay them? and the journey; how pay for that?

The old woman, who had given her what might be called lessons in indigent life, was a pious woman, Marguerite by name, a devotee of genuine devotion, poor, and charitable to the poor, and also to the rich, knowing how to write just enough to sign *Margeritte,* and believing in God, which is knowledge.

There are many of these virtues in low places; some day they will be on high. This life has a morrow.

At first, Fantine was so much ashamed that she did not dare to go out.

When she was in the street, she imagined that people turned behind her and pointed at her; everybody looked at her and no one greeted her; the sharp and cold disdain of the passers-by penetrated her, body and soul, like a north wind.

In small towns an unfortunate woman seems to be laid bare to the sarcasm and the curiosity of all. In Paris, at least, nobody knows you, and that obscurity is a covering. Oh! how she longed to go to Paris! impossible.

She must indeed become accustomed to disrespect as she had to poverty. Little by little she learned her part. After two or three months she shook off her shame and went out as if there were nothing in the way. "It is all one to me," said she.

She went and came, holding her head up and wearing a bitter smile, and felt that she was becoming shameless.

Madame Victurnien sometimes saw her pass her window, noticed the distress of "that creature," thanks to her "put back to her place," and congratulated herself. The malicious have a dark happiness.

Excessive work fatigued Fantine, and the slight dry cough that she had increased. She sometimes said to her neighbour, Marguerite, "just feel how hot my hands are."

In the morning, however, when with an old broken comb she combed her fine hair which flowed down in silky waves, she enjoyed a moment of happiness.

10

FURTHER SUCCESS OF THE GOSSIPS

SHE HAD BEEN discharged towards the end of winter; summer passed away, but winter returned. Short days, less work. In winter there is no heat, no light, no noon, evening touches morning, there is fog, and mist, the window is frosted, and you cannot see clearly. The sky is but the mouth of a cave. The whole day is the cave. The sun has the appearance of a pauper. Frightful season! Winter changes into stone the water of heaven and the heart of man. Her creditors harassed her.

Fantine earned too little. Her debts had increased. The Thénardiers being poorly paid, were constantly writing letters to her, the contents of which disheartened her, while the postage was ruining her. One day they wrote to her that her little Cosette was entirely destitute of clothing for the cold weather, that she needed a woollen skirt, and that her mother must send at least ten francs for that. She received the letter and crushed it in her hand for a whole day. In the evening she went into a barber's shop at the corner of the street, and pulled out her comb. Her beautiful fair hair fell below her waist.

"What beautiful hair!" exclaimed the barber.

"How much will you give me for it?" said she.

"Ten francs."

"Cut it off."

She bought a knit skirt and sent it to the Thénardiers.

This skirt made the Thénardiers furious. It was the money that they wanted. They gave the skirt to Eponine. The poor lark still shivered.

Fantine thought: "My child is no longer cold, I have clothed her with my hair." She put on a little round cap which concealed her shorn head, and with that she was still pretty.

A gloomy work was going on in Fantine's heart.

When she saw that she could no longer dress her hair, she began to look with hatred on all around her. She had long shared in the universal venera-tion for Father Madeleine; nevertheless by dint of repeating to herself that it was he who had turned her away, and that he was the cause of her mis-fortunes, she came to hate him also, and especially. When she passed the factory at the hours in which the labourers were at the door, she forced her-self to laugh and sing.

An old working-woman who saw her once singing and laughing in this way, said: "There is a girl who will come to a bad end."

She took a lover, the first comer, a man whom she did not love, through bravado, and with rage in her heart. He was a wretch, a kind of mendicant musician, a lazy ragamuffin, who beat her, and who left her, as she had taken him, with disgust.

She worshipped her child.

The lower she sank, the more all became gloomy around her, the more the sweet little angel shone out in the bottom of her heart. She would say: "When I am rich, I shall have my Cosette with me," and she laughed. The cough did not leave her, and she had night sweats.

One day she received from the Thénardiers a letter in these words: "Cosette is sick of an epidemic disease. A miliary fever they call it. The drugs necessary are dear. It is ruining us, and we can no longer pay for them. Unless you send us forty francs within a week the little one will die."

She burst out laughing, and said to her old neighbour:

"Oh! they are nice! forty francs! think of that! that is two Napoleons! Where do they think I can get them? How stupid these peasants are."

She went, however, to the staircase, near a dormer window, and read the letter again.

Then she went down stairs and out of doors, running and jumping, still laughing.

Somebody who met her said to her: "What is the matter with you, that you are so gay?"

She answered: "A stupid joke that some country people have just writ-ten me. They ask for forty francs; the louts!"

As she passed through the square, she saw many people gathered about an odd-looking carriage on the top of which stood a man in red clothes, declaiming. He was a juggler and a traveling dentist, and was offering to the public complete sets of teeth, opiates, powders, and elixirs.

Fantine joined the crowd and began to laugh with the rest at this harangue, in which were mingled slang for the rabble and jargon for the better sort. The puller of teeth saw this beautiful girl laughing, and suddenly called out: "You have pretty teeth, you girl who are laughing there. If you will sell me your two incisors, I will give you a gold Napoleon for each of them."

"What is that? What are my incisors?" asked Fantine.

"The incisors," resumed the professor of dentistry, "are the front teeth, the two upper ones."

"How horrible!" cried Fantine.

"Two Napoleons!" grumbled a toothless old hag who stood by. "How lucky she is!"

Fantine fled away and stopped her ears not to hear the shrill voice of the man who called after her: "Consider, my beauty! two Napoleons! how much good they will do you! If you have the courage for it, come this evening to the inn of the *Tillac d'Argent;* you will find me there."

Fantine returned home; she was raving, and told the story to her good neighbour Marguerite: "Do you understand that? isn't he an abominable man? Why do they let such people go about the country? Pull out my two front teeth! why, I should be horrible! The hair is bad enough, but the teeth! Oh! what a monster of a man! I would rather throw myself from the sixth story, head first, to the pavement! He told me that he would be this evening at the *Tillac d'Argent.*"

"And what was it he offered you?" asked Marguerite.

"Two Napoleons."

"That is forty francs."

"Yes," said Fantine, "that makes forty francs."

She became thoughtful and went about her work. In a quarter of an hour she left her sewing and went to the stairs to read again the Thénardiers' letter.

On her return she said to Marguerite, who was at work near her:

"What does this mean, a miliary fever? Do you know?"

"Yes," answered the old woman, "it is a disease."

"Then it needs a good many drugs?"

"Yes; terrible drugs."

"How does it come upon you?"

"It is a disease that comes in a moment."

"Does it attack children?"

"Children especially."

"Do people die of it?"

"Very often," said Marguerite.

Fantine withdrew and went once more to read over the letter on the stairs.

In the evening she went out, and took the direction of the Rue de Paris where the inns are.

The next morning, when Marguerite went into Fantine's chamber before daybreak, for they always worked together, and so made one candle do for the two, she found Fantine seated upon her couch, pale and icy. She had not been in bed. Her cap had fallen upon her knees. The candle had burned all night, and was almost consumed.

Marguerite stopped upon the threshold, petrified by this wild disorder, and exclaimed: "Good Lord! the candle is all burned out. Something has happened."

Then she looked at Fantine, who sadly turned her shorn head.

Fantine had grown ten years older since evening.

"Bless us!" said Marguerite, "what is the matter with you, Fantine?"

"Nothing," said Fantine. "Quite the contrary. My child will not die with that frightful sickness for lack of aid. I am satisfied."

So saying, she showed the old woman two Napoleons that glistened on the table.

"Oh! good God!" said Marguerite. "Why there is a fortune! where did you get these louis d'or?"

"I got them," answered Fantine.

At the same time she smiled. The candle lit up her face. It was a sickening smile, for the corners of her mouth were stained with blood, and a dark cavity revealed itself there.

The two teeth were gone.

She sent the forty francs to Montfermeil.

And this was a ruse of the Thénardiers to get money. Cosette was not sick.

Fantine threw her looking-glass out of the window. Long before she had left her little room on the third story for an attic room with no other fastening than a latch; one of those garret rooms the ceiling of which makes an angle with the floor and hits your head at every moment. The poor cannot go to the end of their chamber or to the end of their destiny, but by bending continually more and more. She no longer had a bed, she retained a rag that she called her coverlid, a mattress on the floor, and a worn-out straw chair. Her little rose-bush was dried up in the corner, forgotten. In the other corner was a butter-pot for water, which froze in the winter, and the different levels at which the water had stood remained marked a long time by circles of ice. She had lost her modesty, she was losing her coquetry. The last sign. She would go out with a dirty cap. Either from want of time or from indifference she no longer washed her linen. As fast as the heels of her stockings wore out she drew them down into her shoes. This was shown by certain perpendicular wrinkles. She mended her old, wornout corsets with bits of calico which were torn by the slightest motion. Her creditors quarrelled with her and gave her no rest. She met them in the street; she met them again on her stairs. She passed whole nights in weeping and thinking. She had a strange brilliancy in her eyes, and a constant pain in her shoulder near the top of her left shoulder-blade. She coughed a great deal. She hated Father Madeleine thoroughly, and never complained. She sewed seventeen hours a day; but a prison contractor, who was working prisoners at a loss, suddenly cut down the price, and this reduced the day's wages of free labourers to nine sous. Seventeen hours of work, and nine sous a day! Her creditors were more pitiless than ever. The second-hand dealer, who had taken back nearly all his furniture, was constantly saying to her: "When will you pay me, wench?"

Good God! what did they want her to do? She felt herself hunted down, and something of the wild beast began to develop within her. About the same time Thénardier wrote to her that really he had waited with too much generosity, and that he must have a hundred francs immediately, or else little Cosette, just convalescing after her severe sickness, would be turned out of doors into the cold and upon the highway, and that she would become what she could, and would perish if she must. "A hundred francs," thought Fantine. "But where is there a place where one can earn a hundred sous a day?"

"Come!" said she, "I will sell what is left."

The unfortunate creature became a woman of the town.

11 (12)

THE IDLENESS OF MONSIEUR BAMATABOIS

THERE IS in all small cities, and there was at M—— sur M—— in particular, a set of young men who nibble their fifteen hundred livres of income in the country with the same air with which their fellows devour two hundred thousand francs a year at Paris. They are beings of the great neuter species, geldings, parasites, nobodies, who have a little land, a little folly, and a little wit, who would be clowns in a drawing-room, and think themselves gentlemen in a bar-room, who talk about "my fields, my woods, my peasants," hiss the actresses at the theatre to prove that they are persons of taste, quarrel with the officers of the garrison to show that they are gallant, hunt, smoke, yawn, drink, take snuff, play billiards, stare at passengers getting out of the coach, live at the café, dine at the inn, have a dog who eats the bones under the table, and a mistress who sets the dishes upon it, hold fast to a sou, overdo the fashions, admire tragedy, despise women, wear out their old boots, copy London as reflected from Paris, and Paris as reflected from Pont-à-Mousson, grow stupid as they grow old, do no work, do no good, and not much harm.

Monsieur Félix Tholomyès, had he remained in his province and never seen Paris, would have been such a man.

It was the time of the war of the South American Republics against the King of Spain, of Bolivar against Morillo. Hats with narrow brims were Royalist, and were called Morillos; the liberals wore hats with wide brims which were called Bolivars.*

Eight or ten months after what has been related in the preceding pages, in the early part of January, 1823, one evening when it had been snowing, one of these dandies, one of these idlers, a "well-intentioned" man, for he wore a morillo, very warmly wrapped in one of those large cloaks which completed the fashionable costume in cold weather, was amusing himself with tormenting a creature who was walking back and forth before the window of the officers' café, in a ball-dress, with her neck and shoulders bare, and flowers upon her head. The dandy was smoking, for that was decidedly the fashion.

Every time that the woman passed before him, he threw out at her, with a puff of smoke from his cigar, some remark which he thought was witty and pleasant as: "How ugly you are!" "Are you trying to hide?" "You have lost your teeth!" etc., etc. This gentleman's name was Monsieur Bamatabois. The woman, a rueful, bedizened spectre, who was walking backwards and forwards upon the snow, did not answer him, did not even look at him, but continued her walk in silence and with a dismal regularity that brought her under his sarcasm every five minutes, like the condemned soldier who at stated periods returns under the rods. This failure to secure attention doubtless piqued the loafer, who, taking advantage of the moment when she turned, came up behind her with a stealthy step and stifling his laughter stooped down, seized a handful of snow from the side walk, and threw it hastily into her back between her naked shoulders. The girl roared with rage, turned, bounded like a panther, and rushed upon the man, burying her nails in his face, and using the most frightful words that ever fell from the off-scouring of a guard-house. These insults were thrown out in a voice roughened by brandy, from a hideous mouth which lacked the two front teeth. It was Fantine.

At the noise which this made, the officers came out of the café, a crowd gathered, and a large circle was formed, laughing, jeering and applauding, around this centre of attraction composed of two beings who could hardly be recognized as a man and a woman, the man defending himself, his hat knocked off, the woman kicking and striking, her head bare, shrieking, toothless, and without hair, livid with wrath, and horrible.

Suddenly a tall man advanced quickly from the crowd, seized the woman by her muddy satin waist, and said: "Follow me!"

The woman raised her head; her furious voice died out at once. Her eyes were glassy, from livid she had become pale, and she shuddered with a shudder of terror. She recognised Javert.

The dandy profited by this to steal away.

---

*The Venezuelan hero Simon Bolívar (1783–1830) devoted his life to trying to create a federation of Latin American countries. Gabriel García Márquez tells his tragic story in *The General in His Labyrinth* (1989).

12 (13)

THE SOLUTION TO SOME MUNICIPAL POLICE ISSUES

JAVERT dismissed the bystanders, broke up the circle and walked off rapidly towards the Police Station at the end of the square, dragging the poor creature after him. She made no resistance, but followed mechanically. Neither spoke a word. The flock of spectators, in a paroxysm of joy, followed with their jokes. The deepest misery, an opportunity for obscenity.

When they reached the station house, which was a low hall warmed by a stove, and guarded by a sentinel, with a grated window looking on the street, Javert opened the door, entered with Fantine, and closed the door behind him, to the great disappointment of the curious crowd who stood upon tiptoe and stretched their necks before the dirty window of the guard-house, in their endeavours to see. Curiosity is a kind of glutton. To see is to devour.

On entering Fantine crouched down in a corner motionless and silent, like a frightened dog.

The sergeant of the guard placed a lighted candle on the table. Javert sat down, drew from his pocket a sheet of stamped paper, and began to write.

Such women are placed by our laws completely under the discretion of the police.* They do what they will with them, punish them as they please, and confiscate at will those two sad things which they call their industry and their liberty. Javert was impassive; his grave face betrayed no emotion. He was, however, engaged in serious and earnest consideration. It was one of those moments in which he exercised without restraint, but with all the scruples of a strict conscience, his formidable discretionary power. At this moment he felt that his policeman's stool was a bench of justice. He was conducting a trial. He was trying and condemning. He called all the ideas of which his mind was capable around the grand thing that he was doing. The more he examined the conduct of this girl, the more he revolted at it. It was clear that he had seen a crime committed. He had seen, there in the street, society represented by a property holder and an elector, insulted and attacked by a creature who was an outlaw and an outcast. A prostitute had assaulted a citizen. He, Javert, had seen that himself. He wrote in silence.

When he had finished, he signed his name, folded the paper, and handed it to the sergeant of the guard, saying: "Take three men, and carry this girl to jail." Then turning to Fantine: "You are in for six months."

---

*For details, see Émile Zola's *Nana* (1880), and Charles Bernheimer's *Figures of Ill Repute* (Harvard University Press, 1989).

The hapless woman shuddered.

"Six months! six months in prison!" cried she. "Six months to earn seven sous a day! but what will become of Cosette! my daughter! my daughter! Why, I still owe more than a hundred francs to the Thénardiers, Monsieur Inspector, do you know that?"

She dragged herself along on the floor, dirtied by the muddy boots of all these men, without rising, clasping her hands, and moving rapidly on her knees.

"Monsieur Javert," said she, "I beg your pity. I assure you that I was not in the wrong. If you had seen the beginning, you would have seen. I swear to you by the good God that I was not in the wrong. That gentleman, whom I do not know, crammed snow down my back. Have they the right to cram snow down our backs when we are going along quietly like that without doing any harm to anybody? That made me wild. I am not very well, you see! and then he had already been saying things to me for some time. 'You are homely!' 'You have no teeth!' I know too well that I have lost my teeth. I did not do anything; I thought: 'He is a gentleman who is amusing himself.' I was not immodest with him, I did not speak to him. It was then that he put the snow on me. Monsieur Javert, my good Monsieur Inspector! was there no one there who saw it and can tell you that this is true! I perhaps did wrong to get angry. You know, at the first moment, we cannot master ourselves. We are excitable. And then, to have something so cold thrown into your back when you are not expecting it. I did wrong to spoil the gentleman's hat. Why has he gone away? I would ask his pardon. Oh! I would beg his pardon. Have pity on me now this once, Monsieur Javert. Stop, you don't know how it is, in the prisons they only earn seven sous; that is not the fault of the government, but they earn seven sous, and just think that I have a hundred francs to pay, or else they will turn away my little one. O my God! I cannot have her with me. What I do is so vile! O my Cosette, O my little angel of the good blessed Virgin, what will she become, poor famished child! I tell you the Thénardiers are inn-keepers, louts, they have no consideration. They must have money. Do not put me in prison! Do you see, she is a little one that they will put out on the highway, to do what she can, in the very heart of winter; you must feel pity for such a thing, good Monsieur Javert. If she were older, she could earn her living, but she cannot at such an age. I am not a bad woman at heart. It is not laziness and appetite that have brought me to this; I have drunk brandy, but it was from misery. I do not like it, but it stupefies. When I was happier, one would only have had to look into my wardrobe to see that I was not a disorderly woman. I had linen, much linen. Have pity on me, Monsieur Javert."

She talked thus, bent double, shaken with sobs, blinded by tears, her neck bare, clenching her hands, coughing with a dry and short cough, stammering very feebly with an agonised voice. Great grief is a divine and terrible radiance which transfigures the wretched. At that moment Fantine had again become beautiful. At certain instants she stopped and tenderly kissed the policeman's coat. She would have softened a heart of granite; but you cannot soften a heart of wood.

"Come," said Javert, "I have heard you. Haven't you got through? March off at once! you have your six months! the Eternal Father in person could do nothing for you."

At those solemn words, *The Eternal Father in person could do nothing for you,* she understood that her sentence was fixed. She sank down murmuring:

"Mercy!"

Javert turned his back.

The soldiers seized her by the arms.

A few minutes before a man had entered without being noticed. He had closed the door, and stood with his back against it, and heard the despairing supplication of Fantine.

When the soldiers put their hands upon the wretched being, who would not rise, he stepped forward out of the shadow and said:

"One moment, if you please!"

Javert raised his eyes and recognised Monsieur Madeleine. He took off his hat, and bowing with a sort of angry awkwardness:

"Pardon, Monsieur Mayor—"

This word, Monsieur Mayor, had a strange effect upon Fantine. She sprang to her feet at once like a spectre rising from the ground, pushed back the soldiers with her arms, walked straight to Monsieur Madeleine before they could stop her, and gazing at him fixedly, with a wild look, she exclaimed:

"Ah! it is you then who are Monsieur Mayor!"

Then she burst out laughing and spit in his face.

Monsieur Madeleine wiped his face and said:

"Inspector Javert, set this woman at liberty."

Javert felt as though he were on the point of losing his senses. He experienced, at that moment, blow on blow, and almost simultaneously, the most violent emotions that he had known in his life. To see a woman of the town spit in the face of a mayor was a thing so monstrous that in his most daring suppositions he would have thought it sacrilege to believe it possible. On the other hand, deep down in his thought, he dimly brought into hideous association what this woman was and what this mayor might be, and then he perceived with horror something indescribably simple in this prodigious assault. But when he saw this mayor, this magistrate, wipe his face quietly and say: *set this woman at liberty,* he was stupefied with amazement; thought and speech alike failed him; the sum of possible astonishment had been overpassed. He remained speechless.

The mayor's words were not less strange a blow to Fantine. She raised her bare arm and clung to the damper of the stove as if she were staggered. Meanwhile she looked all around and began to talk in a low voice, as if speaking to herself:

"At liberty! they let me go! I am not to go to prison for six months! Who was it said that? It is not possible that anybody said that. I misunderstood. That cannot be this monster of a mayor! Was it you, my good Monsieur Javert, who told them to set me at liberty? Oh! look now! I will tell you and you will let me go. This monster of a mayor, this old scoundrel of

a mayor, he is the cause of all this. Think of it, Monsieur Javert, he turned
me away! on account of a parcel of beggars who told stories in the workshop. Was not that horrible! To turn away a poor girl who does her work
honestly. Since then I could not earn enough, and all the wretchedness has
come. To begin with, there is a change that you gentlemen of the police
ought to make—that is, to stop prison contractors from wronging poor
people. I will tell you how it is; listen. You earn twelve sous at shirt making,
that falls to nine sous, not enough to live. Then we must do what we can.
For me, I had my little Cosette, and I had to be a bad woman. You see now
that it is this beggar of a mayor who has done all this, and then, I did stamp
on the hat of this gentleman in front of the officers' café. But he, he had
spoiled my whole dress with the snow. We women, we have only one silk
dress, for evening. See you, I have never meant to do wrong, in truth, Monsieur Javert, and I see everywhere much worse women than I am who are
much more fortunate. Oh, Monsieur Javert, it is you who said that they
must let me go, is it not? Go and inquire, speak to my landlord; I pay my
rent, and he will surely tell you that I am honest. Oh dear, I beg your pardon, I have touched—I did not know it—the damper of the stove, and it's
smoking."

Monsieur Madeleine listened with profound attention. While she was
talking, he had fumbled in his waistcoat, had taken out his purse and opened
it. It was empty. He had put it back into his pocket. He said to Fantine:

"How much did you say that you owed?"

Fantine, who had only looked at Javert, turned towards him:

"Who said anything to you?"

Then addressing herself to the soldiers:

"Say now, did you see how I spit in his face? Oh! you old criminal of a
mayor, you come here to frighten me, but I am not afraid of you. I am
afraid of Monsieur Javert. I am afraid of my good Monsieur Javert!"

As she said this she turned again towards the inspector:

"Now, you see, Monsieur Inspector, you must be just. I know that you
are just, Monsieur Inspector; in fact, it is very simple, a man who plays a
prank by cramming a little snow down a woman's back, that makes them
laugh, the officers, they must divert themselves with something, and we
poor things are only for their amusement. And then, you, you come, you
are obliged to keep order, you arrest the woman who has done wrong, but
on reflection, as you are good, you tell them to set me at liberty, that is for
my little one, because six months in prison, that would prevent my supporting my child. Only never come back again, wretch! Oh! I will never come
back again, Monsieur Javert! They may do anything they like with me now,
I will not stir. Only, to-day, you see, I cried out because that hurt me. I did
not in the least expect that snow from that gentleman, and then, I have told
you, I am not very well, I cough, I have something in my chest like a ball
which burns me, and the doctor tells me: 'be careful.' Stop, feel, give me
your hand, don't be afraid, here it is."

She wept no more; her voice was caressing; she placed Javert's great
coarse hand upon her white and delicate chest, and looked at him smiling.

Suddenly she hastily adjusted the disorder of her garments, smoothed down the folds of her dress, which, in dragging herself about, had been raised almost as high as her knees, and walked towards the door, saying in an undertone to the soldiers, with a friendly nod of the head:

"Boys, Monsieur the Inspector said that you must release me; I am going."

She put her hand upon the latch. One more step and she would be in the street.

Javert until that moment had remained standing, motionless, his eyes fixed on the ground, looking, in the midst of the scene, like a statue which was waiting to be placed in position.

The sound of the latch roused him. He raised his head with an expression of sovereign authority, an expression always the more frightful in proportion as power is vested in beings of lower grade; ferocious in the wild beast, atrocious in the unevolved man.

"Sergeant," exclaimed he, "don't you see that this vagabond is going off? Who told you to let her go?"

"I," said Madeleine.

At the words of Javert, Fantine had trembled and dropped the latch, as a thief who is caught, drops what he has stolen. When Madeleine spoke, she turned, and from that moment, without saying a word, without even daring to breathe freely, she looked by turns from Madeleine to Javert and from Javert to Madeleine, as the one or the other was speaking.

It was clear that Javert must have been, as they say, "thrown off balance," or he would not have allowed himself to address the sergeant as he did, after the direction of the mayor to set Fantine at liberty. Had he forgotten the presence of the mayor? Had he finally decided within himself that it was impossible for "an authority" to give such an order, and that very certainly the mayor must have said one thing when he meant another? Or, in view of the enormities which he had witnessed for the last two hours, did he say to himself that it was necessary to revert to extreme measures, that it was necessary for the little to make itself great, for the detective to transform himself into a magistrate, for the policeman to become a judge, and that in this fearful extremity, order, law, morality, government, society as a whole, were personified in him, Javert?

However this might be, when Monsieur Madeleine pronounced that I which we have just heard, the inspector of police, Javert, turned towards the mayor, pale, cold, with blue lips, a desperate look, his whole body agitated with an imperceptible tremor, and, an unheard-of thing, said to him, with a downcast look, but a firm voice:

"Monsieur Mayor, that cannot be done."

"Why not?" said Monsieur Madeleine.

"This wretched woman has insulted a citizen."

"Inspector Javert," replied Monsieur Madeleine, in a conciliating and calm tone, "listen. You are an honest man, and I have no objection to explaining myself to you. The truth is this. I was passing through the square when you arrested this woman; there was a crowd still there; I learned the circumstances; I know all about it; it is the citizen who was in the wrong, and who, by a faithful police, would have been arrested."

Javert went on:

"This wretch has just insulted Monsieur the Mayor."

"That concerns me," said Monsieur Madeleine. "The insult to me rests with myself, perhaps. I can do what I please about it."

"I beg Monsieur the Mayor's pardon. The insult rests not with him, it rests with justice."

"Inspector Javert," replied Monsieur Madeleine, "the highest justice is conscience. I have heard this woman. I know what I am doing."

"And for my part, Monsieur Mayor, I do not know what I am seeing."

"Then content yourself with obeying."

"I obey my duty. My duty requires that this woman spend six months in prison."

Monsieur Madeleine answered mildly:

"Listen to this. She shall not spend a day."

At these decisive words, Javert had the boldness to look the mayor in the eye, and said, but still in a tone of profound respect:

"I am very sorry to resist Monsieur the Mayor; it is the first time in my life, but he will deign to permit me to observe that I am within the limits of my own authority. I will speak, since the mayor desires it, on the matter of the citizen. I was there. This girl fell upon Monsieur Bamatabois, who is an elector and the owner of that fine house with a balcony, that stands at the corner of the esplanade, three stories high, and all of hewn stone. Indeed, there are some things in this world which must be considered. However that may be, Monsieur Mayor, this matter belongs to the police of the street; that concerns me, and I detain the woman Fantine."

At this Monsieur Madeleine folded his arms and said in a severe tone which nobody in the city had ever yet heard:

"The matter of which you speak belongs to the municipal police. By the terms of articles nine, eleven, fifteen, and sixty-six of the code of criminal law, I am the judge of it. I order that this woman be set at liberty."

Javert endeavoured to make a last attempt.

"But, Monsieur Mayor——"

"I refer *you* to article eighty-one of the law of December 13th, 1799, on illegal imprisonment."

"Monsieur Mayor, permit——"

"Not another word."

"However——"

"Leave," said Monsieur Madeleine.

Javert received the blow, standing head-on, and full in the chest like a Russian soldier. He bowed to the ground before the mayor, and went out.

Fantine stood by the door and looked at him with stupor as he passed before her.

Meanwhile she also was the subject of a strange revolution. She had seen herself somehow fought over by two opposing powers. She had seen struggling before her very eyes two men who held in their hands her liberty, her life, her soul, her child, one of these men was drawing her to the side of darkness, the other was leading her towards the light. In this contest, seen with distortion through the magnifying power of fright, these two men had appeared to her like two giants; one spoke as her demon, the other as her good angel. The angel had vanquished the demon, and the thought of it made her shudder from head to foot, this angel, this deliverer was precisely the man whom she abhorred, this mayor whom she had so long considered as the author of all her woes, this Madeleine! and at the very moment when she had insulted him in a hideous fashion, he had saved her! Had she then been deceived? Ought she then to change her whole heart? She did not know, she trembled. She listened with dismay, she looked around with alarm, and at each word that Monsieur Madeleine uttered, she felt the fearful darkness of her hatred melt within and flow away, while there was born in her heart an indescribable and unspeakable warmth of joy, of confidence, and of love.[*]

When Javert was gone, Monsieur Madeleine turned towards her, and said to her, speaking slowly and with difficulty, like a man who is struggling that he may not weep:

"I have heard you. I knew nothing of what you have said. I believe that it is true. I did not even know that you had left my workshop. Why did you not apply to me? But now: I will pay your debts, I will have your child come to you, or you shall go to her. You shall live here, at Paris, or where you will. I take charge of your child and you. You shall do no more work, if you do not wish to. I will give you all the money that you need. You shall again become honest in again becoming happy. More than that, listen. I declare to you from this moment, if all is as you say, and I do not doubt it, that you have never ceased to be virtuous and holy before God. Oh, poor woman!"

This was more than poor Fantine could bear. To have Cosette! to leave this infamous life! to live free, rich, happy, honest, with Cosette! to see suddenly spring up in the midst of her misery all these realities of paradise! She looked as if she were stupefied at the man who was speaking to her, and could only pour out two or three sobs: "Oh! oh! oh!" Her limbs gave way, she threw herself on her knees before Monsieur Madeleine, and, before he could prevent it, he felt that she had seized his hand and carried it to her lips.

Then she fainted.

---

[*]M. Madeleine's beneficent influence on Fantine illustrates the transference of merit in the Communion of Saints. Bishop Myriel previously imparted redemptive grace to Jean Valjean.

BOOK SIX
JAVERT

1

THE BEGINNING OF REPOSE

Monsieur Madeleine had Fantine taken to the infirmary, which was in his own house. He confided her to the sisters, who put her to bed. A violent fever came on, and she passed a part of the night in delirious ravings. Finally, she fell asleep.

Towards noon the following day, Fantine awoke. She heard a breathing near her bed, drew aside the curtain, and saw Monsieur Madeleine standing gazing at something above his head. His look was full of compassionate and supplicating agony. She followed its direction, and saw that it was fixed upon a crucifix nailed against the wall.

From that moment Monsieur Madeleine was transfigured in the eyes of Fantine; he seemed to her clothed with light. He was absorbed in a kind of prayer. She gazed at him for a long while without daring to interrupt him; at last she said timidly:

"What are you doing?"

Monsieur Madeleine had been in that place for an hour waiting for Fantine to awake. He took her hand, felt her pulse, and said:

"How do you feel?"

"Very well. I have slept," she said. "I think I am getting better—this will be nothing."

Then he said, answering the question she had first asked him, as if she had just asked it:

"I was praying to the martyr who is on high."

And in his thought he added: "For the martyr who is here below."

Monsieur Madeleine had passed the night and morning in informing himself about Fantine. He knew all now, he had learned, even in all its poignant details, the history of Fantine.

He went on:

"You have suffered greatly, poor mother. Oh! do not lament, you have now the portion of the elect. It is in this way that mortals become angels. It is not their fault; they do not know how to set about it otherwise. This hell from which you have come out is the first step towards Heaven. We must begin by that."

He sighed deeply; but she smiled with this sublime smile from which two teeth were gone.

That same night, Javert wrote a letter. Next morning he carried this letter himself to the post-office of M—— sur M——. It was directed to Paris and bore this address: "To Monsieur Chabouillet, Secretary of Monsieur the Prefect of Police."

Because the matter at the police station had become known, the post-mistress and some others who saw the letter before it was sent and who recognized Javert's handwriting in the address, thought he was sending in his resignation.

Monsieur Madeleine wrote immediately to the Thénardiers. Fantine owed them a hundred and twenty francs. He sent them three hundred francs, telling them to pay themselves out of it, and bring the child at once to M—— sur M——, where her mother, who was sick, wanted her.

This astonished Thénardier.

"The Devil!" he said to his wife, "we won't let go of the child. It may be that this lark will become a milk cow. Some silly fellow must have been smitten by the mother."

He replied by a bill of five hundred and some odd francs carefully drawn up. In this bill figured two incontestable items for upwards of three hundred francs, one of a physician and the other of an apothecary who had attended and supplied Eponine and Azelma during two long illnesses. Cosette, as we have said, had not been ill. This was only a slight substitution of names. Thénardier wrote at the bottom of the bill: *"Received on account three hundred francs."*

Monsieur Madeleine immediately sent three hundred francs more, and wrote: "Make haste to bring Cosette."

"Christy!" said Thénardier, "we won't let go of the girl."

Meanwhile Fantine had not recovered. She still remained in the infirmary.

It was not without some repugnance, at first, that the sisters received and cared for "this girl." He who has seen the bas-reliefs at Rheims will recall the distension of the lower lip of the wise virgins beholding the foolish virgins. This ancient contempt of vestals for less fortunate women is one of the deepest instincts of womanly dignity; the sisters had experienced it with the intensification of Religion. But in a few days Fantine had disarmed them. The motherly tenderness within her, with her soft and touching words, moved them. One day the sisters heard her say in her delirium: "I have been a sinner, but when I shall have my child with me, that will mean that God has pardoned me. While I was bad I would not have had my Cosette with me; I could not have borne her sad and surprised looks. It was for her I sinned, and that is why God forgives me. I shall feel this benediction when Cosette comes. I shall gaze upon her; the sight of her innocence will do me good. She knows nothing of it all. She is an angel, you see, my sisters. At her age the wings have not yet fallen."

Monsieur Madeleine came to see her twice a day, and at each visit she asked him:

"Shall I see my Cosette soon?"

He answered:

"Perhaps to-morrow. I expect her every moment."

And the mother's pale face would brighten.

"Ah!" she would say, "how happy I shall be."

We have just said she did not recover: on the contrary, her condition seemed to become worse from week to week. That handful of snow applied to the naked skin between her shoulder-blades, had caused a sudden check of perspiration, in consequence of which the disease, which had been forming for some years, at last attacked her violently. They were just at that time beginning in the diagnosis and treatment of lung diseases to follow the fine theory of Laënnec. The doctor sounded her lungs and shook his head.

Monsieur Madeleine said to him:

"Well?"

"Has she not a child she is anxious to see?" said the doctor.

"Yes."

"Well then, make haste to bring her."

Monsieur Madeleine gave a shudder.

Fantine asked him: "What did the doctor say?"

Monsieur Madeleine tried to smile.

"He told us to bring your child at once. That will restore your health."

"Oh!" she cried, "he is right. But what is the matter with these Thénardiers that they keep my Cosette from me? Oh! She is coming! Here at last I see happiness near me."

The Thénardiers, however, did not "let go of the child;" they gave a hundred bad reasons. Cosette was too delicate to travel in the winter time, and then there were a number of little petty debts, of which they were collecting the bills, etc., etc.

"I will send somebody for Cosette," said Monsieur Madeleine, "if necessary, I will go myself."

He wrote at Fantine's dictation this letter, which she signed. "Monsieur Thénardier:

"You will deliver Cosette to the bearer.

"He will settle all small debts.

"I have the honour to salute you with consideration.

"FANTINE."

At this juncture a serious incident intervened. In vain we chisel, as best we can, the mysterious block of which our life is made, the black vein of destiny reappears continually.

2

HOW JEAN CAN BECOME CHAMP

ONE MORNING Monsieur Madeleine was in his office arranging for some pressing business of the mayoralty, in case he should decide to go to Montfermeil himself, when he was informed that Javert, the inspector of police, wished to speak with him. On hearing this name spoken, Monsieur Madeleine could not repress a disagreeable impression. Since the affair of the Bureau of Police, Javert had more than ever avoided him, and Monsieur Madeleine had not seen him at all.

"Let him come in," said he.

Javert entered.

Monsieur Madeleine remained seated near the fire, looking over a bundle of papers upon which he was making notes, and which contained the reports of the police patrol. He did not disturb himself at all for Javert: he could not but think of poor Fantine, and it was fitting that he should receive him very coldly.

Javert respectfully saluted the mayor, who had his back towards him. The mayor did not look up, but continued to make notes on the papers.

Javert advanced a few steps, and paused without breaking silence.

A physiognomist, had he been familiar with Javert's face, had he made a study for years of this savage in the service of civilisation, this odd mixture of the Roman, Spartan, monk and corporal, this spy, incapable of a lie, this virgin detective—a physiognomist, had he known his secret and inveterate aversion for Monsieur Madeleine, his contest with the mayor on the subject of Fantine, and had he seen Javert at that moment, would have said: "What has happened to him?"*

It was evident to any one who had known this conscientious, straightforward, transparent, sincere, upright, austere, fierce man, that Javert had suffered some great interior commotion. There was nothing in his mind that was not depicted on his face. He was, like all violent people, subject to sudden changes. Never had his face been stranger or more startling. On entering, he had bowed before Monsieur Madeleine with a look in which was neither rancour, anger, nor defiance; he paused some steps behind the mayor's chair, and was now standing in a soldierly attitude with the natural, cold harshness of a man who was never kind, but has always been patient; he waited without speaking a word or making a motion, in genuine humility

---

*Hugo borrows two techniques from Balzac here: allusions to the pseudo-science of physiognomy, and the episodic observer brought in to deliver expert testimony.

and tranquil resignation, until it should please Monsieur the Mayor to turn towards him, calm, serious, hat in hand, and eyes cast down with an expression between that of a soldier before his officer and a prisoner before his judge. All the feeling as well as all the remembrances which we should have expected him to have, disappeared. Nothing was left upon this face, simple and impenetrable as granite, except a gloomy sadness. His whole person expressed abasement and firmness, an indescribably courageous dejection.

At last the mayor laid down his pen and turned partly round:

"Well, what is it? What is the matter Javert?"

Javert remained silent a moment as if collecting himself; then raised his voice with a sad solemnity which did not, however, exclude simplicity: "There has been a criminal act committed, Monsieur Mayor."

"What act?"

"An inferior agent of the government has been wanting in respect to a magistrate, in the gravest manner. I come, as is my duty, to bring the fact to your knowledge."

"Who is this agent?" asked Monsieur Madeleine.

"I," said Javert.

"You?"

"I."

"And who is the magistrate who has to complain of this agent?"

"You, Monsieur Mayor."

Monsieur Madeleine straightened himself in his chair. Javert continued, with serious looks and eyes still cast down.

"Monsieur Mayor, I come to ask you to be so kind as to make charges and procure my dismissal."

Monsieur Madeleine, amazed, opened his mouth. Javert interrupted him:

"You will say that I might tender my resignation, but that is not enough. To resign is honourable; I have done wrong. I ought to be punished. I must be dismissed."

And after a pause he added:

"Monsieur Mayor, you were severe to me the other day, unjustly. Be justly so to-day."

"Ah, indeed! why? What is all this nonsense? What does it all mean? What is the criminal act committed by you against me? What have you done to me? How have you wronged me? You accuse yourself: do you wish to be relieved?"

"Dismissed," said Javert.

"Dismissed it is then. It is very strange. I do not understand you."

"You will understand, Monsieur Mayor," Javert sighed deeply, and continued sadly and coldly:

"Monsieur Mayor, six weeks ago, after that scene about that girl, I was enraged and I denounced you."

"Denounced me?"

"To the Prefecture of Police at Paris."

Monsieur Madeleine, who did not laugh much oftener than Javert, began to laugh:

"As a mayor having encroached upon the police?"

"As a former convict."

The mayor became livid.

Javert, who had not raised his eyes, continued:

"I believed it. For a long while I had had suspicions. A resemblance, information you obtained at Faverolles, your immense strength; the affair of old Fauchelevent; your skill as a marksman; your leg which drags a little—and in fact I don't know what other trivial details; but at last I took you for a man named Jean Valjean."

"Named what? What name did you say?"

"Jean Valjean. He was a convict I saw twenty years ago, when I was adjutant of the galley guard at Toulon. After leaving the galleys this Valjean, it appears, robbed a bishop's palace, then he committed another robbery with weapons in his hands, in a highway, on a little chimneysweep. For eight years his whereabouts have been unknown, and search has been made for him. I fancied—in short, I have done this thing. Anger determined me, and I denounced you to the prefect."

M. Madeleine, who had taken up the file of papers again, a few moments before, said with a tone of perfect indifference: "And what answer did you get?"

"That I was crazy."

"Well!"

"Well; they were right."

"It is fortunate that you admit it!"

"It must be so, for the real Jean Valjean has been found."

The paper that M. Madeleine held fell from his hand; he raised his head, looked steadily at Javert, and said in an inexpressible tone:

"Ah!"

Javert continued:

"I will tell you how it is, Monsieur Mayor. There was, it appears, in the country, near Ailly-le-Haut Clocher, a simple sort of fellow who was called Old Champmathieu. He was very poor. Nobody paid any attention to him. Such folks live, one hardly knows how. Finally, this last fall, Old Champmathieu was arrested for stealing cider apples from——, but that is of no consequence. There was a theft, a wall scaled, branches of trees broken. Our Champmathieu was arrested; he had even then a branch of an apple-tree in his hand. The rogue was caged. So far, it was nothing more than a penitentiary matter. But here comes in the hand of Providence. The jail being in a bad condition, the police justice thought it best to take him to Arras, where the prison of the department is. In this prison at Arras there was a former convict named Brevet, who is there for some trifle, and who, for his good conduct, has been made turnkey. No sooner was Champmathieu set down, than Brevet cried out: 'Ha, ha! I know that man. He is a *fagot*.'*

---

*Former convict.

" 'Look up here, my good man. You are Jean Valjean.' 'Jean Valjean, who is Jean Valjean?' Champmathieu feigns astonishment. 'Don't play ignorance,' said Brevet. 'You are Jean Valjean; you were in the galleys at Toulon. It is twenty years ago. We were there together.' Champmathieu denied it all. Of course! you understand; they investigated it. The case was worked up and this was what they found. This Champmathieu thirty years ago was a pruner in divers places, particularly in Faverolles. There we lose trace of him. A long time afterwards we find him at Auvergne; then at Paris, where he is said to have been a wheelwright and to have had a daughter—a washerwoman, but that is not proven, and finally in this part of the country. Now before going to the galleys for burglary, what was Jean Valjean? A pruner. Where? At Faverolles. Another fact. This Valjean's baptismal name was Jean; his mother's family name, Mathieu. Nothing could be more natural, on leaving the galleys, than to take his mother's name to disguise himself; then he would be called Jean Mathieu. He goes to Auvergne, the pronunciation of that region would make *Chan* of *Jean*—they would call him Chan Mathieu. Our man adopts it, and now you have him transformed into Champmathieu. You follow me, do you not? Search has been made at Faverolles; the family of Jean Valjean are no longer there. Nobody knows where they are. You know in such classes these disappearances of families often occur. You search, but can find nothing. Such people, when they are not mud, are dust. And then as the commencement of this story dates back thirty years, there is nobody now at Faverolles who knew Jean Valjean. But search has been made at Toulon. Besides Brevet there are only two convicts who have seen Jean Valjean. They are convicts for life; their names are Cochepaille and Chenildieu. These men were brought from the galleys and confronted with the so-called Champmathieu. They did not hesitate. To them as well as to Brevet it was Jean Valjean. Same age; fifty-four years old; same height; same appearance, in fact the same man; it is he. At this time it was that I sent my denunciation to the Prefecture at Paris. They replied that I was out of my mind, and that Jean Valjean was at Arras in the hands of justice. You may imagine how that astonished me; I who believed that I had here the same Jean Valjean. I wrote to the examining magistrate; he sent for me and brought Champmathieu before me."

"Well," interrupted Monsieur Madeleine.

Javert replied, with an incorruptible and sad face:

"Monsieur Mayor, truth is truth. I am sorry for it, but that man is Jean Valjean. I recognised him also."

Monsieur Madeleine said in a very low voice:

"Are you sure?"

Javert began to laugh with the suppressed laugh which indicates profound conviction.

"H'm, sure!"

He remained a moment in thought, mechanically taking up pinches of the powdered wood used to dry ink, from the box on the table, and then added:

"And now that I see the real Jean Valjean, I do not understand how

I ever could have believed anything else. I beg your pardon, Monsieur Mayor."

In uttering these serious and supplicating words to him, who six weeks before had humiliated him before the entire squad, and had said "Leave!" Javert, this haughty man, was unconsciously full of simplicity and dignity. Monsieur Madeleine responded to this entreaty only with this abrupt question:

"And what did the man say?"

"Oh, bless me! Monsieur Mayor, the affair is a bad one. If it is Jean Valjean, it is a second offence. To climb a wall, break a branch, and take apples, for a child is only a trespass; for a man it is a misdemeanor; for a convict it is a felony. Scaling a wall and theft includes everything. It is not a case for a police court, but for the circuit court. It is not a few days' imprisonment, but the galleys for life. And then there is the business of the little chimneysweep, whom I hope will be found. The devil! That's a difficult set of charges to elude, isn't it? They would be for anybody but Jean Valjean. But Jean Valjean is a sly fellow. And that is just where I recognise him. Anybody else would know that he was in hot water, and would rave and cry out, as the tea-kettle sings on the fire; he would say that he was not Jean Valjean, et cetera. But this man pretends not to understand, he says: 'I am Champmathieu: I have no more to say.' He puts on an appearance of astonishment; he plays stupid. Oh, the rascal is cunning! But it is all the same, there is the evidence. Four persons have recognised him, and the old villain will be condemned. It has been taken to the circuit court at Arras. I am going to testify. I have been subpoenaed."

Monsieur Madeleine had turned again to his desk, and was quietly looking over his papers, reading and writing alternately, like a man pressed with business. He turned again towards Javert:

"That will do, Javert. Indeed all these details interest me very little. We are wasting time, and we have urgent business, Javert; go at once to the house of the good woman Buseaupied, who sells herbs at the corner of Rue Saint Saulve, tell her to make her complaint against the carman Pierre Chesnelong. He is a brutal fellow, he almost crushed this woman and her child. He must be punished. Then you will go to Monsieur Charcellay, Rue Montre-de-Champigny. He complains that the gutter of the next house when it rains throws water upon his house, and is undermining the foundation. Then you will inquire into the offences that have been reported to me, at the widow Doris's, Rue Guibourg, and Madame Renée le Bossé's, Rue du Garraud Blanc, and make out reports. But I am giving you too much to do. Did you not tell me you were going to Arras in eight or ten days on this matter?"

"Sooner than that, Monsieur Mayor."

"What day then?"

"I think I told monsieur that the case would be tried to-morrow, and that I should leave by the stagecoach to-night."

Monsieur Madeleine made an imperceptible motion.

"And how long will the matter last?"

"One day at longest. Sentence will be pronounced at latest to-morrow evening. But I shall not wait for the sentence, which is certain; as soon as my testimony is given I shall return here."

"Very well," said Monsieur Madeleine.

And he dismissed him with a wave of his hand.

Javert did not go.

"Excuse me, monsieur," said he.

"What more is there?" asked Monsieur Madeleine.

"Monsieur Mayor, there is one thing more to which I desire to call your attention."

"What is it?"

"It is that I ought to be dismissed."

Monsieur Madeleine arose.

"Javert, you are a man of honour and I esteem you. You exaggerate your fault. Besides, this is an offence which concerns me. You are worthy of promotion rather than disgrace. I desire you to keep your place."

Javert looked at Monsieur Madeleine with his calm eyes, in whose depths it seemed that one beheld his conscience, unenlightened, but stern and pure, and said in a tranquil voice:

"Monsieur Mayor, I cannot agree to that."

"I repeat," said Monsieur Madeleine, "that this matter concerns me."

But Javert, with his one idea, continued:

"As to exaggerating, I do not exaggerate. This is the way I reason. I have unjustly suspected you. That is nothing. It is our province to suspect, although it may be an abuse of our right to suspect our superiors. But without proofs and in a fit of anger, with revenge as my aim, I denounced you as a convict—you, a respectable man, a mayor, and a magistrate. This is a serious matter, very serious. I have committed an offence against authority in your person, I, who am the agent of authority. If one of my subordinates had done what I have, I would have pronounced him unworthy of the service, and sent him away. Well, listen a moment, Monsieur Mayor; I have often been severe in my life towards others. It was just. I did right. Now if I were not severe towards myself, all I have justly done would become injustice. Should I spare myself more than others? No. What! if I should be prompt only to punish others and not myself, I should be a wretch indeed!* They who say: 'That blackguard, Javert,' would be right. Monsieur Mayor, I do not wish you to treat me with kindness. Your kindness, when it was for others, enraged me; I do not wish it for myself. That kindness which consists in defending a woman of the town against a citizen, a police agent against the mayor, the inferior against the superior, that is what I call ill-judged kindness. Such kindness disorganizes society. Good God, it is easy to be kind, the difficulty is to be just. Had you been what I thought, I should not have been kind to you; not I. You would have seen, Monsieur Mayor. I ought to treat

---

*Like Jean Valjean elsewhere, Javert here applies the title word *misérable* to himself, in the sense of morally debased.

myself as I would treat anybody else. When I put down malefactors, when I rigorously punished offenders, I often said to myself: 'You, if you ever trip; if ever I catch you doing wrong, look out!' I have tripped, I have caught myself doing wrong. So much the worse! I must be sent away, broken, dismissed, that is right. I have hands: I can till the ground. It is all the same to me. Monsieur Mayor, the good of the service demands an example. I simply ask the dismissal of Inspector Javert."

All this was said in a tone of proud humility, a desperate and resolute tone, which gave an indescribably bizarre grandeur to this oddly honest man.

"We will see," said Monsieur Madeleine.

And he held out his hand to him.

Javert started back, and said fiercely:

"Pardon, Monsieur Mayor, that should not be. A mayor does not give his hand to a spy."

He added between his teeth:

"Spy, yes; from the moment I abused the power of my position, I have been nothing better than a spy!"

Then he bowed profoundly, and went towards the door.

There he turned around: his eyes yet downcast.

"Monsieur Mayor, I will continue in the service until I am relieved."

He went out. Monsieur Madeleine sat musing, listening to his firm and resolute step as it died away along the corridor.

Book Seven
THE CHAMPMATHIEU CASE

1

SISTER SIMPLICE

THE EVENTS which follow were never all known at M—— sur M——. But the few which did leak out have left such memories in that city, that it would be a serious omission in this book if we did not relate them in their minutest details.

Among these details, the reader will meet with two or three improbable circumstances, which we preserve from respect for the truth.

In the afternoon following the visit of Javert, M. Madeleine went to see Fantine as usual.

Before going to Fantine's room, he sent for Sister Simplice.

The two nuns who attended the infirmary, Lazarists as all these Sisters of Charity are, were called Sister Perpétue and Sister Simplice.

Sister Perpétue was an ordinary village-girl, summarily become a Sister of Charity, who entered the service of God as she would have entered service anywhere. She was a nun as others are cooks.

Sister Simplice was white with a waxen clearness. In comparison with Sister Perpétue she was a sacramental taper by the side of a tallow candle. Never to have lied, never to have spoken, for any purpose whatever, even carelessly, a single word which was not the truth, the sacred truth, was the distinctive trait of Sister Simplice; it was the mark of her virtue. She was almost celebrated in the congregation for this imperturbable veracity.

The pious woman had conceived an affection for Fantine, perceiving in her probably some latent virtue, and had devoted herself almost exclusively to her care.

Monsieur Madeleine took Sister Simplice aside and recommended Fantine to her with a singular emphasis, which the sister remembered at a later day.

On leaving the Sister, he approached Fantine.

Fantine awaited each day the appearance of Monsieur Madeleine as one awaits a ray of warmth and of joy. She would say to the sisters: "I live only when the Mayor is here."

That day she had more fever. As soon as she saw Monsieur Madeleine, she asked him:

"Cosette?"

He answered with a smile:

"Very soon."

Monsieur Madeleine, while with Fantine, seemed the same as usual. Only he stayed an hour instead of half an hour, to the great satisfaction of Fantine. He made a thousand charges to everybody that the sick woman

might want for nothing. It was noticed that at one moment his countenance became very sombre. But this was explained when it was known
that the doctor had, bending close to his ear, said to him: "She is sinking
fast."

Then he returned to the mayor's office, and the office boy saw him examine attentively a road-map of France which hung in his room. He made a
few figures in pencil upon a piece of paper.

2

THE SHREWDNESS OF MASTER
SCAUFFLAIRE

FROM THE MAYOR'S OFFICE he went to the outskirts of the city, to a Fleming's, Master Scaufflaer, Frenchified into Scaufflaire, who kept horses to let
and "chaises if desired."

In order to go to Scaufflaire's, the nearest way was by a rarely frequented
street, on which was the parsonage of the parish in which Monsieur
Madeleine lived. The curé was, it was said, a worthy and respectable man,
and a good counsellor. At the moment when Monsieur Madeleine arrived
in front of the parsonage, there was but one person passing in the street,
and he remarked this: the mayor, after passing by the curé's house, stopped,
stood still a moment, then turned back and retraced his steps as far as
the door of the parsonage, which was a large door with an iron knocker.
He seized the knocker quickly and raised it; then he stopped anew, stood
a short time as if in thought, and after a few seconds, instead of letting the
knocker fall smartly, he replaced it gently, and resumed his walk with a
sort of haste that he had not shown before.

Monsieur Madeleine found Master Scaufflaire at home busy repairing
a harness.

"Master Scaufflaire," he asked, "have you a good horse?"

"Monsieur Mayor," said the Fleming, "all my horses are good. What do
you mean by a good horse?"

"I mean a horse that can go fifty miles in a day."

"The devil!" said the Fleming, "fifty miles!"

"Yes."

"Pulling a cabriolet?"

"Yes."

"And how long will he rest after the journey?"

"He must be able to start again the next day in case of need."

"To do the same thing again?"

"Yes."

"The devil! and it is fifty miles?"

Monsieur Madeleine drew from his pocket the paper on which he had pencilled the figures. He showed them to the Fleming. They were the figures 12 1/2, 15, 21.

"You see," said he. "Total, forty-eight and a half, that is to say, fifty miles."

"Monsieur Mayor," resumed the Fleming, "I have just what you want. My little white horse, you must have seen him sometimes passing; he is a little beast from Bas-Boulonnais. He is full of fire. They tried at first to make a saddle horse of him. Bah! he kicked, he threw everybody off. They thought he was vicious, they didn't know what to do. I bought him. I had him pull a cabriolet; Monsieur, that is what he wanted; he is as gentle as a girl, he goes like the wind. But, of course, it won't do to get on his back. It's not his idea to be a saddle horse. Everybody has his peculiar ambition. To draw, but not to carry: we must believe that he has said that to himself."

"And he will make the trip?"

"Your fifty miles, all the way at a trot, in less than eight hours. But there are some conditions."

"Name them."

"First, you must let him rest an hour when you are half way; he will eat and somebody must be by to prevent the tavern boy from stealing his oats, for I have noticed that at taverns oats are oftener drunk by the stable boys than eaten by the horses."

"Somebody shall be there."

"Secondly—is the chaise for Monsieur the Mayor?"

"Yes."

"Monsieur the Mayor knows how to drive?"

"Yes."

"Well, Monsieur the Mayor will travel alone and without baggage, so as not to overload the horse."

"Agreed."

"But Monsieur the Mayor, having no one with him, will be obliged to take the trouble of seeing to the oats himself."

"Agreed."

"I must have thirty francs a day, the days he rests included. Not a penny less, and the fodder of the beast at the expense of Monsieur the Mayor."

Monsieur Madeleine took three Napoleons from his purse and laid them on the table.

"There is two days, in advance."

"Fourthly, for such a trip, a chaise would be too heavy; that would tire the horse. Monsieur the Mayor must consent to travel in a little tilbury that I have."

"I consent to that."

"It is light, but it is open."

"It is all the same to me."

"Has Monsieur the Mayor reflected that it is winter?"

Monsieur Madeleine did not answer; the Fleming went on:
"That it is very cold?"
Monsieur Madeleine kept silence.
Master Scaufflaire continued:
"That it may rain?"
Monsieur Madeleine raised his head and said:
"The horse and the tilbury will be before my door to-morrow at half-past four in the morning."

We have but little to add to what the reader already knows, concerning what had happened to Jean Valjean, since his adventure with Petit Gervais. From that moment, we have seen, he was another man. What the bishop had desired to do with him, that he had executed. It was more than a transformation—it was a transfiguration.

He succeeded in escaping from sight, sold the bishop's silver, keeping only the candlesticks as souvenirs, glided quietly from city to city across France, came to M—— sur M——, conceived the idea that we have described, accomplished what we have related, gained the point of making himself unassailable and inaccessible, and thence forward, established at M—— sur M——, happy to feel his conscience saddened by his past, and the latter half of his existence giving the lie to the first, he lived peaceable, reassured, and hopeful, having but two thoughts: to conceal his name, and to sanctify his life; to escape from men and to return to God.

These two thoughts were associated so closely in his mind, that they formed but a single one; they were both equally absorbing and imperious, and ruled his slightest actions. Ordinarily they were in harmony in the regulation of the conduct of his life, they turned him towards obscurity; they made him benevolent and simple-hearted; they counselled him to do the same things. Sometimes however, there was a conflict between them. In such cases, it will be remembered, the man, whom all the country around M—— sur M—— called Monsieur Madeleine, did not waver in sacrificing the first to the second, his security to his virtue. Thus, in despite of all reserve and of all prudence, he had kept the bishop's candlesticks, worn mourning for him, called and questioned all the little chimneysweeps who passed by, gathered information concerning the families at Faverolles, and saved the life of old Fauchelevent, in spite of the disquieting insinuations of Javert. It would seem, we have already remarked, that he thought, following the example of all who have been wise, holy, and just, that his highest duty was not towards himself.

But of all these occasions, it must be said, none had ever been anything like that which was now presented.

Never had the two ideas that governed the unfortunate man whose sufferings we are relating, engaged in so serious a struggle. He comprehended this confusedly, but thoroughly, from the first words that Javert pronounced on entering his office. At the moment when that name which he had so deeply buried was so strangely uttered, he was seized with stupor, and as if intoxicated by the sinister grotesqueness of his destiny, and through that stupor he felt the shudder which precedes great shocks; he bent like an oak at the approach of a storm, like a soldier at the approach of an assault. He felt clouds full of thunderings and lightnings gathering upon his head. Even while listening to Javert, his first thought was to go, to run, to denounce himself, to drag this Champmathieu out of prison, and to put himself in his place; it was painful and sharp as an incision into the living flesh, but passed away, and he said to himself: "Let us see! Let us see!" He repressed this first generous impulse and recoiled before such heroism.

"Where am I? Am I not in a dream? What have I heard? Is it really true that I saw this Javert, and that he talked to me so? Who can this Champmathieu be? He resembles me then? Is it possible? When I think that yesterday I was so calm, and so far from suspecting anything! What was I doing yesterday at this time? What is there in this matter? How will it turn out? What is to be done?"

Such was the torment he was in. His brain had lost the power of retaining its ideas; they passed away like waves, and he grasped his forehead with both hands to stop them.

Out of this tumult, which overwhelmed his will and his reason, and from which he sought to draw a certainty and a resolution, nothing came clearly forth but anguish.

His head was burning. He went to the window and threw it wide open. Not a star was in the sky. He returned and sat down by the table.

The first hour thus rolled away.

Little by little, however, vague outlines began to take form and to fix themselves in his meditation; he could perceive, with the precision of reality, not the whole of the situation, but a few details.

He began by recognising that, however extraordinary and critical the situation was, he was completely master of it.

His stupor only became the deeper.

Independently of the severe and religious aim that his actions had in view, all that he had done up to this day was only a hole that he was digging in which to bury his name. What he had always most dreaded, in his hours of self-communion, in his sleepless nights, was the thought of ever hearing that name pronounced; he felt that would be for him the end of all; that the day on which that name should reappear would see vanish from around him his new life, and, who knows, even perhaps his new soul from within him. He shuddered at the bare thought that it was possible. Surely, if any one had told him at such moments that an hour would come when that name would resound in his ear, when that hideous word, Jean Valjean, would start forth suddenly from the night and stand before him; when this fearful glare, destined to dissipate the mystery in which he had wrapped himself, would flash suddenly upon his head, and that this name would not menace him, and that this glare would only make his obscurity the deeper, that this rending of the veil would increase the mystery, that this earthquake would consolidate his edifice, that this prodigious event would have no other result, if it seemed good to him, to himself alone, than to render his existence at once more transparent and more impenetrable, and that, from his encounter with the phantom of Jean Valjean, the good and worthy citizen, Monsieur Madeleine, would come forth more honoured, more peaceful and more respected than ever—if any one had said this to him, he would have shaken his head and looked upon the words as nonsense. Well! precisely that had happened; all this grouping of the impossible was now a fact, and God had permitted these absurdities to become real things!

His musings continued to grow clearer. He was getting a wider and wider view of his position.

It seemed to him that he had just awaked from some wondrous slumber, and that he found himself gliding over a precipice in the middle of the night, standing, shivering, recoiling in vain, upon the very edge of an abyss. He perceived distinctly in the gloom an unknown man, a stranger, whom fate had mistaken for him, and was pushing into the gulf in his place. It was necessary, in order that the gulf should be closed, that some one should fall in, he or the other.

He had only to let it alone.

The light became complete, and he recognized this: That his place at the galleys was empty, that do what he could it was always awaiting him, that the robbing of Petit Gervais sent him back there, that this empty place would await him and attract him until he should be there, that this was inevitable and predestined. And then he said to himself: That at this very moment he had a substitute, that it appeared that a man named Champmathieu had that unhappy lot, and that as for himself, present in future at the galleys in the person of this Champmathieu, present in society under the name of Monsieur Madeleine, he had nothing more to fear, provided he did not prevent men from sealing upon the head of this Champmathieu that stone of infamy which, like the stone of the sepulchre, falls once never to rise again.

All this was so violent and so strange that he suddenly felt that kind of indescribable movement that no man experiences more than two or three times in his life, a sort of convulsion of the conscience that stirs up all that is dubious in the heart, which is composed of irony, of joy, and of despair, and which might be called a burst of interior laughter.

He hastily relighted his candle.

"Well, what!" said he, "what am I afraid of? why do I ponder over these things? I am now safe? all is finished. There was but a single half-open door through which my past could make an irruption into my life; that door is now walled up! for ever! This Javert who has troubled me so long, that fearful instinct which seemed to have divined the truth, that had divined it, in fact! and which followed me everywhere, that terrible bloodhound always in pursuit of me, he is thrown off the track, engrossed elsewhere, absolutely baffled. He is satisfied henceforth, he will leave me in quiet, he holds his Jean Valjean fast! Who knows! it is even probable that he will want to leave the city! And all this is accomplished without my aid! And I have nothing to do with it! Ah, yes, but, what is there unfortunate in all this! People who should see me, upon my honour, would think that a catastrophe had befallen me! After all, if there is any harm done to any-body, it is in nowise my fault. Providence has done it all. This is what He wishes apparently. Have I the right to disarrange what He arranges? What is it that I ask for now? Why do I interfere? It does not concern me. How! I am not satisfied! But what would I have then? The aim to which I have aspired for so many years, my nightly dream, the object of my prayers to heaven, security, I have gained it. It is God's will. I must do nothing con-trary to the will of God. And why is it God's will? That I may carry on what I have begun, that I may do good, that I may be one day a grand and encouraging example that it may be said that there was finally some little happiness resulting from this suffering which I have undergone and this virtue to which I have returned! Really I do not understand why I was so much afraid to go to this honest curé and tell him the whole story as a con-fessor, and ask his advice; this is evidently what he would have said to me. It is decided, let the matter alone! let us not interfere with God."

Thus he spoke in the depths of his conscience, hanging over what might be called his own abyss. He rose from his chair, and began to walk the room. "Come," said he, "let us think of it no more. The resolution is formed!" But he felt no joy.

Quite the contrary.

One can no more prevent the mind from returning to an idea than the sea from returning to a shore. In the case of the sailor, this is called the tide; in the case of the guilty, it is called remorse. God upheaves the soul as well as the ocean.

After the lapse of a few moments, he could do no otherwise, he resumed this sombre dialogue, in which it was himself who spoke and himself who listened, saying what he wished to keep silent, listening to what he did not wish to hear, yielding to that mysterious power which said to him: "think!" as it said two thousand years ago to another condemned: "march!"*

He asked himself then where he was. He questioned himself upon this "resolution formed." He confessed to himself that all that he had been arrang-ing in his mind was monstrous, that "to let the matter alone, not to interfere with God," was simply horrible, to let this mistake of destiny and of men be accomplished, not to prevent it, to lend himself to it by his silence, to do noth-ing, finally, was to do all! it was the last degree of hypocritical meanness! it was a base, cowardly, lying, abject, hideous crime!

For the first time within eight years, the unhappy man had just tasted the bitter flavour of a wicked thought and a wicked action.

He spit it out with disgust.

He continued to interrogate himself. He sternly asked himself what he had understood by this: "My object is attained." He declared that his life, in truth, did have an object. But what object? to conceal his name? to deceive the police? was it for so petty a thing that he had done all that he had done?

---

*Hugo compares Jean Valjean to Christ in the Garden of Gethsemane, ordered by God to accept the chalice of fear, pain, and death that is the Crucifixion.

had he no other object, which was the great one, which was the true one? To save, not his body, but his soul. To become honest and good again. To be an upright man! was it not that, above all, that alone, which he had always wished, and which the bishop had enjoined upon him! To close the door on his past? But he was not closing it, great God! he was reopening it by committing an infamous act! for he became a robber again, and the most odious of robbers! he robbed another of his existence, his life, his peace, his place in the sun, he became an assassin! he murdered, he murdered in a moral sense a wretched man, he inflicted upon him that frightful life in death, that living burial, which is called the galleys! on the contrary, to deliver himself up, to save this man stricken by so ghastly a mistake, to reassume his name, to become again from duty the convict Jean Valjean; that was really to achieve his resurrection, and to close for ever the hell from whence he had emerged! to fall back into it in appearance, was to emerge in reality! he must do that! all he had done was nothing, if he did not do that! all his life was useless, all his suffering was lost. He had only to ask the question: "What is the use?" He felt that the bishop was there, that the bishop was present all the more that he was dead, that the bishop was looking fixedly at him, that henceforth Mayor Madeleine with all his virtues would be abominable to him, and the galley slave, Jean Valjean, would be admirable and pure in his sight. That men saw his mask, but the bishop saw his face. That men saw his life, but the bishop saw his conscience. He must then go to Arras, deliver the wrong Jean Valjean, denounce the right one. Alas! that was the greatest of sacrifices, the most poignant of victories, the final step to be taken, but he must do it. Mournful destiny! he could only enter into sanctity in the eyes of God, by returning into infamy in the eyes of men!

"Well," said he, "let us take this course! let us do our duty! Let us save this man!"

He pronounced these words in a loud voice, without perceiving that he was speaking aloud.

He took his books, verified them, and put them in order. He threw into the fire a package of notes which he held against needy small traders. He wrote a letter, which he sealed, and upon the envelope of which might have been read, if there had been any one in the room at the time: *Monsieur Laffitte, banker, Rue d'Artois, Paris.*

He drew from a writing-desk a pocket-book containing some banknotes and the passport that he had used that same year in going to the elections.

Had any one seen him while he was doing these various acts with such serious meditation, he would not have suspected what was passing within him. Still at intervals his lips quivered; at other times he raised his head and fixed his eye on some point of the wall, as if he saw just there something that he wished to clear up or to examine.

The letter to Monsieur Laffitte finished, he put it in his pocket as well as the pocket-book, and began to pace back and forth again.

The current of his thought had not changed. He still saw his duty clearly written in luminous letters which flared out before his eyes, and moved with his gaze: *"Go! avow thy name! denounce thyself!"*

He saw also, and as if they were laid bare before him with sensible forms, the two ideas which had been hitherto the double rule of his life, to conceal his name, and to sanctify his soul. For the first time, they appeared to him absolutely distinct, and he saw the difference which separated them. He recognised that one of these ideas was necessarily good, while the other might become evil; that the former was devotion, and that the latter was selfishness; that the one said: *"the neighbour,"* and that the other said: *"me;"* that the one came from the light, and the other from the night.

They were fighting with each other. He saw them fighting. While he was looking, they had expanded before his mind's eye; they were now colossal; and it seemed to him that he saw struggling within him, in that infinite of which we spoke just now, in the midst of darkness and gloom, a goddess and a giantess.

He was full of dismay, but it seemed to him that the good thought was gaining the victory.

He felt that he had reached the second decisive movement of his conscience, and his destiny; that the bishop had marked the first phase of his new life, and that this Champmathieu marked the second. After a great crisis, a great trial.

At another moment the idea occurred to him that, if he should denounce himself, perhaps the heroism of his action, and his honest life for the past seven years, and what he had done for the country, would be considered, and he would be pardoned.

But this supposition quickly vanished, and he smiled bitterly at the thought, that the robbery of the forty sous from Petit Gervais made him a second offender, that that matter would certainly reappear, and by the precise terms of the law he would be condemned to hard labour for life.

He turned away from all illusion, disengaged himself more and more from the earth, and sought consolation and strength elsewhere. He said to himself that he must do his duty; that perhaps even he should not be more unhappy after having done his duty than after having evaded it; that if he *let matters alone,* if he remained at M—— sur M——, his reputation, his good name, his good works, the deference, the veneration he commanded, his charity, his riches, his popularity, his virtue, would be tainted with a crime, and what pleasure would there be in all these holy things tied to that hideous thing? while, if he carried out the sacrifice, in the galleys, with his chain, with his iron collar, with his green cap, with his perpetual labour, with his pitiless shame, there would be associated a celestial idea.

Finally, he said to himself that it was a necessity, that his destiny was so fixed, that it was not for him to disturb the arrangements of God, that at all events he must choose, either virtue without, and abomination within, or sanctity within, and infamy without.

In revolving so many gloomy ideas, his courage did not fail, but his brain was fatigued. He began in spite of himself to think of other things, of indifferent things.

His blood rushed violently to his temples. He walked back and forth constantly. Midnight was struck first from the parish church, then from the

city hall. He counted the twelve strokes of the two clocks, and he compared the sound of the two bells. It reminded him that, a few days before,
he had seen at a junkshop an old bell for sale, upon which was this name:
Antoine Albin de Romainville.

He was cold. He kindled a fire. He did not think to close the window.

Meanwhile he had fallen into his stupor again. It required not a little
effort to recall his mind to what he was thinking of before the clock struck.
He succeeded at last.

"Ah! yes," said he, "I had formed the resolution to denounce myself."

And then all at once he thought of Fantine.

"Stop!" said he, "this poor woman!"

Here was a new crisis.

Fantine, abruptly appearing in his reverie, was like a ray of unexpected
light. It seemed to him that everything around him was changing its
aspect; he exclaimed:

"Ah! yes, indeed! so far I have only thought of myself! I have only looked
to my own convenience! It is whether I shall keep silent or denounce
myself, conceal my body or save my soul, be a despicable and respected
magistrate, or an infamous and venerable galley slave: it is myself, always
myself, only myself. But, good God! all this is egotism. Different forms of
egotism, but still egotism! Suppose I should think a little of others? The
highest duty is to think of others. Let us see, let us examine! I gone, I taken
away, I forgotten; what will become of all this? I denounce myself? I am
arrested, this Champmathieu is released, I am sent back to the galleys,
very well, and what then? what takes place here? Ah! here, there is a country, city, factories, a business, labourers, men, women, old grandfathers,
children, poor people! I have created all this, I keep it all alive; wherever a
chimney is smoking, I have put the coals on the fire and the meat in the
pot; I have produced well-being, economic activity, credit; before me there
was nothing; I have aroused, vivified, animated, quickened, stimulated,
enriched, all the country; without me, the soul is gone. I take myself away;
it all dies. And this woman who has suffered so much, who is so worthy in
her fall, all whose misfortunes I have unconsciously caused! And that child
which I was going for, which I have promised to the mother! Do I not also
owe something to this woman, in reparation for the wrong that I have
done her? If I should disappear, what happens? The mother dies. The child
becomes what she may. This is what comes to pass if I denounce myself;
and if I do not denounce myself? Let us see, if I do not denounce myself?"

After putting this question, he stopped; for a moment he hesitated and
trembled; but that moment was brief, and he answered with calmness:

"Well, this man goes to the galleys, it is true, but, what of that? He has
stolen! It is useless for me to say he has not stolen, he has stolen! As for
me, I remain here, I go on. In ten years I shall have made ten millions;
I scatter it over the country, I keep nothing for myself; what is it to me?
What I am doing is not for myself. The prosperity of all goes on increasing,
industry is quickened and excited, manufactories and workshops are
multipled, families, a hundred families, a thousand families, are happy; the

country becomes populous; villages spring up where there were only farms, farms spring up where there was nothing; poverty disappears, and with poverty disappear debauchery, prostitution, theft, murder, all vices, all crimes! And this poor mother brings up her child! and the whole country is rich and honest! Ah, yes! How foolish how absurd I was! What was I speaking of in denouncing myself? This demands reflection, surely, and nothing must be precipitate. What! because it would have pleased me to do the grand and the generous! That is melodramatic after all! Because I only thought of myself of myself alone, what! to save from a punishment perhaps a little too severe, but in reality just, nobody knows who, a thief, a scoundrel at any rate. Must an entire region be let go to ruin! must a poor hapless woman perish in the hospital! must a poor little girl perish on the street! like dogs! Ah! that would be abominable! And the mother not even see her child again! and the child hardly have known her mother! And all for this old rascal of an apple-thief who, beyond all doubt, deserves the galleys for something else, if not for this. Fine scruples these, which save an old vagabond who has, after all, only a few years to live, and who will hardly be more unhappy in the galleys than in his hovel, and which sacrifice a whole population, mothers, wives, children! This poor little Cosette who has no one but me in the world, and who is doubtless at this moment all blue with cold in the hut of these Thénardiers! They too are miserable scoundrels! And I should fail in my duty towards all these poor beings! And I should go away and denounce myself! And I should commit this silly blunder! Consider the worst possible case. Suppose there were a misdeed for me in this, and that my conscience should someday reproach me; the acceptance for the good of others of these reproaches which weigh only upon me, of this misdeed which affects only my own soul, why, that is devotion, that is virtue."

He arose and resumed his walk. This time it seemed to him that he was satisfied.

Suddenly his eyes fell upon the two silver candlesticks on the mantel, which were glistening dimly in the reflection.

"Stop!" thought he, "all Jean Valjean is contained in them too. They also must be destroyed."

He took the two candlesticks.

There was fire enough to melt them quickly into an unrecognisable ingot.

He bent over the fire and warmed himself a moment. It felt really comfortable to him. "The pleasant warmth!" said he.

He stirred the embers with one of the candlesticks.

A minute more, and they would have been in the fire.

At that moment, it seemed to him that he heard a voice crying within him: "Jean Valjean!" "Jean Valjean!"

His hair stood on end; he was like a man who hears some terrible thing.

"Yes! that is it, finish!" said the voice, "complete what you are doing! destroy these candlesticks! annihilate this memorial! forget the bishop! forget all! ruin this Champmathieu, yes! very well. Applaud yourself! So it is arranged, it is determined, it is done. Behold a man, a greybeard who knows not what he is accused of, who has done nothing, it may be, an innocent man, whose misfortune is caused by your name, upon whom your name weighs like a crime who will be taken instead of you; will be condemned, will end his days in abjection and in horror! very well. Be an honoured man yourself. Remain, Monsieur Mayor, remain honourable and honoured, enrich the city, feed the poor, bring up the orphans, live happy, virtuous, and admired, and all this time while you are here in joy and in the light, there shall be a man wearing your red smock, bearing your name in ignominy, and dragging your chain in the galleys! Yes! this is a fine arrangement! Oh, wretch!"

The sweat rolled off his forehead. He looked upon the candlesticks with haggard eyes. Meanwhile the voice which spoke within him had not ended. It continued:

"Jean Valjean! there shall be about you many voices which will make great noise, which will speak very loud, and which will bless you; and one only which nobody shall hear, and which will curse you in the darkness. Well, listen, vile sinner! all these blessings shall fall before they reach Heaven; only the curse shall mount into the presence of God!"

This voice, at first quite feeble, and which was raised from the most obscure depths of his conscience, had become by degrees loud and formidable, and he heard it now at his ear. It seemed to him that it had emerged from himself, and that it was speaking now from without. He thought he heard the last words so distinctly that he looked about the room with a kind of terror.

"Is there anybody here?" asked he, aloud and in a startled voice.

Then he continued with a laugh, which was like the laugh of an idiot:

"What a fool I am! there cannot be anybody here."

There was One; but He who was there was not of such as the human eye can see.

He put the candlesticks on the mantel.

Alas! all his irresolutions were again upon him. He was no further advanced than when he began.

So struggled beneath its anguish this unhappy soul. Eighteen hundred years before this unfortunate man, the mysterious being, in whom are aggregated all the sanctities and all the sufferings of humanity, He also, while the olive trees were shivering in the fierce breath of the Infinite, had long put away from his hand the fearful chalice that appeared before him, dripping with shadow and running over with darkness, in the star-filled depths.

3 (4)

FORMS ASSUMED BY SUFFERING DURING SLEEP[9]

THE CLOCK struck three. For five hours he had been walking thus, almost without interruption, when he dropped into his chair.

Exhausted by emotional suffering, Jean Valjean falls asleep and has a nightmare, which he later writes down. He is walking with his long-lost brother in a barren field. They come to an abandoned city filled with motionless, silent men. Without knowing why, he thinks it is "Romainville" (probably through association with the vanished empire of Napoleon, which aped the Roman Empire, and his own industrial empire which conscience forces him to abandon). He realizes he is dead.

He awoke. He was chilly. A wind as cold as the morning wind made the sashes of the still-open window swing on their hinges. The fire had gone out. The candle was low in the holder. The night was yet dark.

He arose and went to the window. There were still no stars in the sky.

From his window he could look into the court-yard and into the street. A harsh, rattling noise that suddenly resounded from the ground made him look down.

He saw below him two red stars, whose rays danced back and forth grotesquely in the shadow.

His mind was still half buried in the mist of his reverie: "Yes!" thought he, "there are none in the sky. They are on the earth now."

This confusion, however, faded away; a second noise like the first awakened him completely; he looked, and he saw that these two stars were the lamps of a carriage. By the light which they emitted, he could distinguish the form of a carriage. It was a tilbury drawn by a small white horse. The noise which he had heard was the sound of the horse's hoofs upon the pavement.

"What carriage is that?" said he to himself. "Who is it that comes so early?"

At that moment there was a low rap at the door of his room.

He shuddered from head to foot and cried in a terrible voice:

"Who is there?"

Some one answered:

"I, Monsieur Mayor."

He recognised the voice of the old woman, his portress.

"Well," said he, "what is it?"

"Monsieur Mayor, it is just five o'clock."

"What is that to me?"

"Monsieur Mayor, it is the chaise."

"What chaise?"

"The tilbury."

"What tilbury?"

"Did not Monsieur the Mayor order a tilbury?"

"No," said he.

"The driver says that he has come for Monsieur the Mayor."

"What driver?"

"Monsieur Scaufflaire's driver."

"Monsieur Scaufflaire?"

That name startled him as if a flash had passed before his face.

"Oh yes!" he said, "Monsieur Scaufflaire!"

Could the old woman have seen him at that moment she would have been frightened.

There was a long silence. He examined the flame of the candle with a dazed air, and took some of the melted wax from around the wick and rolled it in his fingers. The old woman was waiting. She ventured, however, to speak again:

"Monsieur Mayor, what shall I say?"

"Say that it is fine, and I am coming down."

4 (5)

OBSTACLES[10]

THE POSTAL SERVICE from Arras to M—— sur M—— was still performed at this time by the little mail waggons dating from the empire. These mail waggons were two-wheeled cabriolets lined with buckskin, hung upon jointed springs, and having but two seats, one for the driver, the other for the traveller. The wheels were armed with those long threatening hubs which keep other vehicles at a distance, and which are still seen upon the roads of Germany. The letters were carried in a huge oblong box placed behind the cabriolet and forming a part of it. This box was painted black and the cabriolet yellow.

These vehicles, which nothing resembles today, were indescribably misshapen and clumsy, and when they were seen from a distance crawling along some road in the horizon, they were like those insects called, I think, termites, which with a slender body draw a great train behind. They went, however, very fast. The mail that left Arras every night at one o'clock, after the passing of the dispatches from Paris, arrived at M—— sur M—— a little before five in the morning.

That night the mail that came down into M—— sur M—— by the road from Hesdin, at the turn of a street just as it was entering the city, clipped a little tilbury drawn by a white horse, which was going in the opposite direction, and in which there was only one person, a man wrapped in a cloak. The wheel of the tilbury received a very severe blow. The courier cried out to the man to stop, but the traveller did not listen and kept on his way at a rapid trot.

"There is a man in a devilish hurry!" said the courier.

The man who was in such a hurry was he whom we have seen struggling in such pitiable convulsions.

Where was he going? He could not have said. Why was he in haste? He did not know. He went forward as if randomly. Whither? To Arras, doubtless; but perhaps he was going elsewhere also. At moments he felt this, and he shuddered. He plunged into that darkness as into a yawning gulf. Something pushed him, something drew him on. What was happening within him, no one could describe, but all will understand. What man has not entered, at least once in his life, into this dark cavern of the unknown?

But he had resolved upon nothing, decided nothing, determined nothing, done nothing. None of the acts of his conscience had been final. He was more than ever as if at the first moment.

Why was he going to Arras?

He repeated what he had already said to himself when he engaged the cabriolet of Scaufflaire, that, whatever might be the result, there could be no objection to seeing with his own eyes, and judging of the circumstances for himself; that it was even prudent, that he ought to know what took place; that he could decide nothing without having observed and scrutinised; that in the distance every little thing seems a mountain; that after all, when he should have seen this Champmathieu, some wretch probably, his conscience would be very much reconciled to letting him go to the galleys in his place; that it was true that Javert would be there, and Brevet, Chenildieu, Cochepaille, former convicts who had known him; but surely they would not recognise him; bah! what an idea! that Javert was a hundred miles off the track; that all conjectures and all suppositions were fixed upon this Champmathieu, and that nothing is so stubborn as suppositions and conjectures; that there was, therefore, no danger.

That it was no doubt a dark hour, but that he should get through it; that after all he held his destiny, evil as it might be, in his own hand; that he was master of it. He clung to that thought.

In reality, to tell the truth, he would have preferred not to go to Arras.

Still he was on the way.

Although absorbed in thought, he whipped up his horse, which trotted away at that regular and sure full trot that gets over seven miles an hour.

Progressively as the tilbury went forward, he felt something within him which shrank back.

At daybreak he was in the open country, the city of M—— sur M——
was a long way behind. He saw the horizon growing lighter; he beheld,
without seeing them, all the frozen figures of a winter dawn pass before his
eyes. Morning as well as evening has its spectres. He did not see them, but,
unawares, and by a kind of insight which was almost physical, those black
outlines of trees and hills added to the tumultuous state of his soul an
indescribable gloom and apprehension.

Every time he passed one of the isolated houses that stood here and
there by the side of the road, he said to himself: "But yet, there are people
there who are sleeping!"

The trotting of the horse, the rattling of the harness, the wheels upon
the pavement, made a gentle, monotonous sound. These things are charming when one is joyful, and mournful when one is sad.

It was broad day when he arrived at Hesdin. He stopped before an inn
to let his horse breathe and to have some oats given him.

This horse was, as Scaufflaire had said, of that small breed of the Boulon-
nais which has too much head, too much belly, and not enough neck, but
which has an open chest, a large rump, fine and slender legs, and a firm foot,
a homely race, but strong and sound. The excellent animal had made twelve
miles in two hours, without breaking a sweat.

He did not get out of the tilbury. The stable-boy who brought the oats
stooped down suddenly and examined the left wheel.

"Have you gone far so?" said the man.

He answered, almost without breaking up his train of thought:

"Why?"

"Have you come far?" said the boy.

"Twelve miles from here."

"Ah!"

"Why do you say: ah?"

The boy stooped down again, was silent a moment, with his eye fixed
on the wheel, then he rose up saying:

"To think that this wheel has just come twelve miles, that is possible,
but it is very sure that it won't go a half mile now."

He sprang down from the tilbury.

"What are you saying, my friend?"

"I say that it is a miracle that you have come twelve miles without tum-
bling, you and your horse, into some ditch on the way. Look for yourself."

The wheel in fact was badly damaged. The collision with the mail waggon
had broken two spokes and loosened the hub so that the nut no longer held.

"My friend," said he to the stable-boy, "is there a wheelwright here?"

"Certainly, monsieur."

"Do me the favour to go for him."

"There he is, close by. Hallo, Master Bourgaillard!"

Master Bourgaillard the wheelwright was on his own door-step. He
came and examined the wheel, and made such a grimace as a surgeon
makes at the sight of a broken leg.

"Can you mend that wheel on the spot?"

"Yes, monsieur."

"When can I start again?"

"To-morrow."

"To-morrow!"

"It is a good day's work. Is monsieur in a great hurry?"

"A very great hurry. I must leave in an hour at the latest."

"Impossible, monsieur."

"I will pay whatever you like."

"Impossible."

"Well! in two hours."

"Impossible to-day. There are two spokes and a hub to be repaired. Monsieur cannot start again before to-morrow."

He felt an immense joy.

It was evident that Providence was involved. It was Providence that had broken the wheel of the tilbury and stopped him on his way. He had not yielded to this sort of first summons; he had made all possible efforts to continue his journey; he had faithfully and scrupulously exhausted every means, he had shrunk neither before the season, nor from fatigue, nor from expense; he had nothing for which to reproach himself. If he went no further, it no longer concerned him. It was now not his fault; it was, not the act of his conscience, but the act of Providence.[*]

He breathed. He breathed freely and with a full chest for the first time since Javert's visit. It seemed to him that the iron hand which had gripped his heart for twenty hours was relaxed.

It appeared to him that now God was for him, was manifestly for him.

He said to himself that he had done all that he could, and that now he had only to retrace his steps, tranquilly.

If his conversation with the wheelwright had taken place in a room of the inn, it would have had no witnesses, nobody would have heard it, the matter would have rested there, and it is probable that we should not have had to relate any of the events which follow, but that conversation occurred in the street. Every colloquy in the street inevitably gathers a circle. There are always people who ask nothing better than to be spectators. While he was questioning the wheelwright, some of the passers-by had stopped around them. After listening for a few minutes, a young boy whom no one had noticed, had separated from the group and ran away.

At the instant the traveller, after the internal deliberation which we have just indicated, was making up his mind to go back, this boy returned. He was accompanied by an old woman.

"Monsieur," said the woman, "my boy tells me that you are anxious to hire a cabriolet."

---

*This paragraph, in free indirect discourse, faithfully renders Jean Valjean's point of view. The tone is at once sincere, because his rationalizations fully convince him for the moment, and ironic, because the reader can see through them so easily.

This simple speech, uttered by an old woman who was brought there by a boy, made the sweat pour down his back. He thought he saw the hand he was but now freed from reappear in the shadow behind him, all ready to seize him again.

He paid what was asked, left the tilbury to be mended at the blacksmith's against his return, had the white horse harnessed to the carriole, got in, and resumed the route he had followed since morning.

The moment the carriole started, he acknowledged that he had felt an instant before a certain joy at the thought that he should not go where he was going. He examined that joy with a sort of anger, and thought it absurd. Why should he feel joy at going back? After all, he was making a journey of his own accord, nobody forced him to it.

And certainly, nothing could happen which he did not choose to have happen.

He whipped up the horse and started away at a quick trot.

He had lost a good deal of time at Hesdin, he wished to make it up. The little horse was plucky, and pulled enough for two; but it was February, it had rained, the roads were bad. And then, it was no longer the tilbury. The carriole ran hard, and was very heavy. And besides there were many steep hills.

Twilight was falling just as the children coming out of school beheld our traveller entering Tinques. It is true that the days were still short. He did not stop at Tinques. As he was driving out of the village, a worker who was repairing the road, raised his head and said:

"Your horse is very tired."

The poor beast, in fact, was not going faster than a walk.

"Are you going to Arras?" added the countryman.

"Yes."

"If you go at this rate, you won't get there very early."

He stopped his horse and asked the countryman:

"How far is it from here to Arras?"

"Near seventeen miles."

"How is that? the post route only counts thirteen."

"Ah!" replied the workman, "then you don't know that the road is being repaired. You will find it cut off a quarter of an hour from here. There's no means of going further."

"Really!"

"You will take the left, the road that leads to Carency, and cross the river; when you are at Camblin, you will turn to the right; that is the road from Mont Saint-Eloy to Arras."

"But it is night, I shall lose my way."

"You are not from these parts?"

"No."

"Besides, they are all cross-roads."

"Stop, monsieur," the worker continued, "do you want some advice? Your horse is tired; go back to Tinques. There is a good inn there. Sleep there. You can go on to Arras to-morrow."

"I must be there to-night—this evening!"

"That is another matter. Then go back all the same to that inn, and hire an extra horse. The boy who will go with the horse will guide you through the cross-roads."

He followed the road worker's advice, retraced his steps, and a half hour afterwards he again passed the same place, but at a full trot, with a good extra horse. A stable-boy, who called himself a postillion, was sitting upon the shaft of the carriole.

He felt, however, that he was losing time. It was now quite dark.

They took the side road. The road became frightful. The carriole tumbled from one rut to the other. He said to the postillion:

"Keep up a trot, and double drink-money."

In one of the jolts the whiffle-tree broke.*

"Monsieur," said the postillion, "the whiffle-tree is broken; I do not know how to harness my horse now, this road is very bad at night, if you will come back and stop at Tinques, we can be at Arras early to-morrow morning."

He answered: "Have you a piece of string and a knife?"

"Yes, monsieur."

He cut off the limb of a tree and made a whiffle-tree of it.

This was another loss of twenty minutes; but they started off at a gallop.

The plain was dark. A low fog, thick and black, was creeping over the hill-tops and floating away like smoke. There were glimmering flashes from the clouds. A strong wind, which came from the sea, made a sound all around the horizon like the moving of furniture. Everything that he caught a glimpse of had an attitude of terror. How all things shudder under the terrible breath of night!

The cold penetrated him. He had not eaten since the evening before. He recalled vaguely to mind his other night adventure in the great plain near D——, eight years before; and it seemed yesterday to him.

---

*A whiffle-tree or single-tree is a pivoted horizontal crossbar attached to the harness traces of a draft animal and to the vehicle it pulls.

5 (6)

SISTER SIMPLICE PUT TO THE TEST

MEANWHILE, at that very moment, Fantine was in ecstasies.

She had passed a very bad night. Cough frightful, fever redoubled; she had bad dreams. In the morning, when the doctor came, she was delirious. He appeared to be alarmed, and asked to be informed as soon as Monsieur Madeleine came.

All the morning she was low-spirited, spoke little and was making folds in the sheets, murmuring in a low voice over some calculations which appeared to be calculations of distances. Her eyes were hollow and fixed. The light seemed almost gone out, but then, at moments, they would be lighted up and sparkle like stars. It seems as though at the approach of a certain dark hour, the light of heaven fills those who are leaving the light of earth.

Whenever Sister Simplice asked her how she was, she answered invariably: "Well. I would like to see Monsieur Madeleine."

A few months earlier, when Fantine had lost the last of her modesty, her last shame and her last happiness, she was the shadow of herself; now she was the spectre of herself. Physical suffering had completed the work of moral suffering. This creature of twenty-five years had a wrinkled forehead, flabby cheeks, pinched nostrils, shrivelled gums, a leaden complexion, a bony neck, protruding collar-bones, skinny limbs, an earthy skin, and her fair hair was mixed with grey. Alas! how well sickness improvises old age.

At noon the doctor came again, left a few prescriptions, inquired whether the mayor had been at the infirmary, and shook his head.

Monsieur Madeleine usually came at three o'clock to see the sick woman. As promptness was kindness, he was prompt.

About half-past two, Fantine began to be agitated. In the space of twenty minutes, she asked the nun more than ten times: "My sister, what time is it?"

The clock struck three. At the third stroke, Fantine rose up in bed—ordinarily she could hardly turn herself—she joined her two shrunken and yellow hands in a sort of convulsive clasp, and the nun heard from her one of those deep sighs which seem to raise a great weight. Then Fantine turned and looked towards the door.

Nobody came in; the door did not open.

She sat so for a quarter of an hour, her eyes fixed upon the door, motionless, and as if holding her breath. The sister dared not speak. The church clock struck the quarter. Fantine fell back upon her pillow.

She said nothing, and again began to make folds in the sheet.

A half-hour passed, then an hour, but no one came; every time the clock struck, Fantine rose and looked towards the door, then she fell back.

Her thought could be clearly seen, but she pronounced no name, she did not complain, she found no fault. She only coughed mournfully. One would have said that something dark was settling down upon her. She was livid, and her lips were blue. She smiled at times.

The clock struck five. Then the sister heard her speak very low and gently: "But since I am going away to-morrow, he does wrong not to come to-day!"

Sister Simplice herself was surprised at Monsieur Madeleine's delay.

The clock struck six. Fantine did not appear to hear. She seemed no longer to pay attention to anything around her.

Sister Simplice sent a girl to inquire of the portress of the factory if the mayor had come in, and if he would not very soon come to the infirmary. The girl returned in a few minutes.

Fantine was still motionless, and appeared to be absorbed in her own thoughts.

The servant related in a whisper to Sister Simplice that the mayor had gone away that morning before six o'clock in a little tilbury drawn by a white horse, cold as the weather was; that he went alone, without even a driver, that no one knew the road he had taken, that some said he had been seen to turn off by the road to Arras, that others were sure they had met him on the road to Paris. That when he went away he seemed, as usual, very kind, and that he simply said to the portress that he need not be expected that night.

While the two women were whispering, with their backs turned towards Fantine's bed, the sister questioning, the servant conjecturing, Fantine, with that feverish vivacity of certain organic diseases, which unites the free movement of health with the frightful exhaustion of death, had risen to her knees on the bed, her shrivelled hands resting on the bolster, and with her head passing through the opening of the curtains, she listened. All at once she exclaimed:

"You are talking there of Monsieur Madeleine! why do you talk so low? what has he done? why does he not come?"

Her voice was so harsh and rough that the two women thought they heard the voice of a man; they turned towards her affrighted.

"Why don't you answer?" cried Fantine.

The servant stammered out:

"The portress told me that he could not come to-day."

"My child," said the sister, "be calm, lie down again."

Fantine, without changing her attitude, resumed with a loud voice, and in a tone at once piercing and imperious:

"He cannot come. Why not? You know the reason. You were whispering it there between you. I want to know."

The servant whispered quickly in the nun's ear: "Answer that he is busy with the City Council."

Sister Simplice reddened slightly; it was a lie that the servant had proposed to her. On the other hand, it did seem to her that to tell the truth to the sick woman would doubtless be a terrible blow, and that it was dangerous in the state in which Fantine was. This blush did not last long. The sister turned her calm, sad eye upon Fantine, and said:

"The mayor has gone away."

Fantine sprang up and sat upon her feet. Her eyes sparkled. A marvellous joy spread over that mournful face.

"Gone away!" she exclaimed. "He has gone for Cosette!"

Then she stretched her hands towards heaven, and her whole countenance became ineffable. Her lips moved; she was praying in a whisper.

When her prayer was ended: "My sister," said she, "I am quite willing to lie down again, I will do whatever you wish; I was naughty just now, pardon me for having talked so loud; it is very bad to talk loud; I know it, my good sister, but see how happy I am. God is kind, Monsieur Madeleine is good; just think of it, that he has gone to Montfermeil for my little Cosette."

She lay down again, helped the nun to arrange the pillow, and kissed a little silver cross which she wore at her neck, and which Sister Simplice had given her.

"My child," said the sister, "try to rest now, and do not talk any more."

Fantine took the sister's hand between hers; they were moist; the sister was pained to feel it.

"He started this morning for Paris. Indeed he need not even go through Paris. Montfermeil is a little to the left in coming. You remember what he said yesterday, when I spoke to him about Cosette: *Very soon, very soon!* This is a surprise he has for me. You know he had me sign a letter to take her away from the Thénardiers. They will have nothing to say, will they? They will give up Cosette. Because they have their pay. The authorities would not let them keep a child when they are paid. My sister, do not make signs to me that I must not talk. I am very happy, I am doing very well. I have no pain at all, I am going to see Cosette again, I am hungry even. For almost five years I have not seen her. You do not, you cannot imagine what a hold children have upon you! And then she will be so handsome, you will see! If you knew, she has such pretty little rosy fingers! First, she will have very beautiful hands. At a year old she had ridiculous hands,—so! She must be large now. She is seven years old. She is a little lady. I call her Cosette, but her name is Euphrasie. Now, this morning I was looking at the dust on the mantel, and I had an idea that I should see Cosette again very soon! Oh, dear! how wrong it is to be years without seeing one's children! We ought to remember that life is not eternal! Oh! how good it is in the mayor to go—true, it is very cold! He had his cloak, at least! He will be here to-morrow, will he not? That will make to-morrow a fête. To-morrow morning, my sister, you will remind me to put on my little lace cap. Montfermeil is a country place. I made the trip on foot once. It was a long way for me. But the stagecoaches go very fast. He will be here to-morrow with Cosette! How far is it from here to Montfermeil?"

The sister, who had no idea of the distance, answered: "Oh! I feel sure that he will be here to-morrow."

"To-morrow! to-morrow!" said Fantine, "I shall see Cosette to-morrow! See, good Sister of God, I am well now. I am wild; I would dance, if anybody wanted me to."

One who had seen her a quarter of an hour before could not have understood this. Now she was all rosy; she talked in a lively, natural tone; her whole face was only a smile. At times she laughed while whispering to herself. A mother's joy is almost like a child's.

"Well," resumed the nun, "now you are happy, obey me—do not talk any more."

Fantine laid her head upon the pillow, and said in a low voice:

"Yes, lie down again; be prudent now that you are going to have your child. Sister Simplice is right. All here are right."

And then, without moving, or turning her head, she began to look all about with her eyes wide open and a joyous air, and she said nothing more.

The sister closed the curtains, hoping that she would sleep.

Between seven and eight o'clock the doctor came. Hearing no sound, he supposed that Fantine was asleep, went in softly, and approached the bed on tiptoe. He drew the curtains aside, and by the glimmer of the twilight he saw Fantine's large calm eyes looking at him.

She said to him: "Monsieur, you will let her lie by my side in a little bed, won't you?"

The doctor thought she was delirious. She added:

"Look, there is just room."

The doctor took Sister Simplice aside, who explained the matter to him, that Monsieur Madeleine was absent for a day or two, and that, not being certain, they had not thought it best to undeceive the sick woman, who believed the mayor had gone to Montfermeil; that it was possible, after all, that she had guessed aright. The doctor approved of this.

He returned to Fantine's bed again, and she continued:

"Then you see, in the morning, when she wakes, I can say good morning to the poor kitten; and at night, when I am awake, I can hear her sleep. Her little breathing is so sweet it will do me good."

"Give me your hand," said the doctor.

She reached out her hand, and exclaimed with a laugh:

"Oh, stop! Indeed, it is true you don't know! but I am cured. Cosette is coming to-morrow."

The doctor was surprised. She was better. Her languor was less. Her pulse was stronger. A sort of new life was all at once reanimating this poor exhausted being.

"Doctor," she continued, "has the sister told you that Monsieur the Mayor has gone for the little thing?"

The doctor recommended silence, and that she should avoid all painful emotion. He prescribed an infusion of pure quinine, and, in case the fever should return in the night, a soothing potion. As he was going away he said to the sister: "She is better. If by good fortune the mayor should really come back to-morrow with the child, who knows? there are such astonishing crises; we have seen great joy instantly cure diseases; I am well aware that this is an organic disease, and far advanced, but this is all such a mystery! We shall save her perhaps!"

6 (7)

THE TRAVELLER ARRIVES AND
PROVIDES FOR HIS RETURN

IT WAS NEARLY eight o'clock in the evening when the carriole which we left on the road drove into the yard of the Hotel de la Poste at Arras. The man whom we have followed thus far, got out, answered the hospitalities of the inn's people with an absent-minded air, sent back the extra horse, and took the little white one to the stable himself; then he opened the door of a billiard-room on the first floor, took a seat, and leaned his elbows on the table. He had spent fourteen hours in this trip, which he expected to make in six. He did himself the justice to feel that it was not his fault, but at bottom he was not sorry for it.

The landlady entered.

"Will monsieur have a bed? will monsieur have supper?"

He shook his head.

"The stable-boy says that monsieur's horse is very tired!"

Here he broke silence.

"Is not the horse able to start again to-morrow morning?"

"Oh; monsieur! he needs at least two days' rest."

He asked:

"Is not the Post Office here?"

"Yes, sir."

The hostess led him to the Post Office; he showed his passport and inquired if there were an opportunity to return that very night to M—— sur M—— by the mail coach; only one seat was vacant, that by the side of the driver; he retained it and paid for it. "Monsieur," said the booking clerk, "don't fail to be here ready to start at precisely one o'clock in the morning."

This done, he left the hotel and began to walk in the city.

He was not acquainted with Arras, the streets were dark, and he went haphazard. Nevertheless he seemed to refrain obstinately from asking his way. He crossed the little river Crinchon, and found himself in a labyrinth of narrow streets, where he was soon lost. A citizen came along with a lantern. After some hesitation, he determined to speak to this man, but not until he had looked before and behind, as if he were afraid that some-body might overhear the question he was about to ask.

"Monsieur," said he, "the court house, if you please?"

"You are not a resident of the city, monsieur," answered the citizen, who was an old man, "well, follow me, I am going right by the court house, that is to say, the city hall. For they are repairing the court house just now, and the courts are holding the sessions at the city hall, temporarily."

"Is it there," asked he, "that the court sessions are held?"

"Certainly, monsieur; you see, what is the city hall to-day was the bishop's palace before the revolution. Monsieur de Conzié, who was bishop in 'eighty-two, had a large hall built. The court is held in that hall."

As they walked along, the citizen said to him:

"If monsieur wishes to see a trial, he is rather late. Ordinarily the sessions close at six o'clock."

However, when they reached the great square, the citizen showed him four long lighted windows on the front of a vast dark building.

"Faith, monsieur, you are in time, you are fortunate. Do you see those four windows? that is the court. There is a light there. Then they have not finished. The case must have been prolonged and they are having an evening session. Are you interested in this case? Is it a criminal trial? Are you a witness?"

He answered:

"I have no business; I only wish to speak to a lawyer."

"That's another thing," said the citizen. "Stop, monsieur, here is the door. The doorkeeper is up there. You have only to go up the grand stairway."

He followed the citizen's instructions, and in a few minutes found himself in a hall where there were many people, and scattered groups of lawyers in their robes whispering here and there.

This hall, which, though spacious, was lighted by a single lamp, was an ancient hall of the Episcopal palace, and served as a waiting-room. A double folding door, which was now closed, separated it from the large room in which the court was in session.

The darkness was such that he felt no fear in addressing the first lawyer whom he met.

"Monsieur," said he, "how are they getting along?"

"It is finished," said the lawyer.

"Finished!"

The word was repeated in such a tone that the lawyer turned around.

"Pardon me, monsieur, you are a relative, perhaps?"

"No. I know no one here. And was there a sentence?"

"Of course. It was hardly possible for it to be otherwise."

"To hard labour?"

"For life."

He continued in a voice so weak that it could hardly be heard:

"The identity was established, then?"

"What identity?" responded the lawyer. "There was no identity to be established. It was a simple affair. This woman had killed her child, the infanticide was proven, the jury were not satisfied that there was any premeditation; she was sentenced for life."

"It is a woman, then?" said he.

"Certainly. The Limousin girl. What else are you speaking of?"

"Nothing, but if it is finished, why is the hall still lighted up?"

"That is for the other case, which commenced nearly two hours ago."

"What other case?"

"Oh! that is a clear one also. It is a sort of a thief, a second offender, a galley slave; a case of robbery. I forget his name. He looks like a bandit. Were it for nothing but having such a face, I would send him to the galleys."

"Monsieur," asked he, "is there any means of getting into the hall?"

"I think not, really. There is a great crowd. However, they are taking a recess. Some people have come out, and when the session is resumed, you can try."

"How do you get in?"

"Through that wide door."

The lawyer left him. In a few moments, he had undergone, almost at the same time, almost together, all possible emotions. The words of this indifferent man had alternately pierced his heart like icicles and like flames of fire. When he learned that it was not concluded, he drew breath; but he could not have told whether what he felt was satisfaction or pain.

He approached several groups and listened to their talk. The calendar of the term being very heavy, the judge had set down two short, simple cases for that day. They had begun with the infanticide, and now were on the convict, the recidivist, the "habitual offender." This man had stolen some apples, but that did not appear to be very well proven; what was proven, was that he had been in the galleys at Toulon. This was what ruined his case. The examination of the man had been finished, and the testimony of the witnesses had been taken; but there yet remained the argument of the counsel, and the summing up of his prosecuting attorney; it would hardly be finished before midnight. The man would probably be condemned; the prosecuting attorney was very good, and never *failed* with his prisoners; he was a fellow of talent, who wrote poetry.

An officer stood near the door which opened into the court-room. He asked this officer:

"Monsieur, will the door be opened soon?"

"It will not be opened," said the officer.

"How! it will not be opened when the session is resumed? is there not a recess?"

"The session has just been resumed," answered the officer, "but the door will not be opened again."

"Why not?"

"Because the hall is full."

"What! there are no more seats?"

"Not a single one. The door is closed. No one can enter."

The officer added, after a silence: "There are indeed two or three places still behind Monsieur the Judge, but Monsieur the Judge admits none but public officials to them."

So saying, the officer turned his back.

He retired with his head bowed down, crossed the ante-chamber, and walked slowly down the staircase, seeming to hesitate at every step. It is probable that he was holding counsel with himself. The violent combat that had been going on within him since the previous evening was not finished; and, every moment, he fell upon some new turn. When he reached the landing of the stairway, he leaned against the railing and folded his arms. Suddenly he opened his coat, drew out his pocket-book, took out a pencil, tore out a sheet, and wrote rapidly upon that sheet, by the glimmering light, this line: *Monsieur Madeleine, Mayor of M—— sur M——*, then he went up the stairs again rapidly, passed through the crowd, walked straight to the officer, handed him the paper, and said to him with authority: "Take that to Monsieur the Judge."

The officer took the paper, cast his eye upon it, and obeyed.

7 (8)

ADMISSION BY FAVOUR

THE JUDGE OF THE ROYAL COURT of Douai, who was providing over this session at Arras, was familiar, as well as everybody else, with this name so profoundly and so universally honoured. When the officer quietly opening the door which led from the counsel chamber to the court room, bent behind the judge's chair and handed him the paper, on which was written the line we have just read, adding: *"This gentleman desires to witness the trial,"* the judge made a hasty movement of deference, seized a pen, wrote a few words at the bottom of the paper and handed it back to the officer, saying to him: "Let him enter."

The unhappy man, whose story we are telling, had remained near the door of the hall, in the same place and the same posture as when the officer left him. He heard, through his thoughts, some one saying to him: "Will monsieur do me the honour to follow me?" It was the same officer who had turned his back upon him the minute before, and who now bowed to the earth before him. The officer at the same time handed him the paper. He unfolded it, and, as he happened to be near the lamp, he could read:

"The Judge of the Circuit Court presents his respects to Monsieur Madeleine."

He crushed the paper in his hands, as if those few words had left some strange and bitter taste behind.

He followed the officer.

In a few minutes he found himself alone in a kind of panelled cabinet, of a severe appearance, lighted by two wax candles placed upon a table covered with green cloth. The last words of the officer who had left him still rang in his ear: "Monsieur, you are now in the counsel chamber; you have but to turn the brass knob of that door and you will find yourself in the court-room, behind the judge's chair." These words were associated in his thoughts with a vague remembrance of the narrow corridors and dark stairways through which he had just passed.

The officer had left him alone. The decisive moment had arrived. He endeavoured to collect his thoughts, but did not succeed. At those hours especially when we have sorest need of grasping the poignant realities of life do the threads of thought snap off in the brain. He was in the very place where the judges deliberate and pass sentence. He beheld with a stupid tranquillity that silent and formidable room where so many existences had been terminated, where his own name would be heard so soon, and which his destiny was crossing at this moment. He looked at the walls, then he looked at himself, astonished that this could be this room, and that this could be he.

The handle of the door, round and of polished brass, shone out before him like an ominous star. He looked at it as a lamb might look at the eye of a tiger.

His eyes could not move from it.

From time to time, he took another step towards the door.

Had he listened, he would have heard, as a kind of confused murmur, the noise of the neighbouring hall; but he did not listen and he did not hear.

Suddenly, without himself knowing how, he found himself near the door, he seized the knob convulsively; the door opened.

He was in the court-room.

8 (9)

A PLACE FOR ARRIVING AT CONVICTIONS*

HE TOOK A STEP, closed the door behind him, mechanically, and remained standing, noting what he saw.

It was a large hall, dimly lighted, and noisy and silent by turns, where all the machinery of a criminal trial was exhibited, with its petty, yet solemn gravity, before the multitude.

At one end of the hall, that at which he found himself, heedless judges, in threadbare robes, were biting their finger-nails, or closing their eyelids; at the other end was a ragged rabble; there were lawyers in all sorts of

---

*"Convictions" is a pun: the prosecutors and judges want to prove guilt and impose sentence, a social damnation; Jean Valjean, in contrast, comes to realize that his soul's health depends on his accepting his material guilt.

attitudes; soldiers with honest and hard faces; old, stained wainscoting, a dirty ceiling, tables covered with serge, which was more nearly yellow than green; doors blackened by finger-marks; tavern lamps, giving more smoke than light, on nails in the panelling; candles, in brass candlesticks, on the tables; everywhere darkness, unsightliness, and gloom; and from all this there arose an austere and august impression; for men felt therein the presence of that great human thing which is called law, and that great divine thing which is called justice.

No man in this multitude paid any attention to him. All eyes converged on a single point, a wooden bench placed against a little door, along the wall at the left hand of the judge. Upon this bench, which was lighted by several candles, was a man between two gendarmes.

This was the man.

He did not look for him, he saw him. His eyes went towards him naturally, as if they had known in advance where he was.

He thought he saw himself, older, doubtless, not precisely the same in features, but alike in attitude and appearance, with that bristling hair, with those wild and restless eyeballs, with that smock—just as he was on the day he entered D——, full of hatred, and concealing in his soul that hideous hoard of frightful thoughts which he had spent nineteen years in gathering upon the floor of the galleys.

He said to himself, with a shudder: "Great God! shall I again come to this?"

This being appeared at least sixty years old. There was something indescribably rough, stupid, and terrified in his appearance.

At the sound of the door, people had stood aside to make room. The judge had turned his head, and supposing the person who entered to be the mayor of M—— sur M——, greeted him with a bow. The prosecuting attorney, who had seen Madeleine at M—— sur M——, whither he had been called more than once by the duties of his office, recognised him and bowed likewise. He scarcely perceived them. He gazed about him, a prey to a sort of hallucination.

Judges, clerk, gendarmes, a throng of heads, cruelly curious—he had seen all these once before, twenty-seven years ago. He had fallen again upon these fearful things; they were before him, they moved, they had being; it was no longer an effort of his memory, a mirage of his fancy, but real gendarmes and real judges, a real throng, and real men of flesh and bone. It was done; he saw reappearing and living again around him, with all the frightfulness of reality, the monstrous visions of the past.

All this was yawning before him.

Stricken with horror, he closed his eyes, and exclaimed from the depths of his soul: "Never!"

And by a tragic sport of destiny, which was agitating all his ideas and rendering him almost insane, it was another self before him. This man on trial was called by all around him, Jean Valjean!

He had before his eyes an unheard-of vision, a sort of representation of the most horrible moment of his life, played by his shadow.

All, everything was there—the same paraphernalia, the same hour of the night—almost the same faces, judge and assistant judges, soldiers and spectators. But above the head of the judge was a crucifix, a thing which did not appear in court-rooms at the time of his sentence. When he was tried, God was not there.[11]

A chair was behind him; he sank into it, terrified at the idea that he might be observed. When seated, he took advantage of a pile of papers on the judges' desk to hide his face from the whole room. He could now see without being seen. He entered fully into the spirit of the reality; by degrees he recovered his composure, and arrived at that degree of calmness at which it is possible to listen.

Monsieur Bamatabois was one of the jurors.

He looked for Javert, but did not see him. The witnesses' seat was hidden from him by the clerk's table. And then, as we have just said, the hall was very dimly lighted.

At the moment of his entrance, the counsel for the prisoner was finishing his plea. The attention of all was excited to the highest degree; the trial had been in progress for three hours. During these three hours, the spectators had seen a man, an unknown, wretched being, thoroughly stupid or thoroughly artful, gradually bending beneath the weight of a terrible probability. This man, as is already known, was a vagrant who had been found in a field, carrying off a branch, laden with ripe apples, which had been broken from a tree in a neighbouring close called the Pierron inclosure. Who was this man? An examination had been held, witnesses had been heard, they had been unanimous, light had been elicited from every portion of the trial. The prosecution said: "We have here not merely a fruit thief, a marauder; we have here, in our hands, a bandit, a recidivist who has violated his parole, a former convict, a most dangerous wretch, a malefactor, called Jean Valjean, of whom justice has been long in pursuit, and who, eight years ago, on leaving the galleys at Toulon, committed a highway robbery, with force and arms, upon the person of a youth of Savoy, Petit Gervais by name, a crime which is specified in Article 383 of the Penal Code, and for which we reserve the right of further prosecution when his identity shall be judicially established. He has now committed a new theft. It is a second offence. Convict him for the new crime; he will be tried hereafter for the previous one." Before this accusation, before the unanimity of the witnesses, the principal emotion evinced by the accused was astonishment. He made gestures and signs which signified denial, or he gazed at the ceiling. He spoke with difficulty, and answered with embarrassment, but from head to foot his whole person denied the charge. He seemed like an idiot in the presence of all these intellects ranged in battle around him, and like a stranger in the midst of this society by whom he had been seized. Nevertheless, a most threatening future awaited him; probabilities increased every moment; and every spectator was looking with more anxiety than himself for the calamitous sentence which seemed to be hanging over his head with ever increasing surety. One contingency even gave a glimpse of the possibility, beyond the galleys, of a capital penalty should

his identity be established, and the Petit Gervais affair result in his conviction. Who was this man? What was the nature of his apathy? Was it imbecility or artifice? Did he know too much or nothing at all? These were
questions upon which the spectators took sides, and which seemed to
affect the jury. There was something fearful and something mysterious in
the trial; the drama was not merely gloomy, but it was obscure.

The counsel for the defence had made a very good plea. The counsel
established that the theft of the apples was not in fact proved. His client,
whom in his character of counsel he persisted in calling Champmathieu,
had not been seen to scale the wall or break off the branch. He had been
arrested in possession of this branch (which the counsel preferred to call
bough); but he said that he had found it on the ground. Where was the
proof to the contrary? Undoubtedly this branch had been broken and carried off after the scaling of the wall, then thrown away by the alarmed
marauder; undoubtedly, there had been a thief.—But what evidence was
there that this thief was Champmathieu? One single thing. That he was
formerly a convict. The counsel would not deny that this fact unfortunately
appeared to be fully proved; the defendant had resided at Faverolles; the
defendant had been a pruner, the name of Champmathieu might well
have had its origin in that of Jean Mathieu; all this was true, and finally,
four witnesses had positively and without hesitation identified Champmathieu as the galley slave, Jean Valjean; to these circumstances and this
testimony the counsel could oppose nothing but the denial of his client, an
interested denial; but even supposing him to be the convict Jean Valjean,
did this prove that he had stolen the apples? that was a presumption at
most, not a proof. The accused, it was true, and the counsel "in good faith"
must admit it, had adopted "a mistaken system of defence." He had persisted in denying everything, both the theft and the fact that he had been a
convict. An avowal on the latter point would have been better certainly,
and would have secured to him the indulgence of the judges; the counsel
had advised him to this course, but the defendant had obstinately refused,
expecting probably to escape punishment entirely, by admitting nothing. It
was a mistake, but must not the poverty of his intellect be taken into consideration? The man was evidently an imbecile. Long suffering in the galleys, long suffering out of the galleys, had brutalised him, etc., etc.; if he
made a bad defence, was this a reason for convicting him? As to the Petit
Gervais affair, the counsel had nothing to say, it was not in the case. He
concluded by entreating the jury and court, if the identity of Jean Valjean
appeared evident to them, to apply to him the police penalties prescribed
for the breaking of parole, and not the fearful punishment decreed to the
convict found guilty of a second offence.

The prosecuting attorney replied to the counsel for the defence. He
was violent and flowery, like most prosecuting attorneys.

He complimented the counsel for his "frankness," of which he shrewdly
took advantage. He attacked the accused through all the concessions which
his counsel had made. The counsel seemed to admit that the accused was
Jean Valjean. He accepted the admission. This man then was Jean Valjean.

This fact was conceded to the prosecution, and could be no longer contested. Here, by an adroit autonomasia, going back to the sources and causes of crime, the prosecuting attorney thundered against the immorality of the romantic school—then in its dawn, under the name of the *Satanic school,* conferred upon it by the critics of the *Quotidienne* and the *Oriflamme;* and he attributed, not without plausibility, to the influence of this perverse literature, the crime of Champmathieu, or rather of Jean Valjean. These considerations exhausted, he passed to Jean Valjean himself. Who was Jean Valjean? Description of Jean Valjean: a monster vomited, etc. The model of all such descriptions may be found in the story of Théramène, which as tragedy is useless, but which does great service in judicial eloquence every day.* The auditory and the jury "shuddered." This description finished, the prosecuting attorney resumed with an oratorical burst, designed to excite the enthusiasm of the *Journal de la Préfecture* to the highest pitch next morning. "And it is such a man," etc., etc. A vagabond, a mendicant, without means of existence, etc., etc. Accustomed through his existence to criminal acts and profiting little by his past life in the galleys, as is proved by the crime committed upon Petit Gervais, etc., etc. It is such a man who, found on the highway in the very act of theft, a few paces from a wall that had been scaled, still holding in his hand the subject of his crime, denies the act in which he is caught, denies the theft, denies the escalade, denies everything, denies even his name, denies even his identity! Besides a hundred other proofs, to which we will not return, he is identified by four witnesses—Javert—the incorruptible inspector of police. Javert—and three of his former companions in disgrace, the convicts Brevet, Chenildieu, and Cochepaille. What has he to oppose to this overwhelming unanimity? His denial. What depravity! You will do justice, gentlemen of the jury, etc., etc. While the prosecuting attorney was speaking the accused listened opened-mouthed, with a sort of astonishment, not unmingled with admiration. He was evidently surprised that a man could speak so well. From time to time, at the most "forcible" parts of the argument, at those moments when eloquence, unable to contain itself, overflows in a stream of withering epithets, and surrounds the prisoner like a tempest, he slowly moved his head from right to left, and from left to right—a sort of sad, mute protest, with which he contented himself from the beginning of the argument. Two or three times the spectators nearest him heard him say in a low tone: "This all comes from not asking for Monsieur Baloup!" The prosecuting attorney pointed out to the jury this air of stupidity, which was evidently put on, and which denoted, not imbecility, but address, artifice, and the habit of deceiving justice, and which showed in its full light the "deep-rooted perversity" of the man. He concluded by reserving entirely the Petit Gervais affair, and demanding a sentence to the full extent of the law.

---

*By claiming that prosecutors' denunciations of criminals all are derived from Jean Racine's *récit de Théramène* (*Phèdre* V.7), Hugo condemns the poverty of their imagination.

This was, for this offence, as will be remembered, hard labour for life.

The counsel for the prisoner rose, commenced by complimenting "Monsieur, the prosecuting attorney, on his admirable argument," then replied as best he could, but in a weaker tone; the ground was evidently giving way under him.

9 (10)

THE ACCUSED

THE TIME had come for closing the case. The judge commanded the accused to rise, and put the usual question: "Have you anything to add to your defence?"

The man, standing, and twirling in his hands a hideous cap which he had, seemed not to hear.

The judge repeated the question.

This time the man heard, and appeared to comprehend. He started like one awaking from sleep, cast his eyes around him, looked at the spectators, the gendarmes, his counsel, the jurors, and the court, placed his huge fists on the bar before him, looked around again, and suddenly fixing his eyes upon the prosecuting attorney, began to speak. It was like an eruption. It seemed from the manner in which the words escaped his lips, incoherent, impetuous, jostling each other pell-mell, as if they were all eager to find vent at the same time. He said:

"I have this to say: That I have been a wheelwright at Paris; that it was at M. Baloup's too. It is a hard life to be a wheelwright, you always work out-doors, in yards, under sheds when you have good bosses, never in shops, because you must have room, you see. In the winter, it is so cold that you thresh your arms to warm them; but the bosses won't allow that; they say it is a waste of time. It is tough work to handle iron when there is ice on the pavements. It wears a man out quick. You get old when you are young at this trade. A man is used up by forty. I was fifty-three; I was sick a good deal. And then the workmen are so cruel! When a poor fellow isn't young, they always call you old bird, and old beast! I earned only thirty sous a day, they paid me as little as they could—the bosses took advantage of my age. Then I had my daughter, who was a washerwoman at the river. She earned a little for herself; between us two, we got on; she had hard work too. All day long up to the waist in a tub, in rain, in snow, with wind that cuts your face when it freezes, it is all the same, the washing must be done; there are folks who hav'n't much linen and are waiting for it; if you don't

wash you lose your customers. The planks are not well matched, and the
water falls on you everywhere. You get your clothes wet through and
through; the cold bites you to the bone. She washed too in the laundry of
the Enfants-Rouges, where the water comes in through pipes. There you
are not in the tub. You wash in front of you under the pipe, and rinse
behind you in the trough. This is under cover, and you are not so cold. But
there is a steam that is terrible and ruins your eyes. She would come home
at seven o'clock at night, and go to bed right away, she was so tired. Her
husband used to beat her. She is dead. We wasn't very happy. She was a
good girl; she never went to balls, and was very quiet. I remember one Shrove
Tuesday she went to bed at eight o'clock. Look here, I am telling the truth.
You have only to ask if 'tisn't so. Ask! how stupid I am! Paris is a gulf. Who
is there that knows Father Champmathieu? But there is M. Baloup. Go
and see M. Baloup. I don't know what more you want of me."

The man ceased speaking, but did not sit down. He had uttered these sentences in a loud, rapid, hoarse, harsh, and guttural tone, with a sort of angry
and savage simplicity. Once, he stopped to bow to somebody in the crowd.
The sort of affirmations which he seemed to fling out haphazard, came from
him like hiccoughs, and he added to each the gesture of a man chopping
wood. When he had finished, the auditory burst into laughter. He looked
at them, and seeing them laughing and not knowing why, began to laugh
himself.

That was an ill omen.

The judge, considerate and kindly man, raised his voice:

He reminded "gentlemen of the jury" that M. Baloup, the former master wheelwright by whom the prisoner said he had been employed, had
been summoned, but had not appeared. He had become bankrupt, and
could not be found. Then, turning to the accused, he adjured him to listen
to what he was about to say, and added: "You are in a position which
demands reflection. The gravest presumptions are weighing against you,
and may lead to fatal results. Prisoner, on your own behalf, I question you
a second time, explain yourself clearly on these two points. First, did you
or did you not climb the wall of the Pierron close, break off the branch and
steal the apples, that is to say, commit the crime of theft, with the addition
of breaking into an inclosure? Secondly, are you or are you not the discharged convict, Jean Valjean?"

The prisoner shook his head with a knowing look, like a man who
understands perfectly, and knows what he is going to say. He opened his
mouth, turned towards the presiding judge, and said:

"In the first place——"

Then he looked at his cap, looked up at the ceiling, and was silent.

"Prisoner," resumed the prosecuting attorney, in an austere tone, "give
attention. You have replied to nothing that has been asked you. Your agitation condemns you. It is evident that your name is not Champmathieu,
but that you are the convict, Jean Valjean, disguised under the name at
first, of Jean Mathieu, which was that of his mother; that you have lived in
Auvergne; that you were born at Faverolles, where you were a pruner. It is

evident that you have stolen ripe apples from the Pierron close, with the addition of breaking into the inclosure. The gentlemen of the jury will consider this."

The accused had at last resumed his seat; he rose abruptly when the prosecuting attorney had ended, and exclaimed:

"You are a very wicked man, you, I mean. This is what I wanted to say. I couldn't think of it first off. I never stole anything. I am a man who don't get something to eat every day. I was coming from Ailly, walking alone after a shower, which had made the ground all yellow with mud, so that the ponds were running over, and you only saw little sprigs of grass sticking out of the sand along the road, and I found a broken branch on the ground with apples on it; and I picked it up not knowing what trouble it would give me. It is three months that I have been in prison, being knocked about. More'n that, I can't tell. You talk against me and tell me 'answer!' The gendarme, who is a good fellow, nudges my elbow, and whispers, 'answer now.' I can't explain myself; I never studied; I am a poor man. You are all wrong not to see that I didn't steal. I picked up off the ground things that was there. You talk about Jean Valjean, Jean Mathieu—I don't know any such people. They must be villagers. I have worked for Monsieur Baloup, Boulevard de l'Hopital. My name is Champmathieu. You must be very sharp to tell me where I was born. I don't know myself. Everybody can't have houses to be born in; that would be too handy. I think my father and mother were migrant workers, but I don't know. When I was a child they called me Little One; now, they call me Old Man. They're my Christian names. Take them as you like. I have been in Auvergne, I have been at Faverolles. Bless me! can't a man have been in Auvergne and Faverolles without having been at the galleys? I tell you I never stole, and that I am Old Champmathieu. I have been at Monsieur Baloup's; I lived in his house. I am tired of your everlasting nonsense. What is everybody after me for like a mad dog?"

The prosecuting attorney was still standing; he addressed the judge:

"Sir, in the presence of the confused but very adroit denegations of the accused, who endeavours to pass for an idiot, but who will not succeed in it—we will prevent him—we request that it may please you and the court to call again within the bar the convicts, Brevet, Cochepaille, and Chenildieu, and the police-inspector Javert, and to submit them to a final interrogation, concerning the identity of the accused with the convict Jean Valjean."

"I must remind the prosecuting attorney," said the presiding judge, "that police-inspector Javert, recalled by his duties to the chief town of a neighbouring district, left the hall, and the city also as soon as his testimony was taken. We granted him this permission, with the consent of the prosecuting attorney and the counsel of the accused."

"True," replied the prosecuting attorney; "in the absence of Monsieur Javert, I think it a duty to recall to the gentlemen of the jury what he said here a few hours ago. Javert is an estimable man, who does honour to inferior but important functions, by his rigorous and strict probity. These are the terms in which he testified: 'I do not need even moral presumptions and material proofs to contradict the denials of the accused. I recognise him perfectly. This man's name is not Champmathieu; he is a convict, Jean Valjean, very hard, and much feared. He was liberated at the expiration of his term, but with extreme regret. He served out nineteen years at hard labour for burglary; five or six times he attempted to escape. Besides the Petit Gervais and Pierron robberies, I suspect him also of a robbery committed on his highness, the late Bishop of D——. I often saw him when I was adjutant of the galley guard at Toulon. I repeat it; I recognise him perfectly.' "*

This declaration, in terms so precise, appeared to produce a strong impression upon the public and jury. The prosecuting attorney concluded by insisting that, in the absence of Javert, the three witnesses, Brevet, Chenildieu, and Cochepaille, should be heard anew and solemnly interrogated.

The judge gave an order to an officer, and a moment afterwards the door of the witness-room opened, and the officer, accompanied by a gendarme ready to lend assistance, led in the convict Brevet. The audience was in breathless suspense, and all hearts palpitated as if they contained but a single soul.

The old convict Brevet was clad in the black and grey jacket of the central prisons. Brevet was about sixty years old; he had the face of a businessman, and the air of a rogue. They sometimes go together. He had become something like a turnkey in the prison—to which he had been brought by new misdeeds. He was one of those men of whom their superiors are wont to say, "He tries to make himself useful." The chaplain bore good testimony to his religious habits. It must not be forgotten that this happened under the Restoration.†

"Brevet," said the judge, "you have suffered infamous punishment, and cannot take an oath."

Brevet cast down his eyes.

"Nevertheless," continued the judge, "even in the man whom the law has degraded there may remain, if divine justice permit, a sentiment of honour and equity. To that sentiment I appeal in this decisive hour. If it still exist in you, as I hope, reflect before you answer me; consider on the one hand this man, whom a word from you may destroy; on the other hand, justice, which a word from you may enlighten. The moment is a solemn one, and there is still time to retract if you think yourself mistaken. Prisoner, rise. Brevet, look well upon the prisoner; collect your remembrances, and say, on your soul and conscience, whether you still recognise this man as your former comrade in the galleys, Jean Valjean."

---

*Honest Javert is unfair to Jean Valjean, who tried to escape four times, not "five or six." He is innocent of the Pierron robbery and was exonerated by the Bishop.
†The Restoration was so eager to reinstitute state-sponsored Catholicism, the moral basis of divine-right monarchy, that it accepted any manifestation of religious sentiment at face value.

Brevet looked at the prisoner, then turned again to the court.

"Yes, your honour, I was the first to recognise him, and still do so. This man is Jean Valjean, who came to Toulon in 1796, and left in 1815. I left a year after. He looks like a brute now, but he must have grown stupid with age; at the galleys he was sullen. I recognise him now, positively."

"Sit down," said the judge. "Prisoner, remain standing."

Chenildieu was brought in, a convict for life, as was shown by his red cloak and green cap. He was undergoing his punishment in the galleys of Toulon, whence he had been brought for this occasion. He was a little man, about fifty years old, active, wrinkled, lean, yellow, brazen, restless with a sort of sickly feebleness in his limbs and whole person, and great resolve in his eye. His companions in the galleys had nicknamed him Je-nie-Dieu.

The judge addressed nearly the same words to him as to Brevet. When he reminded him that his infamy had deprived him of the right to take an oath, Chenildieu raised his head and looked the spectators in the face. The judge requested him to collect his thoughts, and asked him as he had Brevet, whether he still recognised the prisoner.

Chenildieu burst out laughing.

"Gad! do I recognise him! we were five years on the same chain. You're sulky with me, are you, old boy?"

"Sit down," said the judge.

The officer brought in Cochepaille; this other convict for life, brought from the galleys and dressed in red like Chenildieu, was a peasant from Lourdes, and a semi-bear of the Pyrenees. He had tended flocks in the mountains, and from shepherd had glided into brigandage. Cochepaille was not less uncouth than the accused, and appeared still more stupid. He was one of those unfortunate men whom nature sketches as wild beasts, and society finishes up into galley slaves.

The judge attempted to move him by a few serious and pathetic words, and asked him, as he had the others, whether he still recognised without hesitation or difficulty the man standing before him.

"It is Jean Valjean," said Cochepaille. "The same they called Jean-the-Jack, he was so strong."

Each of the affirmations of these three men, evidently sincere and in good faith, had excited in the audience a murmur of evil augury for the accused—a murmur which increased in force and continuance, every time a new declaration was added to the preceding one. The prisoner himself listened to them with that astonished countenance which, according to the prosecution, was his principal means of defence. At the first, the gendarmes by his side heard him mutter between his teeth: "Ah, well! there is one of them!" After the second, he said in a louder tone, with an air almost of satisfaction, "Good!" At the third, he exclaimed, "Famous!"

The judge addressed him:

"Prisoner, you have listened. What have you to say?"

He replied:

"I say—famous!"

A buzz ran through the crowd and almost invaded the jury. It was evident that the man was lost.

"Officers," said the judge, "enforce order. I am about to sum up the case."

At this moment there was a movement near the judge. A voice was heard exclaiming:

"Brevet, Chenildieu, Cochepaille, look this way!"

So lamentable and terrible was this voice that those who heard it felt their blood run cold. All eyes turned towards the spot whence it came. A man, who had been sitting among the privileged spectators behind the court, had risen, pushed open the low door which separated the tribunal from the bar, and was standing in the centre of the hall. The judge, the prosecuting attorney, Monsieur Bamatabois, twenty persons recognised him, and exclaimed at once:

"Monsieur Madeleine!"

10 (11)

CHAMPMATHIEU MORE AND MORE ASTONISHED

IT WAS HE, indeed. The clerk's lamp lighted up his face. He held his hat in hand; there was no disorder in his dress; his overcoat was carefully buttoned. He was very pale, and trembled slightly. His hair, already grey when he came to Arras, was now perfectly white.*

It had become so during the hour that he had been there. All eyes were strained towards him.

The sensation was indescribable. There was a moment of hesitation in the auditory. The voice had been so poignant, the man standing there appeared so calm, that at first nobody could comprehend it. They asked who had cried out. They could not believe that this tranquil man had uttered that fearful cry.

This indecisiveness lasted but few seconds. Before even the judge and prosecuting attorney could say a word, before the gendarmes and officers could make a sign, the man, whom all up to this moment had called Monsieur Madeleine, had advanced towards the witnesses, Cochepaille, Brevet, and Chenildieu.

---

*To have hair turn white overnight from an emotional shock is a common melodramatic device in nineteenth-century fiction.

"Do you not recognise me?" said he.

All three stood confounded, and indicated by a shake of the head that they did not know him at all. Cochepaille, intimidated, gave the military salute. Monsieur Madeleine turned towards the jurors and court, and said in a mild voice:

"Gentlemen of the jury, release the accused. Your honour, order my arrest. He is not the man whom you seek; it is I. I am Jean Valjean."

Not a breath stirred. To the first commotion of astonishment had succeeded a sepulchral silence. That species of religious awe was felt in the hall which thrills the multitude at the accomplishment of a grand action.

Nevertheless, the face of the judge was marked with sympathy and sadness; he exchanged glances with the prosecuting attorney and a few whispered words with the assistant judges. He turned to the spectators and asked in a tone which was understood by all:

"Is there a physician here?"

The prosecuting attorney continued:

"Gentlemen of the jury, the strange and unexpected incident which disturbs the audience, inspires us, as well as yourselves, with a feeling we have no need to express. You all know, at least by reputation, the honourable Monsieur Madeleine, Mayor of M—— sur M——. If there be a physician in the audience, we unite with his honour the judge in entreating him to be kind enough to lend his assistance to Monsieur Madeleine and conduct him to his residence."

Monsieur Madeleine did not permit the prosecuting attorney to finish, but interrupted him with a tone full of gentleness and authority. These are the words he uttered; we give them literally, as they were written down immediately after the trial, by one of the witnesses of the scene—as they still ring in the ears of those who heard them, now nearly forty years ago.

"I thank you, Monsieur Prosecuting Attorney, but I am not mad. You shall see. You were on the point of committing a great mistake; release that man. I am accomplishing a duty; I am the unhappy convict. I am the only one who sees clearly here, and I tell you the truth. What I do at this moment, God beholds from on high, and that is sufficient. You can take me, since I am here. Nevertheless, I have done my best. I have disguised myself under another name, I have become rich, I have become a mayor, I have desired to reenter the society of honest men. It seems that this cannot be. In short, there are many things which I cannot tell. I shall not relate to you the story of my life: some day you will know it. I did rob Monseigneur the Bishop—that is true; I did rob Petit Gervais—that is true. They were right in telling you that Jean Valjean was a wicked wretch. But all the blame may not belong to him. Listen, your honours; a man so abased as I, has no remonstrance to make with Providence, nor advice to give to society; but, mark you, the infamy from which I have sought to rise is pernicious to men. The galleys make the galley-slave. Receive this in kindness, if you will. Before the galleys, I was a poor peasant, unintelligent, a species of idiot; the galleys changed me. I was stupid, I became wicked; I was a log, I became a firebrand. Later, I was saved by indulgence and kindness, as I had been lost by severity. But, pardon, you cannot comprehend what I say. You will find in my house, among the ashes of the fireplace, the forty-sous coin of which, seven years ago, I robbed Petit Gervais. I have nothing more to add. Take me. Great God! the prosecuting attorney shakes his head. You say 'Monsieur Madeleine has gone mad;' you do not believe me. This is hard to be borne. Do not condemn that man, at least. What! these men do not know me! Would that Javert were here. He would recognise me!"

Nothing could express the kindly yet terrible melancholy of the tone which accompanied these words.

He turned to the three convicts:

"Well! I recognise you, Brevet, do you remember——"

He paused, hesitated a moment, and said:

"Do you remember those checkered, knit suspenders that you had in the galleys?"

Brevet started as if struck with surprise, and gazed wildly at him from head to foot. He continued:

"Chenildieu, surnamed by yourself Je-nie-Dieu, the whole of your left shoulder has been burned deeply, from laying it one day on a chafing dish full of embers, to efface the three letters T. F. P.,* which yet are still to be seen there. Answer me, is this true?"

"It is true!" said Chenildieu.

He turned to Cochepaille:

"Cochepaille, you have on your left arm, near where you have been bled, a date put in blue letters with burnt powder. It is the date of the land-ing of the emperor at Cannes, *March 1st,* 1815. Lift up your sleeve."

Cochepaille lifted up his sleeve; all eyes around him were turned to his naked arm. A gendarme brought a lamp, the date was there.

The unhappy man turned towards the audience and the court with a smile, the thought of which still rends the hearts of those who witnessed it. It was the smile of triumph; it was also the smile of despair.

"You see clearly," said he, "that I am Jean Valjean."

There were no longer either judges, or accusers, or gendarmes in the hall; there were only fixed eyes and beating hearts. Nobody remembered longer the part which he had to play; the prosecuting attorney forgot that he was there to prosecute, the judge that he was there to preside, the coun-sel for the defence that he was there to defend. Strange to say no question was put, no authority intervened. It is the peculiarity of sublime spectacles that they take possession of every soul, and make of every witness a spec-tator. Nobody, perhaps, was positively conscious of what he experienced; and, undoubtedly, nobody said to himself that he there beheld the efful-gence of a great light, yet all felt dazzled at heart.

It was evident that Jean Valjean was before their eyes. That fact shone

---

*The letters are the abbreviation for *travaux forcés à perpétuité*—hard labor for life. Compare the scene in Honoré de Balzac's *Le Père Goriot* (1834) in which slapping the unconscious Vautrin's shoulder reveals his convict's brand.

forth. The appearance of this man had been enough fully to clear up the case, so obscure a moment before. Without need of any further explanation, the multitude, as by a sort of electric revelation, comprehended instantly, and at a single glance, this simple and magnificent story of a man giving himself up that another might not be condemned in his place. The details, the hesitation, the slight reluctance possible were lost in this immense, luminous fact.

It was an impression which quickly passed, but for the moment it was irresistible.

"I will not disturb the proceeding further," continued Jean Valjean. "I am going, since I am not arrested. I have many things to do. Monsieur the prosecuting attorney knows who I am, he knows where I am going, and will have me arrested when he chooses."

He walked towards the outer door. Not a voice was raised, not an arm stretched out to prevent him. All stood aside. There was at this moment an indescribable divinity within him which makes the multitudes fall back and make way before a man. He passed through the throng with slow steps. It was never known who opened the door, but it is certain that the door was open when he came to it. On reaching it he turned and said:

"Monsieur the Prosecuting Attorney, I remain at your disposal."

He then addressed himself to the auditory.

"You all, all who are here, think me worthy of pity, do you not? Great God! when I think of what I have been on the point of doing, I think myself worthy of envy. Still, would that all this had not happened!"

He went out, and the door closed as it had opened, for those who do deeds sovereignly great are always sure of being served by somebody in the throng.

Less than an hour afterwards, the verdict of the jury discharged from all accusation the said Champmathieu; and Champmathieu, set at liberty forthwith, went his way stupefied, thinking all men mad, and understanding nothing of this vision.

BOOK EIGHT
COUNTER-STROKE

1

IN WHAT MIRROR M. MADELEINE
LOOKS AT HIS HAIR

DAY BEGAN to dawn. Fantine had had a feverish and sleepless night, yet full of happy visions; she fell asleep at daybreak. Sister Simplice, who had watched with her, took advantage of this slumber to go and prepare a new potion of quinine. The good sister had been for a few moments in the laboratory of the infirmary, bending over her vials and drugs, looking at them very closely on account of the mist which the dawn casts over all objects, when suddenly she turned her head, and uttered a faint cry. M. Madeleine stood before her. He had just come in silently.

"You, Monsieur the Mayor!" she exclaimed.

"How is the poor woman?" he answered in a low voice.

"Better just now. But we have been very anxious indeed."

She explained what had happened, that Fantine had been very ill the night before, but was now better, because she believed that the mayor had gone to Montfermeil for her child. The sister dared not question the mayor, but she saw clearly from his manner that he had not come from that place.

"That is well," said he. "You did right not to undeceive her."

"Yes," returned the sister, "but now, Monsieur the Mayor, when she sees you without her child, what shall we tell her?"

He reflected for a moment, then said.

"God will inspire us."

"But, we cannot tell her a lie," murmured the sister, in a smothered tone.

The broad daylight streamed into the room, and lighted up the face of M. Madeleine.

The sister happened to raise her eyes.

"O God, monsieur," she exclaimed. "What has befallen you? Your hair is all white!"

"White!" said he.

Sister Simplice had no mirror; she rummaged in a case of instruments, and found a little glass which the physician of the infirmary used to discover whether the breath had left the body of a patient. M. Madeleine took the glass, looked at his hair in it, and said, "Well!"

He spoke the word with indifference, as if thinking of something else.

The sister felt chilled by an unknown something, of which she caught a glimpse in all this.

He asked: "Can I see her?"

"Will not Monsieur the Mayor bring back her child?" asked the sister, scarcely daring to venture a question.

"Certainly, but two or three days are necessary."

"If she does not see Monsieur the Mayor here," continued the sister timidly, "she will not know that he has returned; it will be easy for her to have patience, and when the child comes, she will think naturally that Monsieur the Mayor has just arrived with her. Then we will not have to tell her a falsehood."

Monsieur Madeleine seemed to reflect for a few moments, then said with his calm gravity:

"No, my sister, I must see her. Perhaps I have not much time."

The nun did not seem to notice this "perhaps," which gave an obscure and singular significance to the words of Monsieur the Mayor. She answered, lowering her eyes and voice respectfully:

"In that case, she is asleep, but monsieur can go in."

He made a few remarks about a door that shut with difficulty the noise of which might awaken the sick woman; then entered the chamber of Fantine, approached her bed, and opened the curtains. She was sleeping. Her breath came from her chest with that tragic sound which is peculiar to these diseases, and which rends the heart of unhappy mothers, watching the slumbers of their fated children. But this laboured respiration scarcely disturbed an ineffable serenity, which overshadowed her countenance, and transfigured her in her sleep. Her pallor had become whiteness, and her cheeks were glowing. Her long, fair eyelashes, the only beauty left to her of her maidenhood and youth, quivered as they lay closed upon her cheek. Her whole person trembled as if with the fluttering of wings which were felt, but could not be seen, and which seemed about to unfold and bear her away. To see her thus, no one could have believed that her life was despaired of. She looked more as if about to soar away than to die.

The stem, when the hand is stretched out to pluck the flower, quivers, and seems at once to shrink back, and present itself. The human body has something of this trepidation at the moment when the mysterious fingers of death are about to gather the soul.

Monsieur Madeleine remained for some time motionless near the bed, looking by turns at the patient and the crucifix, as he had done two months before, on the day when he came for the first time to see her in this asylum. They were still there, both in the same attitude, she sleeping, he praying; only now, after these two months had rolled away, her hair was grey and his was white.

The sister had not entered with him. He stood by the bed, with his finger on his lips, as if there were some one in the room to silence. She opened her eyes, saw him, and said tranquilly, with a smile:

"And Cosette?"

2

FANTINE HAPPY

SHE DID NOT start with surprise or joy; she was joy itself. The simple question: "And Cosette?" was asked with such deep faith, with so much certainty, with so complete an absence of disquiet or doubt that he could find no word in reply. She continued:

"I knew that you were there; I was asleep, but I saw you. I have seen you for a long time; I have followed you with my eyes the whole night. You were in a halo of glory, and all manner of celestial forms were hovering around you!"

He raised his eyes towards the crucifix.

"But tell me, where is Cosette?" she resumed. "Why not put her on my bed that I might see her the instant I woke?"

He answered something mechanically, which he could never afterwards recall.

Happily, the physician had come and had been apprised of this. He came to the aid of M. Madeleine.

"My child," said he, "be calm, your daughter is here."

The eyes of Fantine beamed with joy, and lighted up her whole countenance. She clasped her hands with an expression full of the most violent and most gentle entreaty:

"Oh!" she exclaimed, "bring her to me!"

Touching illusion of the mother; Cosette was still to her a little child to be carried in the arms.

"Not yet," continued the physician, "not at this moment. You have some fever still. The sight of your child will agitate you, and make you worse. We must cure you first."

She interrupted him impetuously.

"But I am cured! I tell you I am cured! Is this physician a fool? I will see my child!"

"You see how you are carried away!" said the physician. "So long as you are in this state, I cannot let you have your child. It is not enough to see her, you must live for her. When you are reasonable, I will bring her to you myself."

The poor mother bowed her head.

"Sir, I ask your pardon. I sincerely ask your pardon. Once I would not have spoken as I have now, but so many misfortunes have befallen me that sometimes I do not know what I am saying. I understand, you fear excitement; I will wait as long as you wish, but I am sure that it will not harm me to see my daughter. I see her now, I have not taken my eyes from her since last night. Let them bring her to me now, and I will just speak to her very gently. That is all. Is it not very natural that I should wish to see my child, when they have been to Montfermeil on purpose to bring her to me? I am not angry. I know that I am going to be very happy. All night, I saw figures in white, smiling on me. As soon as the doctor pleases, he can bring Cosette. My fever is gone, for I am cured; I feel that there is scarcely anything the matter with me; but I will act as if I were ill, and do not stir so as to please the ladies here. When they see that I am calm, they will say: 'You must give her the child.'"

M. Madeleine was sitting in a chair by the side of the bed. She turned towards him, and made visible efforts to appear calm and "very good," as she said, in that weakness of disease which resembles childhood, so that, seeing her so peaceful, there should be no objection to bringing her Cosette. Nevertheless, although restraining herself, she could not help addressing a thousand questions to M. Madeleine.

"Did you have a pleasant journey, Monsieur the Mayor? Oh! how good you have been to go for her! Tell me only how she is. Did she bear the journey well? Ah! she will not know me. In all this time, she has forgotten me, poor kitten! Children have no memory. They are like birds. To-day they see one thing, and to-morrow another, and remember nothing. Tell me only, were her clothes clean? Did those Thénardiers keep her neat? How did they feed her? Oh, if you knew how I have suffered in asking myself all these things in the time of my wretchedness! Now, it is past. I am happy. Oh! how I want to see her! Monsieur the Mayor, did you think her pretty? Is not my daughter beautiful? You must have been very cold in the stage-coach? Could they not bring her here for one little moment? they might take her away immediately. Say! you are master here, are you willing?"

He took her hand. "Cosette is beautiful," said he. "Cosette is well; you shall see her soon, but be quiet. You talk too fast; and then you throw your arms out of bed, which makes you cough."

In fact, coughing fits interrupted Fantine at almost every word.

She did not murmur; she feared that by too eager entreaties she had weakened the confidence which she wished to inspire, and began to talk about indifferent subjects.

"Montfermeil is a pretty place, is it not? In summer people go there on pleasure parties. Do the Thénardiers do a good business? Not many great people pass through that country. Their inn is a kind of tavern."

Monsieur Madeleine still held her hand and looked at her with anxiety. It was evident that he had come to tell her things before which his mind now hesitated. The physician had made his visit and retired. Sister Simplice alone remained with them.

But in the midst of the silence, Fantine cried out:—

"I hear her! Oh, darling! I hear her!"

She stretched out her arm to tell the people around her to be quiet, held her breath, and set to listening with rapture.

There was a child playing in the court—the child of the portress or some workwoman. It was one of those coincidences which are always met with, and which seem to form part of the mysterious representation of tragic events. The child, which was a little girl, was running up and down to keep herself warm, singing and laughing in a loud voice. Alas! with what are not the plays of children mingled! Fantine had heard this little girl singing.

"Oh!" said she, "it is my Cosette! I know her voice!"

The child departed as she had come, and the voice died away. Fantine listened for some time. A shadow came over her face, and Monsieur Madeleine heard her whisper, "How wicked it is of that doctor not to let me see my child! That man has a bad face!"

But yet her happy train of thought returned. With her head on the pillow she continued to talk to herself. "How happy we shall be! We will have a little garden in the first place; Monsieur Madeleine has promised it to me. My child will play in the garden. She must know her letters now. I will teach her to spell. She will chase the butterflies in the grass, and I will watch her. Then there will be her first communion. Ah! when will her first communion be?"

She began to count on her fingers.

"One, two, three, four. She is seven years old. In five years. She will have a white veil and open-worked stockings, and will look like a little lady. Oh, my good sister, you do not know how foolish I am; here I am thinking of my child's first communion!"

And she began to laugh.

He had let go the hand of Fantine. He listened to the words as one listens to the wind that blows, his eyes on the ground, and his mind plunged into unfathomable reflections. Suddenly she ceased speaking, and raised her head mechanically. Fantine had become appalling.

She did not speak any longer; she did not breathe any longer; she half-raised herself in the bed, the nightgown slipped from her emaciated shoulder; her countenance, radiant a moment before, became pale, and her eyes, dilated with terror, seemed to fasten on something before her at the other end of the room.

"Good God!" exclaimed he. "What is the matter, Fantine?"

She did not answer; she did not take her eyes from the object which she seemed to see, but touched his arm with one hand, and with the other made a sign to him to look behind him.

He turned, and saw Javert.

3

JAVERT SATISFIED

LET US SEE what had happened.

The half hour after midnight was striking when M. Madeleine left the hall of the Circuit Court of Arras. He had returned to his inn just in time to take the mail-coach, in which it will be remembered he had reserved his seat. A little before six in the morning he had reached M—— sur M——, where his first care had been to post his letter to M. Laffitte, then go to the infirmary and visit Fantine.

Meanwhile he had scarcely left the hall of the Circuit Court when the prosecuting attorney, recovering from his first shock, addressed the court, deploring the insanity of the honourable Mayor of M—— sur M——, declaring that his convictions were in no wise modified by this singular incident, which would be explained hereafter, and demanding the conviction of this Champmathieu, who was evidently the real Jean Valjean. The persistence of the prosecuting attorney was visibly in contradiction to the sentiment of all—the public, the court, and the jury. The counsel for the defence had little difficulty in answering this harangue, and establishing that, in consequence of the revelations of M. Madeleine—that is, of the real Jean Valjean—the aspect of the case was changed, entirely changed, from top to bottom, and that the jury now had before them an innocent man. The counsel drew from this a few passionate appeals, unfortunately not very new, in regard to judicial errors, etc., etc.; the judge, in his summing up, sided with the defence; and the jury, after a few moments' consultation, acquitted Champmathieu.

But yet the prosecuting attorney must have a Jean Valjean, and having lost Champmathieu he took Madeleine.

Immediately upon the discharge of Champmathieu the prosecuting attorney closeted himself with the judge. The subject of their conference was, "Of the necessity of the arrest of the person of Monsieur the Mayor of M—— sur M——." This sentence, in which there is a great deal of *of,* is the prosecuting attorney's, written by his own hand, on the minutes of his report to the Attorney-general.

The first sensation being over, the judge made few objections. Justice must take its course. Then to confess the truth, although the judge was a kind man, and really intelligent, he was at the same time a strong, almost zealous royalist, and had been shocked when the mayor of M—— sur M——, in speaking of the debarkation at Cannes, said the *Emperor* instead of *Buonaparte.**

---

*To say "the Emperor" instead of "Buonaparte" (in four syllables) betrays that M. Madeleine admires or at least respects Napoléon, rather than considers him a

The order of arrest was therefore granted. The prosecuting attorney sent it to M—— sur M—— by a courier, at full speed, to police-inspector Javert.

It will be remembered that Javert had returned to M—— sur M—— immediately after giving his testimony.

Javert was just rising when the courier brought him the warrant and order of arrest.

The courier was himself a policeman, and an intelligent man; who, in few words, acquainted Javert with what had happened at Arras.

The order of arrest, signed by the prosecuting attorney, was couched in these terms:—

"Inspector Javert will seize the body of Sieur Madeleine, Mayor of M—— sur M——, who has this day been identified in court as the discharged convict Jean Valjean."

One who did not know Javert, on seeing him as he entered the hall of the infirmary, could have divined nothing of what was going on, and would have thought his manner the most natural imaginable. He was cool, calm, grave; his grey hair lay perfectly smooth over his temples, and he had ascended the stairway with his customary deliberation. But one who knew him thoroughly and examined him with attention, would have shuddered. The buckle of his leather cravat, instead of being on the back of his neck, was under his left ear. This denoted an unheard-of agitation.*

Javert was a complete character without a wrinkle in his duty or his uniform,[12] methodical with villains, rigid with the buttons of his coat.

For him to misplace the buckle of his cravat, he must have received one of those shocks which may well be the earthquakes of the soul.

He came unostentatiously, had taken a corporal and four soldiers from a station-house near-by, had left the soldiers in the court, had been shown to Fantine's chamber by the portress, without suspicion, accustomed as she was to see armed men asking for the mayor.

On reaching Fantine's room, Javert turned the key, pushed open the door with the gentleness of a sick-nurse, or a police spy, and entered.

Properly speaking, he did not enter. He remained standing in the half-opened door, his hat on his head, and his left hand in his overcoat, which was buttoned to the chin. In the bend of his elbow might be seen the leaden head of his enormous cane, which disappeared behind him.

He remained thus for nearly a minute, unperceived. Suddenly, Fantine raised her eyes, saw him, and caused Monsieur Madeleine to turn round.

At the moment when the glance of Madeleine encountered that of Javert, Javert, without stirring, without moving, without approaching, became terrible. No human feeling can ever be so appalling as joy.

---

foreign usurper, illegitimate and born in Corsica before that island had become French.

*"This denoted" again reflects Balzac's influence in seeing details of a person's features or clothing as revealing deep-seated traits of their personality. The episodic observer (one who knew Javert thoroughly) is used again.

It was the face of a demon who had again found his victim.

The certainty that he had caught Jean Valjean at last brought forth upon his countenance all that was in his soul. The disturbed depths rose to the surface. The humiliation of having lost the scent for a little while, of having been mistaken for a few moments concerning Champmathieu, was lost in the pride of having divined so well at first, and having so long retained a true instinct. The satisfaction of Javert shone forth in his commanding attitude. The deformity of triumph spread over his narrow forehead. It was the fullest development of horror that a gratified face can show.

Javert was at this moment in heaven. Without clearly defining his own feelings, yet notwithstanding with a confused intuition of his necessity and his success, he, Javert, personified justice, light, and truth, in their celestial function as destroyers of evil. He was surrounded and supported by infinite depths of authority, reason, precedent, legal conscience, the vengeance of the law, all the stars in the firmament; he protected order, he hurled forth the thunder of the law, he avenged society, he lent aid to the absolute; he stood erect in a halo of glory; there was in his victory a reminder of defiance and of combat; standing haughty, resplendent, he displayed in full glory the super-human beastliness of a ferocious archangel; the fearful shadow of the deed which he was accomplishing, made visible in his clenched fist, the uncertain flashes of the social sword; happy and indignant, he had set his heel on crime, vice, rebellion, perdition, and hell, he was radiant, exterminating, smiling; there was an incontestable grandeur in this monstrous St. Michael.

Javert, though hideous, was not at all ignoble.

Probity, sincerity, candour, conviction, the idea of duty, are things which, mistaken, may become hideous, but which, even though hideous, remain great; their majesty, peculiar to the human conscience, continues in all their horror; they are virtues with a single vice—error. The pitiless, sincere joy of a fanatic in an act of atrocity preserves an indescribably mournful radiance which inspires us with veneration. Without suspecting it, Javert, in his fear-inspiring happiness, was pitiable, like every ignorant man who wins a triumph. Nothing could be more poignant and terrible than this face, which revealed what we may call all the evil of good.

4

AUTHORITY RESUMES ITS SWAY

FANTINE had not seen Javert since the day the mayor had wrested her from him. Her sick brain accounted for nothing, only she was sure that he had come for her. She could not endure this hideous face, she felt as if she were dying, she hid her face with both hands, and shrieked in anguish:

"Monsieur Madeleine, save me!"

Jean Valjean, we shall call him by no other name henceforth, had risen. He said to Fantine in his gentlest and calmest tone:

"Be composed; it is not for you that he comes."

He then turned to Javert and said:

"I know what you want."

Javert answered:

"Hurry along."

There was in the manner in which these two words were uttered, an inexpressible something which reminded you of a wild beast and of a madman. Javert did not say "Hurry along!" he said: "Hurr-'long!" No orthography can express the tone in which this was pronounced; it ceased to be human speech; it was a howl.

He did not go through the usual ceremony; he made no words; he showed no warrant. To him Jean Valjean was a sort of mysterious and intangible antagonist, a shadowy wrestler with whom he had been struggling for five years, without being able to throw him. This arrest was not a beginning, but an end. He only said: "Hurry along!"

While speaking thus, he did not stir a step, but cast upon Jean Valjean a look like a grappling hook, with which he was accustomed to draw the wretched to him by force.

It was the same look which Fantine had felt penetrate to the very marrow of her bones, two months before.

At the exclamation of Javert, Fantine had opened her eyes again. But the mayor was there, what could she fear?

Javert advanced to the middle of the chamber, exclaiming:

"Hey, there; are you coming?"

The unhappy woman looked around her. There was no one but the nun and the mayor. To whom could this contemptuous familiarity be addressed? To herself alone. She shuddered.

Then she saw a mysterious thing, so mysterious that its like had never appeared to her in the darkest delirium of fever.

She saw the spy Javert seize Monsieur the Mayor by the collar; she saw

Monsieur the Mayor bow his head. The world seemed vanishing before her sight.

Javert, in fact, had taken Jean Valjean by the collar.

"Monsieur Mayor!" shouted Fantine.

Javert burst into a horrid laugh, displaying all his teeth.

"There is no Monsieur the Mayor here any longer!" said he.

Jean Valjean did not attempt to disturb the hand which grasped the collar of his coat. He said:

"Javert——"

Javert interrupted him: "Call me Monsieur the Inspector!"

"Monsieur," continued Jean Valjean, "I would like to speak a word with you in private."

"Aloud, speak aloud," said Javert, "people speak aloud to me."

Jean Valjean went on, lowering his voice.

"It is a request that I have to make of you——"

"I tell you to speak aloud."

"But this should not be heard by any one but yourself."

"What is that to me? I will not listen."

Jean Valjean turned to him and said rapidly and in a very low tone:

"Give me three days! Three days to go for the child of this unhappy woman! I will pay whatever is necessary. You shall accompany me if you like."

"Are you laughing at me!" cried Javert. "Hey! I did not think you so stupid! You ask for three days to get away, and tell me that you are going for this girl's child! Ha, ha, that's good! That is good!"

Fantine shivered.

"My child!" she exclaimed, "going for my child! Then she is not here! Sister, tell me, where is Cosette? I want my child! Monsieur Madeleine, Monsieur the Mayor!"

Javert stamped his foot.

"There goes the other now! Hold your tongue, hussy! Miserable country, where galley slaves are magistrates and women of the town are nursed like countesses! Ha, but all this will be changed; it was time!"

He gazed steadily at Fantine, and added, grasping anew the cravat, shirt, and coat collar of Jean Valjean:

"I tell you that there is no Monsieur Madeleine, and that there is no Monsieur the Mayor. There is a robber, there is a brigand, there is a convict called Jean Valjean, and I have got him! That is what there is!"

Fantine started upright, supporting herself by her rigid arms and hands; she looked at Jean Valjean, then at Javert, and then at the nun; she opened her mouth as if to speak; a rattle came from her throat, her teeth struck together, she stretched out her arms in anguish, convulsively opening her hands, and groping about her like one who is drowning; then sank suddenly back upon the pillow.

Her head struck the head of the bed and fell forward on her breast, the mouth gaping, the eyes open and glazed.

She was dead.

Jean Valjean put his hand on that of Javert which held him, and unclasped it as he would have opened the hand of a child; then he said:

"You have killed this woman."

"Have done with this!" cried Javert, furious. "I am not here to listen to sermons; save all that; the guard is below; come right along, or the handcuffs!"

There stood in a corner of the room an old iron bedstead in a dilapidated condition, which the sisters used as a camp-bed when they watched. Jean Valjean went to the bed, wrenched out the rickety head bar—a thing easy for muscles like his—in the twinkling of an eye, and with the bar in his clenched fist, looked at Javert. Javert recoiled towards the door.

Jean Valjean, his iron bar in hand, walked slowly towards the bed of Fantine. On reaching it, he turned and said to Javert in a voice that could scarcely be heard:

"I advise you not to disturb me now."

Nothing is more certain than that Javert trembled.

He had an idea of calling the guard, but Jean Valjean might profit by his absence to escape. He remained, therefore, grasped the bottom of his cane, and leaned against the framework of the door without taking his eyes from Jean Valjean.

Jean Valjean rested his elbow upon the post, and his head upon his hand, and gazed at Fantine, stretched motionless before him. He remained thus, mute and absorbed, evidently lost to everything of this life. His countenance and attitude bespoke nothing but inexpressible pity.

After a few moments' reverie, he bent down to Fantine, and addressed her in a whisper.

What did he say? What could this condemned man say to this dead woman? What were these words? They were heard by none on earth. Did the dead woman hear them? There are touching illusions which perhaps are sublime realities. One thing is beyond doubt; Sister Simplice, the only witness of what happened, has often related that, at the moment when Jean Valjean whispered in the ear of Fantine, she distinctly saw an ineffable smile beam on those pale lips and in those dim eyes, full of the wonder of the tomb.[13]

Jean Valjean took Fantine's head in his hands and arranged it on the pillow, as a mother would have done for her child, then fastened the string of her night-dress, and replaced her hair beneath her cap. This done, he closed her eyes.

The face of Fantine, at this instant, seemed strangely illumined.

Death is the entrance into the great light.

Fantine's hand hung over the side of the bed. Jean Valjean knelt before this hand, raised it gently, and kissed it.

Then he rose, and, turning to Javert, said:

"Now, I am at your disposal."

5

A FITTING TOMB

JAVERT put Jean Valjean in the city prison.

The arrest of Monsieur Madeleine produced a sensation, or rather an extraordinary commotion, at M—— sur M——. We are sorry not to be able to disguise the fact that, on this single sentence, *he was a galley slave,* almost everybody abandoned him. In less than two hours, all the good he had done was forgotten, and he was "nothing but a galley slave." It is fair to say that the details of the scene at Arras were not yet known. All day long, conversations like this were heard in every part of the town: "Don't you know, he was a discharged convict!" "He! Who?" "The mayor." "Bah! Monsieur Madeleine." "Yes." "Indeed!" "His name was not Madeleine; he has a horrid name, Béjean, Bojean, Bonjean!" "Oh! bless me!" "He has been arrested." "Arrested!" "In prison, in the city prison to await his removal." "His removal! where will he be taken?" "To the Circuit Court for a highway robbery that he once committed." "Well! I always did suspect him. The man was too good, too perfect, too sweet. He refused the Legion of Honor, and gave money to every little blackguard he met. I always thought that there must be something bad at the bottom of all this."

"Society," especially, was entirely of this opinion.

An old lady, a subscriber to the *Drapeau Blanc,* made this remark, the depth of which it is almost impossible to fathom:

"I am not sorry for it. That will teach the Bonapartists!"

In this manner the phantom which had been called Monsieur Madeleine was dissipated at M—— sur M——. Three or four persons alone in the whole city remained faithful to his memory. The old portress who had been his servant was among the number.

On the evening of this same day, the worthy old woman was sitting in her lodge, still quite bewildered and sunk in sad reflections. The factory had been closed all day, the carriage ports were bolted, the street was deserted. There was no one in the house but the two nuns, Sister Perpétue and Sister Simplice, who were watching the corpse of Fantine.

Towards the time when Monsieur Madeleine had been accustomed to return, the honest portress rose mechanically, took the key of his room from a drawer, with the taper-stand that he used at night to light himself up the stairs, then hung the key on a nail from which he had been in the habit of taking it, and placed the taper-stand by its side, as if she were expecting him. She then seated herself again in her chair, and resumed her reflections. The poor old woman had done all this without being conscious of it.

More than two hours had elapsed when she started from her reverie and exclaimed, "Why, bless me! I have hung his key on the nail!"

Just then, the window of her box opened, a hand passed through the opening, took the key and stand, and lighted the taper at the candle which was burning.

The portress raised her eyes; she was transfixed with astonishment; a cry rose to her lips, but she stifled it.

She knew the hand, the arm, the coat-sleeve.

It was M. Madeleine.

She was speechless for some seconds, thunderstruck, as she said herself, afterwards, in giving her account of the affair.

"My God! Monsieur Mayor!" she exclaimed, "I thought you were—"

She stopped; the end of her sentence would not have been respectful to the beginning. To her, Jean Valjean was still Monsieur the Mayor.

He completed her thought.

"In prison," said he. "I was there, I broke a bar from a window, let myself fall from the top of a roof, and here I am. I am going to my room; go for Sister Simplice. She is doubtless beside that poor woman."

The old servant hastily obeyed.

He gave her no warning, very sure she would protect him better than he would protect himself.

It has never been known how he had succeeded in gaining entrance into the court-yard without opening the carriage port. He had, and always carried about him, a pass-key which opened a little side door, but he must have been searched, and this taken from him. This point is not yet cleared up.

He ascended the staircase which led to his room. On reaching the top, he left his taper stand on the upper stair, opened his door with little noise, felt his way to the window and closed the shutter, then came back, took his taper, and went into the chamber.

The precaution was not useless; it will be remembered that his window could be seen from the street.

He cast a glance about him, over his table, his chair, his bed, which had not been slept in for three days. There remained no trace of the disorder of the night before the last. The portress had "put the room to rights." Only, she had picked up from the ashes and laid in order on the table, the ends of the weighted club, and the forty-sous coin, blackened by the fire.

He took a sheet of paper and wrote: *These are the ends of my loaded club and the forty-sous coin stolen from Petit Gervais, of which I spoke at the Court;* then placed the two bits of iron and the piece of silver on the sheet in such a way that it would be the first thing perceived on entering the room. He took from a closet an old shirt which he tore into several pieces and in which he packed the two silver candlesticks. In all this there was neither haste nor agitation. And even while packing the bishop's candlesticks, he was eating a piece of black bread. It was probably prison-bread, which he had brought away in escaping.

This has been established by crumbs of bread found on the floor of the room, when the court afterwards ordered a search.

Two gentle taps were heard at the door.

"Come in," said he.

It was Sister Simplice.

She was pale, her eyes were red, and the candle which she held trembled in her hand. The shocks of destiny have this peculiarity; however subdued or disciplined our feelings may be, they draw out the human nature from the depths of our souls, and compel us to exhibit it to others. In the agitation of this day the nun had again become a woman. She had wept, and she was trembling.

Jean Valjean had written a few lines on a piece of paper, which he handed to the nun, saying: "Sister, you will give this to the curé."

The paper was not folded. She cast her eyes on it.

"You may read it," said he.

She read: "I beg Monsieur the Curé to take charge of all that I leave here. He will please defray therefrom the expenses of my trial, and of the burial of the woman who died this morning. The remainder is for the poor."

The sister attempted to speak, but could scarcely stammer out a few inarticulate sounds. She succeeded, however, in saying:

"Does not Monsieur the Mayor wish to see this poor unfortunate again for the last time?"

"No," said he, "I am pursued; I should only be arrested in her chamber; it would disturb her."*

He had scarcely finished when there was a loud noise on the staircase. They heard a tumult of steps ascending, and the old portress exclaiming in her loudest and most piercing tones:

"My good sir, I swear to you in the name of God, that nobody has come in here the whole day, and the whole evening; that I have not even once been away from my door!"

A man replied: "But yet, there is a light in this room."

They recognised the voice of Javert.

The chamber was so arranged that the door in opening covered the corner of the wall to the right. Jean Valjean blew out the taper, and placed himself in this corner.

Sister Simplice fell on her knees near the table.

The door opened.

Javert entered.

The whispering of several men, and the protestations of the portress were heard in the hall.

The nun did not raise her eyes. She was praying.

The candle was on the mantel, and gave but a dim light.

Javert perceived the sister, and stopped abashed.

It will be remembered that the very foundation of Javert, his element, the medium in which he breathed, was veneration for all authority. He was perfectly homogeneous, and admitted of no objection, or restriction. To

---

*Jean Valjean refers to the dead Fantine, again revealing his faith in immortality.

him, be it understood, ecclesiastical authority was the highest of all; he was devout, superficial, and correct, upon this point as upon all others. In his eyes, a priest was a spirit who was never mistaken, a nun was a being who never sinned. They were souls walled in from this world, with a single door which never opened but for the exit of truth.

On perceiving the sister, his first impulse was to retire.

But there was also another duty which held him, and which urged him imperiously in the opposite direction. His second impulse was to remain, and to venture at least one question.

This was the Sister Simplice, who had never lied in her life. Javert knew this, and venerated her especially on account of it.

"Sister," said he, "are you alone in this room?"

There was a fearful instant during which the poor portress felt her limbs falter beneath her. The sister raised her eyes, and replied:

"Yes."

Then continued Javert—"Excuse me if I persist, it is my duty—you have not seen this evening a person, a man—he has escaped and we are in search of him—Jean Valjean—you have not seen him?"

The sister answered—"No."

She lied. Two lies in succession, one upon another, without hesitation, quickly, as if she were an adept in it.

"Your pardon!" said Javert, and he withdrew, bowing reverently.

Oh, holy maiden! for many years you have been no more in this world; you have joined the sisters, the virgins, and thy brethren, the angels, in glory; may this falsehood be credited to you in Paradise.

The sister's assertion was to Javert something so decisive that he did not even notice the singularity of this taper, just blown out, and smoking on the table.

An hour afterwards, a man was walking rapidly in the darkness beneath the trees from M—— sur M—— in the direction of Paris. This man was Jean Valjean. It has been established, by the testimony of two or three waggoners who met him, that he carried a bundle, and was dressed in a smock. Where did he get this smock? It was never known. Nevertheless, an old artisan had died in the infirmary of the factory a few days before, leaving nothing but his smock. This might have been the one.

A last word in regard to Fantine.

We have all one mother—the earth. Fantine was restored to this mother.

The curé thought best, and did well perhaps, to reserve out of what Jean Valjean had left, the largest amount possible for the poor. After all, who were in question?—a convict and a woman of the town. This was why he simplified the burial of Fantine, and reduced it to that bare necessity called the Potter's field.

And so Fantine was buried in the common grave of the cemetery, which is for everybody and for all, and in which the poor are lost. Happily, God knows where to find the soul. Fantine was laid away in the darkness with bodies which had no name; she suffered the promiscuity of dust. She was thrown into the public pit. Her tomb was like her bed.

COSETTE

BOOK ONE
WATERLOO

1

WHAT YOU MEET IN COMING FROM NIVELLES

Hugo describes himself revisiting the Battlefield of Waterloo, in Belgium, in 1861. There the English had defeated Napoleon for the last time, forcing him to surrender. Hugo recalls the details of the battle. He admires the bravery and gallantry of both sides. Napoleon was a great general facing Wellington, a mediocre one, but Providence wanted Napoleon's tyranny to end so that democracy could progress throughout Europe. Many minor circumstances and unexpected setbacks led to the Emperor's defeat.

Hugo recalls the daring cavalry charge in which Marius's father, Baron and Colonel Pontmercy, fell into a concealed sunken road with his horse, to be buried beneath other horses and men. Their bodies arched over him, preventing him from being crushed. The robber Thénardier inadvertently revived him and thus saved his life while stripping his body of all valuables.

2 (19)

THE FIELD OF BATTLE AT NIGHT

WE RETURN, for it is a requirement of this book, to the fatal field of battle.

On the 18th of June, 1815, the moon was full. Its light favoured the ferocious pursuit of Blücher, disclosed the traces of the fugitives, delivered this helpless mass to the bloodthirsty Prussian cavalry, and aided in the massacre. Night sometimes lends such tragic assistance to catastrophe.

When the last gun had been fired the plain of Mont Saint Jean remained deserted.

The moon was an evil genius on this plain.

Towards midnight a man was prowling or rather crawling along the sunken road of Ohain. He was, to all appearance, one of those whom we have just described, neither English nor French, peasant nor soldier, less a man than a ghoul, attracted by the scent of the corpses, counting theft for victory, coming to rifle Waterloo. He was dressed in a workman's smock which was in part an overcoat, was restless and daring, looking behind and before as he went. Who was this man? Night, probably, knew more of his doings than day! He had no knapsack, but evidently wide pockets under his overcoat. From time to time he stopped, examined the plain around him as if to see if he were observed, stooped down suddenly, stirred on the ground something silent and motionless, then rose up and skulked away. His gliding movement, his attitudes, his rapid and mysterious gestures, made him seem like those twilight spectres which haunt ruins and which the old Norman legends call the Goers.

Certain nocturnal water-birds make such motions in marshes.

An eye which had carefully penetrated all this haze, might have noticed at some distance, standing as it were concealed behind the ruin which is on the Nivelle road at the corner of the route from Mont Saint Jean to Braine l'Alleud, a sort of little canteen owner's waggon, covered with tarred osiers, harnessed to a famished jade browsing nettles through her bit, and in the waggon a sort of woman seated on some trunks and packages. Perhaps there was some connection between this waggon and the prowler.

The night was serene. Not a cloud was in the zenith. What mattered it that the earth was red, the moon retained her whiteness. Such is the indifference of heaven. In the meadows, branches of trees broken by grapeshot, but not fallen, and held by the bark, swung gently in the night wind. A breath, almost a respiration, moved the brushwood. There was a quivering in the grass which seemed like the departure of souls.

The tread of the patrols and sentries of the English camp could be heard dimly in the distance.

Hougomont and La Haie Sainte continued to burn, making, one in the east and the other in the west, two great flames, to which was attached, like a necklace of rubies with two carbuncles at its extremities, the cordon of bivouac fires of the English, extending in an immense semicircle over the hills of the horizon.

We have spoken of the catastrophe of the sunken road to Ohain. The heart almost sinks with terror at the thought of such a death for so many brave men.

There, where this terrible death-rattle had been, all was now silent. The cut of the sunken road was filled with horses and riders inextricably heaped together. Terrible entanglement. There were no longer slopes to the road; dead bodies filled it even with the plain and came to the edge of the banks like a well-measured bushel of barley. A mass of dead above, a river of blood below—such was this road on the evening of the 18th of June, 1815. The blood ran as far as the Nivelles road, and oozed through in a large pool in front of the abattis of trees, which barred that road, at a spot which is still shown. It was, it will be remembered, at the opposite point towards the road from Genappe, that the burying of the cuirassiers took place. The thickness of the mass of bodies was proportioned to the depth of the hollow road. Towards the middle, at a spot where it became shallower, over which Delord's division had passed, this bed of death became thinner.

The night prowler which we have just introduced to the reader went in this direction. He ferreted through this immense grave. He looked about. He passed an indescribably hideous review of the dead. He walked with his feet in blood.

Suddenly he stopped.

A few steps before him, in the sunken road, at a point where the mound of corpses ended, from under this mass of men and horses appeared an open hand, lighted by the moon.

This hand had something upon a finger which sparkled: it was a gold ring.

The man stooped down, remained a moment, and when he rose again there was no ring upon that hand.

He did not rise up precisely; he remained in a sinister and startled attitude, turning his back to the pile of dead, scrutinising the horizon, on his knees, all the front of his body being supported on his two fore-fingers, his head raised just enough to peep above the edge of the hollow road. The four paws of the jackal are adapted to certain actions.

Then, deciding upon his course, he arose.

At this moment he experienced a shock. He felt that he was held from behind.

He turned; it was the open hand, which had closed, seizing the lapel of his overcoat.

An honest man would have been frightened. This man began to laugh.

"Oh," said he, "it's only the dead man. I like a ghost better than a gendarme."

However, the hand relaxed and let go its hold. Strength is soon exhausted in the tomb.

"Ah ha!" returned the prowler, "is this dead man alive? Let us see."

He bent over again, rummaged among the heap, removed whatever impeded him, seized the hand, laid hold of the arm, disengaged the head, drew out the body, and some moments after dragged into the shadow of the hollow road an inanimate man, at least one who was senseless. It was a cavalryman, an officer; an officer, also, of some rank; a great gold epaulet protruded from beneath his cuirass, but he had no helmet. A furious sabre cut had disfigured his face, where nothing but blood was to be seen. It did not seem, however, that he had any limbs broken; and by some happy chance, if the word is possible here, the bodies were arched above him in such a way as to prevent his being crushed. His eyes were closed.

He had on his cuirass the silver cross of the Legion of Honour.

The prowler tore off this cross, which disappeared in one of the gulfs which he had under his coat.

After which he felt the officer's fob, found a watch there, and took it. Then he rummaged in his vest and found a purse, which he pocketed.

When he had reached this phase of the succour he was lending the dying man, the officer opened his eyes.

"Thanks," said he feebly.

The rough movements of the man handling him, the coolness of the night, and breathing the fresh air freely, had roused him from his lethargy.

The prowler answered not. He raised his head. The sound of a foot-step could be heard on the plain; probably it was some patrol who was approaching.

The officer murmured, for there were still signs of suffering in his voice: "Who has won the battle?"

"The English," answered the prowler.

The officer replied:

"Look in my pockets. You will there find a purse and a watch. Take them."

This had already been done.

The prowler made a pretence of executing the command, and said:

"There is nothing there."

"I have been robbed," replied the officer; "I am sorry. They should have been yours."

The step of the patrol became more and more distinct.

"Somebody is coming," said the prowler, making a movement as if he would go.

The officer, raising himself up painfully upon one arm, held him back.

"You have saved my life. Who are you?"

The prowler answered quick and low:

"I belong, like yourself, to the French army. I must go. If I am taken I shall be shot. I have saved your life. Help yourself now."

"What is your rank?"

"Sergeant."

"What is your name?"

"Thénardier."

"I shall not forget that name," said the officer. "And you, remember mine. My name is Pontmercy."

Book Two
THE CONVICT SHIP *ORION*

1

NUMBER 24601 BECOMES NUMBER 9430

JEAN VALJEAN has been recaptured.

We shall be pardoned for passing rapidly over the painful details. We shall merely reproduce a couple of items published in the newspapers of that day, some few months after the remarkable events that occurred at M—— sur M——.

The first item, in the Royalist organ Le Drapeau blanc *of July 25, 1823, tersely reports Valjean's arrest. It acknowledges that he had made a fortune legitimately in the glassworks business, and that the money cannot be found (implying that the law would have cheerfully appropriated it otherwise).*

The second article, which enters a little more into detail, is taken from the *Journal de Paris* of the same date:

"A former convict, named Jean Valjean, has recently been brought before the Var Assizes, under circumstances calculated to attract attention. This villain had succeeded in eluding the vigilance of the police; he had changed his name, and had even been adroit enough to procure the appointment of mayor in one of our small towns in the North. He had established in this town a very considerable business, but was, at length, unmasked and arrested, thanks to the indefatigable zeal of the public authorities. He kept, as his mistress, a prostitute, who died of the shock at the moment of his arrest. This wretch, who is endowed with herculean strength, managed to escape, but, three or four days afterwards, the police recaptured him, in Paris, just as he was getting into one of the small vehicles that ply between the capital and the village of Montfermeil (Seine-et-Oise). It is said that he had availed himself of the interval of these three or four days of freedom, to withdraw a considerable sum deposited by him with one of our principal bankers. The amount is estimated at six or seven hundred thousand francs. According to the minutes of the case, he has concealed it in some place known to himself alone, and it has been impossible to seize it; however that may be, the said Jean Valjean has been brought before the assizes of the Department of the Var under indictment for an assault and armed robbery on the high road committed some eight years ago on the person of one of those honest lads who, as the patriarch of Ferney has written in immortal verse,

> . . . De Savoie arrivent tous les ans,
> Et dont la main légèrement essuie
> Ces longs canaux engorgés par la suie.*

This bandit attempted no defence. It was proven by the able and eloquent representative of the crown that the robbery was shared in by others, and that Jean Valjean formed one of a band of robbers in the South. Consequently, Jean Valjean, being found guilty, was condemned to death. The criminal refused to appeal to the higher courts, and the king, in his inexhaustible clemency, deigned to commute his sentence to that of hard labour in prison for life. Jean Valjean was immediately forwarded to the galleys at Toulon."

It will not be forgotten that Jean Valjean had at M—— sur M—— certain religious habits. Some of the newspapers and, among them, the *Constitutionnel,* held up this commutation as a triumph of the clerical party.[1]

Jean Valjean changed his number at the galleys. He became 9430.

After Jean Valjean's arrest, the town of which he had been mayor rapidly declines, as greedy minor capitalists squabble over the remains of his business. Poverty and misery ensue.

A second chapter tells of the local superstition that the Devil buries treasure in the woods near Montfermeil, where Fantine had left Cosette with the Thénardiers. Glimpsing Jean Valjean there, the drunken road worker Boulatruelle thinks he must have buried treasure there—as he in fact had done—and feverishly searches for it.

---

*. . . Who come from Savoy every year, / And whose hand deftly wipes out / Those long channels choked up with soot.

2 (3)

SHOWING THAT THE CHAIN OF THE SHACKLE MUST NEEDS HAVE UNDERGONE A CERTAIN PREPARATION TO BE THUS BROKEN BY ONE BLOW OF THE HAMMER

TOWARDS THE END of October, in that same year, 1823, the inhabitants of Toulon saw coming back into their port, in consequence of heavy weather, and in order to repair some damages, the ship *Orion,* which was at a later period employed at Brest as a training ship, and which then formed a part of the Mediterranean squadron.

During the operations of the army of the Prince, commander-in-chief, a squadron cruised in the Mediterranean. We have said that the *Orion* belonged to that squadron, and that she had been driven back by bad weather to the port of Toulon.

The presence of a vessel of war in port has about it a certain influence which attracts and engages the multitude. It is because it is something grand, and the crowd likes what is imposing.

The *Orion* was a ship that had long been in bad condition. During her previous voyages, thick layers of shellfish had gathered on her bottom to such an extent as to seriously impede her progress; she had been put on the dry-dock the year before, to be scraped, and then she had gone to sea again. But this scraping had injured her fastening.

In the latitude of the Balearic Isles, her planking had loosened and opened, and as there was in those lays no copper sheathing, the ship had leaked. A fierce equinoctial came on, which had stove in the larboard bows and a porthole, and damaged the fore-chain-wales. In consequence of these injuries, the *Orion* had put back to Toulon.

She was moored near the arsenal. She was in commission, and they were repairing her. The hull had not been injured on the starboard side, but a few planks had been taken off here and there, according to custom, to admit the air to the framework.

One morning, the throng which was gazing at her witnessed an accident.

The crew was engaged in furling sail. The topman, whose duty it was to take in the starboard upper corner of the main top-sail, lost his balance. He was seen tottering; the dense throng assembled on the wharf of the arsenal uttered a cry, the man's head overbalanced his body, and he whirled over the yard, his arms outstretched towards the deep; as he went over, he grasped the man-ropes, first with one hand, and then with the other, and hung suspended in that manner. The sea lay far below him at a giddy depth. The shock of his fall had given to the man-ropes a violent swinging motion, and the poor fellow hung dangling to and fro at the end of this line, like a stone in a sling.

To go to his aid was to run a frightful risk. None of the crew, who were all fishermen of the coast recently taken into service, dared attempt it. In the meantime, the poor topman was becoming exhausted; his agony could not be seen in his countenance, but his increasing weakness could be detected in the movements of all his limbs. His arms twisted about in horrible contortions. Every attempt he made to reascend only increased the oscillations of the man-ropes. He did not cry out, for fear of losing his strength. All were now looking forward to the moment when he should let go of the rope, and, at instants, all turned their heads away that they might not see him fall. There are moments when a rope's end, a pole, the branch of a tree, is life itself, and it is a frightful thing to see a living being lose his hold upon it, and fall like a ripe fruit.

Suddenly, a man was discovered clambering up the rigging with the agility of a wildcat. This man was clad in red—it was a convict; he wore a green cap—it was a convict for life. As he reached the round top, a gust of wind blew off his cap and revealed a head entirely white: it was not a young man.

In fact, one of the convicts employed on board in some prison task, had, at the first alarm, run to the officer of the watch, and, amid the confusion and hesitation of the crew, while all the sailors trembled and shrank back, had asked permission to save the topman's life at the risk of his own. A sign of assent being given, with one blow of a hammer he broke the chain riveted to the iron ring at his ankle, then took a rope in his hand, and flung himself into the shrouds. Nobody, at the moment, noticed with what ease the chain was broken. It was only some time afterwards that anybody remembered it.

In a twinkling he was upon the yard. He paused a few seconds, and seemed to measure it with his glance. Those seconds, during which the wind swayed the sailor to and fro at the end of the rope, seemed ages to the lookers-on. At length, the convict raised his eyes to heaven, and took a step forward. The crowd drew a long breath. He was seen to run along the yard. On reaching its extreme tip, he fastened one end of the rope he had with him, and let the other hang at full length. Thereupon, he began to let himself down by his hands along this rope, and then there was an inexpressible sensation of terror; instead of one man, two were seen dangling at that giddy height.

You would have said it was a spider seizing a fly; only, in this case, the spider was bringing life, and not death. Ten thousand eyes were fixed upon the group. Not a cry; not a word was uttered; the same emotion contracted every brow. Every man held his breath, as if afraid to add the least whisper to the wind which was swaying the two unfortunate men.

However, the convict had, at length, managed to make his way down to the seaman. It was time; one minute more, and the man, exhausted and despairing, would have fallen into the deep. The convict firmly secured him to the rope to which he clung with one hand while he worked with the other. Finally, he was seen reascending to the yard, and hauling the sailor after him; he supported him there, for an instant, to let him recover his strength, and then, lifting him in his arms, carried him, as he walked along the yard, to the crosstrees, and from there to the round-top, where he left him in the hands of his mess-mates.

Then the throng applauded; old galley sergeants wept, women hugged each other on the wharves, and, on all sides, voices were heard exclaiming, with a sort of tenderly subdued enthusiasm:—"This man must be pardoned!"

He, however, had made it a point of duty to descend again immediately, and go back to his work. In order to arrive more quickly he slid down the rigging, and started to run along a lower yard. All eyes were following him. There was a certain moment when every one felt alarmed; whether it was that he felt fatigued, or because his head swam, people thought they saw him hesitate and stagger. Suddenly, the throng uttered a thrilling outcry: the convict had fallen into the sea.

The fall was perilous. The frigate *Algeciras* was moored close to the *Orion,* and the poor convict had plunged between the two ships. It was feared that he would be drawn under one or the other. Four men sprang, at once, into a boat. The people cheered them on, and anxiety again took possession of all minds. The man had not again risen to the surface. He had disappeared in the sea, without making even a ripple, as though he had fallen into a cask of oil. They sounded and dragged the place. It was in vain. The search was continued until night, but not even the body was found.

The next morning, the *Toulon Journal* published the following lines:— "November 17, 1823. Yesterday, a convict at work on board of the *Orion,* on his return from rescuing a sailor, fell into the sea, and was drowned. His body was not recovered. It is presumed that it has been caught under the piles at the pier-head of the arsenal. This man was registered by the number 9430, and his name was Jean Valjean."[*]

---

[*]The newspaper stories at the beginning and end of this book illustrate what Georges May called "the bad conscience of the novel," the desire to be taken seriously that leads it to invent "real" sources (*Le Dilemme du roman français au XVIIIe siècle,* 1963).

BOOK THREE
KEEPING THE PROMISE
TO THE DEAD WOMAN

1

THE WATER PROBLEM AT MONTFERMEIL

MONTFERMEIL IS situated between Livry and Chelles, upon the southern slope of the high plateau which separates the Ourcq from the Marne. At present, it is a considerable town, adorned all the year round with stuccoed villas, and, on Sundays, with citizens in full blossom. In 1823, there were at Montfermeil neither so many white houses nor so many comfortable citizens; it was nothing but a village in the woods. You would find, indeed, here and there a few vacation homes of the last century, recognisable by their grand appearance, their balconies of twisted iron, and those long windows the little panes of which show all sorts of different greens upon the white of the closed shutters. But Montfermeil was none the less a village. Retired dry-goods merchants and amateur villagers had not yet discovered it. It was a peaceful and charming spot, and not upon the road to any place; the inhabitants cheaply enjoyed that rural life which is so luxuriant and so easy of enjoyment. But water was scarce there on account of the height of the plateau.

They had to go a considerable distance for it. The end of the village towards Gagny drew its water from the magnificent ponds in the forest on that side; the other end, which surrounds the church and which is towards Chelles, found drinking-water only at a little spring on the side of the hill, near the road to Chelles, about fifteen minutes' walk from Montfermeil.

It was therefore a serious matter for each household to obtain its supply of water. The great houses, the aristocracy, the Thénardier tavern included, paid a *liard* a bucket-full to an old man who made it his business, and whose income from the Montfermeil water-works was about eight sous per day; but this man worked only till seven o'clock in summer and five in the winter, and when night had come on, and the first-floor shutters were closed, whoever had no drinking-water went after it, or went without.

This was the terror of the poor being whom the reader has not perhaps forgotten—little Cosette. It will be remembered that Cosette was useful to the Thénardiers in two ways, they got pay from the mother and work from the child. Thus when the mother ceased entirely to pay, we have seen why, in the preceding chapters, the Thénardiers kept Cosette. She saved them a servant. In that capacity she ran for water when it was wanted. So the child, always horrified at the idea of going to the spring at night, took good care that water should never be wanting at the house.

On that Christmas evening, several men, waggoners and pedlars were seated at table and drinking around four or five candles in the low hall of the Thénardier tavern. This room resembled all bar-rooms; tables, pewter-mugs, bottles, drinkers, smokers; little light, and much noise.* The date, 1823, was, however, indicated by the two things then in vogue with the middle classes, which were on the table, a kaleidoscope and a fluted tin lamp. Thénardier, the wife, was looking to the supper, which was cooking before a bright blazing fire; the husband, Thénardier, was drinking with his guests and talking politics.

Cosette was at her usual place, seated on the cross-piece of the kitchen table, near the fire-place; she was clad in rags; her bare feet were in wooden shoes, and by the light of the fire she was knitting woollen stockings for the little Thénardiers. A kitten was playing under the chairs. In a neighbouring room the fresh voices of two children were heard laughing and prattling; it was Eponine and Azelma.

In the chimney-corner, a cow-hide hung upon a nail.

At intervals, the cry of a very young child, which was somewhere in the house, was heard above the noise of the bar-room. This was a little boy which the woman had had some winters before—"She didn't know why," she said: "it was the cold weather,"—and which was a little more than three years old. The mother had nursed him, but did not love him. When the hungry clamour of the brat became too much to hear:—"Your boy is squalling," said Thénardier, "why don't you go and see what he wants?" "Bah!" answered the mother; "I am sick of him." And the poor little fellow continued to cry in the darkness.†

2

TWO PORTRAITS COMPLETED

THE THÉNARDIERS have hitherto been seen in this book in profile only; the time has come to turn this couple about and look at them on all sides.

Thénardier has just passed his fiftieth year; Madame Thénardier had reached her fortieth, which is the fiftieth for woman, so that there was an equilibrium of age between the husband and wife.

---

*Hugo knew English and English literature fairly well; one of his sons translated all of Shakespeare's plays into English. Here he alludes to Hamlet's comparison of human life to "a tale told by an idiot, full of sound and fury, signifying nothing."

†This wailing baby will reappear as Gavroche. Mme Thénardier's monstrous nature appears in her total indifference to her three sons. Her cruelty gives the lie to her husband's scruples, the next morning, about giving up Cosette.

The reader has perhaps, since her first appearance, preserved some remembrance of this huge Thénardiess;—for such we shall call the female of this species,—tall, blond, red, fat, brawny, square, enormous, and agile; she belonged, as we have said, to the race of those colossal wild women who pose at fairs with paving-stones hung in their hair. She did everything about the house, the cleaning and bedmaking, the washing, the cooking, anything she pleased, and played the deuce generally. Cosette was her only servant; a mouse in the service of an elephant. Everything trembled at the sound of her voice; windows and furniture as well as people. Her broad face, covered with freckles, had the appearance of a skimmer. She had a beard. She was the ideal of a butcher's boy dressed in petticoats. She swore splendidly; she prided herself on being able to crack a nut with her fist. Apart from the novels she had read, which at times gave you an odd glimpse of the affected lady under the ogress, the idea of calling her a woman never would have occurred to anybody. This Thénardiess seemed like a cross between a wench and a fishwoman. If you heard her speak, you would say it is a gendarme; if you saw her drink, you would say it is a carter; if you saw her handle Cosette, you would say it is the hangman. When she was at rest, a tooth protruded from her mouth.

The other Thénardier was a little man, meagre, pale, angular, bony, and lean, who appeared to be sick, and whose health was excellent; here his knavery began. He smiled habitually as a matter of business, and tried to be polite to everybody, even to the beggar to whom he refused a penny. He had the look of a weazel, and the mien of a man of letters. He had a strong resemblance to the portraits of the Abbé Delille. He affected drinking with waggoners. Nobody ever saw him drunk. He smoked a large pipe. He wore a smock, and under it an old black tuxedo coat. He made pretensions to literature and materialism. There were names which he often pronounced in support of anything whatever that he might say. Voltaire, Raynal, Parny, and, oddly enough, St. Augustine. He professed to have "a system." For the rest, a great swindler. A *filou-sophe*.[*] There is such a variety. It will be remembered, that he pretended to have been in the service; he related with some pomp that at Waterloo, being sergeant in a Sixth or Ninth Light something, he alone, against a squadron of Hussars of Death, had covered with his body, and saved amid a shower of grapeshot, "a general dangerously wounded." Hence the flamboyant picture on his sign, and the name of his inn, which spoken of in the region as the "tavern of the sergeant of Waterloo." He was liberal, classical, and a Bonapartist. He had contributed to the homeless shelter. It was said in the village that he had studied for the priesthood.

We believe[†] that he had only studied in Holland to be an innkeeper. This mongrel cur was, according to all probability, some Fleming of Lille in

---

*Hugo puns by calling Thénardier a *filou-sophe* instead of *philosophe*. *Filou* means "crook"; the whole invented word implies "someone who knows and loves crime."
†Here and in many other places, Hugo portrays himself as an investigative reporter who researches documents and questions witnesses.

Flanders, a Frenchman in Paris, a Belgian in Brussels, conveniently on the fence between the two frontiers. We are acquainted with his prowess at Waterloo. As we have seen, he exaggerated it a little. Ebb and flow, wandering, adventure, was his element; a violated conscience is followed by a loose life; and without doubt, at the stormy epoch of the 18th of June, 1815, Thénardier belonged to that species of marauding canteen owners of whom we have spoken, scouring the country, robbing here and selling there, and travelling in family style, man, woman, and children, in some rickety carry-all, in the wake of marching troops, with the instinct to attach himself always to the victorious army. This campaign over, having, as he said, some funds, he had opened an eatery at Montfermeil.

These funds, composed of purses and watches, gold rings and silver crosses, gathered at the harvest time in the furrows sown with corpses, did not form a great total, and had not lasted this canteen owner, now become a tavern-keeper, very long.

Thénardier had that indescribable stiffness of gesture which, with an oath, reminds you of the barracks, and, with a sign of the cross of the seminary. He was a fine talker. He was fond of being thought learned. Nevertheless, the schoolmaster remarked that he made mistakes in pronunciation. He made out travellers' bills in a superior style, but practised eyes sometimes found them faulty in orthography. Thénardier was sly, greedy, lounging, and clever. He did not disdain servant girls, consequently his wife had no more of them. This giantess was jealous. It seemed to her that this little, lean, and yellow man must be the object of universal desire.

Thénardier, above all a man of astuteness and poise, was a rascal of the subdued order. This is the worst species; there is hypocrisy in it.

Not that Thénardier was not on occasion capable of anger, quite as much as his wife; but that was very rare, and at such times, as if he were at war with the whole human race, as if he had in him a deep furnace of hatred, as if he were of those who are perpetually avenging themselves, who accuse everybody about them of the evils that befall them, and are always ready to throw on the first comer, as legitimate grievance, the sum-total of the deceptions, failures, and calamities of their life—as all this leaven worked in him, and boiled up into his mouth and eyes, he was frightful. Woe to him who came within reach of his fury, then!

Besides all his other qualities, Thénardier was attentive and penetrating, silent or talkative as occasion required, and always with great intelligence. He had somewhat the look of sailors accustomed to squinting the eye in looking through spy-glasses. Thénardier was a statesman.

Every new-comer who entered the tavern said, on seeing the Thénardiess: There is the master of the house. It was an error. She was not even *the mistress.* The husband was both master and mistress. She performed, he created. He directed everything by a sort of invisible and continuous magnetic action. A word sufficed, sometimes a sign; the mastodon obeyed. Thénardier was to her, without her being really aware of it, a sort of being apart and sovereign. She had the virtues of her order of creation; never would she have differed in any detail with "Monsieur Thénardier"—nor—impossible supposition—would she have publicly quarrelled with her husband, on any matter whatever. Never had she committed "before company" that fault of which women are so often guilty, and which is called in parliamentary language: discovering the crown. Although their accord had no other result than evil, there was food for contemplation in the submission of the Thénardiess to her husband. This bustling mountain of flesh moved under the little finger of this frail despot. It was, viewed from its dwarfed and grotesque side, this great universal fact: the homage of matter to spirit; for certain deformities have their origin in the depths even of eternal beauty. There was somewhat of the unknown in Thénardier; hence the absolute empire of this man over this woman. At times, she looked upon him as upon a lighted candle; at others, she felt him like a claw.

This woman was a formidable creation, who loved nothing but her children, and feared nothing but her husband. She was a mother because she was a mammal. Her maternal feelings stopped with her girls, and, as we shall see, did not extend to boys. The man had but one thought—to get rich.

He did not succeed. His great talents had no adequate opportunity. Thénardier at Montfermeil was ruining himself, if ruin is possible at zero. In Switzerland, or in the Pyrenees, this penniless rogue would have become a millionaire. But where fate places the innkeeper he must browse.

It is understood that the word *innkeeper* is employed here in a restricted sense, and does not extend to an entire class.

In this same year, 1823, Thénardier owed about fifteen hundred francs, of pressing debts, which rendered him moody.

However obstinately unjust destiny was to him, Thénardier was one of those men who best understood, to the greatest depth and in the most modern style, that which is a virtue among the barbarous, and an article of commerce among the civilised—hospitality. He was, besides, an admirable poacher, and was counted an excellent shot. He had a certain cool and quiet laugh, which was particularly dangerous.*

His theories of innkeeping sometimes sprang from him by flashes. He had certain professional aphorisms which he inculcated in the mind of his wife. "The duty of the innkeeper," said he to her one day, emphatically, and in a low voice, "is to sell to the first comer, food, rest, light, fire, dirty linen, servants, fleas, and smiles; to stop travellers, empty small purses, and honestly lighten large ones; to receive families who are travelling with respect: scrape the man, pluck the woman, and pick the child; to charge for the open window, the closed window, the chimney corner, the sofa, the chair, the stool, the bench, the feather bed, the mattress, and the straw bed; to know how much the mirror is worn, and to tax that; and, by the five hundred thousand devils, to make the traveller pay for everything, even to the flies that his dog eats!"

This man and this woman were cunning and rage married—a hideous and terrible pair.

---

*The garrulous Thénardier, always lying, contrasts dramatically with the taciturn, invariably truthful Jean Valjean.

While the husband calculated and schemed, the Thénardiess thought not of absent creditors, took no care either for yesterday or the morrow, and lived passionately in the present moment.

Such were these two beings. Cosette was between them, undergoing their double pressure, like a creature who is at the same time being bruised by a millstone, and lacerated with pincers. The man and the woman had each a different way. Cosette was beaten unmercifully; that came from the woman. She went barefoot in winter; that came from the man.

Cosette ran up stairs and down stairs; washed, brushed, scrubbed, swept, ran, slaved, got out of breath, lifted heavy things, and, puny as she was, did the rough work. No pity; a ferocious mistress, a malignant master. The Thénardier tavern was like a snare, in which Cosette had been caught, and was trembling. The ideal of oppression was realised by this dismal servitude. It was something like a fly serving spiders.

The poor child was passive and silent.

When they find themselves in such condition at the dawn of existence, so young, so feeble, among men, what passes in these souls fresh from God!

3

MEN MUST HAVE WINE AND HORSES WATER

FOUR NEW GUESTS had just come in.

Cosette was musing sadly; for, though she was only eight years old, she had already suffered so much that she mused with the mournful air of an old woman.

She had a black eye from a blow of the Thénardiess's fist, which made the Thénardiess say from time to time, "How ugly she is with her bruise."

Cosette was then thinking that it was evening, late in the evening, that she unexpectedly had to fill the bowls and pitchers in the rooms of the travellers who had arrived, and that there was no more water in the cistern.

One thing comforted her a little; they did not drink much water in the Thénardier tavern. There were plenty of people there who were thirsty; but it was that kind of thirst which reaches rather towards the jug than the pitcher. Had anybody asked for a glass of water among these glasses of wine, he would have seemed a savage to all those men. However, there was an instant when the child trembled; the Thénardiess raised the cover of a kettle which was boiling on the range, then took a glass and hastily

approached the cistern. She turned the faucet; the child had raised her
head and followed all her movements. A thin stream of water ran from the
faucet, and filled the glass half full.

"Here," said she, "there is no more water!" Then she was silent for a
moment. The child held her breath.

"Pshaw!" continued the Thénardiess, examining the half-filled glass,
"there is enough of it, such as it is."

Cosette resumed her work, but for more than a quarter of an hour she
felt her heart leaping into her throat like a great ball.

She counted the minutes as they thus rolled away, and eagerly wished it
were morning.

From time to time, one of the drinkers would look out into the street
and exclaim:—"It is as black as an oven!" or, "It would take a cat to go
along the street without a lantern to-night!" And Cosette shuddered.

All at once, one of the pedlars who lodged in the tavern came in, and
said in a harsh voice:

"You have not watered my horse."

"Yes, we have, sure," said the Thénardiess.

"I tell you no, ma'am," replied the pedlar.

Cosette came out from under the table.

"Oh, yes, monsieur!" said she, "the horse did drink; he drank in the bucket,
the bucket full, and 'twas me that carried it to him, and I talked to him."

This was not true. Cosette lied.

"Here is a girl as big as my fist, who can tell a lie as big as a house,"
exclaimed the pedlar. "I tell you that he has not had any water, little wench!
He has a way of blowing when he has not had any water, that I know well
enough."

Cosette persisted, and added in a voice stifled with anguish, and which
could hardly be heard:

"But he did drink a good deal."

"Come," continued the pedlar, in a passion, "that is enough; give my
horse some water, and say no more about it."

Cosette went back under the table.

"Well, of course that is right," said the Thénardiess; "if the beast has not
had any water, she must have some."

Then looking about her:

"Well, what has become of that girl?"

She stooped down and discovered Cosette crouched at the other end of
the table, almost under the feet of the drinkers.

"Aren't you coming?" cried the Thénardiess.

Cosette came out of the kind of hole where she had hidden. The Thénardiess continued:

"Mademoiselle Dog-without-a-name, go and carry some drink to this
horse."

"But, ma'am," said Cosette feebly, "there is no water."

The Thénardiess threw the street door wide open.

"Well, go after some!"

Cosette hung her head, and went for an empty bucket that was by the chimney corner.

The bucket was larger than she, and the child could have sat down in it comfortably.

The Thénardiess went back to her range, and tasted what was in the kettle with a wooden spoon, grumbling the while.

"There is some at the spring. It's as simple as that. I think 'twould have been better if I'd left out the onions."

Then she fumbled in a drawer where there were some pennies, pepper, and scallions.

"Here, Mamselle Toad," added she, "get a big loaf at the baker's, as you come back. Here is fifteen sous."

Cosette had a little pocket in the side of her apron; she took the coin without saying a word, and put it in that pocket.

Then she remained motionless, bucket in hand, the open door before her. She seemed to be waiting for somebody to come to her aid.

"Get along!" cried the Thénardiess.

Cosette went out. The door closed.*

4

A DOLL COMES ONSTAGE

THE ROW of booths extended along the street from the church, the reader will remember, as far as the Thénardier tavern. These booths, on account of the approaching passage of the citizens on their way to the midnight mass, were all illuminated with candles, burning in paper cones, which, as the schoolmaster of Montfermeil, who was at that moment seated at one of Thénardier's tables, said, produced a magical effect. On the other hand, not a star was to be seen in the sky.

The last of these stalls, set up exactly opposite Thénardier's door, was a toy-shop, all glittering with trinkets, glass beads, and magnificent things in tin. In the first rank, and in front, the merchant had placed, upon a bed of white napkins, a great doll nearly two feet high dressed in a robe of pink-crape with golden wheat-ears on its head, and which had real hair and enamel eyes. The whole day, this marvel had been displayed to the

---

*In this scene, frequent notations of posture, gesture, and voice quality reflect Hugo's keen sensitivity to theater.

bewilderment of the passers-by under ten years of age, but there had not been found in Montfermeil a mother rich enough, or prodigal enough to give it to her child. Eponine and Azelma had passed hours in contemplating it, and Cosette herself, furtively, it is true, had dared to look at it.

At the moment when Cosette went out, bucket in hand, all gloomy and overwhelmed as she was, she could not help raising her eyes towards this wonderful doll, towards *the lady* as she called it. The poor child stopped petrified. She had not seen this doll so near before.

This whole booth seemed a palace to her; this doll was not a doll, it was a vision. It was joy, splendour, riches, happiness, and it appeared in a sort of chimerical radiance to this unfortunate little being, buried so deeply in a cold and dismal misery. Cosette was measuring with the sad and simple sagacity of childhood the abyss which separated her from that doll. She was saying to herself that one must be a queen, or at least a princess, to have a "thing" like that. She gazed upon this beautiful pink dress, this beautiful smooth hair, and she was thinking, "How happy must be that doll!" Her eye could not turn away from this fantastic booth. The longer she looked, the more she was dazzled. She thought she saw paradise. There were other dolls behind the large one that appeared to her to be fairies and genii. The merchant walking to and fro in the back part of his stall, suggested the Eternal Father.

In this adoration, she forgot everything, even the errand on which she had been sent. Suddenly, the harsh voice of the Thénardiess called her back to the reality: "How, jade, haven't you gone yet? Hold on; I am coming for you! I'd like to know what she's doing there? Little monster, be off!"

The Thénardiess had glanced into the street, and perceived Cosette in ecstasy.

Cosette fled with her bucket, running as fast as she could.

5

THE LITTLE GIRL ALL ALONE

As the Thénardier tavern was in that part of the village which is near the church, Cosette had to go to the spring in the woods towards Chelles to draw water.

She looked no more at the displays in the booths, so long as she was in the lane Boulanger, and in the vicinity of the church, the illuminated stalls lighted the way, but soon the last gleam from the last stall disappeared. The poor child found herself in darkness. She plunged into it. Only, as she became the prey of a certain sensation, she shook the handle of the bucket as much as she could on her way. That made a noise, which kept her company.

The further she went, the thicker became the darkness. There was no longer anybody in the street. However, she met a woman who turned around on seeing her pass, and remained motionless, muttering between her teeth, "Where in the world can that child be going! Is it a phantom child?" Then the woman recognised Cosette. "Oh," said she, "it is the lark!"

Cosette thus passed through the labyrinth of crooked and deserted streets, which terminates the village of Montfermeil towards Chelles. As long as she had houses, or even walls, on the sides of the road, she went on boldly enough. From time to time, she saw the light of a candle through the cracks of a shutter; it was light and life to her; there were people there; that kept up her courage. However, as she advanced, her speed slackened as if mechanically. When she had passed the corner of the last house, Cosette stopped. To go beyond the last booth had been difficult; to go further than the last house became impossible. She put the bucket on the ground, buried her hands in her hair, and began to scratch her head slowly, a motion peculiar to terrified and hesitating children. It was Montfermeil no longer, it was the open country; dark and deserted space was before her. She looked with despair into this darkness where nobody was, where there were beasts, where there were perhaps ghosts. She looked intensely, and she heard the animals walking in the grass, and she distinctly saw the ghosts moving in the trees.* Then she seized her bucket again; fear gave her boldness: "Pshaw," said she, "I will tell her there isn't any more water!" And she resolutely went back into Montfermeil.

She had scarcely gone a hundred steps when she stopped again, and began to scratch her head. Now, it was the Thénardiess that appeared to her; the hideous Thénardiess, with her hyena mouth and wrath flashing from her eyes. The child cast a pitiful glance before her and behind her. What could she do? What would become of her? Where should she go? Before her, the spectre of the Thénardiess; behind her, all the phantoms of night and of the forest. It was at the Thénardiess that she recoiled. She took the road to the spring again, and began to run. She ran out of the village; she ran into the woods, seeing nothing, hearing nothing. She did not stop running until out of breath, and even then she staggered on. She went right on, desperate.

Even while running, she wanted to cry.

The nocturnal tremulousness of the forest wrapped her about completely.

She thought no more; she saw nothing more. The immensity of night confronted this little creature. On one side, the infinite shadow; on the other, an atom.†

---

*As Cosette proceeds farther into the darkness, her fear ("there were perhaps ghosts") acquires a hallucinatory intensity ("she distinctly saw the ghosts").

†Hugo, typically, contrasts and dramatizes the microcosm (the "atom," the human scale) and the macrocosm (the cosmos, the infinite).

It was only seven or eight minutes' walk from the edge of the woods to the spring. Cosette knew the road, from travelling it several times a day. Strange thing, she did not lose her way. A remnant of instinct guided her blindly. But she neither turned her eyes to the right nor to the left, for fear of seeing things in the trees and in the bushes. Thus she arrived at the spring.

It was a small natural basin, made by the water in the loamy soil, about two feet deep, surrounded with moss and ferns, and paved with a few large stones. A brook escaped from it with a gentle, tranquil murmur.

Cosette did not take time to breathe. It was very dark, but she was accustomed to come to this fountain. She felt with her left hand in the darkness for a young oak which bent over the spring and usually served her as a support, found a branch, swung herself from it, bent down and plunged the bucket in the water. She was for a moment so excited that her strength was tripled. When she was thus bent over, she did not notice that the pocket of her apron emptied itself into the spring. The fifteen-sous coin fell into the water. Cosette neither saw it nor heard it fall. She drew out the bucket almost full and set it on the grass.

This done, she perceived that her strength was exhausted. She was anxious to start at once; but the effort of filling the bucket had been so great that it was impossible for her to take a step. She was compelled to sit down. She fell upon the grass and remained in a crouching posture.

She closed her eyes, then she opened them, without knowing why, without the power of doing otherwise. At her side, the water shaken in the bucket made circles that resembled serpents of white fire.

Above her head, the sky was covered with vast black clouds which were like sheets of smoke. The tragic mask of night seemed to bend vaguely over this child.

Jupiter was setting in the depths of the horizon.

The child looked with a startled eye upon that great star which she did not know and which made her afraid. The planet, in fact, was at that moment very near the horizon and was crossing a dense bed of mist which gave it a horrid redness. The mist, gloomily empurpled, magnified the star. One would have called it a luminous wound.

A cold wind blew from the plain. The woods were dark, without any rustling of leaves, without any of those vague gleams you see in summer. Great branches drew themselves up fearfully. Stunted, shapeless bushes whistled in the glades. The tall grass wriggled under the north wind like eels. The brambles twisted about like long arms seeking to seize their prey in their claws. Some dry weeds driven by the wind passed rapidly by, and appeared to flee with dismay before something that was following. The prospect was dismal.

Without being conscious of what she was experiencing, Cosette felt that she was seized by this black enormity of nature. It was not merely terror that held her, but something more terrible even than terror. She shuddered. Words fail to express the peculiar strangeness of that shudder which chilled her through and through. Her eye had become wild. She felt that perhaps she would be compelled to return there at the same hour the next night.

Then, by a sort of instinct, to get out of this singular state, which she did not understand, but which terrified her, she began to count aloud, one, two, three, four, up to ten, and when she had finished, she began again. This restored her to a real perception of things about her. Her hands, which she had wet in drawing the water, felt cold. She arose. Her fear had returned, a natural and insurmountable fear. She had only one thought, to fly; to fly with all her might, across woods, across fields, to houses, to windows, to lighted candles. Her eyes fell upon the bucket that was before her. Such was the dread with which the Thénardiess inspired her, that she did not dare to go without the bucket of water. She grasped the handle with both hands. She could hardly lift the bucket.

She went a dozen steps in this manner, but the bucket was full, it was heavy, she was compelled to rest it on the ground. She breathed an instant, then grasped the handle again, and walked on, this time a little longer. But she had to stop again. After resting a few seconds, she started on. She walked bending forward, her head down, like an old woman: the weight of the bucket strained and stiffened her thin arms. The iron handle was numbing and freezing her little wet hands; from time to time she had to stop, and every time she stopped, the cold water that splashed from the bucket fell upon her naked knees. This took place in the depth of a wood, at night, in the winter, far from all human sight; it was a child of eight years; there was none but God at that moment who saw this sad thing.

And undoubtedly her mother, alas!

For there are things which open the eyes of the dead in their grave.

She breathed with a kind of mournful rattle; sobs choked her, but she did not dare to weep; so fearful was she of the Thénardiess, even at a distance. She always imagined that the Thénardiess was near.

However, she could not make much headway in this manner, and was getting along very slowly. She tried hard to shorten her resting spells, and to walk as far as possible between them. She remembered with anguish that it would take her more than an hour to return to Montfermeil thus, and that the Thénardiess would beat her. This anguish added to her dismay at being alone in the woods at night. She was worn out with fatigue, and was not yet out of the forest. Arriving near an old chestnut tree which she knew, she made a last halt, longer than the others, to get well rested; then she gathered all her strength, took up the bucket again, and began to walk on courageously. Meanwhile the poor little despairing thing could not help crying: "Oh! my God! my God!"

At that moment she felt all at once that the weight of the bucket was gone. A hand, which seemed enormous to her, had just caught the handle, and was carrying it easily. She raised her head. A large dark form, straight and erect, was walking beside her in the gloom. It was a man who had come up behind her, and whom she had not heard. This man, without saying a word, had grasped the handle of the bucket she was carrying.

There are instincts for all the crises of life.

The child was not afraid.

6

WHICH PERHAPS PROVES THE
INTELLIGENCE OF BOULATRUELLE

IN THE AFTERNOON of that same Christmas-day, 1823, a man walked a long time in the most deserted portion of the Boulevard de l'Hôpital at Paris. This man had the appearance of some one who was looking for lodgings, and seemed to stop by preference before the most modest houses of this dilapidated part of the Faubourg Saint Marceau.

We shall see further on that this man did in fact hire a room in this isolated quarter.

This man, in his dress as in his whole person, realised the type of what might be called the mendicant of good society—extreme misery being combined with extreme neatness. It is a rare coincidence which inspires intelligent hearts with this double respect that we feel for him who is very poor and for him who is very worthy. He wore a round hat, very old and carefully brushed, a long coat, completely threadbare, of coarse yellow cloth, a colour which was in nowise extraordinary at that epoch, a large waistcoat with pockets of antique style, black trousers worn grey at the knees, black woollen stockings, and thick shoes with copper buckles. One would have called him an old preceptor of a good family, returned from the emigration. From his hair, which was entirely white, from his wrinkled brow, from his livid lips, from his face in which everything breathed exhaustion and weariness of life, one would have supposed him considerably over sixty. From his firm though slow step, and the singular vigour impressed upon all his motions, one would hardly have thought him fifty. The wrinkles on his forehead were well disposed, and would have prepossessed in his favour any one who observed him with attention. His lip contracted with a strange expression, which seemed severe and yet which was humble. There was in the depths of his eye an indescribably mournful serenity. He carried in his left hand a small package tied in a handkerchief, with his right he leaned upon a sort of staff cut from a hedge. This staff had been finished with some care, and did not look very badly; the knots were smoothed down, and a coral head had been formed with red wax; it was a cudgel, and it seemed a cane.

There are few people on that boulevard, especially in winter. This man appeared to avoid them rather than seek them, but without affectation.

At a quarter past four, that is to say, after dark, he passed in front of the theatre of the Porte Saint Martin where the play that day was *The Two Convicts*. The poster, lit up by the reflection from the theatre, seemed to strike him, for, although he was walking rapidly, he stopped to read it.

A moment after, he was in the *cul-de-sac* de la Planchette, and entered the
Pewter platter, which was then the office of the Lagny stage. This stage
started at half past four. The horses were harnessed, and the travellers,
who had been called by the driver hastily, were climbing the high iron
steps of the vehicle.

The man asked:

"Have you a seat?"

"Only one, beside me, on the box," said the driver.

"I will take it."

"Get up then."

Before starting, however, the driver cast a glance at the poor apparel of
the traveller, and at the smallness of his bundle, and took his pay.

"Are you going through to Lagny?" asked the driver.

"Yes," said the man.

The traveller paid through to Lagny.

They started off. When they had passed the barrière, the driver tried to
start a conversation, but the traveller answered only in monosyllables. The
driver concluded to whistle, and swear at his horses.

The driver wrapped himself up in his cloak. It was cold. The man did
not appear to notice it. In this way they passed through Gournay and
Neuilly sur Marne. About six o'clock in the evening they were at Chelles.
The driver stopped to let his horses blow, in front of the waggoners' tavern
established in the old buildings of the royal abbey.

"I will get down here," said the man.

He took his bundle and stick, and jumped down from the stage.

A moment afterwards he had disappeared.

He did not go into the tavern.

When, a few minutes afterwards, the stage started off for Lagny, it did
not overtake him in the main street of Chelles.

The man had not sunk into the ground, but he had hurried rapidly in
the darkness along the main street of Chelles; then he had turned to the
left, before reaching the church, into the cross road leading to Montfermeil, like one who knew the country and had been that way before.

He followed this road rapidly. At the spot where it intersects the old
road bordered with trees that goes from Gagny to Lagny, he heard footsteps approaching. He concealed himself hastily in a ditch, and waited
there till the people who were passing were a good distance off. The precaution was indeed almost superfluous, for, as we have already said, it was
a very dark December night. There were scarcely two or three stars to be
seen in the sky.

It is at this point that the ascent of the hill begins. The man did not
return to the Montfermeil road; he turned to the right, across the fields,
and gained the woods with rapid strides.

When he reached the wood, he slackened his pace, and began to look
carefully at all the trees, pausing at every step, as if he were seeking and
following a mysterious route known only to himself. There was a moment
when he appeared to lose himself, and then he stopped, undecided. Finally

he arrived, by continual groping, at a glade where there was a heap of large whitish stones. He made his way quickly towards these stones, and examined them with attention in the dusk of the night, as if he were passing them in review. A large tree, covered with these excrescences which are the warts of vegetation, was a few steps from the heap of stones. He went to this tree, and passed his hand over the bark of the trunk, as if he were seeking to recognise and to count all the warts.

Opposite this tree, which was an ash, there was a chestnut tree wounded in the bark, which had been staunched with a bandage of zinc nailed on. He rose on tip-toe and touched that band of zinc.

Then he stamped for some time upon the ground in the space between the tree and the stones, like one who would be sure that the earth had not been freshly stirred.

This done, he took his course and resumed his walk through the woods.

This was the man who had fallen in with Cosette.

As he made his way through the copse in the direction of Montfermeil, he had perceived that little shadow, struggling along with a groan, setting her burden on the ground, then taking it up and going on again. He had approached her and seen that it was a very young child carrying an enormous bucket of water. Then he had gone to the child, and silently taken hold of the handle of the bucket.

7

COSETTE SIDE BY SIDE WITH THE UNKNOWN, IN THE DARKNESS

COSETTE, we have said, was not afraid.

The man spoke to her. His voice was serious, and was almost a whisper.

"My child, what you are carrying there is very heavy for you."

Cosette raised her head and answered:

"Yes, monsieur."

"Give it to me," the man continued, "I will carry it for you."

Cosette let go of the bucket. The man walked along with her.

"It is very heavy, indeed," said he to himself between his teeth. Then he added:

"Little girl, how old are you?"

"Eight years, monsieur."

"And have you come far in this way?"

"From the spring in the woods."

"And are you going far?"

"A good quarter of an hour from here."

The man remained a moment without speaking, then he said abruptly:

"You have no mother then?"

"I don't know," answered the child.

Before the man had had time to say a word, she added:

"I don't believe I have. All the rest have one. For my part, I have none."

And after a silence, she added:

"I believe I never had any."

The man stopped, put the bucket on the ground, stooped down and placed his hands upon the child's shoulders, making an effort to look at her and see her face in the darkness.

The thin, puny face of Cosette was vaguely outlined in the livid light of the sky.

"What is your name?" said the man.

"Cosette."

It seemed as if the man had an electric shock. He looked at her again, then letting go of her shoulders, took up the bucket, and walked on.

A moment after, he asked:

"Little girl, where do you live?"

"At Montfermeil, if you know it."

"It is there that we are going?"

"Yes, monsieur."

He made another pause, then he began:

"Who is it that has sent you out into the woods after water at this time of night?"

"Madame Thénardier."

The man resumed with a tone of voice which he tried to render indifferent, but in which there was nevertheless a singular tremor:

"What does she do, your Madame Thénardier?"

"She is my mistress," said the child. "She keeps the tavern."

"The tavern," said the man. "Well, I am going there to lodge to-night. Show me the way."

"We are going there," said the child.

The man walked rather fast. Cosette followed him without difficulty. She felt fatigue no more. From time to time, she raised her eyes towards this man with a sort of tranquillity and inexpressible confidence. She had never been taught to turn towards Providence and to pray. However, she felt in her bosom something that resembled hope and joy, and which rose towards heaven.

A few minutes passed. The man spoke:

"Is there no servant at Madame Thénardier's?"

"No, monsieur."

"Are you alone?"

"Yes, monsieur."

There was another interval of silence. Cosette raised her voice:

"That is, there are two little girls."

"What little girls?"

"Ponine and Zelma."

The child simplified in this way the romantic names dear to the mother.

"What are Ponine and Zelma?"

"They are Madame Thénardier's young ladies, you might say her daughters."

"And what do they do?"

"Oh!" said the child, "they have beautiful dolls, things which there's gold in; all kinds of stuff. They play, they amuse themselves."

"All day long?"

"Yes, monsieur."

"And you?"

"Me! I work."

"All day long?"

The child raised her large eyes in which there was a tear, which could not be seen in the darkness, and answered softly:

"Yes, monsieur."

She continued after an interval of silence:

"Sometimes, when I have finished my work and they are willing, I amuse myself also."

"How do you amuse yourself?"

"The best I can. They let me alone. But I have not many playthings. Ponine and Zelma are not willing for me to play with their dolls. I have only a little lead sword, no longer than that."

The child showed her little finger.

"And which does not cut?"

"Yes, monsieur," said the child, "it cuts lettuce and flies' heads."

They reached the village; Cosette guided the stranger through the streets. They passed by the bakery, but Cosette did not think of the bread she was to have brought back. The man questioned her no more, and now maintained a mournful silence. When they had passed the church, the man, seeing all these booths in the street, asked Cosette:

"Is it fair-time here?"

"No, monsieur, it is Christmas."

As they drew near the tavern, Cosette timidly touched his arm:

"Monsieur?"

"What, my child?"

"Here we are close by the house."

"Well?"

"Will you let me take the bucket now?"

"What for?"

"Because, if madame sees that anybody brought it for me, she will beat me."

The man gave her the bucket. A moment after they were at the door of the tavern.

8

INCONVENIENCE OF ENTERTAINING
A POOR MAN WHO IS PERHAPS RICH

COSETTE could not help casting one look towards the grand doll still displayed in the toy-shop, then she rapped. The door opened. The Thénardiess appeared with a candle in her hand.

"Oh! it is you, you little beggar! Lud-a-massy! you have taken your time! she has been playing, the wench!"

"Madame," said Cosette, trembling, "there is a gentleman who is coming to lodge."

The Thénardiess very quickly replaced her fierce air by her amiable grimace, a visible change peculiar to innkeepers, and looked for the newcomer with eager eyes.

"Is it monsieur?" said she.

"Yes, madame," answered the man, touching his hat.

Rich travellers are not so polite. This gesture and the sight of the stranger's costume and baggage which the Thénardiess passed in review at a glance made the amiable grimace disappear and the fierce air reappear. She added drily:

"Enter, goodman."

The "goodman" entered. The Thénardiess cast a second glance at him, examined particularly his long coat which was absolutely threadbare, and his hat which was somewhat broken, and with a nod, a wink, and a turn of her nose, consulted her husband, who was still drinking with the waggoners. The husband answered by that imperceptible shake of the forefinger which, supported by a protrusion of the lips, signifies in such a case: "complete destitution." Upon this the Thénardiess exclaimed:

"Ah! my brave man, I am very sorry, but I have no room."

"Put me where you will," said the man, "in the garret, in the stable. I will pay as if I had a room."

"Forty sous."

"Forty sous. Very well."

"In advance."

"Forty sous," whispered a waggoner to the Thénardiess, "but it is only twenty sous."

"It is forty sous for him," replied the Thénardiess in the same tone. "I don't lodge poor people for less."

"That is true," added her husband softly, "it ruins a house to have this sort of people."

Meanwhile the man, after leaving his stick and bundle on a bench, had seated himself at a table on which Cosette had been quick to place a bottle of wine and a glass. The pedlar, who had asked for the bucket of water, had gone himself to carry it to his horse. Cosette had resumed her place under the kitchen table and her knitting.

The man, who hardly touched his lips to the wine he had poured for himself, was contemplating the child with a strange attentiveness.

Cosette was ugly. Happy, she might, perhaps, have been pretty. We have already sketched this little pitiful face. Cosette was thin and pale; she was nearly eight years old, but one would hardly have thought her six. Her large eyes, sunk in a sort of shadow, were almost completely dulled by continual weeping. The corners of her mouth had that curve of habitual anguish, which is seen in the condemned and in the hopelessly sick. Her hands were, as her mother had guessed, "covered with chilblains." The light of the fire which was shining upon her, made her bones stand out and rendered her thinness fearfully visible. As she was always shivering, she had acquired the habit of drawing her knees together. Her whole dress was nothing but a rag, which would have excited pity in the summer, and which excited horror in the winter. She had on nothing but cotton, and that full of holes; not a rag of woollen. Her skin showed here and there, and black and blue spots could be distinguished, which indicated the places where the Thénardiess had touched her. Her naked legs were red and rough. The hollows under her collar bones would make one weep. The whole person of this child, her gait, her attitude, the sound of her voice, the intervals between one word and another, her looks, her silence, her least motion, expressed and uttered a single idea: fear.

Fear was spread all over her; she was, so to say, covered with it; fear drew back her elbows against her sides, drew her heels under her skirt, made her take the least possible room, prevented her from breathing more than was absolutely necessary, and had become what might be called her bodily habit, without possible variation, except of increase. There was in the depth of her eye an expression of astonishment mingled with terror.

This fear was such that on coming in, all wet as she was, Cosette had not dared go and dry herself by the fire, but had gone silently to her work.

The expression of the countenance of this child of eight years was habitually so sad and sometimes so tragical that it seemed, at certain moments, as if she were in the way of becoming an idiot or a demon.

Never, as we have said, had she known what it is to pray, never had she set foot within a church. "How can I spare the time?" said the Thénardiess.

The man in the yellow coat did not take his eyes from Cosette.

Suddenly, the Thénardiess exclaimed out:

"Oh! I forgot! that bread!"

Cosette, according to her custom whenever the Thénardiess raised her voice, sprang out quickly from under the table.

She had entirely forgotten the bread. She had recourse to the expedient of children who are always terrified. She lied.

"Madame, the baker was shut."

"You ought to have knocked."

"I did knock, madame."

"Well?"

"He didn't open."

"I'll find out to-morrow if that is true," said the Thénardiess, "and if you are lying you will lead a pretty dance. Meantime give me back the fifteen-sous coin."

Cosette plunged her hand into her apron pocket, and turned white. The fifteen-sous coin was not there.

"Come," said the Thénardiess, "didn't you hear me?"

Cosette turned her pocket inside out; there was nothing there. What could have become of that money? The little unfortunate could not utter a word. She was petrified.

"Have you lost it, the fifteen-sous coin?" screamed the Thénardiess, "or do you want to steal it from me?"

At the same time she reached her arm towards the cowhide hanging in the chimney corner.

This menacing movement gave Cosette the strength to cry out:

"Forgive me! Madame! Madame! I won't do so any more!"

The Thénardiess took down the whip.

Meanwhile the man in the yellow coat had been fumbling in his waist-coat pocket, without being noticed. The other travellers were drinking or playing cards, and paid no attention to anything.

Cosette was writhing with anguish in the chimney-corner, trying to gather up and hide her poor half-naked limbs. The Thénardiess raised her arm.

"I beg your pardon, madame," said the man, "but I just now saw something fall out of the pocket of that little girl's apron and roll away. That may be it."

At the same time he stooped down and appeared to search on the floor for an instant.

"Just so, here it is," said he, rising.

And he handed a silver coin to the Thénardiess.

"Yes, that is it," said she.

That was not it, for it was a twenty-sous coin, but the Thénardiess found her profit in it. She put the coin in her pocket, and contented herself with casting a ferocious look at the child and saying:

"Don't let that happen again, ever."

Cosette went back to what the Thénardiess called "her hole," and her large eye, fixed upon the unknown traveller, began to assume an expression that it had never known before. It was still only an artless astonishment, but a sort of blind confidence was associated with it.

"O! you want supper?" asked the Thénardiess of the traveller.

He did not answer. He seemed to be thinking deeply.

"What is that man?" said she between her teeth. "It is some frightful pauper. He hasn't a penny for his supper. Is he going to pay me for his lodging only? It is very lucky, anyway, that he didn't think to steal the money that was on the floor."

A door now opened, and Eponine and Azelma came in.

They were really two pretty little girls, rather city girls than peasants, very charming, one with her well-polished auburn tresses, the other with her long black braids falling down her back and both so lively, neat, plump, fresh, and healthy, that it was a pleasure to see them. They were warmly clad, but with such maternal art, that the thickness of the stuff detracted nothing from the coquetry of the fit. Winter was provided against without effacing spring. These two little girls shed light around them. Moreover, they reigned. In their toilet, in their gaiety, in the noise they made, there was sovereignty. When they entered, the Thénardiess said to them in a scolding tone, which was full of adoration: "Ah! you are here then, you children!"

Then, taking them upon her knees one after the other, smoothing their hair, tying over their ribbons, and finally letting them go with that gentle sort of shake which is peculiar to mothers, she exclaimed:

"Are they dowdies!"

They went and sat down by the fire. They had a doll which they turned backwards and forwards upon their knees with many pretty prattlings. From time to time, Cosette raised her eyes from her knitting, and looked sadly at them as they were playing.

Eponine and Azelma did not notice Cosette. To them she was like the dog. These three little girls could not count twenty-four years among them all, and they already represented all human society; on one side envy, on the other disdain.

The doll of the Thénardier sisters was very much faded, and very old and broken; and it appeared none the less wonderful to Cosette, who had never in her life had a doll, *a real doll,* to use an expression that all children will understand.

All at once, the Thénardiess, who was continually going and coming about the room, noticed that Cosette's attention was distracted, and that instead of working she was watching the little girls who were playing.

"Ah! I've caught you!" cried she. "That is the way you work! I'll make you work with the strap, I will."

The stranger, without leaving his chair, turned towards the Thénardiess.

"Madame," said he, smiling diffidently. "Pshaw! let her play!"

On the part of any traveller who had eaten a slice of mutton, and drunk two bottles of wine at his supper, and who had not had the appearance of *a horrid pauper,* such a wish would have been a command. But that a man who wore that hat should allow himself to have a desire, and that a man who wore that coat should permit himself to have a wish, was what the Thénardiess thought ought not to be tolerated. She replied sharply:

"She must work, for she eats. I don't support her to do nothing."

"What is it she is making?" said the stranger, in that gentle voice which contrasted so strangely with his beggar's clothes and his porter's shoulders.

The Thénardiess deigned to answer.

"Stockings, if you please. Stockings for my little girls who have none, worth speaking of, and will soon be going barefooted."

The man looked at Cosette's poor red feet, and continued:

"When will she finish that pair of stockings?"

"It will take her at least three or four good days, the lazy thing."

"And how much might this pair of stockings be worth, when it is finished?"

The Thénardiess cast a disdained glance at him.

"At least thirty sous."

"Would you take five francs for them?" said the man.

"Goodness!" exclaimed a waggoner who was listening, with a horse-laugh, "five francs? It's a humbug! five bullets!"

Thénardier now thought it time to speak.

"Yes, monsieur, if it is your fancy, you can have that pair of stockings for five francs. We can't refuse anything to travellers."

"You must pay for them now," said the Thénardiess, in her short and peremptory way.

"I will buy that pair of stockings," answered the man, "and," added he, drawing a five-franc coin from his pocket and laying it on the table, "I will pay for them."

Then he turned towards Cosette.

"Now your work belongs to me. Play, my child."

The waggoner was so affected by the five-franc coin, that he left his glass and went to look at it.

"It's so, that's a fact!" cried he, as he looked at it. "A regular hindwheel! and no counterfeit!"

Thénardier approached, and silently put the coin in his pocket.

The Thénardiess had nothing to reply. She bit her lips, and her face assumed an expression of hatred.

Meanwhile Cosette trembled. She ventured to ask:

"Madame, is it true? can I play?"

"Play!" said the Thénardiess in a terrible voice.

"Thank you, madame," said Cosette. And, while her mouth thanked the Thénardiess, all her little soul was thanking the traveller.

Thénardier returned to his drink. His wife whispered in his ear:

"What can that yellow man be?"

"I have seen," answered Thénardier, in a commanding tone, "million-aires with coats like that."

Cosette had left her knitting, but she had not moved from her place. Cosette always stirred as little as was possible. She had taken from a little box behind her a few old rags, and her little lead sword.

Eponine and Azelma paid no attention to what was going on. They had just performed a very important operation; they had caught the kitten. They had thrown the doll on the floor, and Eponine, the elder, was dressing the kitten, in spite of her mewings and contortions, with a lot of clothes and red and blue rags. While she was engaged in this serious and difficult labour, she was talking to her sister in that sweet and charming language of children, the grace of which, like the splendour of the butterfly's wings, escapes when we try to preserve it.

"Look! look, sister, this doll is more amusing than the other. She moves, she cries, she is warm. Come, sister, let us play with her. She shall be my little girl; I will be a lady. I'll come to see you, and you must look at her. By and by you must see her whiskers, and you must be surprised. And then you must see her ears, and then you must see her tail, and that will astonish you. And you must say to me: 'Oh! my stars!' and I will say to you, 'Yes, madame, it is a little girl that I have like that.' Little girls are like that now."

Azelma listened to Eponine with wonder.

Meanwhile, the drinkers were singing an obscene song, at which they laughed enough to shake the room. Thénardier encouraged and accompanied them.

As birds make a nest of anything, children make a doll of no matter what. While Eponine and Azelma were dressing up the cat, Cosette, for her part, had dressed up the sword. That done, she had laid it upon her arm, and was singing it softly to sleep.

The doll is one of the most imperious necessities, and at the same time one of the most charming instincts of female childhood. To care for, to clothe, to adorn, to dress, to undress, to dress over again, to teach, to scold a little, to rock, to cuddle, to put to sleep, to imagine that something is somebody—all the future of woman is there. Even while musing and prattling, while making little wardrobes and little baby-clothes, while sewing little dresses, little bodices, and little jackets, the child becomes a little girl, the little girl becomes a big girl, the big girl becomes a woman. The first baby takes the place of the last doll.

A little girl without a doll is almost as unfortunate and quite as impossible as a woman without children.

Cosette had therefore made a doll of her sword.

The Thénardiess, on her part, approached the *yellow man*. "My husband is right," thought she; "it may be Monsieur Laffitte. Some rich men are so odd."

She came and rested her elbow on the table at which he was sitting.

"Monsieur," said she——

At this word *monsieur,* the man turned. The Thénardiess had called him before only *brave man* or *good man*.

"You see, monsieur," she pursued, putting on her cloying look, which was still more unendurable than her ferocious manner, "I am very willing the child should play, I am not opposed to it; it is well for once, because you are generous. But, you see, she is poor; she must work."

"The child is not yours, then?" asked the man.

"Oh dear! no, monsieur! It is a little pauper that we have taken in through charity. A sort of imbecile child. She must have water on her brain. Her head is big, as you see. We do all we can for her, but we are not rich. It's no use writing to where she comes from; for six months we have had no answer. We think that her mother must be dead."

"Ah!" said the man, and he fell back into his reverie.

"This mother was no great shakes," added the Thénardiess. "She abandoned her child."

During all this conversation, Cosette, as if an instinct had warned her that they were talking about her, had not taken her eyes from the Thénardiess. She listened. She heard a few words here and there.

Meanwhile the drinkers, all three-quarters drunk, were repeating their foul chorus with redoubled gaiety. It was highly spiced with jests, in which the names of the Virgin and the child Jesus were often heard. The Thénardiess had gone to take her part in the hilarity. Cosette, under the table, was looking into the fire, which was reflected from her fixed eye; she was again rocking the sort of rag baby that she had made, and as she rocked it, she sang in a low voice; "My mother is dead! my mother is dead! my mother is dead!"

At the repeated entreaties of the hostess, the yellow man, "the millionaire," finally consented to sup.

"What will monsieur have?"

"Some bread and cheese," said the man.

"Decidedly, it is a beggar," thought the Thénardiess.

The revellers continued to sing their songs, and the child, under the table, also sang hers.

All at once, Cosette stopped. She had just turned and seen the little Thenardiers' doll, which they had forsaken for the cat and left on the floor, a few steps from the kitchen table.

Then she let the bundled-up sword, that only half satisfied her, fall, and ran her eyes slowly around the room. The Thénardiess was whispering to her husband and counting some money, Eponine and Azelma were playing with the cat, the travellers were eating or drinking or singing, nobody was looking at her. She had not a moment to lose. She crept out from under the table on her hands and knees, made sure once more that nobody was watching her, then darted quickly to the doll, and seized it. An instant afterwards she was at her place, seated, motionless, only turned in such a way as to keep the doll that she held in her arms in the shadow. The happiness of playing with a doll was so rare to her that it had all the violence of rapture.

Nobody had seen her, except the traveller, who was slowly eating his meagre supper.

This joy lasted for nearly a quarter of an hour.

But in spite of Cosette's precautions, she did not perceive that one of the doll's feet *stuck out,* and that the fire of the fireplace lighted it up very vividly. This rosy and luminous foot which protruded from the shadow suddenly caught Azelma's eye, and she said to Eponine: "Oh! sister!"

The two little girls stopped, stupefied; Cosette had dared to take the doll.

Eponine got up, and without letting go of the cat, went to her mother and began to pull at her skirt.

"Let me alone," said the mother; "what do you want?"

"Mother," said the child, "look there."

And she pointed at Cosette.

Cosette, wholly absorbed in the ecstasy of her possession, saw and heard nothing else.

The face of the Thénardiess assumed the peculiar expression which is composed of the terrible mingled with the commonplace and which has given this class of women the name of shrews.

This time wounded pride exasperated her anger still more. Cosette had transgressed all social limits. Cosette had laid her hands upon the doll of "those young ladies." A czarina who had seen a moujik trying on the grand cordon of her imperial son would have had the same expression.

She cried with a voice harsh with indignation:

"Cosette!"

Cosette shuddered as if the earth had quaked beneath her. She turned around.

"Cosette!" repeated the Thénardiess.

Cosette took the doll and placed it gently on the floor with a kind of veneration mingled with despair. Then, without taking away her eyes, she joined her hands, and, what is frightful to tell in a child of that age, she wrung them; then, what none of the emotions of the day had drawn from her, neither the run in the wood, nor the weight of the bucket of water, nor the loss of the money, nor the sight of the cowhide, nor even the stern words she had heard from the Thénardiess, she burst into tears. She sobbed.

Meanwhile the traveller arose.

"What is the matter?" said he to the Thénardiess.

"Don't you see?" said the Thénardiess, pointing with her finger to the *corpus delicti* lying at Cosette's feet.

"Well, what is that?" said the man.

"That beggar," answered the Thénardiess, "has dared to touch the children's doll."

"All this noise about that?" said the man. "Well, what if she did play with that doll?"

"She has touched it with her dirty hands!" continued the Thénardiess, "with her horrid hands!"

Here Cosette redoubled her sobs.

"Be still!" cried the Thénardiess.

The man walked straight to the street door, opened it, and went out.

As soon as he had gone, the Thénardiess profited by his absence to give Cosette under the table a severe kick, which made the child shriek.

The door opened again, and the man reappeared, holding in his hands the fabulous doll of which we have spoken, and which had been the admiration of all the youngsters of the village since morning; he stood it up before Cosette, saying:

"Here, this is for you."

It is probable that during the time he had been there—more than an hour—in the midst of his reverie, he had caught confused glimpses of this toy-shop, lighted up with lamps and candles so splendidly that it shone through the bar-room window like an illumination.

Cosette raised her eyes; she saw the man approach her with that doll as she would have seen the sun approach her, she heard those astounding words: *This is for you.* She looked at him, she looked at the doll, then she drew back slowly, and went and hid as far as she could under the table in the corner of the room.

She wept no more, she cried no more, she had the appearance of no longer daring to breathe.

The Thénardiess, Eponine, and Azelma were so many statues. Even the drinkers stopped. There was a solemn silence in the whole bar-room.

The Thénardiess, petrified and mute, recommenced her conjectures anew: "What is this old fellow? is he a pauper? is he a millionaire? Perhaps he's both, that is a robber."

The face of the husband Thénardier presented that expressive wrinkle which marks the human countenance whenever the dominant instinct appears in it with all its brutal power. The innkeeper contemplated by turns the doll and the traveller; he seemed to be scenting this man as he would have scented a bag of money. This only lasted for a moment. He approached his wife and whispered to her:

"That gadget cost at least thirty francs. No nonsense. Down on your knees before the man!"

Coarse natures have this in common with artless natures, that they have no transitions.

"Well, Cosette," said the Thénardiess in a voice which was meant to be sweet, and which was entirely composed of the sour honey of vicious women, "a'n't you going to take your doll?"

Cosette ventured to come out of her hole.

"My little Cosette," said Thénardier with a caressing air, "Monsieur gives you a doll. Take it. It is yours."

Cosette looked upon the wonderful doll with a sort of terror. Her face was still flooded with tears, but her eyes began to fill, like the sky in the breaking of the dawn, with strange radiations of joy. What she experienced at that moment was almost like what she would have felt if some one had said to her suddenly: Little girl, you are queen of France.

It seemed to her that if she touched that doll, thunder would spring forth from it.

Which was true to some extent, for she thought that the Thénardiess would scold and beat her.

However, the attraction overcame her. She finally approached and timidly murmured, turning towards the Thénardiess:

"Can I, madame?"

No expression can describe her look, at once full of despair, dismay, and transport.

"Good Lord!" said the Thénardiess, "it is yours. Since monsieur gives it to you."

"Is it true, is it true, monsieur?" said Cosette; "is the lady for me?"

The stranger appeared to have his eyes full of tears. He seemed to be at that stage of emotion in which one does not speak for fear of weeping. He nodded assent to Cosette, and put the hand of "the lady" in her little hand.

Cosette withdrew her hand hastily, as if that of *the lady* burned her, and looked down at the floor. We are compelled to add, that at that instant she thrust out her tongue enormously. All at once she turned, and seized the doll eagerly.

"I will call her Catharine," said she.

It was a strange moment when Cosette's rags met and pressed against the ribbons and the fresh pink muslins of the doll.

"Madame," said she, "may I put her in a chair?"

"Yes, my child," answered the Thénardiess.

It was Eponine and Azelma now who looked upon Cosette with envy.

Cosette placed Catharine on a chair, then sat down on the floor before her, and remained motionless, without saying a word, in the attitude of contemplation.

"Why don't you play, Cosette?" said the stranger.

"Oh! I am playing," answered the child.

This stranger, this unknown man, who seemed like a visit from Providence to Cosette, was at that moment the being which the Thénardiess hated more than aught else in the world. However, she was compelled to restrain herself. Her emotions were more than she could endure, accustomed as she was to dissimulation, by endeavouring to copy her husband in all her actions. She sent her daughters to bed immediately, then asked the yellow man's *permission* to send Cosette to bed—*who is very tired to-day,* added she, with a motherly air. Cosette went to bed, holding Catharine in her arms.

The Thénardiess went from time to time to the other end of the room, where her husband was, *to vent her feelings,* she said. She exchanged a few words with him, which were the more furious that she did not dare to speak them aloud:—

"The old fool! what has he got into his head, to come here to disturb us! to want that little monster to play! to give her dolls! to give forty-franc dolls to a slut that I wouldn't give forty sous for. A little more, and he would say your majesty to her, as they do to the Duchess of Berry! Is he in his senses? he must be crazy, the strange old fellow!"

"Why? It is very simple," replied Thénardier. "If it amuses him! It amuses you for the girl to work; it amuses him for her to play. He has the right to do it. A traveller can do as he likes, if he pays. If this old fellow is a philanthropist, what is that to you? if he is crazy it don't concern you. What do you interfere for, as long as he has money?"

Language of a master and reasoning of an innkeeper, which neither in one case nor the other admits of reply.

The man had leaned his elbows on the table, and resumed his attitude of reverie. All the other travellers, pedlars, and waggoners, had drawn back a little, and sung no more. They looked upon him from a distance with a sort of respectful fear.

This solitary man, so poorly clad, who took five-franc coins from his pocket with so much indifference, and who lavished gigantic dolls on little brats in wooden shoes, was certainly a magnificent and formidable "good-fellow."

Several hours passed away. The midnight mass was said, the revel was finished, the drinkers had gone, the house was closed, the room was deserted, the fire had gone out, the stranger still remained in the same place and in the same posture. From time to time he changed the elbow on which he rested. That was all. But he had not spoken a word since Cosette was gone.

The Thénardiers alone out of propriety and curiosity, had remained in the room.

"Is he going to spend the night like this?" grumbled the Thénardiess. When the clock struck two in the morning, she acknowledged herself beaten, and said to her husband: "I am going to bed, you may do as you like." The husband sat down at a table in a corner, lighted a candle, and began to read the *Courrier Français*.

A good hour passed thus. The worthy innkeeper had read the *Courrier Français* at least three times, from the date of the number to the name of the printer. The stranger did not stir.

Thénardier moved, coughed, spit, blew his nose, and creaked his chair. The man did not stir. "Is he asleep?" thought Thénardier. The man was not asleep, but nothing could arouse him.

Finally, Thénardier took off his cap, approached softly, and ventured to say:—

"Is monsieur not going to repose?"

Not going to bed would have seemed to him too much and too familiar. To *repose* implied luxury, and there was respect in it. Such words have the mysterious and wonderful property of swelling the bill in the morning. A room in which you go *to bed* costs twenty sous; a room in which you *repose* costs twenty francs.

"Yes," said the stranger, "you are right. Where is your stable?"

"Monsieur," said Thénardier, with a smile, "I will conduct monsieur."

He took the candle, the man took his bundle and his staff, and Thénardier led him into a room on the first floor, which was very showy, furnished all in mahogany, with a high-post bedstead and red calico curtains.

"What is this?" said the traveller.

"It is properly our bridal chamber," said the innkeeper. "We occupy another like this, my spouse and I; this is not open more than three or four times in a year."

"I should have liked the stable as well," said the man, bluntly.

Thénardier did not appear to hear this not very civil answer.

He lighted two entirely new wax candles, which were displayed upon the mantel; a good fire was blazing in the fireplace. There was on the mantel, under a glass case, a woman's head-dress of silver thread and orange-flowers.

"What is this?" said the stranger.

"Monsieur," said Thénardier, "it is my wife's bridal cap."

The traveller looked at the object with a look which seemed to say: "there was a moment, then, when this monster was a virgin."

Thénardier lied, however. When he hired this shanty to turn it into a tavern, he found the room thus furnished, and bought this furniture, and purchased at second-hand these orange-flowers, thinking that this would cast a gracious light over "his spouse," and that the house would derive from them what the English call respectability.

When the traveller turned again the host had disappeared. Thénardier had discreetly taken himself out of the way without daring to say good-night, not desiring to treat with a disrespectful cordiality a man whom he proposed to skin royally in the morning.

The innkeeper retired to his room; his wife was in bed, but not asleep. When she heard her husband's step, she turned towards him and said:

"You know that I am going to kick Cosette out doors to-morrow."

Thénardier coolly answered:

"You are, indeed!"

They exchanged no further words, and in a few moments their candle was blown out.

For his part, the traveller had put his staff and bundle in a corner. The host gone, he sat down in an arm-chair, and remained some time thinking. Then he drew off his shoes, took one of the two candles, blew out the other, pushed open the door, and went out of the room, looking about him as if he were searching for something. He passed through a hall, and came to the stairway. There he heard a very soft little sound, which resembled the breathing of a child. Guided by this sound he came to a sort of triangular nook built under the stairs, or, rather, formed by the staircase itself. This hole was nothing but the space beneath the stairs. There, among all sorts of old baskets and old rubbish, in the dust and among the cobwebs, there was a bed; if a mattress so full of holes as to show the straw, and a covering so full of holes as to show the mattress, can be called a bed. There were no sheets. This was placed on the floor immediately on the tiles. In this bed Cosette was sleeping.

The man approached and looked at her.

Cosette was sleeping soundly; she was dressed. In the winter she did not undress on account of the cold. She held the doll clasped in her arms; its large open eyes shone in the obscurity. From time to time she heaved a deep sigh, as if she were about to wake, and she hugged the doll almost convulsively. There was only one of her wooden shoes at the side of her bed. An open door near Cosette's nook disclosed a large dark room. The stranger entered. At the further end, through a glass window, he perceived two little beds with very white spreads. They were those of Azelma and Eponine. Half hid behind these beds was a willow cradle without curtains, in which the little boy who had cried all the evening was sleeping.

The stranger conjectured that this room communicated with that of the Thénardiers. He was about to withdraw when his eye fell upon the fireplace, one of those huge tavern fireplaces where there is always so little fire, when there is a fire, and which are so cold to look upon. In this one there was no fire, there were not even any ashes. What there was, however, attracted the traveller's attention. It was two little children's shoes, of coquettish shape and of different sizes. The traveller remembered the graceful and immemorial custom of children putting their shoes in the fireplace on Christmas night, to wait there in the darkness in expectation of some shining gift from their good fairy. Eponine and Azelma had taken good care not to forget this, and each had put one of her shoes in the fireplace.

The traveller bent over them.

The fairy—that is to say, the mother—had already made her visit, and shining in each shoe was a beautiful new ten-sous coin.

The man rose up and was on the point of going away, when he perceived further along, by itself, in the darkest corner of the fireplace, another object. He looked, and recognised a shoe, a horrid wooden shoe of the clumsiest sort, half broken and covered with ashes and dried mud. It was Cosette's shoe. Cosette, with that touching confidence of childhood which can always be deceived without ever being discouraged, had also placed her shoe in the fireplace.

What a sublime and sweet thing is hope in a child who has never known anything but despair!

There was nothing in this wooden shoe.

The stranger fumbled in his waistcoat, bent over, and dropped into Cosette's shoe a gold Louis.

Then he went back to his room with stealthy tread.

9

THÉNARDIER MANŒUVRING

ON THE following morning, at least two hours before day, Thénardier, seated at a table in the bar-room, a candle by his side with pen in hand, was making out the bill of the traveller in the yellow coat.

His wife was standing, half bent over him, following him with her eyes. Not a word passed between them. It was, on one side, a profound meditation, on the other that religious admiration with which we observe a marvel of the human mind spring up and expand. A noise was heard in the house; it was the lark, sweeping the stairs.

After a good quarter of an hour and some erasures, Thénardier produced this masterpiece.

Bill of Monsieur in No. 1.

Supper	3 frs.
Room	10 frs.
Candle	5 frs.
Fire	4 frs.
Service	1 frs.
Total.	23 frs.

Service was written *servisse.*

"Twenty-three francs!" exclaimed the woman, with an enthusiasm which was mingled with some hesitation.

Like all great artists, Thénardier was not satisfied.

"Pooh!" said he.

It was the accent of Castlereagh drawing up for the Congress of Vienna the bill which France was to pay.

"Monsieur Thénardier, you are right, he deserves it," murmured the woman, thinking of the doll given to Cosette in the presence of her daughters; "it is right! but it's too much. He won't pay it."

Thénardier put on his cold laugh, and said: "He will pay it."

This laugh was the highest sign of certainty and authority. What was thus said, must be. The woman did not insist. She began to arrange the tables; the husband walked back and forth in the room. A moment after he added:

"I owe, at least, fifteen hundred francs!"

He seated himself thoughtfully in the chimney corner, his feet in the warm ashes.

"Ah ha!" replied the woman, "you don't forget that I kick Cosette out of the house to-day? The monster! it tears my vitals to see her with her doll! I would rather marry Louis XVIII, than keep her in the house another day!"

Thénardier lighted his pipe, and answered between two puffs:

"You'll give the bill to the man."

Then he went out.

He was scarcely out of the room when the traveller came in.

Thénardier reappeared immediately behind him, and remained motionless in the half-open door, visible only to his wife.

The yellow man carried his staff and bundle in his hand.

"Up so soon!" said the Thénardiess; "is monsieur going to leave us already?"

While speaking, she turned the bill in her hands with an embarrassed look, and made creases in it with her nails. Her hard face exhibited a shade of timidity and doubt that was not habitual.

To present such a bill to a man who had so perfectly the appearance of "a pauper" seemed too awkward to her.

The traveller appeared pre-occupied and absent-minded.

He answered:

"Yes, madame, I am going away."

"Monsieur, then, had no business at Montfermeil?" replied she.

"No, I am passing through; that is all. Madame," added he, "what do I owe?"

The Thénardiess, without answering, handed him the folded bill.

The man unfolded the paper and looked at it; but his thoughts were evidently elsewhere.

"Madame," replied he, "do you do a good business in Montfermeil?"

"So-so, monsieur," answered the Thénardiess, stupefied at seeing no other explosion.

She continued in a mournful and lamenting strain:

"Oh! monsieur, the times are very hard, and then we have so few rich people around here! It is a very little place, you see. If we only had rich travellers now and then, like monsieur! We have so many expenses! Why, that little girl eats us out of house and home."

"What little girl?"

"Why, the little girl you know! Cosette! the Lark, as they call her about here!"

"Ah!" said the man.

She continued:

"How stupid these peasants are with their nicknames! She looks more like a bat than a lark. You see, monsieur, we don't ask charity, but we are not able to give it. We make nothing, and have a great deal to pay. The licence, the excise, the doors and windows, the tax on everything! Monsieur knows that the government demands a deal of money. And then I have my own girls. I have nothing to spend on other people's children."

The man replied in a voice which he endeavoured to render indifferent, and in which there was a slight tremulousness.

"Suppose you were relieved of her?"

"Who? Cosette?"

"Yes."

The red and violent face of the woman became illumined with a hideous expression.

"Ah, monsieur! my good monsieur! take her, keep her, take her away, carry her off, sugar her, stuff her, drink her, eat her, and be blessed by the holy Virgin and all the saints in Paradise!"

"Agreed."

"Really! you will take her away?"

"I will."

"Immediately?"

"Immediately. Call the child."

"Cosette!" cried the Thénardiess.

"In the meantime," continued the man, "I will pay my bill. How much is it?"

He cast a glance at the bill, and could not repress a movement of surprise.

"Twenty-three francs?"

He looked at the hostess and repeated:

"Twenty-three francs?"

There was, in the pronunciation of these two sentences, thus repeated, the accent which lies between the point of exclamation and the point of interrogation.

The Thénardiess had had time to prepare herself for the shock. She replied with assurance:

"Yes, of course, monsieur! it is twenty-three francs."

The stranger placed five five-franc coins upon the table.

"Go for the little girl," said he.

At this moment Thénardier advanced into the middle of the room and said:

"Monsieur owes twenty-six sous."[2]

"Twenty-six sous!" exclaimed the woman.

"Twenty sous for the room," continued Thénardier coldly, "and six for supper. As to the little girl, I must have some talk with monsieur about that. Leave us, wife."

The Thénardiess was dazzled by one of those unexpected flashes which emanate from talent. She felt that the great actor had entered upon the scene, answered not a word, and went out.

As soon as they were alone, Thénardier offered the traveller a chair. The traveller sat down, but Thénardier remained standing and his face assumed a singular expression of good-nature and simplicity.

"Monsieur," said he, "listen, I must say that I adore this child."

The stranger looked at him steadily.

"What child?"

Thénardier continued:

"How strangely we become attached! What is all this silver? Take back your money. This child I adore."

"Who is that?" asked the stranger.

"Oh, our little Cosette! And you wish to take her away from us? Indeed, I speak frankly, as true as you are an honourable man, I cannot consent to it. I should miss her. I have had her since she was very small. It is true, she costs us money; it is true she has her faults, it is true we are not rich, it is true I paid four hundred francs for medicines at one time when she was sick. But we must do something for God. She has neither father nor mother; I have brought her up. I have bread enough for her and for myself. In fact, I must keep this child. You understand, we have affections; I am a good beast; myself, I do not reason; I love this little girl; my wife is impulsive, but she loves her also. You see, she is like our own child. I feel the need of her prattle in the house."

The stranger was looking steadily at him all the while. He continued:

"Pardon me, excuse me, monsieur, but one does not give his child like that to a traveller. Isn't it true that I am right? After that, I don't say—you are rich and have the appearance of a very fine man—if it is for her advantage,—but I must know about it. You understand? On the supposition that I should let her go and sacrifice my own feelings, I should want to know where she is going. I would not want to lose sight of her, I should want to know who she was with, that I might come and see her now and then, and that she might know that her good foster-father was still watching over her. Finally, there are things which are not possible. I do not know even your name. If you should take her away, I should say, alas for the little Lark, where has she gone? I must, at least, see some poor rag of paper, a bit of a passport, something."

The stranger, without removing from him this gaze which went, so to speak, to the bottom of his conscience, answered in a severe and firm tone.

"Monsieur Thénardier, people do not take a passport to come five leagues from Paris. If I take Cosette, I take her, that is all. You will not know my name, you will not know my abode, you will not know where she goes, and my intention is that she shall never see you again in her life. I'll cut the rope she's tethered by, and off she goes. Do you agree to that? Yes or no?"

As demons and genii recognise by certain signs the presence of a superior God, Thénardier comprehended that he was to deal with one who was very powerful. It came like an intuition; he understood it with his clear and quick sagacity; although during the evening he had been drinking with the waggoners, smoking, and singing bawdy songs, still he was observing the stranger all the while, watching him like a cat, and studying him like a mathematician. He had been observing him on his own account, for pleasure and by instinct, and at the same time lying in wait as if he had been paid for it. Not a gesture, not a movement of the man in the yellow coat had escaped him. Before even the stranger had so clearly shown his interest in Cosette, Thénardier had divined it. He had surprised the searching glances of the old man constantly returning to the child. Why this interest? What was this man? Why, with so much money in his purse, this miserable dress? These were questions which he put to himself without being able to answer them, and they irritated him. He had been thinking it over all night. This could not be Cosette's father. Was it a grandfather? Then why did he not make himself known at once? When a man has a right, he shows it. This man evidently had no right to Cosette. Then who was he? Thénardier was lost in conjectures. He caught glimpses of everything, but saw nothing. However it might be, when he commenced the conversation with this man, sure that there was a secret in all this, sure that the man had an interest in remaining unknown, he felt himself strong; at the stranger's clear and firm answer, when he saw that this mysterious personage was mysterious and nothing more, he felt weak. He was expecting nothing of the kind. His conjectures were put to flight. He rallied his ideas. He weighed all in a second. Thénardier was one of those men who comprehend a situation at a glance. He decided that this was the moment to advance straightforward and swiftly. He did what great captains do at that decisive instant which they alone can recognise; he unmasked his battery at once.

"Monsieur," said he, "I must have fifteen hundred francs."

The stranger took from his side-pocket an old black leather pocket-book, opened it, and drew forth three bank bills which he placed upon the table. He then rested his large thumb on these bills, and said to the tavern-keeper.

"Bring Cosette."

While this was going on what was Cosette doing?

Cosette, as soon as she awoke, had run to her wooden shoe. She had found the gold coin in it. It was not a Napoleon, but one of those new twenty-franc coins of the Restoration, on the face of which the little Prussian queue had replaced the laurel crown. Cosette was dazzled. Her destiny began to intoxicate her. She did not know that it was a coin of gold; she had never seen one before; she hastily concealed it in her pocket as if she had stolen it. Nevertheless she felt it boded good to her. She divined whence the gift came, but she experienced a joy that was filled with awe.

She was gratified; she was moreover stupefied. Such magnificent and beautiful things seemed unreal to her. The doll made her afraid, the gold coin made her afraid. She trembled with wonder before these magnificences. Only the stranger did not make her afraid. On the contrary, he reassured her. Since the previous evening, amid all her astonishment, and in her sleep, she was thinking in her little child's mind of this man who had such an old, and poor, and sad appearance, and who was so rich and so kind. Since she had met this goodman in the wood, it seemed as though all things were changed about her. Cosette, less happy than the least swallow of the sky, had never known what it is to take refuge under a mother's wing. For five years, that is to say, as far back as she could remember, the poor child had shivered and shuddered. She had always been naked under the biting north wind of misfortune, and now it seemed to her that she was clothed. Before her soul was cold, now it was warm. Cosette was no longer afraid of the Thénardiers; she was no longer alone; she had somebody to look to.

She hurriedly set herself to her morning task. This louis, which she had placed in the same pocket of her apron from which the fifteen-sous coin had fallen the night before, distracted her attention from her work. She did not dare to touch it, but she spent five minutes at a time contemplating it, and we must confess, with her tongue thrust out. While sweeping the stairs, she stopped and stood there, motionless, forgetting her broom, and the whole world besides, occupied in looking at this shining star at the bottom of her pocket.

It was in one of these reveries that the Thénardiess found her.

At the command of her husband, she had gone to look for her. Wonderful to tell, she did not give her a slap nor even call her a hard name. "Cosette," said she, almost gently, "come quick."

An instant after, Cosette entered the bar-room.

The stranger took the bundle he had brought and untied it. This bundle contained a little woollen frock, an apron, a coarse cotton under-garment, a petticoat, a scarf, woollen stockings, and shoes—a complete dress for a girl of seven years. It was all in black.

"My child," said the man, "take this and go and dress yourself quick."

The day was breaking when those of the inhabitants of Montfermeil who were beginning to open their doors, saw pass on the road to Paris a poorly clad goodman leading a little girl dressed in mourning who had a pink doll in her arms. They were going towards Livry.

It was the stranger and Cosette.

No one recognised the man; as Cosette was not now in tatters, few recognised her.

Cosette was going away. With whom? She was ignorant. Where? She knew not. All she understood was, that she was leaving behind the Thénardier tavern. Nobody had thought of bidding her good-by, nor had she of bidding good-by to anybody. She went out from that house, hated and hating.

Poor gentle being, whose heart had only been crushed hitherto.

Cosette walked seriously along, opening her large eyes, and looking at the sky. She had put her louis in the pocket of her new apron. From time to time she bent over and cast a glance at it, and then looked at the goodman. She felt somewhat as if she were near God.

10

WHO SEEKS THE BEST MAY FIND THE WORST

THE THÉNARDIESS, according to her custom, had left her husband alone. She was expecting great events. When the man and Cosette were gone, Thénardier, after a good quarter of an hour, took her aside, and showed her the fifteen hundred francs.

"Is *that* all?" said she.

It was the first time, since the beginning of their living together, that she had dared to criticise the act of her master.

He felt the blow.

"True you are right," said he; "I am a fool. Give me my hat."

He folded the three banknotes, thrust them into his pocket, and started in all haste, but he missed the direction and took the road to the right. Some neighbours of whom he inquired put him on the track; the Lark and the man had been seen to go in the direction of Livry. He followed this indication, walking rapidly and talking to himself.

"This man is evidently a millionaire dressed in yellow, and as for me, I am an idiot. He first gave twenty sous, then five francs, then fifty francs, then fifteen hundred francs, all so readily. He would have given fifteen thousand francs. But I shall catch him."

And then this bundle of clothes, made ready beforehand for the little girl; all that was strange, there was a good deal of mystery under it. When one gets hold of a mystery, he does not let go of it. The secrets of the rich are sponges full of gold; a man ought to know how to squeeze them. All these thoughts were whirling in his brain. "I am an idiot," said he.

On leaving Montfermeil and reaching the turn made by the road to Livry, the road may be seen for a long distance on the plateau. On reaching this point he counted on being able to see the man and the little girl. He looked as far as his eye could reach, but saw nothing. He inquired again. In the meanwhile he was losing time. The passers-by told him that the man and child whom he sought had travelled towards the wood in the direction of Gagny. He hastened in this direction.

They had the start of him, but a child walks slowly, and he went rapidly. And then the country was well known to him.

Suddenly he stopped and struck his forehead like a man who has forgotten the main thing, and who thinks of retracing his steps.

"I ought to have taken my gun!" said he.

Thénardier was one of those double natures who sometimes appear among us without our knowledge, and disappear without ever being known, because destiny has shown us but one side of them. It is the fate of many men to live thus half submerged. In a quiet ordinary situation, Thénardier had all that is necessary to make—we do not say to be—what passes for an honest tradesman, a good citizen. At the same time, under certain circumstances, under the operation of certain occurrences exciting his baser nature, he had in him all that was necessary to be a villain. He was a shopkeeper in which lay hidden a monster. At times, Satan must have squatted in some corner of the hole in which Thénardier lived and daydreamed at the spectacle of this hideous masterpiece.

After hesitating an instant:

"Bah!" thought he, "they would have time to escape!"

And he continued on his way, going rapidly forward, and almost as if he were certain, with the sagacity of the fox scenting a flock of partridges.

In fact, when he had passed the ponds, and crossed obliquely the large meadow at the right of the avenue de Bellevue, as he reached the grassy path which nearly encircles the hill, and which covers the arch of the old aqueduct of the abbey of Chelles, he perceived above a bush, the hat on which he had already built so many conjectures. It was the man's hat. The bushes were low. Thénardier perceived that the man and Cosette were seated there. The child could not be seen, she was so short, but he could see the head of the doll.

Thénardier was not mistaken. The man had sat down there to give Cosette a little rest. The tavern-keeper turned aside the bushes, and suddenly appeared before the eyes of those whom he sought.

"Pardon me, excuse me, monsieur," said he, all out of breath; "but here are your fifteen hundred francs."

So saying, he held out the three bank bills to the stranger.

The man raised his eyes:

"What does that mean?"

Thénardier answered respectfully:

"Monsieur, that means that I'm taking back Cosette."

Cosette shuddered, and hugged close to the goodman.

He answered, looking Thénardier straight in the eye, and spacing his syllables.

"You're—taking—back—Cosette?"

"Yes, monsieur, I'm taking her back. I tell you I have thought it over. Indeed, I haven't the right to give her to you. I am an honest man, you see. This little girl is not mine. She belongs to her mother. Her mother has confided her to me; I can only give her up to her mother. You will tell me: But her mother is dead. Well. In that case, I can only give up the child to a person who shall bring me a written order, signed by the mother, stating I should deliver the child to him. That is clear."

The man, without answering, felt in his pocket, and Thénardier saw the pocket-book containing the bank bills reappear.

The tavern-keeper felt a thrill of joy.

"Good!" thought he; "hold on. He is going to bribe me!"

Before opening the pocket-book, the traveller cast a look about him. The place was entirely deserted. There was not a soul either in the wood, or in the valley. The man opened the pocket-book, and drew from it, not the handful of bankbills which Thénardier expected, but a little piece of paper, which he unfolded and presented open to the innkeeper, saying:

"You are right. Read that!"

Thénardier took the paper and read.

"M—— sur M——, March 25, 1823.

"Monsieur Thénardier:

"You will deliver Cosette to the bearer. He will settle all small debts.

"I have the honour to salute you with consideration.

FANTINE."

"You know that signature?" replied the man.

It was indeed the signature of Fantine. Thénardier recognised it.

There was nothing to say. He felt doubly enraged, enraged at being compelled to give up the bribe which he hoped for, and enraged at being beaten. The man added:

"You can keep this paper as your receipt."

Thénardier retreated in good order.

"This signature is very well imitated," he grumbled between his teeth. "Well, so be it!"

Then he made a desperate effort.

"Monsieur," said he, "it is all right. Then you are the person. But you must settle 'all small debts.' There is a large amount due to me."

The man rose to his feet, and said at the same time, snapping with his thumb and finger some dust from his threadbare sleeve:

"Monsieur Thénardier, in January the mother reckoned that she owed you a hundred and twenty francs; you sent her in February a memorandum of five hundred francs; you received three hundred francs at the end of February, and three hundred at the beginning of March. There has since elapsed nine months which, at fifteen francs per month, the price agreed upon, amounts to a hundred and thirty-five francs. You had received a hundred francs in advance. There remain thirty-five francs due you. I have just given you fifteen hundred francs."

Thénardier felt what the wolf feels the moment when he finds himself seized and crushed by the steel jaws of the trap.

"What is this devil of a man?" thought he.

He did what the wolf does, he gave a spring. Audacity had succeeded with him once already.

"Monsieur-I-don't-know-your-name," said he resolutely, and putting aside this time all show of respect. "I shall take back Cosette or you must give me a thousand crowns."*

The stranger said quietly:

"Come, Cosette."

He took Cosette with his left hand, and with the right picked up his staff, which was on the ground.

Thénardier noted the enormous size of the cudgel, and the solitude of the place.

The man disappeared in the wood with the child, leaving the tavern-keeper motionless and non-plussed.

As they walked away, Thénardier observed his broad shoulders, a little rounded, and his big fists.

Then his eyes fell back upon his own puny arms and thin hands. "I must have been a fool indeed," thought he, "not to have brought my gun, as I was going on a hunt."

However, the innkeeper did not abandon the pursuit.

"I must know where he goes," said he; and he began to follow them at a distance. There remained two things in his possession, one a bitter mockery, the piece of paper signed Fantine, and the other a consolation, the fifteen hundred francs.

The man was leading Cosette in the direction of Livry and Bondy. He was walking slowly, his head bent down, in an attitude of reflection and sadness. The winter had bereft the wood of foliage, so that Thénardier did not lose sight of them, though remaining at a considerable distance behind. From time to time the man turned, and looked to see if he were followed. Suddenly he perceived Thénardier. He at once entered a coppice with Cosette, and both disappeared from sight. "The devil!" said Thénardier. And he redoubled his pace.

The density of the thicket compelled him to approach them. When the man reached the thickest part of the wood, he turned again. Thénardier had endeavoured to conceal himself in the branches in vain, he could not prevent the man from seeing him. The man cast an uneasy glance at him, then shook his head, and resumed his journey. The innkeeper again took up the pursuit. They walked thus two or three hundred paces. Suddenly the man turned again. He perceived the innkeeper. This time he looked at him so forbiddingly that Thénardier judged it "unprofitable" to go further. Thénardier went home.

---

*A thousand crowns is 3,000 francs, double the amount agreed on.

11

NUMBER 9430 COMES UP AGAIN, AND COSETTE DRAWS IT

JEAN VALJEAN was not dead.

When he fell into the sea, or rather when he threw himself into it, he was, as we have seen, free from his irons. He swam under water to a ship at anchor to which a boat was fastened.

He found means to conceal himself in this boat until evening. At night he betook himself again to the water, and reached the land a short distance from Cape Brun.

There, as he did not lack for money, he could procure clothes. A little public-house in the environs of Balaguier was then the place which supplied clothing for escaped convicts, a lucrative business. Then Jean Valjean, like all those joyless fugitives who are endeavouring to throw off the track the spy of the law and social fatality, followed an obscure and wandering path. He found an asylum first in Pradeaux, near Beausset. Then he went towards Grand Villard near Briançon, in the Hautes Alpes. Groping and restless flight, threading the mazes of the mole whose windings are unknown. There were afterwards found some trace of his passage in Ain, on the territory of Civrieux, in the Pyrenees at Accons, at a place called the Grange-de-Domecq, near the hamlet of Chavailles, and in the environs of Périgneux, at Brunies, a canton of Chapelle Gonaguet. He finally reached Paris. We have just seen him at Montfermeil.

His first care, on reaching Paris, had been to purchase a mourning dress for a little girl of seven years, then to procure lodgings. That done, he had gone to Montfermeil.

It will be remembered that, at the time of his former escape, or near that time, he had made a mysterious journey of which justice had had some glimpse.

Moreover, he was believed to be dead, and that thickened the obscurity which surrounded him. At Paris there fell into his hands a paper which chronicled the fact. He felt reassured, and almost as much at peace as if he really had been dead.

On the evening of the same day that Jean Valjean had rescued Cosette from the clutches of the Thénardiess, he entered Paris again. He entered the city at night-fall, with the child, by the barriere de Monceaux. There he took a cabriolet, which carried him as far as the esplanade of the Observatory. There he got out, paid the driver, took Cosette by the hand, and both in the darkness of the night, through the deserted streets in the vicinity of l'Ourcine and la Glacière, walked towards the boulevard de l'Hôpital.

The day had been strange and full of emotion for Cosette; they had eaten behind hedges bread and cheese bought at isolated taverns; they had often changed carriages, and had travelled short distances on foot. She did not complain; but she was tired, and Jean Valjean perceived it by her pulling more heavily at his hand while walking. He took her in his arms; Cosette, without letting go of Catharine, laid her head on Jean Valjean's shoulder, and went to sleep.

BOOK FOUR
THE OLD GORBEAU HOUSE

1

MASTER GORBEAU

FORTY YEARS AGO, the solitary stroller who ventured into the unknown regions of La Salpêtrière and went up along the Boulevard as far as the Barrière d'Italie, reached certain points where it might be said that Paris disappeared. It was not deserted, for there were people passing; it was not the country, for there were houses and streets; it was not a city, the streets had ruts in them, like the highways, and grass grew along their borders; it was not a village, the houses were too tall. What was it then? It was an inhabited place where there was nobody, it was a deserted place where there was somebody; it was a boulevard of the great city, a street of Paris, wilder, at night, than a forest, and gloomier, by day, than a graveyard.

It was the old quarter of the Horse Market.

Our pedestrian, if he trusted himself beyond the four crumbling walls of this Horse Market, if willing to go even further than the Rue du Petit Banquier, leaving on his right a courtyard shut in by lofty walls, then a meadow studded with stacks of tanbark that looked like the gigantic beaver dams, then an enclosure half filled with lumber and piles of stumps, sawdust and shavings, from the top of which a huge dog was baying, then a long, low, ruined wall with a small dark-coloured and decrepit gate in it, covered with moss, which was full of flowers in spring-time, then, in the loneliest spot, a frightful broken-down structure on which could be read in large letters: POST NO BILLS; this bold promenader, we say, would reach the corner of the Rue des Vignes-Saint-Marcel, a latitude not much explored. There, near a manufactory and between two garden walls, could be seen at the time of which we speak an old ruined dwelling that, at first sight, seemed as small as a cottage, yet was, in reality, as vast as a cathedral. It stood with its gable end towards the highway, and hence its apparent diminutiveness. Nearly the whole house was hidden. Only the door and one window could be seen.

This old dwelling had but one story.

On examining it, the peculiarity that first struck the beholder was that the door could never have been anything but the door of a hovel, while the window, had it been cut in quarrystone instead of fieldstone, might have been the casement of a lordly residence.

The door was merely a collection of worm-eaten boards crudely tacked together with cross-pieces that looked like pieces of firewood clumsily split out. It opened directly on a steep staircase with high steps covered with mud, plaster, and dust, and of the same breadth as the door, and which seemed from the street to rise perpendicularly like a ladder, and disappear in the shadow between two walls. The top of the shapeless opening which this door closed upon was disguised by a thin plank, in the middle of which had been sawed a three-cornered orifice that served both for skylight and ventilator when the door was shut. On the inside of the door a brush dipped in ink had, in a couple of strokes of the hand, traced the number 52, and above the plank, the same brush had daubed the number 50, so that a new-comer would hesitate, asking: Where am I?

2

A NEST FOR OWL AND WREN

BEFORE THIS Gorbeau tenement Jean Valjean stopped. Like the birds of prey, he had chosen this lonely place to make his nest.

He fumbled in his waistcoat and took from it a sort of master key, opened the door, entered, then carefully closed it again and ascended the stairway, still carrying Cosette.

At the top of the stairway he drew from his pocket another key, with which he opened another door. The room which he entered and closed again immediately was a sort of garret, rather spacious, furnished only with a mattress spread on the floor, a table, and a few chairs. A stove containing a fire, the coals of which were visible, stood in one corner. The street lamp of the boulevards shed a dim light through this poor interior. At the further extremity there was a little room containing a cot. On this Jean Valjean laid the child without waking her.

He struck a light with a flint and steel and lit a candle, which, with his tinder-box, stood ready, beforehand, on the table; and, as he had done on the preceding evening, he began to gaze upon Cosette with a look of ecstasy, in which the expression of goodness and tenderness went almost to the verge of insanity. The little girl, with that tranquil confidence which belongs only to extreme strength or extreme weakness, had fallen asleep without knowing with whom she was, and continued to slumber without knowing where she was.

Jean Valjean bent down and kissed the child's hand.

Nine months before, he had kissed the hand of the mother, who also had just fallen asleep.

The same mournful, pious, agonising feeling now filled his heart.

He knelt down by the bedside of Cosette.

It was broad daylight, and yet the child slept on. A pale ray from the December sun struggled through the garret window and traced upon the ceiling long streaks of light and shade. Suddenly a quarry waggon, heavily laden, trundled over the cobble-stones of the boulevard, and shook the old building like the rumbling of a tempest, jarring it from cellar to roof-tree.

"Yes, madame!" cried Cosette, starting up out of sleep, "here I am! here I am!"

And she threw herself from the bed, her eyelids still half closed with the weight of slumber, stretching out her hand towards the corner of the wall.

"Oh! what shall I do? Where is my broom?" said she.

By this time her eyes were fully open, and she saw the smiling face of Jean Valjean.

"Oh! yes—so it is!" said the child. "Good morning, monsieur."

Children at once accept joy and happiness with quick familiarity, being themselves naturally all happiness and joy.

Cosette noticed Catharine at the foot of the bed, laid hold of her at once, and, playing the while, asked Jean Valjean a thousand questions.—Where was she? Was Paris a big place? Was Madame Thénardier really very far away? Wouldn't she come back again, etc., etc. All at once she exclaimed, "How pretty it is here!"

It was a frightful hovel, but she felt free.

"Must I sweep?" she continued at length.

"Play!" replied Jean Valjean.

And thus the day passed by. Cosette, without troubling herself with trying to understand anything about it, was inexpressibly happy with her doll and her good friend.

3

TWO MISFORTUNES MINGLED MAKE HAPPINESS

THE DAWN of the next day found Jean Valjean again near the bed of Cosette. He waited there, motionless, to see her wake.

Something new was entering his soul.

Jean Valjean had never loved anything. For twenty-five years he had been alone in the world. He had never been a father, lover, husband, or friend. At the galleys, he was cross, sullen, abstinent, ignorant, and intractable. The old convict had a virginal heart. His sister and her children had left in his memory only a vague and distant impression, which had finally almost entirely vanished. He had made every exertion to find them again, and, not succeeding, had forgotten them. Human nature is thus constituted. The other tender emotions of his youth, if any such he had, were lost in an abyss.

When he saw Cosette, when he had taken her, carried her away, and rescued her, he felt his heart moved. All that he had of feeling and affection was aroused and vehemently attracted towards this child. He would approach the bed where she slept, and would tremble there with delight; he felt inward stirrings, like a mother, and knew not what they were; for it is something very incomprehensible and very sweet, this grand and strange emotion of a heart in its first love.

Poor old heart, so young!

But, as he was fifty-five and Cosette was but eight years old, all that he might have felt of love in his entire life melted into a sort of ineffable radiance.[3]

This was the second white vision he had seen. The bishop had caused the dawn of virtue on his horizon; Cosette evoked the dawn of love.

The first few days rolled by amid this bewilderment.

For her part, Cosette, too, unconsciously underwent a change, poor little creature! She was so small when her mother left her, that she could not recollect her now. As all children do, like the young shoots of the vine that cling to everything, she had tried to love. She had not been able to succeed. Everybody had rejected her—the Thénardiers, their children, other children. She had loved the dog; it died, and after that no person and no thing would have aught to do with her. Mournful thing to tell, and one which we have already hinted, at the age of eight her heart was cold. This was not her fault; it was not the faculty of love that she lacked; alas! it was the possibility. And so, from the very first day, all that thought and felt in her began to love this kind old friend. She now felt sensations utterly unknown to her before—a sensation of budding and of growth.

Her kind friend no longer impressed as old and poor. In her eyes Jean Valjean was handsome, just as the garret had seemed pretty.

Such are the effects of the aurora-glow of childhood, youth, and joy. The newness of earth and of life has something to do with it. Nothing is so charming as the ruddy tints that happiness can shed around a garret room. We all, in the course of our lives, have had our rose-coloured attics.

Nature had placed a wide chasm—fifty years' interval of age—between Jean Valjean and Cosette. This chasm fate filled up. Fate abruptly brought together, and wedded with its resistless power, these two shattered lives, dissimilar in years, but similar in sorrow. The one, indeed, was the complement of the other. The instinct of Cosette sought for a father, as the instinct of Jean Valjean sought for a child. To meet, was to find one another. In that mysterious moment, when their hands touched, they were welded together. When their two souls saw each other, they recognised that they were mutually needed, and they closely embraced.

Taking the words in their most comprehensive and most absolute sense, it might be said that, separated from everything by the walls of the tomb, Jean Valjean was the Widower, as Cosette was the Orphan. This position made Jean Valjean become, in a celestial sense, the father of Cosette.

And, in truth, the mysterious impression produced upon Cosette, in the depths of the woods at Chelles, by the hand of Jean Valjean grasping her own in the darkness, was not an illusion but a reality. The coming of this man and his participation in the destiny of this child had been the advent of God.

Moreover, Jean Valjean had chosen his hiding-place well. He was there in a state of security that seemed to be complete.

The apartment with the side chamber which he occupied with Cosette, was the one whose window looked out upon the boulevard. This window being the only one in the house, there was no neighbour's prying eye to fear either from that side or opposite.

The lower floor of No. 50-52 was a sort of dilapidated shed; it served as a sort of stable for market gardeners, and had no communication with the upper floor. It was separated from it by the flooring, which had neither stairway nor trap-door, and was, as it were, the diaphragm of the old building. The upper floor contained, as we have said, several rooms and a few lofts, only one of which was occupied—by an old woman, who was maid of all work to Jean Valjean. All the rest was uninhabited.

It was this old woman, honoured with the title of landlady, but, in reality, entrusted with the functions of portress, who had rented him these lodgings on Christmas Day. He had passed himself off to her as a gentleman of means, ruined by the Spanish Bonds, who was going to live there with his grand-daughter. He had paid her for six months in advance, and engaged the old dame to furnish the chamber and the little bedroom, as we have described them. This old woman it was who had kindled the fire in the stove and made everything ready for them, on the evening of their arrival.

Weeks rolled by. In that wretched shelter these two beings led a happy life.

From the earliest dawn, Cosette laughed, prattled, and sang. Children have their morning song, like birds.

Sometimes it happened that Jean Valjean would take her little red hand, all chapped and frost-bitten as it was, and kiss it. The poor child, accustomed only to blows, had no idea what this meant, and would draw back ashamed.

At times, she grew serious and looked musingly at her little black dress. Cosette was no longer in rags; she was in mourning. She was issuing from utter poverty and was entering upon life.

Jean Valjean had begun to teach her to read. Sometimes, while teaching the child to spell, he would remember that it was with the intention of accomplishing evil that he had learned to read, in the galleys. This intention had now been changed into teaching a child to read. Then the old convict would smile with the pensive smile of angels.

He felt in this a pre-ordination from on high, a volition of some one more than man, and he would lose himself in reverie. Good thoughts as well as bad have their abysses.

To teach Cosette to read, and to watch her playing, was nearly all Jean Valjean's life. And then, he would talk to her about her mother, and teach her to pray.

She called him *Father,* and knew him by no other name.

He spent hours seeing her dress and undress her doll, and listening to her song and prattle. From that time on, life seemed full of interest to him, men seemed good and just; he no longer, in his thoughts, reproached any one with any wrong; he saw no reason, now, why he should not live to grow very old, since his child loved him. He looked forward to a long future illuminated by Cosette with charming light. The very best of us are not altogether exempt from some tinge of egotism. At times, he thought with a sort of joy, that she would be ugly.

This is but personal opinion; but in order to express our idea thoroughly, at the point Jean Valjean had reached, when he began to love Cosette, it is not clear to us that he did not require this fresh supply of goodness to enable him to persevere in the right path. He had just seen the wickedness of men and the moral depravity of society under new aspects—aspects incomplete and, unfortunately, showing forth only one side of the truth—the lot of woman summed up in Fantine, public authority personified in Javert; he had been sent back to the galleys this time for doing good; new waves of bitterness had overwhelmed him; disgust and weariness had once more resumed their sway; the recollection of the bishop, even, was perhaps eclipsed, sure to reappear afterwards, luminous and triumphant; yet, in fact, this blessed remembrance was growing feebler. Who knows whether Jean Valjean was not on the point of becoming discouraged and falling back to evil ways? Love came, and he again grew strong. Alas! he was no less feeble than Cosette. He protected her, and she gave strength to him. Thanks to him, she could walk upright in life; thanks to her, he could persist in virtuous deeds. He was the support of his child, and this child was his prop and staff. Oh, divine and unfathomable mystery of the compensations of Destiny!

4

WHAT THE LANDLADY DISCOVERED

JEAN VALJEAN was prudent enough never to go out in the daytime. Every evening, however, about twilight, he would walk for an hour or two, sometimes alone, often with Cosette, selecting the most unfrequented side alleys of the boulevards and going into the churches at nightfall. He was fond of going to St. Médard, which is the nearest church. When he did not take Cosette, she remained with the old woman; but it was the child's delight to go out with her kind old friend. She preferred an hour with him even to her delicious tête-à-têtes with Catharine. He would walk along holding her by the hand, and telling her pleasant things.

It turned out that Cosette was very playful.

The old woman was housekeeper and cook, and did the marketing.

They lived frugally, always with a little fire in the stove, but like people in embarrassed circumstances. Jean Valjean made no change in the furniture described on the first day, excepting that he caused a solid door to be put in place of the glass door of Cosette's little bed-chamber.

He still wore his yellow coat, his black trousers, and his old hat. On the street he was taken for a beggar. It sometimes happened that kind-hearted dames, in passing, would turn and hand him a penny. Jean Valjean accepted the penny and bowed humbly. It chanced sometimes, also, that he would meet some wretched creature begging alms, and then, glancing about him to be sure no one was looking, he would stealthily approach the beggar, slip a coin, often silver, into his hand, and walk rapidly away. This had its drawbacks. He began to be known in the neighbourhood as *the beggar who gives alms*.

The old landlady, a crabbed creature, fully possessed with that keen observation as to all that concerned her neighbours, which is peculiar to the suburbs, watched Jean Valjean closely without exciting his suspicion. She was a little deaf, which made her talkative. She had but two teeth left, one in the upper and one in the lower jaw, and these she was continually rattling together. She had questioned Cosette, who, knowing nothing, could tell nothing, further than that she came from Montfermeil. One morning this old female spy saw Jean Valjean go, with an appearance which seemed peculiar to the old busybody, into one of the uninhabited apartments of the building. She followed him with the steps of an old cat, and could see him without herself being seen, through the chink of the door directly opposite. Jean Valjean had, doubtless for greater caution, turned his back towards the door in question. The old woman saw him fumble in his pocket, and take from it a sewing case, scissors, and thread, and then proceed to rip open the lining of one lapel of his coat and take from under it a piece of yellowish paper, which he unfolded. The beldame remarked with dismay, that it was a bank bill for a thousand francs. It was the second or third one only that she had ever seen. She ran away very much frightened.

A moment afterwards, Jean Valjean accosted her, and asked her to get this thousand-franc bill changed for him, adding that it was the half-yearly interest on his property which he had received on the previous day. "Where?" thought the old woman. He did not go out until six o'clock, and the government treasury is certainly not open at that hour. The old woman got the note changed, all the while forming her conjectures. This bill of a thousand francs, commented upon and multiplied, gave rise to a host of breathless conferences among the gossips of the Rue des Vignes Saint Marcel.

Some days afterwards, it chanced that Jean Valjean, in his shirt-sleeves, was sawing wood in the entry. The old woman was in his room doing the cleaning. She was alone. Cosette was intent upon the wood he was sawing. The woman saw the coat hanging on a nail, and examined it. The lining had been sewed over. She felt it carefully and thought she could detect in the lapels and in the padding, thicknesses of paper. Other thousand-franc bills beyond a doubt!

She noticed, besides, that there were all sorts of things in the pockets. Not only were there the needles, scissors, and thread which she had already seen, but a large wallet, a very big knife, and, most suspicious of all, several wigs of different colours. Every pocket of this coat had the appearance of containing something to be provided with against sudden emergencies.

Thus, the occupants of the old building reached the closing days of winter.

5

A FIVE-FRANC COIN FALLING ON
THE FLOOR MAKES A NOISE

THERE WAS, in the neighbourhood of Saint Médard, a mendicant who sat crouching over the edge of a condemned public well near by, and to whom Jean Valjean often gave alms. He never passed this man without giving him a few pennies. Sometimes he spoke to him. Those who were envious of this poor creature said he was in the pay of the police. He was an old church beadle of seventy-five, who was always mumbling prayers.

One evening, as Jean Valjean was passing that way, unaccompanied by Cosette, he noticed the beggar sitting in his usual place, under the street lamp which had just been lighted. The man, according to custom, seemed to be praying and was bent over. Jean Valjean walked up to him, and put a coin in his hand, as usual. The beggar suddenly raised his eyes, gazed intently at Jean Valjean, and then quickly dropped his head. This movement was like a flash; Jean Valjean shuddered; it seemed to him that he had just seen, by the light of the street lamp, not the calm, sanctimonious face of the aged beadle, but a terrible and well-known countenance. He experienced the sensation one would feel on finding himself suddenly face to face, in the gloom, with a tiger. He recoiled, horror-stricken and petrified, daring neither to breathe nor to speak, to stay nor to fly, but gazing upon the beggar who had once more bent down his head, with its tattered covering, and seemed to be no longer conscious of his presence. At this singular moment, an instinct, perhaps the mysterious instinct of self-preservation, prevented Jean Valjean from uttering a word. The beggar had the same form, the same rags, the same general appearance as on every other day. "Pshaw!" said Jean Valjean to himself, "I am mad! I am dreaming! It cannot be!" And he went home, anxious and ill at ease.

He scarcely dared to admit, even to himself, that the countenance he thought he had seen was the face of Javert.

That night, upon reflection, he regretted that he had not questioned the man so as to compel him to raise his head a second time. On the morrow, at nightfall, he went thither, again. The beggar was in his place. "Good day! Good day!" said Jean Valjean, with firmness, as he gave him the accustomed alms. The beggar raised his head and answered in a whining voice: "Thanks, kind sir, thanks!" It was, indeed, only the old beadle.

Jean Valjean now felt fully reassured. He even began to laugh. "What the deuce was I about to fancy that I saw Javert," thought he; "is my sight growing poor already?" And he thought no more about it.

Some days after, it might be eight o'clock in the evening, he was in his room, giving Cosette her spelling lesson, which the child was repeating in a loud voice, when he heard the door of the building open and close again. That seemed odd to him. The old woman, the only occupant of the house besides himself and Cosette, always went to bed at dark to save candles. Jean Valjean made a sign to Cosette to be silent. He heard some one coming up the stairs. Possibly, it might be the old woman who had felt unwell and had been to the druggist's. Jean Valjean listened. The footstep was heavy, and sounded like a man's; but the old woman wore heavy shoes, and there is nothing so much like the step of a man as the step of an old woman. However, Jean Valjean blew out his candle.

He sent Cosette to bed, telling her in a suppressed voice to lie down very quietly—and, as he kissed her forehead, the footsteps stopped. Jean Valjean remained silent and motionless, his back turned towards the door, still seated on his chair from which he had not moved, and holding his breath in the darkness. After a considerable interval, not hearing anything more, he turned round without making any noise, and as he raised his eyes towards the door of his room, he saw a light through the keyhole. This ray of light was an evil star in the black background of the door and the wall. There was, evidently, somebody outside with a candle who was listening.

A few minutes elapsed, and the light disappeared. But he heard no sound of footsteps, which seemed to indicate that whoever was eavesdropping had taken off his shoes.

Jean Valjean threw himself on his bed without undressing, but could not shut his eyes that night.

At daybreak, as he was sinking into slumber from fatigue, he was aroused, again, by the creaking of the door of some room at the end of the hall, and then he heard the same footstep which had ascended the stairs, on the preceding night. The step approached. He started from his bed and placed his eye to the keyhole, which was quite a large one, hoping to get a glimpse of the person, whoever it might be, who had made his way into the building in the night-time and had listened at his door. It was a man, indeed, who passed by Jean Valjean's room, this time without stopping.

The hall was still too dark for him to make out his features; but, when the man reached the stairs, a ray of light from without made his figure stand out like a profile, and Jean Valjean had a full view of his back. The man was tall, wore a long frock-coat, and had a cudgel under his arm. It was the redoubtable form of Javert.

Jean Valjean might have tried to get another look at him through his window that opened on the boulevard, but he would have had to raise the sash, and that he dared not do.

It was evident that the man had entered by means of a key, as if at home. "Who, then, had given him the key?—and what was the meaning of this?"

At seven in the morning, when the old lady came to clear up the rooms, Jean Valjean eyed her sharply, but asked her no questions. The good dame appeared as usual.

While she was doing her sweeping, she said:——

"Perhaps monsieur heard some one come in, last night?"

At her age and on that boulevard, eight in the evening is the very darkest of the night.

"Ah! yes, by the way, I did," he answered in the most natural tone. "Who was it?"

"It's a new lodger," said the old woman, "who has come into the house."

"And his name—?"

"Well, I hardly recollect now. Dumont or Daumont.—Some such name as that."

"And what is he—this M. Daumont?"

The old woman studied him, a moment, through her little foxy eyes, and answered:

"He's a gentleman living on his income like you."

She may have intended nothing by this, but Jean Valjean thought he could make out that she did.

When the old woman was gone, he made a roll of a hundred francs he had in a drawer and put it into his pocket. Do what he would to manage this so that the clinking of the silver should not be heard, a five-franc coin escaped his grasp and rolled jingling away over the floor.

At dusk, he went to the street-door and looked carefully up and down the boulevard. No one was to be seen. The boulevard seemed to be utterly deserted. It is true that there might have been someone hidden behind a tree.

He went upstairs again.

"Come," said he to Cosette.

He took her by the hand and they both went out.

BOOK FIVE
A SINISTER HUNT REQUIRES
A SILENT PACK

1

STRATEGIC ZIGZAGS

JEAN VALJEAN had immediately left the boulevard and began to thread the streets, making as many turns as he could, returning sometimes upon his track to make sure that he was not followed.

This manœuvre is peculiar to the hunted stag. On ground where the foot leaves a mark, it has, among other advantages, that of deceiving the hunters and the dogs by doubling back. It is what is called in venery *false reimbushment*.

The moon was full. Jean Valjean was not sorry for that. The moon, still near the horizon, cut large prisms of light and shade in the streets. Jean Valjean could glide along the houses and the walls on the dark side and observe the light side. He did not, perhaps, sufficiently realise that the shadowy side escaped him. However, in all the deserted alleys in the neighbourhood of the Rue de Poliveau, he felt sure that no one was behind him.

Cosette walked without asking any questions. The sufferings of the first six years of her life had introduced something of the passive into her nature.[4] Besides—and this is a remark to which we shall have more than one occasion to return—she had become familiar, without being fully conscious of them, with the peculiarities of her good friend and the eccentricities of destiny. And then, she felt safe, being with him.

Jean Valjean knew, no more than Cosette, where he was going. He trusted in God, as she trusted in him. It seemed to him that he also held some one greater than himself by the hand; he believed he felt a being leading him, invisible. Finally, he had no definite idea, no plan, no project. He was not even absolutely sure that this was Javert, and then it might be Javert, and Javert not know that he was Jean Valjean. Was he not disguised? was he not supposed to be dead? Nevertheless, singular things had happened within the last few days. He wanted no more of them. He was determined not to enter Gorbeau House again. Like the animal hunted from his den, he was looking for a hole to hide in until he could find one to remain in.

Jean Valjean described many and varied labyrinths in the Quartier Mouffetard, which was asleep already as if it were still under the discipline of the middle age and the yoke of the curfew; he produced different combinations, in wise strategy, with the Rue Censier and the Rue Copeau, the Rue du Battoir Saint Victor and the Rue du Puits l'Ermite. There are lodgings in that region, but he did not even enter them, not finding what suited him. He had no doubt whatever that if, perchance, they had sought his track, they had lost it.

As eleven o'clock struck in the tower of Saint Etienne du Mont, he crossed the Rue de Pontoise in front of the Police Station, which is at No. 14. Some moments afterwards, the instinct of which we have already spoken made him turn his head. At this moment he saw distinctly—thanks to the station house lamp which revealed them—three men following him quite near, pass one after another under this lamp on the dark side of the street. One of these men entered the passage leading to the station house. The one in advance appeared to him decidedly suspicious.

"Come, child!" said he to Cosette, and he made haste to get out of the Rue de Pontoise.

He made a circuit, went round the arcade des Patriarches, which was closed on account of the lateness of the hour, walked rapidly through the Rue de l'Epée-de-Bois and the Rue de l'Arbalète, and plunged into the Rue des Postes.

There was a square there, where the Collège Rollin now is, and from which branches off the Rue Neuve-Sainte-Geneviève.

The moon lighted up this square brightly. Jean Valjean concealed himself in a doorway, calculating that if these men were still following him, he could not fail to get a good view of them when they crossed this lighted space.

In fact, three minutes had not elapsed when the men appeared. There were now four of them; all were tall, dressed in long brown coats, with bowler hats, and great clubs in their hands. They were not less fearfully forbidding by their size and their large fists than by their stealthy tread in the darkness. One would have taken them for four spectres in civilian dress.

They stopped in the centre of the square and formed a group like people consulting. They appeared undecided. The man who seemed to be the leader turned and energetically pointed in the direction in which Jean Valjean was; one of the others seemed to insist with some obstinacy on the contrary direction. At the instant when the leader turned, the moon shone full in his face. Jean Valjean recognised Javert perfectly.

2

IT IS FORTUNATE THAT VEHICLES CAN CROSS THE BRIDGE OF AUSTERLITZ

UNCERTAINTY was at an end for Jean Valjean; happily, it still continued with these men. He took advantage of their hesitation; it was time lost for them, gained for him. He came out from the doorway in which he was concealed, and made his way into the Rue des Postes towards the region of the Jardin des Plantes. Cosette began to be tired; he took her in his arms, and carried her. There was nobody in the streets, and the lamps had not been lighted on account of the moon.

He doubled his pace.

He arrived at the bridge of Austerlitz.

It was still a toll-bridge at this period.

He presented himself at the toll-house and gave a sou.

"It is two sous," said the toll-keeper. "You are carrying a child who can walk. Pay for two."

He paid, annoyed that his passage should have attracted observation. All flight should be gliding.

A large cart was passing the Seine at the same time, and like him was going towards the right bank. This could be made of use. He could go the whole length of the bridge in the shadow of this cart.

Towards the middle of the bridge, Cosette, her feet becoming numb, desired to walk. He put her down and took her by the hand.

The bridge passed, he perceived some wood-yards a little to the right and walked in that direction. To get there, he must venture into a large clear open space. He did not hesitate. Those who followed him were evidently thrown off his track, and Jean Valjean believed himself out of danger. Sought for, he might be, but followed he was not.

A little street, the Rue de Chemin Vert Saint Antoine, opened between two wood-yards inclosed by walls. This street was narrow, obscure, and seemed made expressly for him. Before entering it, he looked back.

From the point where he was, he could see the whole length of the bridge of Austerlitz.

Four shadows, at that moment, entered upon the bridge.

These shadows were coming from the Jardin des Plantes towards the right bank.

These four shadows were the four men.

Jean Valjean felt a shudder like that of the deer when he sees the hounds again upon his track.

One hope was left him; it was that these men had not entered upon the bridge, and had not perceived him when he crossed the large square clear space leading Cosette by the hand.

In that case, by plunging into the little street before him, if he could succeed in reaching the wood-yards, the marshes, the fields, the open ground, he could escape.

It seemed to him that he might trust himself to this silent little street. He entered it.

3

SEE THE MAP OF PARIS IN 1727

SOME three hundred paces on, he reached a point where the street forked. It divided into two streets, the one turning off obliquely to the left, the other to the right. Jean Valjean had before him the two branches of a Y. Which should he choose?

He did not hesitate, but took the right.

Why?

Because the left branch led towards the faubourg—that is to say, towards the inhabited region, and the right branch towards the country— that is, towards the uninhabited region.

But now, they no longer walked very fast. Cosette's step slackened Jean Valjean's pace.

He took her up and carried her again. Cosette rested her head upon the goodman's shoulder, and did not say a word.

He turned, from time to time, and looked back. He took care to keep always on the dark side of the street. The street was straight behind him. The two or three first times he turned, he saw nothing; the silence was complete, and he kept on his way somewhat reassured. Suddenly, on turning again, he thought he saw in the portion of the street through which he had just passed, far off in the darkness, something which stirred.

He plunged forward rather than walked, hoping to find some side street by which to escape, and once more to elude his pursuers.

He came to a wall.

This wall, however, did not prevent him from going further; it was a wall forming the side of a cross alley, in which the street Jean Valjean was then in came to an end.

Here again he must decide; should he take the right or the left?

He looked to the right. The alley ran out to a space between some buildings that were mere sheds or barns, then terminated abruptly. The end of this blind alley was plain to be seen—a great white wall.

He looked to the left. The alley on this side was open, and, about two hundred paces further on, ran into a street. In this direction lay safety.

The instant Jean Valjean decided to turn to the left, to try to reach the street which he saw at the end of the alley, he perceived, at the corner of the alley and the street towards which he was just about going, a sort of black, motionless statue.

It was a man, who had just been posted there, evidently, and who was waiting for him, guarding the passage.

Jean Valjean was startled.

There was no doubt. He was watched by this shadow.

What should he do?

There was now no time to turn back. What he had seen moving in the obscurity some distance behind him, the moment before, was undoubtedly Javert and his squad. Javert probably had already reached the beginning of the street of which Jean Valjean was at the end. Javert, to all appearance, was acquainted with this little trap, and had taken his precautions by sending one of his men to guard the exit. These conjectures, so like certainties, whirled about wildly in Jean Valjean's troubled brain, as a handful of dust flies before a sudden blast. He scrutinised the Cul-de-sac Genrot; there were high walls. He scrutinised the Petite Rue Picpus; there was a sentinel. He saw the dark form stand out in black against the white pavement flooded with the moonlight. To advance, was to fall upon that man. To go back, was to throw himself into Javert's hands. Jean Valjean felt as if caught in a net that was slowly tightening. He looked up at the sky in despair.

4

GROPING FOR ESCAPE

IN ORDER to understand what follows, it is necessary to form an exact idea of the little Rue Droit Mur, and particularly the angle which it makes at the left as you leave the Rue Polonceau to enter this alley. The little Rue Droit Mur was almost entirely lined on the right, as far as the Petite Rue Picpus, by houses of poor appearance; on the left by a single building of severe outline, composed of several structures which rose gradually a story or two, one above another, as they approached the Petite Rue Picpus, so that the building, very high on the side of the Petite Rue Picpus, was quite low on the side of the Rue Polonceau. There, at the corner of which we have spoken, it became so low as to be nothing more than a wall. This wall did not abut squarely on the corner, which was cut off diagonally, leaving a considerable space that was shielded by the two angles thus formed from observers at a distance in either the Rue Polonceau, or the Rue Droit Mur.

From these two angles of the truncated corner, the wall extended along the Rue Polonceau as far as a house numbered 49, and along the Rue Droit Mur, where its height was much less, to the sombre-looking building of which we have spoken, cutting its gable, and thus making a new re-entering angle in the street. This gable had a gloomy aspect; there was but one window to be seen, or rather two shutters covered with a sheet of zinc, and always closed.

This truncated corner was entirely filled by a thing which seemed like a colossal and miserable door. It was a vast shapeless assemblage of perpendicular planks, broader above than below, bound together by long transverse iron bands. At the side there was a porte-cochère of the ordinary dimensions, which had evidently been cut in within the last fifty years.

A lime-tree lifted its branches above this corner, and the wall was covered with ivy towards the Rue Polonceau.

In the imminent peril of Jean Valjean, this sombre building had a solitary and uninhabited appearance which attracted him. He glanced over it rapidly. He thought if he could only succeed in getting into it, he would perhaps be safe. Hope came to him with the idea.

Midway of the front of this building on the Rue Droit Mur, there were at all the windows of the different stories old leaden waste-pipes. The varied branchings of the tubing which was continued from a central conduit to each of these waste-pipes, outlined on the façade a sort of tree. These branching pipes with their hundred elbows seemed like those old closely-pruned grape-vines which twist about over the front of ancient farm-houses.

This grotesque espalier, with its sheet-iron branches, was the first object which Jean Valjean saw. He seated Cosette with her back against a post, and, telling her to be quiet, ran to the spot where the conduit came to the pavement. Perhaps there was some means of scaling the wall by that and entering the house. But the conduit was dilapidated and out of use, and scarcely held by its fastening. Besides, all the windows of this silent house were protected by thick bars of iron, even the dormer windows. And then the moon shone full upon this façade, and the man who was watching from the end of the street would have seen Jean Valjean making the climb. And then what should he do with Cosette? How could he raise her to the top of a three-story house?

He gave up climbing by the conduit, and crept along the wall to the Rue Polonceau.

5

WHICH WOULD BE IMPOSSIBLE WERE THE STREETS LIGHTED WITH GAS

AT THIS MOMENT a muffled and regular sound began to make itself heard at some distance. Jean Valjean ventured to thrust his head a little way around the corner of the street. Seven or eight soldiers, formed in platoon, had just turned into the Rue Polonceau. He saw the gleam of their bayonets. They were coming towards him.

The soldiers, at whose head he distinguished the tall form of Javert, advanced slowly and with precaution. They stopped frequently. It was plain they were exploring all the recesses of the walls and all the entrances of doors and alleys.

It was—and here conjecture could not be deceived—some patrol which Javert had met and which he had put in requisition.

Javert's two assistants marched in the ranks.

At the rate at which they were marching, and the stops they were making, it would take them about a quarter of an hour to arrive at the spot where Jean Valjean was. It was a frightful moment. A few minutes separated Jean Valjean from that awful precipice which was opening before him for the third time. And the galleys now were no longer simply the galleys, they were Cosette lost for ever; that is to say, they seemed like the interior of a tomb.

There was now only one thing possible.

Jean Valjean had this peculiarity, that he might be said to carry two knapsacks; in one he had the thoughts of a saint, in the other the formidable talents of a convict. He helped himself from one or the other as occasion required.

Among other resources, thanks to his numerous escapes from the galleys at Toulon, he had, it will be remembered, become master of that incredible art of raising himself, in the right angle of a wall, if need to be to the height of a sixth story; an art without ladders or props, by mere muscular strength, supporting himself by the back of his neck, his shoulders, his hips, and his knees, hardly making use of the few projections of the stone, which rendered so terrible and so celebrated the corner of the yard of the Conciergerie of Paris by which, some twenty years ago, the convict Battemolle made his escape.

Jean Valjean measured with his eyes the wall above which he saw the lime-tree. It was about eighteen feet high. The angle that it made with the gable of the great building was filled in its lower part with a pile of masonry of triangular shape, probably intended to preserve this too convenient recess from a too public use. This preventive filling-up of the corners of a wall is very common in Paris.

This pile was about five feet high. From its top the space to climb to get upon the wall was hardly more than fourteen feet.

The wall was capped by a flat stone without any projection.

The difficulty was Cosette. Cosette did not know how to scale a wall. Abandon her? Jean Valjean did not think of it. To carry her was impossible. The whole strength of a man is necessary to accomplish these strange ascents. The least burden would make him lose his centre of gravity and he would fall.

He needed a cord. Jean Valjean had none. Where could he find a cord, at midnight, in the Rue Polonceau? Truly at that instant, if Jean Valjean had had a kingdom, he would have given it for a rope.

All extreme situations have their flashes which sometimes make us blind, sometimes illuminate us.

The despairing gaze of Jean Valjean encountered the lamp-post in the Cul-de-sac Genrot.

At this epoch there were no gas-lights in the streets of Paris. At nightfall they lighted the street lamps, which were placed at intervals, and were raised and lowered by means of a rope traversing the street from end to end, running through the grooves of posts. The reel on which this rope was wound was inclosed below the lantern in a little iron box, the key of which was kept by the lamp-lighter, and the rope itself was protected by a casing of metal.

Jean Valjean, with the energy of a final struggle, crossed the street at a bound, entered the cul-de-sac, sprang the bolt of the little box with the point of his knife, and an instant after was back at the side of Cosette. He had a rope. These desperate inventors of expedients, in their struggles with fatality, move electrically in case of need.

We have explained that the street lamps had not been lighted that night. The lamp in the Cul-de-sac Genrot was then, as a matter of course, extinguished like the rest, and one might pass by without even noticing that it was not in its place.

Meanwhile the hour, the place, the darkness, the preoccupation of Jean Valjean, his singular actions, his going to and fro, all this began to disturb Cosette. Any other child would have uttered loud cries long before. She contented herself with pulling Jean Valjean by the skirt of his coat. The sound of the approaching patrol was constantly becoming more and more distinct.

"Father," said she, in a whisper, "I am afraid. Who is it that is coming?"

"Hush!" answered the unhappy man, "it is the Thénardiess."

Cosette shuddered. He added:

"Don't say a word; I'll take care of her. If you cry, if you make any noise, the Thénardiess will hear you. She is coming to catch you."

Then, without any haste, but without doing anything a second time, with a firm and rapid decisiveness, so much the more remarkable at such a moment when the patrol and Javert might come upon him at any instant, he took off his cravat, passed it around Cosette's body under the arms, taking care that it should not hurt the child, attached this cravat to an end of the rope by means of the knot which seamen call a swallow-knot, took the other end of the rope in his teeth, took off his shoes and stockings and threw them over the wall, climbed upon the pile of masonry and began to raise himself in the angle of the wall and the gable with as much solidity and certainty as if he had the rounds of a ladder under his heels and his elbows. Half a minute had not passed before he was on his knees on the wall.

Cosette watched him, stupefied, without saying a word. Jean Valjean's charge and the name of the Thénardiess had made her dumb.

All at once, she heard Jean Valjean's voice calling to her in a low whisper:

"Put your back against the wall."

She obeyed.

"Don't speak, and don't be afraid," added Jean Valjean.

And she felt herself lifted from the ground.

Before she had time to think where she was she was at the top of the wall.

Jean Valjean seized her, put her on his back, took her two little hands in his left hand, lay down flat and crawled along the top of the wall as far as the cut-off corner. As he had supposed, there was a building there, the roof of which sloped from the top of the wooden casing we have mentioned very nearly to the ground, with a gentle inclination, and just reaching to the lime-tree.

A fortunate circumstance, for the wall was much higher on this side than on the street. Jean Valjean saw the ground beneath him at a great depth.

He had just reached the inclined plane of the roof, and had not yet left the crest of the wall, when a violent uproar proclaimed the arrival of the patrol. He heard the thundering voice of Javert:

"Search the cul-de-sac! The Rue Droit Mur is guarded, the Petite Rue Picpus also. I'll bet he's in the cul-de-sac."

The soldiers rushed into the Cul-de-sac Genrot.

Jean Valjean slid down the roof, keeping hold of Cosette, reached the lime-tree, and jumped to the ground. Whether from terror, or from courage, Cosette had not uttered a whisper. Her hands were a little scraped.

6

A MYSTERY BEGINS

JEAN VALJEAN found himself in a sort of garden, very large and of a singular appearance; one of those gloomy gardens which seem made to be seen in the winter and at night. This garden was oblong, with a row of tall poplars at the far end, some tall forest trees in the corners, and a clear space in the centre, where stood a very large isolated tree, then a few fruit trees, contorted and shaggy, like big bushes, some vegetable plots, a melon patch the glass covers of which shone in the moonlight, and an old well. There were here and there stone benches which seemed black with moss. The walks were bordered with sorry little shrubs perfectly straight. The grass covered half of them, and a green moss covered the rest.

Jean Valjean had on one side the building, down the roof of which he had come, a wood-pile, and behind the wood, against the wall, a stone statue, the mutilated face of which was now nothing but a shapeless mask which was seen dimly through the darkness.

The building was in ruins, but some unfurnished rooms could be distinguished in it, one of which was cluttered, and appeared to serve as a shed.

Jean Valjean's first care had been to find his shoes, and put them on; then he entered the shed with Cosette. A man trying to escape never thinks himself sufficiently concealed. The child, thinking constantly of the Thénardiess, shared his instinct, and cowered down as low as she could.

Cosette trembled, and pressed closely to his side. They heard the tumultuous clamour of the patrol ransacking the cul-de-sac and the street, the clatter of their muskets against the stones, the calls of Javert to the watchmen he had stationed, and his curses mingled with words which they could not distinguish.

At the end of a quarter of an hour it seemed as though this stormy rumbling began to recede. Jean Valjean did not breathe.

He had placed his hand gently upon Cosette's mouth.

But the solitude about him was so strangely calm that that frightful din, so furious and so near, did not even cast over it a shadow of disturbance. It seemed as if these walls were built of the deaf stones spoken of in Scripture.

Suddenly, in the midst of this deep calm, a new sound arose; a celestial, divine, ineffable sound, as ravishing as the other was horrible. It was a hymn which came forth from the darkness, a bewildering mingling of prayer and harmony in the obscure and fearful silence of the night; voices of women, but voices with the pure accents of virgins, and artless accents of children; those voices which are not of earth, and which resemble those that the newborn still hear, and the dying hear already. This song came from the gloomy building which overlooked the garden. At the moment when the uproar of the demons receded, one would have said, it was a choir of angels approaching in the darkness.

Cosette and Jean Valjean fell on their knees.

They knew not what it was; they knew not where they were; but they both felt, the man and the child, the penitent and the innocent, that they ought to be on their knees.

These voices had this strange effect; they did not prevent the building from appearing deserted. It was like a supernatural song in an uninhabited dwelling.

While these voices were singing Jean Valjean was entirely absorbed in them. He no longer saw the night, he saw a blue sky. He seemed to feel the spreading of these wings which we all have within us.

The chant ceased. Perhaps it had lasted a long time. Jean Valjean could not have told. Hours of ecstasy are never more than a moment.

All had again relapsed into silence. There was nothing more in the street, nothing more in the garden. That which threatened, that which reassured, all had vanished. The wind rattled the dry grass on the top of the wall, which made a low, soft, and mournful noise.

7

THE MYSTERY CONTINUED

THE COLD NIGHT WIND had risen, which indicated that it must be between one and two o'clock in the morning. Poor Cosette did not speak. As she had sat down at his side and leaned her head on him, Jean Valjean thought that she was asleep. He bent over and looked at her. Her eyes were wide open, and she had a thoughtful look that gave Jean Valjean pain.

She was still trembling.

"Are you sleepy?" said Jean Valjean.

"I am very cold," she answered.

A moment after she added:

"Is she there yet?"

"Who?" said Jean Valjean.

"Madame Thénardier."

Jean Valjean had already forgotten the means he had employed to secure Cosette's silence.

"Oh!" said he. "She has gone. Don't be afraid any longer."

The child sighed as if a weight were lifted from her breast.

The ground was damp, the shed open on all sides, the wind freshened every moment. The goodman took off his coat and wrapped Cosette in it.

"Are you warmer, so?"

"Oh! yes, father!"

"Well, wait here a moment for me. I shall soon be back."

He went out of the ruin, and along by the large building, in search of some better shelter. He found doors, but they were all closed. All the windows of the ground-floor were barred.

Where was he? who would ever have imagined anything equal to this species of sepulchre in the midst of Paris? what was this strange house? A building full of nocturnal mystery, calling to souls in the shade with the voice of angels, and, when they came, abruptly presenting to them this frightful vision—promising to open the radiant gate of Heaven and opening the horrible door of the tomb. And that was in fact a building, a house which had its number in a street? It was not a dream? He had to touch the walls to believe it.

The cold, the anxiety, the agitation, the anguish of the night, were giving him a veritable fever, and all his ideas were jostling in his brain.

He went to Cosette. She was sleeping.

8

THE MYSTERY REDOUBLES

THE CHILD had laid her head upon a stone and gone to sleep.

He sat down near her and looked at her. Little by little, as he beheld her, he grew calm, and regained possession of his clearness of mind.

He plainly perceived this truth, the basis of his life henceforth, that so long as she should be alive, so long as he should have her with him, he should need nothing except for her, and fear nothing save on her account. He did not even realise that he was very cold, having taken off his coat to cover her.

Meanwhile, through the reverie into which he had fallen, he had heard for some time a singular noise. It sounded like a little bell that some one was shaking. This noise was in the garden. It was heard distinctly though feebly. It resembled the dimly heard tinkling of cow-bells in the pastures at night.

This noise made Jean Valjean turn.

He looked, and saw that there was some one in the garden.

Something which resembled a man was walking among the glass covers of the melon patch, rising up, stooping down, stopping, with a regular motion, as if he were drawing or stretching something upon the ground. This being appeared to limp.

Jean Valjean shuddered with the continual tremor of the outcast. To them everything is hostile and suspicious. They distrust the day because it helps to reveal them, and the night because it helps others to catch them. A moment ago he was shuddering because the garden was empty, now he shuddered because there was some one in it.

He fell again from chimerical terrors into real terrors. He said to himself that perhaps Javert and his spies had not gone away, that they had doubtless left somebody on the watch in the street; that, if this man should discover him in the garden, he would cry thief, and would deliver him up. He took the sleeping Cosette gently in his arms and carried her into the furthest corner of the shed behind a heap of old furniture that was out of use. Cosette did not stir.

From there he watched the strange motions of the man in the melon patch. It seemed very singular, but the sound of the bell followed every movement of the man. When the man approached, the sound approached; when he moved away, the sound moved away; if he made some sudden motion, a trill accompanied the motion; when he stopped, the noise ceased. It seemed evident that the bell was fastened to this man; but then what could that mean? what was this man to whom a bell was hung as to a ram or a cow?

While he was resolving these questions, he touched Cosette's hands. They were icy.

"Oh! God!" said he.

He called to her in a low voice:

"Cosette!"

She did not open her eyes.

He shook her smartly.

She did not wake.

"Could she be dead?" said he, and he sprang up, shuddering from head to foot.

The most frightful thoughts rushed through his mind in confusion. There are moments when hideous suppositions besiege us like a throng of furies and violently force the portals of our brain. When those whom we love are in danger, our solicitude invents all sorts of crazy ideas. He remembered that sleep may be fatal in the open air in a cold night.

Cosette was pallid; she had fallen prostrate on the ground at his feet, making no sign.

He listened for her breathing; she was breathing; but with a respiration that appeared feeble and about to stop.

How should he get her warm again? how rouse her? All else was banished from his thoughts. He rushed desperately out of the ruin.

It was absolutely necessary that in less than a quarter of an hour Cosette should be in bed and before a fire.

9

THE MAN WITH THE BELL

HE WALKED straight to the man whom he saw in the garden. He had taken in his hand the roll of money which was in his vest-pocket.

This man had his head down, and did not see him coming. A few strides, Jean Valjean was at his side.

Jean Valjean approached him, exclaiming:

"A hundred francs!"

The man started and raised his eyes.

"A hundred francs for you," continued Jean Valjean, "if you will give me refuge to-night."

The moon shone full in Jean Valjean's bewildered face.

"What, it is you, Father Madeleine!" said the man.

This name, thus pronounced, at this dark hour, in this unknown place, by this unknown man, made Jean Valjean start back.

He was ready for anything but that. The speaker was an old man, bent and lame, dressed much like a peasant, who had on his left knee a leather knee-cap from which hung a rather large bell. His face was in the shade, and could not be distinguished.

Meanwhile the goodman had taken off his cap, and was exclaiming, tremulously:

"Ah! my God! how did you come here, Father Madeleine? How did you get in, O Lord? Did you fall from the sky? There is no doubt, if you ever do fall, you will fall from there. And what has happened to you? You have no cravat, you have no hat, you have no coat? Do you know that you would have frightened anybody who did not know you? No coat? Merciful heavens! are the saints all crazy now? But how did you get in?"

One word did not wait for another. The old man spoke with a rustic volubility in which there was nothing disquieting. All this was said with a mixture of astonishment, and frank good nature.

"Who are you? and what is this house!" asked Jean Valjean.

"Oh! indeed, that is good now," exclaimed the old man. "I am the one you got the place for here, and this house is the one you got me the place in. What! you don't remember me?"

"No," said Jean Valjean. "And how does it happen that you know me?"

"You saved my life," said the man.

He turned, a ray of the moon lighted up his side face, and Jean Valjean recognised old Fauchelevent.

"Ah!" said Jean Valjean, "it is you? yes, I remember you."

"That is very fortunate!" said the old man, in a reproachful tone.

"And what are you doing here?" added Jean Valjean.

"Oh! I am covering my melons."

Old Fauchelevent had in his hand, indeed, at the moment when Jean Valjean accosted him, the end of a piece of awning which he was stretching out over the melon patch. He had already spread out several in this way during the hour he had been in the garden. It was this work which made him go through the peculiar motions observed by Jean Valjean from the shed.

He continued:

"I said to myself: the moon is bright, there is going to be a frost. Suppose I put their jackets on my melons? And," added he, looking at Jean Valjean, with a loud laugh, "you would have done well to do as much for yourself? but how did you come here?"

Jean Valjean, finding that he was known by this man, at least under his name of Madeleine, went no further with his precautions. He multiplied questions. Oddly enough their parts seemed reversed. It was he, the intruder, who put questions.

"And what is this bell you have on your knee?"

"That!" answered Fauchelevent, "that is so that they may keep away from me."

"How! keep away from you?"

Old Fauchelevent winked in an indescribable manner.

"Ah! Bless me! there's nothing but women in this house; plenty of young girls. It seems that I am dangerous to meet. The bell warns them. When I come they go away."

"What is this house?"

"Why, you know very well."

"No, I don't."

"Why, you got me this place here as gardener."

"Answer me as if I didn't know."

"Well, it is the Convent of the Petit Picpus, then."

Jean Valjean remembered. Chance, that is to say, Providence, had thrown him precisely into this convent of the Quartier Saint Antoine, to which old Fauchelevent, crippled by his fall from his cart, had been admitted, upon his recommendation, two years before. He repeated as if he were talking to himself:

"The Convent of the Petit Picpus!"

"But now, really," resumed Fauchelevent, "how the deuce did you manage to get in, you, Father Madeleine? It is no use for you to be a saint, you are a man; and no men come in here."

"But you are here."

"There is none but me."

"But," resumed Jean Valjean, "I must stay here."

"Oh! my God," exclaimed Fauchelevent.

Jean Valjean approached the old man, and said to him in a grave voice:

"Father Fauchelevent, I saved your life."

"I was first to remember it," answered Fauchelevent.

"Well, you can now do for me what I once did for you."

Fauchelevent grasped in his old wrinkled and trembling hands the robust hands of Jean Valjean, and it was some seconds before he could speak; at last he exclaimed:

"Oh! that would be a blessing of God if I could do something for you, in return for that! I save your life! Monsieur Mayor, the old man is at your disposal."

A wonderful joy had, as it were, transfigured the old gardener. A radiance seemed to shine forth from his face.[*]

"What do you want me to do?" he added.

---

[*]Hugo suggests that Fauchelevent has been transformed by divine grace.

"I will explain. You have a room?"

"I have a solitary shanty, over there, behind the ruins of the old convent, in a corner that nobody ever sees. There are three rooms."

The shanty was in fact so well concealed behind the ruins, and so well arranged, that no one should see it—that Jean Valjean had not seen it.

"Good," said Jean Valjean. "Now I ask of you two things."

"What are they, Monsieur Madeleine?"

"First, that you will not tell anybody what you know about me. Second, that you will not attempt to learn anything more."

"As you please. I know that you can do nothing dishonourable, and that you have always been a man of God. And then, besides, it was you that put me here. It is your place, I am yours."

"Very well. But now come with me. We will go for the child."

"Ah!" said Fauchelevent, "there is a child!"

He said not a word more, but followed Jean Valjean as a dog follows his master.

In half an hour Cosette, again become rosy before a good fire, was asleep in the old gardener's bed. Jean Valjean had put on his cravat and coat; his hat, which he had thrown over the wall, had been found and brought in. While Jean Valjean was putting on his coat, Fauchelevent had taken off his knee-cap with the bell attached, which now, hanging on a nail near a shutter, decorated the wall. The two men were warming themselves, with their elbows on a table, on which Fauchelevent had set a piece of cheese, some brown bread, a bottle of wine, and two glasses, and the old man said to Jean Valjean, putting his hand on his knee:

"Ah! Father Madeleine! you didn't know me at first? You save people's lives and then you forget them? Oh! that's bad; they remember you. You are ungrateful!"

10

IN WHICH IS EXPLAINED HOW
JAVERT LOST HIS PREY

THE EVENTS, the reverse side of which, so to speak, we have just seen, had been brought about under the simplest conditions.

When Jean Valjean, on the night of the very day that Javert arrested him at the death-bed of Fantine, escaped from the municipal prison of M——sur M——, the police supposed that the escaped convict would start for Paris. Paris is a maelstrom in which everything is lost; and everything disappears in this navel of the world as in the whirlpool of the sea. No forest conceals a man like this multitude. Fugitives of all kinds know this. They go to Paris to be swallowed up; there are swallowings-up which save. The police know it also, and it is in Paris that they search for what they have lost elsewhere. They searched there for the ex-mayor of M—— sur M——. Javert was summoned to Paris to aid in the investigation. Javert, in fact, was of great aid in the recapture of Jean Valjean. The zeal and intelligence of Javert on this occasion were remarked by M. Chabouillet, Secretary of the Prefecture, under Count Anglès. M. Chabouillet, who had already helped to advance Javert's career, secured the transfer of the inspector of M—— sur M—— to the police of Paris. There Javert rendered himself in various ways, and, let us say, although the word seems unusual for such service, honourably, useful.

He thought no more of Jean Valjean—with these hounds always upon the scent, the wolf of to-day banishes the memory of the wolf of yesterday—when, in December, 1823, he read a newspaper, he who never read the newspapers; but Javert, as a monarchist, made a point of knowing the details of the triumphal entry of the "Prince generalissimo" into Bayonne. Just as he finished the article which interested him, a name—the name of Jean Valjean—at the bottom of the page attracted his attention. The newspaper announced that the convict Jean Valjean was dead, and published the fact in terms so explicit, that Javert had no doubt of it. He merely said: *"That settles it."** Then he threw aside the paper, and thought no more of it.

Some time afterwards it happened that a police notice was transmitted by the Prefecture of Seine-et-Oise to the Prefecture of Police of Paris in relation to the kidnapping of a child, which had taken place, it was said, under peculiar circumstances in the commune of Montfermeil. A little girl, seven or eight years old, the notice said, who had been confided by her mother to an innkeeper of the country, had been stolen by an unknown man; this little girl answered to the name of Cosette, and was the child of a young woman named Fantine, who had died at the Hôpital, nobody knew when or where. This notice came under the eyes of Javert, and set him to thinking.

The name of Fantine was well known to him. He remembered that Jean Valjean had actually made him—Javert—laugh aloud by asking of him a respite of three days, in order to go for the child of this creature. He recalled the fact that Jean Valjean had been arrested at Paris, at the moment he was getting into the Montfermeil stage. Some indications had even led him to think then that it was the second time that he had taken it, and that he had already, the night previous, made another excursion to the environs of this village, for he had not been seen in the village itself. What was he doing in this region of Montfermeil? Nobody could guess. Javert understood it. The daughter of Fantine was there. Jean Valjean was going after her. Now this child had been stolen by an unknown man! Who could this man be? Could

---

*In French, *c'est là le bon écrou:* that [death] is the best lock-up.

it be Jean Valjean? But Jean Valjean was dead. Javert, without saying a word to any one, took the stage at the Plat d'Etain, cul-de-sac de Planchette, and took a trip to Montfermeil.

He expected to find great developments there; he found great obscurity.

For the first few days, the Thénardiers, in their spite, had blabbed the story about. The disappearance of the Lark had made some noise in the village. There were soon several versions of the story, which ended by becoming a case of kidnapping. Hence the police notice. However, when the first ebullition was over, Thénardier, with admirable instinct, very soon arrived at the conclusion that it is never useful to set in motion the Procureur du Roi; that the first result of his complaints in regard to the *kidnapping* of Cosette would be to fix upon himself, and on many business troubles which he had, the keen eye of justice. The last thing that owls wish is a candle. And first of all, how should he explain the fifteen hundred francs he had received? He stopped short, and enjoined secrecy upon his wife, and professed to be astonished when anybody spoke to him of the *stolen child*. He knew nothing about it; undoubtedly he had made some complaint at the time that the dear little girl should be "taken away" so suddenly; he would have liked, for affection's sake, to keep her two or three days; but it was her "grandfather" who had come for her, the most natural thing in the world. He had added the grandfather, which sounded well. It was upon this story that Javert fell on reaching Montfermeil. The grandfather put Jean Valjean out of the question.

Javert, however, dropped a few questions like plummets into Thénardier's story. Who was this grandfather, and what was his name? Thénardier answered with simplicity: "He is a rich farmer. I saw his passport. I believe his name is M. Guillaume Lambert."

Lambert is a very respectable reassuring name. Javert returned to Paris. "Jean Valjean is really dead," said he, "and I am a fool."

He had begun to forget all this story, when, in the month of March, 1824, he heard an odd person spoken of who lived in the parish of Saint Médard, and who was called "the beggar who gives alms." This person was, it was said, a man living on his income whose name nobody knew exactly, and who lived alone with a little girl eight years old, who knew nothing of herself except that she came from Montfermeil. Montfermeil! This name constantly recurring, excited Javert's attention anew. An old begging police spy, formerly a beadle, to whom this person had extended his charity, added some other details. "This man was very unsociable, never going out except at night, speaking to nobody, except to the poor sometimes, and allowing nobody to get acquainted with him. He wore a horrible old yellow coat which was worth millions, being lined all over with bank bills." This decidedly piqued Javert's curiosity. That he might get a near view of this fantastic rich man without frightening him away, he borrowed one day of the beadle his old frock, and the place where the old spy squatted every night droning out his orisons and playing the spy as he prayed.

"The suspicious individual" did indeed come to Javert thus disguised, and gave him alms; at that moment Javert raised his head and the shock which Jean Valjean received, thinking that he recognised Javert, Javert received, thinking that he recognised Jean Valjean.

However, the obscurity might have deceived him, the death of Jean Valjean was officially certified; Javert had still serious doubts; and in case of doubt, Javert, scrupulous as he was, never collared any man.

He followed the old man to Gorbeau House, and set "the old woman" talking, which was not at all difficult. The old woman confirmed the story of the coat lined with millions, and related to him the episode of the thousand-franc note. She had seen it! she had touched it! Javert hired a room. That very night he installed himself in it. He listened at the door of the mysterious lodger, hoping to hear the sound of his voice, but Jean Valjean perceived his candle through the key-hole and thwarted the spy by keeping silence.

The next day Jean Valjean decamped. But the noise of the five-franc coin which he dropped was noticed by the old woman, who hearing money clinking, suspected that he was going to move out, and hastened to forewarn Javert. At night, when Jean Valjean went out, Javert was waiting for him behind the trees of the boulevard with two men.

Javert had called for assistance from the Prefecture, but he had not given the name of the person he hoped to seize. That was his secret; and he kept it for three reasons; first, because the least indiscretion might give the alarm to Jean Valjean; next, because the arrest of an old escaped convict who was reputed dead, a criminal whom the records of justice had already classed for ever *among malefactors of the most dangerous kind,* would be a magnificent success which the senior members of the Parisian police certainly would never leave to a new-comer like Javert, and he feared they would take his galley-slave away from him; finally, because Javert, being an artist, had a liking for surprises. He hated these boasted successes which are deflowered by talking of them long in advance. He liked to elaborate his masterpieces in the shade, and then to unveil them suddenly afterwards.

Javert had followed Jean Valjean from tree to tree, then from street corner to street corner, and had not lost sight of him a single instant; even in the moments when Jean Valjean felt himself most secure, the eye of Javert was upon him. Why did not Javert arrest Jean Valjean? Because he was still in doubt.

It must be remembered that at that time the police was not exactly at its ease; it was cramped by a free press. Some arbitrary arrests, denounced by the newspapers, had been re-echoed even in the Chambers, and rendered the Prefecture timid. To attack individual liberty was a serious thing. The officers were afraid of making mistakes, the Prefect held them responsible; an error meant the loss of their place. Imagine the effect which this brief paragraph, repeated in twenty papers, would have produced in Paris. "Yesterday, an old white-haired grandsire, a respectable person living on his income, who was taking a walk with his grand-daughter, eight years old, was arrested and taken to the Station of the Prefecture as an escaped convict!"

Let us say, in addition, that Javert had his own personal scruples; the injunctions of his conscience were added to the injunctions of the Prefect. He was really in doubt.

Jean Valjean turned his back, and walked away in the darkness.

Sadness, trouble, anxiety, weight of cares, this new sorrow of being obliged to fly by night, and to seek a chance asylum in Paris for Cosette and himself, the necessity of adapting his pace to the pace of a child, all this, without his knowing it even, had changed Jean Valjean's gait, and impressed upon his carriage such an appearance of old age that the police itself, incarnated in Javert, could be deceived. The impossibility of approaching too near, his dress of an old preceptor of the emigration, the declaration of Thénardier, who made him a grandfather; finally, the belief in his death at the galleys, added yet more to the uncertainty which was increasing in Javert's mind.

For a moment he had an idea of asking him abruptly for his papers. But if the man were not Jean Valjean, and if the man were not a good old honest man of means, he was probably some sharper profoundly and skilfully adept in the obscure web of Parisian crime, some dangerous chief of bandits, giving alms to conceal his other talents, an old trick. He had comrades, accomplices, retreats on all hands, in which he would take refuge without doubt. All these windings which he was making in the streets seemed to indicate that he was not a simple honest man. To arrest him too soon would be "to kill the goose that laid the golden eggs." What inconvenience was there in waiting? Javert was very sure that he would not escape.

He walked on, therefore, in some perplexity, questioning himself continually in regard to this mysterious personage.

It was not until quite late, in the Rue de Pontoise, that, thanks to the bright light which streamed from a bar-room, he decidedly recognised Jean Valjean.

There are in this world two beings who can be deeply thrilled: the mother, who finds her child, and the tiger, who finds his prey. Javert felt this profound thrill.

As soon as he had positively recognised Jean Valjean, the formidable convict, he perceived that there were only three of them, and sent to the commissary of police, of the Rue de Pontoise, for additional aid. Before grasping a thorny stick, men put on gloves.

This delay and stopping at the Rollin square to arrange with his men almost made him lose the scent. However, he had very soon guessed that Jean Valjean's first wish would be to put the river between his pursuers and himself. He bowed his head and reflected, like a hound who put his nose to the ground to be sure of the way. Javert, with his straightforward power of instinct, went directly to the bridge of Austerlitz. A word to the toll-keeper set him right. "Have you seen a man with a little girl?" "I made him pay two sous," answered the tollman. Javert reached the bridge in time to see Jean Valjean on the other side of the river leading Cosette across the space lighted by the moon. He saw him enter the Rue de Chemin Vert Saint Antoine, he thought of the Cul-de-sac Genrot placed there like a trap, and of the only outlet from the Rue Droit Mur into the Petite Rue Picpus. He *put out beaters,* as hunters say; he sent one of his men hastily by a detour to guard that outlet. A patrol passing on its return to the station at the arsenal, he put it in requisition and took it along with him. In such games soldiers are trumps. Moreover, it is a maxim that, to take the boar requires the know-how of the hunter, and the strength of the dogs. These combinations being effected, feeling that Jean Valjean was caught between the Cul-de-sac Genrot on the right, his officer on the left, and himself, Javert, in the rear, he took a pinch of snuff.

Then he began to play. He enjoyed a ravishing and infernal moment; he let his man go before him, knowing that he had him, but desiring to put off as long as possible the moment of arresting him, delighting to feel that he was caught, and to see him free, fondly gazing upon him with the rapture of the spider which lets the fly buzz, or the cat which lets the mouse run. The paw and the talon find a monstrous pleasure in the quivering of the animal imprisoned in their grasp. What delight there is in this suffocation!

Javert was rejoicing. The links of his chain were solidly welded. He was sure of success; he had now only to close his hand.

Escorted as he was, the very idea of resistance was impossible, however energetic, however vigorous, and however desperate Jean Valjean might be.

Javert advanced slowly, sounding and ransacking on his way all the recesses of the street as he would the pockets of a thief.

When he reached the centre of the web, the fly was no longer there. Imagine his exasperation.

He questioned his sentinel at the corner of the Rue Droit Mur and Rue Picpus; this officer, who had remained motionless at his post, had not seen the man pass.

His disappointment had a moment of despair and fury.

However this may be, even at the moment when he perceived that Jean Valjean had escaped him, Javert did not lose his presence of mind. Sure that the convict who had broken his ban could not be far away, he set watches, arranged traps and ambushes, and beat the quarter the night through. The first thing that he saw was the displacement of the lamp that had been tampered with; its rope was cut. A precious clue, which led him astray, however, by directing all his researches towards the Cul-de-sac Genrot. There are in that cul-de-sac some rather low walls which face upon gardens the limits of which extend to some very large uncultivated grounds. Jean Valjean evidently must have fled that way. The fact is that, if he had penetrated into the Cul-de-sac Genrot a little farther, he would have done so, and would have been lost. Javert explored these gardens and these grounds, as if he were searching for a needle.

At daybreak, he left two intelligent men on the watch, and returned to the Prefecture of Police, crestfallen as a spy who has been caught by a thief.

[Book Six, "Petit Picpus," and Book Seven, "A Parenthesis," do not appear in this abridged edition.]

BOOK EIGHT
CEMETERIES TAKE WHAT IS GIVEN THEM

1

WHICH TELLS HOW TO ENTER THE CONVENT

INTO THIS HOUSE it was that Jean Valjean had, as Fauchelevent said, "fallen from heaven."

He had crossed the garden wall at the corner of the Rue Polonceau. That angels' hymn which he had heard in the middle of the night was the nuns chanting matins; that hall of which he had caught a glimpse in the obscurity, was the chapel; that phantom which he had seen stretched out on the floor was the sister performing the reparation; that bell the sound of which had so strangely surprised him was the gardener's bell fastened to old Fauchelevent's knee.

When Cosette had been put to bed, Jean Valjean and Fauchelevent had, as we have seen, taken a glass of wine and a piece of cheese before a blazing fire; then, the only bed in the shanty being occupied by Cosette, they had thrown themselves each upon a bundle of straw. Before closing his eyes, Jean Valjean had said: "Henceforth I must remain here." These words were chasing one another through Fauchelevent's head the whole night.

To tell the truth, neither of them had slept.

Jean Valjean, feeling that he was discovered and Javert was upon his track, knew full well that he and Cosette were lost should they return into the city. Since the new blast which had burst upon him had thrown him into this cloister, Jean Valjean had but one thought, to remain there. Now, for one in his unfortunate position, this convent was at once the safest and the most dangerous place, the most dangerous, for, no man being allowed to enter, if he should be discovered, it was a flagrant crime, and Jean Valjean would take but one step from the convent to prison; the safest, for if he succeeded in getting permission to remain, who would come there to look for him? To live in an impossible place; that would be safety.

For his part, Fauchelevent was racking his brains. He began by deciding that he was utterly bewildered. How did Monsieur Madeleine come there, with such walls! The walls of a cloister are not so easily crossed. How did he happen to be with a child? A man does not scale a steep wall with a child in his arms. Who was this child? Where did they both come from? Since Fauchelevent had been in the convent, he had not heard a word from M—— sur M——, and he knew nothing of what had taken place. Father Madeleine wore that air which discourages questions; and moreover, Fauchelevent said to himself: "One does not cross-examine a saint." To him Monsieur Madeleine had preserved all his prestige. From some words that escaped from Jean Valjean, however, the gardener thought he might conclude that Monsieur Madeleine had probably gone bankrupt on account of the hard times, and that he was pursued by his creditors; or it might be that he was compromised in some political affair and was concealing himself; which did not at all displease Fauchelevent, who, like many of our peasants of the north, had an old Bonapartist heart. Being in concealment, Monsieur Madeleine had taken the convent for an asylum, and it was natural that he should wish to remain there. But the mystery to which Fauchelevent constantly returned and over which he was racking his brains was, that Monsieur Madeleine should be there, and that this little girl should be with him. Fauchelevent saw them, touched them, spoke to them, and yet did not believe it. An incomprehensibility had made its way into Fauchelevent's hut. Fauchelevent was groping amid conjectures, but saw nothing clearly except this: Monsieur Madeleine has saved my life. This single certainty was sufficient, and determined him. He said aside to himself: It is my turn now. He added in his conscience: Monsieur Madeleine did not deliberate so long when the question was about squeezing himself under the waggon to draw me out. He decided that he would save Monsieur Madeleine.

He however put several questions to himself and made several answers: "After what he has done for me, if he were a thief, would I save him? just the same. If he were an assassin, would I save him? just the same. Since he is a saint, shall I save him? just the same."

But to have him remain in the convent, what a problem was that! Before that almost chimerical attempt, Fauchelevent did not recoil; this poor Picardy peasant, with no other ladder than his devotion, his goodwill, a little of that old country cunning, engaged for once in the service of a generous intention, undertook to scale the impossibilities of the cloister and the craggy escarpments of the rules of St. Benedict. Fauchelevent was an old man who had been selfish throughout his life, and who, near the end of his days, crippled, infirm, having no interest longer in the world, found it sweet to be grateful, and seeing a virtuous action to be done, threw himself into it like a man who, at the moment of death, finding at hand a glass of some good wine which he had never tasted, should drink it greedily. We might add that the atmosphere which he had been breathing now for several years in this convent had destroyed his former personality, and had at last rendered some good action necessary to him.*

He formed his resolution then: to devote himself to Monsieur Madeleine.

We have just described him as a *poor Picardy peasant.* The description is true, but incomplete. At the point of this story at which we now are, a closer acquaintance with Fauchelevent becomes necessary. He was a peasant, but he had been a notary, which added craft to his cunning, and penetration to his simplicity. Having, from various causes, failed in his business, from a notary he had fallen to a cartman and labourer. But, in spite of the oaths and blows which seem necessary with horses, he had retained something of the notary. He had some natural wit; he said neither I is nor I has;

---

*The Communion of Saints has transferred merit from both the nuns and M. Madeleine to Fauchelevent.

he could carry on a conversation, a rare thing in a village; and the other peasants said of him: he talks almost like a gentleman. Fauchelevent belonged in fact to that class which the flippant and impertinent vocabulary of the last century termed half-middle-class, half-rustic; and which the metaphors ranging from the castle to the hovel pigeonhole among the commoners as a bit cloddish, a bit citified, *pepper-and-salt*. Fauchelevent, although sorely tried and sorely used by Fortune; a sort of poor old soul worn threadbare, was nevertheless an impulsive man, and had a very willing heart; a precious quality, which prevents one from ever being wicked. His faults and his vices, for such he had had, were superficial; and finally, his physiognomy was one of those which attract the observer. That old face had none of those ugly wrinkles in the upper part of the forehead which indicate wickedness or stupidity.

At daybreak, having dreamed enormously, old Fauchelevent opened his eyes, and saw Monsieur Madeleine, who, seated upon his bunch of straw, was looking at Cosette as she slept. Fauchelevent half arose, and said:——

"Now that you are here, how are you going to manage to come in?"

This question summed up the situation, and wakened Jean Valjean from his reverie.

The two men took counsel.

"To begin with," said Fauchelevent, "you will not set foot outside of this room, neither the little girl nor you. One step in the garden, we are ruined."

"That is true."

"Monsieur Madeleine," resumed Fauchelevent, "you have arrived at a very good time; I mean to say very bad; there is one of these ladies dangerously sick. On that account they do not look this way much. She must be dying. They are saying the forty-hour prayers. The whole community is in disarray. That takes up their attention. She who is about departing is a saint. In fact, we are all saints here; all the difference between them and me is, that they say: our cell, and I say: my shanty. They are going to have the rites for the dying, and then for the dead. For to-day we shall be quiet here; but I cannot answer for to-morrow."

"However," observed Jean Valjean, "this shanty is under the corner of the wall; it is hidden by a sort of ruin; there are trees; they cannot see it from the convent."

"And I add, that the nuns never come near it."

"Well?" said Jean Valjean.

The question mark which followed that "well" meant: it seems to me that we can remain here concealed. This Fauchelevent answered:——

"There are the little girls."

"What little girls?" asked Jean Valjean.

As Fauchelevent opened his mouth to explain the words he had just uttered, a single stroke of a bell was heard.

"The nun is dead," said he. "There is the knell."

And he motioned to Jean Valjean to listen.

The bell sounded a second time.

"It is the knell, Monsieur Madeleine. The bell will strike every minute, for twenty-four hours, until the body goes out of the church. You see they play. During their recess, if a ball rolls here, that is enough for them to come after it, in spite of the rules, and rummage all about here. Those cherubs are little devils."

"Who?" asked Jean Valjean.

"The little girls. You would be found out very soon. They would cry, 'What! a man!' But there is no danger to-day. There will be no recreation. The day will be all prayers. You hear the bell. As I told you, a stroke every minute. It is the knell."

"I understand, Father Fauchelevent. There are student boarders."

And Jean Valjean thought within himself:——

"Here, then, Cosette can be educated, too."

Fauchelevent exclaimed:——

"Zounds! they are the little girls for you! And how they would scream at sight of you! and how they would run! Here, to be a man, is to have the plague. You see how they fasten a bell to my leg, as they would to a wild beast."

Jean Valjean was studying more and more deeply. "The convent would save us," murmured he. Then he raised his voice:

"Yes, the difficulty is in remaining."

"No," said Fauchelevent, "it is to get out."

Jean Valjean felt his blood run cold.

"To get out?"

"Yes, Monsieur Madeleine, in order to come in, it is necessary that you should get out."

And, after waiting for a sound from the tolling bell to die away, Fauchelevent pursued:——

"It would not do to have you found here like this. Whence do you come? for me you have fallen from heaven, because I know you; but for the nuns, you must come in at the door."

Suddenly they heard a complicated ringing upon another bell.

"Oh!" said Fauchelevent, "that is the ring for the nuns who have a voice in the affairs of the convent. They are going to the assembly. They always hold one when anybody dies. She died at daybreak. It is usually at day-break that people die. But cannot you go out the way you came in? Let us see; this is not to question you, but where did you come in?"

Jean Valjean became pale; the bare idea of climbing down again into that formidable street, made him shudder. Make your way out of a forest full of tigers, and when out, fancy yourself advised by a friend to return. Jean Valjean imagined all the police still swarming in the quarter, officers on the watch, sentries everywhere, frightful fists stretched out towards his collar,—Javert, perhaps, at the corner of the square.

"Impossible," said he. "Father Fauchelevent, let it go that I fell from on high."

"Ah! I believe it, I believe it," replied Fauchelevent. "You have no need to tell me so. God must have taken you into his hand, to have a close look at you, and then put you down. Only he meant to put you into a monastery; he made a mistake. Hark! another ring; that is to warn the porter to go and notify the municipality, so that they may go and notify the coroner, so that he may come and see that there is really a dead woman. All that is the ceremony of dying. These good ladies do not like this visit very much. A physician believes in nothing. He lifts the veil. He even lifts something else, sometimes. How soon they have notified the inspector, this time! What can be the matter? Your little one is asleep yet. What is her name?"

"Cosette."

"She is your girl? that is to say: you should be her grandfather?"

"Yes."

"For her, to get out will be easy. I have my door, which opens into the court. I knock; the porter opens. I have my basket on my back; the little girl is inside; I go out. Old Fauchelevent goes out with his basket—that is all simple. You will tell the little girl to keep very still. She will be under cover. I will leave her as soon as I can, with a good old friend of mine, a fruit merchant, in the Rue du Chemin Vert, who is deaf, and who has a little bed. I will scream into her ear that Cosette is my niece, and she must keep her for me till to-morrow. Then the little girl will come back with you; for I shall bring you back. It must be done. But how are you going to manage to get out?"

Jean Valjean shook his head.

"Let nobody see me, that is all, Father Fauchelevent. Find some means to get me out, like Cosette, in a basket, and under cover."

Fauchelevent scratched the tip of his ear with the middle finger of his left hand—a sign of serious embarrassment.

A third ring made a diversion.

"That is the coroner leaving," said Fauchelevent. "He has looked, and said she is indeed dead. When the inspector has stamped the passport for paradise, the undertaker sends a coffin. If it is a Holy Mother, the Mothers wrap her in the shroud; if it is a Holy Sister, the Sisters do. After which, I nail it up. That's a part of my gardening. A gardener is something of a gravedigger. They put her in a low room in the church which communicates with the street, and where no man can enter except the coroner. I do not count the bearers and myself as men. In that room I nail the coffin. The bearers come and take her, and giddy-up, driver: that is the way they go to heaven. They bring in a box with nothing in it, they carry it away with something inside. That is what an interment is. *De profundis.*"

A ray of the rising sun beamed upon the face of the sleeping Cosette, who half-opened her mouth dreamily, seeming like an angel drinking in the light. Jean Valjean was looking at her. He no longer heard Fauchelevent.

Not being heard is no reason for silence. The good old gardener peaceably continued his garrulous account.

"The grave is at the Vaugirard cemetery. They claim that this Vaugirard cemetery is going to be suppressed. It is an ancient cemetery, which is exempt from the regulations, which does not wear the uniform, and which is going to be retired. I am sorry for it, for it is convenient. I have a friend there—Father Mestienne, the gravedigger. The nuns here have the privilege of being carried to that cemetery at night-fall. There is an order of the

Police Headquarters, expressly for them. But how many events since yesterday! Mother Crucifixion is dead, and Father Madeleine"——

"Is buried," said Jean Valjean, sadly smiling.

Fauchelevent echoed the word.

"Really, if you were here for good, it would be a genuine burial."

A fourth time the bell rang out. Fauchelevent quickly took down the knee-piece and bell from the nail, and buckled it on his knee.

"This time, it is for me. The mother prioress wants me. Well! I am pricking myself with the tongue of my buckle. Monsieur Madeleine, do not stir, but wait for me. There is something new. If you are hungry, there is the wine, and bread and cheese."

And he went out of the hut, saying: "I am coming, I am coming."

Jean Valjean saw him hasten across the garden, as fast as his crooked leg would let him, with side glances at his melons the while.

In less than ten minutes, Father Fauchelevent, whose bell put the nuns to flight as he went along, rapped softly at a door, and a gentle voice answered—*Forever, Forever!* that is to say, *Come in.*

This door was that of the parlour allotted to the gardener, for use when it was necessary to communicate with him. This parlour was near the hall of the chapter. The prioress, seated in the only chair in the parlour, was waiting for Fauchelevent.

2

FAUCHELEVENT FACING THE DIFFICULTY

A SERIOUS and troubled bearing is peculiar, on critical occasions, to certain characters and certain professions, especially priests and monastics. At the moment when Fauchelevent entered, this double sign of preoccupation marked the countenance of the prioress, the charming and learned Mademoiselle de Blemeur, Mother Innocent, who was ordinarily cheerful.

The gardener made a timid bow, and stopped at the threshold of the cell. The prioress, who was saying her rosary, raised her eyes and said:

"Ah! it is you, Father Fauvent."

This abbreviation had been adopted in the convent.

Fauchelevent again began his bow.

"Father Fauvent, I have called you."

"I am here, reverend mother."

"I wish to speak to you."

"And I, for my part," said Fauchelevent, with a boldness at which he was alarmed himself, "I have something to say to the most reverend mother."

The prioress looked at him.

"Ah, you have a communication to make to me."

"A petition!"

"Well, what is it?"

The goodman, with the assurance of one who feels that he is appreciated, began before the reverend prioress a rustic harangue, quite diffuse and very profound. He spoke at length of his age, his infirmities, of the weight of years henceforth doubly heavy upon him, of the growing demands of his work, of the size of the garden, of the nights to be spent, like last night for example, when he had to put awnings over the melons on account of the moon; and finally ended with this: "that he had a brother—(the prioress gave a start)—a brother not young—(second start of the prioress, but a reassured start)—that if it was desired, this brother could come and live with him and help him; that he was an excellent gardener; that the community would get good services from him, better than his own; that, otherwise, if his brother were not admitted, as he, the oldest, felt that he was broken down, and unequal to the labour, he would be obliged to leave, though with much regret; and that his brother had a little girl that he would bring with him, who would be reared under God in the house, and who, perhaps,—who knows?—would some day become a nun.

When he had finished, the prioress stopped the sliding of her rosary through her fingers, and said:

"Can you, between now and nightfall, procure a strong iron bar?"

"For what work?"

"To be used as a lever."

"Yes, reverend mother," answered Fauchelevent.

The prioress, without adding a word, arose, and went into the next room, which was the hall of the chapter, where the voting mothers were probably assembled: Fauchelevent remained alone.

3

MOTHER INNOCENT

ABOUT a quarter of an hour elapsed. The prioress returned and resumed her seat.

Both parties seemed preoccupied. We are transcribing as well as we can the dialogue that followed.

"Father Fauvent?"

"Reverend mother?"

"You are familiar with the chapel?"

"I have a little box there to go to mass, and the offices."

"And you have been in the choir about your work?"

"Two or three times."

"A stone is to be raised."

"Heavy?"

"The slab of the pavement at the side of the altar."

"The stone that covers the vault?"

"Yes."

"That is a piece of work where it would be well to have two men."

"Mother Ascension, who is as strong as a man, will help you."

"A woman is never a man."

"And then you will have a lever."

"That is the only kind of key that fits that kind of door."

"There is a ring in the stone."

"I will pass the lever through it."

"And the stone is arranged to turn on a pivot."

"Very well, reverend mother, I will open the vault."

"And the four mother choristers will assist you."

"And when the vault is opened?"

"It must be shut again."

"Is that all?"

"No."

"Give me your orders, most reverend mother."

"Fauvent, we have confidence in you."

"I am here to do everything."

"And to keep silent about everything."

"Yes, reverend mother."

"When the vault is opened——"

"I will shut it again."

"But before——"

"What, reverend mother?"

"Something must be let down."

There was silence. The prioress, after a quivering of the underlip which resembled hesitation, spoke:

"Father Fauvent?"

"Reverend mother?"

"You know that a mother died this morning."

"No."

"You have not heard the bell then?"

"Nothing is heard at the further end of the garden."

"Really?"

"I can hardly distinguish my ring."

"She died at daybreak."

"And then, this morning, the wind didn't blow my way."

"It is Mother Crucifixion. One of the blest."

The prioress was silent, moved her lips a moment as in a mental orison, and resumed:

"Father Fauvent, the community has been blessed in Mother Crucifixion. Doubtless, it is not given to everybody to die like Cardinal de Bérulle, saying the holy mass, and to breathe out his soul to God, pronouncing these words: *Hanc igitur oblationem*. But without attaining such great happiness, Mother Crucifixion had a very precious death. She had her consciousness to the last. She spoke to us, then she spoke to the angels. She gave us her last commands. If you had a little more faith, and if you could have been in her cell, she would have cured your leg by touching it. She smiled. We felt that she was returning to life in God. There was something of Paradise in that death."

Fauchelevent thought that he had been listening to a prayer.

"Amen!" said he.

"Father Fauvent, we must do what the dead wish."

The prioress counted a few beads on her chaplet. Fauchelevent was silent. She continued:

"I have consulted upon this question several ecclesiastics labouring in Our Lord, who are engaged in the exercise of clerical functions, and with admirable results.

"We must obey the dead. To be buried in the vault under the altar of the chapel, not to go into profane ground, to remain in death where she prayed in life; this was the last request of Mother Crucifixion. She has asked it, that is to say, commanded it."

"But it is forbidden."

"Forbidden by men, enjoined by God."

"If it should come to be known?"

"We have confidence in you."

"Oh! as for me, I am like a stone in your wall."

"The chapter has assembled. The vocal mothers, whom I have just consulted again and who are now deliberating, have decided that Mother Crucifixion should be, according to her desire, buried in her coffin under our altar. Think, Father Fauvent, if there should be miracles performed here! what glory under God for the community! Miracles spring from tombs."

"But, reverend Mother, if the agent of the Health Commission——"

"St. Benedict II, in the matter of burial, resisted Constantine Pogonatus."

"However, the Commissary of Police——"

"Chonodemaire, one of the seven German kings who entered Gaul in the reign of Constantius, expressly recognised the right of conventuals to be inhumed in religion, that is to say, under the altar."

"But the Inspector of the Prefecture——"

"The world is nothing before the cross. Martin, eleventh general of the Carthusians, gave to his order this device: *Stat crux dum volvitur orbis*."

"Amen," said Fauchelevent, imperturbable in this method of extricating himself whenever he heard any Latin.

The prioress drew breath, then turning towards Fauchelevent:

"Father Fauvent, is it settled?"

"It is settled, reverend mother."

"Can we count upon you?"

"I shall obey."

"It is well."

"I am entirely devoted to the convent."

"Agreed, you will close the coffin. The sisters will carry it into the chapel. The office for the dead will be said. Then they will return to the cloister. Between eleven o'clock and midnight, you will come with your iron bar. All will be done with the greatest secrecy. There will be in the chapel only the four mother choristers, Mother Ascension, and you."

"And the sister who will be on watch."

"She will not turn around."

"But she will hear."

"She will not listen; moreover, what the cloister knows the world does not know."

There was a pause again. The prioress continued:

"You will take off your bell. It is unnecessary for the sister on watch to notice that you are there."

"Reverend mother?"

"What, Father Fauvent?"

"Has the coroner made his visit?"

"He is going to make it at four o'clock to-day. The bell has been sounded which summons the coroner. But you do not hear any ring then?"

"I only pay attention to my own."

"That is right, Father Fauvent."

"Reverend mother, I shall need a lever at least six feet long."

"Where will you get it?"

"Where there are gratings there are always iron bars. I have my heap of old iron at the back of the garden."

"About three-quarters of an hour before midnight; do not forget."

"Reverend mother?"

"What?"

"If you should ever have any other work like this, my brother is very strong. A Turk."

"You will do it as quickly as possible."

"I cannot go very fast. I am infirm; it is on that account I need help. I limp."

"To limp is not a crime, and it may be a blessing. The Emperor Henry II, who fought the Antipope Gregory, and re-established Benedict VIII, has two surnames: the Saint and the Lame."

"Two overcoats are very good," murmured Fauchelevent, who, in reality, was a little hard of hearing.*

"Father Fauvent, now I think of it, we will take a whole hour. It is not

---

*Fauchelevent mishears *surnoms* as *surtouts*.

too much. Be at the high altar with the iron bar at eleven o'clock. The office commences at midnight. It must all be finished a good quarter of an hour before."

"I will do everything to prove my zeal for the community. This is the arrangement. I shall nail up the coffin. At eleven o'clock precisely I will be in the chapel. The mother choristers will be there. Mother Ascension will be there. Two men would be better. But no matter! I shall have my lever. We shall open the vault, let down the coffin, and close the vault again. After which, there will be no trace of anything. The government will suspect nothing. Reverend mother, is everything arranged then?"

"No."

"What more is there?"

"There is still the empty coffin."

This brought them to a stand. Fauchelevent pondered. The prioress pondered.

"Father Fauvent, what shall be done with the coffin?"

"It will be put in the ground."

"Empty?"

Another silence. Fauchelevent made with his left hand that peculiar gesture, which dismisses an unpleasant question.

"Reverend mother, I nail up the coffin in the lower room in the church, and nobody can come in there except me, and I will cover the coffin with the pall."

"Yes, but the bearers, in putting it into the hearse and in letting it down into the grave, will surely perceive that there is nothing inside."

"Ah! the de—!" exclaimed Fauchelevent.

The prioress began to cross herself, and looked fixedly at the gardener. *Vil* stuck in his throat.

He made haste to think of an expedient to make her forget the oath.

"Reverend mother, I will put some earth into the coffin. That will have the effect of a body."

"You are right. Earth is the same thing as man. So you will prepare the empty coffin?"

"I will attend to that."

The face of the prioress, till then dark and anxious, became again serene. She made him the sign of a superior dismissing an inferior. Fauchelevent moved towards the door. As he was going out, the prioress gently raised her voice.

"Father Fauvent, I am satisfied with you; to-morrow after the burial, bring your brother to me, and tell him to bring his daughter."

4

IN WHICH JEAN VALJEAN HAS QUITE
THE APPEARANCE OF HAVING
READ AUSTIN CASTILLEJO

THE STRIDES of the lame are like the glances of the one-eyed: they do not speedily reach their aim. Furthermore, Fauchelevent was perplexed. It took him nearly a quarter of an hour to get back to the shanty in the garden. Cosette was awake. Jean Valjean had seated her near the fire. At the moment when Fauchelevent entered, Jean Valjean was showing her the gardener's basket hanging on the wall and saying to her:

"Listen attentively to me, my little Cosette. We must go away from this house, but we shall come back, and we shall be very well off here. The good man here will carry you out on his back inside there. You will wait for me at a lady's. I shall come and find you. Above all, if you do not want the Thénardiess to take you back, obey and say nothing."

Cosette nodded her head with a serious look.

At the sound of Fauchelevent opening the door, Jean Valjean turned.

"Well?"

"All is arranged, and nothing is," said Fauchelevent. "I have permission to bring you in; but before bringing you in, it is necessary to get you out. That is where the cart is blocked! For the little girl, it is easy enough."

"You will carry her out?"

"And she will keep quiet?"

"I will answer for it."

"But you, Father Madeleine?"

And, after an anxious silence, Fauchelevent exclaimed:

"But why not go out the way you came in?"

Jean Valjean, as before, merely answered: "Impossible."

Fauchelevent talking more to himself than to Jean Valjean, grumbled:

"There is another thing that torments me. I said I would put in some earth. But I think that earth inside, instead of a body, will not be like it; that will not do, it will shake about; it will move. The men will feel it. You understand, Father Madeleine, the government will find it out."

Jean Valjean stared at him, and thought that he was raving.

Fauchelevent resumed:

"How the d—ickens are you going to get out? For all this must be done to-morrow. To-morrow I am to bring you in. The prioress expects you."

Then he explained to Jean Valjean that this was a reward for a service that he, Fauchelevent, was rendering to the community. That it was a part of his duties to assist in burials, that he nailed up the coffins, and attended the grave-digger at the cemetery. That the nun who died that morning had requested to be buried in the coffin which she had used as a bed, and interred in the vault under the altar of the chapel. That this was forbidden by the regulations of the police, but that she was one of those departed ones to whom nothing is refused. That the prioress and the vocal mothers intended to carry out the will of the deceased. So much the worse for the government. That he, Fauchelevent, would nail up the coffin in the cell, raise the stone in the chapel, and let down the body into the vault. And that, in return for this, the prioress would admit his brother into the house as gardener and his niece as boarder. That his brother was M. Madeleine, and that his niece was Cosette. That the prioress had told him to bring his brother the next evening, after the fictitious burial at the cemetery. But that he could not bring M. Madeleine from the outside, if M. Madeleine were not outside. That that was the first difficulty. And then that he had another difficulty; the empty coffin.

"What is the empty coffin?" asked Jean Valjean.

Fauchelevent responded:

"The coffin from the administration."

"What coffin? and what administration?"

"A nun dies. The municipality physician comes and says: there is a nun dead. The government sends a coffin. The next day it sends a hearse and some bearers to take the coffin and carry it to the cemetery. The bearers will come and take up the coffin; there will be nothing in it."

"Put somebody in it."

"A dead body? I have none."

"No."

"What then?"

"A living body."

"What living body?"

"Me," said Jean Valjean.

Fauchelevent, who had taken a seat, sprang up as if a firecracker had burst under his chair.

"You!"

"Why not?"

Jean Valjean had one of those rare smiles which came over him like the aurora in a winter sky.

"You know, Fauchelevent, that you said: Mother Crucifixion is dead, and that I added: and Father Madeleine is buried. It will be so."

"Ah! good, you are laughing, you are not talking seriously."

"Very seriously. I must get out!"

"Undoubtedly."

"And I told you to find a basket and a cover for me also."

"Well!"

"The basket will be of pine, and the cover will be of black cloth."

"In the first place, a white cloth. The nuns are buried in white."

"Well, a white cloth."

"You are not like other men, Father Madeleine."

To see such devices, which are nothing more than the savage and fool-hardy inventions of the galleys, appear in the midst of the peaceful things that surrounded him and mingled with what he called the "little jog-jog of the convent," was to Fauchelevent an astonishment comparable to that of a person who should see a seagull fishing in the gutter in the Rue St. Denis.

Jean Valjean continued:

"The question is, how to get out without being seen. This is the means. But in the first place tell me, how is it done? where is this coffin?"

"The empty one?"

"Yes."

"Down in what is called the dead-room. It is on two sawhorses and under the pall."

"How long is the coffin?"

"Six feet."

"What is the dead-room?"

"It is a room on the ground floor, with a grated window towards the garden, closed on the outside with a shutter, and two doors; one leading to the convent, the other to the church."

"What church?"

"The church on the street, the church for everybody."

"Have you the keys of those two doors?"

"No. I have the keys of the door that opens into the convent; the porter has the key of the door that opens into the church."

"When does the porter open that door?"

"Only to let in the undertaker's helpers, who come after the coffin; as soon as the coffin goes out, the door is closed again."

"Who nails up the coffin?"

"I do."

"Who puts the cloth on it?"

"I do."

"Are you alone?"

"No other man, except the police physician, can enter the dead-room. That is even written upon the wall."

"Could you, to-night, when all are asleep in the convent, hide me in that room?"

"No. But I can hide you in a little dark closet which opens into the dead-room, where I keep my burial tools, and of which I have the care and the key."

"At what hour will the hearse come after the coffin to-morrow?"

"About three o'clock in the afternoon. The burial takes place at the Vaugirard cemetery, a little before night. It is not very near."

"I shall remain hidden in your tool-closet all night and all the morning. And about eating? I shall be hungry."

"I will bring you something."

"You can come and nail me up in the coffin at two o'clock."

Fauchelevent started back, and began to snap his fingers.

"But it is impossible!"

"Pshaw! to take a hammer and drive some nails into a board?"

What seemed unheard-of to Fauchelevent was, we repeat, simple to Jean Valjean. Jean Valjean had been in worse straits. He who has been a prisoner knows the art of making himself small according to the dimensions of the place for escape. The prisoner is subject to flight as the sick man is to the crisis which cures or kills him. An escape is a cure. What does not one undergo to be cured? To be nailed up and carried out in a chest like a bundle, to live a long time in a box, to find air where there is none, to economise the breath for entire hours, to know how to be stifled without dying—that was one of the somber talents of Jean Valjean.

Moreover, a coffin in which there is a living being, that convict's expedient, is also an emperor's expedient. If we can believe the monk Austin Castillejo, this was the means which Charles V, desiring after his abdication to see La Plombes again a last time, employed to bring her into the monastery of St. Juste and to take her out again.

Fauchelevent, recovering a little, exclaimed:

"But how will you manage to breathe?"

"I shall breathe."

"In that box? Only to think of it suffocates me."

"You surely have a drill, you can make a few little holes about the mouth here and there, and you can nail it without drawing the upper board tight."

"Good! But if you happen to cough or sneeze?"

"He who is escaping never coughs and never sneezes."

And Jean Valjean added:

"Father Fauchelevent, I must decide: either to be arrested here, or to be willing to go out in the hearse."

Everybody has noticed the taste which cats have for stopping and loitering in a half-open door. Who has not said to a cat: Why don't you come in? There are men who, with an opportunity half-open before them, have a similar tendency to remain undecided between two resolutions, at the risk of being crushed by destiny abruptly closing the opportunity. The overly prudent, cats as they are, and because they are cats, sometimes run more danger than the bold. Fauchelevent was of this hesitating nature. However, Jean Valjean's coolness won him over in spite of himself. He grumbled:

"It is true, there is no other way."

Jean Valjean resumed:

"The only thing that I am anxious about, is what will be done at the cemetery."

"That is just what does not embarrass me," exclaimed Fauchelevent. "If you are sure of getting yourself out of the coffin, I am sure of getting you out of the grave. The gravedigger is a drunkard and a friend of mine. He is Father Mestienne. An old son of the old vine. The gravedigger puts the dead in the grave, and I put the gravedigger in my pocket. I will tell you what will take place. We shall arrive a little before dusk, three-quarters of an hour before the cemetery gates are closed. The hearse will go to the grave. I shall follow: that is my business. I will have a hammer, a chisel, and some pincers in my pocket. The hearse stops, the bearers tie a rope around your coffin and let you down. The priest says the prayers, makes the sign of the cross, sprinkles the holy water, and is off. I remain alone with Father Mestienne. He is my friend, I tell you. One of two things; either he will be drunk, or he will not be drunk. If he is not drunk, I say to him: come and take a drink before the *Good Quince* is shut. I get him away, I fuddle him; Father Mestienne is not long in getting fuddled, he is always half way. I lay him under the table, I take his card from him to return to the cemetery with! and I come back without him. You will have only me to deal with. If he is drunk, I say to him: be off. I'll do your work. He goes away, and I pull you out of the hole."

Jean Valjean extended his hand, upon which Fauchelevent threw himself with a rustic outburst of touching devotion.

"It is settled, Father Fauchelevent. All will go well."

"Provided nothing goes amiss," thought Fauchelevent. "How terrible that would be!"

5

IT IS NOT ENOUGH TO BE A DRUNKARD
TO BE IMMORTAL

NEXT DAY, as the sun was declining, the scattered passers-by on the Boulevard du Maine took off their hats at the passage of an old-fashioned hearse, adorned with death's-heads, cross-bones, and tear-drops. In this hearse there was a coffin covered with a white cloth upon which was displayed a large black cross like a great dummy with hanging arms. A draped carriage, in which might be seen a priest in a surplice, and a choir-boy in a red skullcap, followed. Two bearers in grey uniform with black trimmings walked on the right and left of the hearse. In the rear came an old man dressed like a labourer, who limped. The procession moved towards the Vaugirard cemetery.

Sticking out of the man's pocket were the handle of a hammer, the blade of a cold chisel, and the double handles of a pair of pincers.

The Vaugirard cemetery was an exception among the cemeteries of Paris. It had its peculiar usages, as it had its porte-cochère, and its small door which, in the neighbourhood, old people faithful to archaic words called the horseman's door and the pedestrian door. The Bernardine-Benedictines of the Petit Picpus had obtained the right, as we have said, to be buried in a corner apart and at night, this ground having formerly belonged to their community. The gravediggers, having thus to work in the cemetery in the evening in summer, and at night in winter, were subject to a special regulation. The gates of the cemeteries of Paris closed at that epoch at sunset, and, this being a measure of municipal order, the Vaugirard cemetery was subject to it like the rest.* The gatehouse door and the pedestrian door were two contiguous gratings; near which was a pavilion built by the architect Perronet, in which the guardian of the cemetery lived. These gratings therefore inexorably turned upon their hinges the instant the sun disappeared behind the dome of the Invalides. If any gravedigger, at that moment, had lingered in the cemetery his only resource for getting out was his gravedigger's card, given him by the administration of funeral ceremonies. A sort of letterbox was arranged in the shutter of the gate-keeper's window. The gravedigger dropped his card into this box, the gate-keeper heard it fall, pulled the string, and the pedestrian door opened. If the gravedigger did not have his card, he gave his name; the gate-keeper, sometimes in bed and asleep, got up, went to identify the gravedigger, and open the door with the key; the gravedigger went out, but paid fifteen francs fine.

This cemetery, with its peculiar procedures, violated the symmetry of the administration. It was suppressed shortly after 1830. The Mont Parnasse Cemetery, called the Cemetery of the East, has succeeded it, and has inherited this famous drinking house let into the Vaugirard cemetery, which was surmounted by a quince painted on a board, which looked on one side upon the tables of the drinkers, and on the other upon graves, with this inscription: *The Good Quince.*†

The Vaugirard cemetery was what might be called a decayed cemetery. It was falling into disuse. Mould was invading it, flowers were leaving it. The well-to-do citizens little cared to be buried at Vaugirard; it sounded poor. Père Lachaise is very fine! to be buried in Père Lachaise is like having mahogany furniture. That says elegance to everyone. The Vaugirard cemetery was a venerable inclosure, laid out like an old French garden. Straight walks, box, evergreens, hollies, old tombs under old yews, very high grass. Night there was terrible. There were some very dismal outlines there.

The sun had not yet set when the hearse with the white pall and the black cross entered the avenue of the Vaugirard cemetery. The lame man who followed it was no other than Fauchelevent.

The burial of Mother Crucifixion in the vault under the altar, the departure of Cosette, the introduction of Jean Valjean into the dead-room, all had been carried out without obstruction, and nothing had gone wrong.

We will say, by the way, the inhumation of Mother Crucifixion under the convent altar is, to us, a perfectly venial thing. It is one of those faults which resemble a duty. The nuns had accomplished it, not only without

---

*Cemeteries are locked at night to prevent grave robbing, desecration of tombs, and the sale of cadavers for dissection.
†*Le Bon Coing* in French; puns with *Le Bon Coin,* meaning the cozy corner.

discomposure, but with an approving conscience. In the cloister, what is called the "government" is only an interference with authority, an interference which is always questionable. First the rule of the order; as to the law, we will see. Men, make as many laws as you please, but keep them for yourselves. The tribute to Cæsar is never more than the remnant of the tribute to God. A prince is nothing in the presence of a principle.

Fauchelevent limped behind the hearse, very well satisfied. His two twin plots, one with the nuns, the other with M. Madeleine, one for the convent, the other against it, had succeeded equally well. Jean Valjean's calmness had that powerful tranquillity which is contagious. Fauchelevent had now no doubt of success. What remained to be done was nothing. Within two years he had fuddled the gravedigger ten times, good Father Mestienne, a rubicund old fellow. Father Mestienne was play for him. He did what he liked with him. He controlled him at will and at his fancy. Mestienne saw through Fauchelevent's eyes.* Fauchelevent's security was complete.

At the moment the convoy entered the avenue leading to the cemetery, Fauchelevent, happy, looked at the hearse and rubbed his big hands together, saying in an undertone:

"Here's a farce!"

Suddenly the hearse stopped; they were at the gate. It was necessary to exhibit the burial permit. The undertaker whispered with the porter of the cemetery. During this colloquy, which always causes a delay of a minute or two, somebody, an unknown man, came and placed himself behind the hearse at Fauchelevent's side. He was a working-man, who wore a vest with large pockets, and had a pick under his arm.

Fauchelevent looked at this unknown man.

"Who are you?" he asked.

The man answered:

"The gravedigger."

Should a man survive a cannon-shot through his breast, he would present the appearance that Fauchelevent did.

"The gravedigger?"

"Yes."

"You!"

"Me."

"The gravedigger is Father Mestienne."

"He was."

"What! he was?"

"He is dead."

Fauchelevent was ready for anything but this, that a gravedigger could die. It is, however, true; gravediggers themselves die. By dint of digging graves for others, they open their own.

---

*In French, *il le coiffait*—literally, "he did his hair"; figuratively it means "he seduced him [into drinking] by putting the idea in his head."

Fauchelevent remained speechless. He had hardly the strength to stammer out:

"But it's not possible!"

"It is so."

"But," repeated he, feebly, "the gravedigger is Father Mestienne."

"After Napoleon, Louis XVIII. After Mestienne, Gribier. Peasant, my name is Gribier."

Fauchelevent grew pale; he stared at Gribier.

He was a long, thin, livid man, perfectly funereal. He had the appearance of a broken-down doctor turned gravedigger.

Fauchelevent burst out laughing.

"Ah! what droll things happen! Old Mestienne is dead. Little old Mestienne is dead, but hurrah for little old Lenoir! You know what little old Lenoir is? It is the mug of red wine on the counter for a six spot. It is the mug of Surêne, zounds! real Paris Surêne. So he is dead, old Mestienne! I am sorry for it; he was a jolly fellow. But you too, you are a jolly fellow. Isn't that so, comrade? we will go and take a drink together, right away."

The man answered: "I have studied, I have graduated. I never drink."

The hearse had started moving again, and was rolling along the main avenue of the cemetery.

Fauchelevent had slackened his pace. He limped still more from anxiety than from infirmity.

The gravedigger walked before him.

Fauchelevent again scrutinised the unexpected Gribier.

He was one of those men who, though young, have an old appearance, and who, though thin, are very strong.

"Comrade!" cried Fauchelevent.

The man turned.

"I am the gravedigger of the convent."

"My colleague," said the man.

Fauchelevent, illiterate, but very keen, understood that he had to do with a very formidable species, a good talker.

He mumbled out:

"Is it so, Father Mestienne is dead?"

The man answered:

"Perfectly. The good God consulted his list of bills payable. It was Father Mestienne's turn. Father Mestienne is dead."

Fauchelevent repeated mechanically.

"The good God."

"The good God," said the man authoritatively. "What the philosophers call the Eternal Father; the Jacobins, the Supreme Being."

"Are we not going to make each other's acquaintance?" stammered Fauchelevent.

"It is made. You are a peasant, I am a Parisian."

"We are not acquainted as long as we have not drunk together. He who empties his glass empties his heart. Come and drink with me. You can't refuse."

"Business first."

Fauchelevent said to himself: I am lost.

They were now only a few turns of the wheel from the path that led to the nuns' corner.

The gravedigger continued:

"Peasant, I have seven youngsters that I must feed. As they must eat, I must not drink."

And he added with the satisfaction of a serious being who is making a sententious phrase:

"Their hunger is the enemy of my thirst."

The hearse turned a huge cypress, left the main path, took a little one, entered upon the grounds, and was lost in a thicket. This indicated the immediate proximity of the grave. Fauchelevent slackened his pace, but could not slacken that of the hearse. Luckily the mellow soil, wet by the winter rains, stuck to the wheels, and made the track heavy.

He approached the gravedigger.

"They have such a good little Argenteuil wine," suggested Fauchelevent.

"Villager," continued the man, "I ought not to be a gravedigger. My father was porter at the Prytanée.* He intended me for literature. But he was unfortunate. He lost his money on stocks. I was obliged to renounce the condition of an author. However, I am still a public scribe."

"But then you are not the gravedigger?" replied Fauchelevent, catching at a straw, feeble as it was.

"One does not prevent the other. I cumulate."

Fauchelevent did not understand this last word.

"Let us go and drink," said he.

Here an observation is necessary. Fauchelevent, whatever was his anguish, proposed to drink, but did not explain himself on one point; who should pay? Ordinarily Fauchelevent proposed, and Father Mestienne paid. A proposal to drink resulted evidently from the new situation produced by the fact of the new gravedigger, and this proposal he must make; but the old gardener left, not unintentionally, the proverbial quarter of an hour of Rabelais unclear.† As for himself, Fauchelevent, however excited he was, did not care to pay.

The gravedigger went on, with a smile of superiority:

"We must live. I accepted the succession of Father Mestienne. When one has almost finished his classes, he is a philosopher. To the labour of my hand, I have added the labour of my arm. I have my little writer's shop at the Market in the Rue de Sèvre. You know? the umbrella market. All the cooks of the Croix Rouge come to me; I patch up their declarations to their true loves. In the morning I write love letters; in the evening I dig graves. Such is life, peasant."

---

*Le Prytanée was a military academy.
†Idiom for "he didn't say who was going to pay."

The hearse advanced; Fauchelevent, full of anxiety, looked about him on all sides. Great drops of sweat were falling from his forehead.

"However," continued the gravedigger, "one cannot serve two mistresses; I must choose between the pen and the pick. The pick hurts my hand."

The hearse stopped.

The choir-boy got out of the hearse, then the priest.

One of the forward wheels of the hearse was lifted a little by a heap of earth, beyond which was seen an open grave.

"This is a laugh!" repeated Fauchelevent in consternation.

6

DEAD AND BURIED*

WHO WAS in the coffin? We know. Jean Valjean.

Jean Valjean had arranged it so that he could live in it, and could breathe, if only barely.

It is a strange thing to what extent an easy conscience gives calmness in other respects. The entire strategem pre-arranged by Jean Valjean had been working, and working well, since the night before. He counted, as did Fauchelevent, upon Father Mestienne. He had no doubt of the result. Never was a situation more critical, never calmness more complete.

The four boards of the coffin exhaled a kind of terrible peace. It seemed as if something of the repose of the dead had entered into the tranquillity of Jean Valjean.

From within that coffin he had been able to follow, and he had followed, all the phases of the fearful drama which he was playing with Death.

Soon after Fauchelevent had finished nailing down the upper board, Jean Valjean had felt himself carried out, then wheeled along. By the diminished jolting, he had felt that he was passing from the pavement to the hard ground; that is to say, that he was leaving the streets and entering upon the boulevards. By a dull sound, he had divined that they were crossing the bridge of Austerlitz. At the first stop he had comprehended that they were entering the cemetery; at the second stop he had said: here is the grave.

---

*"Dead and Buried" translates the idiom *[être cloué] entre quatre planches*, "to be nailed up inside four planks" (four sometimes is an indefinite number in French).

He felt that hands hastily seized the coffin, then a harsh scraping upon the boards; he concluded that that was a rope which they were tying around the coffin to let it down into the excavation.

Then he felt a kind of dizziness.

Probably the bearer and the gravedigger had tipped the coffin and let the head down before the feet. He returned fully to himself on feeling that he was horizontal and motionless. He had touched the bottom.

He felt a certain chill.

A voice arose above him, icy and solemn. He heard pass away, some Latin words which he did not understand, pronounced so slowly that he could catch them one after another:

"Qui dormiunt in terræ pulvere, evigilabunt; alii in vitam æternam, et alii in opprobrium, ut videant semper."*

A child's voice said:

"De profundis."

The deep voice recommenced:

"Requiem æternam dona ei, Domine."

The child's voice responded:

"Et lux perpetua luceat ei."

He heard upon the board which covered him something like the gentle patter of a few drops of rain. It was probably the holy water.

He thought: "This will soon be finished. A little more patience. The priest is going away. Fauchelevent will take Mestienne away to drink. They will leave me. Then Fauchelevent will come back alone, and I shall get out. That will take a good hour."

The deep voice resumed.

"Requiescat in pace."

And the child's voice said:

"Amen."

Jean Valjean, intently listening, perceived something like receding steps.

"Now there they go," thought he. "I am alone."

All at once he heard a sound above his head which seemed to him like a clap of thunder.

It was a spadeful of earth falling upon the coffin.

A second spadeful of earth fell.

One of the holes by which he breathed was stopped up.

A third spadeful of earth fell.

Then a fourth.

There are things stronger than the strongest man. Jean Valjean lost consciousness.

---

*They who were sleeping in the dust of the earth, shall awake; some into the life eternal, and others into disgrace, that they shall see forever.

7

THE MISSING CARD

LET US SEE what occurred over the coffin in which Jean Valjean lay.

When the hearse had departed and the priest and the choir-boy had got into the carriage, and were gone, Fauchelevent, who had never taken his eyes off the gravedigger, saw him stoop, and grasp his spade, which was standing upright in the heap of earth.

Hereupon, Fauchelevent formed a supreme resolve.

Placing himself between the grave and the gravedigger, and folding his arms, he said:

"I'll pay for it!"

The gravedigger eyed him with amazement, and replied:

"What, peasant?"

Fauchelevent repeated:

"I'll pay for it!"

"For what?"

"For the wine."

"What wine?"

"The Argenteuil."

"Where's the Argenteuil?"

"At the Good Quince."

"Go to the devil!" said the gravedigger.

And he threw a spadeful of earth upon the coffin.

The coffin gave back a hollow sound. Fauchelevent felt himself stagger, and nearly fell into the grave. In a voice in which the strangling sound of the death-rattle began to be heard he cried:

"Come, comrade, before the Good Quince closes!"

The gravedigger took up another spadeful of earth. Fauchelevent continued:

"I'll pay," and he seized the gravedigger by the arm.

"Hark ye, comrade," he said, "I am the gravedigger of the convent, and have come to help you. It's a job we can do at night. Let us take a drink first."

And as he spoke, even while clinging desperately to this urgent effort, he asked himself, with some misgiving: "And even should he drink—will he get tipsy?"

"Good rustic," said the gravedigger, "if you insist, I consent. We'll have a drink but after my work, never before it."

And he tossed his spade again. Fauchelevent held him.

"It is Argenteuil at six sous the pint!"

"Ah, bah!" said the gravedigger, "you're a bore. Ding-dong, ding-dong, the same thing over and over again; that's all you can say. Be off, about your business."

And he threw in the second spadeful.

Fauchelevent had reached that point where a man knows no longer what he is saying. "Oh! come on, and take a glass, since I'm the one to pay," he again repeated.

"When we've put the child to bed," said the gravedigger.

He tossed in the third spadeful: then, plunging his spade into the earth, he added:

"You see, now, it's going to be cold to-night, and the dead one would cry out after us, if we were to plant her there without good covering."

At this moment, in the act of filling his spade, the gravedigger stooped low and the pocket of his vest gaped open.

The bewildered eye of Fauchelevent rested mechanically on this pocket, and remained fixed.

The sun was not yet hidden behind the horizon, and there was still light enough to distinguish something white in the gaping pocket.

All the lightning which the eye of a Picardy peasant can contain flashed into the pupils of Fauchelevent. A new idea had struck him.

Without the gravedigger, who was occupied with his spadeful of earth, perceiving him, he slipped his hand from behind into the pocket, and took from him the white object it contained.

The gravedigger flung into the grave the fourth spadeful.

Just as he was turning to take the fifth, Fauchelevent, looking at him with imperturbable calmness, asked:

"By the way, my new friend, have you your card?"

The gravedigger stopped.

"What card?"

"The sun is setting."

"Well, let him put on his night-cap."

"The cemetery-gate will be closed."

"Well, what then?"

"Have you your card?"

"Oh! my card!" said the gravedigger, and he felt in his pocket.

Having rummaged one pocket, he tried another. From these, he proceeded to try his watch-fobs, exploring the first, and turning the second inside out.

"No!" said he, "no! I haven't got my card. I must have forgotten it."

"Fifteen francs fine!" said Fauchelevent.

The gravedigger turned green. Green is the paleness of people naturally livid.

"Oh, good-gracious God, what a fool I am!" he exclaimed. "Fifteen francs fine!"

"Three hundred-sou coins," said Fauchelevent.

The gravedigger dropped his spade.

Fauchelevent's turn had come.

"Come! come, recruit," said Fauchelevent, "never despair; there's nothing to kill oneself about, and feed the worms. Fifteen francs are fifteen francs, and besides, you may not have them to pay. I am an old hand, and you a new one. I know all the tricks and traps and turns and twists of the business. I'll give you a friend's advice. One thing is clear—the sun is setting—and the graveyard will be closed in five minutes."

"That's true," replied the gravedigger.

"Five minutes is not time enough for you to fill the grave—it's as deep as the very devil—and get out of this before the gate is shut."

"You're right."

"In that case, there is fifteen francs fine."

"Fifteen francs!"

"But you have time. . . . Where do you live?"

"Just by the barrière. Fifteen minutes' walk. Number 87 Rue de Vaugirard."

"You have time, if you make it snappy, to get out at once."

"That's true."

"Once outside of the gate, you scamper home, get your card, come back, and the gatekeeper will let you in again. Having your card, there's nothing to pay. Then you can bury your dead man. I'll stay here, and watch him while you're gone, to see that he doesn't run away."

"I owe you my life, peasant!"

"Be off, then, quick!" said Fauchelevent.

The gravedigger, overcome with gratitude, shook his hands, and started at a run.

When the gravedigger had disappeared through the bushes, Fauchelevent listened until his footsteps died away, and then, bending over the grave, called out in a low voice:

"Father Madeleine!"

No answer.

Fauchelevent shuddered. He dropped rather than clambered down into the grave, threw himself upon the head of the coffin, and cried out:

"Are you there?"

Silence in the coffin.

Fauchelevent, no longer able to breathe for the shiver that was on him, took his cold chisel and hammer, and wrenched off the top board. The face of Jean Valjean could be seen in the twilight, his eyes closed and his cheeks colourless.

Fauchelevent's hair stood erect with alarm; he rose to his feet, and then tottered with his back against the side of the grave, ready to sink down upon the coffin. He looked upon Jean Valjean.

Jean Valjean lay there pallid and motionless.

Fauchelevent murmured in a voice low as a whisper:

"He is dead!"

Then straightening himself, and crossing his arms so violently that his clenched fists sounded against his shoulders, he exclaimed:

"This is the way I have saved him!"

Then the poor old man began to sob, talking aloud to himself the while, for it is a mistake to think that talking to one's self is not natural. Powerful emotions often speak aloud.

"It's Father Mestienne's fault. What did he die for, the fool? What was the use of going off in that way, just when no one expected it? It was he who killed poor M. Madeleine. Father Madeleine! He is in the coffin. He's settled. There's an end of it. Now, what's the sense of such things? Good God! he's dead! Yes, and his little girl—what am I to do with her? What will the fruit-woman say? That such a man could die in that way. Good Heaven, is it possible! When I think that he put himself under my care! . . . Father Madeleine! Father Madeleine! Mercy, he's suffocated, I said so—but, he wouldn't believe me. Now, here's a pretty piece of business! He's dead—one of the very best men God ever made; aye, the best, the very best! And his little girl! I'm not going back there again. I'm going to stay here. To have done such a thing as this! It's well worth while to be two old greybeards, in order to be two old fools. But, to begin with, how did he manage to get into the convent—that's where it started. Such things shouldn't be done. Father Madeleine! Father Madeleine! Father Madeleine! Madeleine! Monsieur Madeleine! Monsieur Mayor! He doesn't hear me. Get yourself out of this now, if you please."

And he tore his hair.

At a distance, through the trees, a harsh grating sound was heard. It was the gate of the cemetery closing.

Fauchelevent again bent over Jean Valjean, but suddenly jumped back as far as one can in a grave. Jean Valjean's eyes were open, and gazing at him.

To behold death is terrifying, and to see a sudden resurrection is nearly as much so. Fauchelevent became cold and white as a stone, wild-eyed and utterly disconcerted by all these powerful emotions, and not knowing whether he had the dead or the living to deal with, stared at Jean Valjean, who in turn stared at him.

"I was falling asleep," said Jean Valjean.

And he rose to a sitting posture.

Fauchelevent dropped on his knees.

"Oh, blessed Virgin! How you frightened me!"

Then, springing again to his feet, he cried:

"Thank you, Father Madeleine!"

Jean Valjean had merely swooned. The open air had revived him.

Joy is the reflex of terror. Fauchelevent had nearly as much difficulty as Jean Valjean in coming to himself.

"Then you're not dead! Oh, what good sense you have! I called you so loudly that you got over it. When I saw you with your eyes shut, I said, 'Well, there now! he's suffocated!' I would have gone raving mad—mad enough for a strait-jacket. They'd have put me in the Bicêtre. What would you have had me do, if you had been dead? And your little girl! the fruit-woman would have understood nothing about it! A child dropped into her lap, and its grandfather dead! What a story to tell! By all the saints in heaven, what a story! Ah! but you're alive—that's the best of it."

"I am cold," said Jean Valjean.

These words recalled Fauchelevent completely to the real state of affairs, which were urgent. These two men, even when restored, felt without knowing it, a peculiar agitation and a strange inward trouble, which was but the sinister bewilderment of the place.

"Let us get away from here at once," said Fauchelevent.

He thrust his hand into his pocket, and drew from it a flask with which he was provided.

"But a drop of this first!" said he.

The flask completed what the open air had begun. Jean Valjean took a swallow of brandy, and felt thoroughly restored.

He got out of the coffin, and assisted Fauchelevent to nail down the lid again. Three minutes afterwards, they were out of the grave.

After this, Fauchelevent was calm enough. He took his time. The cemetery was closed. There was no fear of the return of Gribier the gravedigger. That recruit was at home, hunting up his "card," and rather unlikely to find it, as it was in Fauchelevent's pocket. Without his card, he could not get back into the cemetery.

Fauchelevent took the spade and Jean Valjean the pick, and together they buried the empty coffin.

When the grave was filled, Fauchelevent said to Jean Valjean:

"Come, let us go; I'll keep the spade, and you take the pick."

Night was coming on rapidly.

Jean Valjean found it hard to move and walk. In the coffin he had stiffened considerably, somewhat in reality like a corpse. The anchylosis of death had seized him in that narrow wooden box. He had, in some sort, to thaw himself out of the sepulchre.

"You are benumbed," said Fauchelevent; "and what a pity that I'm lame, or we'd run a bit."

"No matter!" replied Jean Valjean, "a few steps will put my legs into walking order."

They went out by the avenues the hearse had followed. When they reached the closed gate and the porter's lodge, Fauchelevent, who had the gravedigger's card in his hand, dropped it into the box, the porter drew the cord, the gate opened, and they went through.

"How well everything goes!" said Fauchelevent; "what a good plan that was of yours, Father Madeleine!"

They passed the Barrière Vaugirard in the easiest way in the world. In the neighbourhood of a graveyard, a pick and spade are two passports.

The Rue de Vaugirard was deserted.

"Father Madeleine," said Fauchelevent, as he went along, looking up at the houses, "you have better eyes than mine—which is number 87?"

"Here it is, now," said Jean Valjean.

"There's no one in the street," resumed Fauchelevent. "Give me the pick, and wait for me a couple of minutes."

Fauchelevent went in at number 87, ascended to the topmost flight, guided by the instinct which always leads the poor to the garret, and knocked, in the dark, at the door of a little attic room. A voice called:

"Come in!"

It was Gribier's voice.

Fauchelevent pushed open the door. The lodging of the gravedigger was, like all these shelters of the needy, an unfurnished but much littered loft. A packing-case of some kind—a coffin, perhaps—supplied the place of a bureau, a straw pallet the place of a bed, a butter-pot the place of water-cooler, and the floor served alike for chairs and table. In one corner, on a ragged old scrap of carpet, was a haggard woman, and a number of children were huddled together. The whole of this wretched interior bore the traces of recent overturn. One would have said that there had been an earthquake served up there "for one." The coverlets were displaced, the ragged garments scattered about, the pitcher broken, the mother had been weeping, and the children probably beaten; all traces of a headlong and violent search. It was plain that the gravedigger had been looking, wildly, for his card, and had made everything in the attic, from his pitcher to his wife, responsible for the loss. He had a desperate appearance.

But Fauchelevent was in too great a hurry for the end of his adventure, to notice this gloomy side of his triumph.

As he came in, he said:

"I've brought your spade and pick."

Gribier looked at him with stupefaction.

"What, it is you, peasant?"

"And, to-morrow morning, you will find your card with the gatekeeper of the cemetery."

And he set down the pick and the spade on the floor.

"What does all this mean?" asked Gribier.

"Why, it means that you let your card drop out of your pocket; that I found it on the ground when you had gone; that I buried the corpse; that I filled in the grave; that I finished your job; that the porter will give you your card, and that you will not have to pay the fifteen francs. That's what it means, recruit!"

"Thanks, villager!" exclaimed Gribier, in amazement. "The next time I will treat."

8

SUCCESSFUL EXAMINATION

AN HOUR LATER, in the depth of night, two men and a child stood in front of No. 62, Petite Rue Picpus. The elder of the men lifted the knocker and rapped.

It was Fauchelevent, Jean Valjean, and Cosette.

The two men had gone to look for Cosette at the shop of the fruiteress of the Rue de Chemin Vert, where Fauchelevent had left her on the preceding evening. Cosette had passed the twenty-four hours wondering what it all meant and trembling in silence. She trembled so much that she had not wept, nor had she tasted food nor slept. The worthy fruit-woman had asked her a thousand questions without obtaining any other answer than a sad look that never varied. Cosette did not let a word of all she had heard and seen, in the last two days, escape her. She divined that a crisis had come. She felt, in her very heart, that she must be "good." Who has not experienced the supreme effect of these two words pronounced in a certain tone in the ear of some little frightened creature, "Don't speak!" Fear is mute. Besides, no one ever keeps a secret so well as a child.

But when, after those mournful four-and-twenty hours, she again saw Jean Valjean, she uttered such a cry of joy that any thoughtful person hearing her would have divined in it an escape from some yawning gulf.[*]

Fauchelevent belonged to the convent and knew all the pass-words. Every door opened before him.

Thus was that doubly fearful problem solved of getting out and getting in again.

The porter, who had his instructions, opened the little side door which served to communicate between the court and the garden, and which, twenty years ago, could still be seen from the street, in the wall at the extremity of the court, facing the porte-cochère. The porter admitted all three by this door, and from that point they went to this private inner parlour, where Fauchelevent had, on the previous evening, received the orders of the prioress.

The prioress, rosary in hand, was awaiting them. A mother, with her veil down, stood near her. A modest taper lighted, or one might almost say, pretended to light up the parlour.

---

[*]Hugo characteristically introduces an episodic observer here, but this time not an expert one. Such figures anchor the story in a social nexus, a human community, that connects readers and characters.

The prioress scrutinised Jean Valjean. Nothing scans so carefully as a downcast eye.

Then she proceeded to question:

"You are the brother?"

"Yes, reverend mother," replied Fauchelevent.

"What is your name?"

Fauchelevent replied:

"Ultimus Fauchelevent!"

He had, in reality, had a brother named Ultimus, who was dead.

"From what part of the country are you?"

Fauchelevent answered:

"From Picquigny, near Amiens."

"What is your age?"

Fauchelevent answered:

"Fifty."

"What is your business?"

Fauchelevent answered:

"Gardener."

"Are you a true Christian?"

Fauchelevent answered:

"All of our family are such."

"Is this your little girl?"

Fauchelevent answered:

"Yes, reverend mother."

"You are her father?"

Fauchelevent answered:

"Her grandfather."

The mother said to the prioress in an undertone:

"He answers well."

Jean Valjean had not spoken a word.

The prioress looked at Cosette attentively, and then said, aside to the mother——

"She will be homely."

The two mothers talked together very low for a few minutes in a corner of the parlour, and then the prioress turned and said——

"Father Fauvent, you will have another knee-cap and bell. We need two, now."

So, next morning, two little bells were heard tinkling in the garden and the nuns could not keep from lifting a corner of their veils. They saw two men digging side by side, in the lower part of the garden under the trees—Fauvent and another. Immense event! The silence was broken, so far as to say——

"It's an assistant-gardener!"

The mothers added:

"He is Father Fauvent's brother."

In fact, Jean Valjean was regularly installed; he had the leather kneecap and the bell; henceforth he had his commission. His name was Ultimus Fauchelevent.

The strongest recommendation for Cosette's admission had been the remark of the prioress: *She will be homely.*

The prioress having uttered this prediction, immediately took Cosette into her friendship and gave her a place in the school building as a charity pupil.

There is nothing not entirely logical in this.

It is all in vain to have no mirrors in convents; women are conscious of their own appearance; young girls who know that they are pretty do not readily become nuns; the inclination to the calling being in inverse proportion to good looks, more is expected from the homely than from the handsome ones. Hence a marked preference for the homely.

This whole affair elevated good old Fauchelevent greatly; he had achieved a triple success;—in the eyes of Jean Valjean whom he had rescued and sheltered; with the gravedigger, Gribier, who said he had saved him from a fine; and, at the convent, which, thanks to him, in retaining the coffin of Mother Crucifixion under the altar, eluded Cæsar and satisfied God. There was a coffin with a body in it at the Petit Picpus, and a coffin without a body in the Vaugirard cemetery. Public order was greatly disturbed thereby, undoubtedly, but nobody perceived it. As for the convent, its gratitude to Fauchelevent was deep. Fauchelevent became the best of servants and the most precious of gardeners.

9

THE CLOSE

COSETTE, at the convent, still kept silent. She very naturally thought herself Jean Valjean's daughter. Moreover, knowing nothing, there was nothing she could tell, and then, in any case, she would not have told anything. As we have remarked, nothing habituates children to silence like misfortune. Cosette had suffered so much that she was afraid of everything, even to speak, even to breathe. A single word had so often brought down an avalanche on her head! She had hardly begun to feel re-assured since she had been with Jean Valjean. She soon became accustomed to the convent. Still, she longed for Catharine,* but dared not say so. One day, however, she said to Jean Valjean, "If I had known it, father, I would have brought her with me."

---

*Catharine was Cosette's magnificent doll, purchased by Jean Valjean. This paragraph again explains the origins of the girl's timid, self-effacing character.

Cosette, in becoming a pupil at the convent, had to assume the dress of the school girls. Jean Valjean succeeded in having the garments which she laid aside given to him. It was the same mourning suit he had carried for her to put on when she left the Thénardiers. It was not much worn. Jean Valjean rolled up these garments, as well as the woollen stockings and shoes, with much camphor and other aromatic substances of which there is such an abundance in convents, and packed them in a small valise which he managed to procure. He put this valise in a chair near his bed, and always kept the key of it in his pocket.

"Father," Cosette one day asked him, "what is that box there that smells so good?"

Father Fauchelevent, besides the "glory" we have just described, and of which he was unconscious, was recompensed for his good deed; in the first place it made him happy, and then he had less work to do, as it was divided. Finally, as he was very fond of tobacco, he found the presence of M. Madeleine advantageous in another point of view; he took three times as much tobacco as before and that too in a manner infinitely more voluptuous, since M. Madeleine paid for it. The nuns did not adopt the name of *Ultimus;* they called Jean Valjean *the other Fauvent.*

If those holy women had possessed aught of the discrimination of Javert, they might have remarked, in course of time, that when there was any little errand to run outside for on account of the garden, it was always the elder Fauchelevent, old, infirm, and lame as he was, who went, and never the other; but, whether it be that eyes continually fixed upon God cannot play the spy, or whether they were too constantly employed in watching one another, they noticed nothing.

However, Jean Valjean was well advised to lay low. Javert watched the quarter for a good long month.

The convent was to Jean Valjean like an island surrounded by wide waters. These four walls were, henceforth, the world to him. Within them he could see enough of the sky to be calm, and enough of Cosette to be happy.

A very pleasant life began again for him.

He lived with Fauchelevent in the out-building at the foot of the garden.

Jean Valjean worked every day in the garden, and was very useful there. He had formerly been a pruner, and now found it quite in his way to be a gardener. It may be remembered that he knew all kinds of techniques and secrets of horticulture. These he turned to account. Nearly all the orchard trees were wild stock; he grafted them and made them bear excellent fruit.

Cosette was allowed to come every day, and pass an hour with him. As the sisters were melancholy, and he was kind, the child compared him with them, and worshipped him. Every day, at the hour appointed, she would hurry to the little building. When she entered the old place, she filled it with Paradise. Jean Valjean basked in her presence and felt his own happiness increase by reason of the happiness he conferred on Cosette. The delight we inspire in others has this enchanting peculiarity that, far from being diminished like every other reflection, it returns to us more radiant than ever. At the hours of recreation, Jean Valjean from a distance watched her playing and romping, and he could distinguish her laughter from the laughter of the rest.

For, now, Cosette laughed.

Even Cosette's countenance had, in a measure, changed. The gloomy cast had disappeared. Laughter is sunshine; it chases winter from the human face.

When the recreation was over and Cosette went in, Jean Valjean watched the windows of her schoolroom, and, at night, would rise from his bed to take a look at the windows of the room in which she slept.

God has his own ways. The convent contributed, like Cosette, to confirm and complete, in Jean Valjean, the work of the bishop. It cannot be denied that one of virtue's phases ends in pride. Therein is a bridge built by the Evil One. Jean Valjean was, perhaps, without knowing it, near that very phase of virtue, and that very bridge, when Providence flung him into the convent of the Petit Picpus. So long as he compared himself only with the bishop, he found himself unworthy and remained humble; but, for some time past, he had been comparing himself with the rest of men, and pride was springing up in him. Who knows? He might have finished by going gradually back to hate.

The convent halted him on this descent.*

It was the second place of captivity he had seen. In his youth, in what had been for him the commencement of life, and, later, quite recently too, he had seen another, a frightful place, a terrible place, the severities of which had always seemed to him to reflect the iniquity of public justice and the crime of the law. Now, after having seen the galleys, he saw the cloister, and reflecting that he had been an inmate of the galleys, and that he now was, so to speak, a spectator of the cloister, he anxiously compared them in his meditations with anxiety.

Sometimes he would lean upon his spade and descend slowly along the endless spirals of reverie.†

He recalled his former companions, and how wretched they were. They rose at dawn and toiled until night. Scarcely allowed to sleep they lay on camp-beds, and were permitted to have mattresses but two inches thick in halls which were warmed only during the most inclement months. They were attired in hideous red sacks, and had given to them, as a favour, a pair of canvas trousers in the heats of midsummer, and a square of woollen stuff to throw over their shoulders, during the bitterest frosts of winter. They had no wine to drink, no meat for food excepting when sent upon "extra hard work." They lived without names, distinguished solely by numbers, and reduced to

---

*As he does in dozens of other places in the novel, Hugo strongly implies that Providence has intervened to help redeem Jean Valjean.

†The spiral is a common image in nineteenth-century French literature to signal the presence and effects of altered states of consciousness.

numbers themselves, lowering their eyes, lowering their voices, with their hair cropped close, under the rod, and plunged in shame.

Then, his thoughts reverted to the beings before his eyes.

These beings, also, lived with their hair cut close, their eyes bent down, their voices hushed, not in shame indeed, but amid the mockery of the world; not with their backs bruised by the gaoler's staff, but with their shoulders lacerated by self-inflicted penance. Their names, too, had perished from among men, and they now existed under austere designations alone. They never ate meat and never drank wine; they often remained until evening without food. They were attired not in red sacks, but in black habits of woollen, heavy in summer, light in winter, unable to increase or diminish them, without even the privilege, according to the season, of substituting a linen dress or a woollen cloak, and then, for six months of the year, they wore underclothing of serge which fevered them. They dwelt not in dormitories warmed only in the bitterest frost of winter, but in cells where fire was never kindled. They slept not on mattresses two inches thick, but upon straw. Moreover, they were not even allowed to sleep, for, every night, after a day of labour, they were, when overwhelmed beneath the weight of the first sleep, at the moment when they were just beginning to slumber, and, with difficulty, to collect a little warmth, required to waken, rise and assemble for prayers in an icy-cold, gloomy chapel, with their knees on the stone pavement.

On certain days, each one of these beings, in her turn, had to remain twelve hours in succession kneeling upon the flagstones, or prostrate on her face, with her arms crossed.

The others were men, these were women. What had these men done? They had robbed, raped, plundered, killed, assassinated. They were highwaymen, forgers, poisoners, arsonists, murderers, parricides. What had these women done? They had done nothing.

On one side, robbery, fraud, chicanery, violence, lust, homicide, every species of sacrilege, every kind of offence; on the other, one thing only,— innocence.

A perfect innocence almost borne upwards in a mysterious Assumption, clinging still to Earth through virtue, already touching Heaven through holiness.*

On the one hand, the mutual avowal of crimes detailed with bated breath; on the other, faults confessed aloud. And oh! what crimes! and oh! what faults!

On one side foul miasma, on the other, ineffable perfume. On the one side, a moral pestilence, watched day and night, held in subjection at the cannon's mouth, and slowly consuming its infected victims; on the other, chaste kindling of every soul together on the same hearthstone. There,

---

*The Assumption of the Blessed Virgin Mary, a national holiday on August 15, refers to her being taken up directly into Heaven at the moment of her death, and before her mortal body could suffer any corruption (decay).

utter gloom; here, the shadow, but a shadow full of light, and the light full of glowing rays.

Two places of slavery; but, in the former, rescue possible, a legal limit always in view, and, then, escape. In the second, perpetuity, the only hope at the most distant boundary of the future, that gleam of liberty which men call death.

In the former, the captives were enchained by chains only; in the other, they were enchained by faith alone.

What resulted from the first? One vast curse, the gnashing of teeth, hatred, desperate depravity, a cry of rage against human society, sarcasm against heaven.

What issued from the second? Benediction and love.

And, in these two places, so alike and yet so different, these two species of beings so dissimilar were performing the same work of expiation.

Jean Valjean thoroughly comprehended the expiation of the first; personal expiation, expiation for oneself. But, he did not understand that of the others, of these blameless, spotless creatures, and he asked himself with a tremor: "Expiation of what? What expiation?"

A voice responded in his conscience: the most divine of all human generosity, expiation for others.

Here we withhold all theories of our own: we are but the narrator; we adopt Jean Valjean's point of view and we merely reproduce his impressions.*

He had before his eyes the sublime summit of self-denial, the loftiest possible height of virtue; innocence forgiving men their sins and expiating them in their stead; servitude endured, torture accepted, chastisement and misery invoked by souls that had not sinned in order that these might not fall upon souls which had; the love of humanity losing itself in the love of God, but remaining there, distinct and suppliant; sweet, feeble beings supporting all the torments of those who are punished, yet retaining the smile of those who are rewarded. And then he remembered that he had dared to complain.

When he thought of these things, all that was in him gave way before this mystery of sublimity. In these meditations, pride vanished. He reverted, again and again, to himself; he felt his own pitiful unworthiness, and often wept. All that had occurred in his existence, for the last six months, led him back towards the holy injunctions of the bishop; Cosette through love, the convent through humility.

Sometimes, in the evening, about dusk, at the hour when the garden was solitary, he was seen kneeling, in the middle of the walk that ran along the chapel, before the window through which he had looked, on the night of his first arrival, turned towards the spot where he knew that the sister who was performing the reparation was prostrate in prayer. Thus he prayed kneeling before this sister.

---

*The disclaimer means that Hugo feels more skeptical and critical than Jean Valjean. He admires many nuns as individuals, but condemns the monastic life.

It seemed as though he dared not kneel directly before God.

Everything around him, this quiet garden, these balmy flowers, these children, shouting with joy, these meek and simple women, this silent cloister, gradually entered into all his being, and, little by little, his soul subsided into silence like this cloister, into fragrance like these flowers, into peace like this garden, into simplicity like these women, into joy like these children. And then he reflected that two houses of God had received him in succession at the two critical moments of his life, the first when every door was closed and human society repelled him; the second, when human society again howled upon his track, and the galleys once more gaped for him; and that, had it not been for the first, he should have fallen back into crime, and had it not been for the second, into punishment.

His whole heart melted in gratitude, and he loved more and more.*
Several years passed thus. Cosette was growing.

---

*Such spiritual development characterizes the Idealistic Novel; compare Flaubert's tale "A Simple Heart," or several of George Sand's novels.

MARIUS

Book One
Paris Studied Through
Its Microcosm

1

PARVULUS

PARIS has a child and the forest has a bird; the bird is called the sparrow; the child is called the *gamin*.*

Couple these two ideas, the one containing all the heat of the furnace, the other all the light of the dawn; strike together these two sparks, Paris and infancy; and there leaps forth from them a little creature. Homuncio, Plautus would say.†

This little creature is full of joy. He has not food to eat every day, yet he goes to the show every evening, if he sees fit. He has no shirt to his back, no shoes to his feet, no roof over his head; he is like the flies in the air who have none of all these things. He is from seven to thirteen years of age, lives in troops, ranges the streets, sleeps in the open air, wears an old pair of his father's trousers down about his heels, an old hat of some other father, which covers his ears, and a single suspender of coarse yellow cloth, runs about, is always on the watch and on the search, kills time, breaks in pipes, swears like an imp, hangs about the wine-shop, knows thieves and robbers, is hand in glove with the street-girls, rattles off slang, sings smutty songs, and, withal, has nothing bad in his heart. This is because he has a pearl in his soul, innocence; and pearls do not dissolve in mire. So long as man is a child, God wills that he be innocent.

If one could ask of this vast city: what is that creature? She would answer: "it is my little one."

Gamin is "street urchin," a meaning that is now archaic.
†Plautus and Terence, ancient Roman writers of comedies, use the word "homuncio," as does the satirist Juvenal; the most famous example, in the sense of "test tube baby" that we find here, appears in part II of Johann Wolfgang von Goethe's *Faust* (the Homunculus).

2

SOME OF HIS PRIVATE MARKS

THE gamin of Paris is the dwarf of the giantess.

We will not exaggerate. This cherub of the gutter sometimes has a shirt, but then he has only one; sometimes he has shoes, but then they have no soles; sometimes he has a shelter, and he loves it, for there he finds his mother; but he prefers the street for there he finds his liberty. He has games of his own, roguish tricks of his own, of which a hearty hatred of the bourgeois is the basis; he has his own metaphors; to be dead he calls eating dandelions by the root; he has his own occupations, such as running for hacks, letting down carriage-steps, sweeping the rain away from the cross-walks in rainy weather, creating dryer walkways which he charges pedestrians to cross—he calls them "Ponts des Arrhes,"* shouting out the speeches often made by the authorities on behalf of the French people, and digging out the grout between the flagstones; he has his own kind of money, consisting of all the little bits of wrought copper that can be found on the public thoroughfares. This curious currency, which takes the name of scraps, has an unvarying and well-regulated circulation throughout this little gipsy-land of children.

He has a fauna of his own, which he studies carefully in the corners; the ladybug, the death's head grub, the reaper, and the "devil," a black insect that threatens you by twisting about its tail which is armed with two horns. He has his fabulous monster which has scales on its belly, and yet is not a lizard, has warts on its back, and yet is not a toad, which lives in the crevices of old lime-kilns and dry-cisterns, a black, velvety, slimy, crawling creature, sometimes swift and sometimes slow of motion, emitting no cry, but which stares at you, and is so terrible that nobody has ever seen it; this monster he calls the "deaf thing." Hunting for deaf things among the stones is a pleasure which is thrillingly dangerous. Another enjoyment is to raise a slab of the sidewalk suddenly and see the wood-lice. Every region of Paris is famous for the discoveries which can be made in it. There are earwigs in the wood-yards of the Ursulines, there are wood-lice at the Pantheon, and tadpoles in the ditches of the Champ-de-Mars.

In repartee, this youngster is as gifted as Talleyrand. He is equally cynical, but he is more sincere. He is gifted with an odd kind of unpremeditated

---

*A pun: Pont des Arts is a bridge in Paris; *arrhes* is earnest money paid to bind a contract.

jollity; he stuns the shopkeeper with his wild laughter. His gamut slides merrily from high comedy to farce.

A funeral is passing. There is a doctor in the procession. "Hullo!" shouts a gamin, "how long is it since the doctors began to take home their work?"

Another happens to be in a crowd. A grave-looking man, who wears spectacles and trinkets, turns upon him indignantly: "You scamp, you've been seizing my wife's waist!"

"I, sir! search me!"

3

HE IS AGREEABLE*

IN THE EVENING, by means of a few pennies which he always manages to scrape together, the *homuncio* goes to some theatre. By the act of passing that magic threshold, he becomes transfigured; he was a *gamin*, he becomes a *titi*. Theatres are a sort of vessel turned upside down with the hold at the top; in this hold the *titi* gather in crowds.† The *titi* is to the *gamin* what the butterfly is to the grub; the same creature on wings and sailing through the air. It is enough for him to be there with his radiance of delight, his fulness of enthusiasm and joy and his clapping of hands like the clapping of wings, to make that hold, close, dark, fœtid, filthy, unwholesome, hideous, and detestable as it is, to be called the "Paradise."‡

Give to a being the useless, and deprive him of the needful, and you have the *gamin*.

The *gamin* is not without a certain inclination towards literature. His tendency, however—we say it with the befitting quantum of regret— would not be considered as towards the classic. He is, in his nature, but

---

*"Agreeable" in conjunction with the word "useful" in the next chapter title alludes to the ancient Roman definition of the desiderata for literary satire: the *gamin* Gavroche is satire personified.

†A ship's cheapest cabins are in the hold, below the decks; a theater's are in the top balcony.

‡A term jokingly used for the upper balconies of a theater, because they seem so close to Heaven.

slightly academic. For instance, the popularity of Mademoiselle Mars among this little public of children was spiced with a touch of irony. The *gamin* called her Mademoiselle *Muche*.*

This being jeers, wrangles, sneers, jangles, has frippery like a baby and rags like a philosopher, fishes in the gutter, hunts in the sewer, extracts gaiety from filth, lashes the street corners with his wit, sneers and bites, hisses and sings, applauds and hoots, tempers Hallelujah with tralalas, chants all sorts of rhythms from De Profundis to the Shit-in-the-bed, finds without searching, knows what he does not know, is Spartan even to roguery, is witless even to wisdom, is lyric even to impurity, would squat upon Olympus, wallows in the dung-heap and comes out of it covered with stars. The gamin of Paris is Rabelais as a child.

He is never satisfied with his trousers unless they have a watch-fob.

He is seldom astonished, is frightened still less frequently, turns superstitions into doggerel verses and sings them, deflates exaggerations, makes light of mysteries, sticks out his tongue at ghosts, lowers everything that is on stilts, and introduces caricature into all epic pomposities. This is not because he is prosaic, far from it; but he substitutes the phantasmagoria of fun for solemn dreams. Were the giant Adamaster to appear to him, he would shout out: "Hallo, there, old Bug-a-boo!"†

4

HE MAY BE USEFUL

PARIS BEGINS with the curious onlooker and ends with the *gamin,* two beings of which no other city is capable; passive acceptance satisfied with merely looking on, and exhaustless enterprise; Prudhomme and Fouillou. Paris alone comprises this in its natural history. All monarchy is comprised in the onlooker; all anarchy in the *gamin*.

This pale child of the Paris suburbs lives, develops, and gets into and out of "scrapes," amid suffering, a thoughtful witness of our social realities.

Muche is perhaps from the variant form of *musse-pot,* "in hiding." Hugo disliked the famous actress Mlle Mars, who complained of and sometimes refused to use the informal language in his plays.

†The last two paragraphs characterize the *gamin* as an *eiron* (debunker, deflator of pretentions), and thus as the natural enemy of the bourgeois *alazon,* or self-satisfied braggart.

5 (13)

LITTLE GAVROCHE

ABOUT eight or nine years after the events narrated in the second part of this story, there was seen, on the Boulevard du Temple, and in the neighbourhood of the Château d'Eau, a little boy of eleven or twelve years of age, who would have realised with considerable accuracy the ideal of the gamin previously sketched, if, with the laughter of his youth upon his lips, his heart had not been absolutely dark and empty. This child was well muffled up in a man's pair of trousers, but he had not got them from his father, and in a woman's chemise, which was not an inheritance from his mother. Strangers had clothed him in these rags out of charity. Still, he had a father and a mother. But his father never thought of him, and his mother did not love him. He was one of those children so deserving of pity from all, who have fathers and mothers, and yet are orphans.

This little boy never felt so happy as when in the street. The pavement was not so hard to him as the heart of his mother.

His parents had thrown him out into life with a kick.

He had quite ingenuously spread his wings, and taken flight.

He was a boisterous, pallid, nimble, wide-awake, roguish urchin, with an air at once vivacious and sickly. He went, came, sang, played pitch and toss, scraped the gutters, stole a little, but he did it gaily like the cats and the sparrows, laughed when people called him an errand-boy, and got angry when they called him a juvenile delinquent. He had no shelter, no food, no fire, no love, but he was light-hearted because he was free.

When these poor creatures are men, the millstone of our social system almost always comes in contact with them, and grinds them, but while they are children they escape because they are little. The smallest hole saves them.

However, deserted as this lad was, it happened sometimes, every two or three months, that he would say to himself: "Come, I'll go and see my mother!" Then he would leave the Boulevard, the Cirque, the Porte Saint Martin, go down along the quays, cross the bridges, reach the suburbs, walk as far as the Salpêtrière, and arrive—where? Precisely at that double number, 50–52, which is known to the reader, the Gorbeau building.

At the period referred to, the tenement No. 50–52, usually empty, and permanently decorated with the placard "Rooms to let," was, for a wonder, tenanted by several persons who, in all other respects as is always the case at Paris, had no relation to or connection with each other. They all belonged to that indigent class which begins with the petit bourgeois in straitened circumstances, and descends, from grade to grade of wretchedness, through the lower strata of society, until it reaches those two beings in whom all the material things of civilisation terminate, the scavenger and the ragpicker.

·The "landlady" of the time of Jean Valjean was dead, and had been replaced by another exactly like her. I do not remember what philosopher it was who said: "There is never any lack of old women."

The new old woman was called Madame Burgon, and her life had been remarkable for nothing except a dynasty of three paroquets, which had in succession ruled over her affections.

Among those who lived in the building, the wretchedest of all were a family of four persons, father, mother, and two daughters nearly grown, all four lodging in the same garret room, one of those cells of which we have already spoken.

This family at first sight presented nothing very peculiar but its extreme destitution; the father, in renting the room, had given his name as Jondrette. Some time after his moving in, which had singularly resembled, to borrow the memorable expression of the landlady, the entrance of nothing at all, this Jondrette said to the old woman, who, like her predecessor, was, at the same time, portress and swept the stairs: "Mother So-and-So, if anybody should come and ask for a Pole or an Italian or, perhaps, a Spaniard, that is for me."

Now, this family was the family of our sprightly little bare-footed urchin. When he came there, he found distress and, what is sadder still, no smile; a cold hearthstone and cold hearts. When he came in, they would ask: "Where have you come from?" He would answer: "From the street." When he was going away they would ask him: "Where are you going to?" He would answer: "Into the street." His mother would say to him: "What have you come here for?"

The child lived, in this absence of affection, like those pale plants that spring up in cellars. He felt no suffering from this mode of existence, and bore no ill-will to anybody. He did not know how a father and mother ought to be.

But yet his mother loved his sisters.

We had forgotten to say that on the Boulevard du Temple this boy went by the name of little Gavroche. Why was his name Gavroche? Probably because his father's name was Jondrette.

To break all links seems to be the instinct of some wretched families.

The room occupied by the Jondrettes in the Gorbeau tenement was the last at the end of the hall. The adjoining cell was tenanted by a very poor young man who was called Monsieur Marius.

Let us see who and what Monsieur Marius was.

[Book Two, "The Grand Bourgeois," does not appear in this abridged edition.]

BOOK THREE
THE GRANDFATHER AND THE GRANDSON

1 (2)

ONE OF THE RED SPECTRES OF THAT TIME*

WHOEVER, at that time, had passed through the little town of Vernon, and walked over that beautiful monumental bridge which will be very soon replaced, let us hope, by some horrid wire bridge, would have noticed, as his glance fell from the top of the parapet, a man of about fifty, with a leather cap on his head, dressed in trousers and waistcoat of coarse grey cloth, to which something yellow was stitched which had been a red ribbon, shod in wooden shoes, browned by the sun, his face almost black and his hair almost white, a large scar upon his forehead extending down his cheek, bent, bowed down, older than his years, walking nearly every day with a spade and a pruning knife in his hand, in one of those walled compartments, in the vicinity of the bridge, which, like a chain of terraces border the left bank of the Seine,—charming inclosures full of flowers of which one would say, if they were much larger, they are gardens, and if they were a little smaller, they are bouquets. All these inclosures are bounded by the river on one side and by a house on the other. The man in the waistcoat and wooden shoes of whom we have just spoken lived, about the year 1817, in the smallest of these inclosures and the humblest of these houses. He lived there solitary and alone, in silence and in poverty, with a woman who was neither young nor old, neither beautiful nor ugly, neither peasant nor bourgeois, who waited upon him. The square of earth which he called his garden was celebrated in the town for the beauty of the flowers which he cultivated in it. Flowers were his occupation.

By dint of labour, perseverance, attention, and pails of water, he had succeeded in creating after the Creator, and had invented certain tulips and dahlias which seemed to have been forgotten by Nature. He was ingenious; he anticipated Soulange Bodin in the use of raised beds of peat moss for the culture of rare and precious shrubs from America and China. By break of day, in summer, he was in his walks, digging, pruning, weeding, watering, walking in the midst of his flowers with an air of kindness, sadness, and gentleness, sometimes dreamy and motionless for whole hours listening to the song of a bird in a tree, the prattling of a child in a house, or oftener with his eyes fixed on some drop of dew at the end of a spear of grass, of which the sun was making a carbuncle. His table was very frugal, and he drank more milk than wine. An urchin would make him give way,

---

*The term "red spectre" described a bloodthirsty revolutionary, in the eyes of the Royalists; the reference is to Colonel Pontmercy, Marius's gentle, courageous, devoted father, an idealization of Hugo's.

his servant scolded him. He was timid, so much so as to seem unsociable; he rarely went out, and saw nobody but the poor who rapped at his window, and his curé Abbé Mabeuf, a good old man. Still, if any of the inhabitants of the city or strangers, whoever they might be, curious to see his tulips and roses, knocked at his little house, he opened his door with a smile. This was the brigand of the Loire.

We have already seen something of his history. After Waterloo, Pontmercy, drawn out, as will be remembered, from the heap of bodies on the sunken road of Ohain, succeeded in regaining the army, and was passed along from ambulance to ambulance to the cantonments of the Loire.

The Restoration put him on half-pay, then sent him to a residence, that is to say under surveillance at Vernon. The king, Louis XVIII, discounting all that had been done in the Hundred Days, recognised neither his position of officer of the Legion of Honour, nor his rank of colonel, nor his title of baron.* He, on his part, neglected no opportunity to sign himself *Colonel Baron Pontmercy*. He had only one old blue coat, and he never went out without putting on the rosette of an officer of the Legion of Honour. The *procureur du roi* notified him that he would be prosecuted for "illegally" wearing this decoration. When this notice was given to him by a friendly intermediary, Pontmercy answered with a bitter smile: "I do not know whether it is that I no longer understand French, or you no longer speak it; but the fact is I do not understand you." Then he went out every day for a week with his rosette. Nobody dared to disturb him. Two or three times the minister of war or the general commanding the department wrote to him with this address: *Monsieur Commandant Pontmercy*. He returned the letters unopened. At the same time, Napoleon at St. Helena was treating Sir Hudson Lowe's missives addressed to General Bonaparte in the same way. Pontmercy at last, excuse the expression, came to have in his mouth the same saliva as his emperor.

So too, there were in Rome a few Carthaginian soldiers, taken prisoners, who refused to bow to Flaminius, and who had a little of Hannibal's soul.

One morning, he met the *procureur du roi* in one of the streets of Vernon, went up to him and said: "Monsieur *procureur du roi,* am I allowed to wear my scar?"

He had nothing but his very scanty half-pay as chief of squadron. He hired the smallest house he could find in Vernon. He lived there alone; how we have just seen. Under the empire, between two wars he had found time to marry Mademoiselle Gillenormand. The old bourgeois, who really felt outraged, consented with a sigh, saying: *"The greatest families are forced to it."* In 1815, Madame Pontmercy, an admirable woman in every respect, noble and rare, and worthy of her husband, died, leaving a child. This child

---

Baron was an honorific title ranking just above *chevalier* and just below *vicomte* (the lowest rank of land-owning nobility). Napoléon awarded it widely to honor meritorious achievement; his enemies, the Royalists, therefore had no inclination to honor it.

would have been the colonel's joy in his solitude; but the grandfather had imperiously demanded his grandson, declaring that, unless he were given up to him, he would disinherit him. The father yielded for the sake of the little boy, and not being able to have his child he set about loving flowers.

He had moreover given up everything, making no movement nor conspiring with others. He divided his thoughts between the innocent things he was doing, and the grand things he had done. He passed his time hoping for a pink to bloom or remembering Austerlitz.

M. Gillenormand had no intercourse with his son-in-law. The colonel was to him "a bandit," and he was to the colonel "a blockhead." M. Gillenormand never spoke of the colonel, unless sometimes to make mocking allusions to "his barony." It was expressly understood that Pontmercy should never endeavour to see his son or speak to him, under pain of the boy being turned away, and disinherited. To the Gillenormands, Pontmercy was pestiferous. They intended to bring up the child to their liking. The colonel did wrong perhaps to accept these conditions, but he submitted to them, thinking that he was doing right, and sacrificing himself alone.

The inheritance from the grandfather Gillenormand was a small affair, but the inheritance from Mlle Gillenormand the elder was considerable. This aunt, who had remained single, was very rich from the maternal side, and the son of her sister was her natural heir. The child, whose name was Marius, knew that he had a father, but nothing more. Nobody spoke a word to him about him. However, in the society into which his grandfather took him, the whisperings, the hints, the winks, enlightened the little boy's mind at length; he finally comprehended something of it, and as he naturally imbibed by a sort of infiltration and slow penetration the ideas and opinions which formed, so to say, the air he breathed, he came little by little to think of his father only with shame and with a closed heart.

While he was thus growing up, every two or three months the colonel would escape, come furtively to Paris like a fugitive from justice breaking his ban, and go to Saint Sulpice, at the hour when Aunt Gillenormand took Marius to mass. There, trembling lest the aunt should turn round, concealed behind a pillar, motionless, not daring to breathe, he saw his child. The scarred veteran was afraid of the old maid.

Twice a year, on the first of January and on St. George's Day, Marius wrote filial letters to his father, which his aunt dictated, and which, one would have said, were copied from some Complete Letter Writer; this was all that M. Gillenormand allowed; and the father answered with very tender letters, which the grandfather thrust into his pocket without reading.

2 (3)

REQUIESCANT

THE SALON of Madame de T. was all that Marius Pontmercy knew of the world. It was the only opening by which he could look out into life. This opening was sombre, and through this porthole there came more cold than warmth, more night than day. The child, who was nothing but joy and light on entering this strange world, in a little while became sad, and, what is still more unusual at his age, grave. Surrounded by all these imposing and singular persons, he looked about him with a serious astonishment. Everything united to increase his amazement. There were in Madame de T.'s salon some very venerable noble old ladies whose names were Mathan, Noah, Lévis which was pronounced Lévi, Cambis which was pronounced Cambyse. These antique faces and these biblical names mingled in the child's mind with his Old Testament, which he was learning by heart, and when they were all present, seated in a circle about a dying fire, dimly lighted by a green-shaded lamp, with their stern profiles, their grey or white hair, their long dresses of another age, in which mournful colours only could be distinguished, at rare intervals dropping a few words which were at once majestic and austere, the little Marius looked upon them with startled eyes thinking that he saw, not women, but patriarchs and magi, not real beings, but phantoms.

Marius Pontmercy went, like all children, through various studies. When he left the hands of Aunt Gillenormand, his grandfather entrusted him to a worthy professor, of the purest classic innocence. This young, unfolding soul passed from a prude to a pedant. Marius had his years at college, then he entered the law-school. He was royalist, fanatical, and austere. He had little love for his grandfather, whose gaiety and cynicism wounded him, and the place of his father was a dark void.

For the rest, he was an ardent but cool lad, noble, generous, proud, religious, lofty; honourable even to harshness, pure even to unsociableness.

3 (4)

END OF THE BRIGAND

THE COMPLETION of Marius' classical studies was coincident with M. Gillenormand's retirement from the world. The old man bade farewell to the Faubourg Saint Germain, and to Madame de T.'s salon, and established himself in the Marais, at his house in the Rue des Filles du Calvaire. His servants were, in addition to the porter, this chambermaid Nicolette who had succeeded Magnon, and this short-winded, pot-bellied Basque whom we have already mentioned.

In 1827, Marius had just attained his eighteenth year. On coming in one evening, he saw his grandfather with a letter in his hand.

"Marius," said M. Gillenormand, "you will set out tomorrow for Vernon."

"What for?" said Marius.

"To see your father."

Marius shuddered. He had thought of everything but this, that a day might come, when he would have to see his father. Nothing could have been more unlooked for, more surprising, and, we must say, more disagreeable. It was aversion compelled to intimacy. It was not affliction; no, it was pure drudgery.

Marius, besides his feelings of political antipathy, was convinced that his father, the bloodthirsty brute, as M. Gillenormand called him in the gentler moments, did not love him; that was clear, since he had abandoned him and left him to others. Feeling that he was not loved at all, he had no love. Nothing more natural, said he to himself.

He was so astounded that he did not question M. Gillenormand. The grandfather continued:

"It appears that he is sick. He is asking for you."

And after a moment of silence he added:

"Start to-morrow morning. I think there is at the Cour des Fontaines a coach which starts at six o'clock and arrives at night. Take it. He says it's urgent."

Then he crumpled up the letter and put it in his pocket. Marius could have started that evening and been with his father the next morning. A stagecoach then made the trip to Rouen from the Rue du Bouloi by night passing through Vernon. Neither M. Gillenormand nor Marius thought of inquiring.

The next day at dusk, Marius arrived at Vernon. Candles were just beginning to be lighted. He asked the first person he met for *the house of Monsieur Pontmercy*. For in his feelings he agreed with the Restoration, and he, too, recognised his father neither as baron nor as colonel.

The house was pointed out to him. He rang; a woman came and opened the door with a small lamp in her hand.

"Monsieur Pontmercy?" said Marius.

The woman remained motionless.

"Is it here?" asked Marius.

The woman gave an affirmative nod of the head.

"Can I speak with him?"

The woman gave a negative sign.

"But I am his son!" resumed Marius. "He expects me."

"He expects you no longer," said the woman.

Then he perceived that she was in tears.

She pointed to the door of a low room; he entered.

In this room, which was lighted by a tallow candle on the mantel, there were three men, one of them standing, one on his knees, and one stripped to his shirt and lying at full length upon the floor. The one upon the floor was the colonel.

The two others were a physician and a priest who was praying.

The colonel had been three days before attacked with a brain fever. At the beginning of the sickness, having a presentiment of ill, he had written to Monsieur Gillenormand to ask for his son. He had grown worse. On the very evening of Marius' arrival at Vernon, the colonel had had a fit of delirium; he sprang out of his bed in spite of the servant, crying: "My son has not come! I am going to meet him!" Then he had gone out of his room and fallen upon the floor of the hall. He had just died.

The doctor and the curé had been sent for. The doctor had come too late, the curé had come too late. The son also had come too late.

By the dim light of the candle, they could distinguish upon the cheek of the pale and prostrate colonel a big tear which had fallen from his death-stricken eye. The eye was glazed, but the tear was not dry. This tear was for his son's delay.

Marius looked upon this man, whom he saw for the first time, and for the last—this venerable and manly face, these open eyes which saw not, this white hair, these robust limbs upon which he distinguished here and there brown lines which were sabre-cuts, and a species of red stars which were bullet-holes. He looked upon that gigantic scar which imprinted heroism upon this face on which God had impressed goodness. He thought that this man was his father and that this man was dead, and he remained unmoved.

The sorrow which he experienced was the sorrow which he would have felt before any other man whom he might have seen stretched out in death.

Mourning, bitter mourning was in that room. The servant was lamenting by herself in a corner, the curé was praying, and his sobs were heard; the doctor was wiping his eyes; the corpse itself wept.

This doctor, this priest, and this woman, looked at Marius through their affliction without saying a word; it was he who was the stranger. Marius, too little moved, felt ashamed and embarrassed at his attitude; he had his hat in his hand, he let it fall to the floor, to make them believe that grief deprived him of strength to hold it.

At the same time he felt something like remorse, and he despised himself for acting thus. But was it his fault? He did not love his father, indeed!

The colonel left nothing. The sale of his furniture hardly paid for his burial. The servant found a scrap of paper which she handed to Marius. It contained this, in the handwriting of the colonel:

"*For my Son.*—The emperor made me a baron upon the battlefield of Waterloo. Since the Restoration contests this title which I have bought with my blood, my son will take it and bear it. I need not say that he will be worthy of it." On the back, the colonel had added: "At this same battle of Waterloo, a sergeant saved my life. This man's name is Thénardier. Not long ago, I believe he was keeping a little tavern in a village in the suburbs of Paris, at Chelles or at Montfermeil. If my son meets him, he will do Thénardier all the service he can."

Not from duty towards his father, but on account of that vague respect for death which is always so imperious in the heart of man, Marius took this paper and pressed it.

No trace remained of the colonel. Monsieur Gillenormand had his sword and uniform sold to a second-hand dealer. The neighbours stripped the garden and carried off the rare flowers. The other plants became briery and scraggy, and died.

Marius remained only forty-eight hours at Vernon. After the burial, he returned to Paris and went back to his law, thinking no more of his father than if he had never lived. In two days the colonel had been buried, and in three days forgotten. Marius wore crape on his hat. That was all.

4 (5)

THE USEFULNESS OF GOING TO MASS TO BECOME A REVOLUTIONARY

MARIUS had preserved the religious habits of his childhood. One Sunday he had gone to hear mass at Saint Sulpice, at this same chapel of the Virgin to which his aunt took him when he was a little boy, and being that day more absent-minded and dreamy than usual, he took his place behind a pillar and knelt down, without noticing it, before a Utrecht velvet chair, on the back of which this name was written: *Monsieur Mabeuf, churchwarden.* The mass had hardly commenced when an old man presented himself and said to Marius:

"Monsieur, this is my place."

Marius moved away readily, and the old man took his chair.

After mass, Marius remained absorbed in thought a few steps distant; the old man approached him again and said: "I beg your pardon, monsieur, for having disturbed you a little while ago, and for disturbing you again now; but you must have thought me impertinent, and I must explain myself."

"Monsieur," said Marius, "it is unnecessary."

"Yes!" resumed the old man; "I do not wish you to have a bad opinion of me. You see I think a great deal of that place. It seems to me that the mass is better there. Why? I will tell you. To that place I have seen for ten years, regularly, every two or three months, a poor, brave father come, who had no other opportunity and no other way of seeing his child, being prevented through some family arrangements. He came at the hour when he knew his son was brought to mass. The little one never suspected that his father was here. He did not even know, perhaps, that he had a father, the innocent boy! The father, for his part, kept behind a pillar, so that nobody should see him. He looked at his child, and wept. This poor man worshipped this little boy. I saw that. This place has become sanctified, as it were, for me, and I have acquired the habit of coming here to hear mass. I prefer it to the bench, where I have a right to be as a warden. I was even acquainted slightly with this unfortunate gentleman. He had a father-in-law, a rich aunt, relatives, I do not remember exactly, who threatened to disinherit the child if he, the father, should see him. He had sacrificed himself that his son might some day be rich and happy. They were separated by political opinions. Certainly I approve of political opinions, but there are people who do not know where to stop. Bless me! because a man was at Waterloo he is not a monster; a father is not separated from his child for that. He was one of Bonaparte's colonels. He is dead, I believe. He lived at Vernon, where my brother is curé, and his name is something like Pontmarie, Montpercy. He had a handsome sabre cut."

"Pontmercy," said Marius, turning pale.

"Exactly; Pontmercy. Did you know him?"

"Monsieur," said Marius, "he was my father."

The old churchwarden clasped his hands, and exclaimed——

"Ah! you are the child! Yes, that is it; he ought to be a man now. Well! poor child, you can say that you had a father who loved you well."

Marius offered his arm to the old man, and walked with him to his house. Next day he said to Monsieur Gillenormand:——

"We have arranged a hunting party with a few friends. Will you permit me to be absent for three days?"

"Four," answered the grandfather; "go; amuse yourself."

And, with a wink he whispered to his daughter——

"Some love affair!"

5 (6)

WHAT IT IS TO HAVE MET
A CHURCHWARDEN

WHERE MARIUS WENT we shall see a little further on.

Marius was absent three days, then he returned to Paris, went straight to the library of the law-school, and asked for the file of the *Moniteur.*

He read the *Moniteur;* he read all the histories of the republic and the empire; the *Memorial de Sainte-Hélène;* all the memoirs, journals, bulletins, proclamations; he devoured everything. The first time he met his father's name in the bulletins of the grand army he had a fever for a whole week. He went to see the generals under whom George Pontmercy had served—among others, Count H. The churchwarden, Mabeuf, whom he had gone to see again, gave him an account of the life at Vernon, the colonel's retreat, his flowers and his solitude. Marius came to understand fully this rare, sublime, and gentle man, this sort of lion-lamb who was his father.

In the meantime, engrossed in this study, which took up all his time, as well as all his thoughts, he hardly saw the Gillenormands more. At the hours of meals he appeared; then when they looked for him, he was gone. The aunt grumbled. The grandfather smiled. "Poh, poh! it is the age for the lasses!" Sometimes the old man added: "The devil! I thought that it was some flirtation. It seems to be a passion."

It was a passion, indeed. Marius was on the way to adoration for his father.

The republic, the empire, had been to him, till then, nothing but monstrous words. The republic, a guillotine in a twilight; the empire, a sabre in the night. He had looked into them, and there, where he expected to find only a chaos of darkness, he had seen, with a sort of astounding surprise, mingled with fear and joy, stars shining, Mirabeau, Vergniaud, Saint-Just, Robespierre, Camille Desmoulins, Danton, and a sun rising, Napoleon. He knew not where he was. He recoiled blinded by the splendours. Little by little, the astonishment passed away, he accustomed himself to this radiance; he looked upon acts without dizziness, he examined personages without error; the revolution and the empire set themselves in luminous perspective before his straining eyes; he saw each of these two groups of events and men arrange themselves into two enormous facts: the republic into the sovereignty of the civic right restored to the masses, the empire into the sovereignty of the French idea imposed upon Europe; he saw spring out of the revolution the grand figure of the people, and out of the empire the grand figure of France. He declared to himself that all that had been good.

He perceived then that up to that time he had comprehended his country no more than he had his father. He had known neither one nor the other, and he had had a sort of voluntary night over his eyes. He now saw, and on the one hand he admired, on the other he worshipped.

He was full of regret and remorse and he thought with despair that all he had in his soul he could say now only to a tomb. Oh! if his father were living, if he had had him still, if God in his mercy and in his goodness had permitted that his father might be still alive, how he would have run, how he would have plunged headlong, how he would have cried to his father: "Father! I am here! it is I! my heart is the same as yours! I am your son!" How he would have embraced his white head, wet his hair with tears, gazed upon his scar, pressed his hands, worshipped his garments, kissed his feet! oh! why had this father died so soon, before the maturation, before the justice, before the love of his son! Marius had a continual sob in his heart which said at every moment: "Alas!" At the same time he became more truly serious, more truly grave, surer of his faith and his thought. Gleams of the true came at every instant to complete his reasoning. It was like an interior growth. He felt a sort of natural aggrandisement which these two new things, his father and his country, brought to him.

As when one has a key, everything opened; he explained to himself what he had hated, he penetrated what he had abhorred; he saw clearly henceforth the providential, divine, and human meaning of the great things which he had been taught to detest, and the great men whom he had been instructed to curse. When he thought of his former opinions, which were only of yesterday, but which seemed so ancient to him already, he became indignant at himself, and he smiled. From the rehabilitation of his father he had naturally passed to the rehabilitation of Napoleon.

This, however, we must say, was not accomplished without labour.

From childhood he had been imbued with the judgment of the party of 1814 in regard to Bonaparte. Now, all the prejudices of the Restoration, all its interests, all its instincts, tended to the disfigurement of Napoleon. It execrated him still more than it did Robespierre. It made skilful use of the fatigue of the nation and the hatred of mothers [who had lost their sons in war]. Bonaparte had become a sort of monster almost fabulous, and to depict him to the imagination of the people, which, as we have already said, resembles the imagination of children, the party of 1814 revealed in succession every terrifying mask, from that which is terrible, while yet it is grand, to that which is terrible in the grotesque, from Tiberius to Bugaboo. Thus, in speaking of Bonaparte, you might either weep, or burst with laughter, provided hatred was the basis. Marius had never had—about that man, as he was called—any other ideas in his mind. They had grown together with the tenacity of his nature. There was in him a complete little man who was devoted to hatred of Napoleon.

On reading his history, especially in studying it in documents and other materials, the veil which covered Napoleon from Marius' eyes gradually fell away. He perceived something immense, and suspected that he had been deceiving himself up to that moment about Bonaparte as well as about everything else; each day he saw more clearly; and he began to mount slowly, step by step, in the beginning almost with regret, afterwards with rapture, and as if drawn by an irresistible fascination, at first the sombre stages, then the dimly lighted stages, finally the luminous and splendid stages of enthusiasm.

The emperor had been to his father only the beloved captain, whom one admires, and for whom one devotes himself; to Marius he was something more. He was the predestined constructor of the French group, succeeding the Roman group in the mastery of the world. He was the stupendous architect of a downfall, the successor of Charlemagne, of Louis XI, of Henry IV, of Richelieu, of Louis XIV, and of the Committee of Public Safety, having doubtless his blemishes, his faults, and even his crimes, that is to say being man; but august in his faults, brilliant in his blemishes, mighty in his crimes.

He was the man foreordained to force all nations to say: the Grand Nation. He was better still; he was the very incarnation of France, conquering Europe by the sword which he held, and the world by the light which he shed. Marius saw in Bonaparte the flashing spectre which will always rise upon the frontier, and which will guard the future. Despot, but dictator; despot resulting from a republic and summing up a revolution. Napoleon became to him the people-man as Jesus is the God-man.[1]

We see that, as for all converts to a religion, his conversion intoxicated him, he plunged headlong into adhesion, and he went too far. His nature was such; once on a slope it was almost impossible for him to hold back. Fanaticism for the sword took possession of him, and became complicated in his mind with enthusiasm for the idea. He did not perceive that along with genius, and indiscriminately, he was admiring force, that is to say that he was installing in the two compartments of his idolatry, on one side what is divine, and on the other what is brutal. In several respects he began to deceive himself in other matters. He accepted everything. There is a way of meeting error while on the road of truth. He had a sort of wilful implicit faith which swallowed everything en masse. On the new path upon which he had entered, in judging the crimes of the ancient régime as well as in measuring the glory of Napoleon, he neglected the extenuating circumstances.

However this might be, a great step had been taken. Where he had formerly seen the fall of the monarchy, he now saw the advent of France. His pole-star was changed. What had been the setting, was now the rising of the sun. He had turned around.

All these revolutions were accomplished in him without a suspicion of it in his family.

When, in this mysterious labour, he had entirely cast off his old Bourbon and ultra skin, when he had shed the aristocrat, the jacobite, and the royalist, when he was fully revolutionary, thoroughly democratic, and almost republican, he went to an engraver on the Quai des Orfévres, and ordered a hundred cards bearing this name: *Baron Marius Pontmercy.*

This was but a very logical consequence of the change which had taken place in him, a change in which everything gravitated about his father.

However, as he knew nobody, and could not leave his cards at anybody's door, he put them in his pocket.

By another natural consequence, in proportion as he drew nearer to his father, his memory, and the things for which the colonel had fought for twenty-five years, he drew away from his grandfather. As we have mentioned, for a long time M. Gillenormand's capriciousness had been disagreeable to him. There was already between them all the distaste of a serious young man for a frivolous old man. Geront's gaiety shocks and exasperates Werther's melancholy. So long as the same political opinions and the same ideas had been common to them, Marius had met M. Gillenormand by means of them as if upon a bridge. When this bridge fell, the abyss appeared. And then, above all, Marius felt inexpressibly revolted when he thought that M. Gillenormand, from stupid motives, had pitilessly torn him from the colonel, thus depriving the father of the child, and the child of the father.

Through affection and veneration for his father, Marius had almost reached aversion for his grandfather.

Nothing of this, however, as we have said, was betrayed externally. Only he was more and more frigid; laconic at meals, and scarcely ever in the house. When his aunt scolded him for it, he was very mild, and gave as an excuse his studies, courts, examinations, dissertations, etc. The grandfather did not change his infallible diagnosis: "In love? I understand it."

Marius was absent for a while from time to time.

"Where can he go to?" asked the aunt.

On one of these journeys, which were always very short, he went to Montfermeil in obedience to the injunction which his father had left him, and sought for the former sergeant of Waterloo, the innkeeper Thénardier. Thénardier had failed, the inn was closed, and nobody knew what had become of him. While making these researches, Marius was away from the house four days.

"Decidedly," said the grandfather, "he is going astray."

They thought they noticed that he wore something, upon his breast and under his shirt, hung from his neck by a black ribbon.

Lieutenant Théodule Gillenormand, M. Gillenormand's great-nephew, is a vain, handsome lancer (a member of a cavalry unit armed with lances: they existed from 1801–1871), and a potential rival to Marius for the old man's affections and fortune. He is a favorite of Mlle Gillenormand, his aunt. Curious about Marius's mysterious appearances, and thinking that he is having an affair with "a creature," she persuades Théodule to spy on him when the two young men happen to be traveling the same way. Théodule discovers that Marius's assignation is with his father's tomb.

Marius returned from Vernon early in the morning of the third day, was set down at his grandfather's, and, fatigued by the two nights passed in the coach, feeling the need of making up for his lack of sleep by an hour at the swimming school, ran quickly up to his room, took only time enough to lay off his travelling coat and the black ribbon which he wore about his neck, and went away to the bath.

M. Gillenormand, who had risen early like all old persons who are in good health, had heard him come in, and hastened as fast as he could with his old legs, to climb to the top of the stairs where Marius' room was, that he might embrace him, question him while embracing him, and find out something about where he came from.

But the youth had taken less time to go down than the octogenarian to go up, and when Grandfather Gillenormand entered the garret room, Marius was no longer there.

The bed was not disturbed, and upon the bed were displayed without distrust the coat and the black ribbon.

"I like that better," said M. Gillenormand.

And a moment afterwards he entered the parlour where Mademoiselle Gillenormand the elder was already seated, embroidering her cab wheels.

The entrance was triumphal.

M. Gillenormand held in one hand the coat and in the other the neck ribbon, and cried:

"Victory! We are going to penetrate the mystery! we shall know the end of the end, we shall feel of the libertinism of our trickster! here we are with the romance even. I have the portrait."

In fact, a black shagreen box, much like to a medallion, was fastened to the ribbon.

The old man took this box and looked at it some time without opening it, with that air of desire, ravishment, and anger, with which a poor, hungry devil sees an excellent dinner pass under his nose, when it is not for him.

"For it is evidently a portrait. I know all about that. This is worn tenderly upon the heart. What fools they are! Some abominable trollop, enough to make one shudder probably! Young folks have such bad taste in these days!"

"Let us see, father," said the old maid.

The box opened by pressing a spring. They found nothing in it but a piece of paper carefully folded.

"*From the same to the same,*" said M. Gillenormand, bursting with laughter. "I know what that is. A love-letter!"

"Ah! then let us read it!" said the aunt.

And she put on her spectacles. They unfolded the paper and read this:

"*For my son.*—The emperor made me a baron upon the battlefield of Waterloo. Since the Restoration contests this title which I have bought with my blood, my son will take it and bear it. I need not say that he will be worthy of it."

The feelings of the father and daughter cannot be described. They felt chilled as by the breath of a death's head. They did not exchange a word. M. Gillenormand, however, said in a low voice, and as if talking to himself:

"It is the handwriting of that butcher."

The aunt examined the paper, turned it on all sides, then put it back in the box.

Just at that moment, a little oblong package, wrapped in blue paper, fell from a pocket of the coat. Mademoiselle Gillenormand picked it up and unfolded the blue paper. It was Marius' hundred cards. She passed one of them to M. Gillenormand, who read: *Baron Marius Pontmercy.*

The old man rang. Nicolette came. M. Gillenormand took the ribbon, the box, and the coat, threw them all on the floor in the middle of the parlour, and said:

"Take away those things."

A full hour passed in complete silence. The old man and the old maid sat with their backs turned to one another, and were probably, each on their side, thinking over the same things. At the end of that hour, aunt Gillenormand said:

"Pretty!"

A few minutes afterwards, Marius made his appearance. He came in. Even before crossing the threshold of the parlour, he perceived his grandfather holding one of his cards in his hand, who, on seeing him, exclaimed with his crushing air of sneering, bourgeois superiority:

"Stop! stop! stop! stop! stop! you are a baron now. I present you my compliments. What does this mean?"

Marius coloured slightly, and answered:

"It means that I am my father's son."

M. Gillenormand checked his laugh, and said harshly:

"Your father; I am your father."

"My father," resumed Marius with downcast eyes and stern manner, "was a humble and heroic man, who served the Republic and France gloriously, who was great in the greatest history that men have ever made, who lived a quarter of a century in the camp, by day under fire, by night in the snow, in the mud, and in the rain, who captured colours, who received twenty wounds, who died forgotten and abandoned, and who had but one fault; that was in loving too dearly two ingrates, his country and me."

This was more than M. Gillenormand could listen to. At the word, *Republic,* he rose, or rather, sprang to his feet. Every one of the words which Marius had pronounced, had produced the effect upon the old royalist's face, of a blast from a bellows upon a burning coal. From dark he had become red, from red purple, and from purple glowing.

"Marius!" exclaimed he, "abominable child! I don't know what your father was! I don't want to know! I know nothing about him and I don't know him! but what I do know is, that there was never anything but miserable wretches among all that rabble! that they were all beggars, assassins, red caps, thieves! I say all! I say all! I know nobody! I say all! do you hear, Marius? Look you, indeed, you are as much a baron as my slipper! they were all bandits who served Robespierre! all brigands who served B-u-o-naparte! all traitors who betrayed, betrayed, betrayed! their legitimate king! all cowards who ran from the Prussians and English at Waterloo! That is what I know. If your father is among them I don't know him, I am sorry for it, so much the worse, your servant!"

In his turn, Marius now became the coal, and M. Gillenormand the bellows. Marius shuddered in every limb, he knew not what to do, his head burned. He was the priest who sees all his wafers thrown to the winds, the fakir who sees a passer-by spit upon his idol. He could not allow such things to be said before him unanswered. But what could he do? His father had been trodden under foot and stamped upon in his presence, but by whom? by his grandfather. How should he avenge the one without outraging the other? It was impossible for him to insult his grandfather, and it was equally impossible for him not to avenge his father. On one hand a sacred tomb, on the other white hairs. He was for a few moments dizzy and staggering with all this whirlwind in his head; then he raised his eyes, looked straight at his grandfather, and cried in a thundering voice:

"Down with the Bourbons, and the great hog Louis XVIII!"

Louis XVIII had been dead for four years; but it was all the same to him.

The old man, scarlet as he was, suddenly became whiter than his hair. He turned towards a bust of the Duke de Berry which stood upon the mantel, and bowed to it profoundly with a sort of peculiar majesty. Then he walked twice, slowly and in silence, from the fireplace to the window and from the window to the fireplace, traversing the whole length of the room and making the floor crack as if an image of stone were walking over it. The second time, he bent towards his daughter, who was enduring the shock with the stupor of an aged sheep, and said to her with a smile that was almost calm:

"A baron like Monsieur and a bourgeois like me cannot remain under the same roof."

And all at once straightening up, pallid, trembling, terrible, his forehead swelling with the fearful radiance of anger, he stretched his arm towards Marius and cried to him:

"Be off."

Marius left the house.

The next day, M. Gillenormand said to his daughter:

"You will send sixty pistoles every six months to this blood-drinker, and never speak of him to me again."*

Having an immense residuum of fury to expend, and not knowing what to do with it, he spoke to his daughter with coldness for more than three months.

Marius, for his part, departed in indignation. A circumstance, which we must mention, had aggravated his exasperation still more. There are always such little fatalities complicating domestic dramas. Feelings are embittered by them, although in reality the faults are none the greater. In hurriedly carrying away, at the old man's command, Marius' "things" to his room, Nicolette had, without perceiving it, dropped, probably on the garret stairs, which were dark, the black shagreen medallion which contained the paper written by the colonel. Neither the paper nor the medallion could be

---

Pistoles were 10-franc coins.

found. Marius was convinced that "Monsieur Gillenormand"—from that day forth he never named him otherwise—had thrown "his father's will" into the fire. He knew by heart the few lines written by the colonel, and consequently nothing was lost. But the paper, the writing, that sacred relic, all that was his heart itself. What had been done with it?

Marius went away without saying where he was going, and without knowing where he was going, with thirty francs, his watch, and a few clothes in a carpet-bag. He hired a cabriolet by the hour, jumped in, and drove at random towards the Latin quarter.

What was Marius to do?

BOOK FOUR
THE FRIENDS OF THE A B C

1

A GROUP WHICH ALMOST BECAME HISTORIC

AT THAT PERIOD, apparently unimportant, something of a revolutionary thrill was vaguely felt. Whispers coming from the depths of '89 and of '92 were in the air. Young Paris was, excuse the expression, in the process of moulting. People were transformed almost without suspecting it, by the very movement of the time. The hand which moves over the dial moves also among souls. Each one took the step forward which was before him. Royalists became liberals, liberals became democrats.

It was like a rising tide, complicated by a thousand ebbs; the peculiarity of the ebb is to make mixtures; thence very singular combinations of ideas; men worshipped at the same time Napoleon and liberty.

At that time there were not yet in France any of those underlying organisations like the German Tugenbund and the Italian Carbonari; but here and there obscure excavations were branching out. La Cougourde was assuming form at Aix; there was in Paris, among other affiliations of this kind, the Society of the Friends of the A B C.

Who were the Friends of the A B C? A society having as its aim, in appearance, the education of children; in reality, the elevation of men.

They declared themselves the Friends of the A B C.* The *abaissé* were the people. They wished to raise them up.

The Friends of the A B C were not numerous, it was a secret society in the embryonic state; we should almost say a coterie, if coteries produced heroes. They met in Paris, at two places, near the Halles, in a wine shop called *Corinthe*, which will be referred to hereafter, and near the Pantheon, in a little coffeehouse on the Place Saint Michel, called *Le Café Musain*, now torn down; the first of these two places of rendezvous was near the working-men, the second near the students.[2]

The ordinary conventicles of the Friends of the A B C were held in a back room of the Café Musain.

This room, quite distant from the café, with which it communicated by a very long passage, had two windows, and an exit by a private stairway upon the little Rue des Grès. They smoked, drank, played, and laughed there. They talked very loud about everything, and in whispers about something else. On the wall was nailed, an indication sufficient to awaken the suspicion of a police officer, an old map of France under the republic.

---

*"A B C" in French is pronounced ah-bay-say, exactly like the French word *abaissé*, "the abased."

Most of the Friends of the A B C were students, in thorough understanding with a few working-men. The names of the principal are as follows. They belong to a certain extent to history; Enjolras, Combeferre, Jean
Prouvaire, Feuilly, Courfeyrac, Bahorel, Lesgle or Laigle, Joly, Grataire.

These young men constituted a sort of family among themselves, by
force of friendship. All except Laigle were from the South.

This was a remarkable group. It has vanished into the invisible depths
which are behind us. At the point of this drama which we have now
reached, it may not be useless to throw a ray of light upon these young
heads before the reader sees them sink into the shadow of a tragic fate.

Enjolras, whom we have named first, the reason why will be seen by-
and-by, was an only son and was rich.

Enjolras was a charming young man, who was capable of being terrible.
He was angelically beautiful. He was Antinous wild. You would have said,
to see the thoughtful reflection of his eye, that he had already, in some preceding existence, passed through the revolutionary apocalypse. He had the
tradition of it like an eye-witness. He knew all the little details of the grand
thing, a pontifical and warrior nature, strange in a youth. He was officiating and militant; from the immediate point of view, a soldier of democracy;
above the movement of the time, a priest of the ideal. He had a deep eye,
lids a little red, thick under lip, easily becoming disdainful, and a high forehead. Much forehead in a face is like much sky in a horizon. Like certain
young men of the beginning of this century and the end of the last century,
who became illustrious in early life, he had an exceedingly youthful look,
as fresh as a young girl's, although he had periods of pallor. He was now a
man, but he seemed a child still. His twenty-two years of age appeared
seventeen; he was serious, he did not seem to know that there was on the
earth a being called woman.

Beside Enjolras who represented the logic of the revolution, Combeferre represented its philosophy. Between the logic of the revolution and
its philosophy, there is this difference—that its logic could conclude with
war, while its philosophy could only end in peace. Combeferre completed
and corrected Enjolras. He was lower and broader. His desire was to instil
into all minds the broad principles of general ideas; he said "Revolution,
but civilisation;" and about the steep mountain he spread the vast blue
horizon. Hence, in all Combeferre's views, there was something attainable
and practicable. Revolution with Combeferre was more breathable than
with Enjolras. Enjolras expressed its divine right, and Combeferre its natural right. The first went as far as Robespierre; the second stopped at Condorcet. Combeferre more than Enjolras lived the life of the world generally.
Had it been given to these two young men to take a place in history, one
would have been the upright man, the other would have been the wise man.
Enjolras was more manly. Combeferre was more humane. *Homo* and *Vir*
indeed express the exact shade of difference. Combeferre was gentle, as
Enjolras was severe, from natural purity. He loved the word citizen, but he
preferred the word man. He believed in all the dreams: railroads, the sup-
pression of suffering in surgical operations, the fixing of the image in the

camera obscura, the electric telegraph, the steering of balloons. Little dismayed, moreover, by the citadels built upon all sides against the human race by superstitions, despotisms, and prejudices, he was one of those who think that science will at last turn the position. Enjolras was a chief; Combeferre was a guide. You would have preferred to fight with the one and march with the other. Not that Combeferre was not capable of fighting; he did not refuse to close with an obstacle, and to attack it by main strength and by explosion, but to put, gradually, by the teaching of axioms and the promulgation of positive laws, the human race in harmony with its destinies, pleased him better; and of the two lights, his inclination was rather for illumination than for conflagration. A fire would cause a dawn, undoubtedly, but why not wait for the break of day? A volcano enlightens, but the morning enlightens still better. *"The good must be innocent,"* he repeated incessantly. And in fact, if it is the grandeur of the revolution to gaze steadily upon the dazzling ideal, and to fly to it through the lightnings, with blood and fire in its talons, it is the beauty of progress to be without a stain; and there is between Washington, who represents the one, and Danton, who incarnates the other, the difference which separates the angel with the wings of a swan, from the angel with the wings of an eagle.

Jean Prouvaire was yet a shade more subdued than Combeferre. He called himself Jehan, from that little momentary fancifulness which mingled with the deep and powerful movement from which arose the study of the Middle Ages, then so necessary. Jean Prouvaire was addicted to love; he cultivated a pot of flowers, played on the flute, made verses, loved the people, mourned over woman, wept over childhood, confounded the future and God in the same faith and blamed the revolution for having cut off a royal head, that of André Chénier. His voice was usually delicate, but at times suddenly became masculine. He was well read, even to erudition, and almost an orientalist. Above all, he was good, and, a very natural thing to one who knows how near goodness borders upon grandeur, in poetry he preferred the grand. He understood Italian, Latin, Greek, and Hebrew; and that served him only to read four poets: Dante, Juvenal, Æschylus, and Isaiah. In French, he preferred Corneille to Racine, and Agrippa d'Aubigné to Corneille. He was fond of strolling in fields of wild oats and blue-bells, and paid almost as much attention to the clouds as to passing events. His mind had two attitudes—one towards man, the other towards God; he studied, or he contemplated. All day he pondered over social questions: wages, capital, credit, marriage, religion, liberty of thought, liberty of love, education, punishment, misery, association, property, production and distribution, the lower enigma which covers the human ant-hill with a shadow; and at night he gazed upon the stars, those enormous beings. Like Enjolras, he was rich, and an only son. He spoke gently, bent his head, cast down his eyes, smiled with embarrassment, dressed badly, had an awkward air, blushed at nothing, was very timid, still intrepid.

Feuilly was a fan-maker, an orphan, who with difficulty earned three francs a day, and who had but one thought, to deliver the world. He had still another desire—to instruct himself; which he also called deliverance. He had taught himself to read and write; all that he knew, he had learned alone. Feuilly was a generous heart. He had an immense embrace. This orphan had adopted the people. Being without a mother, he had meditated upon his mother country. He was not willing that there should be any man upon the earth without a country. He nurtured within himself, with the deep divination of the man of the people, what we now call *the idea of nationality*. He had learned history expressly that he might base his indignation upon a knowledge of its cause. In this new upper room of utopists particularly interested in France, he represented the foreign nations. His specialty was Greece, Poland, Hungary, the Danubian Provinces, and Italy. He uttered these names incessantly, in season and out of season, with the tenacity of the right. Turkey upon Greece and Thessaly, Russia upon Warsaw, Austria upon Venice, these violations exasperated him. The grand highway robbery of 1772 excited him above all. There is no more sovereign eloquence than the truth in indignation; he was eloquent with this eloquence. He was never done with that infamous date, 1772, that noble and valiant people blotted out by treachery, that threefold crime, that monstrous ambush, prototype and pattern of all those terrible suppressions of states which, since, have stricken several noble nations, and have, so to say, erased the record of their birth. All the contemporary assaults upon society date from the partition of Poland. Such was the usual text of Feuilly. This poor working man had made himself a teacher of justice, and she rewarded him by making him grand. For there is in fact eternity in the right. Warsaw can no more be Tartar than Venice can be Teutonic. The kings lose their labour at this, and their honour. Sooner or later, the submerged country floats to the surface and reappears. Greece again becomes Greece, Italy again becomes Italy. The protest of the right against the fact, persists forever. The robbery of a people never becomes prescriptive. These lofty swindles have no future. You cannot pick the mark out of a nation as you can out of a handkerchief.[3]

Courfeyrac had a father whose name was M. de Courfeyrac. One of the false ideas of the restoration in point of aristocracy and nobility was its faith in the particle. The particle, we know, has no significance. But the bourgeois of the time of *La Minerve* considered this poor *de* so highly that men thought themselves obliged to renounce it. M. de Chauvelin called himself M. Chauvelin, M. de Caumartin, M. Caumartin, M. de Constant de Rebecque, Benjamin Constant, M. de Lafayette, M. Lafayette. Courfeyrac did not wish to be behind, and called himself briefly Courfeyrac.

We might almost, in what concerns Courfeyrac, stop here, and content ourselves with saying as to the remainder: Courfeyrac, see Tholomyès.

Courfeyrac had in fact that youthful animation which we might call the diabolic beauty of mind. In later life, this dies out, like the playfulness of the kitten, and all that grace ends, on two feet in the bourgeois, and on four paws in the mouser.

This style of mind is transmitted from generation to generation of students, passed from hand to hand by the successive groups of youth, *quasi cursores,* nearly always the same: so that, as we have just indicated, any person who has listened to Courfeyrac in 1828, would have thought he was hearing Tholomyès in 1817. But Courfeyrac was a decent fellow. Beneath the apparent similarities of the exterior mind, there was great dissimilarity between Tholomyès and him. The latent man which existed in each, was in the first altogether different from what it was in the second. There was in Tholomyès an attorney, and in Courfeyrac a paladin.

Enjolras was the chief, Combeferre was the guide, Courfeyrac was the centre. The others gave more light, he gave more heat; the truth is, that he had all the qualities of a centre, roundness and radiance.

Bahorel had figured in the bloody tumult of June, 1822, on the occasion of the burial of young Lallemand.

Bahorel was a creature of good humour and bad company, brave, a spendthrift, prodigal almost to generosity, talkative almost to eloquence, bold almost to effrontery; the best possible devil's-pie; with fool-hardy waistcoats and scarlet opinions; a wholesale blusterer, that is to say, liking nothing so well as a quarrel unless it were a riot, and nothing so well as a riot unless it were a revolution; always ready to break a paving-stone, then to tear up a street, then to demolish a government, to see the effect of it; a student of the eleventh year. He had adopted for his motto: *never a lawyer,* and for his coat of arms a bedroom table on which you might discern a square cap. Whenever he passed by the law-school, which rarely happened, he buttoned up his overcoat, the short winter jacket was not yet invented, and he took hygienic precautions. He said of the portal of the school: what a fine old man! and of the dean, M. Delvincourt: what a monument! He saw in his studies subjects for ditties, and in his professors opportunities for caricatures. He ate up in doing nothing a considerable allowance, something like three thousand francs. His parents were peasants, in whom he had succeeded in inculcating a respect for their son.

He said of them: "They are peasants and not bourgeois; which explains their intelligence."

Bahorel, a capricious man, was scattered over several cafés; the others had habits, he had none. He loafed. To err is human. To loaf is Parisian. At bottom, a penetrating mind and more of a thinker than he seemed.

He served as a bond between the Friends of the A B C and some other groups which were without definite shape, but which were to take form afterwards.

In this conclave of young heads there was one bald member.

The Marquis d'Avaray, whom Louis XVIII made a duke for having helped him into a cab the day that he emigrated, related that in 1814, on his return to France, as the king landed at Calais, a man presented a petition to him.

"What do you want?" said the king.

"Sire, a post-office."

"What is your name?"

"L'Aigle." [The eagle].

The king scowled, looked at the signature of the petition and saw the name written thus: LESGLE. This orthography, anything but Bonapartist, pleased the king, and he began to smile. "Sire," resumed the man with the petition, "my ancestor was a dog-trainer surnamed Lesgueules [The Chaps]. This surname has become my name. My name is Lesgueules, by contraction Lesgle, and by corruption L'Aigle." This made the king finish his smile. He afterwards gave the man the post-office at Meaux, either intentionally or inadvertently.

The bald member of the club was son of this Lesgle, or Lègle, and signed his name Lègle (de Meaux). His comrades, for the sake of brevity, called him Bossuet.

Bossuet was a cheery fellow who was unlucky. His specialty was to succeed in nothing. On the other hand, he laughed at everything. At twenty-five he was bald. His father had died owning a house and some land, but he, the son, had found nothing more urgent than to lose this house and land in a bad speculation. He had nothing left. He had considerable knowledge and wit, but he always miscarried. Everything failed him, everything deceived him; whatever he built up fell upon him. If he split wood, he cut his finger. If he had a mistress, he very soon discovered that he had also a friend. Every moment some misfortune happened to him; hence his joviality. He said: *I live under the roof of the falling tiles.* Rarely astonished since he was always expecting some accident, he took ill luck with serenity and smiled at the vexations of destiny like one who hears a jest. He was poor, but his fund of good-humour was inexhaustible. He soon reached his last sou, never his last burst of laughter. When met by adversity, he saluted that acquaintance cordially, he patted catastrophes on the back; he was so familiar with fatality as to call it by its nick-name. "Good morning, old Genius," he would say.

These persecutions of fortune had made him inventive. He was full of resources. He had no money, but he found means, when it seemed good to him, to go to "reckless expenses." One night, he even spent a hundred francs on a supper with a trollop, which inspired him in the midst of the orgy with this memorable saying: *"Daughter of five louis, pull off my boots."*

Bossuet was slowly making his way towards the legal profession; he was doing his law, in the manner of Bahorel. Bossuet had never much domicile, sometimes none at all. He lodged sometimes with one, sometimes with another, oftenest with Joly. Joly was studying medicine. He was two years younger than Bossuet.

Joly was a young Malade Imaginaire. What he had learned in medicine was rather to be a patient than a physician. At twenty-three, he thought himself a valetudinarian, and passed his time in looking at his tongue in a mirror. He declared that man is a magnet, like the needle, and in his room he placed his bed with the head to the south and the foot to the north, so that at night the circulation of the blood should not be interfered with by the grand magnetic current of the globe. In stormy weather, he felt his pulse. Nevertheless, the gayest of all. All these incoherences, young, notional, sickly, joyous, got along very well together, and the result was an

eccentric and agreeable person whom his comrades, prodigal of conso-
nants, called Jolllly. "You can fly upon four L's," [*ailes,* wings] said Jean
Prouvaire.

Joly had the habit of rubbing his nose with the end of his cane which is
an indication of a sagacious mind.

All these young men, diverse as they were, and of whom, as a whole we
ought only to speak seriously, had the same religion: Progress.

All were legitimate sons of the French Revolution. The giddiest became
solemn when pronouncing this date: '89. Their fathers according to the
flesh, were, or had been Feuillants, Royalists, Doctrinaires; it mattered little; this hurly-burly which antedated them, had nothing to do with them;
they were young; the pure blood of principles flowed in their veins. They
attached themselves without an intermediate shade to incorruptible right
and to absolute duty.

Affiliated and initiated, they secretly sketched out their ideas.

Among all these passionate hearts and all these undoubting minds
there was one sceptic. How did he happen to be there? from juxtaposition.
The name of this sceptic was Grantaire, and he usually signed with the
rebus: R [*grand R,* capital R]. Grantaire was a man who took good care
not to believe anything. He was, moreover, one of the students who had
learned most during their course in Paris; knew that the best coffee was at
the Café Lemblin, and the best billiard table at the Café Voltaire; that you
could find good rolls and good girls at the hermitage on the Boulevard du
Maine, broiled chickens at Mother Saguet's, excellent chowders at the
Barrière de la Cunette, and a peculiar light white wine at the Barrière du
Combat. He knew the good places for everything; furthermore, boxing,
tennis, a few dances, and he was a profound cudgel-player. A great drinker
to boot. He was frightfully ugly; the prettiest shoebinder of that period,
Irma Boissy, revolting at his ugliness, had uttered this sentence: "Grantaire
is impossible," but Grantaire's self-conceit was not disconcerted. He
looked tenderly and fixedly upon every woman, appearing to say of them
all: *if I only would;* and trying to make his comrades believe that he was in
general demand.

All these words: rights of the people, rights of man, social contract,
French Revolution, republic, democracy, humanity, civilisation, religion,
progress, were, to Grantaire, very nearly meaningless. He smiled at them.
Scepticism, that cries of the intellect, had not left one entire idea in his
mind. He lived in irony. This was his axiom: There is only one certainty, my
full glass. He ridiculed all devotion, under all circumstances, in the brother
as well as the father, in Robespierre the younger as well as Loizerolles.
"Much good it does them to be dead," he exclaimed. He said of the cross:
"There is a gibbet which has made a success." A rover, a gambler, a libertine, and often drunk, he displeased these young thinkers by singing incessantly: *"I loves the girls and I loves good wine."* Tune: Vive Henri IV.

Still, this sceptic had a fanaticism. This fanaticism was neither an idea,
nor a dogma, nor an art, nor a science; it was a man: Enjolras. Grantaire
admired, loved, and venerated Enjolras. To whom did this anarchical

doubter ally himself in this phalanx of absolute minds? To the most absolute. In what way did Enjolras subjugate him? By ideas? No. By character. A phenomenon often seen. A sceptic adhering to a believer; that is as simple as the law of the complementary colours. What we lack attracts us. Nobody loves the light like the blind man. The dwarf adores the drum-major. The toad is always looking up at the sky; why? To see the bird fly. Grantaire, in whom doubt was creeping, loved to see faith soaring in Enjolras. He had need of Enjolras. Without understanding it himself clearly, and without trying to explain it, that chaste, healthy, firm, direct, hard, candid nature charmed him. He admired, by instinct, his opposite. His soft, wavering, disjointed, diseased, deformed ideas, attached themselves to Enjolras as to a backbone. His moral spine leaned upon that firmness. Grantaire, by the side of Enjolras, became somebody again. He was himself, moreover, composed of two apparently incompatible elements. He was ironical and cordial. His indifference was loving. His mind dispensed with belief, yet his heart could not dispense with friendship. A thorough contradiction; for an affection is a conviction. His nature was so. There are men who seem born to be the opposite, the reverse, the counterpart.

Grantaire, a true satellite of Enjolras, lived in this circle of young people; he dwelt in it; he took pleasure only in it; he followed them everywhere. His delight was to see these forms coming and going in the fumes of the wine. He was tolerated for his good-humour.

Enjolras, being a believer, disdained this sceptic, and being sober, scorned this drunkard. He granted him a little haughty pity. Grantaire was an unaccepted Pylades. Always rudely treated by Enjolras, harshly repelled, rejected, yet returning, he said of Enjolras: "What a fine statue!"

2

FUNERAL ORATION UPON BLONDEAU, BY BOSSUET

ON A CERTAIN AFTERNOON, which had, as we shall see, some coincidence with events before related, Laigle de Meaux was leaning lazily back against the doorway of the Café Musain. He had the appearance of a caryatid on vacation; he was supporting nothing but his reverie. He was looking at the Place Saint Michel. Leaning back is a way of lying down standing which is not disliked by dreamers. Laigle de Meaux was thinking, without melancholy, of a little mishap which had befallen him the day before at the law-school, and which modified his personal plans for the future—plans which were, moreover, rather indefinite.

Reverie does not hinder a carriage from going by, nor the dreamer from noticing the carriage. Laigle de Meaux, whose eyes were wandering in a sort of general stroll, perceived, through all his somnambulism, a two-wheeled vehicle turning into the square, which was moving at a walk, as if undecided. What did this carriage want? why was it moving at a walk? Laigle looked at it. There was inside, beside the driver, a young man, and before the young man, a large carpet-bag. The bag exhibited to the passers-by this name, written in big black letters upon a card sewed to the cloth: MARIUS PONTMERCY.

This name changed Laigle's attitude. He straightened up and addressed this apostrophe to the young man in the cabriolet:

"Monsieur Marius Pontmercy?"

The cabriolet, thus called upon, stopped.

The young man, who also seemed to be profoundly musing, raised his eyes.

"Well?" said he.

"You are Monsieur Marius Pontmercy?"

"Certainly."

"I was looking for you," said Laigle de Meaux.

"How is that?" inquired Marius; for he it was, in fact he had just left his grandfather's, and he had before him a face which he saw for the first time. "I do not know you."

"Nor I either. I do not know you," answered Laigle.

Marius thought he had met a buffoon, and that this was the beginning of a mystification in the middle of the street. He was not in a pleasant humour just at that moment. He knit his brows; Laigle de Meaux, imperturbable, continued:

"You were not at school yesterday."

"It is possible."

"It is certain."

"You are a student?" inquired Marius.

"Yes, Monsieur. Like you. The day before yesterday I happened to go into the school. You know, one sometimes has such notions. The professor was about to call the roll. You know that they are very ridiculous just at that time. If you miss the third call, they erase your name. Sixty francs gone."

Marius began to listen. Laigle continued:

"It was Blondeau who was calling the roll. You know Blondeau; he has a very sharp and very malicious nose, and delights in smelling out the absent. He slily commenced with the letter P. I was not listening, not being concerned in that letter. The roll went on well, no erasure, the universe was present, Blondeau was sad. I said to myself, Blondeau, my love, you won't do the slightest execution to-day. Suddenly, Blondeau calls *Marius Pontmercy;* nobody answers. Blondeau, full of hope, repeats louder: *Marius*

Pontmercy? And he seizes his pen. Monsieur, I have bowels. I said to myself rapidly: Here is a brave fellow who is going to be erased. Attention. This is a real live fellow who is not punctual. He is not a good boy. He is not a book-worm, a student who studies, a white-billed pedant strong on science, letters, theology, and wisdom, one of those numskulls drawn out with four pins, a pin for each faculty. He is an honourable idler who loafs, who likes to rusticate, who cultivates the grisette, who pays his court to beauty, who is perhaps, at this very moment, with my mistress. Let us save him. Death to Blondeau! At that moment Blondeau dipped his pen, black with erasures into the ink, cast his tawny eye over the room, and repeated for the third time: *Marius Pontmercy!* I answered: *Present!* In that way you were not erased."

"Monsieur!—" said Marius.

"And I was," added Laigle de Meaux.

"I do not understand you," said Marius.

Laigle resumed:

"Nothing more simple. I was near the chair to answer, and near the door to escape. The professor was looking at me with a certain fixedness. Suddenly, Blondeau, who must be the malignant nose of which Boileau speaks, leaps to the letter L. L is my letter; I am of Meaux, and my name is Lesgle."

"L'Aigle!" interrupted Marius, "what a fine name."

"Monsieur, the Blondeau re-echoes this fine name and cries: *'Laigle!'* I answer: *Present!* Then Blondeau looks at me with the gentleness of a tiger, smiles, and says: If you are Pontmercy, you are not Laigle. A phrase which is uncomplimentary to you, but which brought me only to grief. So saying, he erases me."

Marius exclaimed:

"Monsieur, I am mortified——"

"First of all," interrupted Laigle, "I beg leave to embalm Blondeau in a few words of feeling eulogy. I suppose him dead. There wouldn't be much to change in his thinness, his paleness, his coldness, his stiffness, and his odour. And I say: *Erudimini qui judicatis terram.* Here lies Blondeau, Blondeau the Nose, Blondeau Nasica, the ox of discipline, *bos disciplinæ,* the Molossus of his orders, the angel of the roll, who was straight, square, exact, rigid, honest, and hideous. God has erased him as he erased me."

Marius resumed:

"I am very sorry——"

"Young man," said Laigle of Meaux, "let this be a lesson to you. In future, be punctual."

"I really must give a thousand excuses."

"Never expose yourself again to having your neighbour erased."

"I am very sorry."

Laigle burst out laughing.

"And I, in raptures; I was on the brink of being a lawyer. This rupture saves me. I renounce the triumphs of the bar. I shall not defend the widow, and I shall not attack the orphan. No more toga, no more probation. Here is my erasure obtained. It is to you that I owe it, Monsieur Pontmercy. I intend to pay you a solemn visit of thanks. Where do you live?"

"In this cabriolet," said Marius.

"A sign of opulence," replied Laigle calmly. "I congratulate you. You have here rent of nine thousand francs a year."

Just then Courfeyrac came out of the café.

Marius smiled sadly.

"I have been paying this rent for two hours, and I hope to get out of it; but, it is the usual story, I do not know where to go."

"Monsieur," said Courfeyrac, "come home with me."

"I should have priority," observed Laigle, "but I have no home."

"Silence, Bossuet," replied Courfeyrac.

"Bossuet," said Marius, "but I thought you called yourself Laigle.

"Of Meaux," answered Laigle; "metaphorically, Bossuet."

Courfeyrac got into the cabriolet.

"Driver," said he, "Hôtel de la Porte Saint Jacques."

And that same evening, Marius was installed in a room at the Hôtel de la Porte Saint Jacques, side by side with Courfeyrac.

3

THE ASTONISHMENTS OF MARIUS

IN A FEW DAYS, Marius was the friend of Courfeyrac. Youth is the season of prompt weldings and rapid cicatrisations. Marius, in Courfeyrac's presence, breathed freely, a new thing for him. Courfeyrac asked him no questions. He did not even think of it. At that age, the countenance tells all at once. Speech is useless. There are some young men of whom we might say their physiognomies are talkative. They look at one another, they know one another.

One morning, however, Courfeyrac abruptly put this question to him.

"By the way, have you any political opinions?"

"What do you mean?" said Marius, almost offended at the question.

"What are you?"

"Bonapartist democrat."

"Grey shade of quiet mouse colour," said Courfeyrac.

The next day, Courfeyrac introduced Marius to the Café Musain. Then he whispered in his ear with a smile: "I must give you your admission into the revolution." And he took him into the room of the Friends of the A B C. He presented him to the other members, saying in an undertone this simple word which Marius did not understand: "A pupil."

Marius had fallen into a mental wasps' nest. Still, although silent and serious, he was not the less winged, nor the less armed.

Marius, up to this time solitary and inclined to speak in soliloquies and asides by habit and by taste, was a little bewildered at this flock of young men about him. All these different progressives attacked him at once, and perplexed him. The tumultuous sweep and sway of all these minds at liberty and at work set his ideas in a whirl. Sometimes, in the confusion, they went so far from him that he had some difficulty in finding them again. He heard talk of philosophy, of literature, of art, of history, of religion, in a style he had not looked for. He caught glimpses of strange appearances; and, as he did not bring them into perspective, he was not sure that it was not a chaos that he saw. On abandoning his grandfather's opinions for his father's he had thought himself settled; he now suspected, with anxiety, and without daring to confess it to himself, that he was not. The angle under which he saw all things was beginning to change anew. A certain oscillation shook the whole horizon of his brain. A strange internal moving-day. He almost suffered from it.

It seemed that there were to these young men no "sacred things." Marius heard, upon every subject, singular ways of speaking that were awkward for his still timid mind.

A theatre poster presented itself, decorated with the title of a tragedy of the old repertory, called classic: "Down with tragedy dear to the bourgeois!" cried Bahorel. And Marius heard Combeferre reply.

"You are wrong, Bahorel. The bourgeoisie love tragedy, and upon that point we must let the bourgeoisie alone. Tragedy in a wig has its reason for being, and I am not one of those who, in the name of Æschylus, deny it the right of existence. There are rough drafts in nature; there are, in creation, ready-made parodies; a bill which is not a bill, wings which are not wings, fins which are not fins, claws which are not claws, a mournful cry which inspires us with the desire to laugh, there is the duck. Now, since the fowl exists along with the bird, I do not see why classic tragedy should not exist in the face of antique tragedy."

At another time Marius happened to be passing through the Rue Jean Jacques Rousseau between Enjolras and Courfeyrac.

Courfeyrac took his arm:

"Pay attention. This is the Rue Plâtrière, now called Rue Jean Jacques Rousseau, on account of a singular household which lived on it sixty years ago. It consisted of Jean Jacques and Thérèse. From time to time, little creatures were born in it. Thérèse brought them forth. Jean Jacques turned them forth."*

And Enjolras replied with severity:

"Silence before Jean Jacques! I admire that man. He disowned his children; very well; but he adopted the people."

---

*Enlightenment philosopher Jean Jacques Rousseau, harbinger of the Revolution, put all five of his children up for adoption. (The evil Thénardiers also will have five, but they at least keep two.)

None of these young men uttered this word: the emperor. Jean Prouvaire alone sometimes said Napoleon; all the rest said Bonaparte. Enjolras pronounced *Buonaparte*.

Marius became confusedly astonished. *Initium sapientiæ.**

4

THE BACK ROOM OF THE CAFÉ MUSAIN

OF THE CONVERSATIONS among these young men which Marius frequented and in which he sometimes took part, one shocked him severely.

This was held in the back room of the Café Musain. Nearly all the Friends of the A B C were together that evening. The large lamp was ceremoniously lighted. They talked of one thing and another without passion and with noise. Save Enjolras and Marius, who were silent! each one harangued a little at random. The talk of comrades does sometimes amount to these harmless tumults. It was a play and a fracas as much as a conversation. One threw out words which another caught up. They were talking in each of the four corners.

5

ENLARGEMENT OF THE HORIZON

THE JOSTLINGS of young minds against each other have this wonderful attribute, that one can never foresee the spark, nor predict the flash. What may spring up in a moment? Nobody knows. A burst of laughter follows a scene of tenderness. In a moment of buffoonery, the serious makes its entrance. Impulses depend upon a chance word. The wit of each is sovereign. A jest suffices to open the door to the unlooked for. These are conferences with

---

*The beginning of wisdom (Latin).

sharp turns, where the perspective suddenly changes. Chance is the director of these conversations.

A stern thought, oddly brought out of a clatter of words, suddenly crossed the tumult of speech in which Grantaire, Bahorel, Prouvaire, Bossuet, Combeferre, and Courfeyrac were confusedly fencing.

How does a phrase make its way into a dialogue? whence comes it that it makes its mark all at once upon the attention of those who hear it? We have just said, nobody knows. In the midst of the uproar Bossuet suddenly ended some apostrophe to Combeferre with this date:

"The 18th of June, 1815: Waterloo."

At this name, Waterloo, Marius, who was leaning on a table with a glass of water by him, took his hand away from under his chin and began to look earnestly about the room.

"Bygod," exclaimed Courfeyrac (*Bygosh,* at that period, was falling into disuse), "that number 18 is strange, and striking to me. It is the fatal number of Bonaparte. Put Louis before and Brumaire behind, you have the whole destiny of the man, with this expressive peculiarity, that the beginning is hard pressed by the end."

Enjolras, till now dumb, broke the silence, and thus addressed Courfeyrac: "You mean the crime by the expiation."

This word, *crime,* exceeded the limits of the endurance of Marius, already much excited by the abrupt evocation of Waterloo.

He rose, he walked slowly towards the map of France spread out upon the wall, at the bottom of which could be seen an island in a separate compartment; he laid his finger upon this compartment and said:

"Corsica. A little island which has made France truly great."

This was a breath of freezing air. All was silent. They felt that now something was to be said.

Bahorel, replying to Bossuet, was just assuming a pet attitude. He gave it up to listen.

Enjolras, whose blue eye was not fixed upon anybody, and seemed staring into space, answered without looking at Marius:

"France needs no Corsica to be great. France is great because she is France. *Quia nominor leo.*"*

Marius felt not the slightest desire to retreat, he turned towards Enjolras, and his voice rang with a vibration which came from the quivering of his nerves:

"God forbid that I should diminish France! but it is not lessening her to join her with Napoleon. Come, let us talk then. I am a new-comer among you, but I confess that you astound me. Where are we? who are we? who are you? who am I? Let us explain ourselves about the emperor. I hear you say Buonaparte, accenting the *u* like the royalists. I can tell you that my grandfather does better yet; he says Buonaparté. I thought you were

---

*Because my name is lion (Latin; the implication is "I am entitled to the largest share"): a well-known proverb taken from a fable.

young men. Where is your enthusiasm then? and what do you do with it?
whom do you admire, if you do not admire the emperor? and what more
must you have? If you do not like that great man, what great men would
you have? He was everything. He was complete. He had in his brain the
cube of human faculties. He made codes like Justinian, he dictated like
Cæsar, his conversation joined the lightning of Pascal to the thunderbolt
of Tacitus, he made history and he wrote it, his bulletins are Iliads, he combined the figures of Newton with the metaphors of Mahomet, he left
behind him in the Orient words as grand as the pyramids, at Tilsit he
taught majesty to emperors, at the Academy of Sciences he replied to
Laplace, in the Council of State he held his ground with Merlin, he gave a
soul to the geometry of those and to the trickery of these, he was legal with
the attorneys and sidereal with the astronomers; like Cromwell blowing
out one candle when two were lighted, he went to the Temple to cheapen
a curtain tassel; he saw everything; he knew everything; which did not prevent him from laughing a goodman's laugh by the cradle of his little child;
and all at once, startled Europe listened, armies set themselves in march,
parks of artillery rolled along, bridges of boats stretched over the rivers,
clouds of cavalry galloped in the hurricane, cries, trumpets, a trembling of
thrones everywhere, the frontiers of the kingdoms oscillated upon the
map, the sound of a superhuman blade was heard leaping from its sheath,
men saw him, him, standing erect in the horizon with a flame in his hands
and a resplendence in his eyes, unfolding in the thunder his two wings, the
Grand Army and the Old Guard, and he was the archangel of war!"

All were silent, and Enjolras bowed his head. Silence always has something of the effect of an acquiescence or of a sort of pushing to the wall.
Marius, almost without taking breath, continued with a burst of enthusiasm:

"Be just, my friends! to be the empire of such an emperor, what a splendid destiny for a people, when that people is France, and when it adds its
genius to the genius of such a man! To appear and to reign, to march and to
triumph, to have every capital for a stage in the journey, to take his
grenadiers and make kings of them, to decree the downfall of dynasties,
to transfigure Europe at a double quickstep, so that men feel, when you
threaten, that you lay your hand on the hilt of the sword of God, to follow, as
a single man, Hannibal, Cæsar, and Charlemagne, to be the people of one
who mingles with your every dawn the glorious announcement of a battle
won, to be wakened in the morning by the cannon of the Invalides, to hurl
into the vault of day mighty words which blaze for ever, Marengo, Arcola,
Austerlitz, Jena, Wagram! to call forth at every moment constellations of
victories in the zenith of the centuries, to make the French Empire, the successor of the Roman Empire, to be the grand nation and to bring forth the
grand army, to send your legions flying over the whole earth as a mountain
sends its eagles upon all sides, to vanquish, to rule, to thunderstrike, to be in
Europe a kind of gilded people through much glory, to sound through history a Titan trumpet call, to conquer the world twice, by conquest and by
resplendence, this is sublime, and what can be more grand?"

"To be free," said Combeferre.

Marius in his turn bowed his head: these cold and simple words had pierced his epic effusion like a blade of steel, and he felt it vanish within him. When he raised his eyes, Combeferre was there no longer. Satisfied probably with his reply to the apotheosis, he had gone out, and all, except Enjolras, had followed him. The room was empty. Enjolras, remaining alone with Marius, was looking at him gravely. Marius, meanwhile, having rallied his ideas a little, did not consider himself beaten; there was still something left of the ebullition within him, which doubtless was about to find expression in syllogisms arrayed against Enjolras, when suddenly they heard somebody singing as he was going downstairs. It was Combeferre, and what he was singing is this:

> *Si César m'avait donné*
> *   La gloire et la guerre,*
> *Et qu'il me fallût quitter*
> *L'amour de ma mère,*
> *   Je dirais au grand César:*
> *Reprends ton sceptre et ton char,*
> *J'aime mieux ma mère, ô gué!*
> *J'aime mieux ma mère.**

The wild and tender accent with which Combeferre sang, gave to this stanza a strange grandeur. Marius, thoughtful and with his eyes directed to the ceiling, repeated almost mechanically: "my mother——"

At this moment, he felt Enjolras' hand on his shoulder.

"Citizen," said Enjolras to him, "my mother is the republic."

6

ANGUISH

THAT EVENING left Marius in a profound agitation, with a sorrowful darkness in his soul. He was experiencing what perhaps the earth experiences at the moment when it is sliced with the iron blade so that the grains of wheat may be sown; it feels the wound alone; the thrill of the germ and the joy of the fruit do not come until later.

---

*If Caesar had given me / Glory and war / And I had to abandon / The love of my mother, / I would say to great Caesar: / Take thy sceptre and car, / I prefer my mother, ah me! / I prefer my mother.

Marius was gloomy. He had but just attained a faith; could he so soon reject it? He decided within himself that he could not. He declared to himself that he would not doubt, and he began to doubt in spite of himself. To be between two religions, one which you have not yet abandoned, and another which you have not yet adopted, is unbearable; and twilight is pleasant only to bat-like souls. Marius was an open eye, and he needed the true light. To him the dusk of doubt was harmful. Whatever might be his desire to stop where he was, and to hold fast there, he was irresistibly compelled to continue, to advance, to examine, to think, to go forward. Where was that going to lead him? he feared, after having taken so many steps which had brought him nearer to his father, to take now any steps which should separate them. His dejection increased with every reflection which occurred to him. Steep cliffs rose about him. He was on good terms neither with his grandfather nor with his friends; rash towards the former, backward towards the others; and he felt doubly isolated, from old age, and also from youth. He went no more to the Café Musain.

In this agitation in which his mind was plunged he scarcely gave a thought to certain serious matters of existence. The realities of life do not allow themselves to be forgotten. They came and jogged his memory sharply.

One morning, the manager of the lodging house entered Marius' room, and said to him:

"Monsieur Courfeyrac is responsible for you."

"Yes."

"But I am in need of money."

"Ask Courfeyrac to come and speak with me," said Marius.

Courfeyrac came; the host left them. Marius related to him what he had not thought of telling him before, that he was, so to speak, alone in the world, without any relatives.

"What are you going to become?" said Courfeyrac.

"I have no idea," answered Marius.

"What are you going to do?"

"I have no idea."

"Have you any money?"

"Fifteen francs."

"Do you wish me to lend you some?"

"Never."

"Have you any clothes?"

"What you see."

"Have you any jewellery?"

"A watch."

"A silver one?"

"Gold, here it is."

"I know a dealer in clothing who will take your overcoat and one pair of trousers."

"That is good."

"You will then have but one pair of trousers, one waistcoat, one hat, and one coat."

"And my boots."

"What? you will not go barefoot? what opulence!"

"That will be enough."

"I know a watchmaker who will buy your watch."

"That is good."

"No, it is not good. What will you do afterwards?"

"What I must. Anything honourable at least."

"Do you know English?"

"No."

"Do you know German?"

"No."

"That is bad."

"Why?"

"Because a friend of mine, a bookseller, is making a sort of encyclopædia, for which you could have translated German or English articles. It
doesn't pay well, but you can live on it."

"I will learn English and German."

"And in the meantime?"

"In the meantime I will eat my coats and my watch."

The clothes dealer was sent for. He gave twenty francs for the clothes.
They went to the watchmaker. He gave forty-five francs for the watch.

"That is not bad," said Marius to Courfeyrac, on returning to the house;
"with my fifteen francs, this makes eighty francs."

"The hotel bill?" observed Courfeyrac.

"Ah! I forgot," said Marius.

The host presented his bill, which had to be paid on the spot. It amounted
to seventy francs.

"I have ten francs left," said Marius.

"The devil," said Courfeyrac, "you will have five francs to eat while you
are learning English, and five francs while you are learning German. That
will be swallowing a language very rapidly or a hundred-sous coin very
slowly."

Meanwhile Aunt Gillenormand, who was really a kind person on sad
occasions, had finally unearthed Marius' lodgings.

One morning when Marius came home from the school, he found a letter from his aunt, and the *sixty pistoles,* that is to say, six hundred francs in
gold, in a sealed box.

Marius sent the thirty louis back to his aunt, with a respectful letter, in
which he told her that he had enough to live on, and that he could provide
henceforth for all his necessities. At that time he had three francs left.

The aunt did not inform the grandfather of this refusal, lest she should
exasperate him. Indeed, had he not said: "Let nobody ever speak to me of
this blood-drinker?"

Marius left the Porte Saint Jacques Hôtel, unwilling to contract debt.

BOOK FIVE
THE EXCELLENCE OF MISFORTUNE

1

MARIUS INDIGENT

LIFE BECAME STERN for Marius. To eat his coats and his watch was nothing. He chewed that inexpressible thing which is called *the cud of bitterness*. A horrible thing, which includes days without bread, nights without sleep, evenings without a candle, a hearth without a fire, weeks without labour, a future without hope, a coat out at the elbows, an old hat which makes young girls laugh, the door found shut against you at night because you have not paid your rent, the insolence of the porter and the landlord, the jibes of neighbours, humiliations, self-respect outraged, any drudgery acceptable, disgust, bitterness, prostration—Marius learned how one swallows down all these things, and how they are often the only things that one has to swallow. At that period of existence, when man has need of pride, because he has need of love, he felt that he was mocked at because he was badly dressed, and ridiculed because he was poor. At the age when youth swells the heart with an imperial pride, he more than once dropped his eyes upon his worn-out boots, and experienced the undeserved shame and the poignant blushes of misery. Wonderful and terrible trial, from which the feeble come out infamous, from which the strong come out sublime. Crucible into which destiny casts a man whenever she desires a scoundrel or a demi-god.

For there are many great deeds done in the small struggles of life. There is a determined though unseen bravery, which defends itself foot to foot in the darkness against the fatal invasions of need and degradation. Noble and mysterious triumphs which no eye sees, which no renown rewards, which no flourish of triumph salutes. Life, misfortunes, isolation, abandonment, poverty, are battlefields which have their heroes; obscure heroes, sometimes greater than the illustrious heroes.[*]

Strong and rare natures are thus created; extreme poverty, almost always a cruel stepmother, is sometimes a mother; privation gives birth to power of soul and mind; distress is the nurse of self-respect; misfortune is a good breast for great souls.

There was a period in Marius' life when he swept his own hall, when he bought a pennyworth of Brie cheese at the market-woman's, when he waited for nightfall to make his way to the baker's and buy a loaf of bread, which he carried furtively to his garret, as if he had stolen it. Sometimes there was seen to glide into the corner meat-market, in the midst of the jeering cooks who elbowed him, an awkward young man, with books

---

[*]Throughout the novel Hugo emphasizes the grandeur of moral courage, which may show itself in obscure deeds and in humble lives.

under his arm, who had a timid and frightened appearance, and who, as he entered, took off his hat from his forehead, which was dripping with sweat, made a low bow to the astonished butcher, another bow to the butcher's boy, asked for a mutton cutlet, paid six or seven sous for it, wrapped it up in paper, put it under his arm between two books, and went away. It was Marius. On this cutlet, which he cooked himself, he lived three days.

The first day he ate the meat; the second day he ate the fat; the third day he gnawed the bone. On several occasions, Aunt Gillenormand made overtures, and sent him the sixty pistoles. Marius always sent them back, saying that he had no need of anything.

He was still in mourning for his father, when the revolution which we have described was accomplished in his ideas. Since then, he had never left off black clothes. His clothes left him, however. A day came, at last, when he had no coat. His trousers were going also. What was to be done? Courfeyrac, for whom he also had done some good turns, gave him an old coat. For thirty sous, Marius had it turned by some porter or other, and it was a new coat. But this coat was green. Then Marius did not go out till after nightfall. That made his coat black. Desiring always to be in mourning, he clothed himself with night.

Through all this, he procured admission to the bar. He was reputed to occupy Courfeyrac's room, which was decent, and where a certain number of law books, supported and filled out by some odd volumes of novels, made up the library required by the rules.

When Marius had become a lawyer, he informed his grandfather of it, in a letter which was frigid, but full of submission and respect. M. Gillenormand took the letter with trembling hands, read it, and threw it torn in pieces, into the basket. Two or three days afterwards, Mademoiselle Gillenormand overheard her father, who was alone in his room, talking aloud. This was always the case when he was much excited. She listened: the old man said: "If you were not a fool, you would know that a man cannot be a baron and a lawyer at the same time."

2

MARIUS POOR

It is with great poverty as with everything else. It gradually becomes endurable. It ends by taking form and becoming fixed. You vegetate, that is to say you develop in some wretched fashion, but sufficient for existence. This is the way in which Marius Pontmercy's life was arranged.

He had got out of the narrowest place; the pass widened a little before him. By dint of hard work, courage, perseverance, and will, he had succeeded in earning by his labour about seven hundred francs a year. He had learned German and English; thanks to Courfeyrac, who introduced him to his friend the publisher, Marius filled, in the literary department of the bookhouse, the useful rôle of *utility*. He made out prospectuses, translated from the journals, annotated republications, compiled biographies, etc., net result, year in and year out, seven hundred francs. He lived on this.

For Marius to arrive at this flourishing condition had required years. Hard years, and difficult ones; those to get through, these to climb. Marius had never given up for a single day. He had undergone everything, in the shape of privation; he had done everything, except get into debt. He gave himself this credit, that he had never owed a sou to anybody. For him a debt was the beginning of slavery. He felt even that a creditor is worse than a master; for a master owns only your person, a creditor owns your dignity and can belabour that. Rather than borrow, he did not eat. He had had many days of fasting. Feeling that all extremes meet and that if we do not take care, abasement of fortune may lead to baseness of soul, he watched jealously over his pride. Such a habit or such a carriage as, in any other condition, would have appeared deferential, seemed humiliating, and he braced himself against it. He risked nothing, not wishing to take a backward step. He had a kind of stern blush upon his face. He was timid even to rudeness.

In all his trials he felt encouraged and sometimes even upborne by a secret force within. The soul helps the body, and at certain moments uplifts it. It is the only bird which sustains its cage.

By the side of his father's name, another name was engraven upon Marius' heart, the name of Thénardier. Marius, in his enthusiastic yet serious nature, surrounded with a sort of halo the man to whom, as he thought, he owed his father's life, that brave sergeant who had saved the colonel in the midst of the balls and bullets of Waterloo. He never separated the memory of this man from the memory of his father, and he associated them in his veneration. It was a sort of worship with two steps, the high altar for the colonel, the low one for Thénardier. The idea of the misfortune into which he knew that Thénardier had fallen and been engulfed, intensified his feeling of gratitude. Marius had learned at Montfermeil of the ruin and bankruptcy of the unlucky innkeeper. Since then, he had made untold effort to get track of him, and to endeavour to find him, in that dark abyss of misery in which Thénardier had disappeared. Marius had beaten the whole country; he had been to Chelles, to Bondy, to Gournay, to Nogent, to Lagny. For three years he had been devoted to this, spending in these explorations what little money he could spare. Nobody could give him any news of Thénardier; it was thought he had gone abroad. His creditors had sought for him, also, with less love than Marius, but with as much zeal, and had not been able to put their hands on him. Marius blamed and almost hated himself for not succeeding in his researches. This was the only debt which the colonel had left him, and

Marius made it a point of honour to pay it. "What," thought he, "when my father lay dying on the field of battle, Thénardier could find him through the smoke and the grapeshot, and carry him away on his shoulders, and yet he owed him nothing; while I, who owe so much to Thénardier, I cannot reach him in that darkness in which he is suffering, and restore him, in my turn, from death to life. Oh! I will find him!" Indeed, to find Thénardier, Marius would have given one of his arms, and to save him from his wretchedness, all his blood. To see Thénardier, to render some service to Thénardier, to say to him—"You do not know me, but I do know you. Here I am, dispose of me!" This was the sweetest and most magnificent dream of Marius.

3

MARIUS GROWN

MARIUS WAS NOW twenty years old. It was three years since he had left his grandfather. They remained on the same terms on both sides, without attempting a reconciliation, and without seeking to meet. And, indeed, what was the use of meeting? to come in conflict? Which would have had the best of it? Marius was a vase of brass, but M. Gillenormand was an iron pot.

To tell the truth, Marius was mistaken as to his grandfather's heart. He imagined that M. Gillenormand had never loved him, and that this crusty and harsh yet smiling old man, who swore, screamed, stormed, and lifted his cane, felt for him at most only the affection, at once slight and severe, of the old men of comedy. Marius was deceived. There are fathers who do not love their children; there is no grandfather who does not adore his grandson. In reality, we have said, M. Gillenormand worshipped Marius. He worshipped him in his own way, with an accompaniment of cuffs, and even of blows; but, when the child was gone, he felt a dark void in his heart; he ordered that nobody should speak of him again, and regretted that he was so well obeyed. At first he hoped that this Buonapartist, this Jacobin, this terrorist, this Septembrist, would return. But weeks passed away, months passed away, years passed away; to the great despair of M. Gillenormand, the blood-drinker did not reappear! "But I could not do anything else than turn him away," said the grandfather, and he asked himself: "If it were to be done again, would I do it?" His pride promptly answered Yes, but his old head, which he shook in silence, sadly answered, No. He had his hours of dejection. He missed Marius. Old men need affection as they do sunshine. It is warmth. However strong his nature might be, the absence of Marius had changed something in him. For nothing in the world would he have taken a step towards the "little rogue;" but he suffered. He never inquired after him, but he thought of him constantly. He lived, more and more retired, in the Marais. He was still, as formerly, gay and violent, but his gaiety had a convulsive harshness as if it contained grief and anger, and his bursts of violence always terminated by a sort of placid and gloomy exhaustion. He said sometimes: "Oh! if he would come back, what a good box of the ear I would give him."

As for the aunt, she thought too little to love very much; Marius was now nothing to her but a sort of dim, dark outline; and she finally busied herself a good deal less about him than with the cat or the paroquet which she probably had.

What increased the secret suffering of Grandfather Gillenormand, was that he shut her entirely out, and let her suspect nothing of it. His grieving was like those newly invented furnaces which consume their own smoke. Sometimes it happened that some blundering, officious body would speak to him of Marius, and ask: "What is your grandson doing, or what has become of him?" The old bourgeois would answer, with a sigh if he was too sad, or giving his ruffle a tap, if he wished to seem gay. "Monsieur the Baron Pontmercy is pettifogging in some hole."

While the old man was regretting, Marius was congratulating himself. As with all good hearts, suffering had taken away his bitterness. He thought of M. Gillenormand only with kindness, but he had determined to receive nothing more from the man *who had been cruel to his father.* This was now the softened translation of his first indignation. Moreover, he was happy in having suffered, and in suffering still. It was for his father. His hard life satisfied him, and pleased him. He said to himself with a sort of pleasure that—*it was the very least;* that it was—an expiation; that—save for this, he would have been punished otherwise and later, for his unnatural indifference towards his father, and towards such a father;—that it would not have been just that his father should have had all the suffering, and himself none;—what were his efforts and his privation, moreover, compared with the heroic life of the colonel? that finally his only way of drawing near his father, and becoming like him, was to be valiant against indigence as he had been brave against the enemy; and that this was doubtless what the colonel meant by the words: *"He will be worthy of it."* Words which Marius continued to bear, not upon his breast, the colonel's paper having disappeared, but in his heart.

And then, when his grandfather drove him away, he was but a child; now he was a man. He felt it. Poverty, we must insist, had been good to him. Poverty in youth, when it succeeds, is so far magnificent that it turns the whole will towards effort, and the whole soul towards aspiration. Poverty strips the material life entirely bare, and makes it hideous; thence arise inexpressible yearnings towards the ideal life.

This is what had taken place in Marius. He had even, to tell the truth, gone a little too far on the side of contemplation. The day on which he had arrived at the point of being almost sure of earning his living, he stopped there, preferring to be poor, and retrenching from labour to give to thought. That is to say, he passed sometimes whole days in thinking, plunged and swallowed up like a visionary, in the mute joys of ecstasy and interior radiance. He had put the problem of his life thus: to work as little as possible at material labour, that he might work as much as possible at impalpable labour; in other words, to give a few hours to real life, and to cast the rest into the infinite. He did not perceive, thinking that he lacked nothing, that contemplation thus obtained comes to be one of the forms of sloth, that he was content with subduing the primary necessities of life, and that he was resting too soon.

It was clear that, given his energetic and generous nature, this could only be a transitory state, and that at the first shock against the inevitable complications of destiny, Marius would arouse.

Meantime, although he was a lawyer, and whatever Grandfather Gillenormand might think, he was not pleading, he was not even pettifogging. Reverie had turned him away from the law. To consort with attorneys, to attend courts, to hunt up cases, was wearisome. Why should he do it? He saw no reason for changing his business. This cheap and obscure book-making had procured him sure work, work with little labour, which, as we have explained, was sufficient for him.

It was Marius' delight to take long walks alone on the outer boulevards, or in the Champ de Mars, or in the less frequented walks of the Luxembourg Gardens. He sometimes spent half a day in looking at a vegetable garden, at the beds of salad, the fowls on the dung-heap and the horse turning the wheel of the pump. The passers-by looked at him with surprise, and some thought that he had a suspicious appearance and an ill-omened manner. He was only a poor young man, dreaming without an object.

It was in one of these walks that he had discovered the Gorbeau tenement, and its isolation and cheapness being an attraction to him, he had taken a room in it. He was only known in it by the name of Monsieur Marius.

All passions, except those of the heart, are dissipated by reverie. Marius' political fevers were over. The revolution of 1830, by satisfying him, and soothing him, had aided in this. He remained the same, with the exception of his passionateness. He had still the same opinions. But they were softened. Properly speaking, he held opinions no longer; he had sympathies. Of what party was he? of the party of humanity. Out of humanity he chose France; out of the nation he chose the people; out of the people he chose woman. To her, above all, his pity went out. He now preferred an idea to a fact, a poet to a hero, and he admired a book like Job still more than an event like Marengo. And then, when, after a day of meditation, he returned at night along the boulevards, and saw through the branches of the trees the fathomless space, the nameless lights, the depths, the darkness, the mystery, all that which is only human seemed to him very pretty.

Marius thought he had, and he had perhaps in fact arrived at the truth of life and of human philosophy, and he had finally come hardly to look at anything but the sky, the only thing that truth can see from the bottom of her well.

This did not hinder him from multiplying plans, combinations, scaffoldings, projects for the future. In this condition of reverie, an eye which could have looked into Marius' soul would have been dazzled by its purity. In fact, were it given to our eye of flesh to see into the consciences of others, we should judge a man much more surely from what he dreams than from what he thinks. There is will in the thought, there is none in the dream. The dream, which is completely spontaneous, takes and keeps, even in the gigantic and the ideal, the form of our mind. Nothing springs more directly and more sincerely from the very bottom of our souls than our unreflected and indefinite aspirations towards the splendours of destiny. In these aspirations, much more than in ideas which are combined, studied, and compared, we can find the true character of each man. Our chimeras are what most resemble ourselves. Each one dreams the unknown and the impossible according to his own nature.

Towards the middle of this year, 1831, the old woman who waited upon Marius told him that his neighbours, the wretched Jondrette family, were to be turned into the street. Marius, who passed almost all his days out of doors, hardly knew that he had any neighbours.

"Why are they turned out?" said he.

"Because they do not pay their rent; they owe for two terms."

"How much is that?"

"Twenty francs," said the old woman.

Marius had thirty francs in reserve in a drawer.

"Here," said he to the old woman, "there are twenty-five francs. Pay for these poor people, give them five francs, and do not tell them that it is from me."

Book Six
THE CONJUNCTION OF TWO STARS

1

THE NICKNAME: MODE OF FORMATION
OF FAMILY NAMES*

MARIUS WAS now a fine-looking young man, of medium height, with heavy jet black hair, a high intelligent brow, large and passionate nostrils, a frank and calm expression, and a indescribable something beaming from every feature, which was at once lofty, thoughtful and innocent.

At the time of his most wretched poverty, he noticed that girls turned when he passed, and with a deathly feeling in his heart he fled or hid himself. He thought they looked at him on account of his old clothes, and that they were laughing at him; the truth is, that they looked at him because of his graceful appearance, and that they dreamed over it.

For more than a year Marius had noticed in a retired walk of the Luxembourg Gardens, the walk which borders the parapet of the Pépinière, a man and a girl quite young, nearly always sitting side by side, on the same bench, at the most retired end of the walk, near the Rue de l'Ouest. Whenever that chance which controls the promenades of men whose eye is turned within, led Marius to this walk, and it was almost every day, he found this couple there. The man might be sixty years old; he seemed sad and serious; his whole person presented the robust but wearied appearance of a soldier retired from active service. Had he worn a decoration, Marius would have said: it is an old officer. His expression was kind, but it did not invite approach, and he never returned a look. He wore a blue coat and trousers, and a broad-brimmed hat, which always appeared to be new, a black cravat, and Quaker linen, that is to say, brilliantly white, but of coarse texture. A grisette passing near him one day, said: There is a very nice widower. His hair was perfectly white.

The first time the young girl that accompanied him sat down on the bench which they seemed to have adopted, she looked like a girl of about thirteen or fourteen, thin to the extent of being almost ugly, awkward, insignificant, yet promising, perhaps, to have rather fine eyes. But they were always looking about with a disagreeable assurance. She wore the dress at once aged and childish, peculiar to the convent school-girl, an ill-fitting garment of coarse black wool. They appeared to be father and daughter.

---

*Note Hugo's tidy construction: the meeting of Marius and Cosette, whose story will dominate the remainder of the novel, occurs exactly in the middle of the third of five parts.

For two or three days Marius scrutinised this old man, who was not yet an aged man, and this little girl, not yet a woman; then he paid no more attention to them. For their part they did not even seem to see him. They talked with each other peacefully, and with indifference to all else. The girl chatted incessantly and gaily. The old man spoke little, and at times looked upon her with an unutterable expression of fatherliness.

Marius had acquired a sort of mechanical habit of strolling on this walk. He always found them there.

It was usually thus:

Marius would generally reach the walk at the end opposite their bench, stroll the whole length of it, passing before them, then return to the end by which he entered, and so on. He performed this turn five or six times in his promenade, and this promenade five or six times a week, but they and he had never come to exchange bows.

2

A LIGHT DAWNS

THE SECOND YEAR, at the precise point of this history to which the reader has arrived, it so happened that Marius broke off this habit of going to the Luxembourg Gardens, without really knowing why himself, and there were nearly six months during which he did not set foot in his walk. At last he went back there again one day; it was a serene summer morning, Marius was as happy as one always is when the weather is fine. It seemed to him as if he had in his heart all the bird songs which he heard, and all the bits of blue sky which he saw through the trees.

He went straight to "his walk," and as soon as he reached it, he saw, still on the same bench, this well known pair. When he came near them, however, he saw that it was indeed the same man, but it seemed to him that it was no longer the same girl. The woman whom he now saw was a tall, beautiful creature, with all the most bewitching outlines of woman, at the precise moment at which they are yet combined with all the most charming graces of childhood,—that pure and fleeting moment which can only be translated by these two words: sweet fifteen. Beautiful chestnut hair, shaded with veins of gold, a brow which seemed chiselled marble, cheeks which seemed made of roses, a pale incarnadine, a flushed whiteness, an exquisite mouth, whence came a smile like a gleam of sunshine, and a voice like music, a head which Raphael would have given to Mary, on a neck which Jean Goujon would have given to Venus.* And that nothing might be wanting to this ravishing form, the nose was not beautiful, it was pretty; neither straight nor curved, neither Italian nor Greek; it was the Parisian nose; that is, something sprightly, fine, irregular, and pure, the despair of painters and the charm of poets.

When Marius passed near her, he could not see her eyes, which were always cast down. He saw only her long chestnut lashes, eloquent of mystery and modesty.

But that did not prevent the beautiful girl from smiling as she listened to the white-haired man who was speaking to her, and nothing was so transporting as this maidenly smile with these downcast eyes.

At the first instant Marius thought it was another daughter of the same man, a sister doubtless of her whom he had seen before. But when the invariable habit of his stroll led him for the second time near the bench, and he had looked at her attentively, he recognised that she was the same. In six months the little girl had become a young woman; that was all. Nothing is more frequent than this phenomenon. There is a moment when girls bloom out in a twinkling and become roses all at once. Yesterday we left them children, to-day we find them dangerous.

She had not only grown; she had become idealised. As three April days are enough for certain trees to put on a covering of flowers, so six months had been enough for her to put on a mantle of beauty.

We sometimes see people, poor and stingy, who seem to awaken, pass suddenly from indigence to luxury, incur expenses of all sorts, and become all at once splendid, prodigal, and magnificent. That comes from interest received; yesterday the quarterly statement had arrived. The young girl had received her dividend.

And then she was no longer the school-girl with her plush hat, her wool dress, her shapeless shoes, and her red hands; taste had come to her with beauty. She was a woman well dressed, with a sort of simple and rich elegance without any particular style. She wore a dress of black damask, a mantle of the same, and a white crape hat. Her white gloves showed the delicacy of her hand which played with the Chinese ivory handle of her parasol, and her silk boot betrayed the smallness of her foot. When you passed near her, her whole toilet exhaled the penetrating fragrance of youth.

As to the man, he was still the same.

The second time that Marius came near her, the young girl raised her eyes; they were of a deep celestial blue, but in this veiled azure was nothing yet beyond the look of a child. She looked at Marius with indifference, as she would have looked at any little monkey playing under the sycamores,

---

*The Italian painter Raphael (1483–1520) captures the ideal spirituality of woman; the French sculptor and architect Jean Goujon, her material beauty: Cosette—at least in Marius's eyes, combines both.

or the marble vase which cast its shadow over the bench; and Marius also continued his stroll thinking of something else.

He passed four or five times more by the bench where the young girl was, without even turning his eyes towards her.

On the following days he came as usual to the Luxembourg Gardens, as usual he found "the father and daughter" there, but he paid no attention to them. He thought no more of this girl now that she was handsome than he had thought of her when she was homely. He passed very near the bench on which she sat, because that was his habit.

3

AN EFFECT OF SPRING

ONE DAY the air was mild, the Luxembourg Gardens were flooded with sunshine and shadow, the sky was as clear as if the angels had washed it that morning, the sparrows were twittering in the depths of the chestnut trees, Marius had opened his whole soul to nature, he was thinking of nothing, he was living and breathing, he passed near this bench, the young girl raised her eyes, their glances met.

But what was there now in the glance of the young girl? Marius could not have told. There was nothing, and there was everything. It was a strange flash.

She cast down her eyes, and he continued on his way.

What he had seen was not the simple, artless eye of a child; it was a mysterious abyss, half-opened, then suddenly closed.

There is a time when every young girl looks thus. Woe to him upon whom she looks!

This first glance of a soul which does not yet know itself is like the dawn in the sky. It is the awakening of something radiant and unknown. Nothing can express the dangerous chasm of this unlooked-for gleam which suddenly suffuses adorable mysteries, and which is made up of all the innocence of the present, and of all the passion of the future. It is a kind of irresolute lovingness which is revealed by chance, and which is waiting. It is a snare which Innocence unconsciously spreads, and in which she catches hearts without intending to, and without knowing it. It is a maiden glancing like a woman.

It is rare that deep reverie is not born of this glance wherever it may fall. All that is pure, and all that is vestal, is concentrated in this celestial and mortal glance, which more than the most studied ogling of the coquette, has the magic power of suddenly forcing into bloom in the depths of a heart this flower of the shade full of perfumes and poisons, which is called love.

At night, on returning to his garret, Marius cast a look upon his dress, and for the first time perceived that he had the slovenliness, the indecency, and the unheard-of stupidity, to stroll in the Luxembourg Gardens with his "every-day" suit, a hat broken near the band, coarse teamsters' boots, black trousers shiny at the knees, and a black coat threadbare at the elbows.

4

COMMENCEMENT OF A SERIOUS ILLNESS

THE NEXT DAY, at the usual hour, Marius took from his closet his new coat, his new trousers, his new hat, and his new boots; he dressed himself in this panoply complete, put on his gloves, prodigious prodigality, and went to the Luxembourg Gardens.

On the way, he met Courfeyrac, and pretended not to see him. Courfeyrac, on his return home, said to his friends:

"I have just met Marius' new hat and coat, with Marius inside. Probably he was going to an examination. He looked stupid enough."

On reaching the Luxembourg Gardens, Marius took a turn round the fountain and looked at the swans; then he remained for a long time in contemplation before a statue, the head of which was black with moss, and which was minus a hip. Near the fountain was a big-bellied bourgeois of forty, holding a little boy of five by the hand, to whom he was saying: "Beware of extremes, my son. Keep thyself equally distant from despotism and from anarchy." Marius listened to this good bourgeois. Then he took another turn around the fountain. Finally, he went towards "his walk;" slowly, and as if with regret. One would have said that he was at once compelled to go and prevented from going. He was unconscious of all this, and thought he was doing as he did every day.

When he entered the walk he saw M. Leblanc and the young girl at the other end "on their bench." He buttoned his coat, stretched it down that there might be no wrinkles, noticed with some complaisance the lustre of his trousers, and marched upon the bench. There was something of attack in this march, and certainly a desire of conquest. I say, then, he marched upon the bench, as I would say: Hannibal marched upon Rome.

Beyond this there was nothing which was not mechanical in all his movements, and he had in no wise interrupted the customary preoccupations of his mind and his labour. He was thinking at that moment that the *Manual du Baccalauréat* was a stupid book, and that it must have been compiled by rare old fools, to give an analysis, as of masterpieces of the human mind, of three tragedies of Racine and only one of Molière's comedies. He had a sharp whistling sound in his ear. While approaching the bench, he was smoothing the wrinkles out of his coat, and his eyes were fixed on the young girl. It seemed to him as though she filled the whole extremity of the walk with a pale, bluish light.[*]

As he drew nearer, his step became slower and slower. At some distance from the bench, long before he had reached the end of the walk, he stopped, and he did not know himself how it happened, but he turned back. He did not even say to himself that he would not go to the end. It was doubtful if the young girl could see him so far off, and notice his fine appearance in his new suit. However, he held himself very straight, so that he might look well, in case anybody who was behind should happen to notice him.

He reached the opposite end and then returned, and this time he approached a little nearer to the bench. He even came to within about three trees of it, but there he felt an indescribable lack of power to go further, and he hesitated. He thought he had seen the young girl's face bent towards him. Still he made a great and manly effort, conquered his hesitation, and continued his advance. In a few seconds, he was passing before the bench, erect and firm, blushing to his ears, without daring to cast a look to the right or the left, and with his hand in his coat like a statesman. At the moment he passed under the guns of the fortress, he felt a frightful palpitation of the heart. She wore, as on the previous day, her damask dress and her crape hat. He heard the sound of an ineffable voice, which might be "her voice." She was talking quietly. She was very pretty. He felt it, though he made no effort to see her. "She could not, however," thought he, "but have some esteem and consideration for me, if she knew that I was the real author of the dissertation on Marcos Obregon de la Ronda, which Monsieur François de Neufchâteau has put, as his own, at the beginning of his edition of *Gil Blas!*"[†]

He passed the bench, went to the end of the walk, which was quite near, then turned and passed again before the beautiful girl. This time he was very pale. Indeed, he was experiencing nothing that was not very disagreeable. He walked away from the bench and from the young girl, and although his back was turned, he imagined that she was looking at him, and that made him stumble.

He made no effort to approach the bench again, he stopped midway

---

[*]The "pale, bluish light" represents a perception of the ideal. Flaubert had fiercely satirized this association in *Madame Bovary* (1857).

[†]An autobiographical reference: at age fifteen, Hugo himself had allowed the much older Neufchâteau, a member of the Académie Française, to take credit for Hugo's brilliant article on Alain-René Lesage's early eighteenth-century novel, in exchange for patronage in his nascent literary career.

along the walk, and sat down there—a thing which he never did—casting many side glances, and thinking, in the most indistinct depths of his mind, that after all it must be difficult for persons whose white hat and black dress he admired, to be absolutely insensitive to his glossy trousers and his new coat.

At the end of a quarter of an hour, he rose, as if to recommence his walk towards this bench, which was encircled by a halo. He, however, stood silent and motionless. For the first time in fifteen months, he said to himself, that this gentleman, who sat there every day with his daughter, had undoubtedly noticed him, and probably thought his assiduity very strange. For the first time, also, he felt a certain irreverence in designating this unknown man, even in the silence of his thought, by the nickname of M. Leblanc.

He remained thus for some minutes with his head down tracing designs on the ground with a little stick which he had in his hand.

Then he turned abruptly away from the bench, away from Monsieur Leblanc and his daughter, and went home.

That day he forgot to go to dinner. At eight o'clock in the evening he discovered it, and as it was too late to go down to the Rue Saint Jacques, "No matter," said he, and he ate a piece of bread.

He did not retire until he had carefully brushed and folded his coat.

5

SUNDRY THUNDERBOLTS FALL UPON MA'AM BOUGON

NEXT DAY, Ma'am Bougon,—thus Courfeyrac designated the old portress-landlady of the Gorbeau tenement,—Ma'am Bougon—her name was in reality Madame Bougon, as we have stated, but this terrible fellow Courfeyrac respected nothing,—Ma'am Bougon was stupefied with astonishment to see Monsieur Marius go out again with his new coat.

He went again to the Luxembourg Gardens, but did not get beyond his bench midway along the walk. He sat down there as on the day previous, gazing from a distance and seeing distinctly the white hat, the black dress, and especially the bluish light. He did not stir from the bench, and did not go home until the gates of the gardens were shut. He did not see Monsieur Leblanc and his daughter retire. He concluded from that that they left the garden by the gate on the Rue de l'Ouest. Later, some weeks afterwards, when he thought of it, he could not remember where he had dined that night.

The next day, for the third time, Ma'am Bougon was thunderstruck. Marius went out with his new suit. "Three days running!" she exclaimed.

She made an attempt to follow him, but Marius walked briskly and with immense strides; it was a hippopotamus undertaking to catch a chamois. In two minutes she lost sight of him, and came back out of breath three quarters choked by her asthma, and furious. "The silly fellow," she muttered, "to put on his handsome clothes every day and make people run like that!"

Marius had gone to the Luxembourg Gardens.

The young girl was there with Monsieur Leblanc. Marius approached as near as he could, seeming to be reading a book, but he was still very far off, then he returned and sat down on his bench, where he spent four hours watching the artless little sparrows as they hopped along the walk; they seemed to him to be mocking him.

Thus a fortnight rolled away. Marius went to the Luxembourg Gardens, no longer to stroll, but to sit down, always in the same place, and without knowing why. Once there he did not stir. Every morning he put on his new suit, not to be conspicuous, and he began again the next morning.

She was indeed of a marvelous beauty. The only remark which could be made, that would resemble a criticism, is that the contradiction between her look, which was sad, and her smile, which was joyous, gave to her countenance something a little wild, which produced this effect, that at certain moments this sweet face became strange without ceasing to be charming.

6

TAKEN PRISONER

ON ONE OF the last days of the second week, Marius was as usual sitting on his bench, holding in his hand an open book of which he had not turned a page for two hours. Suddenly he trembled. A great event was commencing at the end of the walk. Monsieur Leblanc and his daughter had left their bench, the daughter had taken the arm of the father, and they were coming slowly towards the middle of the walk where Marius was. Marius closed his book, then he opened it, then he made an attempt to read. He trembled. The halo was coming straight towards him. "O dear!" thought he, "I shall not have time to take an attitude." However, the man with the white hair and the young girl were advancing. It seemed to him that it would last a century, and that it was only a second. "What are they coming by here for?" he asked himself. "What! is she going to pass this place! Are her feet to press this ground in this walk, but a step from me?" He was overwhelmed, he would gladly have been very handsome, he would gladly have worn the cross of the Legion of Honour. He heard the gentle and measured sound of their steps approaching. He imagined that Monsieur Leblanc was hurling angry looks upon him. "Is he going to speak to me?" thought he. He bowed his head; when he raised it they were quite near him. The young girl passed, and in passing she looked at him. She looked at him steadily, with a sweet and thoughtful look which made Marius tremble from head to foot. It seemed to him that she reproached him for having been so long without coming to her, and that she said: "It is I who come." Marius was bewildered by these eyes full of flashing light and fathomless abysses.

He felt as though his brain were on fire. She had come to him, what happiness! And then, how she had looked at him! She seemed more beautiful than she had ever seemed before. Beautiful with a beauty which combined all of the woman with all of the angel, a beauty which would have made Petrarch sing and Dante kneel. He felt as though he was swimming in the deep blue sky. At the same time he was horribly disconcerted, because he had a little dust on his boots.

He felt sure that she had seen his boots in this condition.

He followed her with his eyes till she disappeared, then he began to walk in the Luxembourg Gardens like a madman. It is probable that at times he laughed, alone as he was, and spoke aloud. He was so strange and dreamy when near the children's nurses that every one thought he was in love with her.

He went out of the gardens to find her again in some street.

He met Courfeyrac under the arches of the Odeon, and said: "Come and dine with me." They went to Rousseau's and spent six francs. Marius ate like an ogre. He gave six sous to the waiter. At dessert he said to Courfeyrac: "Have you read the paper? What a fine speech Audry de Puyraveau has made!"

He was desperately in love.

After dinner he said to Courfeyrac, "Come to the theatre with me." They went to the Porte Saint Martin to see Frederick in *L'Auberge des Adrets*. Marius was hugely amused.*

At the same time he became still more strange and incomprehensible. On leaving the theatre, he refused to look at the garter of a little milliner who was crossing a gutter, and when Courfeyrac said: *"I would not object to putting that woman in my collection,"* it almost horrified him.

Courfeyrac invited him to breakfast next morning at the Café Voltaire. Marius went and ate still more than the day before. He was very thoughtful, and yet very gay. One would have said that he seized upon all possible occasions to burst out laughing. To every country-fellow who was introduced to

---

*Marius is so emotionally overwrought by being in love that he responds intensely to the most banal potboiler of the popular boulevard theater.

him he gave a tender embrace. A circle of students gathered round the table, and there was talk of the flummery paid for by the government, which was retailed at the Sorbonne; then the conversation fell upon the faults and gaps in the dictionaries and prosodies of Quicherat. Marius interrupted the discussion by exclaiming: "However, it is a very pleasant thing to have the Cross."*

"He is a comical fellow!" said Courfeyrac, aside to Jean Prouvaire.

"No," replied Jean Prouvaire, "he is serious."

He was serious, indeed. Marius was in this first vehement and fascinating period which the grand passion commences.

One glance had done all that.

When the mine is loaded, and the match is ready, nothing is simpler. A glance is a spark.

It was all over with him. Marius loved a woman. His destiny was entering upon the unknown.

7

ADVENTURES OF THE LETTER *U*
ABANDONED TO CONJECTURE

ISOLATION, separation from all things, pride, independence, a taste for nature, lack of everyday material activity, life in one's self, the secret struggles of chastity, and an ecstasy of goodwill towards the whole creation, had prepared Marius for this possession which is called love. His worship for his father had become almost a religion, and, like all religion, had retired into the depths of his heart. He needed something above that. Love came.

A whole month passed during which Marius went every day to the Luxembourg Gardens. When the hour came, nothing could keep him away. "He is on duty," said Courfeyrac. Marius lived in transports. It is certain that the girl was looking at him.

He finally grew bolder, and approached nearer to the bench. However he passed before it no more, obeying at once the instinct of timidity and the instinct of prudence, peculiar to lovers. He thought it better not to attract the "attention of the father." He formed his combinations of sentry duty behind trees and the pedestals of statues with consummate art, so as

---

*Marius would love to be able to flaunt some distinction so as to impress Cosette.

to be seen as much as possible by the young girl and as little as possible by the old gentleman. Sometimes he would stand for half an hour motionless behind some Leonidas or Spartacus with a book in his hand, over which his eyes, timidly raised, were looking for the young girl, while she, for her part, was turning her charming profile towards him, suffused with a smile. While yet talking in the most natural and quiet way in the world with the white-haired man, she rested upon Marius all the dreams of a maidenly and passionate eye. Ancient and immemorial art which Eve knew from the first day of the world, and which every woman knows from the first day of her life! Her tongue replied to one and her eyes to the other.

We must, however, suppose that M. Leblanc perceived something of this at last, for often when Marius came, he would rise and begin to stroll. He had left their accustomed place, and had taken the bench at the other end of the walk, near the Gladiator, as if to see whether Marius would follow them. Marius did not understand, and committed that blunder. "The father" began to be less punctual and did not bring "his daughter" every day. Sometimes he came alone. Then Marius did not stay. Another blunder.

Marius took no note of these symptoms. From the phase of timidity he had passed, a natural and inevitable progress, to the phase of blindness. His love grew. He dreamed of her every night. And then there came to him a good fortune for which he had not even hoped, oil upon the fire, double darkness upon his eyes. One night, at dusk, he found on the bench, which "M. Leblanc and his daughter" had just left, a handkerchief, a plain handkerchief without embroidery, but white, fine, and which appeared to him to exhale ineffable odours. He seized it in transport. This handkerchief was marked with the letters U. F.: Marius knew nothing of this beautiful girl, neither her family, nor her name, nor her dwelling; these two letters were the first thing he had caught of her, adorable initials upon which he began straightway to build his castle. It was evidently her first name. Ursula, thought he, what a sweet name! He kissed the handkerchief, inhaled its perfume, put it over his heart, on his flesh in the day-time, and at night went to sleep with it on his lips.

"I feel her whole soul in it!" he exclaimed.

This handkerchief belonged to the old gentleman, who had simply let it fall from his pocket.

For days and days after this piece of good fortune, he always appeared at the Luxembourg Gardens kissing this handkerchief and placing it on his heart. The beautiful child did not understand this at all, and indicated it to him by signs, which he did not perceive.

"Oh, modesty!" said Marius.*

---

*Marius imagines the handkerchief to be a love token left for him by Cosette: in fact, it is a trap set by Jean Valjean, to test the young man's feelings.

8

EVEN DISABLED VETERANS
MAY BE LUCKY

SINCE WE HAVE PRONOUNCED the word *modesty,* and since we are conceal-
ing nothing, we must say that once, however, through all his ecstasy "his
Ursula" gave him a very serious pang. It was upon one of the days when she
prevailed upon M. Leblanc to leave the bench and to stroll along the walk.
A brisk north wind was blowing, which swayed the tops of the plane trees.
Father and daughter, arm in arm, had just passed before Marius' bench.
Marius had risen behind them and was following them with his eyes, as it
was natural that he should in this desperate situation of his heart.

Suddenly a gust of wind, rather more lively than the rest, and probably
entrusted with the little affairs of Spring, flew down from La Pépinière,
rushed upon the walk, enveloped the young girl in a transporting tremor
worthy of the nymphs of Virgil and the fauns of Theocritus, and raised her
skirt, this skirt more sacred than that of Isis, almost to the height of the
garter. A limb of exquisite mould was seen. Marius saw it. He was exasperated and furious.

The young girl had put down her dress with a divinely startled movement, but he was outraged none the less. True, he was alone in the walk.
But there might have been somebody there. And if anybody had been
there! could one conceive of such a thing? what she had done was horrible!
Alas, the poor child had done nothing; there was but one culprit, the wind;
and yet Marius in whom all the Bartholo which there is in Cherubin was
confusedly trembling, was determined to be dissatisfied, and was jealous of
his shadow. For it is thus that is awakened in the human heart, and imposed
upon man, even unjustly, the bitter and strange jealousy of the flesh.
Besides, and throwing this jealousy out of consideration, there was nothing
that was agreeable to him in the sight of that beautiful limb; the white stock-
ing of the first woman that came along would have given him more pleasure.

When "his Ursula," reaching the end of the walk, returned with
M. Leblanc, and passed before the bench on which Marius had again sat
down, Marius threw at her a cross and cruel look. The young girl slightly
straightened back, with that elevation of the eyelids, which says: "Well,
what is the matter with him?"

That was "their first quarrel."

Marius had hardly finished this scene with her when somebody came
down the walk. It was a disabled veteran, very much bent, wrinkled and
pale with age, in the uniform of Louis XV, with the little oval patch of red
cloth with crossed swords on his back, the soldier's Cross of Saint Louis,

and decorated also by a coat sleeve in which there was no arm, a silver chin, and a wooden leg. Marius thought he could discern that this man appeared to be very much pleased. It seemed to him even that the old cynic, as he hobbled along by him, had addressed to him a very fraternal and very merry wink, as if by some chance they had been put into communication and had enjoyed some dainty bit of good fortune together. What had he seen to be so pleased, this relic of Mars? What had happened between this leg of wood and the other? Marius had a paroxysm of jealousy. "Perhaps he was by!" said he; "perhaps he saw!" And he would have been glad to exterminate the crippled veteran.

Time lending his aid, every point is blunted. This anger of Marius against "Ursula," however just and proper it might be, passed away. He forgave her at last; but it was a great effort; he pouted at her three days.

Meanwhile, in spite of all that, and because of all that, his passion was growing, and was growing insane.

9

AN ECLIPSE

WE HAVE SEEN how Marius discovered, or thought he discovered, that her name was Ursula.

Hunger comes with love.* To know that her name was Ursula had been much; it was little. In three or four weeks Marius had devoured this piece of good fortune. He desired another. He wished to know where she lived.

He had committed one blunder in falling into the snare of the bench by the Gladiator. He had committed a second by not remaining at the Luxembourg Gardens when Monsieur Leblanc came there alone. He committed a third, a monstrous one. He followed "Ursula."

She lived in the Rue de l'Ouest, in the least frequented part of it, in a new four-story house, of modest appearance.

From that moment Marius added to his happiness in seeing her at the Luxembourg Gardens, the happiness of following her home.

His hunger increased. He knew her name, her first name, at least, the charming name, the real name of a woman; he knew where she lived; he desired to know who she was.

---

*Hugo alludes to the French proverb *l'appétit vient en mangeant,* "eating gives you an appetite"—that is, having a little makes you want more.

One night after he had followed them home, and seen them disappear at the porte-cochère, he entered after them, and said boldly to the porter:——

"Is it the gentleman on the second floor who has just come in?"*

"No," answered the porter. "It is the gentleman on the fourth."

Another fact. This success made Marius still bolder.

"In front?" he asked.

"Faith!" said the porter, "the house is only built on the street."

"And what is this gentleman?"

"He lives on his income, monsieur. A very kind man, who does a great deal of good among the poor, though not rich."

"What is his name?" continued Marius.

The porter raised his head, and said:——

"Is monsieur a detective?"

Marius retired, much abashed, but still in great transports. He was making progress.

"Good," thought he. "I know that her name is Ursula, that she is the daughter of a retired gentleman, and that she lives there, in the third story, in the Rue de l'Ouest."

Next day Monsieur Leblanc and his daughter made but a short visit to the Luxembourg Gardens; they went away while it was yet broad daylight. Marius followed them into the Rue de l'Ouest, as was his custom. On reaching the porte-cochère, Monsieur Leblanc passed his daughter in, and then stopped, and before entering himself, turned and looked steadily at Marius. The day after that they did not come to the gardens. Marius waited in vain all day.

At nightfall he went to the Rue de l'Ouest, and saw a light in the windows of the fourth story. He walked beneath these windows until the light was put out.

The next day nobody at the Luxembourg Gardens. Marius waited all day, and then went to perform his night duty under the windows. That took him till ten o'clock in the evening. His dinner took care of itself. Fever supports the sick man, and love the lover.

He passed a week in this way. Monsieur Leblanc and his daughter appeared at the Luxembourg Gardens no more. Marius made melancholy conjectures; he dared not watch the porte-cochère during the day. He limited himself to going at night to gaze upon the reddish light of the windows. At times he saw shadows moving, and his heart beat high.

On the eighth day when he reached the house, there was no light in the windows. "What!" said he, "the lamp is not yet lighted. But yet it is dark. Or they have gone out?" He waited till ten o'clock. Till midnight. Till one o'clock in the morning. No light appeared in the fourth story windows, and nobody entered the house. He went away very gloomy.

On the morrow—for he lived only from morrow to morrow; there was

---

*Idealizing Cosette and her "father," Marius assumes that they must be rich; lodgings on the lower floors above ground level cost more.

no longer any to-day, so to speak, to him—on the morrow he found nobody at the Luxembourg Gardens, he waited; at dusk he went to the house. No light in the windows; the blinds were closed; the fourth story was entirely dark.

Marius knocked at the porte-cochère; went in and said to the porter:——

"The gentleman on the fourth floor?"

"Moved," answered the porter.

Marius tottered, and said feebly:

"Since when?"

"Yesterday."

"Where does he live now?"

"I don't know anything about it."

"He has not left his new address, then?"

"No."

And the porter, looking up, recognised Marius.

"What! it is you!" said he, "so then you're really on the look-out."

BOOK SEVEN
PATRON-MINETTE

1

THE MINES AND THE MINERS

EVERY HUMAN SOCIETY has what is called in the theatres a *third substage*. The social soil is mined everywhere, sometimes for good, sometimes for evil. These works are in strata; there are upper mines and lower mines. There is a top and a bottom in this dark sub-soil which sometimes sinks beneath civilisation, and which our indifference and our carelessness trample underfoot. The Encyclopædia, in the last century, was a mine almost on the surface. The dark caverns, these gloomy protectors of primitive Christianity, were awaiting only an opportunity to explode beneath the Cæsars, and to flood the human race with light. For in these sacred shades there is latent light. Volcanoes are full of a blackness, capable of flashing flames. All lava begins at midnight. The catacombs, where the first mass was said, were not merely the cave of Rome; they were the cavern of the world.

The deeper we sink, the more mysterious are the workers. To a degree which social philosophy can recognise, the work is good; beyond this degree it is doubtful and mixed; below, it becomes terrible. At a certain depth, the excavations become impenetrable to the soul of civilisation, the respirable limit of man is passed; the existence of monsters becomes possible.

The descending ladder is a strange one;[4] each of its rounds corresponds to a step whereupon philosophy can set foot, and where we discover some one of her workers, sometimes divine, sometimes monstrous. Below John Huss is Luther; below Luther is Descartes; below Descartes is Voltaire; below Voltaire is Condorcet; below Condorcet is Robespierre; below Robespierre is Marat; below Marat is Babeuf. And that continues. Lower still, in dusky confusion, at the limit which separates the indistinct from the invisible, glimpses are caught of other men in the gloom, who perhaps no longer exist. Those of yesterday are spectres; those of to-morrow are goblins. The embryonary work of the future is one of the visions of the philosopher.

A fœtus world in limbo, an unheard-of silhouette!

Saint Simon, Owen, Fourier, are there also, in lateral galleries.

Indeed, although an invisible divine chain links together all these subterranean pioneers, who almost always believe they are alone, yet are not, their labours are very diverse, and the glow of some is in contrast with the flame of others. Some are paradisaic, others are tragic. Nevertheless, be the contrast what it may, all these workers, from the highest to the darkest, from the wisest to the silliest, have one thing in common, and that is disinterestedness. Marat, like Jesus, forgets himself. They throw self aside; they omit self; they do not think of self. They see something other than themselves. They have a light in their eyes, and this light is searching for the absolute. The highest has all heaven in his eyes; the lowest, enigmatical as he may be, has yet beneath his brows the pale glow of the infinite. Venerate him, whatever he may do, who has this sign, the star-eye.

The shadow-eye is the other sign.

With it evil commences. Before him whose eye has no light, reflect and tremble. Social order has its black miners.

There is a point where undermining becomes burial, and where light is extinguished.

Below all these mines which we have pointed out, below all these galleries, below all this immense underground venous system of progress and of utopia, far deeper in the earth, lower than Marat, lower than Babeuf, lower, much lower, and without any connection with the upper galleries, is the last tunnel. A fear-inspiring place. This is what we have called the third substage. It is the grave of the depths. It is the cave of the blind *Inferi*.

This connects with the abyss.

2

THE LOWEST DEPTH

THERE disinterestedness vanishes. The demon is dimly rough-hewn; every one for himself. The eyeless I howls, searches, gropes, and gnaws. The social Ugolino is in this gulf.*

The savage silhouettes which prowl over this grave, half brute, half phantom, have no thought for universal progress, they ignore ideas and words, they have no care but for individual glut. They are almost unconscious, and there is in them a horrible defacement. They have two mothers, both stepmothers, ignorance and misery. They have one guide, want; and their only form of satisfaction is appetite. They are voracious as beasts, that is to say ferocious, not like the tyrant but like the tiger. From suffering these goblins pass to crime; fated filiation, giddy procreation, the logic of darkness. What crawls in the third substage is no longer the stifled demand for the absolute, it is the protest of matter. Man there becomes dragon.

---

*Ugolino, in Dante's early-fourteenth-century *Inferno*, was punished for having devoured his children to survive when he and they were imprisoned together. Thénardier, who sacrifices his own children for paltry profits, illustrates the social form of such supreme egotism.

Hunger and thirst are the point of departure: Satan is the point of arrival. From this cave comes Lacenaire.*

We have just seen, in the fourth book, one of the compartments of the upper mine, the great political, revolutionary, and philosophic tunnel. There, as we have said, all is noble, pure, worthy, and honourable. There, it is true, men may be deceived and are deceived, but there error is venerable, so much heroism does it imply. For the sum of all work which is done there, there is one name: Progress.

The time has come to open other depths, the depths of horror.

There is beneath society, we must insist upon it, and until the day when ignorance shall be no more, there will be, the great cavern of evil.

This cave is beneath all, and is the enemy of all. It is hate universal. This cave knows no philosophers; its dagger has never trimmed a pen. Its blackness has no relation to the sublime blackness of script. Never have the fingers of night, which are clutching beneath this asphyxiating vault, turned the leaves of a book, or unfolded a newspaper. Babeuf is a speculator to Cartouche; Marat is an aristocrat to Schinderhannes.† The object of this cave is the ruin of all things.

Of all things. Including therein the upper mineshafts, which it execrates. It does not undermine, in its hideous swarming, merely the social order of the time; it undermines philosophy, it undermines science, it undermines law, it undermines human thought, it undermines civilisation, it undermines revolution, it undermines progress. It goes by the naked names of theft, prostitution, murder, and assassination. It is darkness, and it desires chaos. It is vaulted over with ignorance.‡

All the others, those above it, have but one object—to suppress it. To that end philosophy and progress work through all their organs at the same time, through amelioration of the real as well as through contemplation of the absolute. Destroy the cave Ignorance, and you destroy the mole Crime.§

We will condense in a few words a portion of what we have just said. The only social peril is darkness.

---

*Lacenaire was a famous contemporary criminal and murderer.

†François-Noël Babeuf (1760–1797) and Jean-Paul Marat (1743–1793) both justified massacres with their egalitarian theories, before they themselves died in the Revolution. Cartouche and Schinderhannes were criminals who killed from pure hate.

‡For Hugo's understanding of Satan's rebellion, his fall, and Hell, see his long visionary poem *La Fin de Satan* (unfinished; c.1859–1860), which correlates the cosmic drama with the phases of the French Revolution.

§"The cave Ignorance" and "the mole Crime" are further examples of Hugo's *métaphore maxima* (maximal metaphor) that modifies one noun with another—contrary to French grammar—to produce a synthetic concept that reflects supernatural truths.

Humanity is identity. All men are the same clay. No difference, here below at least, in predestination. The same darkness before, the same flesh during, the same ashes after life. But ignorance, mixed with the human composition, blackens it. This incurable ignorance possesses the heart of man, and there becomes Evil.

3

BABET, GUEULEMER, CLAQUESOUS, AND MONTPARNASSE

A QUARTETTE of bandits, Claquesous, Gueulemer, Babet, and Montparnasse, ruled from 1830 to 1835 over the third substage of Paris.

Gueulemer was a Hercules who has come down in the world. His cave was the Arche-Marion sewer. He was six feet high, and had a marble chest, brazen biceps, cavernous lungs, a colossus' body, and a bird's skull. You would think you saw the Farnese Hercules dressed in cotton trousers and a cotton-velvet waistcoat. Gueulemer, built in this sculptural fashion, could have subdued monsters; he found it easier to become one. Low forehead, large temples, less than forty, squinting eyes, coarse short hair, a bushy cheek, a wild boar's beard; from this you see the man. His muscles asked for work, his stupidity would have none. This was a huge lazy force. He was an assassin through nonchalance. He was thought to be a creole. Probably there was a little of Marshal Brown in him, he having been a porter at Avignon in 1815. After this he had become a bandit.

The diaphaneity of Babet contrasted with the meatiness of Gueulemer. Babet was thin and shrewd. He was transparent, but impenetrable. You could see the light through his bones, but nothing through his eye. He professed to be a chemist. He had been bar-keeper for Bobèche, and clown for Bobino. He had played vaudeville at Saint Mihiel. He was an affected man, a great talker, who italicised his smiles and quoted his gestures. His business was to sell plaster busts and portraits of the "head of the Government" in the street. Moreover, he pulled teeth. He had exhibited monstrosities at fairs, and had a booth with a trumpet and this placard: "Babet, dental artist, member of the Academies, physical experimenter on metals and metalloids, extirpates teeth, removes stumps left by other dentists. Price: one tooth, one franc fifty centimes; two teeth, two francs; three teeth, two francs fifty centimes. Improve your opportunity." (This "improve your opportunity," meant: "get as many pulled as possible.") He had been married, and had had children. What had become of his wife and children, he did not know. He had lost them as one loses his pocket-handkerchief. A remarkable exception in the dark world to which he belonged, Babet read the papers. One day during the time he had his family with him in his travelling booth he had read in the *Messenger* that a woman had been delivered of a child, likely to live, which had the face of a calf, and he had exclaimed: *"There is a piece of good luck! My wife hasn't the sense to bring me a child like that."* Since then, he had left everything, "to take on Paris hand to hand." His own expression.*

What was Claquesous? He was night. Before showing himself he waited till the sky was daubed with black. At night he came out of a hole, which he went into again before day. Where was this hole? Nobody knew. In the most perfect darkness, and to his accomplices, he always turned his back when he spoke. Was his name Claquesous? No. He said: "My name is Nothing-at-all." If a candle was brought he put on a mask. He was a ventriloquist. Babet said: *"Claquesous is a night-bird with two voices."* Claquesous was restless, roving, terrible. It was not certain that he had a name, Claquesous being a nickname; it was not certain that he had a voice, his chest speaking oftener than his mouth; it was not certain that he had a face, nobody having ever seen anything but this mask. He disappeared as if he sank into the ground; he came like an apparition.

A mournful sight was Montparnasse. Montparnasse was a child; less than twenty, with a pretty face, lips like cherries, charming black locks, the glow of spring in his eyes; he had all the vices and aspired to all the crimes. The digestion of what was bad gave him an appetite for what was worse. He was the *gamin* turned vagabond and the vagabond become an assassin. He was genteel, effeminate, graceful, robust, weak, and ferocious. He wore his hat turned upon the left side, to make room for the tuft of hair, according to the fashion of 1829. He lived by robbery. His coat was the most fashionable cut, but threadbare. Montparnasse was a fashion-plate living in distress and committing murders. The cause of all the crimes of this young man was his desire to be well dressed. The first grisette who had said to him: "You are handsome," had thrown the stain of darkness into his heart, and had made a Cain of this Abel. Thinking that he was handsome, he had desired to be elegant; now the first of elegances is idleness: idleness for a poor man is crime. Few prowlers were so much feared as Montparnasse. At eighteen, he had already left several corpses on his track. More than one traveller lay in the shadow of this wretch, with extended arms and with his face in a pool of blood. Frizzled, pomaded, with slender waist, hips like a woman, the chest of a Prussian officer, a buzz of admiration about him from the girls of the boulevard, an elaborately-tied cravat, a blackjack in his pocket, a flower in his button-hole; such was this charmer of the sepulchre.

---

*"To take on Paris hand to hand" imitates the challenge that Honoré de Balzac's flawed hero Eugène de Rastignac cries out to the city at the end of *Le Père Goriot* (1834): *à nous deux maintenant*, "the two of us will have it out now."

4

COMPOSITION OF THE BAND

THESE FOUR BANDITS formed a sort of Proteus, winding through the police and endeavouring to escape from the indiscreet glances of Vidocq "under various form, tree, flame, and fountain," lending each other their names and their tricks, concealing themselves in their own shadow, each a refuge and a hiding-place for the others, throwing off their personalities, as one takes off a false nose at a masked ball, sometimes simplifying themselves till they are but one, sometimes multiplying themselves till Coco Lacour himself took them for a multitude.

These four men were not four men; it was a sort of mysterious robber with four heads preying upon Paris by wholesale; it was the monstrous polyp of evil which inhabits the crypt of society.

By means of their ramifications and the underlying network of their relations, Babet, Gueulemer, Claquesous, and Montparnasse controlled the general ambush business of the Department of the Seine. Originators of ideas in this line, men of midnight imagination came to them for the execution. The four villains being furnished with the single draft they took charge of putting it on the stage. They worked upon scenario. They were always in condition to furnish a company proportioned and suitable to any enterprise which stood in need of aid, and was sufficiently lucrative. A crime being in search of arms, they sublet accomplices to it. They had a company of actors of darkness at the disposition of every cavernous tragedy.

They usually met at nightfall, their waking hour, in the waste grounds near La Salpêtrière. There they conferred. They had the twelve dark hours before them; they allotted their employ.

Patron-Minette, such was the name which was given in subterranean society to the association of these four men. In the old, popular, fantastic language, which now is dying out every day, *Patron-Minette* means morning, just as *entre chien et loup* [between dog and wolf], means night. This appellation, Patron-Minette, probably came from the hour at which their work ended, the dawn being the moment for the disappearance of phantoms and the separation of bandits. These four were known by this title. When the Chief Judge of the Circuit Court visited Lacenaire in prison, he questioned him in relation to some crime which Lacenaire denied. "Who did do it?" asked the judge. Lacenaire made this reply, enigmatic to the magistrate, but clear to the police: "Patron-Minette, perhaps."

BOOK EIGHT
THE CRIMINAL POOR

1 (2)

A FIND

MARIUS still lived in the Gorbeau tenement. He paid no attention to anybody there.

At this time, it is true, there were no occupants remaining in the house but himself and those Jondrettes whose rent he had once paid, without having ever spoken, however, either to the father, or to the mother, or to the daughters. The other tenants had moved away or died, or had been turned out for not paying their rent.

One day, in the course of this winter, the sun shone a little in the afternoon, but it was the second of February, that ancient Candlemas-day whose treacherous sun, the precursor of six weeks of cold, inspired Matthew Laensberg with these two lines, which have deservedly become classic:

> Qu'il luise ou qu'il luiserne,
> L'ours rentre en sa caverne.*

Marius had just left his; night was falling. It was his dinner hour; for it was still necessary for him to go to dinner, alas! oh, infirmity of the ideal passions.†

He had just crossed his door-sill which Ma'am Bougon was sweeping at that very moment, muttering at the same time this memorable monologue:

"What is there that is cheap now? everything is expensive. There is nothing but people's trouble that is cheap; that comes for nothing, people's trouble."

Marius went slowly up the boulevard towards the barrière,‡ on the way to the Rue Saint Jacques. He was walking thoughtfully, with his head down.

Suddenly he felt that he was elbowed in the dusk; he turned, and saw two young girls in rags, one tall and slender, the other a little shorter, passing rapidly by, breathless, frightened, and apparently in flight; they had met him, had not seen him, and had jostled him in passing. Marius could see in the twilight their livid faces, their hair tangled and flying, their frightful bonnets, their tattered skirts, and their naked feet. As they

---

*Let it gleam or let it glimmer, / The bear returns into his cave. The equivalent of Ground Hog Day is a long-standing international tradition.

†Marius's point of view, gently mocked by Hugo; to attend to his material needs seems unworthy of his devotion to Cosette.

‡The city gate, where tolls (*l'octroi*) were levied for importing certain merchandise; these entrance duties were suppressed throughout France in 1949.

ran they were talking to each other. The taller one said in a very low voice:

"The *cognes* came. They just missed *pincer* me at the *demi-cercle*."

The other answered: "I saw them. I *cavalé, cavalé, cavalé*."*

Marius understood, through this dismal argot, that the gendarmes, or the city police, had not succeeded in seizing these two girls, and that the girls had escaped.

They plunged in under the trees of the boulevard behind him, and for a few seconds made a kind of dim whiteness in the darkness which soon faded out.

Marius stopped for a moment.

He was about to resume his course when he perceived a little greyish packet on the ground at his feet. He stooped down and picked it up. It was a sort of envelope which appeared to contain papers.

"Well," said he, "those poor creatures must have dropped this!"

He retraced his steps, he called, he did not find them; he concluded they were already beyond hearing, put the packet in his pocket and went to dinner.

On his way, in an alley on the Rue Mouffetard, he saw a child's coffin covered with a black cloth, placed upon three chairs and lighted by a candle. The two girls of the twilight returned to his mind.

"Poor mothers," thought he. "There is one thing sadder than to see their children die—to see them lead evil lives."

Then these shadows which had distracted his sadness left his thoughts, and he fell back into his customary musings. He began to think of his six months of love and happiness in the open air and the broad daylight under the beautiful trees of the Luxembourg Gardens.

"How dark my life has become!" said he to himself. "Girls still pass before me. Only formerly they were angels; now they are ghouls."

---

*"The cops came. They just missed nabbing me at the half-circle [-shaped road intersection]." "I saw them. I beat it out of there."

2 (3)

THE MAN WITH FOUR FACES

IN THE EVENING, as he was undressing to go to bed, he happened to feel in his coat-pocket the packet which he had picked up on the boulevard. He had forgotten it. He thought it might be well to open it, and that the packet might perhaps contain the address of the young girls, if, in reality, it belonged to them, or at all events the information necessary to restore it to the person who had lost it.

He opened the envelope.

It was unsealed and contained four letters, also unsealed.

The addresses were upon them.

All four exhaled an odour of wretched tobacco.

The first letter was addressed: *To Madame, Madame the Marchioness de Grucheray, Square opposite the Chamber of Deputies, No.——*

Marius said to himself that he should probably find in this letter the information of which he was in search, and that, moreover, as the letter was not sealed, probably it might be read without impropriety.

It was in these words:

"Madame the Marchioness:
"The virtue of kindness and piety is that which binds sosiety most closely. Call up your christian sentiment, and cast a look of compassion upon this unfortunate Spanish victim of loyalty and attachment to the sacred cause of legitimacy, which he has paid for with his blood, consecrated his fortune, wholy, to defend this cause, and to-day finds himself in the greatest povarty. He has no doubt that your honourable self will furnish him assistance to preserve an existence extremely painful for a soldier of education and of honour full of wounds, reckons in advance upon the humanity which animmates you and upon the interest which Madame the Marchioness feels in a nation so unfortunate. Their prayer will not be in vain, and their memory will retain herr charming souvenir.
"From my respectful sentiments with which I have the honour to be

"Madame,
"DON ALVARÈS, Spanish captain of cabalry, royalist refuge in France, who finds himself traveling for his country and ressources fail him to continue his travells."

No address was added to the signature. Marius hoped to find the address in the second letter the superscription of which ran: *to Madame, Madame the Countess de Montvernet, Rue Cassette, No. 9.* Marius read as follows:

"Madame the Comtess,
    "It is an unfortunat mothur of a family of six children the last of whom is only eight months old. I sick since my last lying-in, abandoned by my husband for five months haveing no ressources in the world in the most frightful indigance.
    "In the hope of Madame the Comtesse, she has the honour to be, Madame, with profound respect,

"MOTHER BALIZARD."

Marius passed to the third letter, which was, like the preceding, a begging one; it read:

"Monsieur Pabourgeot, elector, wholesale merchant-milliner, Rue Saint Denis, corner of the Rue aux Fers.
    "I take the liberty to address you this letter to pray you to accord me the pretious favour of your simpathies and to interest you in a man of letters who has just sent a drama to the Théatre Français. Its subject is historical, and the action takes place in Auvergne in the time of the empire: its style, I believe, is natural, laconic and perhaps has some merit. There are verses to be sung in four places. The comic, the serious, the unforeseen, mingle themselves with the variety of the characters and with a tint of romance spread lightly over all the plot which advances misteriously, ånd by striking unixpectit terns, to a denouement in the midst of several hits of splendid scenes.
    "My principal object is to satisfie the desire which animates progressively the man of our century, that is to say, fashion, that caprisious and grotesque weathercock which changes almost with every new wind.
    "In spite of these qualities I have reason to fear that jealousy, the selfishness of the privileged authors, may secure my exclusion from the theatre, for I am not ignorant of the distaste with which newcomers are swollowed.
    "Monsieur Pabourgeot, your just reputation as an enlightened protector of literary fokes emboldens me to send my daughter to you, who will expose to you our indigant situation, wanting bread and fire in this wynter season. To tell you that I pray you to accept the homage which I desire to offer you in my drama and in all those which I will make, is to prove to you how ambicious I am of the honour of sheltering myself under your aegis, and of adorning my writings with your name. If you deign to honour me with the most modest offering, I shall occupy myself immediately a piese of verse for you to pay my tribut of recognition. This piese, which I shall endeavour to render as

perfect as possible, will be sent to you before being inserted in the beginning of the drama and recited upon the stage.

"To Monsieur and Madame Pabourgeot,
My most respectful homage,
GENFLOT, MAN OF LETTERS.

"P.S. Were it only forty sous.

"Excuse me for sending my daughter and for not presenting myself, but sad motives of dress do not permit me, alas! to go out——"

Marius finally opened the fourth letter. There was on the address: *To the beneficent gentleman of the church of Saint Jaques du Haut Pas.* It contained these few lines:

"Beneficent man.

"If you will deign to accompany my daughter, you will see a misserable calamity, and I will show you my certificates.

"At the sight of these writings your generous soul will be moved with a sentiment of lively benevolence, for true philosophers always experience vivid emotions.

"Agree, compassionate man, that one must experience the most cruel necessity, and that it is very painful, to obtain relief, to have it attested by authority, as if we were not free to suffer and to die of inanition while waiting for some one to relieve our missery. The fates are very cruel to some and too lavish or too protective to others.

"I await your presence or your offering, if you deign to make it, and I pray you to have the kindness to accept the respectful sentiments with which I am proud to be,

"Truly magnanimous man,
"Your very humble
And very obedient servant,
"P. FABANTOU, DRAMATIC ARTIST."

After reading these four letters, Marius did not find himself much wiser than before.

In the first place none of the signers gave his address.

Then they seemed to come from four different individuals, Don Alvarès, Mother Balizard, the poet Genflot, and the dramatic artist Fabantou; but, strangely enough, these letters were all four written in the same hand.

What could one conclude from that, except that they came from the same person?

Moreover, and this rendered the conjecture still more probable, the paper, coarse and yellow, was the same in all four, the odour of tobacco was the same, and although there was an evident endeavour to vary the style, the same faults of orthography were reproduced with unruffled assurance, and Genflot, the man of letters, was no more free from them than the Spanish captain.

To endeavour to unriddle this little mystery was a useless labour. If it had not been a lost object, it would have had the appearance of a mystification. Marius was too sad to take a joke kindly even from chance, or to lend himself to the game which the street pavement seemed to wish to play with him. It appeared to him that he was like Colin Maillard among the four letters, which were mocking him.*

Nothing, however, indicated that these letters belonged to the girls whom Marius had met on the boulevard. After all, they were but waste paper evidently without value.

Marius put them back into the envelope, threw it into a corner, and went to bed.

About seven o'clock in the morning, he had got up and breakfasted, and was trying to set about his work when there was a gentle rap at his door.

As he owned nothing, he never locked his door, except sometimes, and that very rarely, when he was about some pressing piece of work. And, indeed, even when absent, he left his key in the lock. "You will be robbed," said Ma'am Bougon. "Of what?" said Marius. The fact is, however, that one day somebody had stolen an old pair of boots, to the great triumph of Ma'am Bougon.

There was a second rap, very gentle like the first.

"Come in," said Marius.

The door opened.

"What do you want, Ma'am Bougon?" asked Marius, without raising his eyes from the books and papers which he had on his table.

A voice, which was not Ma'am Bougon's, answered:

"I beg your pardon, Monsieur——"

It was a hollow, cracked, rasping voice, the voice of a congested old man, roughened by brandy and by strong liquors.

Marius turned quickly and saw a girl.

3 (4)

A ROSE IN DIRE POVERTY

A GIRL who was quite young, was standing in the half-opened door. The little round window through which the light found its way into the garret was exactly opposite the door, and lit up this form with a pallid light. It was a pale, puny, meagre creature, nothing but a chemise and a skirt covered a shivering and chilly nakedness. A string for a belt, a string for a head-dress,

---

*"Colin Maillard," who is "it" in the child's game Blind-Man's Buff, tries to catch and identify one of the other players. Marius can't figure out who they are.

sharp shoulders protruding from the chemise, a blond and lymphatic pallor, dirty shoulder-blades, red hands, the mouth open and sunken, some teeth gone, the eyes dull, bold, and drooping, the form of an unripe young girl and the look of a corrupted old woman; fifty years joined with fifteen; one of those beings who are both feeble and horrible at once, and who make those shudder whom they do not make weep.*

Marius arose and gazed with a kind of astonishment upon this being, so much like the shadowy forms which pass across our dreams.

The most poignant thing about it was that this young girl had not come into the world to be ugly. In her early childhood, she must have even been pretty. The grace of her youth was still struggling against the hideous, premature old age brought on by debauchery and poverty. A remnant of beauty was dying out upon this face of sixteen, like the pale sun which is extinguished by frightful clouds at the dawn of a winter's day.

The face was not absolutely unknown to Marius. He thought he remembered having seen it somewhere.

"What do you wish, mademoiselle?" asked he.

The young girl answered with her voice like a drunken galley-slave's:

"Here is a letter for you, Monsieur Marius."

She called Marius by his name; he could not doubt that her business was with him; but what was this girl? how did she know his name?

Without waiting for an invitation, she entered. She entered resolutely, looking at the whole room and the unmade bed with a sort of assurance which chilled the heart.† She was barefooted. Great holes in her skirt revealed her long limbs and her sharp knees. She was shivering.

She indeed had in her hand a letter which she presented to Marius.

Marius, in opening this letter, noticed that the enormously large seal was still wet. The message could not have come far. He read:

"My amiable neighbour, young man!

"I have lerned your kindness towards me, that you have paid my rent six months ago. I bless you, young man. My eldest daughter will tell you that we have been without a morsel of bread for two days, four persons, and my spouse sick. If I am not desseived by my thoughts, I think I may hope that your generous heart will soften at this account and that the desire will subjugate you of being propitious to me by deigning to lavish upon me some slight gift.

"I am with the distinguished consideration which is due to the benefactors of humanity,

"JONDRETTE

"P.S. My daughter will await your orders, dear Monsieur Marius."

---

*Eponine, once favored over Cosette, now contrasts dramatically with Jean Valjean's radiant ward, having become prematurely aged, ill, and morally degraded.
†That she feels at home in a man's bedroom suggests that she has engaged in prostitution. What follows makes it clear that her father is offering to sell her body.

This letter, in the midst of the obscure accident which had occupied Marius' thoughts since the previous evening, was a candle in a cave. Everything was suddenly cleared up.

This letter came from the same source as the other four. It was the same writing, the same style, the same orthography, the same paper, the same odour of tobacco.

There were five missives, five stories, five names, five signatures and a single signer. The Spanish Captain Don Alvarès, the unfortunate mother Balizard, the dramatic poet Genflot, the old comedy writer Fabantou, were all four named Jondrette, if indeed the name of Jondrette himself was Jondrette.

During the now rather long time that Marius had lived in the tenement, he had had, as we have said, but very few opportunities to see, or even catch a glimpse of his very few neighbours. His mind was elsewhere, and where the mind is, thither the eyes are directed. He must have met the Jondrettes in the passage and on the stairs, more than once, but to him they were only shadows; he had taken so little notice that on the previous evening he had brushed against the Jondrette girls upon the boulevard without recognising them; for it was evidently they; and it was with great difficulty that this girl, who had just come into his room, had awakened in him beneath his disgust and pity, a vague remembrance of having met with her elsewhere.

Now he saw everything clearly. He understood that the occupation of his neighbour Jondrette in his distress was to work upon the sympathies of benevolent persons; that he procured their addresses, and that he wrote under assumed names letters to people whom he deemed rich and compassionate, which his daughters carried, at their risk and peril; for this father was one who risked his daughters; he was playing a game with destiny, and he added them to the stake. Marius understood, to judge by their flight in the evening, by their breathlessness, by their terror, by those words of argot which he had heard, that probably these unfortunate things were carrying on also some of the secret trades of darkness, and that from all this the result was, in the midst of human society constituted as it is, two miserable beings who were neither children, nor girls, nor women, a species of impure yet innocent monsters produced by misery.

Sad creatures without name, without age, without sex, to whom neither good nor evil were any longer possible, and for whom, on leaving childhood, there is nothing more in this world, neither liberty, nor virtue, nor responsibility. Souls blooming yesterday, faded to-day, like those flowers which fall in the street and are bespattered by the mud before a wheel crushes them.

Meantime, while Marius fixed upon her an astonished and sorrowful look, the young girl was walking to and fro in the room with the boldness of a spectre. She bustled about regardless of her nakedness. At times, her chemise, unfastened and torn, fell almost to her waist. She moved the chairs, she disarranged the toilet articles on the bureau, she felt of Marius' clothes, she searched over what there was in the corners.

"Ah," said she, "you have a mirror!"

And she hummed, as if she had been alone, snatches of songs, light refrains which were made dismal by her harsh and guttural voice. Beneath this boldness could be perceived an indescribable constraint, restlessness, and humility. Effrontery is a form of shame.

Nothing was more sorrowful than to see her amusing herself, and, so to speak, fluttering about the room with the movements of a bird which is startled by the light, or which has a wing broken. One felt that under other conditions of up-bringing and of destiny, the gay and free manner of this young girl might have been something sweet and charming. Never among animals does the creature which is born to be a dove change into an osprey. That is seen only among men.

Marius was reflecting, and let her go on.

She went to the table.

"Ah!" said she, "books!"

A light flashed through her glassy eye. She resumed, and her tone expressed that happiness of being able to boast of something, to which no human creature is insensitive:

"I can read, I can."

She hastily caught up the book which lay open on the table, and read fluently:

"——General Bauduin received the order to take five battalions of his brigade and carry the château of Hougomont, which is in the middle of the plain of Waterloo——"

She stopped:

"Ah, Waterloo! I know that. It is a battle in old times. My father was there; my father served in the armies. We are jolly good Bonapartists at home, that we are. Against the English, Waterloo was."

She put down the book, took up a pen, and exclaimed:

"And I can write, too!"

She dipped the pen in the ink, and turning towards Marius:

"Would you like to see? Here, I am going to write a bit to show you."

And before he had had time to answer, she wrote upon a sheet of blank paper which was on the middle of the table: *The cops are here.*

Then, throwing down the pen:

"There are no mistakes in spelling. You can look. We have received an education, my sister and I. We have not always been what we are. We were not made——"

Here she stopped, fixed her faded eye upon Marius, and burst out laughing, saying in a tone which contained complete anguish stifled by complete cynicism:

"Bah!"

And she began to hum these words, to a lively air:

> *J'ai faim, mon père.*
> *Pas de fricot.*
> *J'ai froid, ma mère.*

Pas de tricot.
Grelotte,
Lolotte!
Sanglote,
Jacquot. *

Hardly had she finished this stanza when she exclaimed:

"Do you ever go to the theatre, Monsieur Marius? I do. I have a little brother who is a friend of some artists, and who gives me tickets sometimes. Now, I do not like the seats in the galleries. You are crowded, you are uncomfortable. There are sometimes coarse people there; there are also people who smell bad."

Then she looked at Marius, put on a strange manner, and said to him:

"Do you know, Monsieur Marius, that you are a very pretty boy?"

And at the same time the same thought occurred to both of them, which made her smile and made him blush.

She went to him, and laid her hand on his shoulder: "You pay no attention to me, but I know you, Monsieur Marius. I meet you here on the stairs, and then I see you visiting a man named Father Mabeuf, who lives out by Austerlitz, sometimes, when I am walking that way. That becomes you very well, your tangled hair."

Her voice tried to be very soft, but succeeded only in being very low. Some of her words were lost in their passage from the larynx to the lips, as upon a key-board in which some notes are missing.

Marius had drawn back quietly.

"Mademoiselle," said he, with his cold gravity, "I have here a packet, which is yours, I think. Permit me to return it to you."

And he handed her the envelope, which contained the four letters.

She clapped her hands and exclaimed:

"We have looked everywhere!"

Then she snatched the packet, and opened the envelope, saying:

"Lordy, Lordy, haven't we looked, my sister and I? And you have found it! on the boulevard, didn't you? It must have been on the boulevard? You see, this dropped when we ran. It was my brat of a sister who made the stupid blunder. When we got home we could not find it. As we did not want to be beaten, since that is pointless, since that is entirely pointless, since that is absolutely pointless, we said at home that we had carried the letters to the persons, and that they told us: Nix! Now here they are, these poor letters. And how did you know they were mine? Ah, yes! by the writing! It was you, then, that we knocked against last evening. We did not see you, really! I said to my sister: Is that a gentleman. My sister said:—I think it is a gentleman!"

---

*I'm hungry, dad. / The food is gone. / I'm cold, ma. / No coat to put on. / Shiver, girl! / Cry, little boy.

Meanwhile she had unfolded the petition addressed "to the beneficent gentleman of the church Saint Jacques du Haut Pas."

"Here!" said she, "this is for the old fellow who goes to mass. And this too is the hour. I am going to carry it to him. He will give us something perhaps for breakfast."

Then she began to laugh, and added:

"Do you know what it will be if we have breakfast to-day? It will be that we shall have had our breakfast for day before yesterday, our dinner for day before yesterday, our breakfast for yesterday, our dinner for yesterday, all that at one time this morning. Yes! zounds! if you're not satisfied, die, dogs!"

This reminded Marius of what the poor girl had come to his room for.

He felt in his waistcoat, he found nothing there.

The young girl continued, seeming to talk as if she were no longer conscious that Marius was there present.

"Sometimes I go away at night. Sometimes I do not come back. Before coming to this place, last winter, we lived under the arches of the bridges. We hugged close to each other so as not to freeze. My little sister cried. How chilly the water is! When I thought of drowning myself, I said: No; it is too cold. I go all alone when I want to, I sleep in the ditches sometimes. Do you know, at night, when I walk on the boulevards, I see the trees like gibbets, I see all the black houses as large as the towers of Notre Dame, I imagine that the white walls are the river, I say to myself: Here, there is water there! The stars are like spotlights, one would say that they are smoking, and that the wind is blowing them out, I am confused, as if I had horses panting in my ear; though it is night, I hear hand-organs and spinning wheels, I don't know what. I think that somebody is throwing stones at me, I run without knowing it, it is all a whirl, all a whirl. When one has not eaten, it is very queer."[5]

And she looked at him with a wandering eye.

After a thorough exploration of his pockets, Marius had at last got together five francs and sixteen sous. This was at the time all that he had in the world. "That is enough for my dinner to-day," thought he, "to-morrow we will see." He took the sixteen sous, and gave the five francs to the young girl.

She took the coin eagerly.

"Good," said she, "there is some sunshine!"

And as if the sun had had the effect to loosen an avalanche of argot in her brain, she continued:

"Five francs! a shiner! a monarch! in this *piolle!* it is *chenâtre!* You are a good *mion.* I give you my *palpitant.* Bravo for the *fanandels!* Two days of *pivois!* and of *viandemuche!* and of *frictomar!* we shall *pitancer chenument!* and *bonne mouise!*"

She drew her chemise up over her shoulders, made a low bow to Marius, then a familiar wave of the hand, and moved towards the door, saying:

"Good morning, monsieur. It is all the same. I am going to find my old man."

On her way she saw on the bureau a dry crust of bread mouldering there in the dust; she sprang upon it, and bit it, muttering:

"That is good! it is hard! it breaks my teeth!"

Then she went out.

4 (5)

THE PROVIDENTIAL SPYHOLE

FOR FIVE YEARS Marius had lived in poverty, in privation, in distress even, but he perceived that he had never known true want. True want he had just seen. It was this phantom which had just passed before his eyes. In fact, he who has seen the misery of man only has seen nothing, he must see the misery of woman; he who has seen the misery of woman only has seen nothing, he must see the misery of childhood.

When man has reached the last extremity, he comes, at the same time, to the last expedients. Woe to the defenceless beings who surround him! Work, wages, bread, fire, courage, willingness, all fail him at once. The light of day seems to die away without, the moral light dies out within; in this gloom, man meets the weakness of woman and childhood, and puts them by force to ignominious uses.

Then all horrors are possible. Despair is surrounded by fragile partitions which all open into vice or crime.

Health, youth, honour, the holy and passionate delicacies of the still tender flesh, the heart, virginity, modesty, that epidermis of the soul, are fatally disposed of by that blind groping which seeks for aid, which meets degradation, and which accommodates itself to it. Fathers, mothers, children, brothers, sisters, men, women, girls, cling together, and almost grow together like a mineral formation, in that dark promiscuity of sexes, of relationships, of ages, of infancy, of innocence. They crouch down, back to back, in a kind of fate-hovel.* They glance at one another sorrowfully. Oh, the unfortunate! how pallid they are! how cold they are! It seems as though they were on a planet much further from the sun than we.

This young girl was to Marius a sort of messenger from the night.

She revealed to him an entire and hideous aspect of the darkness.

Marius almost reproached himself with the fact that he had been so

---

*The agrammatical *métaphore maxima*, modifying one noun with another, indicates the effects of supernatural intervention.

absorbed in his reveries and passion that he had not until now cast a glance upon his neighbours. Paying their rent was a mechanical impulse; everybody would have had that impulse; but he, Marius, should have done better. What! a mere wall separated him from these abandoned beings, who lived by groping in the night without the pale of the living; he came in contact with them, he was in some sort the last link of the human race which they touched, he heard them live or rather breathe beside him, and he took no notice of them! every day at every moment, he heard them through the wall, walking, going, coming, talking, and he did not lend his ear! and in these words there were groans, and he did not even listen, his thoughts were elsewhere, upon dreams, upon impossible glimmerings, upon loves in the sky, upon infatuations; and all the while human beings, his brothers in Jesus Christ, his brothers in the people, were suffering death agonies beside him! agonising uselessly; he even caused a portion of their suffering, and aggravated it. For had they had another neighbour, a less chimerical and more observant neighbour, an ordinary and charitable man, it was clear that their poverty would have been noticed, their signals of distress would have been seen, and long ago perhaps they would have been gathered up and saved! Undoubtedly they seemed very depraved, very corrupt, very vile, very hateful, even, but those are rare who fall without becoming degraded; there is a point, moreover, at which the unfortunate and the infamous are associated and confounded in a single word, a fatal word, *Les Misérables;* whose fault is it? And then, is it not when the fall is lowest that charity ought to be greatest?

While he thus preached to himself, for there were times when Marius, like all truly honest hearts, was his own monitor, and scolded himself more than he deserved, he looked at the wall which separated him from the Jondrettes, as if he could send his pitying glance through that partition to warn those unfortunate beings. The wall was a thin layer of plaster, upheld by laths and joists, through which, as we have just seen, voices and words could be distinguished perfectly. None but the dreamer, Marius, would not have perceived this before. There was no paper hung on this wall either on the side of the Jondrettes, or on Marius' side; its coarse construction was bare to the eye. Almost unconsciously, Marius examined this partition; sometimes reverie examines, observes, and scrutinises, as thought would do. Suddenly he arose, he noticed towards the top, near the ceiling, a triangular hole, where three laths left a space between them. The plaster which should have stopped this hole was gone, and by getting upon the bureau he could see through that hole into the Jondrettes' garret. Pity has and should have its curiosity. This gap made a kind of spyhole. It is lawful to look upon misfortune like a betrayer for the sake of relieving it. "Let us see what these people are," thought Marius, "and to what they are reduced."

He climbed upon the bureau, put his eye to the crevice, and looked.

5 (6)

THE WILD MAN IN HIS LAIR

CITIES, like forests, have their dens in which hide all their most evil and terrible monsters. But in cities, what hides thus is ferocious, unclean, and small, that is to say, ugly; in forests, what hides is ferocious, savage, and large, that is to say, beautiful. Den for den, those of beasts are preferable to those of men. Caverns are better than the wretched holes which shelter humanity.

What Marius saw was a hole.

Marius was poor and his room was poorly furnished, but even as his poverty was noble, his garret was clean. The den into which his eyes were at that moment directed, was abject, filthy, fetid, infectious, gloomy, sordid. All the furniture was a straw chair, a rickety table, a few old broken dishes, and in two of the corners two indescribable pallets; all the light came from a dormer window of four panes, curtained with spiders' webs. Just enough light came through that loophole to make a man's face appear like the face of a phantom. The walls had a leprous look, and were covered with seams and scars like a face disfigured by some horrible malady; a putrid moisture oozed from them. Obscene pictures could be discovered upon them coarsely sketched in charcoal.

The room which Marius occupied had a broken brick pavement; this one was neither paved nor floored; the inmates walked immediately upon the old plastering of the ruinous tenement, which had grown black under their feet. Upon this uneven soil where the dust was, as it were, incrusted, and which was virgin soil in respect only of the broom, were grouped at random constellations of socks, old shoes, and hideous rags; however, this room had a fireplace; so it rented for forty francs a year. In the fireplace there was a little of everything, a chafing-dish, a kettle, some broken boards, rags hanging on nails, a bird cage, some ashes, and even a little fire. Two embers were smoking sullenly.

The size of this garret added still more to its horror. It had projections, angles, black holes, recesses under the roof, bays, and promontories. Beyond were hideous, unfathomable corners, which seemed as if they must be full of spiders as big as one's fist, centipedes as large as one's foot, and perhaps even some unknown monsters of humanity.

One of the pallets was near the door, the other near the window. Each had one end next the fireplace and both were opposite Marius. In a corner near the opening through which Marius was looking, hanging upon the wall in a black wooden frame, was a coloured engraving at the bottom of which was written in large letters: THE DREAM. It represented a sleeping woman and a sleeping child, the child upon the woman's lap, an eagle in a cloud with a crown in his beak, and the woman pushing away the crown from the child's head, but without waking; in the background Napoleon in a halo, leaning against a large blue column with a yellow capital adorned with this inscription:

MARINGO
AUSTERLITS
IENA
WAGRAMME
ELOT*

Below this frame a sort of wooden panel longer than it was wide was standing on the floor and leaning at an angle against the wall. It had the appearance of a picture set against the wall, of a frame probably daubed on the other side, of a pier glass taken down from a wall and forgotten there while waiting to be hung again.

By the table, upon which Marius saw a pen, ink, and paper, was seated a man of about sixty, small, thin, livid, haggard, with a keen, cruel, and restless air; a hideous harpy.

Lavater, if he could have studied this face, would have found in it a mixture of vulture and shyster; the bird of prey and the con man rendering each other ugly and complete, the con man making the bird of prey ignoble, the bird of prey making the con man horrible.

This man had a long grey beard. He was dressed in a woman's chemise, which showed his shaggy chest and his naked arms bristling with grey hairs. Below this chemise were a pair of muddy trousers and boots from which the toes stuck out.

He had a pipe in his mouth, and was smoking. There was no more bread in the den, but there was still tobacco.

He was writing, probably some such letter as those which Marius had read.

On one corner of the table was an old odd volume with a reddish cover, the size of which, the old duodecimo of series of books, betrayed that it was a novel. On the cover was displayed the following title, printed in huge capitals: GOD, THE KING, HONOUR AND THE LADIES, BY DUCRAY DUMINIL, 1814.

As he wrote, the man talked aloud, and Marius heard his words:

"To think that there is no equality even when we are dead! Look at Père Lachaise! The great, those who are rich, are in the upper part, in the avenue of the acacias, which is paved. They can go there in a carriage. The low, the poor, the unfortunate, they are put in the lower part, where

---

*Thénardier has misspelled four of the five names of Napoléon's great victories—he wants to imply that he fought in them, but his spelling exposes his lack of familiarity with those campaigns.

there is mud up to the knees, in holes, in the wet. They are put there so that they may rot sooner! You cannot go to see them without sinking into the ground."

Here he stopped, struck his fist on the table, and added, gnashing his teeth:

"Oh! I could eat the world!"

A big woman, who might have been forty years old or a hundred, was squatting near the fireplace, upon her bare feet.

She also was dressed only in a chemise and a knit skirt patched with pieces of old cloth. A coarse tow apron covered half the skirt. Although this woman was bent and drawn up into herself, it could be seen that she was very tall. She was a kind of giantess by the side of her husband. She had hideous hair, light red sprinkled with grey, that she pushed back from time to time with her huge shining hands which had flat nails.

Lying on the ground, at her side, wide open, was a volume of the same appearance as the other, and probably of the same novel.

Upon one of the pallets Marius could discern a sort of slender little wan girl seated, almost naked, with her feet hanging down, having the appearance neither of listening, nor of seeing, nor of living.

The younger sister, doubtless, of the one who had come to his room.

She appeared to be eleven or twelve years old. On examining her attentively, he saw that she must be fourteen. It was the child who, the evening before, on the boulevard, said: *"I cavalé, cavalé, cavalé!"*

She was of that sickly species which long remain backward, then pushes forward rapidly, and all at once. These sorry human plants are produced by want. These poor creatures have neither childhood nor youth. At fifteen they appear to be twelve; at sixteen they appear to be twenty. To-day a little girl, to-morrow a woman. One would say that they leap through life, to have done with it sooner.

This being now had the appearance of a child.

Nothing, moreover, indicated the performance of any labour in this room; not a loom, not a spinning wheel, not a tool. In one corner a few dubious-looking scraps of iron. It was that gloomy idleness which follows despair, and which precedes the death-agony.

Marius looked for some time into that funereal interior, more fearful than the interior of a tomb; for here were felt the movements of a human soul, and the palpitation of life.

The garret, the cellar, the deep ditch, in which some of the wretched crawl at the bottom of the social edifice, are not the sepulchre itself; they are its antechamber; but like those rich men who display their greatest magnificence at the entrance of their palace, death, who is close at hand, seems to display his greatest wretchedness in this vestibule.

The man became silent, the woman did not speak, the girl did not seem to breathe. Marius could hear the pen scratching over the paper.

The man muttered out, without ceasing to write:—"Rabble! rabble! all is rabble!"

This variation upon the ejaculation of Solomon* drew a sigh from the woman.

"My darling, be calm," said she. "Do not hurt yourself, dear. You are too good to write to all those people, my man."

In poverty bodies hug close to each other as in the cold, but hearts grow distant. This woman, according to all appearance, must have loved this man with as much love as was in her; but probably, in the repeated mutual reproaches which grew out of the frightful distress that weighed upon them all, this love had become extinguished. She now felt towards her husband nothing more than the ashes of affection. Still the words of endearment, as often happens, had survived. She said to him: *Dear; my darling; my man,* etc., with her lips, her heart was silent.

The man returned to his writing.

6 (7)

STRATEGY AND TACTICS

MARIUS, with a heavy heart, was about to get down from the sort of observatory which he had improvised, when a sound attracted his attention, and induced him to remain in his place.

The door of the garret was hastily opened. The eldest daughter appeared upon the threshold. On her feet she had coarse men's shoes, covered with mud, which had been spattered as high as her red ankles, and she was wrapped in a ragged old gown which Marius had not seen upon her an hour before, but which she had probably left at his door that she might inspire the more pity, and which she must have put on upon going out. She came in, pushed the door to behind her, stopped to take breath, for she was quite breathless, then cried with an expression of joy and triumph:

"He is coming!"

The father turned his eyes, the woman turned her head, the younger sister did not stir.

"Who?" asked the father.

"The gentleman!"

---

*"Vanity of vanity, says the preacher; all *is* vanity," Ecclesiastes 12:8. The Bible rejects attachment to worldly things; Thénardier, in contrast, bitterly resents not having received more recognition from the world of men.

"The philanthropist?"

"Yes."

"Of the church of Saint Jacques?"

"Yes."

"That old man?"

"Yes."

"He is going to come?"

"He is behind me."

"You are sure?"

"I am sure."

"There, true, he is coming?"

"He is coming in a fiacre."

"In a fiacre. It is Rothschild?"

The father arose.

"How are you sure? if he is coming in a fiacre, how is it that you get here before him? you gave him the address, at least? you told him the last door at the end of the hall on the right? provided he does not make a mistake? you found him at the church then? did he read my letter? what did he say to you?"

"Tut, tut, tut!" said the girl, "how you run on, goodman! I'll tell you: I went into the church, he was at his usual place, I made a curtsey to him, and I gave him the letter, he read it and said to me: Where do you live, my child? I said: Monsieur, I will show you. He said to me: No, give me your address; my daughter has some purchases to make, I am going to take a carriage and I will get to your house as soon as you do. I gave him the address. When I told him the house, he appeared surprised and hesitated an instant, then he said: It is all the same, I will go. When mass was over, I saw him leave the church with his daughter. I saw them get into a fiacre. And I told him plainly the last door at the end of the hall on the right."

"And how do you know that he will come?"

"I just saw the fiacre coming into the Rue du Petit Banquier. That is what made me run."

"How do you know it is the same fiacre?"

"Because I had noticed the number."

"What is the number?"

"Four hundred and forty."

"Good, you are a clever girl."

The girl looked resolutely at her father, and showing the shoes which she had on, said:

"A clever girl that may be, but I tell you that I shall never put on these shoes again, and that I will not do it, for health first, and then for hygiene. I know nothing more irritating than soles that squeak and go ghee, ghee, ghee, all along the street. I would rather go barefoot."

"You are right," answered the father, in a mild tone which contrasted with the rudeness of the young girl, "but they would not let you go into the churches; the poor must have shoes. People do not go to God's house

barefooted," added he bitterly. Then returning to the subject which occupied his thoughts——

"And you are sure then, sure that he is coming?"

"He is at my heels," said she.

The man sprang up. There was a sort of illumination on his face.

"Wife!" cried he, "you hear. Here is the philanthropist. Put out the fire."

The astounded woman did not stir.

The father, with the agility of a mountebank, caught a broken pot
which stood on the mantel, and threw some water upon the embers.

Then turning to his elder daughter:

"You! unbottom the chair!"

His daughter did not understand him at all.

He seized the chair, and with a kick he ruined the seat. His leg went
through it.

As he drew out his leg, he asked his daughter:

"Is it cold?"

"Very cold. It's snowing."

The father turned towards the younger girl, who was on the pallet near
the window, and cried in a thundering voice:

"Quick! off the bed, good-for-nothing! will you never do anything?
break a pane of glass!"

The little girl sprang off the bed trembling.

"Break a pane of glass!" said he again.

The child was speechless.

"Do you hear me?" repeated the father, "I tell you to break a pane!"

The child, with a sort of terrified obedience, rose upon tiptoe and struck
her fist into a pane. The glass broke and fell with a crash.

"Good," said the father.

He was serious, yet rapid. His eye ran hastily over all the nooks and
corners of the garret.

You would have said he was a general, making his final preparations at
the moment when the battle was about to begin.

The mother, who had not yet said a word, got up and asked in a slow,
muffled tone, her words seeming to come out as if curdled:

"Dear, what is it you want to do?"

"Get into bed," answered the man.

His tone admitted of no deliberation. The mother obeyed, and threw
herself heavily upon one of the pallets.

Meanwhile a sob was heard in a corner.

"What is that?" cried the father.

The younger daughter, without coming out of the darkness into which
she had shrunk, showed her bleeding fist. In breaking the glass she had cut
herself; she had gone to her mother's bed, and she was weeping in silence.

It was the mother's turn to rise and cry out.

"You see now! what stupid things you are doing? breaking your glass,
she has cut herself!"

"So much the better!" said the man. "I knew she would."

"How! so much the better?" resumed the woman.

"Silence!" replied the father. "I suppress the liberty of the press."

Then tearing the chemise which he had on, he made a bandage with which he hastily wrapped up the little girl's bleeding wrist.

That done, his eye fell upon the torn chemise with satisfaction.

"And the chemise too," said he, "all this looks convincing."

An icy wind whistled at the window and came into the room. The mist from without entered and spread about like a whitish wadding picked apart by invisible fingers. Through the broken pane the falling snow was seen. The cold promised the day before by the Candlemas sun had come indeed.

The father cast a glance about him as if to assure himself that he had forgotten nothing. He took an old shovel and spread ashes over the moistened embers in such a way as to hide them completely.

Then rising and standing with his back to the chimney:

"Now," said he, "we can receive the philanthropist."

7 (8)

THE SUNBEAM IN THE HOLE

THE LARGE GIRL went to her father and laid her hand on his.

"Feel how cold I am," said she.

"Pshaw!" answered the father. "I am a good deal colder than that."

The mother cried impetuously:

"You always have everything better than the rest, even pain."

"Down!" said the man.

The mother, after a peculiar look from the man, held her peace.

There was a moment of silence in the den. The eldest daughter was scraping the mud off the bottom of her dress with a careless air, the young sister continued to sob; the mother had taken her head in both hands and was covering her with kisses, saying to her in a low tone:

"My treasure, I beg of you, it will be nothing, do not cry, you will make your father angry."

"No!" cried the father, "on the contrary! sob! sob! that creates a good effect."

Then turning to the eldest:

"Ah! but where is he! if he is not coming, I shall have put out my fire, knocked the bottom out of my chair, torn my chemise, and broken my window for nothing."

"And cut the little girl!" murmured the mother.

"Do you know," resumed the father, "that it's damn cold in this devilish garret? If this man should not come! Oh! that is it! he makes us wait for him! he says: Well! they will wait for me! that is what they are for!—Oh! how I hate them, and how I would strangle them with joy and rejoicing, enthusiasm and satisfaction, these rich men! all the rich! these so-called charitable men, who act so pious, who go to mass, who act like priests, preachy, preachy, and who think themselves above us, and who come to humiliate us, and to bring us clothes! as they call them! rags which are not worth four sous, and bread! that is not what I want of the rabble! I want money! But money, never! because they say that we would go and drink it, and that we are drunkards and do-nothings! And what then are they, and what have they been in their time? Thieves! they would not have got rich without that! Oh! somebody ought to take society by the four corners of the sheet and toss it all into the air! Everything would smash, it is likely, but at least nobody would have anything, there would be so much gained! But what now is he doing, your mug of a benevolent gentleman? is he coming? The brute may have forgotten the address! I will bet that the old fool——"

Just then there was a light rap at the door, the man rushed forward and opened it, exclaiming with many low bows and smiles of adoration:

"Come in, monsieur! deign to come in, my noble benefactor, as well as your charming young lady."

A man of mature age and a young girl appeared at the door of the garret.

Marius had not left his place. What he felt at that moment escapes human language.

It was She.

Whoever has loved, knows all the radiant meaning contained in the three letters of this word: She.

It was indeed she. Marius could hardly discern her through the luminous vapour which suddenly spread over his eyes. It was that sweet absent being, that star which had been his light, for six months, it was that eye, that brow, that mouth, that beautiful vanished face which had produced night when it went away. The vision had been in an eclipse, it was reappearing.

She appeared again in this gloom, in this garret, in this shapeless den, in this horror!

Marius shuddered desperately. What! it was she! the beating of his heart disturbed his sight. He felt ready to melt into tears. What! at last he saw her again after having sought for her so long! it seemed to him that he had just lost his soul and that he had just found it again.

She was still the same, a little paler only; her delicate face was set in a violet velvet hat, her form was hidden under a black satin pelisse, below her long dress he caught a glimpse of her little foot squeezed into a silk buskin.

She was still accompanied by Monsieur Leblanc.

She stepped into the room and laid a large package on the table.

The elder Jondrette girl had retreated behind the door and was looking upon that velvet hat, that silk dress, and that charming happy face, with an evil eye.

8 (9)

JONDRETTE WEEPS ALMOST

THE DEN was so dark that people who came from outdoors felt as if they were entering a cellar on coming in. The two new-comers stepped forward, therefore, with some hesitation, hardly discerning the dim forms about them, while they were seen and examined with perfect ease by the tenants of the garret, whose eyes were accustomed to this twilight.

Monsieur Leblanc approached with his kind and compassionate look, and said to the father:

"Monsieur, you will find in this package some new clothes, some stockings, and some new blankets."

"Our angelic benefactor overwhelms us," said Jondrette, bowing down to the floor. Then, stooping to his eldest daughter's ear, while the two visitors were examining this lamentable abode, he added rapidly in a whisper:

"Well! what did I tell you? rags? no money. They are all alike! Tell me, how was the letter to this old blubber-lip signed?"

"Fabantou," answered the daughter.

"The dramatic artist, good!"

This was lucky for Jondrette, for at that very moment Monsieur Leblanc turned towards him and said to him, with the appearance of one who is trying to recollect a name:

"I see that you are indeed to be pitied, Monsieur——"

"Fabantou," said Jondrette quickly.

"Monsieur Fabantou, yes, that is it. I remember."

"Dramatic artist, monsieur, and who has had his successes."

Here Jondrette evidently thought the moment come to make an impression upon the "philanthropist." He exclaimed in a tone of voice which belongs to the braggadocio of the juggler at a fair, and, at the same time, to the humility of a beggar on the highway: "Pupil of Talma! Monsieur! I am a pupil of Talma! Fortune once smiled on me. Alas! now it is the turn of misfortune. Look, my benefactor, no bread, no fire. My poor darlings have no fire! My only chair unseated! A broken window! in such weather as is this! My spouse in bed! sick!"

"Poor woman!" said Monsieur Leblanc.

"My child injured!" added Jondrette.

The child, whose attention had been diverted by the arrival of the strangers, was staring at "the young lady," and had ceased her sobbing.

"Why don't you cry? why don't you scream?" said Jondrette to her in a whisper.

At the same time he pinched her injured hand. All this with the skill of a juggler.

The little one uttered loud cries.

The adorable young girl whom Marius in his heart called "his Ursula" went quickly to her:

"Poor, dear child!" said she.

"Look, my beautiful young lady," pursued Jondrette, "her bleeding wrist! It is an accident which happened in working at a machine by which she earned six sous a day. It may be necessary to cut off her arm."

"Indeed!" said the old gentleman alarmed.

The little girl, taking this seriously, began to sob again beautifully.

"Alas, yes, my benefactor!" answered the father.

For some moments, Jondrette had been looking at "the philanthropist" in a strange manner. Even while speaking, he seemed to scrutinise him closely as if he were trying to recall some reminiscence. Suddenly, taking advantage of a moment when the new-comers were anxiously questioning the smaller girl about her mutilated hand, he passed over to his wife who was lying in her bed, appearing to be overwhelmed and stupid, and said to her quickly and in a very low tone:

"Get a good look at that man!"

Then turning towards M. Leblanc, and continuing his lamentation:

"You see, monsieur! my only clothes are nothing but a chemise of my wife's! and that all torn! in the heart of winter. I cannot go out, for lack of a coat. If I had any kind of a coat, I should go to see Mademoiselle Mars, who knows me, and of whom I am a great favourite. She is still living in the Rue de la Tour des Dames, is not she? You know, monsieur, we have acted together in the provinces. I shared her laurels. Celimène would come to my relief, monsieur! Elmira would give alms to Belisarius! But no, nothing! And not a sou in the house! My wife sick, not a sou! My daughter dangerously injured, not a sou! My spouse has choking fits. It is her time of life, and then the nervous system has something to do with it. She needs aid, and my daughter also! But the doctor! but the druggist! how can I pay them! not a penny! I would fall on my knees before a penny, monsieur! You see how the arts are fallen! And do you know, my charming young lady, and you, my generous patron, do you know, you who breathe virtue and goodness, and who perfume that church where my daughter, in going to say her prayers, sees you every day? For I bring up my daughters religiously, monsieur. I have not allowed them to take to the theatre. Ah! the rogues! if I should see them slip! I do not jest! I fortify them with sermons about honour, about morals, about virtue! Ask them! They must walk straight. They have a father. They are none of those unfortunates, who begin by having no family, and who end by marrying the public. They are Mamselle Nobody, and become Madame Everybody. Thank heaven! none of that in the Fabantou family! I mean to educate them virtuously, and that they may be honest, and that they may be genteel, and that they may believe in God's sacred name! Well, monsieur, my worthy monsieur, do you know what is going to happen to-morrow? To-morrow is the 4th of February, the fatal day, the last delay that my landlord will give me; if I do not pay him this evening, tomorrow my eldest daughter, myself, my spouse with her fever, my child with her wound, we shall all four be turned out of doors, and driven off into the street, upon the boulevard, without shelter, into the rain, upon the snow. You see, monsieur, I owe four quarters, a year! that is sixty francs."

Jondrette lied. Four quarters would have made but forty francs, and he could not have owed for four, since it was not six months since Marius had paid for two.

M. Leblanc took five francs from his pocket and threw them on the table.

Jondrette had time to mutter into the ear of his elder daughter:

"The whelp! what does he think I am going to do with his five francs? That will not pay for my chair and my window! I must make my expenses!"

Meantime, M. Leblanc had taken off a large brown overcoat, which he wore over his blue overcoat, and hung it over the back of the chair.

"Monsieur Fabantou," said he, "I have only these five francs with me; but I am going to take my daughter home, and I will return this evening; is it not this evening that you have to pay?"

Jondrette's face lighted up with a strange expression. He answered quickly:

"Yes, my noble monsieur. At eight o'clock, I must be at my landlord's."

"I will be here at six o'clock, and I will bring you the sixty francs."

"My benefactor!" cried Jondrette, distractedly.

And he added in an undertone:

"Take a good look at him, wife!"

M. Leblanc took the arm of the beautiful young girl, and turned towards the door:

"Till this evening, my friends," said he.

"Six o'clock," said Jondrette.

"Six o'clock precisely."

Just then the overcoat on the chair caught the eye of the elder daughter.

"Monsieur," said she, "you forget your coat."

Jondrette threw a crushing glance at his daughter, accompanied by a terrible shrug of the shoulders.

M. Leblanc turned and answered with a smile:

"I do not forget it, I leave it."

"O my patron," said Jondrette, "my noble benefactor, I am melting into tears! Allow me to conduct you to your carriage."

"If you go out," replied M. Leblanc, "put on this overcoat. It is really very cold."

Jondrette did not make him say it twice. He put on the brown overcoat very quickly.

And they went out all three, Jondrette preceding the two strangers.

9 (10)

PRICE OF CABS: TWO FRANCS AN HOUR

MARIUS had lost nothing of all this scene, and yet in reality he had seen nothing of it. His eyes had remained fixed upon the young girl, his heart had, so to speak, seized upon her and enveloped her entirely, from her first step into the garret. During the whole time she had been there, he had lived that life of ecstasy which suspends material perceptions and precipitates the whole soul upon a single point. He contemplated, not that girl, but that light in a satin pelisse and a velvet hat. Had the star Sirius entered the room he would not have been more dazzled.

While the young girl was opening the bundle, unfolding the clothes and the blankets, questioning the sick mother kindly and the little injured girl tenderly, he watched all her motions, he endeavoured to hear her words. He knew her eyes, her forehead, her beauty, her stature, her gait, he did not know the sound of her voice. He thought he had caught a few words of it once at the Luxembourg Gardens, but he was not absolutely sure. He would have given ten years of his life to hear it, to be able to carry a little of that music in his soul. But all was lost in the wretched displays and trumpet blasts of Jondrette. This added a real anger to the transport of Marius. He brooded her with his eyes. He could not imagine that it really was that divine creature which he saw in the midst of the misshapen beings of this monstrous den. He seemed to see a humming-bird among toads.

When he went out, he had but one thought, to follow her, not to give up her track, not to leave her without knowing where she lived, not to lose her again, at least, after having so miraculously found her! He leaped down from the bureau and took his hat. As he was putting his hand on the bolt, and was just going out, he reflected and stopped. The hall was long, the stairs steep, Jondrette a great talker, M. Leblanc doubtless had not yet got into his carriage; if he should turn round in the passage, or on the stairs, or on the doorstep, and perceive him, Marius, in that house, he would certainly be alarmed and would find means to escape him anew, and it would be all over at once. What was to be done? wait a little? but during the delay the carriage might go. Marius was perplexed. At last he took the risk and went out of his room.

There was nobody in the hall. He ran to the stairs. There was nobody on the stairs. He hurried down, and reached the boulevard in time to see a fiacre turn the corner of the Rue du Petit Banquier and return into the city.

Marius rushed in that direction. When he reached the corner of the boulevard, he saw the fiacre again going rapidly down the Rue Mouffetard;

it was already far off, there was no means of reaching it, what should he do? run after it? impossible; and then from the carriage they would certainly notice a man running at full speed in pursuit of them, and the father would recognise him. Just at this moment, marvellous and unheard-of good fortune, Marius saw a public cab passing along the boulevard, empty. There was but one course to take, to get into this cab, and follow the fiacre. That was sure, effectual, and without danger.

Marius made a sign to the driver to stop, and cried to him:

"Right away!"

Marius had no cravat, he had on his old working coat, some of the buttons of which were missing, and one of the front pleats of his shirt was torn.

The driver stopped, winked, and reached his left hand towards Marius, rubbing his forefinger gently with his thumb.

"What?" said Marius.

"Pay in advance," said the driver.

Marius remembered that he had only sixteen sous with him.

"How much?" he asked.

"Forty sous."

"I will pay when I get back."

The driver made no reply, but to whistle an air from La Palisse and whip up his horse.

Marius saw the cab move away with a bewildered air. For the want of twenty-four sous he was losing his joy, his happiness, his love! he was falling back into night! he had seen, and he was again becoming blind. He thought bitterly, and it must indeed be said, with deep regret, of the five francs he had given that very morning to that miserable girl. Had he had those five francs he would have been saved, he would have been born again, he would have come out of limbo and darkness, he would have come out of his isolation, his spleen, his bereavement; he would have again knotted the black thread of his destiny with that beautiful golden thread which had just floated before his eyes and broken off once more. He returned to the old tenement in despair.

He might have thought that M. Leblanc had promised to return in the evening, and that he had only to take better care to follow him then; but in his wrapt contemplation he had hardly understood it.

Just as he went up the stairs, he noticed on the other side of the boulevard, beside the deserted wall of the Rue de la Barrière des Gobelins, Jondrette in the "philanthropist's" overcoat, talking to one of those men of dangerous appearance, who, by common consent, are called *prowlers of the barrières;* men of equivocal faces, suspicious speech, who have an appearance of evil intentions, and who usually sleep by day, which leads us to suppose that they work by night.

These two men quietly talking while the snow was whirling about them in its fall made a picture which a policeman certainly would have observed, but which Marius hardly noticed.

Nevertheless, however mournful was the subject of his reflections, he could not help saying to himself that this prowler of the barrières with whom Jondrette was talking, resembled a certain Panchaud, alias Printanier, alias Bigrenaille, whom Courfeyrac had once pointed out to him, and who passed in the neighbourhood for a very dangerous night-wanderer. We have seen this man's name in the preceding book. This Panchaud, alias Printanier, alias Bigrenaille, figured afterwards in several criminal trials, and has since become a celebrated scoundrel.

10 (11)

OFFERS OF SERVICE BY POVERTY TO GRIEF

MARIUS mounted the stairs of the old tenement with slow steps; just as he was going into his cell, he perceived in the hall behind him the elder Jondrette girl, who was following him. This girl was odious to his sight; it was she who had his five francs, it was too late to ask her for them, the cab was there no longer, the fiacre was far away. Moreover she would not give them back to him. As to questioning her about the address of the people who had just come, that was useless; it was plain that she did not know, since the letter signed Fabantou was addressed *to the beneficent gentleman of the Church Saint Jacques du Haut Pas.*

Marius went into his room and pushed to his door behind him.

It did not close; he turned and saw a hand holding the door partly open.

"What is it?" he asked, "who is there?"

It was the Jondrette girl.

"Is it you?" said Marius almost harshly, "you again? What do you want of me?"

She seemed thoughtful and did not look at him. She had lost the assurance which she had had in the morning. She did not come in but stopped in the dusky hall, where Marius perceived her through the half-open door.

"Come now, will you answer?" said Marius. "What is it you want of me?"

She raised her mournful eyes, in which a sort of faint light seemed to shine dimly, and said to him:

"Monsieur Marius, you look sad. What is the matter with you?"

"With me?"

"Yes, you."

"There is nothing the matter with me."

"Yes!"

"No."

"I tell you there is!"

"Leave me alone!"

Marius pushed the door anew, she still held it back.

"Stop," said she, "you are wrong. Though you may not be rich, you were good this morning. Be so again now. You gave me something to eat, tell me now what ails you. You are troubled at something, that is plain. I do not want you to be troubled. What must be done for that? Can I serve you in anything? Let me. I do not ask your secrets, you need not tell them to me, but yet I may be useful. I can certainly help you, since I help my father. When it is necessary to carry letters, go into houses, inquire from door to door, find out an address, follow somebody, I do it. Now, you can certainly tell me what is the matter with you. I will go and speak to the persons; sometimes for somebody to speak to the persons is enough to help them understand things, and everything works out. Make use of me."

An idea came into Marius' mind. What branch won't we clutch when we feel ourselves falling?

He approached the girl.

"Listen," said he to her, kindly.

She interrupted him with a flash of joy in her eyes.

"Oh! yes, say *tu* with me! I like that better."

"Well," resumed he, "you brought this old gentleman here with his daughter."

"Yes."

"Do you know their address?"

"No."

"Find it for me."

The girl's eyes, which had been gloomy, had become joyful; they now became dark.

"Is that what you want?" she asked.

"Yes."

"Do you know them?"

"No."

"That is to say," said she hastily, "you do not know her, but you want to know her."

This *them* which had become *her* had an indescribable significance and bitterness.

"Well, can you do it?" said Marius.

"You shall have the beautiful young lady's address."

There was again, in these words "the beautiful young lady," an expression which made Marius uneasy. He continued:

"Well, no matter! the address of the father and daughter. Their address, yes!"

She looked steadily at him.

"What will you give me?"

"Anything you wish!"

"Anything I wish?"

"Yes."

"You shall have the address."

She looked down, and then with a hasty movement closed the door.

Marius was alone.

He dropped into a chair, with his head and both elbows on the bed swallowed up in thoughts which he could not grasp, and as if he were in a fit of vertigo. All that had taken place since morning, the appearance of the angel, her disappearance, what this poor creature had just said to him, a gleam of hope floating in an ocean of despair,—all this was confusedly crowding his brain.

Suddenly he was violently awakened from his reverie.

He heard the loud, harsh voice of Jondrette pronounce these words for him, full of the strangest interest:

"I tell you that I am sure of it, and that I recognised him!"

Of whom was Jondrette talking? he had recognised whom? M. Leblanc? the father of "his Ursula"? What! did Jondrette know him? was Marius just about to get in this sudden and unexpected way all the information the lack of which made his life obscure to himself? was he at last to know whom he loved, who that young girl was? who her father was? was the thick shadow which enveloped them to be rolled away? was the veil to be rent? Oh! heavens!

He sprang, rather than mounted, upon the bureau, and resumed his place near the little aperture in the partition.

He again saw the interior of the Jondrette den.

11 (12)

THE USE OF M. LEBLANC'S FIVE-FRANC COIN

NOTHING HAD CHANGED in the appearance of the family, except that the wife and daughters had opened the package, and put on the woollen stockings and underclothes. Two new blankets were thrown over the two beds.

Jondrette had evidently just come in. He was still out of breath from the cold outdoors. His daughters were sitting on the floor near the fireplace, the elder binding up the hand of the younger. His wife lay as if exhausted upon the pallet near the fireplace with an astonished countenance. Jondrette was walking up and down the garret with rapid strides. His eyes had an extraordinary look.

The woman, who seemed timid and stricken with stupor before her husband, ventured to say to him:

"What, really? you are sure?"

"Sure! It was eight years ago! but I recognise him! Ah! I recognise him! I recognised him immediately. What! it did not strike you?"

"No."

"And yet I told you to pay attention. But it is the same height, the same face, hardly any older; there are some men who do not grow old; I don't know how they do it; it is the same tone of voice. He is better dressed, that is all! Ah! mysterious old devil, I have got you, all right!"

He checked himself, and said to his daughters:

"You go out! It is queer that it did not strike your eye."

They got up to obey.

The mother stammered out:

"With her sore hand?"

"The air will do her good," said Jondrette. "Go along."

It was clear that this man was one of those to whom there is no reply. The two girls went out.

Just as they were passing the door, the father caught the elder by the arm, and said with a peculiar tone:

"You will be here at five o'clock precisely. Both of you. I shall need you."

Marius redoubled his attention.

Alone with his wife, Jondrette began to walk the room again, and took two or three turns in silence. Then he spent a few minutes in tucking the bottom of the woman's chemise which he wore into the waist of his trousers.

Suddenly he turned towards the woman, folded his arms, and exclaimed:

"And do you want to know something? the young lady——"

"Well, what?" said the woman, "the young lady?"

Marius could doubt no longer, it was indeed of her that they were talking. He listened with an intense anxiety. His whole life was concentrated in his ears.

But Jondrette stooped down, and whispered to his wife. Then he straightened up and finished aloud:

"It is she!"

"That girl?" said the wife.

"That girl!" said the husband.

No words could express what there was in the *that girl* of the mother. It was surprise, rage, hatred, anger, mingled and combined in a monstrous intonation. The few words that had been spoken, some name, doubtless, which her husband had whispered in her ear had been enough to rouse this huge drowsy woman and to change her repulsiveness to hideousness.

"Impossible!" she exclaimed, "when I think that my daughters go barefoot and have not a dress to put on! What! a satin pelisse, a velvet hat, buskins, and all! more than two hundred francs' worth! one would think she was a lady! no, you are mistaken! why, in the first place she was horrid, this one is not bad! she is really not bad! it cannot be she!"

"I tell you it is she. You will see."

At this absolute affirmation, the woman raised her big red and blond face and looked at the ceiling with a hideous expression. At that moment she appeared to Marius still more terrible than her husband. She was a swine with the look of a tigress.

"What!" she resumed, "this horrible beautiful young lady who looked at my girls with an appearance of pity, can she be that beggar! Oh, I would like to stamp her heart out!"

She sprang off the bed, and remained a moment standing, her hair flying, her nostrils distended, her mouth half open, her fists clenched and drawn back. Then she fell back upon the pallet. The man still walked back and forth, paying no attention to his female.

After a few moments of silence, he approached her and stopped before her, with folded arms, as before.

"And do you want to know something?"

"What?" she asked.

He answered in a quick and low voice:

"My fortune is made."

The woman stared at him with that look which means: Has the man who is talking to me gone crazy?

He continued:

"Thunder! it is a good long time now that I have been a parishioner of the die-of-hunger-if-you-have-any-fire-and-die-of-cold-if-you-have-any-bread parish! I have had misery enough! my burden and the burden of other people! It's not time for jokes anymore, it's not funny anymore, enough puns, good God! No more farces, Father Eternal! I want food for my hunger, I want drink for my thirst! to stuff! to sleep! to do nothing! I want to have my turn, I do! before I burst! I want to be a bit of a millionaire!"

He took a turn about the garret and added:

"Like other people."

"What do you mean?" asked the woman.

He shook his head, winked and lifted his voice like a street doctor about to make a demonstration:

"What do I mean? listen!"

"Hist!" muttered the woman, "not so loud! if it means business nobody must hear."

"Pshaw! who is there to hear? our neighbour? I saw him go out just now. Besides, does he hear, that big dummy? and then I tell you that I saw him go out."

Nevertheless, by a sort of instinct, Jondrette lowered his voice, not enough, however, for his words to escape Marius. A favourable circumstance, and one which enabled Marius to lose nothing of this conversation, was that the fallen snow muffled the sound of the carriages on the boulevard.

Marius heard this:

"Listen up. He is caught, the Crœsus! or he might as well be. It is already done. Everything is arranged. I have seen the men. He will come this evening at six o'clock. To bring his sixty francs, the rascal! did you see how I got that out, my sixty francs, my landlord, my 4th of February! it is not even a quarter! was that stupid! He will come then at six o'clock! our neighbour is gone to dinner then. Mother Bougon is washing dishes in the city. There is nobody in the house. Our neighbour never comes back before eleven o'clock. The girls will stand watch. You shall help us. He will comply."

"And if he should not be his own executor," asked the wife.

Jondrette made a sinister gesture and said:

"We will execute him."*

And he burst into a laugh.

It was the first time that Marius had seen him laugh. This laugh was cold and soft, and made him shudder.

Jondrette opened a closet near the chimney, took out an old cap and put it on his head after brushing it with his sleeve.

"Now," said he, "I am going out. I have still some men to see. Some good ones. You will see how it is going to work. I shall be back as soon as possible, it is a great hand to play, watch the house."

And with his two fists in the two pockets of his trousers, he stood a moment in thought, then exclaimed:

"Do you know that it is very lucky indeed that he did not recognise me? If he had been the one to recognise me he would not have come back. He would escape us! It is my beard that saved me! my romantic goatee! my pretty little romantic beard!"

And he began to laugh again.

He went to the window. The snow was still falling, and blotted out the grey sky.

"What villainous weather!" said he.

Then folding his coat:

"The skin is too large. It doesn't matter," added he, "he did devilish well to leave it for me, the old scoundrel! Without this I should not have been able to go out and the whole thing would have been spoiled! But on what do things hang!"

And pulling his cap over his eyes, he went out.

Hardly had he had time to take a few steps in the hall, when the door opened and his tawny and cunning face again appeared.

"I forgot," said he. "You will have a charcoal fire."

And he threw into his wife's apron the five-franc coin which the "philanthropist" had left him.

"A charcoal fire?" asked the woman.

"Yes."

"How many bushels?"

"Two good ones."

"That will be thirty sous. With the rest, I will buy something for dinner."

"The devil, no."

---

*A pun on the French *s'exécuter* (comply) and *exécuter* (kill).

"Why?"

"The coin of a hundred sous is not to be spent."

"Why?"

"Because I shall have something to buy."

"What?"

"Something."

"How much will you need?"

"Where is there a hardware store near here?"

"Rue Mouffetard."

"Oh! yes, at the corner of some street; I remember the shop."

"But tell me now how much you will need for what you have to buy?"

"Fifty sous or three francs."

"There won't be much left for dinner."

"Don't bother about eating to-day. There is better business."

"All right, my jewel."

At this word from his wife, Jondrette closed the door, and Marius heard his steps recede along the hall and go rapidly down the stairs.

Just then the clock of Saint Médard struck one.

12 (13)

SOLUS CUM SOLO, IN LOCO REMOTO, NON COGITABANTUR ORARE PATER NOSTER*

MARIUS, all dreamer as he was, was, as we have said, of a firm and energetic nature. His habits of solitary meditation, while developing sympathy and compassion in him, had perhaps diminished his liability to become irritated, but left intact the faculty of indignation; he had the benevolence of a brahmin and the severity of a judge; he would have pitied a toad, but he would have crushed a viper. Now it was into a viper's hole that he had just been looking; it was a nest of monsters that he had before his eyes.

"I must put my foot on these wretches," said he.

None of the enigmas which he hoped to see unriddled were yet cleared up; on the contrary, all had perhaps become still darker; he knew nothing more of the beautiful child of the Luxembourg Gardens or of the man whom he called M. Leblanc, except that Jondrette knew them. Across the

---

*Two people don't get together in an isolated place in order to say the rosary (Latin).

dark words which had been uttered, he saw distinctly but one thing, that an ambush was in the works, obscure, but terrible; that they were both running a great risk, she probably, her father certainly; that he must foil the hideous schemes of the Jondrettes and break the web of these spiders.

He looked for a moment at the female Jondrette. She had pulled an old sheet-iron furnace out of a corner and she was fumbling among the old scraps of iron.

He got down from the bureau as quietly as he could, taking care to make no noise.

In the midst of his dread at what was in preparation, and the horror with which the Jondrettes had inspired him, he felt a sort of joy at the idea that it would perhaps be given to him to render so great a service to her whom he loved.

But what was he to do? warn the persons threatened? where should he find them? He did not know their address. They had reappeared to his eyes for an instant, then they had again plunged into the boundless depths of Paris. Wait at the door for M. Leblanc at six o'clock in the evening, the time when he would arrive, and warn him of the plot? But Jondrette and his men would see him watching, the place was solitary, they would be stronger than he, they would find means to seize him or get him out of the way, and he whom Marius wished to save would be lost. One o'clock had just struck, the ambush was to be carried out at six. Marius had five hours before him.

There was but one thing to be done.

He put on his presentable coat, tied a cravat about his neck, took his hat, and went out, without making any more noise than if he had been walking barefooted upon moss.

Besides the Jondrette woman was still fumbling with her old scrap iron.

Once out of the house, he went to the Rue du Petit Banquier.

He was about midway of that street near a very low wall which he could have stepped over in some places and which bordered a broad field, he was walking slowly, absorbed in his thoughts as he was, and the snow deafened his steps; all at once he heard voices talking very near him. He turned his head, the street was empty, there was nobody in it, it was broad daylight, and yet he heard voices distinctly.

It occurred to him to look over this wall.

There were in fact two men there with their backs to the wall, seated in the snow, and talking in a low tone.

These two forms were unknown to him, one was a bearded man in a smock, and the other a long-haired man in tatters. The bearded man had on a Greek cap, the other was bare-headed, and there was snow in his hair.

By bending his head over above them, Marius could hear.

The long-haired one jogged the other with his elbow, and said:

"With Patron-Minette, it can't fail."

"Do you think so?" said the bearded one; and the long-haired one replied:

"It will be a *fafiot* of five hundred *balles* for each of us, and the worst that can happen: five years, six years, ten years at most!"*

The other answered hesitatingly, shivering under his Greek cap:

"Yes, that's real money. We can't pass it up."

"I tell you that the deal can't fail," replied the long-haired one. "We'll fix Old What's-his-name's waggon for him."

Then they began to talk about a melodrama which they had seen the evening before at La Gaîté.

Marius went on his way.

It seemed to him that the obscure words of these men, so strangely hidden behind that wall, and crouching down in the snow, were not perhaps without some connection with Jondrette's terrible projects. That must be *the deal*.

He went towards the Faubourg Saint Marceau, and asked at the first shop in his way where he could find a chief of police.

Number 14, Rue de Pontoise, was pointed out to him.

Marius went thither.

Passing a baker's shop, he bought a two-sou loaf and ate it, foreseeing that he would have no dinner.

On his way he rendered to Providence its due. He thought that if he had not given his five francs to the Jondrette girl in the morning, he would have followed M. Leblanc's fiacre, and consequently known nothing of this, so that there would have been no obstacle to the ambush of the Jondrettes, and M. Leblanc would have been lost, and doubtless his daughter with him.

13 (14)

IN WHICH A POLICE OFFICER GIVES A LAWYER TWO *COUPS DE POIGN*

ON REACHING Number 14, Rue de Pontoise, he went upstairs and asked for the chief of police.

"The chief of police is not in," said one of the office boys; "but there is an inspector who answers for him. Would you like to speak to him? is it urgent?"

---

*Thénardier, who plans to blackmail Jean Valjean for 200,000 francs, apparently plans to try to get away with giving only 500 to each of his accomplices.

"Yes," said Marius.

The office boy introduced him into the chief's office. A man of tall stature was standing there, behind a railing, in front of a stove, and holding up with both hands the flaps of a huge overcoat with three layered flaps. He had a square face, a thin and firm mouth, very fierce, bushy, greyish whiskers, and an eye that would turn your pockets inside out. You might have said of this eye, not that it penetrated, but that it ransacked.

This man's appearance was not much less ferocious or formidable than Jondrette's; it is sometimes no less startling to meet the dog than the wolf.

"What do you wish?" said he to Marius, without adding monsieur.

"The chief of police?"

"He is absent. I answer for him."

"It is a very secret affair."

"Speak, then."

"And very urgent."

"Then speak quickly."

This man, calm and abrupt, was at the same time alarming and reassuring. He inspired fear and confidence. Marius related his adventure.—That a person whom he only knew by sight was to be drawn into an ambush that very evening; that occupying the room next the place, he, Marius Pontmercy, attorney, had heard the whole plot through the partition; that the scoundrel who had contrived the plot was named Jondrette; that he had accomplices, probably prowlers of the barrières, among others a certain Panchaud, alias Printanier, alias Bigrenaille; that Jondrette's daughters would stand watch; that there was no means of warning the threatened man, as not even his name was known; and finally, that all this was to be done at six o'clock that evening, at the most desolate spot on the Boulevard de l'Hôpital, in the house numbered 50–52.

At that number the inspector raised his head, and said coolly:

"It is then in the room at the end of the hall?"

"Exactly," said Marius, and he added, "Do you know that house?"

The inspector remained silent a moment, then answered, warming the heel of his boot at the door of the stove:

"It seems so."

He continued between his teeth, speaking less to Marius than to his cravat.

"There ought to be a dash of Patron-Minette in this."

That word struck Marius.

"Patron-Minette," said he. "Indeed, I heard that word pronounced."

And he related to the inspector the dialogue between the long-haired man and the bearded man in the snow behind the wall on the Rue du Petit Banquier.

The inspector muttered:

"The long-haired one must be Brujon, and the bearded one must be Demi-Liard, alias Deux-Milliards."

He had dropped his eyes again, and was considering.

"As to the Father What's-his-name, I have a suspicion of who he is.

There, I have burnt my coat. They always make too much fire in these cursed stoves. Number 50–52. Old Gorbeau property."

Then he looked at Marius:

"You have seen only this bearded man and this long-haired man?"

"And Panchaud."

"You did not see a sort of little devilish rat prowling about there?"

"No."

"Nor a great, big, clumsy heap, like the elephant in the Jardin des Plantes?"

"No."

"Nor a villain who has the appearance of an old red cue?"

"No."

"As to the fourth nobody sees him, not even his helpers, clerks, and agents. It is not very surprising that you did not see him."

"No. What are all these beings?" inquired Marius.

The inspector answered:

"And then it is not their hour."

He relapsed into silence, then resumed:

"No. 50–52. I know the shanty. Impossible to hide ourselves in the interior without the artists perceiving us, then they would leave and break up the play. They are so modest! the public bothers them. No way, no way. I want to hear them sing, and make them dance."

This monologue finished, he turned towards Marius and asked him looking steadily at him:

"Will you be afraid?"

"Of what?" said Marius.

"Of these men?"

"No more than of you!" replied Marius rudely, who began to notice that this police spy had not yet called him monsieur.

The inspector looked at Marius still more steadily and continued with a sententious solemnity:

"You speak now like a brave man and an honest man. Courage does not fear crime, and honesty does not fear authority."

Marius interrupted him:

"That is well enough; but what are you going to do?"

The inspector merely answered:

"The lodgers in that house have latch-keys to get in with at night. You must have one?"

"Yes," said Marius.

"Do you have it with you?"

"Yes."

"Give it to me," said the inspector.

Marius took his key from his waistcoat, handed it to the inspector, and added:

"If you trust me you will come in force."

The inspector threw a glance upon Marius such as Voltaire would have thrown upon a provincial academician who had proposed a rhyme to him;

with a single movement he plunged both his hands, which were enormous, into the two immense pockets of his overcoat, and took out two small steel pistols, of the kind called fisticuffs. He presented them to Marius, saying hastily and abruptly:

"Take these. Go back home. Hide yourself in your room; let them think you have gone out. They are loaded. Each with two balls. You will watch; there is a hole in the wall, as you have told me. The men will come. Let them go on a little. When you deem the affair at a point, and when it is time to stop it, you will fire off a pistol. Not too soon. The rest is my affair. A pistol shot in the air, into the ceiling, no matter where. Above all, not too soon. Wait till they start committing the felony; you are a lawyer, you know what that is."

Marius took the pistols and put them in the side pocket of his coat.

"They make a bulge that way, they show," said the inspector. "Put them in your vest pockets rather."

Marius hid the pistols in his vest pockets.

"Now," pursued the inspector, "there is not a minute to be lost by any-body. What time is it? Half past two. It is at seven?"

"Six o'clock," said Marius.

"I have time enough," continued the inspector, "but I have only enough. Forget nothing of what I have told you. Bang. A pistol shot."

"Be assured," answered Marius.

And as Marius placed his hand on the latch of the door to go out, the inspector called to him:

"By the way, if you need me between now and then, come or send here. You will ask for Inspector Javert."

14 (15)

JONDRETTE MAKES HIS PURCHASE

ON THE WAY HOME, Marius had in fact seen Jondrette passing along the Rue Mouffetard, and followed him.

Jondrette went straight on without suspecting that there was now an eye fixed upon him.

He left the Rue Mouffetard, and Marius saw him go into one of the most wretched places on the Rue Gracieuse; he stayed there about a quarter of an hour, and then returned to the Rue Mouffetard. He stopped at a hard-ware store, which there was in those times at the corner of the Rue Pierre Lombard, and, a few minutes afterwards, Marius saw him come out of the shop holding in his hand a large cold chisel with a pine handle which he concealed under his coat. At the upper end of the Rue de Petit Gentilly, he turned to the left and walked rapidly to the Rue du Petit Banquier. Night was falling; the snow which had ceased to fall for a moment was beginning again; Marius hid just at the corner of the Rue du Petit Banquier, which was deserted, as usual, and did not follow Jondrette further. It was fortunate that he did, for, on reaching the low wall where Marius had heard the long-haired man and the bearded man talking, Jondrette turned around, made sure that nobody was following him or saw him, then stepped over the wall, and disappeared.

The grounds which this wall bounded communicated with the rear court of an old livery stable-keeper of bad repute, who had failed, but who had still a few old vehicles under his sheds.

Marius thought it best to take advantage of Jondrette's absence to get home; besides it was getting late; every evening, Ma'am Burgon, on going out to wash her dishes in the city, was in the habit of closing the house door, which was always locked at dusk; Marius had given his key to the inspector of police; it was important, therefore, that he should make haste.

Evening had come; night had almost closed in; there was now but one spot in the horizon or in the whole sky which was lighted by the sun; that was the moon.

She was rising red behind the low dome of La Salpêtrière.

Marius returned to No. 50–52 with rapid strides. The door was still open, when he arrived. He ascended the stairs on tiptoe, and glided along the wall of the hall as far as his room. This hall, it will be remembered, was lined on both sides by garrets, which were all at that time empty and to let. Ma'am Burgon usually left the doors open. As he passed by one of these doors, Marius thought he perceived in the unoccupied cell four motionless heads, which were made dimly visible by a remnant of daylight falling through the little window. Marius, not wishing to be seen, did not endeavour to see. He succeeded in getting into his room without being perceived and without any noise. It was time. A moment afterwards, he heard Ma'am Burgon going out and closing the door of the house.

15 (16)

IN WHICH WILL BE FOUND THE SONG SET TO AN ENGLISH AIR IN FASHION IN 1832

MARIUS sat down on his bed. It might have been half-past five o'clock. A half-hour only separated him from what was to come. He heard his arteries beat as one hears the ticking of a watch in the dark. He thought of this double march that was going on that moment in the darkness, crime advancing on the one hand, justice coming on the other. He was not afraid, but he could not think without a sort of shudder of the things which were so soon to take place. To him, as to all those whom some surprising adventure has suddenly befallen, this whole day seemed but a dream; and, to assure himself that he was not the prey of a nightmare, he had to feel the chill of the two steel pistols in his vest pockets.

It was not now snowing; the moon, growing brighter and brighter, was getting clear of the haze, and its light, mingled with the white reflection from the fallen snow, gave the room a twilight appearance.

There was a light in the Jondrette den. Marius saw the hole in the partition shine with a red gleam which appeared to him bloody.

He was sure that this gleam could hardly be produced by a candle. However, there was no movement in their room, nobody was stirring there, nobody spoke, not a breath, the stillness was icy and deep, and save for that light he could have believed that he was beside a sepulchre.

Marius took his boots off softly, and pushed them under his bed.

Some minutes passed. Marius heard the lower door turn on its hinges; a heavy and rapid step ascended the stairs and passed along the corridor, the latch of the garret was noisily lifted; Jondrette came in.

Several voices were heard immediately. The whole family was in the garret. Only they kept silence in the absence of the master, like the cubs in the absence of the wolf.

"It is me," said he.

"Good evening, *pèremuche*," squeaked the daughters.

"Well!" said the mother.

"Everything's going like a charm," answered Jondrette, "but my feet are as cold as a dog's. Good, that is right, you are dressed up. You must be able to inspire confidence."

"All ready to go out."

"You will forget nothing of what I told you! you will do the whole of it?"

"Rest assured about that."

"Because—" said Jondrette. And he did not finish his sentence. Marius heard him put something heavy on the table, probably the chisel which he had bought.

"Ah, ha!" said Jondrette, "have you been eating here?"

"Yes," said the mother, "I have had three big potatoes and some salt. I took advantage of the fire to cook them."

"Well," replied Jondrette, "to-morrow I will take you to dine with me. There will be a duck and the accompaniments. You shall dine like Charles X; everything is going well?"

Then he added, lowering his voice:

"The mouse-trap is open. The cats are ready."

He lowered his voice still more, and said:

"Put that into the fire."

Marius heard a sound of charcoal, as if somebody were striking it with pincers or some iron tool, and Jondrette continued:

"Have you greased the hinges of the door, so that they shall not make any noise?"

"Yes," answered the mother.

"What time is it?"

"Six o'clock, almost. The half has just struck on Saint Médard."

"The devil!" said Jondrette, "the girls must go and stand watch. Come here, you children, and listen to me."

There was a whispering.

Jondrette's voice rose again:

"Has Burgon gone out?"

"Yes," said the mother.

"Are you sure there is nobody at home in our neighbour's room?"

"He has not been back to-day, and you know that it is his dinner time."

"You are sure?"

"Sure."

"It is all the same," replied Jondrette; "there is no harm in going to see whether he is at home. Daughter, take the candle and go."

Marius dropped on his hands and knees, and crept noiselessly under the bed.

Hardly had he concealed himself, when he perceived a light through the cracks of his door.

"P'pa," cried a voice, "he has gone out."

He recognised the voice of the elder girl.

"Have you gone in?" asked the father.

"No," answered the girl; "but as his key is in the door, he has gone out."

The father cried:

"Go in just the same."

The door opened, and Marius saw the tall girl come in with a candle. She had the same appearance as in the morning, except that she was still more horrible in this light.

She walked straight towards the bed. Marius had a moment of

inexpressible anxiety, but there was a mirror nailed on the wall near the bed; it was to that she was going. She stretched up on tiptoe and looked at herself in it. A sound of old iron rattling was heard in the next room.

She smoothed her hair with the palm of her hand, and smiled at the mirror, singing the while in her broken sepulchral voice:

> *Nos amours ont duré tout une semaine,*
> *Mais que du bonheur les instants sont courts!*
> *S'adorer huit jours,'était bien la peine!*
> *Le temps des amours devrait durer toujours!*
> *Devrait durer toujours! devrait durer toujours!*[6]

Meanwhile Marius was trembling. It seemed impossible to him that she should not hear his breathing.

She went to the window and looked out, speaking aloud in her half-crazy way.

"How ugly Paris is when he puts a white shirt on!" said she.

She returned to the mirror and renewed her grimaces, taking alternately front and the three-quarter views of herself.

"Well," cried her father, "what are you doing now?"

"I am looking under the bed and the furniture," answered she, continuing to arrange her hair; "there is nobody here."

"Booby!" howled the father. "Here immediately, and let us lose no time."

"I am coming! I am coming!" said she. "One has no time for anything in their shanty."

She hummed:

> *Vous me quittez pour aller à la gloire,*
> *Mon triste cœur suivra partout vos pas.*

She cast a last glance at the mirror, and went out, shutting the door after her.

A moment afterwards, Marius heard the sound of the bare feet of the two young girls in the passage, and the voice of Jondrette crying to them.

"Pay attention, now! one towards the barrière, the other at the corner of the Rue du Petit Banquier. Don't lose sight of the house door a minute, and if you see the least thing, here immediately! tumble along! You have a key to come in with."

The elder daughter muttered:

"To stand sentry barefoot in the snow!"

"To-morrow you shall have boots of scarab colour silk!" said the father.

They went down the stairs, and, a few seconds afterwards, the sound of the lower door shutting announced that they had gone out.

There were now in the house only Marius and the Jondrettes, and probably also the mysterious beings of whom Marius had caught a glimpse in the twilight behind the door of the untenanted garret.

16 (17)

USE OF MARIUS' FIVE-FRANC COIN

Marius judged that the time had come to resume his place at his observatory. In a twinkling, and with the agility of his age, he was at the hole in the partition.

He looked in.

The interior of the Jondrette apartment presented a singular appearance, and Marius found the explanation of the strange light which he had noticed. A candle was burning in a verdigrised candlestick, but it was not that which really lighted the room. The entire den was, as it were, illuminated by the reflection of a large sheet iron furnace in the fireplace, which was filled with lighted charcoal. The fire which the female Jondrette had made ready in the daytime. The charcoal was burning and the furnace was red hot, a blue flame danced over it and helped to show the form of the chisel bought by Jondrette in the Rue Pierre Lombard, which was growing ruddy among the coals. In a corner near the door, and arranged as if for anticipated use, were two heaps which appeared to be, one a heap of old iron, the other a heap of ropes. All this would have made one, who had known nothing of what was going forward, waver between a very sinister idea and a very simple idea. The room thus lighted up seemed rather a smithy than a mouth of hell; but Jondrette, in that glare, had rather the appearance of a demon than of a blacksmith.

The heat of the glowing coals was such that the candle upon the table melted on the side towards the furnace and was burning fastest on that side. An old copper dark lantern, worthy of Diogenes turned Cartouche, stood upon the mantel.

The furnace, which was set into the fireplace, beside the almost extinguished embers, sent its smoke into the flue of the chimney and exhaled no odour.

The moon, shining through the four panes of the window, threw its whiteness into the ruddy and flaming garret; and to Marius' poetic mind, a dreamer even in the moment of action, it was like a thought of heaven mingled with the shapeless nightmares of earth.

A breath of air, coming through the broken pane, helped to dissipate the charcoal odour and to conceal the furnace.

The Jondrette lair was, if the reader remembers what we have said of the Gorbeau house, admirably chosen for the theatre of a deed of darkness and violence, and for the concealment of a crime. It was the most retired room of the most isolated house of the most solitary boulevard in Paris. If ambush had not existed, it would have been invented there.

The whole depth of a house and a multitude of untenanted rooms separated this hole from the boulevard and its only window opened upon
waste fields inclosed with walls and palisade fences.

Jondrette had lighted his pipe, sat down on the dismantled chair, and
was smoking. His wife was speaking to him in a low tone.

Suddenly Jondrette raised his voice:

"By the way, now, I think of it. In such weather as this he will come in a
fiacre. Light the lantern, take it, and go down. You will stay there behind
the lower door. The moment you hear the carriage stop, you will open
immediately, he will come up, you will light him up the stairs and above
the hall, and when he comes in here, you will go down again immediately,
pay the driver, and send the fiacre away."

"And the money?" asked the woman.

Jondrette fumbled in his trousers, and handed her five francs.

"What is that?" she exclaimed.

Jondrette answered with dignity:——

"It is the monarch which our neighbour gave this morning."

And he added:——

"Do you know? we must have two chairs here."

"What for?"

"To sit in."

Marius felt a shiver run down his back on hearing the woman make this
quiet reply:——

"Pardieu! I will get our neighbour's."

And with rapid movement she opened the door of the den, and went
out into the hall.

Marius physically had not the time to get down from the bureau, and
go and hide himself under the bed.

"Take the candle," cried Jondrette.

"No," said she, "that would bother me; I have two chairs to bring. It is
moonlight."

Marius heard the heavy hand of mother Jondrette groping after his key
in the dark. The door opened. He stood nailed to his place by apprehension and stupor.

The woman came in.

The gable window let in a ray of moonlight, between two great sheets
of shadow. One of these sheets of shadow entirely covered the wall against
which Marius was leaning, so as to conceal him.

Mother Jondrette raised her eyes, did not see Marius, took the two
chairs, the only chairs which Marius had, and went out, slamming the door
noisily behind her.

She went back into the den.

"Here are the two chairs."

"And here is the lantern," said the husband. "Go down quick."

She hastily obeyed, and Jondrette was left alone.

He arranged the two chairs on the two sides of the table, turned the chisel
over in the fire, put an old screen in front of the fireplace, which concealed

the furnace, then went to the corner where the heap of ropes was, and stooped down, as if to examine something. Marius then perceived that what he had taken for a shapeless heap, was a rope ladder, very well made, with wooden rounds, and two large hooks to hang it by.

This ladder and a few big tools, actual masses of iron, which were thrown upon the pile of old iron heaped up behind the door, were not in the Jondrette den in the morning, and had evidently been brought there in the afternoon, during Marius' absence.

"Those are metalworkers' tools," thought Marius.

Had Marius been a little better informed in this line, he would have recognised, in what he took for metalworkers' tools, certain instruments capable of picking a lock or forcing a door and others capable of cutting or hacking,—the two families of sinister tools, which thieves call jimmies and bolt-cutters.

The fireplace and the table, with the two chairs, were exactly opposite Marius. The furnace was hidden; the room was now lighted only by the candle; the least thing upon the table or the mantel made a great shadow. A broken water-pitcher masked the half of one wall. There was in the room a calm which was inexpressibly hideous and threatening. The approach of some appalling thing could be felt.

Jondrette had let his pipe go out—a sure sign that he was intensely absorbed—and had come back and sat down. The candle made the savage ends and corners of his face stand out prominently. There were contractions of his brows, and abrupt openings of his right hand, as if he were replying to the last counsels of a dark interior monologue. In one of these obscure replies which he was making to himself, he drew the table drawer out quickly towards him, took out a long carving knife which was hidden there, and tried its edge on his nail. This done, he put the knife back into the drawer, and shut it.

Marius, for his part, grasped the pistol on his right side, pulled it out, and cocked it.

The pistol in cocking gave a little, clear, sharp sound.

Jondrette started, and half rose from his chair.

"Who is there?" cried he.

Marius held his breath; Jondrette listened a moment, then began to laugh, saying:—

"What a fool I am! It is the partition cracking."

Marius kept the pistol in his hand.

MARIUS' TWO CHAIRS FACE EACH OTHER

JUST THEN the distant and melancholy vibration of a bell shook the windows. Six o'clock struck on Saint Médard.

Jondrette marked each stroke with a nod of his head. At the sixth stroke, he snuffed the candle with his fingers.

Then he began to walk about the room, listened in the hall, walked, listened again: "Provided he comes!" muttered he; then he returned to his chair.

He had hardly sat down when the door opened.

The mother Jondrette had opened it, and stood in the hall making a horrible, amiable grimace, which was lighted up from beneath by one of the holes of the dark lantern.

"Come in," said she.

"Come in, my benefactor," repeated Jondrette, rising precipitately.

Monsieur Leblanc appeared.

He had an air of serenity which made him singularly venerable.

He laid four louis upon the table.

"Monsieur Fabantou," said he, "that is for your rent and your pressing wants. We will see about the rest."

"God reward you, my generous benefactor!" said Jondrette, and rapidly approaching his wife:

"Send away the fiacre!"

She slipped away, while her husband was lavishing bows and offering a chair to Monsieur Leblanc. A moment afterwards she came back and whispered in his ear:

"It is done."

The snow which had been falling ever since morning, was so deep that they had not heard the fiacre arrive, and did not hear it go away.

Meanwhile Monsieur Leblanc had taken a seat.

Jondrette had taken possession of the other chair opposite Monsieur Leblanc.

Now, to form an idea of the scene which follows, let the reader call to mind the chilly night, the solitudes of La Salpêtrière covered with snow, and white in the moonlight, like immense shrouds, the flickering light of the street lamps here and there reddening these tragic boulevards and the long rows of black elms, not a passer-by perhaps within a mile around, the Gorbeau tenement at its deepest degree of silence, horror, and night, in that tenement, in the midst of these solitudes, in the midst of this darkness, the vast Jondrette garret lighted by a candle, and in this den two men seated at a table, Monsieur Leblanc tranquil, Jondrette smiling and terrible, his wife, the she-wolf, in a corner, and, behind the partition, Marius, invisible, alert, losing no word, missing no movement, his eye on the watch, the pistol in his grasp.

Marius, moreover, was experiencing nothing but an emotion of horror, not fear. He clasped the butt of the pistol, and felt reassured. "I shall stop this wretch when I please," thought he.

He felt that the police was somewhere near by in ambush, awaiting the signal agreed upon, and all ready to stretch out its arm.

He hoped, moreover, that from this terrible meeting between Jondrette and Monsieur Leblanc some light would be thrown upon all that he was interested to know.

18 (19)

THE DISTRACTIONS OF DARK CORNERS

NO SOONER was Monsieur Leblanc seated than he turned his eyes towards the empty pallets.

"How is the poor little injured girl?" he inquired.

"Badly," answered Jondrette with a doleful yet grateful smile, "very badly, my worthy monsieur. Her eldest sister has taken her to the Bourbe to have her arm dressed. You will see them, they will be back directly."

"Madame Fabantou appears to me much better?" resumed Monsieur Leblanc, casting his eyes upon the grotesque accoutrement of the female Jondrette, who, standing between him and the door, as if she were already guarding the exit, was looking at him in a threatening and almost a defiant posture.

"She is dying," said Jondrette. "But you see, monsieur! she has so much courage, that woman! She is not a woman, she is an ox."

The woman, touched by the compliment, retorted with the smirk of a flattered monster:

"You are always too kind to me, Monsieur Jondrette."

"Jondrette!" said M. Leblanc, "I thought that your name was Fabantou?"

"Fabantou or Jondrette!" replied the husband hastily. "Stage name as an artist!"

And, directing a shrug of the shoulders towards his wife, which M. Leblanc did not see, he continued with an emphatic and caressing tone of voice:

"Ah! how long we have always got along together, this poor dear and I!

What would be left to us, if it were not for that? We are so unfortunate, my respected monsieur! We have arms, no work! We have courage, no employment! I do not know how the government arranges it, but, upon my word of honour, I am no jacobin, monsieur, I am no brawler, I wish them no harm, but if I were the ministers, upon my most sacred word, it would go differently. Now, for example, I wanted to have my girls learn the trade of making cardboard boxes. You will say: What! a trade? Yes! a trade! a simple trade! a living! What a fall, my benefactor! What a degradation, when one has been what we were! Alas! we have nothing left from our days of prosperity! Nothing but one single thing, a painting, to which I cling, but yet which I shall have to part with, for we must live! item, we must live!"

While Jondrette was talking, with an apparent disorder which detracted nothing from the crafty and cunning expression of his physiognomy, Marius raised his eyes, and perceived at the back of the room somebody whom he had not before seen. A man had come in so noiselessly that nobody had heard the door turn on its hinges. This man had a knit woollen waistcoat of violet colour, old, worn-out, stained, cut, and showing gaps at all its folds, full trousers of cotton velvet, socks on his feet, no shirt, his neck bare, his arms bare and tattooed, and his face stained black. He sat down in silence and with folded arms on the nearest bed, and as he kept behind the woman, he was only dimly visible.

That kind of magnetic instinct which warns the eye made M. Leblanc turn almost at the same time with Marius. He could not help a movement of surprise, which did not escape Jondrette:

"Ah! I see!" exclaimed Jondrette, buttoning up his coat with a complacent air, "you are looking at your overcoat. It's a fit! my faith, it's a fit!"

"Who is that man?" said M. Leblanc.

"That man?" said Jondrette, "that is a neighbour. Pay no attention to him."

The neighbour had a singular appearance. However, factories of chemical products abound in Faubourg Saint Marceau. Many machinists might have their faces blacked. The whole person of M. Leblanc, moreover, breathed a candid and intrepid confidence. He resumed:

"Pardon me; what were you saying to me, Monsieur Fabantou?"

"I was telling you, monsieur and dear patron," replied Jondrette, leaning his elbows on the table, and gazing at M. Leblanc with fixed and tender eyes, similar to the eyes of a boa constrictor, "I was telling you that I had a picture to sell."

A slight noise was made at the door. A second man entered, and sat down on the bed behind the female Jondrette. He had his arms bare, like the first, and a mask of ink or of soot.

Although this man had, literally, slipped into the room, he could not prevent M. Leblanc from perceiving him.

"Do not mind them," said Jondrette. "They are people of the house. I was telling you, then, that I have a valuable painting left. Here, monsieur, look."

He got up, went to the wall, at the foot of which stood the panel of which we have spoken, and turned it round, still leaving it resting against the wall. It was something, in fact, that resembled a picture, and which the candle scarcely revealed. Marius could make nothing out of it, Jondrette being between him and the picture; he merely caught a glimpse of a coarse daub, with a sort of principal personage, coloured in the crude and glaring style of strolling panoramas and paintings upon screens.

"What is that?" asked M. Leblanc.

Jondrette exclaimed:

"A painting by a master; a picture of great price, my benefactor! I cling to it as to my two daughters, it calls up memories to me! but I have told you, and I cannot unsay it, I am so unfortunate that I would part with it."

Whether by chance, or whether there was some beginning of distrust, while examining the picture, M. Leblanc glanced towards the back of the room. There were now four men there, three seated on the bed, one standing near the door-casing; all four bare-armed, motionless, and with blackened faces. One of those who were on the bed was leaning against the wall, with his eyes closed, and one would have said he was asleep. This one was old; his white hair over his black face was horrible. The two others appeared young; one was bearded, the other had long hair. None of them had shoes on; those who did not have socks were barefooted.

Jondrette noticed that M. Leblanc's eye was fixed upon these men.

"They are friends. They live near by," said he. "They are dark because they work in charcoal. They are chimney doctors.* Do not occupy your mind with them, my benefactor, but buy my picture. Take pity on my misery. I shall not sell it to you at a high price. How much do you estimate it worth?"

"But," said M. Leblanc, looking Jondrette full in the face and like a man who puts himself on his guard, "this is some tavern sign, it is worth about three francs."

Jondrette answered calmly:

"Have you your wallet here? I will be satisfied with a thousand crowns."

M. Leblanc rose to his feet, placed his back to the wall, and ran his eye rapidly over the room. He had Jondrette at his left on the side towards the window, and his wife and the four men at his right on the side towards the door. The four men did not stir, and had not even the appearance of seeing him; Jondrette had begun again to talk in a plaintive key, with his eyes so wild and his tones so mournful that M. Leblanc might have thought that he had before his eyes nothing more nor less than a man gone crazy from misery.

"If you do not buy my picture, dear benefactor," said Jondrette, "I am without resources, I have only to throw myself into the river. When I think that I wanted to have my two girls learn to work on cardboard demi-fine,

---

Fumistes also means cruel tricksters.

cardboard work for gift-boxes. Well! they must have a table with a board at the bottom so that the glasses shall not fall on the ground, they must have a furnace made on purpose, a pot with three compartments for the different degrees of strength which the paste must have according to whether it is used for wood, for paper, or for cloth, a knife to cut the paste-board, a gauge to adjust it, a hammer for the stamps, pincers, the devil, how do I know what else? and all this to earn four sous a day! and work four-teen hours! and every box passes through the girl's hands thirteen times! and wetting the paper! and to stain nothing! and to keep the paste warm! the devil! I tell you! four sous a day! how do you think one can live?"

While speaking Jondrette did not look at M. Leblanc, who was watch-ing him. M. Leblanc's eye was fixed upon Jondrette, and Jondrette's eye upon the door, Marius' breathless attention went from one to the other. M. Leblanc appeared to ask himself, "Is this an idiot?" Jondrette repeated two or three times with all sorts of varied inflections in the drawling and begging style: "I can only throw myself into the river! I went down three steps for that the other day by the side of the bridge of Austerlitz!"

Suddenly his dull eye lighted up with a hideous glare, this little man straightened up and became horrifying, he took a step towards M. Leblanc and cried to him in a voice of thunder:

"But all this is not the question! do you know me?"

19 (20)

THE AMBUSH

THE DOOR of the garret had been suddenly flung open, disclosing three men in blue smocks with black paper masks. The first was spare and had a long iron-bound cudgel; the second, who was a sort of colossus, held by the middle of the handle, with the blade down, a butcher's pole-axe. The third, a broad-shouldered man, not so thin as the first, nor so heavy as the sec-ond, held in his clenched fist an enormous key stolen from some prison door.

It appeared that it was the arrival of these men for which Jondrette was waiting. A rapid dialogue commenced between him and the man with the cudgel, the spare man.

"Is everything ready?" said Jondrette.

"Yes," answered the spare man.

"Where is Montparnasse then?"

"The pretty boy stopped to chat with your daughter."

"Which one?"

"The elder."

"Is there a fiacre below?"

"Yes."

"The waggon is ready?"

"Ready."

"With two good horses?"

"Excellent."

"It is waiting where I said it should wait?"

"Yes."

"Good," said Jondrette.

M. Leblanc was very pale. He looked over everything in the room about him like a man who understands into what he has fallen, and his head, directed in turn towards all the heads which surrounded him, moved on his neck with an attentive and astonished slowness, but there was nothing in his manner which resembled fear. He had made an extemporised intrenchment of the table; and this man who, the moment before, had the appearance only of a good old man, had suddenly become a sort of athlete, and placed his powerful fist upon the back of his chair with a surprising and formidable gesture.

This old man, so firm and so brave before so great a peril, seemed to be one of those natures who are courageous as they are good, simply and naturally. The father of a woman that we love is never a stranger to us. Marius felt proud of this unknown man.

Three of the men of whom Jondrette had said: they are *chimney doctors*, had taken from the heap of old iron, one a large pair of shears, another a steelyard tongs, the third a hammer, and placed themselves before the door without saying a word. The old man was still on the bed, and had merely opened his eyes. The woman Jondrette was sitting beside him.

Marius thought that in a few seconds more the time would come to interfere, and he raised his right hand towards the ceiling, in the direction of the hall, ready to let off his pistol-shot.

Jondrette, after his colloquy with the man who had the cudgel, turned again towards M. Leblanc and repeated his question, accompanying it with that low, smothered, and terrible laugh of his:

"You do not recognise me, then?"

M. Leblanc looked him in the face, and answered:

"No."

Then Jondrette came up to the table. He leaned forward over the candle, folding his arms, and pushing his angular and ferocious jaws up towards the calm face of M. Leblanc, as nearly as he could without forcing him to draw back, and in that posture, like a wild beast just about to bite, he cried:

"My name is not Fabantou, my name is not Jondrette, my name is Thénardier! I am the innkeeper of Montfermeil! do you understand me? Thénardier! now do you know me?"

An imperceptible flush passed over M. Leblanc's forehead, and he answered without a tremor or elevation of voice, and with his usual placidness:

"No more than before."[7]

Marius did not hear this answer. Could anybody have seen him at that moment in that darkness, he would have seen that he was haggard, astounded, and thunderstruck. When Jondrette had said: *My name is Thénardier,* Marius had trembled in every limb, and supported himself against the wall as if he had felt the chill of a swordblade through his heart. Then his right arm, which was just ready to fire the signal shot, dropped slowly down, and at the moment that Jondrette had repeated: *Do you understand me, Thénardier?* Marius' nerveless fingers had almost dropped the pistol. Jondrette, in unveiling who he was, had not moved M. Leblanc, but he had completely unnerved Marius. That name of Thénardier, which M. Leblanc did not seem to know, Marius knew. Remember what that name was to him! that name he had worn on his heart, written in his father's will! he carried it in the innermost place of his thoughts, in the holiest spot of his memory, in that sacred command: "A man named Thénardier saved my life. If my son should meet him, he will do him all the good he can." That name, we remember, was one of the devotions of his soul; he mingled it with the name of his father in his worship. What! here was Thénardier, here was that Thénardier, here was that innkeeper of Montfermeil, for whom he had so long and so vainly sought! He had found him at last, and how? this saviour of his father was a bandit! this man, to whom he, Marius, burned to devote himself, was a monster! this deliverer of Colonel Pontmercy was in the actual commission of a crime, the shape of which Marius did not yet see very distinctly, but which looked like an assassination! and upon whom, Great God! what a fatality! what a bitter mockery of Fate! His father from the depths of his coffin commanded him to do all the good he could to Thénardier; for four years Marius had had no other thought than to acquit this debt of his father, and the moment that he was about to cause a brigand to be seized by justice, in the midst of a crime, destiny called to him: that is Thénardier! his father's life, saved in a storm of grapeshot upon the heroic field of Waterloo, he was at last about to reward this man for, and to reward him with the scaffold! He had resolved, if ever he found this Thénardier, to accost him in no other wise than by throwing himself at his feet, and now he found him indeed, but to deliver him to the executioner! his father said to him: Aid Thénardier! and he was answering that adored and holy voice by crushing Thénardier! presenting as a spectacle to his father in his tomb, the man who had snatched him from death at the peril of his life, executed in the Place St. Jacques by the act of his son, this Marius to whom he had bequeathed this man! And what a mockery to have worn so long upon his breast the last wishes of his father, written by his hand, only to act so frightfully contrary to them! but on the other hand, to see him ambush and not prevent it! to condemn the victim and spare the assassin, could he be bound to any gratitude towards such a wretch? all the ideas which Marius had had for the last four years were, as it were, pierced through and through by this unexpected blow. He shuddered. Everything depended upon him. He held in his hand, they all unconscious, those beings who were moving there before his eyes. If he fired the pistol, M. Leblanc was saved and Thénardier was lost; if he did not, M. Leblanc was sacrificed, and, perhaps, Thénardier escaped. To hurl down the one or to let the other fall! remorse on either hand. What was to be done? which should he choose? be wanting to his most imperious memories, to so many deep resolutions, to his most sacred duty, to that most venerated paper! be wanting to his father's will, or suffer a crime to be accomplished? He seemed on the one hand to hear "his Ursula" entreating him for her father, and on the other the colonel commending Thénardier to him. He felt that he was mad. His knees gave way beneath him; and he had not even time to deliberate, with such fury was the scene which he had before his eyes rushing forward. It was like a whirlwind, which he had thought himself master of, and which was carrying him away. He was on the point of fainting.

Meanwhile Thénardier, we will call him by no other name henceforth, was walking to and fro before the table in a sort of insane and frenzied triumph.

He clutched the candle and put it on the mantel with such a shock that the flame was almost extinguished and the tallow was spattered upon the wall.

Then he turned towards M. Leblanc, and with a frightful look, spit out this:

"Singed! smoked! basted! spitted!"

And he began to walk again, in full explosion.

"Ha!" cried he, "I have found you again at last, monsieur philanthropist! monsieur threadbare millionaire! monsieur giver of dolls! old marrow-bones! ha! you do not know me? no, it was not you who came to Montfermeil, to my inn, eight years ago, the night of Christmas, 1823! it was not you who took away Fantine's child from my house! the Lark! it was not you who had a yellow coat! no! and a package of clothes in your hand just as you came here this morning! say now, wife! it is his mania it appears, to carry packages of woollen stockings into houses! old benevolence, get out! Are you a hosier, monsieur millionaire? you give the poor your shop sweepings, holy man! what a charlatan! Ha! you do not know me? Well, I knew you! I knew you immediately as soon as you stuck your nose in here. Ah! you are going to find out at last that it is not all roses to go into people's houses like that, under pretext of their being inns, with worn-out clothes, with the appearance of a pauper, to whom anybody would have given a sou, to deceive persons, to act the generous, take their help away, and threaten them in the woods, and that you do not get quit of it by bringing back afterwards, when people are ruined, an overcoat that is too large and two paltry hospital blankets, old beggar, child-stealer!"

He stopped, and appeared to be talking to himself for a moment. One would have said that his fury dropped like the Rhone into some hole; then, as if he were finishing aloud something that he had been saying to himself, he struck his fist on the table and cried:

"With his wishy-washy look!"

And apostrophising M. Leblanc:

"Zounds! you made a mock of me once! You are the cause of all my misfortunes! For fifteen hundred francs you got a girl that I had and who certainly belonged to rich people, and who had already brought me in a good deal of money, and from whom I ought to have got enough to live on all my life! A girl who would have made up all that I lost in that abominable tavern where they had such royal sprees and where I devoured my all like a fool! Oh! I wish that all the wine that was drunk in my house had been poison to those who drank it! But no matter! Say, now! you must have thought me green when you went away with the Lark? you had your club in the woods! you were the stronger! Revenge! The trumps are in my hand to-day. You are skunked, my good man! Oh! but don't I laugh! Indeed, I do! Didn't he fall into the trap? I told him that I was an actor, that my name was Fabantou, that I had played comedy with Mamselle Mars, with Mamselle Muche, that my landlord must be paid to-morrow the 4th of February, and he did not even think that the 8th of January is quarter day and not the 4th of February! The ridiculous fool! And these four paltry philippes that he brings me! Rascal! He had not even heart enough to go up to a hundred francs! And how he swallowed my platitudes! The fellow amused me. I said to myself: Blubber-lips! Go on, I have got you, I lick your paws this morning! I will gnaw your heart to-night!"

Thénardier stopped. He was out of breath. His little narrow chest was blowing like a blacksmith's bellows. His eye was full of the base delight of a feeble, cruel, and cowardly animal, which can finally prostrate that of which it has stood in awe, and insult what it has flattered, the joy of a dwarf putting his heel upon the head of Goliath, the joy of a jackal beginning to tear a sick bull, dead enough not to be able to defend himself, alive enough yet to suffer.

M. Leblanc did not interrupt him but said when he stopped:

"I do not know what you mean. You are mistaken. I am a very poor man and anything but a millionaire. I do not know you; you mistake me for another."

"Ha!" screamed Thénardier, "good mountebank! You stick to that joke yet! You are in the fog, my old boy! Ah! you do not remember! You do not see who I am!"

"Pardon me, monsieur," answered M. Leblanc, with a tone of politeness which, at such a moment, had a peculiarly strange and powerful effect, "I see that you are a bandit."

Who has not noticed it, hateful beings have their tender points; monsters are easily annoyed. At this word bandit, the Thénardiess sprang off the bed. Thénardier seized his chair as if he were going to crush it in his hands: "Don't you stir," cried he to his wife, and turning towards M. Leblanc:

"Bandit! Yes, I know that you call us so, you rich people! Yes! it is true I'm bankrupt; I am in concealment, I have no bread; I have not a sou, I am a bandit. Here are three days that I have eaten nothing, I am a bandit! Ah!

you warm your feet; you have Sacoski pumps, you have wadded overcoats like archbishops, you live on the second floor in houses with a porter, you eat truffles, you eat forty-franc bunches of asparagus in the month of January, and green peas, you stuff yourselves, and when you want to know if it is cold you look in the newspaper to see at what degree the thermometer of the inventor, Chevalier, stands. But we are our own thermometers! We have no need to go to the quai at the corner of the Tour de l'Horloge, to see how many degrees below freezing it is; we feel the blood stiffen in our veins and the ice reach our hearts, and we say 'There is no God!' And you come into our caverns, yes, into our caverns, to call us bandits. But we will eat you! but we will devour you, poor little things! Monsieur Millionaire! know this:—I have been a man established in business, I have been licensed, I have been an elector, I am a citizen, I am! And you, perhaps, are not one?"

Here Thénardier took a step towards the men who were before the door, and added, trembling with rage:

"When I think that he dares to come and talk to me, as if I were a cobbler!"

Then addressing M. Leblanc with a fresh burst of frenzy:

"And know this, too, monsieur philanthropist! I am no shady man. I am not a man whose name nobody knows, and who comes into houses to carry off children. I am a combat veteran; I ought to be decorated. I was at Waterloo, I was, and in that battle I saved a general, named the Comte de Pontmercy. This picture which you see, and which was painted by David at Bruqueselles, do you know who it represents? It represents me. David desired to immortalise that feat of arms.[8] I have General Pontmercy on my back, and I am carrying him through the storm of grapeshot. That is history. He has never done anything at all for me, this general; he is no better than other people. But, nevertheless, I saved his life at the risk of my own, and I have my pockets full of certificates. I am a soldier at Waterloo— damn it all! And now that I have had the goodness to tell you all this, let us make an end of it; I must have some money; I must have a good deal of money, I must have an immense deal of money, or I will exterminate you, by God's lightning!"

Marius had regained some control over his distress, and was listening. The last possibility of doubt had now vanished. It was indeed the Thénardier of the will. Marius shuddered at that reproach of ingratitude flung at his father, and which he was on the point of justifying so fatally. His perplexities were redoubled. Moreover, there was in all these words of Thénardier, in his tone, in his gestures, in his look which flashed out flames at every word, there was in this explosion of an evil nature exposing its entire self, in this mixture of braggadocio and abjectness, of pride and pettiness, of rage and folly in this chaos of real grievances and false sentiments, in this shamelessness of a wicked man tasting the sweetness of violence, in this brazen nakedness of a deformed soul, in this conflagration of every suffering combined with every hatred, something which was as hideous as evil and as sharp and bitter as the truth.

The picture by a master, the painting by David, the purchase of which he had proposed to M. Leblanc, was, the reader has guessed, nothing more than the sign of his tavern, painted, as will be remembered, by himself, the only relic which he had saved from his shipwreck at Montfermeil.

As he had ceased to intercept Marius' line of vision, Marius could now look at the thing, and in this daub he really made out a battle, a background of smoke, and one man carrying off another. It was the group of Thénardier and Pontmercy; the saviour sergeant, the colonel saved. Marius was as it were intoxicated; this picture in some sort restored his father to life; it was not now the sign of the Montfermeil inn, it was a resurrection; in it a tomb half opened, from it a phantom arose. Marius heard his heart ring in his temples, he had the cannon of Waterloo sounding in his ears; his bleeding father dimly painted upon this dusky panel startled him, and it seemed to him that that shapeless shadow was gazing steadily upon him.

When Thénardier had taken breath he fixed his bloodshot eyes upon Monsieur Leblanc, and said in a low and abrupt tone:

"What have you to say before we begin to go to work on you?"

Monsieur Leblanc said nothing. In the midst of this silence a hoarse voice threw in this ghastly sarcasm from the hall:

"If there is any wood to split, I am on hand!"

It was the man with the pole-axe who was making merry.

At the same time a huge face, bristly and dirty, appeared in the doorway, with a hideous laugh, which showed not teeth, but fangs.

It was the face of the man with the pole-axe.

"What have you taken off your mask for?" cried Thénardier, furiously.

"To laugh," replied the man.

For some moments, Monsieur Leblanc had seemed to follow and to watch all the movements of Thénardier, who, blinded and bewildered by his own rage, was walking to and fro in the den with the confidence inspired by the feeling that the door was guarded, having armed possession of a disarmed man, and being nine to one, even if the Thénardiess should count but for one man. In his apostrophe to the man with the pole-axe, he turned his back on Monsieur Leblanc.

Monsieur Leblanc seized this opportunity, pushed the chair away with his foot, the table with his hand, and at one bound, with a marvellous agility, before Thénardier had had time to turn around he was at the window. To open it, get up and step through it, was the work of a second. He was half outside when six strong hands seized him, and drew him forcibly back into the room. The three "chimney doctors" had thrown themselves upon him. At the same time the Thénardiess had clutched him by the hair.

At the disturbance which this made, the other bandits ran in from the hall. The old man, who was on the bed, and who seemed overwhelmed with wine, got off the pallet, and came tottering along with a road-mender's hammer in his hand.

One of the "chimney doctors," whose blackened face was lighted up by the candle, and in whom Marius, in spite of this colouring, recognised

Panchaud, alias Printanier, alias Bigrenaille, raised a sort of loaded club made of a bar of iron with a knob of lead at each end, over Monsieur Leblanc's head.

Marius could not endure this sight. "Father," thought he, "pardon me!" And his finger sought the trigger of the pistol. The shot was just about to be fired, when Thénardier's voice cried:

"Do him no harm!"

This desperate attempt of the victim, far from exasperating Thénardier, had calmed him. There were two men in him, the ferocious man and the crafty man. Up to this moment, in the first flush of triumph, before his prey stricken down and motionless, the ferocious man had been predominant; when the victim resisted, and seemed to desire a struggle, the crafty man reappeared and resumed control.

"Do him no harm!" he repeated, and without suspecting it, the first result of this was to stop the pistol which was just ready to go off, and paralyse Marius, to whom the urgency seemed to disappear, and who, in view of this new phase of affairs, saw no impropriety in waiting longer. Who knows but some chance may arise which will save him from the fearful alternative of letting the father of Ursula perish, or destroying the saviour of the colonel!

A herculean struggle had commenced. With one blow full in the chest M. Leblanc had sent the old man sprawling into the middle of the room, then with two back strokes had knocked down two other assailants, whom he held one under each knee; the wretches screamed under the pressure as if they had been under a granite mill-stone; but the four others had seized the formidable old man by the arms and the back, and held him down over the two prostrate "chimney doctors." Thus, master of the latter and mastered by the former, crushing those below him and suffocating under those above him, vainly endeavouring to shake off all the violence and blows which were heaped upon him, M. Leblanc disappeared under the horrible group of the bandits, like a wild boar under a howling pack of hounds and mastiffs.

They succeeded in throwing him over upon the bed nearest to the window and held him there at bay. The Thénardiess had not let go of his hair.

"Here," said Thénardier, "stay out of it. You will tear your shawl."

The Thénardiess obeyed, as the she-wolf obeys her mate, with a growl.

"Now, the rest of you," continued Thénardier, "search him."

M. Leblanc seemed to have given up all resistance. They searched him. There was nothing upon him but a leather purse which contained six francs, and his handkerchief.

Thénardier put the handkerchief in his pocket.

"What! no pocket-book?" he asked.

"Nor any watch," answered one of the "chimney doctors."

"It is all the same," muttered, with the voice of a ventriloquist, the masked man who had the big key, "he is a tough old bird."

Thénardier went to the corner by the door and took a bundle of ropes which he threw to them.

"Tie him to the foot of the bed," said he, and perceiving the old fellow who lay motionless, when he was stretched across the room by the blow of M. Leblanc's fist:

"Is Boulatruelle dead?" asked he.

"No," answered Bigrenaille, "he is drunk."

"Sweep him into a corner," said Thénardier.

Two of the "chimney doctors" pushed the drunkard up to the heap of old iron with their feet.

"Babet, what did you bring so many for?" said Thénardier in a low tone to the man with the cudgel, "it was needless."

"What would you have?" replied the man with the cudgel, "they all wanted to be in. The season is bad. There is nothing doing."

The pallet upon which M. Leblanc had been thrown was a sort of hospital bed supported by four big roughly squared wooden posts. M. Leblanc made no resistance. The brigands bound him firmly, standing, with his feet to the floor, by the bed-post furthest from the window and nearest to the chimney.

When the last knot was tied, Thénardier took a chair and came and sat down nearly in front of M. Leblanc. Thénardier looked no longer like himself, in a few seconds the expression of his face had passed from unbridled violence to tranquil and crafty mildness. Marius hardly recognised in that polite, clerkly smile, the almost beastly mouth which was foaming a moment before; he looked with astonishment upon this fantastic and alarming metamorphosis, and he experienced what a man would feel who should see a tiger change itself into an attorney.

"Monsieur," said Thénardier.

And with a gesture dismissing the brigands who still had their hands upon M. Leblanc:

"Move off a little, and let me talk with monsieur."

They all retired towards the door. He resumed:

"Monsieur, you were wrong in trying to jump out the window. You might have broken your leg. Now, if you please, we will talk quietly. In the first place I must inform you of a circumstance I have noticed, which is that you have not yet made the least outcry."

Thénardier was right; this detail was true, although it had escaped Marius in his anxiety. M. Leblanc had only uttered a few words without raising his voice, and, even in his struggle by the window with the six bandits, he had preserved the most profound and the most remarkable silence. Thénardier continued:

"Indeed! you might have cried thief a little, for I should not have found it inconvenient. Murder! that is said upon occasion, and, as far as I am concerned, I should not have taken it in bad part. It is very natural that one should make a little noise when he finds himself with persons who do not inspire him with as much confidence as they might; you might have done it, and we should not have disturbed you. We would not even have gagged you. And I will tell you why. It is because this room is very deaf. That is all I can say for it, but I can say that. It is like a cellar. We could set off a bomb here, and at the nearest guardhouse it would sound like a drunkard's snore. Here a cannon would go boom, and thunder would go puff. It is a convenient apartment. But, in short, you did not cry out, that was better, I make you my compliments for it, and I will tell you what I conclude from it: my dear monsieur, when a man cries out, who is it that comes? The police. And after the police? Justice. Well! you did not cry out; because you were no more anxious than we to see justice and the police come. It is because,—I suspected as much long ago,—you have some interest in concealing something. For our part we have the same interest. Now we can come to an understanding."

While speaking thus, it seemed as though Thénardier, with his gaze fixed upon Monsieur Leblanc, was endeavouring to thrust the daggers which he looked, into the very conscience of his prisoner. His language, moreover, marked by a sort of subdued and sullen insolence, was reserved and almost select, and in this wretch who was just before nothing but a brigand, one could now perceive "the man who studied to be a priest."

The silence which the prisoner had preserved, this precaution which he had carried even to the extent of endangering his life, this resistance to the first impulse of nature, which is to utter a cry, all this, it must be said, since it had been remarked, was awkward for Marius, and painfully astonished him.[9]

Thénardier's remark, well founded as it was, added in Marius' eyes still more to the obscurity of the mysterious cloud that enveloped this strange and serious face to which Courfeyrac had given the nickname of Monsieur Leblanc. But whatever he might be, bound with ropes, surrounded by assassins, half buried so to speak, in a grave which was deepening beneath him every moment, before the fury as well as before the mildness of Thénardier, this man remained impassive; and Marius could not repress at such a moment his admiration for that superbly melancholy face.

Here was evidently a soul inaccessible to fear, and ignorant of dismay. Here was one of those men who are superior to astonishment in desperate situations. However extreme the crisis, however inevitable the catastrophe, there was nothing there of the agony of the drowning man, staring with horrified eyes as he sinks to the bottom.

Thénardier quietly got up, went to the fireplace, took away the screen which he leaned against the nearest pallet, and thus revealed the furnace full of glowing coals in which the prisoner could plainly see the chisel at a white heat, spotted here and there with little scarlet stars.

Then Thénardier came back and sat down by Monsieur Leblanc.

"I continue," said he. "Now we can come to an understanding. Let us arrange this amicably. I was wrong to fly into a passion just now. I do not know where my wits were, I went much too far, I talked extravagantly. For instance, because you are a millionaire, I told you that I wanted money, a good deal of money, an immense deal of money. That would not be reasonable. My God, rich as you may be, you have your expenses; who does not have them? I do not want to ruin you, I am not a cannibal, after all. I am not one of those people who, because they have the advantage, use it to be ridiculous. Here, I am willing to go half way and make some sacrifice on my part. I need only two hundred thousand francs."

Monsieur Leblanc did not breathe a word. Thénardier went on:

"You see that I water my wine pretty well.* I do not know the state of your fortune, but I know that you do not care much for money and a benevolent man like you can certainly give two hundred thousand francs to a father of a family who is unfortunate. Certainly you are reasonable also, you do not imagine that I would take the trouble I have to-day, and that I would organise the affair of this evening, which is a very fine piece of work, in the opinion of these gentlemen, to end off by asking you for enough to go and drink fifteen sou red wine and eat veal at Desnoyers'. Two hundred thousand francs, it is worth it. That trifle once out of your pocket, I assure you that all is said, and that you need not fear a snap of the finger. You will say: but I have not two hundred thousand francs with me. Oh! I am not exacting. I do not require that I only ask one thing. Have the goodness to write what I shall dictate."

Here Thénardier paused, then he added, emphasising each word and casting a smile towards the furnace:

"I give you notice that I shall not accept that you cannot write."

A grand inquisitor might have envied that smile.

Thénardier pushed the table close up to Monsieur Leblanc, and took the inkstand, a pen, and a sheet of paper from the drawer, which he left partly open, and in which gleamed the long blade of the knife.

He laid the sheet of paper before Monsieur Leblanc.

"Write," said he.

The prisoner spoke at last:

"How do you expect me to write? I am tied."

"That is true, pardon me!" said Thénardier, "you are quite right."

And turning towards Bigrenaille:

"Untie monsieur's right arm."

Panchaud, alias Printanier, alias Bigrenaille, executed Thénardier's order. When the prisoner's right hand was free, Thénardier dipped the pen into the ink, and presented it to him.

"Remember, monsieur, that you are in our power, at our discretion, that no human power can take you away from here, and that we should be really grieved to be obliged to proceed to unpleasant extremities. I know neither your name nor your address, but I give you notice that you will remain tied until the person whose duty it will be to carry the letter which you are about to write, has returned. Have the kindness now to write."

"What?" asked the prisoner.

"I will dictate."

M. Leblanc took the pen.

Thénardier began to dictate:

"My daughter——"

The prisoner shuddered and lifted his eyes to Thénardier.

---

*The French uses the idiom *Je mets de l'eau dans mon vin* ("I'm watering down my wine").

"Put 'my dear daughter,'" said Thénardier. M. Leblanc obeyed. Thénardier continued:

"Come immediately——"

He stopped.

"You call her daughter, do you not?"

"Who?" asked M. Leblanc.

"Zounds!" said Thénardier, "the little girl, the Lark."

M. Leblanc answered without the least sign of emotion:

"I do not know what you mean."

"Well, go on," said Thénardier, and he began to dictate again.

"Come immediately, I have imperative need of you. The person who will give you this note is directed to bring you to me. I am waiting for you. Come with confidence."

M. Leblanc had written the whole. Thénardier added:

"Ah! strike out *come with confidence,* that might lead her to suppose that the thing is not quite clear and that distrust is possible."

M. Leblanc erased the three words.

"Now," continued Thénardier, "sign it. What is your name?"

The prisoner laid down the pen and asked:

"For whom is this letter?"

"You know very well," answered Thénardier, "for the little girl, I have just told you."

It was evident that Thénardier avoided naming the young girl in question. He said "the Lark," he said "the little girl," but he did not pronounce the name. The precaution of a shrewd man preserving his own secret before his accomplices. To speak the name would have been to reveal the whole "affair" to them, and to tell them more than they needed to know.

He resumed:

"Sign it. What is your name?"

"Urbain Fabre," said the prisoner.

Thénardier, with the movement of a cat, thrust his hand into his pocket and pulled out the handkerchief taken from M. Leblanc. He looked for the mark upon it and held it up to the candle.

"U. F. That is it. Urbain Fabre. Well, sign U. F."

The prisoner signed.

"As it takes two hands to fold the letter, give it to me, I will fold it."

This done, Thénardier resumed:

"Put on the address, *Mademoiselle Fabre,* at your house. I know that you live not very far from here, in the neighbourhood of Saint Jacques du Haut Pas, since you go there to mass every day, but I do not know in what street. I see that you understand your situation. As you have not lied about your name, you will not lie about your address. Put it on yourself."

The prisoner remained thoughtful for a moment, then he took the pen and wrote:

"Mademoiselle Fabre, at Monsieur Urbain Fabre's, Rue Saint Dominique d'Enfer, No. 17."

Thénardier seized the letter with a sort of feverish convulsive movement.

"Wife!" cried he.

The Thénardiess sprang forward.

"Here is the letter. You know what you have to do. There is a fiacre below. Go right away, and come back ditto."

And addressing the man with the pole-axe:

"Here, since you have taken off your mask, go with the woman. You will ride behind the fiacre. You know where you left the *maringotte?*"

"Yes," said the man.

And, laying down his pole-axe in a corner, he followed the Thénardiess. As they were going away, Thénardier put his head through the half-open door and screamed into the hall:

"Above all things do not lose the letter! remember that you have two hundred thousand francs with you."

The harsh voice of the Thénardiess answered:

"Rest assured, I have put it in my bosom."

A minute had not passed when the snapping of a whip was heard, which grew fainter and rapidly died away.

"Good!" muttered Thénardier. "They are going good speed. At that speed the bourgeoise will be back in three quarters of an hour."*

He drew a chair near the fireplace and sat down, folding his arms and holding his muddy boots up to the furnace.

"My feet are cold," said he.

There were now but five bandits left in the den with Thénardier and the prisoner. These men, through the masks or the black varnish which covered their faces and made of them, as fear might suggest, charcoal men, negroes, or demons, had a heavy and dismal appearance, and one felt that they would execute a crime as they would any drudgery, quietly, without anger and without mercy, with a sort of irksomeness. They were heaped together in a corner like brutes, and were silent. Thénardier was warming his feet. The prisoner had relapsed into his taciturnity. A gloomy stillness had succeeded the savage tumult which filled the garret a few moments before.

The candle, on which a large mushroom had formed, hardly lighted up the enormous den, the fire had grown dull, and all these monstrous heads made huge shadows on the walls and on the ceiling.

No sound could be heard save the quiet breathing of the drunken old man, who was asleep.

Marius was waiting in an anxiety which everything increased. The riddle was more impenetrable than ever. Who was this "little girl," whom Thénardier had also called the Lark? was it his "Ursula"? The prisoner had not seemed to be moved by this word, the Lark, and answered in the most natural way in the world: I do not know what you mean. On the other hand, the two letters U. F. were explained; it was Urbain Fabre, and Ursula's name was no longer Ursula. This Marius saw most clearly. A sort

La bourgeoise is equivalent to "my old lady."

of hideous fascination held him spellbound to the place from which he observed and commanded the whole scene. There he was, almost incapable of reflection and motion, as if annihilated by such horrible things in so close proximity. He was waiting, hoping for some movement, no matter what, unable to collect his ideas and not knowing what course to take.

"At all events," said he, "if the Lark is she, I shall certainly see her, for the Thénardiess is going to bring her here. Then all will be plain. I will give my blood and my life if need be, but I will deliver her. Nothing shall stop me."

Nearly half an hour passed thus. Thénardier appeared absorbed in a dark meditation, the prisoner did not stir. Nevertheless Marius thought he had heard at intervals and for some moments a little dull noise from the direction of the prisoner.

Suddenly Thénardier addressed the prisoner:

"Monsieur Fabre, here, I may as well tell you this much right away."

These few words seemed to promise a clearing up. Marius listened closely. Thénardier continued:

"My spouse is coming back, do not be impatient. I think the Lark is really your daughter, and I find it quite natural that you should keep her. But listen a moment; with your letter, my wife is going to find her. I told my wife to dress up, as you saw, so that your young lady would follow her without hesitation. They will both get into the fiacre with my comrade behind. There is somewhere outside one of the barriers a *maringotte* with two very good horses harnessed. They will take your young lady there. She will get out of the carriage. My comrade will get into the *maringotte* with her, and my wife will come back here to tell us: 'It is done.' As to your young lady, no harm will be done her; the *maringotte* will take her to a place where she will be quiet, and as soon as you have given me the little two hundred thousand francs, she will be sent back to you. If you have me arrested, my comrade will take care of the Lark, that is all."

The prisoner did not utter a word. After a pause, Thénardier continued:

"It is very simple, as you see. There will be no harm done unless you wish there should be. That is the whole story. I tell you in advance so that you may know."

He stopped; the prisoner did not break the silence, and Thénardier resumed:

"As soon as my spouse has got back and said: 'The Lark is on her way,' we will release you, and you will be free to go home to bed. You see that we have no bad intentions."

Appalling images passed before Marius' mind. What! this young girl whom they were kidnapping, they were not going to bring her here? One of those monsters was going to carry her off into the gloom? where?— And if it were she! And it was clear that it was she. Marius felt his heart cease to beat. What was he to do? Fire off the pistol? put all these wretches into the hands of justice? But the hideous man of the pole-axe would none the less be out of all reach with the young girl, and Marius remembered these words of Thénardier, the bloody signification of which he divined: *If you have me arrested, my comrade will take care of the Lark.*

Now it was not by the colonel's will alone, it was by his love itself, by the peril of her whom he loved, that he felt himself held back.

This fearful situation, which had lasted now for more than an hour, changed its aspect at every moment. Marius had the strength to pass in review successively all the most heart-rending conjectures, seeking some hope and finding more. The tumult of his thoughts strangely contrasted with the deathly silence of the den.

In the midst of this silence they heard the sound of the door of the stairway which opened, then closed.

The prisoner made a movement in his bonds.

"Here is the bourgeoise," said Thénardier.

He had hardly said this, when in fact the Thénardiess burst into the room, red, breathless, panting, with glaring eyes, and cried, striking her hands upon her hips both at the same time:

"False address!"

The bandit whom she had taken with her, came in behind her and picked up his pole-axe again:

"False address?" repeated Thénardier.

She continued:

"Nobody! Rue Saint Dominique, number seventeen, no Monsieur Urbain Fabre! They do not know who he is!"

She stopped for lack of breath, then continued:

"Monsieur Thénardier! this old fellow has cheated you! you are too kind, do you see! I would have sliced up his mug, to begin with! And if he had acted up, I would have cooked him alive! Then he would have had to talk, and had to tell where the girl is, and had to tell where the rhino [dough] is! That is how I would have fixed it! No wonder that they say men are stupider than women! Nobody! number seventeen! It is a large porte-cochère! No Monsieur Fabre! Rue Saint Dominique, full gallop, and drink-money to the driver, and all! I spoke to the porter and the portress, who is a fine stout woman, they did not know the fellow."

Marius breathed. She, Ursula or the Lark, she whom he no longer knew what to call, was safe.

While his exasperated wife was vociferating, Thénardier had seated himself on the table; he sat a few seconds without saying a word, swinging his right leg, which was hanging down, and gazing upon the furnace with a look of savage reverie.

At last he said to the prisoner with a slow and singularly ferocious inflexion:

"A false address! what did you hope for by that?"

"To gain time!" cried the prisoner with a ringing voice.

And at the same moment he shook off his bonds; they were cut. The prisoner was no longer fastened to the bed save by one leg.

Before the seven men had had time to recover themselves and spring upon him he had bent over to the fireplace, reached his hand towards the furnace, then rose up, and now Thénardier, the Thénardiess, and the bandits, thrown by the shock into the back part of the room, beheld him with stupefaction, holding above his head the glowing chisel, from which fell an ominous light, almost free and in a formidable attitude.

At the judicial inquest, to which the ambush in the Gorbeau tenement gave rise in the sequel, it appeared that a big sou, cut and worked in a peculiar fashion, was found in the garret, when the police made a descent upon it; this big sou was one of those marvels of labour which the patience of the galleys produces in the darkness and for the darkness, marvels which are nothing else but instruments of escape. These hideous and delicate products of a wonderful art are to jewellery what the metaphors of argot are to poetry. There are Benvenuto Cellinis in the galleys, even as there are Villons in language. The unhappy man who aspires to deliverance, finds the means, sometimes without tools, with a folding knife, with an old case knife, to split a sou into two thin plates, to hollow out these two plates without touching the stamp of the mint, and to cut a screw-thread upon the edge of the sou, so as to make the plates adhere anew. This screws and unscrews at will; it is a box. In this box, they conceal a watch-spring, and this watch-spring, well handled, cuts through thick leg-irons and iron bars. The unfortunate convict seems to possess only a sou; no, he possesses liberty. A big sou of this kind, on subsequent examination by the police, was found open and in two pieces in the room under the pallet near the window. There was also discovered a little saw of blue steel which could be concealed in the big sou. It is probable that when the bandits were searching the prisoner's pockets, he had this big sou upon him and succeeded in hiding it in his hand; and that afterwards, having his right hand free, he unscrewed it and used the saw to cut the ropes by which he was fastened, which would explain the slight noise and the imperceptible movements which Marius had noticed.

Being unable to stoop down for fear of betraying himself, he had not cut the cords on his left leg.

The bandits had recovered their first surprise.

"Be easy," said Bigrenaille to Thénardier. "He holds yet by one leg, and he will not go off, I answer for that. I tied that shank for him."

The prisoner now raised his voice:

"You are pitiable, but my life is not worth the trouble of so long a defence. As to your imagining that you could make me speak, that you could make me write what I do not wish to write, that you could make me say what I do not wish to say——"

He pulled up the sleeve of his left arm, and added:

"Here."

At the same time he extended his arm, and laid upon the naked flesh the glowing chisel, which he held in his right hand, by the wooden handle.

They heard the hissing of the burning flesh; the odour peculiar to chambers of torture spread through the den. Marius staggered lost in horror; the brigands themselves felt a shudder; the face of the wonderful old man hardly contracted, and while the red iron was sinking into the smoking, impassable, and almost august wound, he turned upon Thénardier his fine face, in which there was no hatred, and in which suffering was swallowed up in a serene majesty.

With great and lofty natures the revolt of the flesh and the senses against the assaults of physical pain, brings out the soul, and makes it appear on the countenance, in the same way as mutinies of the soldiery force the captain to show himself.

"Wretches," said he, "have no more fear for me than I have of you."

And drawing the chisel out of the wound, he threw it through the window, which was still open; the horrible glowing tool disappeared, whirling into the night, and fell in the distance, and was quenched in the snow.

The prisoner resumed:

"Do with me what you will."

He was disarmed.

"Lay hold of him," said Thénardier.

Two of the brigands laid their hands upon his shoulders, and the masked man with the ventriloquist's voice placed himself in front of him, ready to knock out his brains with a blow of the key, at the least motion.

At the same time Marius heard beneath him, at the foot of the partition, but so near that he could not see those who were talking, this colloquy, exchanged in a low voice:

"There is only one thing more to do."

"Do him in!"

"That is it."

It was the husband and wife who were holding counsel.

Thénardier walked with slow steps towards the table, opened the drawer, and took out the knife.

Marius was tormenting the trigger of his pistol. Unparalleled perplexity! For an hour there had been two voices in his conscience, one telling him to respect the will of his father, the other crying to him to succour the prisoner. These two voices, without interruption, continued their struggle, which threw him into agony. He had vaguely hoped up to that moment to find some means of reconciling these two duties but no possible way had arisen. The peril was now urgent, the last limit of hope was passed; at a few steps from the prisoner, Thénardier was reflecting, with the knife in his hand.

Marius cast his eyes wildly about him; the last mechanical resource of despair.

Suddenly he started.

At his feet, on the table, a clear ray of the full moon illuminated and seemed to point out to him a sheet of paper. Upon that sheet he read this line, written in large letters that very morning, by the elder of the Thénardier girls:

"THE COPS ARE HERE."

An idea, a flash crossed Marius' mind; that was the means which he sought; the solution of this dreadful problem which was torturing him, to spare the assassin and to save the victim. He knelt down upon his bureau, reached out his arm, caught up the sheet of paper, quietly detached a bit of plaster from the partition, wrapped it in the paper, and threw the whole through the crevice into the middle of the den.

It was time. Thénardier had conquered his last fears, or his last scruples, and was moving towards the prisoner.

"Something fell!" cried the Thénardiess.

"What is it?" said the husband.

The woman had sprung forward, and picked up the piece of plaster wrapped in the paper. She handed it to her husband.

"How did this come in?" asked Thénardier.

"Egad!" said the woman, "how do you suppose it got in? It came through the window."

"I saw it pass," said Bigrenaille.

Thénardier hurriedly unfolded the paper, and held it up to the candle.

"It is Eponine's writing. The devil!"

He made a sign to his wife, who approached quickly, and he showed her the line written on the sheet of paper; then he added in a hollow voice:

"Quick! the ladder! leave the meat in the trap, and clear the camp!"

"Without cutting the man's throat?" asked the Thénardiess.

"We have not the time."

"Which way?" inquired Bigrenaille.

"Through the window," answered Thénardier. "As Ponine threw the stone through the window, that shows that the house is not watched on that side."

The mask with the ventriloquist's voice laid down his big key, lifted both arms into the air, and opened and shut his hands rapidly three times, without saying a word. This was like the signal to clear the decks in a fleet. The brigands, who were holding the prisoner, let go of him; in the twinkling of an eye, the rope ladder was unrolled out of the window, and firmly fixed to the casing by the two iron hooks.

The prisoner paid no attention to what was passing about him. He seemed to be dreaming or praying.

As soon as the ladder was fixed, Thénardier cried:

"Come, old lady!"

And he rushed towards the window.

But as he was stepping out, Bigrenaille seized him roughly by the collar.

"No way, old joker! after us."

"After us!" howled the bandits.

"You are children," said Thénardier. "We are losing time. The fuzz is at our heels."

"Well," said one of the bandits, "let us draw lots who shall go out first."

Thénardier exclaimed:

"Are you fools? are you cracked? You are a mess of bunglers! Losing time, isn't it? drawing lots, isn't it? with a wet finger! for the short straw! write our names! put them in a cap!——"

"Would you like my hat?" cried a voice from the door.

They all turned round. It was Javert.

He had his hat in his hand, and was holding it out smiling.

20 (21)

THE VICTIMS SHOULD ALWAYS
BE ARRESTED FIRST

JAVERT, at nightfall, had posted his men and hid himself behind the trees on the Rue de la Barrière des Gobelins, which fronts the Gorbeau tenement on the other side of the boulevard. He commenced by opening "his pocket," to put into it the two young girls, who were charged with watching the approaches to the den. But he only "bagged" Azelma. As for Eponine, she was not at her post; she had disappeared and he could not take her. Then Javert held off, and listened for the signal agreed upon. The going and coming of the fiacre made him very anxious. At last, he became impatient, and, *sure that there was a nest there,* sure of being *"in good luck,"* having recognised several of the bandits who had gone in, he finally decided to go up without waiting for the pistol shot.

It will be remembered that he had Marius' pass-key.

He had come at the right time.

The frightened bandits rushed for the weapons which they had thrown down anywhere when they had attempted to escape. In less than a second, these seven men, terrible to look upon, were grouped in a posture of defence; one with his pole-axe, another with his key, a third with his club, the others with the shears, the pincers, and the hammers, Thénardier grasping his knife. The Thénardiess seized a huge paving-stone which was in the corner of the window, and which served her daughters for a stool.

Javert put on his hat again, and stepped into the room, his arms folded, his cane under his arm, his sword in its sheath.

"Halt there," said he. "You will not pass out through the window, you will pass out through the door. It is less unwholesome. There are seven of you, fifteen of us. Don't let us collar you like peasants. Let's be nice."

Bigrenaille took a pistol which he had concealed under his smock, and put it into Thénardier's hand, whispering in his ear:

"It is Javert. I dare not fire at that man. Dare you?"

"Damn right!" answered Thénardier.

"Well, fire."

Thénardier took the pistol, and aimed at Javert.

Javert, who was within three paces, looked at him steadily, and contented himself with saying:

"Don't fire, now! It will flash in the pan."

Thénardier pulled the trigger. The pistol flashed in the pan.

"I told you so!" said Javert.

Bigrenaille threw his tomahawk at Javert's feet.

"You are the emperor of the devils! I surrender."

"And you?" asked Javert of the other bandits.

They answered:

"We, too."

Javert replied calmly:

"That is it, that is well, I said so, we're being nice."

"I only ask one thing," said Bigrenaille, "that is, that I shan't be refused tobacco while I am in solitary."

"Granted," said Javert.

And turning round and calling behind him:

"Come in now!"

A squad of sergents de ville with drawn swords, and officers armed with axes and clubs, rushed in at Javert's call. They bound the bandits. This crowd of men, dimly lighted by a candle, filled the den with shadow.

"Handcuffs on all!" cried Javert.

"Come on, then!" cried a voice which was not a man's voice, but of which nobody could have said: "It is the voice of a woman."

The Thénardiess had intrenched herself in one of the corners of the window, and it was she who had just uttered this roar.

The sergents de ville and officers fell back.

She had thrown off her shawl, but kept on her hat; her husband, crouched down behind her, was almost hidden beneath the fallen shawl, and she covered him with her body, holding the paving-stone with both hands above her head with the poise of a giantess who is going to hurl a rock.

"Take care!" she cried.

They all crowded back towards the hall. A wide space was left in the middle of the garret.

The Thénardiess cast a glance at the bandits who had allowed themselves to be tied, and muttered in a harsh and guttural tone:

"The cowards!"

Javert smiled, and advanced into the open space which the Thénardiess was watching with all her eyes.

"Don't come near! get out," cried she, "or I will crush you!"

"What a grenadier!" said Javert; "mother, you have a beard like a man, but I have claws like a woman."

And he continued to advance.

The Thénardiess, her hair flying wildly and terrible, braced her legs, bent backwards, and threw the paving-stone wildly at Javert's head. Javert stooped, the stone passed over him, hit the wall behind, from which it knocked down a large piece of the plastering, and returned, bounding from corner to corner across the room, luckily almost empty, finally stopping at Javert's heels.

At that moment Javert reached the Thénardier couple. One of his huge hands fell upon the shoulder of the woman, and the other upon her husband's head.

"The handcuffs!" cried he.

The police officers returned in a body, and in a few seconds Javert's order was executed.

The Thénardiess, completely crushed, looked at her manacled hands and those of her husband, dropped to the floor and exclaimed, with tears in her eyes:

"My daughters!"

"They are provided for," said Javert.

Meanwhile the officers had found the drunken fellow who was asleep behind the door, and shook him. He awoke stammering.

"Is it over, Jondrette?"

"Yes," answered Javert.

The six manacled bandits were standing; however, they still retained their spectral appearance, three blackened, three masked.

"Keep on your masks," said Javert.

And, passing them in review with the eye of a Frederic II at parade at Potsdam, he said to the three "chimney doctors:"

"Good day, Bigrenaille. Good day, Brujon. Good day, Deux Milliards."

Then, turning towards the three masks, he said to the man with the pole-axe:

"Good day, Gueulemer."

And to the man of the cudgel:

"Good day, Babet."

And to the ventriloquist:

"Your health, Claquesous."

Just then he perceived the prisoner of the bandits, who, since the entrance of the police, had not uttered a word, and had held his head down.

"Untie monsieur!" said Javert, "and let nobody go out."

This said, he sat down with authority before the table, on which the candle and the writing materials still were, drew a stamped sheet from his pocket, and commenced his procès verbal.

When he had written the first lines, a part of the formula, which is always the same, he raised his eyes:

"Bring forward the gentleman whom these gentlemen had bound."

The officers looked about them.

"Well," asked Javert, "where is he now?"

The prisoner of the bandits, M. Leblanc, M. Urbain Fabre, the father of Ursula, or the Lark, had disappeared.

The door was guarded, but the window was not. As soon as he saw that he was unbound, and while Javert was writing, he had taken advantage of the disturbance, the tumult, the confusion, the darkness, and a moment when their attention was not fixed upon him, to leap out of the window.

An officer ran to the window, and looked out; nobody could be seen outside.

The rope ladder was still trembling.

"The devil!" said Javert, between his teeth, "that must have been the best one."

THE EPIC ON THE RUE SAINT-DENIS

AND THE IDYLL OF

THE RUE PLUMET

BOOK ONE
A FEW PAGES OF HISTORY

1

WELL CUT

THE YEARS 1831 AND 1832, the two years immediately connected with the Revolution of July, are one of the most peculiar and most striking periods in history. These two years, among those which precede and those which follow them, are like two mountains. They have revolutionary grandeur. In them we discern precipices. In them the social masses, the very strata of civilisation, the consolidated group of superimposed and cohering interests, the venerable profile of the old French formation, appear and disappear at every instant through the stormy clouds of systems, passions, and theories. These appearances and disappearances have been named resistance and movement. At intervals we see truth gleaming forth, that daylight of the human soul.

This remarkable period is short enough, and is beginning to be far enough from us, so that it is henceforth possible to catch its principal outlines.

We will make the endeavour.

The Restoration had been one of those intermediate phases, hard to define, in which there are fatigue, buzzings, murmurs, slumber, tumult, and which are nothing more nor less than a great nation making a temporary halt. These periods are peculiar, and deceive the politicians who would take advantage of them. At first, the nation asks only for repose; men have but one thirst, for peace; they have but one ambition, to be little. That is a translation of being quiet. Great events, great fortunes, great ventures, great men, thank God, they have seen enough of them; they have been submerged in them. They would exchange Cæsar for Prusias, and Napoleon for the king of Yvetot. "What a good little king he was!" They have walked since daybreak, it is the evening of a long, hard day; they made the first relay with Mirabeau, the second with Robespierre, the third with Bonaparte, they are thoroughly exhausted. Every one of them asks for a bed.

Devotions wearied, heroisms grown old, ambitions sated, fortunes made, all seek, demand, implore, solicit, what? A place to lie down? They have it. They take possession of peace, quietness, and leisure; they are content. At the same time, however, certain facts arise, compel recognition, and knock at the door on their side, also. These facts have sprung from revolutions and wars; they exist, they live, they have a right to instal themselves in society, and they do instal themselves; and the most of the time the facts are pioneers and quartermasters that merely prepare a bivouac for principles.

Then, this is what appears to the political philosopher.

At the same time that weary men demand repose, accomplished facts demand guarantees. Guarantees to facts are the same thing as repose to men.

This is what England demanded of the Stuarts after the Protector; this is what France demanded of the Bourbons after the empire.

These guarantees are a necessity of the times. They must be accorded. The princes "grant" them, but in reality it is the force of circumstances which gives them. A profound truth, and a piece of useful knowledge, of which the Stuarts had no suspicion in 1662, and of which the Bourbons had not even a glimpse in 1814.

The predestined family which returned to France when Napoleon fell, had the fatal simplicity to believe that it was it that gave, and that what it had given it could take back; that the house of Bourbon possessed Divine Right, that France possessed nothing, and that the political rights conceded in the Charter of Louis XVIII were only a branch of the divine right, detached by the house of Bourbon and graciously given to the people until such day as it should please the king to take it back again. Still, by the regret which the gift cost them, the Bourbons should have felt that it did not come from them.

They were surly with the nineteenth century. They made a sour face at every development of the nation. To adopt a commonplace word, that is to say, a popular and a true one, they looked glum. The people saw it.

They believed that they were strong, because the empire had been swept away before them like a stage set. They did not perceive that they themselves had been brought in in the same way. They did not see that they also were in that hand which had taken off Napoleon.*

They believed that they were rooted because they were the past. They were mistaken; they were a portion of the past, but the whole past was France. The roots of French society were not in Bourbons but in the nation. These obscure, undying roots did not constitute the right of a family, but the history of a people. They were everywhere except under the throne.

The house of Bourbon was to France the illustrious and bloodstained knot of her history, but it was not the principal element of her destiny, or the essential basis of her politics. She could do without the Bourbons; she had done without them for twenty-two years; there had been a break; they did not suspect it. And how should they suspect it, they who imagined that Louis XVII reigned on the 9th of Thermidor, and that Louis XVIII reigned on the day of Marengo.† Never, since the beginning of history, have princes been so blind in the presence of facts, and of the portion of divine authority which facts contain and promulgate. Never had that earthly pretension which is called the right of kings, denied the divine right to such an extent.

---

*The Hand of Providence, which willed that democracy would ultimately triumph in France.

†Days of triumph for the Revolution and for Napoléon, respectively.

A capital error which led that family to lay its hand upon the guarantees "granted" in 1814, upon the concessions, as it called them. Sad thing! what they called their concessions were our conquests; what they called our encroachments were our rights.[1]

When its hour seemed come, the Restoration, supposing itself victorious over Bonaparte, and rooted in the country, that is to say, thinking itself strong and thinking itself deep, made up its mind and risked its throw.[*] One morning it rose in the face of France, and, lifting up its voice, it denied the collective title and the individual title, sovereignty to the nation, liberty to the citizen. In other words, it denied to the nation what made it a nation, and to the citizen what made him a citizen.

This is the essence of those famous acts which are called the ordinances of July.

The Restoration fell.

It fell justly. We must say, however, that it had not been absolutely hostile to all forms of progress. Some grand things were done in its presence.

Under the Restoration the nation became accustomed to discussion with calmness, which was wanting in the republic; and to grandeur in peace, which was wanting in the empire. France, free and strong, had been an encouraging spectacle to the other peoples of Europe. The Revolution had had its say under Robespierre; the cannon had had its say under Bonaparte; under Louis XVIII and Charles X intelligence in its turn had a chance to speak. The wind ceased, the torch was relighted. The pure light of mind was seen trembling upon the serene summits. A magnificent spectacle, instructive and charming. For fifteen years there were seen at work, in complete peace, and openly in public places, these great principles, so old to the thinker, so new to the statesman: equality before the law, freedom of conscience, freedom of speech, freedom of the press, the accessibility of every talent to every employment. This went on thus until 1830. The Bourbons were an instrument of civilisation, which broke in the hands of Providence.

The fall of the Bourbons was full of grandeur, not on their part but on the part of the nation. They left the throne with gravity, but without authority; their descent into the night was not one of those solemn disappearances which leave a dark emotion to history; it was neither the spectral calmness of Charles I, nor the eagle cry of Napoleon. They went away, that is all. They laid off the crown, and did not keep the halo. They were worthy, but they were not august. They fell short, to some extent, of the majesty of their misfortune. Charles X, during the voyage from Cherbourg, having a round table[†] cut into a square table, appeared more solicitous of imperilled etiquette than of the falling monarchy. This pettiness saddened the devoted

---

[*]Alludes to Julius Caesar's famous *alea jacta est* ("the die is cast") when he crossed the Rubicon with his troops, in defiance of a standing order by the Senate.
[†]A round table did not allow for one person to sit at the head, symbolically superior to the others seated there.

men who loved them, and the serious men who honoured their race. The people, for its part, was wonderfully noble. The nation, attacked one morning by force and arms, by a sort of royal insurrection, felt so strong that it had no anger. It defended itself, restrained itself, put things into their places, the government into the hands of the law, the Bourbons into exile, alas! and stopped. It took the old king, Charles X, from under that dais which had sheltered Louis XIV, and placed him gently on the ground. It touched the royal personages sadly and with precaution. It was not a man, it was not a few men, it was France, all France, France victorious and intoxicated with her victory, seeming to remember herself, and putting in practice before the eyes of the whole world these grave words of Guillaume du Vair after the day of the barricades: "It is easy for those who are accustomed to gather the favours of the great, and to leap, like a bird, from branch to branch, from a grievous to a flourishing fortune, to show themselves bold towards their prince in his adversity; but to me the fortune of my kings will always be venerable, and principally when they are in distress."

The Bourbons left us with respect, but not regret. As we have said, their misfortune was greater than they. They faded away on the horizon.

The Revolution of July immediately found friends and enemies throughout the world. The former rushed towards it with enthusiasm and joy, the latter turned away; each according to his own nature. The princes of Europe, at the first moment, owls in this dawn, closed their eyes, shocked and stupefied, and opened them only to threaten. A fright which can be understood, an anger which can be excused. This strange revolution had hardly been a shock; it did not even do vanquished royalty the honour of treating it as an enemy and shedding its blood. In the eyes of the despotic governments, always interested that liberty should calumniate herself, the Revolution of July had the fault of being formidable and yet being mild. Nothing, however, was attempted, or plotted against it. The most dissatisfied, the most irritated, the most horrified, bowed to it; whatever may be our selfishness and our prejudices, a mysterious respect springs from events in which we feel the intervention of a hand higher than that of man.

The Revolution of July is the triumph of the Right prostrating the fact. A thing full of splendour.

The right prostrating the fact. Thence the glory of the Revolution of 1830, thence its mildness also. The right, when it triumphs, has no need to be violent.

The right is the just and the true.

The peculiarity of the right is that it is always beautiful and pure. The fact, even that which is most necessary in appearance, even that most accepted by its contemporaries, if it exist only as fact, and if it contain too little of the right, or none at all, is destined infallibly to become, in the lapse of time, deformed, unclean, perhaps even monstrous. If you would ascertain at once what degree of ugliness the fact may reach, seen in the distance of the centuries, look at Machiavelli. Machiavelli is not an evil genius, nor a demon, nor a cowardly and miserable writer; he is nothing but the fact. And he is not merely the Italian fact, he is the European fact, the fact of the sixteenth century. He seems hideous, and he is so, in presence of the moral idea of the nineteenth.

This conflict of the right and the fact endures from the origin of society. To bring the duel to an end, to amalgamate the pure ideal with the human reality, to make the right peacefully interpenetrate the fact, and the fact the right, this is the work of the wise.

2

BADLY SEWED TOGETHER

BUT THE WORK of the wise is one thing, the work of the clever another.

The Revolution of 1830 soon ran aground.

As soon as a revolution strikes a reef, clever people carve up the wreck.

The clever, in our day, have arrogated for themselves the title of statesmen, so that this word, statesman, has come to be somewhat of a slang word. Indeed, let no one forget that wherever one finds cleverness only, there is inevitably pettiness. To say "the clever ones" amounts to saying "mediocrity."

Just as saying "statesmen" is sometimes tantamount to saying "traitors."

According to the clever, therefore, revolutions such as the Revolution of July [1830] are severed arteries; prompt ligature is needed. Rights, too grandly proclaimed, are disquieting. So once those rights have been affirmed, the State must be reaffirmed. Liberty having been assured, we must think about power.

Up to this point, the wise do not think differently from the clever, but they begin to feel distrust. Power, very well. But first, what is power? Second, where does it come from?

The clever seem not to hear the murmurs of objection, and they continue their work.

According to these politicians, ingenious in putting a mask of necessity upon profitable fictions, the first need of a people after a revolution, if this people forms part of a monarchical continent, is to procure a dynasty. In this way, say they, it can have peace after its revolution, that is to say, time to staunch its wounds and to repair its house. The dynasty hides the scaffolding and covers the ambulance.

Now, it is not always easy to procure a dynasty.

In case of necessity, the first man of genius, or even the first adventurer you meet, suffices for a king. You have in the first place Bonaparte, and in the second Iturbide.*

But the first family you meet with does not suffice to make a dynasty. There must be a certain amount of antiquity in a race, and the wrinkles of centuries cannot be improvised.

If we adopt at the statesmen's point of view, of course with every reservation, after a revolution, what are the qualities of the king who springs from it? He may be, and it is well that he should be, revolutionary, that is to say, a participant in his own person in this revolution, that he should have taken part in it, that he should be compromised in it, or made illustrious, that he should have touched the axe or handled the sword.

What are the qualities of a dynasty? It should be national; that is to say, revolutionary at a distance, not by acts performed, but by ideas accepted. It should be composed of the past and be historic, of the future and be sympathetic.

All this explains why the first revolutions content themselves with finding a man, Cromwell or Napoleon; and why the second absolutely insist on finding a family, the house of Brunswick or the house of Orleans.

Royal houses resemble those banyan trees of India, each branch of which, by bending to the ground, takes root there and becomes a banyan. Each branch may become a dynasty. On the sole condition that it bend to the people.

Such is the theory of the clever.

This, then, is the great art, to give a success something of the sound of a catastrophe, in order that those who profit by it may tremble also, to moderate a step in advance with fear, to enlarge the curve of transition to the extent of retarding progress, to tame down this work, to denounce and restrain the ardours of enthusiasm, to cut off the corners and the claws, to put protective padding over triumph, to swaddle rights, to wrap the people-giant up in flannel and hurry him off to bed, to impose a diet on this excessive health, to put Hercules in a convalescent home, to dilute the event within the expedient, to offer minds thirsting for the ideal this nectar stretched with barley-water, to take precautions against too much success, to provide the revolution with a sunscreen.

The year 1830 carried out this theory, already applied to England by 1688.

The year 1830 is a revolution arrested in mid career.† Half progress, partial right. Now logic ignores the Almost, just as the sun ignores the candle.

Who stops revolutions half way? The bourgeoisie.

Why?

---

*Agostín Iturbide (1783–1824), a Mexican general, was proclaimed Emperor of Mexico in 1822, and executed by firing squad two years later.

†This revolution imposed a new constitution, but retained the king and limited suffrage to 1 percent of potentially eligible voters—the wealthiest males.

Because the bourgeoisie is the interest which has attained to satisfaction. Yesterday it was hungry, to-day it has been fed, to-morrow it will be sated.

The phenomenon of 1814 after Napoleon was reproduced in 1830 after Charles X.

There has been an attempt, an erroneous one, to make a special class of the bourgeoisie. The bourgeoisie is simply the contented portion of the people. The bourgeois is the man who has now time to sit down. A chair is not a caste.

But, by wishing to sit down, we may stop the progress even of the human race. That has often been the fault of the bourgeois.

The commission of a fault does not constitute a class. Egotism is not one of the divisions of the social order.

Besides, we must be just even towards egotism. The state to which, after the shock of 1830, that part of the nation which is called bourgeoisie aspired, was not inertia, which is a complication of indifference and idleness, and which contains something of shame; it was not slumber, which supposes a momentary forgetfulness accessible to dreams; it was a halt.

Halt is a word formed with a singular and almost contradictory double meaning: a troop on the march, that is to say, movement; a stopping, that is to say, repose.

Halt is the regaining of strength, it is armed and watchful repose; it is the accomplished fact which plants sentinels and keeps itself upon its guard. Halt supposes battle yesterday and battle to-morrow.

This is the interval between 1830 and 1848.

What we here call battle may also be called progress.

The bourgeoisie, then, as well as the statesmen, felt the need of a man who should express this word: Halt! An Although Because. A composite individuality, signifying revolution and signifying stability; in other words, assuring the present through the evident compatibility of the past with the future.

This man was "ready to hand." His name was Louis-Philippe d'Orleans.

The 221 electors made Louis-Philippe king. Lafayette undertook the coronation. He called it *the best of republics*. The City Hall of Paris replaced the Cathedral of Rheims.*

This substitution of a demi-throne for the complete throne was "the work of 1830."

When the clever had finished their work, the immense defect of their solution became apparent. All this was done without reference to absolute right. The absolute right cried "I protest!" then, a fearful thing, it retreated into darkness.

---

*To hold the coronation ceremony in a secular building instead was symbolically to diminish the influence of the Catholic Church in the government.

3 (4)

CRACKS UNDER THE FOUNDATION

AT THE MOMENT the drama which we are relating is about to penetrate into the depths of one of the tragic clouds which cover the first years of the reign of Louis-Philippe, we could not be ambiguous, and it was necessary that this book should be explicit in regard to this king.

Louis-Philippe entered into the royal authority without violence, without direct action on his part, by the action of a revolutionary transfer, evidently very distinct from the real aim of the revolution, but in which he, the Duke d'Orleans, had no personal initiative. He was a born prince, and believed himself elected king. He had not given himself this command; he had not taken it; it had been offered to him and he had accepted it; convinced, wrongly in our opinion, but convinced, that the offer was consistent with right, and that the acceptance was consistent with duty. Hence a possession in good faith. Now, we say it in all conscience, Louis-Philippe being in good faith in his possession, and the democracy being in good faith in their attack, the terror which arises from social struggles is chargeable neither to the king nor to the democracy.

The government of 1830 had from the first a hard life. Born yesterday, it was obliged to fight to-day.

It was hardly installed when it began to feel on all sides vague movements directed against the machinery of July, still so newly set up, and so far from secure.

Resistance was born on the morrow, perhaps even it was born on the eve.

From month to month the hostility increased, and from dumb it became outspoken.

The Revolution of July, tardily accepted, as we have said, outside of France by the kings, had been diversely interpreted in France.

To the old parties, who are attached to hereditary right by the grace of God, revolutions having arisen from the right of revolt, there is a right of revolt against them. An error. For in revolutions the revolted party is not the people, it is the king. Revolution is precisely the opposite of revolt. Every revolution, being a normal accomplishment, contains in itself its own legitimacy, which false revolutionists sometimes dishonour, but which persists, even when sullied, which survives, even when stained with blood. Revolutions spring, not from an accident, but from necessity. A revolution is a return from the factitious to the real. It is, because it must be.

The old legitimist parties none the less assailed the Revolution of 1830 with all the violence which springs from false reasoning. Errors are excellent projectiles. They struck it skilfully just where it was vulnerable, at the defect in its cuirass, its want of logic; they attacked this revolution in its royalty. They cried to it: Revolution, why this king? Factions are blind men who aim straight.

This cry was uttered also by the republicans. But, coming from them, this cry was logical. What was blindness with the legitimists was clear-sightedness with the democrats. The year 1830 had become bankrupt with the people. The democracy indignantly reproached it with its failure.

In civilisation such as it is constituted to a small extent by God, to great by man, interests are combined, aggregated, and amalgamated in such a manner as to form actual hard rock, according to a dynamic law patiently studied by the economists, those geologists of politics.

These men who grouped themselves under different appellations but who may all be designated by the generic title of socialists, endeavoured to pierce this rock and to make the living waters of human felicity gush forth from it.

From the question of the scaffold to the question of war, their labours embraced everything. To the rights of man, proclaimed by the French Revolution, they added the rights of woman and the rights of childhood.

No one will be astonished that, for various reasons, we do not here treat fundamentally, from the theoretic point of view, the questions raised by socialism. We limit ourselves to indicating them.

All the problems which the socialists propounded, aside from the cosmogonic visions, dreams, and mysticism, may be reduced to two principal problems.

First problem:

To produce wealth.

Second problem:

To distribute it.

The first problem contains the question of labour.

The second contains the question of wages.

In the first problem the question is of the employment of force.

In the second of the distribution of enjoyment.

From the good employment of force results public power.

From the good distribution of enjoyment results individual happiness.

By good distribution, we must understand not equal distribution, but equitable distribution. The highest equality is equity.

From these two things combined, public power without, individual happiness within, results social prosperity.

Social prosperity means, man happy, the citizen free, the nation great.

England solves the first of these two problems. She creates wealth wonderfully; she distributes it badly. This solution, which is complete only on one side, leads her inevitably to these two extremes: monstrous opulence, monstrous misery. All the enjoyment to a few, all the privation to the rest, that is to say, to the people; privilege, exception, monopoly, feudality, springing from labour itself; a false and dangerous situation which founds public power upon private misery, which plants the grandeur of the state in the suffering of the individual. A grandeur ill constituted, in which all the material elements are combined, and into which no moral element enters.

Communism and agarian law think they have solved the second problem. They are mistaken. Their distribution kills production. Equal division abolishes emulation. And consequently labour. It is a distribution made by the butcher, who kills what he divides. It is therefore impossible to stop at these professed solutions. To kill wealth is not to distribute it.

The two problems must be solved together to be well solved. The two solutions must be combined and form but one.

Solve the two problems, encourage the rich, and protect the poor, suppress misery, put an end to the unjust speculation upon the weak by the strong, put a bridle upon the iniquitous jealousy of him who is on the road, against him who has reached his end, adjust mathematically and fraternally wages to labour, join gratuitous and obligatory instruction to the growth of childhood, and make science the basis of manhood, develop the intelligence while you occupy the arm, be at once a powerful people and a family of happy men, democratise property, not by abolishing it, but by universalising it, in such a way that every citizen without exception may be a proprietor, an easier thing than it is believed to be; in two words, learn to produce wealth and learn to distribute it, and you shall have material grandeur and moral grandeur combined; and you shall be worthy to call yourselves France.

This, above and beyond a few sects which ran wild, is what socialism said; that is what it sought to realise; this is what it outlined in men's minds.

Admirable efforts! sacred attempts!

These doctrines, these theories, these resistances, the unforeseen necessity for the statesman to consult with the philosopher, confused evidences half seen, a new politics to create, accordant with the old world, and yet not too discordant with the ideal of the revolution; a state of affairs in which Lafayette must be used to oppose Polignac, the intuition of progress transparent in the émeute, the chambers, and the street, competitions to balance about him, his faith in the revolution, perhaps some uncertain eventual resignation arising from the vague acceptance of a definitive superior right, his desire to remain in his race, his family pride, his sincere respect for the people, his own honesty, pre-occupied Louis-Philippe almost painfully, and at moments, strong and as courageous as he was, overwhelmed him under the difficulties of being king.

He felt beneath his feet a terrible disaggregation which was not, however, a crumbling into dust—France being more France than ever.

Dark drifts covered the horizon. A strange shadow approaching nearer and nearer, was spreading little by little over men, over things, over ideas; a shadow which came from indignations and from systems. All that had been hurriedly stifled was stirring and fermenting. Sometimes the conscience of the honest man caught its breath, there was so much confusion in that air in which sophisms were mingled with truths. Minds trembled in the social anxiety like leaves at the approach of the storm. The electric tension was so great that at certain moments any chance-comer, though unknown, flashed out. Then the twilight darkness fell again. At intervals, deep and sullen mutterings enabled men to judge of the amount of lightning in the cloud.

BOOK TWO
EPONINE

1 (2)

EMBRYONIC FORMATION OF CRIMES
IN THE INCUBATION OF PRISONS

JAVERT'S TRIUMPH in the Gorbeau tenement had seemed complete, but it was not so.

In the first place, and this was his principal regret, Javert had not made the prisoner prisoner. The victim who slips away is more suspicious than the assassin; and it was probable that this personage, so precious a capture to the bandits, would be a not less valuable prize to the authorities.

And then, Montparnasse had escaped Javert.

He must await another occasion to lay his hand upon "that devilish dandy." Montparnasse, in fact, having met Eponine, who was standing sentry under the trees of the boulevard, had led her away, liking rather to be Némorin with the daughter than to be Schinderhannes with the father. Well for him that he did so. He was free. As to Eponine, Javert "nabbed" her; trifling consolation. Eponine had rejoined Azelma at Les Madelonnettes.

Finally, on the trip from the Gorbeau tenement to La Force, one of the principal prisoners, Claquesous, had been lost. Nobody knew how it was done, the officers and sergeants "didn't understand it," he had changed into vapour, he had glided out of the handcuffs, he had slipped through the cracks of the carriage, the fiacre was leaky, and had fled; nothing could be said, save that on reaching the prison there was no Claquesous. There were either fairies or police in the matter. Had Claquesous melted away into the darkness like a snowflake in the water? Was there some secret connivance of the officers? Did this man belong to the double enigma of disorder and of order? Was he concentric with infraction and with repression? Had this sphinx forepaws in crime and hind-paws in authority? Javert in no wise accepted these combinations, and his hair rose on end in view of such an exposure; but his squad contained other inspectors besides himself, more deeply initiated, perhaps, than himself, although his subordinates, in the secrets of the precinct, and Claquesous was so great a scoundrel that he might be a very good officer. To be on such intimate juggling relations with darkness is excellent for brigandage and admirable for the police. There are such two-edged rascals. However it might be, Claquesous was lost, and was not found again. Javert appeared more irritated than astonished at it.

As to Marius, "that dolt of a lawyer," who was "probably frightened," and whose name Javert had forgotten, Javert cared little for him. Besides he was a lawyer, they are always found again. But was he a lawyer merely?

The trial commenced.

The police judge thought it desirable not to put one of the men of the Patron-Minette band into solitary confinement, hoping for some blabbing. This was Brujon, the long-haired man of the Rue du Petit Banquier. He was left in the Charlemagne court, and the watchmen kept their eyes upon him.

This name, Brujon, is one of the traditions of La Force. In the hideous court in what was called the New Building, which the administration named Court Saint Bernard, and which the robbers named La Fosse aux Lions, upon that wall covered with filth and with mould, which rises on the left to the height of the roofs, near an old rusty iron door which leads into the former chapel of the ducal hotel of La Force, now become a dormitory for brigands, a dozen years ago there could still be seen a sort of bastille coarsely cut in the stone with a nail, and below it this signature:

BRUJON, 1811.

The Brujon of 1811 was the father of the Brujon of 1832.

The last, of whom only a glimpse was caught in the Gorbeau ambush was a sprightly young fellow, very cunning and very adroit, with a flurried and plaintive appearance. It was on account of this flurried air that the judge had selected him, thinking that he would be of more use in the Charlemagne court than in a solitary cell.

Robbers do not cease operations because they are in the hands of justice. They are not disconcerted so easily. Being in prison for one crime does not prevent starting another crime. They are artists who have a picture in the parlour, and who labour none the less for that on a new work in their studio.

Brujon seemed stupefied by the prison. He was sometimes seen whole hours in the Charlemagne court, standing near the canteen, and staring like an idiot at that dirty list of prices of supplies which began with: *garlic, 62 centimes,* and ended with: *cigars, cinq centimes.* Or instead, he would pass his time in trembling and making his teeth chatter, saying that he had a fever, and inquiring if one of the twenty-eight beds in the fever ward was not vacant.

Suddenly, about the second fortnight in February, 1832, it was discovered that Brujon, that sleepy fellow, had arranged, through the agents of the house, not in his own name, but in the name of three of his comrades, three different errands, which had cost him in all fifty sous, a tremendous expense which attracted the attention of the prison brigadier.

He inquired into it, and by consulting the price list for errands hung up in the convicts' waiting-room, he found that the fifty sous were made up thus: three errands; one to the Pantheon, ten sous; one to the Val de Grâce, fifteen sous; and one to the Barrière de Grenelle, twenty-five sous. This was the most expensive of the whole list. Now the Pantheon, the Val de Grâce, and the Barrière de Grenelle happened to be the residences of three of the most dreaded prowlers of the barriers, Kruideniers alias Bizarro, Glorieux, a liberated convict, and Barrecarrosse, upon whom this incident fixed the eyes of the police. They thought they divined that these men were affiliated with Patron-Minette, two of whose chiefs, Babet and Gueulemer, were secured. It was supposed that Brujon's messages sent, not addressed to any houses, but to persons who were waiting for them in the street, must have been notices of some projected crime. There were still other indications; they arrested the three prowlers, and thought they had foiled Brujon's machination whatever it was.

About a week after these measures were taken, one night, a watchman, who was watching the dormitory in the lower part of the New Building, at the instant of putting his chestnut into the chestnut-box—this is the means employed to make sure that the watchmen do their duty with exactness; every hour a chestnut must fall into every box nailed on the doors of the dormitories—a watchman then saw through the peep-hole of the dormitory, Brujon sitting up in his bed and writing something by the light of the reflector. The warden entered, Brujon was put in solitary for a month, but they could not find what he had written. The police knew nothing more.

It is certain, however, that the next day "a postman" was thrown from the Charlemagne court into the Fosse aux Lions, over the five-story building which separates the two courts.

Prisoners call a ball of bread artistically kneaded, which is sent *into Ireland,* that is to say, over the roof of a prison from one court to the other, a postman. Etymology: over England; from one county to the other; *into Ireland*. This ball falls in the court. He who picks it up opens it, and finds a letter in it addressed to some prisoner in the court. If it be a convict who finds it, he hands the letter to its destination; if it be a warden, or one of those secretly bribed prisoners who are called sheep in the prisons and foxes in the galleys, the letter is carried to the office and delivered to the police.

This time the postman reached its address, although he for whom the message was destined was then *in solitary*. Its recipient was none other than Babet, one of the four heads of Patron-Minette.

The postman contained a paper rolled up, on which there were only these two lines:

"Babet, there is an affair on hand in the Rue Plumet. A grating in a garden."

This was the thing that Brujon had written in the night.

In spite of spies, both male and female, Babet found means to send the letter from La Force to La Salpêtrière to "a friend" of his who was shut up there. This girl in her turn transmitted the letter to another whom she knew, named Magnon, who was closely watched by the police, but not yet arrested. This Magnon, whose name the reader has already seen, had some relations with the Thénardiers which will be related hereafter, and could, by going to see Eponine, serve as a bridge between La Salpêtrière and Les Madelonnettes.

It happened just at that very moment, the proofs in the prosecution of Thénardier failing in regard to his daughters, that Eponine and Azelma were released.

When Eponine came out, Magnon, who was watching for her at the

door of Les Madelonnettes, handed her Brujon's note to Babet, charging
her to scout out the affair.

Eponine went to the Rue Plumet, reconnoitred the grating and the garden, looked at the house, spied, watched, and, a few days after, carried to
Magnon, who lived in the Rue Clocheperce, a biscuit, which Magnon
transmitted to Babet's mistress at La Salpêtrière. A biscuit, in the dark
symbolism of the prisons, signifies: *nothing to do.*

So that in less than a week after that, Babet and Brujon, meeting on the
way from La Force, as one was going "to examination," and the other was
returning from it: "Well," asked Brujon, "the Rue P.?" "Biscuit," answered
Babet.

This was the end of that fœtus of crime, engendered by Brujon in La Force.

This abortion, however, led to results entirely foreign to Brujon's programme. We shall see them.

Often, when thinking to knot one thread, we tie another.

2 (4)

AN APPARITION TO MARIUS

*Distracted by Cosette's disappearance, and unable to concentrate on the
translation work Marius does to survive, he goes out nearly every day to sit
on a bench in "The Field of the Lark," which reminds him of her because
of the coincidence of that name with Cosette's nickname.*

One day, a few days after this visit of a "spirit" to Father Mabeuf, one
morning—it was Monday, the day on which Marius borrowed the hundred-
sous coin of Courfeyrac for Thénardier—Marius had put this hundred-sous
coin into his pocket and before carrying it to the prison once, he had gone
"to take a little walk," hoping that it would enable him to work on his
return. It was eternally so. As soon as he rose in the morning, he sat down
before a book and a sheet of paper to work upon some translation; the
work he had on hand at that time was the translation into French of a celebrated quarrel between two Germans, the controversy between Gans and
Savigny; he took Savigny, he took Gans, read four lines, tried to write one of
them, could not, saw a star between his paper and his eyes, and rose from
his chair, saying: "I will go out. That will put me in trim."

And he would go to the Field of the Lark.

There he saw the star more than ever, and Savigny and Gans less than
ever.

He returned, tried to resume his work, and did not succeed; he found no means of tying a single one of the broken threads in his brain; then he would say: "I will not go out to-morrow. It prevents my working." Yet he went out every day.

He lived in the Field of the Lark rather than in Courfeyrac's room. This was his real address: Boulevard de la Santé, seventh tree from the Rue Croulebarbe.

That morning, he had left this seventh tree, and sat down on the bank of the brook of the Gobelins. The bright sun was gleaming through the new and glossy leaves.

He was thinking of "Her!" And his dreaminess, becoming reproachful, fell back upon himself; he thought sorrowfully of the idleness, the paralysis of the soul, which was growing up within him, and of that night which was thickening before him hour by hour so rapidly that he had already ceased to see the sun.

Meanwhile, through this painful evolution of indistinct ideas which were not even a soliloquy, so much had action become enfeebled within him, and he no longer had even strength to develop his grief—through this melancholy distraction, the sensations of the world without reached him. He heard behind and below him, on both banks of the stream, the washer-women of the Gobelins beating their linen; and over his head, the birds chattering and singing in the elms. On the one hand the sound of liberty, of happy unconcern, of winged leisure; on the other, the sound of labour. A thing which made him muse profoundly, and almost reflect, these two joyous sounds.

All at once, in the midst of his ecstasy of exhaustion, he heard a voice which was known to him, say:

"Ah! there he is!"

He raised his eyes and recognised the unfortunate child who had come to his room one morning, the elder of the Thénardier girls, Eponine; he now knew her name. Singular fact, she had become more wretched and more beautiful, two steps which seemed impossible. She had accomplished a double progress towards the light, and towards distress. She was barefooted and in rags, as on the day when she had so resolutely entered his room, only her rags were two months older; the holes were larger, the tatters dirtier. It was the same rough voice, the same forehead tanned and wrinkled by exposure; the same free, wild, and wandering gaze. She had, in addition to her former expression, that mixture of fear and sorrow which the experience of a prison adds to misery.

She had spears of straw and grass in her hair, not like Ophelia from having gone mad through the contagion of Hamlet's madness but because she had slept in some stable loft.

And with all this, she was beautiful. What a star thou art, O youth!

Meantime, she had stopped before Marius, with an expression of pleasure upon her livid face, and something which resembled a smile.

She stood for a few seconds, as if she could not speak.

"I have found you, then?" said she at last. "Father Mabeuf was right; it was on this boulevard. How I have looked for you! if you only knew! Do you know? I have been in the jug. A fortnight! They have let me out! seeing that there was nothing against me and then I was not of the age of discernment. It lacked two months. Oh! how I have looked for you! it is six weeks now. You don't live down there any longer?"

"No," said Marius.

"Oh! I understand. On account of the affair. Such scares are disagreeable. You have moved. What! why do you wear such an old hat as that? a young man like you ought to have fine clothes. Do you know, Monsieur Marius? Father Mabeuf calls you Baron Marius, I forget what more. It's not true that you are a baron? barons are old fellows, they go to the Luxembourg Gardens in front of the château where there is the most sun, they read the *Quotidienne* for a sou. I went once for a letter to a baron's like that. He was more than a hundred years old. But tell me, where do you live now?"

Marius did not answer.

"Ah!" she continued, "you have a hole in your shirt. I must mend it for you."

She resumed with an expression which gradually grew darker:

"You don't seem to be glad to see me?"

Marius said nothing; she herself was silent for a moment, then exclaimed:

"But if I would, I could easily make you glad!"

"How?" inquired Marius. "What does that mean?"

"Ah! you used to speak more kindly to me!" replied she.

"Well, what is it that you mean?"

She bit her lip; she seemed to hesitate, as if passing through a kind of interior struggle. At last, she appeared to decide upon her course.

"So much the worse, it makes no difference. You look sad, I want you to be glad. But promise me that you will laugh, I want to see you laugh and hear you say: Ah, well! that is good. Poor Monsieur Marius! you know, you promised me that you would give me whatever I should ask——"

"Yes! but tell me!"

She looked into Marius' eyes and said:

"I have the address."

Marius turned pale. All his blood flowed back to his heart.

"What address?"

"The address you asked me for."

She added as if she were making an effort:

"The address—you know well enough!"

"Yes!" stammered Marius.

"Of the young lady!"

Having pronounced this word, she sighed deeply.

Marius sprang up from the bank on which he was sitting, and took her wildly by the hand.

"Oh! come! show me the way, tell me! ask me for whatever you will! Where is it?"

"Come with me," she answered. "I am not sure of the street and the number; it is away on the other side from here, but I know the house very well. I will show you."

She withdrew her hand and added in a tone which would have pierced the heart of an observer, but which did not even touch the intoxicated and transported Marius:

"Oh! how glad you are!"

A cloud passed over Marius' brow. He seized Eponine by the arm:

"Swear to me one thing!"

"Swear?" said she, "what does that mean? Ah! you want me to swear?" And she laughed.

"Your father! promise me, Eponine! swear to me that you will not give this address to your father!"

She turned towards him with an astounded appearance.

"Eponine! How do you know that my name is Eponine?"

"Promise what I ask you!"

But she did not seem to understand.

"That is nice! you called me Eponine!"

Marius caught her by both arms at once.

"But answer me now, in heaven's name! pay attention to what I am saying, swear to me that you will not give the address you know to your father!"

"My father?" said she. "Oh! yes, my father! Do not be concerned on his account. He is in solitary. Besides, do I busy myself about my father!"

"But you don't promise me!" exclaimed Marius.

"Let me go then!" said she, bursting into a laugh, "how you shake me! Yes! yes! I promise you that! I swear to you that! What is it to me? I won't give the address to my father. There! will that do? is that it?"

"Nor to anybody?" said Marius.

"Nor to anybody."

"Now," added Marius, "show me the way."

"Right away?"

"Right away."

"Come. Oh! how glad he is!" said she.

After a few steps, she stopped.

"You follow too near me, Monsieur Marius. Let me go forward, and follow me like that, without seeming to. It won't do for a fine young man, like you, to be seen with a woman like me."

No tongue could tell all that there was in that word, woman, thus uttered by this child.

She went on a few steps, and stopped again; Marius rejoined her. She spoke to him aside and without turning:

"By the way, you know you have promised me something?"

Marius fumbled in his pocket. He had nothing in the world but the five francs intended for Thénardier. He took it, and put it into Eponine's hand.

She opened her fingers and let the coin fall on the ground, and, looking at him with a gloomy look:

"I don't want your money," said she.

BOOK THREE
THE HOUSE IN THE RUE PLUMET

1

THE SECRET HOUSE

TOWARDS THE MIDDLE of the last century, a velvet-capped president of the Parlement of Paris having a mistress and concealing it, for in those days the great lords exhibited their mistress and the bourgeois concealed theirs, had *"une petite maison"* built in the Faubourg Saint Germain, in the deserted Rue de Blomet, now called the Rue Plumet, not far from the spot which then went by the name of the *Combat des Animaux*.

This was a summer-house of but two stories; two rooms on the ground floor, two rooms in the second story, a kitchen below, a boudoir above, a garret next the roof, the whole fronted by a garden with a large iron grated gate opening on the street. This garden contained about an acre. This was all that the passers-by could see; but in the rear of the house there was a small yard, at the further end of which there was a low building, two rooms only and a cellar, a convenience intended to conceal a child and nurse in case of need. This building communicated, from the rear, by a masked door opening secretly, with a long narrow passage, paved, winding, open to the sky, bordered by two high walls, and which, concealed with wonderful art, and as it were lost between the inclosures of the gardens and fields, all the corners and turnings of which it followed, came to an end at another door, also concealed, which opened a third of a mile away, almost in another neighbourhood, upon the unbuilt end of the Rue de Babylone.

The president came in this way, so that those even who might have watched and followed him, and those who might have observed that the president went somewhere mysteriously every day, could not have suspected that going to the Rue de Babylone was going to the Rue Blomet. By skilful purchases of land, the ingenious magistrate was enabled to have this secret route to his house made upon his own ground, and consequently without supervision. He had afterwards sold off the lots of ground bordering on the passage in little parcels for flower and vegetable gardens, and the proprietors of these lots of ground supposed on both sides that what they saw was a partition wall, and did not even suspect the existence of that long ribbon of pavement winding between two walls among their beds and fruit trees. The birds alone saw this curiosity. It is probable that the larks and the sparrows of the last century had a good deal of chattering about the president.

The house, built of stone in the Mansard style, wainscoted, and furnished in the Watteau style, rococo within, old-fashioned without, walled about with a triple hedge of flowers, had a discreet, coquettish, and solemn appearance about it, suitable to a caprice of love and of magistracy.

This house and this passage, which have since disappeared, were still in existence fifteen years ago. In '93, a coppersmith bought the house to pull it down, but not being able to pay the price for it, the nation sent him into bankruptcy. So that it was the house that pulled down the coppersmith. Thereafter the house remained empty, and fell slowly into ruin, like all dwellings to which the presence of man no longer communicates life. It remained, furnished with its old furniture, and always for sale or to let, and the ten or twelve persons who passed through the Rue Plumet in the course of a year were notified of this by a yellow and illegible piece of paper which had hung upon the railing of the garden since 1810.

Towards the end of the Restoration, these same passers-by might have noticed that the paper had disappeared, and that, also, the shutters of the upper story were open. The house was indeed occupied. The windows had "little curtains," a sign that there was a woman there.

In the month of October, 1829, a man of a certain age had appeared and hired the house as it stood, including, of course, the building in the rear, and the passage which ran out to the Rue de Babylone. He had the secret openings of the two doors of this passage repaired. The house, as we have just said, was still nearly furnished with the president's old furniture. The new tenant had ordered a few repairs, added here and there what was lacking, put in a few flags in the yard, a few bricks in the basement, a few steps in the staircase, a few tiles in the floors, a few panes in the windows, and finally came and installed himself with a young girl and an aged servant, without any noise, rather like somebody stealing in than like a man who enters his own house. The neighbours did not gossip about it, for the reason that there were no neighbours.

This tenant, to partial extent, was Jean Valjean; the young girl was Cosette. The servant was a spinster named Toussaint, whom Jean Valjean had saved from the poorhouse and misery, and who was old, stuttering, and a native of a province, three qualities which had determined Jean Valjean to take her with him. He hired the house under the name of Monsieur Fauchelevent, gentleman. In what has been related hitherto, the reader doubtless recognised Jean Valjean even before Thénardier did.

Why had Jean Valjean left the convent of the Petit Picpus? What had happened?

Nothing had happened.

As we remember, Jean Valjean was happy in the convent, so happy that his conscience at last began to be troubled. He saw Cosette every day, he felt paternity springing up and developing within him more and more, he brooded this child with his soul, he said to himself that she was his, that nothing could take her from him, that this would be so indefinitely, that certainly she would become a nun, being every day gently led on towards it, that thus the convent was henceforth the universe to her as well as to him, that he would grow old there and she would grow up there, that she would grow old there and he would die there; that finally, ravishing hope, no separation was possible. In reflecting upon this, he at last began to find difficulties. He questioned himself. He asked himself if all this happiness were really his own, if it were not made up of the happiness of another, of the happiness of this child whom he was appropriating and plundering, he, an old man; if this was not a robbery? He said to himself that this child had a right to know what life was before renouncing it; that to cut her off, in advance, and, in some sort, without consulting her, from all pleasure, under pretence of saving her from all trial, to take advantage of her ignorance and isolation to give her an artificial vocation, was to outrage a human creature and to lie to God. And who knows but, thinking over all this some day, and being a nun with regret, Cosette might come to hate him? a final thought, which was almost selfish and less heroic than the others, but which was unbearable to him. He resolved to leave the convent.

He resolved it, he recognised with despair that it must be done. As to objections, there were none. Five years of sojourn between those four walls, and of absence from among men, had necessarily destroyed or dispersed the elements of alarm. He might return tranquilly among men. He had grown old, and all had changed. Who would recognise him now? And then, to look at the worst, there was no danger save for himself, and he had no right to condemn Cosette to the cloister for the reason that he had been condemned to the galleys. What, moreover, is danger in presence of duty? Finally, nothing prevented him from being prudent, and taking proper precautions.

As to Cosette's education, it was almost finished and complete.

His determination once formed, he awaited an opportunity. It was not slow to present itself. Old Fauchelevent died.

Jean Valjean asked an audience of the reverend prioress, and told her that having received a small inheritance on the death of his brother, which enabled him to live henceforth without labour, he would leave the service of the convent, and take away his daughter; but that, as it was not just that Cosette, not taking her vows, should have been educated gratuitously, he humbly begged the reverend prioress to allow him to offer the community, as indemnity for the five years which Cosette had passed there, the sum of five thousand francs.

Thus Jean Valjean left the convent of the Perpetual Adoration.

On leaving the convent, he took in his own hands, and would not entrust to any assistant, the little box, the key of which he always had about him. This box puzzled Cosette, on account of the odour of embalming which came from it.

Let us say at once, that henceforth this box never left him more. He always had it in his room. It was the first, and sometimes the only thing that he carried away in his changes of abode. Cosette laughed about it, and called this box *the inseparable,* saying: "I am jealous of it."

Jean Valjean nevertheless did not appear again in the open city without deep anxiety.

He discovered the house in the Rue Plumet, and buried himself in it. He was henceforth in possession of the name of Ultimus Fauchelevent.

At the same time he hired two other lodgings in Paris, in order to attract less attention than if he always remained in the same neighbourhood, to be able to change his abode on occasion, at the slightest anxiety which he might feel, and finally, that he might not again find himself in such a strait as on the night when he had so miraculously escaped from Javert. These two lodgings were two very humble dwellings, and of a poor appearance, in two neighbourhoods widely distant from each other, one in the Rue de l'Ouest, the other in the Rue de l'Homme Armé.

He went from time to time, now to the Rue de l'Homme Armé and now to the Rue de l'Ouest, to spend a month or six weeks, with Cosette, without taking Toussaint. He was waited upon by the porters, and gave himself out for a man of some means of the suburbs, having a foothold in the city. This lofty virtue had three domiciles in Paris in order to escape from the police.

2 (5)

THE ROSE DISCOVERS THAT SHE
IS AN ENGINE OF WAR

ONE DAY Cosette happened to look in her mirror, and she said to herself: "What!" It seemed to her almost that she was pretty. This threw her into strange anxiety. Up to this moment she had never thought of her face. She had seen herself in her glass, but she had not looked at herself. And then, she had often been told that she was homely; Jean Valjean alone would quietly say: "Why no! why! no!" However that might be, Cosette had always thought herself homely, and had grown up in that idea with the pliant resignation of childhood. And now suddenly her mirror said like Jean Valjean: "Why no!" She had no sleep that night. "If I were pretty!" thought she, "how funny it would be if I should be pretty!" And she called to mind those of her companions whose beauty had made an impression in the convent, and said: "What! I should be like Mademoiselle Such-a-one!"

The next day she looked at herself, but not by chance, and she doubted. "Where were my wits gone?" said she, "no, I am homely." She had merely slept badly, her eyes were dark and she was pale. She had not felt very happy the evening before, in the thought that she was beautiful, but she was sad at thinking so no longer. She did not look at herself again, and for more than a fortnight she tried to dress her hair with her back to the mirror.

In the evening after dinner, she regularly made tapestry or did some convent work in the parlour, while Jean Valjean read by her side. Once, on raising her eyes from her work, she was very much surprised at the anxious way in which her father was looking at her.

At another time, she was passing along the street, and it seemed to her that somebody behind her, whom she did not see, said: "Pretty woman! but badly dressed." "Pshaw!" thought she, "that is not me. I am well dressed and homely." She had on at the time her plush hat and merino dress.

At last, she was in the garden one day, and heard poor old Toussaint saying: "Monsieur, do you notice how pretty mademoiselle is growing?" Cosette did not hear what her father answered. Toussaint's words threw her into a sort of commotion. She ran out of the garden, went up to her room, hurried to the glass, it was three months since she had looked at herself, and uttered a cry. She was dazzled by herself.

She was beautiful and handsome; she could not help being of Toussaint's and her mirror's opinion. Her form was complete, her skin had become white, her hair had grown lustrous, an unknown splendour was lighted up in her blue eyes. The consciousness of her beauty came to her entire, in a moment, like broad daylight when it bursts upon us; others noticed it moreover, Toussaint said so, it was of her evidently that the passer-by had spoken, there was no more doubt; she went down into the garden again, thinking herself a queen, hearing the birds sing, it was in winter, seeing the sky golden, the sunshine in the trees, flowers among the shrubbery, wild, mad, in an inexpressible rapture.

For his part, Jean Valjean felt a deep and undefinable anguish in his heart.

He had in fact, for some time past, been contemplating with terror that beauty which appeared every day more radiant upon Cosette's sweet face. A dawn, charming to all others, ominous to him.

Cosette had been beautiful for some time before she perceived it. But, from the first day, this unexpected light which slowly rose and by degrees enveloped the young girl's whole person, wounded Jean Valjean's gloomy eyes. He felt that it was a change in a happy life, so happy that he dared not stir for fear of disturbing something. This man who had passed through every distress, who was still all bleeding from the lacerations of his destiny, who had been almost evil, and who had become almost holy, who, after having dragged the chain of the galleys, now dragged the invisible but heavy chain of indefinite infamy, this man whom the law had not released, and who might be at any instant retaken, and led back from the darkness of his virtue to the broad light of public shame, this man accepted all, excused all, pardoned all, blessed all, wished well to all, and only asked of Providence, of men, of the laws, of society, of nature, of the world, this one thing, that Cosette should love him!

That Cosette should continue to love him! That God would not prevent the heart of this child from coming to him, and remaining his! Loved by Cosette, he felt himself healed, refreshed, soothed, satisfied, rewarded, crowned. Loved by Cosette, he was content! he asked nothing more. Had anybody said to him: "Do you desire anything better?" he would have answered: "No." Had God said to him: "Do you desire heaven?" he would have answered: "I should be the loser."

Whatever might affect this condition, were it only on the surface, made him shudder as if it were the commencement of another. He had never known very clearly what the beauty of a woman was; but, by instinct, he understood, that it was terrible.

This beauty which was blooming out more and more triumphant and superb beside him, under his eyes, upon the ingenuous and fearful brow of this child—he looked upon it, from the depths of his ugliness, his old age, his misery, his reprobation, and his dejection, with dismay.

He said to himself: "How beautiful she is! What will become of me?"

Here in fact was the difference between his tenderness and the tenderness of a mother. What he saw with anguish, a mother would have seen with delight.

The first symptoms were not slow to manifest themselves.

From the morrow of the day on which she had said: "Really, I am handsome!" Cosette gave attention to her dress. She recalled the words of the passer-by: "Pretty, but badly dressed," breath of an oracle which had passed by her and vanished after depositing in her heart one of the two seeds which must afterwards fill the whole life of the woman, coquetry. Love is the other.

With faith in her beauty, the entire feminine soul blossomed within her. She was horrified at the wool and ashamed of the plush. Her father had never refused her anything. She knew at once the whole science of the hat, the dress, the cloak, the boot, the cuff, the stuff which sits well, the colour which is becoming, that science which makes the Parisian woman something so charming, so deep, and so dangerous. The phrase *heady woman* was invented for her.

In less than a month little Cosette was, in that Thebaid of the Rue de Babylone, not only one of the prettiest women, which is something, but one of "the best dressed" in Paris, which is much more. She would have liked to meet "her passer-by" to hear what he would say, and "to show him!" The truth is that she was ravishing in every point, and that she distinguished marvellously well between a Gérard hat and an Herbaut hat.

Jean Valjean beheld these ravages with anxiety. He, who felt that he could never more than creep, or walk at the most, saw wings growing on Cosette.

Still, merely by simple inspection of Cosette's toilette, a woman would have recognised that she had no mother. Certain little proprieties, certain special conventionalities, were not observed by Cosette. A mother, for instance, would have told her that a young girl does not wear damask.

The first day that Cosette went out with her dress and mantle of black damask and her white crape hat she came to take Jean Valjean's arm, gay, radiant, rosy, proud, and brilliant. "Father," said she, "how do you like this?" Jean Valjean answered in a voice which resembled the bitter voice of envy: "Charming!" He seemed as usual during the walk. When they came back he asked Cosette:

"Are you not going to wear your dress and hat any more?"

This occurred in Cosette's room. Cosette turned towards the wardrobe where her boarding-school dress was hanging.

"That disguise!" said she. "Father, what would you have me do with it?

Oh! to be sure, no, I shall never wear those horrid things again. With that machine on my head, I look like Madame Mad-dog."

Jean Valjean sighed deeply.

From that day, he noticed that Cosette, who previously was always asking to stay in, saying: "Father, I enjoy myself better here with you," was now always asking to go out. Indeed, what is the use of having a pretty face and a delightful dress, if you do not show them?

He also noticed that Cosette no longer had the same taste for the back-yard. She now preferred to stay in the garden, walking even without displeasure before the grating. Jean Valjean, unsociably, did not set his foot in the garden. He stayed in his back-yard, like a dog.

Cosette, by learning that she was beautiful, lost the grace of not knowing it; an exquisite grace, for beauty heightened by artlessness is ineffable, and nothing is so adorable as dazzling innocence, going on her way, and holding in her hand, all unconscious, the key of a paradise. But what she lost in ingenuous grace, she gained in pensive and serious charm. Her whole person, pervaded by the joys of youth, innocence, and beauty, breathed a splendid melancholy.

It was at this period that Marius, after the lapse of six months, saw her again at the Luxembourg Gardens.

3 (6)

THE BATTLE COMMENCES

COSETTE, in her seclusion, like Marius in his, was all ready to take fire. Destiny, with its mysterious and fatal patience, was slowly bringing these two beings near each other, fully charged and all languishing with the stormy electricities of passion,—these two souls which held love as two clouds hold lightning, and which were to meet and mingle in a glance like clouds in a flash.

The power of a glance has been so much abused in love stories, that it has come to be disbelieved in. Few people dare now to say that two beings have fallen in love because they have looked at each other. Yet it is in this way that love begins, and in this way only. The rest is only the rest, and comes afterwards. Nothing is more real than these great shocks which two souls give each other in exchanging this spark.

At that particular moment when Cosette unconsciously looked with this glance which so affected Marius, Marius had no suspicion that he also had a glance which affected Cosette.

She received from him the same harm and the same blessing.

For a long time now she had seen and scrutinised him as young girls scrutinise and see, while looking another way. Marius still thought Cosette ugly, while Cosette already began to think Marius beautiful. But as he paid no attention to her, this young man was quite indifferent to her.

Still she could not help saying to herself that he had beautiful hair, beautiful eyes, beautiful teeth, a charming voice, when she heard him talking with his comrades; that he walked with an awkward gait, if you will, but with a grace of his own; that he didn't appear altogether stupid; that his whole person was noble, gentle, natural, and proud, and finally that he had a poor appearance, but that he had a good appearance.

On the day their eyes met and at last said abruptly to both those first obscure and ineffable things which the glance stammers out, Cosette at first did not comprehend. She went back pensively to the house in the Rue de l'Ouest, to which Jean Valjean, according to his custom, had gone to spend six weeks. The next day, on waking, she thought of this unknown young man, so long indifferent and icy, who now seemed to give some attention to her, and it did not seem to her that this attention was in the least degree pleasant. She was rather a little angry at this disdainful beau. An under-current of war was excited in her. It seemed to her, and she felt a pleasure in it still altogether childish, that at last she should be avenged.

Knowing that she was beautiful, she felt thoroughly, although in an indistinct way, that she had a weapon. Women play with their beauty as children do with their knives. They wound themselves with it.

We remember Marius' hesitations, his palpitations, his terrors. He remained at his seat and did not approach, which vexed Cosette. One day she said to Jean Valjean: "Father, let us walk a little this way." Seeing that Marius was not coming to her, she went to him. In such a case, every woman resembles Mahomet. And then, oddly enough, the first symptom of true love in a young man is timidity, in a young woman, boldness. This is surprising, and yet nothing is more natural. It is the two sexes tending to unite, and each acquiring the qualities of the other.

That day Cosette's glance made Marius mad, Marius' glance made Cosette tremble. Marius went away confident, and Cosette anxious. From that day onward, they adored each other.

The first thing that Cosette felt was a vague yet deep sadness. It seemed to her that since yesterday her soul had become black. She no longer recognised herself. The whiteness of soul of young girls, which is composed of coldness and gaiety, is like snow. It melts before love, which is its sun.

Cosette did not know what love was. She had never heard the word uttered in its earthly sense. In the books of profane music which came into the convent, *amour* was replaced by *tambour,* or *Pandour.* This made puzzles which exercised the imagination of the great girls, such as: *Oh! how delightful is the tambour!* or: *Pity is not a Pandour!* But Cosette had left while yet too young to be much concerned about the "tambour." She did not know, therefore, what name to give to what she now experienced. Is one less sick for not knowing the name of the disease?

4 (7)

FOR SADNESS, SADNESS REDOUBLED

THERE IS ANOTHER LAW of these young years of suffering and care, of these sharp struggles of the first love against the first obstacles, the young girl does not allow herself to be caught in any toil, the young man falls into all. Jean Valjean had commenced a sullen war against Marius, which Marius, with the sublime folly of his passion and his age, did not guess. Jean Valjean spread around him a multitude of snares; he changed his hours, he changed his bench, he forgot his handkerchief, he went to the Luxembourg Gardens alone; Marius fell headlong into every trap; and to all these question marks planted upon his path by Jean Valjean he answered ingenuously, yes. Meanwhile Cosette was still walled in in her apparent unconcern and her imperturbable tranquillity, so that Jean Valjean came to this conclusion: "This booby is madly in love with Cosette, but Cosette does not even know of his existence!"

There was nevertheless a painful tremor in the heart. The moment when Cosette would fall in love might come at any instant. Does not everything begin by indifference?

Once only Cosette made a mistake, and startled him. He rose from the bench to go, after sitting there three hours, and she said: "So soon!"

Jean Valjean had not discontinued the strolls in the Luxembourg Gardens, not wishing to do anything singular, and above all dreading to excite any suspicion in Cosette; but during those hours so sweet to the two lovers, while Cosette was sending her smile to the intoxicated Marius, who perceived nothing but that, and now saw nothing in the world save one radiant, adored face, Jean Valjean fixed upon Marius glaring and terrible eyes. He who had come to believe that he was no longer capable of a malevolent feeling, had moments in which, when Marius was there, he thought that he was again becoming savage and ferocious, and felt opening and upheaving against this young man those old depths of his soul where there had once been so much wrath. It seemed to him almost as if the unknown craters were forming within him again.

What? he was there, that creature. What did he come for? He came to pry, to scent, to examine, to attempt: he came to say, "Eh, why not?" he came to prowl about his, Jean Valjean's life!—to prowl about his happiness, to clutch it and carry it away!

Jean Valjean added: "Yes, that is it! what is he looking for? an adventure? What does he want? an amour! An amour!—and as for me! What! I, after having been the most miserable of men, shall be the most unfortunate; I shall have spent sixty years of life upon my knees; I shall have suffered all that a man can suffer; I shall have grown old without having been young; I shall have lived with no family, no relatives, no friends, no wife, no children! I shall have left my blood on every stone, on every thorn, on every post, along every wall; I shall have been mild, although the world was harsh to me, and good, although it was evil; I shall have become an honest man in spite of all; I shall have repented of the wrong which I have done, and pardoned the wrongs which have been done to me and the moment that I am rewarded, the moment that it is over, the moment that I reach the end, the moment that I have what I desire, rightfully and justly; I have paid for it, I have earned it; it will all disappear, it will all vanish, and I shall lose Cosette, and I shall lose my life, my joy, my soul, because a great booby has been pleased to come and lounge about the Luxembourg Gardens."

Then his eyes filled with a strange and dismal light. It was no longer a man looking upon a man; it was not an enemy looking upon an enemy. It was a dog looking upon a robber.

We know the rest. The insanity of Marius continued. One day he followed Cosette to the Rue de l'Ouest. Another day he spoke to the porter: the porter in his turn spoke, and said to Jean Valjean: "Monsieur, who is that curious young man who has been asking for you?" The next day, Jean Valjean cast that glance at Marius which Marius finally perceived. A week after, Jean Valjean had moved. He resolved that he would never set his foot again either in the Luxembourg Gardens, or in the Rue de l'Ouest. He returned to the Rue Plumet.

Cosette did not complain, she said nothing, she asked no questions, she did not seek to know any reason; she was already at that point at which one fears discovery and self-betrayal. Jean Valjean had no experience of this misery, the only misery which is charming, and the only misery which he did not know; for this reason, he did not understand the deep significance of Cosette's silence. He noticed only that she had become sad, and he became gloomy. There was on either side an armed inexperience.

Once he made a trial. He asked Cosette:

"Would you like to go to the Luxembourg Gardens?"

A light illumined Cosette's pale face.

"Yes," said she.

They went. Three months had passed. Marius went there no longer. Marius was not there.

The next day, Jean Valjean asked Cosette again:

"Would you like to go to the Luxembourg Gardens?"

She answered sadly and quietly:

"No!"

Jean Valjean was hurt by this sadness, and harrowed by this gentleness.

For her part, Cosette was languishing. She suffered from the absence of Marius, as she had rejoiced in his presence, in a peculiar way, without really knowing it. When Jean Valjean ceased to take her on their usual walk, her woman's instinct murmured confusedly in the depths of her heart, that she must not appear to cling to the Luxembourg Gardens; and that if it were indifferent to her, her father would take her back there. But days, weeks, and months passed away. Jean Valjean had tacitly accepted Cosette's tacit consent. She regretted it. It was too late. The day she returned to the Luxembourg Gardens, Marius was no longer there. Marius then had disappeared; it was all over; what could she do? Would she ever find him again? She felt a constriction of her heart, which nothing relaxed, and which was increasing every day; she no longer knew whether it was winter or summer, sunshine or rain, whether the birds sang, whether it was the season for dahlias or daisies, whether the Luxembourg Gardens were more charming than the Tuileries, whether the linen which the washer-woman brought home was starched too much, or not enough, whether Toussaint did "her marketing" well or ill, and she became dejected, absorbed, intent upon a single thought, her eye wild and fixed, as when one looks into the night at the deep black place where an apparition has vanished.

Still she did not let Jean Valjean see anything, except her paleness. She kept her face sweet for him.

This paleness was more than sufficient to make Jean Valjean anxious. Sometimes he asked her:

"What is the matter with you?"

She answered:

"Nothing."

And after a silence, as she felt that he was sad also, she continued: "And you, father, is not something the matter with you?"

"Me? nothing," said he.

These two beings, who had loved each other so exclusively, and with so touching a love, and who had lived so long for each other, were now suffering by each other and through each other; without speaking of it, without harsh feeling, and smiling the while.

BOOK FOUR
AID FROM BELOW MAY BE AID
FROM ABOVE

1

WOUND WITHOUT, CURE WITHIN

THUS THEIR LIFE gradually darkened.

There was left to them but one distraction, and this had formerly been a pleasure: that was to carry bread to those who were hungry, and clothing to those who were cold. In these visits to the poor, in which Cosette often accompanied Jean Valjean, they found some remnant of their former light-heartedness; and, sometimes, when they had had a good day, when many sorrows had been relieved and many little children revived and made warm, Cosette, in the evening, was a little gay. It was at this period that they visited the Jondrette den.

The day after that visit, Jean Valjean appeared in the cottage in the morning, with his ordinary calmness, but with a large wound on his left arm, very much inflamed and infected, which resembled a burn, and which he explained in some fashion. This wound confined him within doors more than a month with fever. He would see no physician. When Cosette urged it: "Call the veterinarian," said he.

Cosette dressed it night and morning with so divine a grace and so angelic a pleasure in being useful to him, that Jean Valjean felt all his old happiness return, his fears and his anxieties dissipate, and he looked upon Cosette, saying: "Oh! the good wound! Oh! the kind hurt!"

Cosette, as her father was sick, had deserted the summer-house and regained her taste for the little lodge and the back-yard. She spent almost all her time with Jean Valjean, and read to him the books which he liked. In general, books of travels. Jean Valjean was born anew; his happiness revived with inexpressible radiance; the Luxembourg Gardens, the unknown young prowler, Cosette's coldness, all these clouds of his soul faded away. He now said to himself: "I imagined all that. I am an old fool."

His happiness was so great, that the frightful discovery of the Thénardiers, made in the Jondrette den, and so unexpectedly, had in some sort glided over him. He had succeeded in escaping; his trace was lost, what mattered the rest! he thought of it only to grieve over those wretches. "They are now in prison, and can do no harm in future," thought he, "but what a pitiful family in distress!"

BOOK FIVE
THE END OF WHICH IS UNLIKE
THE BEGINNING

1 (2)

FEARS OF COSETTE

IN THE FIRST FORTNIGHT in April, Jean Valjean went on a journey. This, we know, happened with him from time to time, at very long intervals. He remained absent one or two days at the most. Where did he go? nobody knew, not even Cosette. Once only, on one of these trips, she had accompanied him in a fiacre as far as the corner of a little cul-de-sac, on which she read: *Impasse de la Planchette*. There he got out, and the fiacre took Cosette back to the Rue de Babylone. It was generally when money was needed for the household expenses that Jean Valjean made these little journeys.

Jean Valjean then was absent. He had said: "I shall be back in three days."

In the evening, Cosette was alone in the parlour. To amuse herself, she had opened her piano and began to sing, playing an accompaniment, the chorus from *Euryanthe: Hunters wandering in the woods!* which is perhaps the finest piece in all music.*

All at once it seemed to her that she heard a step in the garden.

It could not be her father, he was absent; it could not be Toussaint, she was in bed. It was ten o'clock at night.

She went to the window shutter which was closed and put her ear to it.

It appeared to her that it was a man's step, and that he was treading very softly.

She ran immediately up to the first story, into her room, opened a slide in her blind, and looked into the garden. The moon was full. She could see as plainly as in broad day.

There was nobody there.

She opened the window. The garden was absolutely silent and all that she could see of the street was as deserted as it always was.

Cosette thought she had been mistaken. She had imagined she heard this noise. It was a hallucination produced by Weber's sombre and majestic chorus, which opens before the mind startling depths, which trembles before the eye like a bewildering forest, and in which we hear the crackling of the dead branches beneath the anxious step of the hunters dimly seen in the twilight.

She thought no more about it.

Euryanthe was composed by the German Romantic artist Carl Maria von Weber (1786–1826), who was quite popular in France and particularly distinguished in his work for the piano.

Moreover, Cosette by nature was not easily startled. There was in her veins the blood of the gipsy and of the adventuress who goes barefoot. It must be remembered she was rather a lark than a dove. She was wild and brave at heart.

The next day, not so late, at nightfall, she was walking in the garden. In the midst of the confused thoughts which filled her mind, she thought she heard for a moment a sound like the sound of the evening before, as if somebody were walking in the darkness under the trees, not very far from her, but she said to herself that nothing is more like a step in the grass than the rustling of two limbs against each other, and she paid no attention to it. Moreover, she saw nothing.

She left "the bush;" she had to cross a little green grass-plot to reach the steps. The moon, which had just risen behind her, projected, as Cosette came out from the shrubbery, her shadow before her upon this grass-plot.

Cosette stood still, terrified.

By the side of her shadow, the moon marked out distinctly upon the sward another shadow singularly frightful and terrible, a shadow with a round hat.

It was like the shadow of a man who might have been standing in the edge of the shrubbery, a few steps behind Cosette.

For a moment she was unable to speak, or cry, or call, or stir, or turn her head.

At last she summoned up all her courage and resolutely turned round. There was nobody there.

She looked upon the ground. The shadow had disappeared.

She returned into the shrubbery, boldly hunted through the corners, went as far as the gate, and found nothing.

She felt her blood run cold. Was this also a hallucination? What! two days in succession? One hallucination may pass, but two hallucinations? What made her most anxious was that the shadow was certainly not a phantom. Phantoms never wear round hats.

The next day Jean Valjean returned. Cosette narrated to him what she thought she had heard and seen. She expected to be reassured, and that her father would shrug his shoulders and say: "You are a foolish little girl."

Jean Valjean became anxious.

"It may be nothing," said he to her.

He left her under some pretext and went into the garden, and she saw him examining the gate very closely.

In the night she awoke; now she was certain, and she distinctly heard somebody walking very near the steps under her window. She ran to her slide and opened it. There was in fact a man in the garden with a big club in his hand. Just as she was about to cry out, the moon lighted up the man's face. It was her father!

She went back to bed, saying: "So he is really anxious!"

Jean Valjean passed that night in the garden and the two nights following. Cosette saw him through the hole in her shutter.

The third night the moon was smaller and rose later, it might have been one o'clock in the morning, she heard a loud burst of laughter and her father's voice calling her:

"Cosette!"

She sprang out of bed, threw on her dressing-gown, and opened her window.

Her father was below on the grass-plot.

"I woke you up to show you," said he. "Look, here is your shadow in a round hat." And he pointed to a shadow on the sward made by the moon, and which really bore a close resemblance to the appearance of a man in a round hat. It was a figure produced by a sheet-iron stove-pipe with a cap, which rose above a neighbouring roof.

Cosette also began to laugh, all her gloomy suppositions fell to the ground, and the next day, while breakfasting with her father, she made merry over the mysterious garden haunted by shadows of stove-pipes.

Jean Valjean became entirely calm again; as to Cosette, she did not notice very carefully whether the stove-pipe was really in the direction of the shadow which she had seen, or thought she saw, and whether the moon was in the same part of the sky. She made no question about the oddity of a stove-pipe which is afraid of being caught in the act, and which retires when you look at its shadow, for the shadow had disappeared when Cosette turned round, and Cosette had really believed that she was certain of that. Cosette was fully reassured. The demonstration appeared to her complete, and the idea that there could have been anybody walking in the garden that evening, or that night, no longer entered her head.

A few days afterwards, however, a new incident occurred.

2 (3)

ENRICHED BY THE COMMENTARIES OF TOUSSAINT

IN THE GARDEN, near the grated gate, on the street, there was a stone bench protected from the gaze of the curious by a hedge, but which, nevertheless, by an effort, the arm of a passer-by could reach through the grating and the hedge.

One evening in this same month of April, Jean Valjean had gone out; Cosette, after sunset, had sat down on this bench. The wind was freshening in the trees, Cosette was musing; a vague sadness was coming over her little by little, that invincible sadness which evening gives and which comes perhaps, who knows? from the mystery of the tomb half-opened at that hour.

Fantine was perhaps in that shadow.

Cosette rose, slowly made the round of the garden, walking in the grass which was wet with dew, and saying to herself through the kind of melancholy somnambulism in which she was enveloped: "One really needs wooden shoes for the garden at this hour. I shall catch cold."

She returned to the bench.

Just as she was sitting down, she noticed in the place she had left a stone of considerable size which evidently was not there the moment before.

Cosette reflected upon this stone, asking herself what it meant. Suddenly, the idea that this stone did not come upon the bench of itself, that somebody had put it there, that an arm had passed through that grating, this idea came to her and made her afraid. It was a genuine fear this time; there was the stone. No doubt was possible, she did not touch it, fled without daring to look behind her, took refuge in the house, and immediately shut the glass-door of the stairs with shutter, bar, and bolt. She asked Toussaint:

"Has my father come in?"

"Not yet, mademoiselle."

(We have noted once for all Toussaint's stammering. Let us be permitted to indicate it no longer. We dislike the musical notation of an infirmity.)

Jean Valjean, a man given to thought and a night-walker, frequently did not return till quite late.

"Toussaint," resumed Cosette, "you are careful in the evening to bar the shutters well, upon the garden at least, and to really put the little iron things into the little rings which fasten?"

"Oh! never fear, mademoiselle."

Toussaint did not fail, and Cosette well knew it, but she could not help adding:

"Because it is so solitary about here!"

"For that matter," said Toussaint, "that is true. We would be assassinated before we would have time to say Boo! And then, monsieur doesn't sleep in the house. But don't be afraid, mademoiselle, I fasten the windows like Bastilles. Lone women! I am sure it is enough to make us shudder! Just imagine it! to see men come into the room at night and say to you: Hush! and set themselves to cutting your throat. It isn't so much the dying, people die, that is all right, we know very well that we must die, but it is the horror of having such people touch you. And then their knives, they must cut badly! O God!"

"Be still," said Cosette. "Fasten everything well."

Cosette, dismayed by the melodrama improvised by Toussaint, and perhaps also by the memory of the apparitions of the previous week which came back to her, did not even dare to say to her: "Go and look at the stone which somebody has laid on the bench!" for fear of opening the garden door again, and lest "the men" would come in. She had all the doors and windows carefully closed, made Toussaint go over the whole house from cellar to garret, shut herself up in her room, drew her bolts, looked under her bed, lay down, and slept badly. All night she saw the stone big as a mountain and full of caves.

At sunrise—the peculiarity of sunrise is to make us laugh at all our terrors of the night, and our laugh is always proportioned to the fear we have had—at sunrise Cosette, on waking, looked upon her fright as upon a nightmare, and said to herself: "What have I been dreaming about? This is like those steps which I thought I heard at night last week in the garden! It is like the shadow of the stove-pipe! And am I going to be a coward now!"

The sun, which shone through the cracks of her shutters, and made the damask curtains purple, reassured her to such an extent that it all vanished from her thoughts, even the stone.

"There was no stone on the bench, any more than there was a man with a round hat in the garden; I dreamed the stone as I did the rest."

She dressed herself, went down to the garden, ran to the bench, and felt a cold sweat. The stone was there.

But this was only for a moment. What is fright by night is curiosity by day.

"Pshaw!" said she, "now let us see."

She raised the stone, which was pretty large. There was something underneath which resembled a letter.

It was a white paper envelope. Cosette seized it; there was no address on the one side, no seal on the other. Still the envelope, although open, was not empty. Papers could be seen in it.

Cosette examined it. There was no more fright, there was curiosity no more; there was a beginning of anxious interest.

Cosette took out of the envelope what it contained, a quire of paper, each page of which was numbered and contained a few lines written in a rather pretty hand-writing, thought Cosette, and very fine.

Cosette looked for a name, there was none; a signature, there was none. To whom was it addressed? to her probably, since a hand had placed the packet upon her seat. From whom did it come? An irresistible fascination took possession of her, she endeavoured to turn her eyes away from these leaves which trembled in her hand, she looked at the sky, the street, the acacias all steeped in light, some pigeons which were flying about a neighbouring roof, then all at once her eye eagerly sought the manuscript, and she said to herself that she must know what there was in it.

This is what she read:

3 (4)

A HEART UNDER A STONE

THE REDUCTION of the universe to a single being, the expansion of a single being even to God, this is love

———————

Love is the angels' greeting.

———————

How sad is the soul when it is sad from love!

What a void is the absence of the being who alone fills the world! Oh! how true it is that the beloved being becomes God! One would conceive that God would be jealous if the Father of all had not evidently made creation for the soul, and the soul for love!

———————

A glimpse of a smile under a white crape hat with a lilac coronet is enough, for the soul to enter into the palace of dreams.

———————

God is behind all things, but all things hide God. Things are black, creatures are opaque. To love a being, is to render her transparent.*

———————

Certain thoughts are prayers. There are moments when, whatever be the posture of the body, the soul is on its knees.

———————

Separated lovers deceive absence by a thousand chimerical things which still have their reality. They are prevented from seeing each other, they cannot write to each other; they find a multitude of mysterious means of correspondence. They commission the song of the birds, the perfume of flowers, the laughter of children, the light of the sun, the sighs of the wind, the beams of the stars, the whole creation. And why not? All the works of God were made to serve love. Love is powerful enough to charge all nature with its messages.

———————

*Hugo alludes to the Cabalist doctrine of "Occultation": to preserve the free will and moral responsibility of humans, who would be overwhelmed by a direct view of God's glory, he "withdraws" behind the masks of the sun and stars.

O Spring! thou art a letter which I write to her.

———————

The future belongs still more to the heart than to the mind. To love is the only thing which can occupy and fill up eternity. The infinite requires the inexhaustible.

———————

Love partakes of the soul itself. It is of the same nature. Like it, it is a divine spark; like it, it is incorruptible, indivisible, imperishable. It is a point of fire which is within us, which is immortal and infinite, which nothing can limit and which nothing can extinguish. We feel it burn even in the marrow of our bones, and we see it radiate even to the depths of the sky.

Becoming increasingly religious and mystical, but also alluding increasingly to his brief encounters with Cosette, Marius's effusions continue for another four pages.

4 (5)

COSETTE AFTER THE LETTER

DURING THE READING, Cosette entered gradually into reverie. At the moment she raised her eyes from the last line of the last page, the handsome officer, it was his hour, passed triumphant before the grating. Cosette thought him hideous.

She began again to contemplate the letter. It was written in a ravishing hand-writing, thought Cosette; in the same hand, but with different inks, sometimes very black, sometimes pale, as ink is put into the ink-stand, and consequently on different days. It was then a thought which had poured itself out there, sigh by sigh, irregularly, without order, without choice, without aim, at hazard. Cosette had never read anything like it. This manuscript, in which she found still more clearness than obscurity, had the effect upon her of a half-opened sanctuary. Each of these mysterious lines was resplendent to her eyes, and flooded her heart with a strange light. The education which she had received had always spoken to her of the soul and never of love, almost like one who should speak of the ember and not of the flame. This manuscript of fifteen pages revealed to her suddenly and sweetly the whole of love, the sorrow, the destiny, the life, the eternity, the beginning, the end. It was like a hand which had opened and thrown suddenly upon her a handful of sunbeams. She felt in these few lines a passionate, ardent, generous, honest nature, a consecrated will, an immense sorrow and a boundless hope, an oppressed heart, a glad ecstasy. What was this manuscript? a letter. A letter with no address, no name, no date, no signature, intense and disinterested, an enigma composed of truths, a message of love made to be brought by an angel and read by a virgin, a rendezvous given beyond the earth, a love-letter from a phantom to a shade. He was a calm yet exhausted absent one, who seemed ready to take refuge in death, and who sent to the absent Her the secret of destiny, the key of life, love. It had been written with the foot in the grave and the finger in Heaven. These lines, fallen one by one upon the paper, were what might be called drops of soul.

Now these pages, from whom could they come? Who could have written them?

Cosette did not hesitate for a moment. One single man.

He!

Day had revived in her mind; all had appeared again. She felt a wonderful joy and deep anguish. It was he! he who wrote to her! he who was there! he whose arm had passed through that grating! While she was forgetting him, he had found her again! But had she forgotten him? No, never! She was mad to have thought so for a moment. She had always loved him, always adored him. The fire had been covered and had smouldered for a time, but she clearly saw it had only sunk in the deeper, and now it burst out anew and fired her whole being. This letter was like a spark dropped from that other soul into hers. She felt the conflagration rekindling. She was penetrated by every word of the manuscript: "Oh, yes!" said she, "how I recognise all this! This is what I had already read in his eyes."

As she finished it for the third time, Lieutenant Théodule returned before the grating, and rattled his spurs on the pavement. Cosette mechanically raised her eyes. She thought him flat, stupid, silly, useless, conceited, odious, impertinent, and very ugly. The officer thought it his duty to smile. She turned away insulted and indignant. She would have been glad to have thrown something at his head.

She fled, went back to the house and shut herself up in her room to read over the manuscript again, to learn it by heart, and to muse. When she had read it well, she kissed it, and put it in her bosom.

It was done. Cosette had fallen back into the profound seraphic love. The abyss of Eden had reopened.

5 (6)

THE OLD ARE MADE TO GO OUT WHEN CONVENIENT

WHEN EVENING CAME, Jean Valjean went out; Cosette dressed herself. She arranged her hair in the manner which best became her, and she put on a dress the neck of which, as it had received one cut of the scissors too much, and as, by this slope, it allowed the turn of the neck to be seen, was, as young girls say, "a little immodest." It was not the least in the world immodest, but it was prettier than otherwise. She did all this without knowing why.

Did she expect a visit? no.

At dusk, she went down to the garden. Toussaint was busy in her kitchen, which looked out upon the back-yard.

She began to walk under the branches, putting them aside with her hand from time to time, because there were some that were very low.

She thus reached the bench.

The stone was still there.

She sat down, and laid her soft white hand upon that stone as if she would caress it and thank it.

All at once, she had that indefinable impression which we feel, though we see nothing, when there is somebody standing behind us.

She turned her head and arose.

It was he.

He was bareheaded. He appeared pale and thin. She hardly discerned his black dress. The twilight dimmed his fine forehead, and covered his eyes with darkness. He had, under a veil of incomparable sweetness, something of death and of night. His face was lighted by the light of a dying day, and by the thought of a departing soul.

It seemed as if he was not yet a phantom, and was now no longer a man.

His hat was lying a few steps distant in the shrubbery.

Cosette, ready to faint, did not utter a cry. She drew back slowly, for she felt herself attracted forward. He did not stir. Through the sad and ineffable something which enwrapped him, she felt the look of his eyes, which she did not see.

Cosette, in retreating, encountered a tree, and leaned against it. But for this tree, she would have fallen.

Then she heard his voice, that voice which she had never really heard, hardly rising above the rustling of the leaves, and murmuring:

"Forgive me, I am here. My heart is bursting, I could not live as I was, I have come. Have you read what I placed there, on this bench? do you recognise me at all? do not be afraid of me. It is a long time now, do you remember the day when you looked upon me? it was at the Luxembourg Gardens, near the Gladiator. And the day when you passed before me? it was the 16th of June and the 2nd of July. It will soon be a year. For a very long time now, I have not seen you at all. I asked the chairkeeper, she told me that she saw you no more. You lived in the Rue de l'Ouest, on the fourth floor front, in a new house, you see that I know! I followed you. What was I to do? And then you disappeared. I thought I saw you pass once when I was reading the papers under the arches of the Odéon. I ran. But no. It was a person who had a hat like yours. At night, I come here. Do not be afraid, nobody sees me. I come for a near look at your windows. I walk very softly that you may not hear, for perhaps you would be afraid. The other evening I was behind you, you turned round, I fled. Once I heard you sing. I was happy. Does it disturb you that I should hear you sing through the shutter? it can do you no harm. It cannot, can it? See, you are my angel, let me come sometimes; I believe I am going to die. If you but knew! I adore you! Pardon me, I am talking to you, I do not know what I am saying to you, perhaps I annoy you, do I annoy you?"

"O mother!" said she.

And she sank down upon herself as if she were dying.

He caught her, she fell, he caught her in his arms, he grasped her tightly, unconscious of what he was doing. He supported her even while tottering himself. He felt as if his head were enveloped in smoke; flashes of light passed through his eyelids; his ideas vanished; it seemed to him that he was performing a religious act, and that he was committing a profanation. Moreover, he did not feel one passionate emotion for this ravishing woman, whose form he felt against his heart. He was lost in love.

She took his hand and laid it on her heart. He felt the paper there, and stammered:

"You love me, then?"

She answered in a voice so low that it was no more than a breath which could scarcely be heard:

"Hush! you know it!"

And she hid her blushing head in the bosom of the proud and intoxicated young man.

He fell upon the bench, she by his side. There were no more words. The stars were beginning to shine. How was it that their lips met? How is it that the birds sing, that the snow melts, that the rose opens, that May blooms, that the dawn whitens behind the black trees on the shivering summit of the hills?

One kiss, and that was all.

Both trembled, and they looked at each other in the darkness with brilliant eyes.

They felt neither the fresh night, nor the cold stone, nor the damp ground, nor the wet grass, they looked at each other, and their hearts were full of thought. They had clasped hands, without knowing it.

She did not ask him, she did not even think of it, in what way and by what means he had succeeded in penetrating into the garden. It seemed so natural to her that he should be there.

From time to time Marius' knee touched Cosette's knee, which gave them both a thrill.

At intervals, Cosette faltered out a word. Her soul trembled upon her lips like a drop of dew upon a flower.

Gradually they began to talk. Overflow succeeded to silence, which is fulness. The night was serene and splendid above their heads. These two beings, pure as spirits, told each other all their dreams, their frenzies, their ecstasies, their chimeras, their despondencies, how they had adored each other from afar, how they had longed for each other, their despair when they had ceased to see each other. They confided to each other in an intimacy of the ideal, which even now nothing could have increased, all that was most hidden and most mysterious of themselves. They related to each other, with a candid faith in their illusions, all that love, youth, and that remnant of childhood was theirs, suggested to their thought. These two hearts poured themselves out into each other, so that at the end of an hour, it was the young man who had the young girl's soul and the young girl who had the soul of the young man. They inter-penetrated, they enchanted, they dazzled each other.

When they had finished, when they had told each other everything, she laid her head upon his shoulder, and asked him:

"What is your name?"

"My name is Marius," said he. "And yours?"

"My name is Cosette."

BOOK SIX
LITTLE GAVROCHE

1

A MALEVOLENT TRICK OF THE WIND

SINCE 1823, and while the Montfermeil tavern was gradually foundering and being swallowed up, not in the abyss of a bankruptcy, but in the sink of petty debts, the Thénardier couple had had two more children; both male. This made five; two girls and three boys. It was a good many.

The Thénardiess had gotten rid of the two last, while yet at an early age and quite small, with singular good fortune.

Gotten rid of is the right expression. There was in this woman but a fragment of nature. A phenomenon, moreover, of which there is more than one example. Like Madame la Maréchale de La Mothe Houdancourt, the Thénardiess was a mother only to her daughters. Her maternity ended there. Her hatred of the human race began with her boys. On the side towards her sons, her malignity was precipitous, and her heart had at that spot a fearful escarpment. As we have seen, she detested the eldest; she execrated the two others. Why? Because. The most terrible of motives and the most unanswerable of responses: Because. "I have no use for a squalling pack of children," said this mother.

We must explain how the Thénardiers had succeeded in disencumbering themselves of their two youngest children, and even in deriving a profit from them.

This Magnon girl, spoken of some pages back, was the same who had succeeded in getting her two children endowed by goodman Gillenormand. She lived on the Quai des Célestins, at the corner of that ancient Rue du Petit Musc which has done what it could to change its evil renown into good odour. Many will remember that great epidemic of croup which desolated, thirty-five years ago, the quarters bordering on the Seine at Paris, and of which science took advantage to experiment on a large scale as to the efficacy of insufflations of alum, now so happily replaced by the tincture of iodine externally applied. In that epidemic, Magnon lost her two boys, still very young, on the same day, one in the morning, the other at night. This was a blow. These children were precious to their mother; they represented eighty francs a month. These eighty francs were paid with great exactness, in the name of M. Gillenormand, by his rent-agent, M. Barge, retired constable, Rue du Roi de Sicile. The children dead, the income was buried. Magnon sought for an expedient. In that dark masonry of evil of which she was a part, everything is known, secrets are kept, and each aids the other. Magnon needed two children! the Thénardiess had two. Same sex, same age. Good arrangement for one, good investment for the other. The little Thénardiers became the little Magnons. Magnon left the Quai des Célestins and went to live in the Rue

Clocheperce. In Paris, the identity which binds an individual to himself is broken from one street to another.

The government, not being notified, did not object, and the substitution took place in the most natural way in the world. Only Thénardier demanded, for this loan of children, ten francs a month, which Magnon promised, and even paid. It need not be said that Monsieur Gillenormand continued to pay. He came twice a year to see the little ones. He did not perceive the change. "Monsieur," said Magnon to him, "how much they look like you."

Thénardier, to whom reincarnations were easy, seized this opportunity to become Jondrette. His two girls and Gavroche had hardly had time to perceive that they had two little brothers. At a certain depth of misery, men are possessed by a sort of spectral indifference, and look upon their fellow beings as upon goblins. Your nearest relatives are often but vague forms of shadow for you, hardly distinct from the nebulous background of life, and easily reblended with the invisible.

On the evening of the day she had delivered her two little ones to Magnon, expressing her willingness freely to renounce them forever, the Thénardiess had, or feigned to have, a scruple. She said to her husband: "But this is abandoning one's children!" Thénardier, magisterial and phlegmatic, cauterised the scruple with this phrase: "Jean Jacques Rousseau did better!" From scruple the mother passed to anxiety: "But suppose the police come to torment us? What we have done here, Monsieur Thénardier, say now, is it lawful?" Thénardier answered: "Everything is lawful. Nobody will see it but the sky. Moreover, with children who have not a sou, nobody has any interest to look closely into it."

Magnon had a kind of elegance in crime. She dressed with care. She shared her rooms, furnished in a gaudy yet wretched style, with a shrewd Frenchified English thief. This naturalised Parisian English woman, recommendable by very rich connections, intimately acquainted with the medals of the Bibliothèque and the diamonds of Mademoiselle Mars, afterwards became famous in the judicial records. She was called *Mamselle Miss*.

The two little ones who had fallen to Magnon had nothing to complain of. Recommended by the eighty francs, they were taken care of, as everything is which is a matter of business; not badly clothed, not badly fed, treated almost like "little gentlemen," better with the false mother than with the true. Magnon acted the lady and did not talk argot before them.

They passed some years thus: Thénardier augured well of it. It occurred to him one day to say to Magnon who brought him his monthly ten francs, "*The father* must give them an education."

Suddenly, these two poor children, till then well cared for, even by their ill fortune, were abruptly thrown out into life, and compelled to begin it.

A numerous arrest of malefactors like that of the Jondrette garret, necessarily complicated with ulterior searches and seizures, is really a disaster for this hideous occult counter-society which lives beneath public society; an event like this involves every description of misfortune in that gloomy world. The catastrophe of the Thénardiers produced the catastrophe of Magnon.

One day, a short time after Magnon handed Eponine the note relative to the Rue Plumet, there was a sudden descent of the police in the Rue Clocheperce. Magnon was arrested as well as Mamselle Miss, and the whole household, which was suspicious, was included in the haul. The two little boys were playing at the time in a back-yard, and saw nothing of the raid. When they wanted to go in, they found the door closed and the house empty. A cobbler, whose shop was opposite, called them and handed them a paper which "their mother" had left for them. On the paper there was an address: M. Barge, rent-agent, Rue du Roi de Sicile, No. 8. The man of the shop said to them: "You don't live here any more. Go there—it is near by—the first street to the left. Ask your way with this paper."

The children started, the elder leading the younger, and holding in his hand the paper which was to be their guide. He was cold, and his benumbed little fingers had but an awkward grasp, and held the paper loosely. As they were turning out of the Rue Clocheperce, a gust of wind snatched it from him, and, as night was coming on, the child could not find it again. They began to wander, as chance led them, in the streets.

2

IN WHICH LITTLE GAVROCHE TAKES
ADVANTAGE OF NAPOLEON THE GREAT

SPRING IN PARIS is often accompanied with keen and sharp north winds, by which one is not exactly frozen, but frost-bitten; these winds, which mar the most beautiful days, have precisely the effect of those currents of cold air which enter a warm room through the cracks of an ill-closed window or door. It seems as if the dreary door of winter were partly open and the wind were coming in at it. In the spring of 1832, the time when the first great epidemic of this century broke out in Europe, these winds were sharper and more piercing than ever. A door still more icy than that of winter was ajar. The door of the sepulchre. The breath of the cholera was felt in those cold north winds.

In the meteorological point of view, these winds had this peculiarity, that they did not exclude a strong electric tension. Storms accompanied by thunder and lightning were frequent during this time.

One evening when these winds were blowing harshly, to that degree that January seemed returned, and the bourgeois had resumed their cloaks, little Gavroche, always shivering cheerfully under his rags, was standing, as if in ecstasy, before a wig-maker's shop in the neighbourhood of the Orme Saint Gervais. He was adorned with a woman's woollen shawl, picked up nobody knows where, of which he had made a muffler. Little Gavroche appeared to be intensely admiring a wax bride, with a décolleté and a head-dress of orange flowers, which was revolving behind the sash, exhibiting between two lamps, its smile to the passers-by; but in reality he was watching the shop to see if he could not "filch" a cake of soap from the front, which he would afterwards sell for a sou to a hairdresser in the banlieue. It often happened that he breakfasted upon one of these cakes. He called this kind of work, for which he had some talent, "shaving the barbers."

As he was contemplating the bride and squinting at the cake of soap, he muttered between his teeth: "Tuesday. It isn't Tuesday. Is it Tuesday? Perhaps it is Tuesday. Yes, it is Tuesday."

Nobody ever discovered to what this monologue related.

If, perchance, this soliloquy referred to the last time he had dined it was three days before, for it was then Friday.

The barber in his shop, warmed by a good stove, was shaving a customer and casting from time to time a look towards this enemy, this frozen and brazen *gamin*, who had both hands in his pockets, but his wits evidently out of their sheath.

While Gavroche was examining the bride, the windows, and the Windsor soap, two children of unequal height, rather neatly dressed, and still smaller than he, one appearing to be seven years old, the other five, timidly turned the knob of the door and entered the shop, asking for something, charity, perhaps, in a plaintive manner which rather resembled a groan than a prayer. They both spoke at once and their words were unintelligible because sobs choked the voice of the younger, and the cold made the elder's teeth chatter. The barber turned with a furious face, and without leaving his razor, crowding back the elder with his left hand and the little one with his knee, pushed them into the street and shut the door saying:

"Coming and freezing people for nothing!"

The two children went on, crying. Meanwhile a cloud had come up; it began to rain.

Little Gavroche ran after them and accosted them:

"What is the matter with you, little brats?"

"We don't know where to sleep," answered the elder.

"Is that all?" said Gavroche. "That is nothing. Does anybody cry for that? You aren't lost puppies."

And assuming, through his slightly bantering superiority, a tone of softened authority and gentle protection:

"*Momacques*, come with me."

"Yes, monsieur," said the elder.

And the two children followed him as they would have followed an archbishop. They had stopped crying.

Gavroche led them up the Rue Saint Antoine in the direction of the Bastille.

Gavroche, as he travelled on, cast an indignant and retrospective glance at the barber's shop.

"He has no heart, that *merlan*," he muttered. "He is an *Angliche*."*

A girl, seeing them all three marching in a row, Gavroche at the head, broke into a loud laugh. This laugh was lacking in respect for the group.

"Good day, Mamselle Omnibus,"† said Gavroche to her.

Meanwhile, continuing up the street, he saw, quite frozen under a porte-cochère, a beggar girl of thirteen or fourteen, whose clothes were so short that her knees could be seen. The little girl was beginning to be too big a girl for that. Growth plays you such tricks. The skirt becomes short at the moment that nudity becomes indecent.

"Poor girl!" said Gavroche. "She hasn't even any underwear. But here, take this."

And, taking off all that good woollen scarf which he had about his neck, he threw it upon the bony and purple shoulders of the beggar girl, where the muffler became a shawl again.

The little girl looked at him with an astonished appearance, and received the shawl in silence. At a certain depth of distress, the poor, in their stupor, groan no longer over evil, and are no longer thankful for good.

This done:

"Brrr!" said Gavroche, shivering worse than St. Martin, who, at least, kept half his cloak.‡

At this brrr! the storm, redoubling its fury, became violent. These malignant skies punish good actions.

"Ah," exclaimed Gavroche, "what does this mean? It's raining again! Good God, if this continues, I withdraw my subscription."

And he started walking again.

"It's all the same," added he, casting a glance at the beggar girl who was cuddling herself under the shawl, "there is somebody who has some great duds."

And, looking at the cloud, he cried:

"Gotcha!"

The two children limped along behind him.

As they were passing by one of those thick grated lattices which indicate a baker's shop, for bread like gold is kept behind iron gratings, Gavroche turned:

"Ah, ha, *mômes*, have we dined?"

"Monsieur," answered the elder, "we have not eaten since early this morning."

---

*Figuratively means "hairdresser," but literally, "codfish."

†"Omnibus" because anybody can ride on her.

‡Saint Martin, bishop of Tours (ca. 316–397), cut his warm winter cloak in half to give part to a freezing beggar.

"You are then without father or mother?" resumed Gavroche, majestically.

"Excuse us, monsieur, we have a papa and mamma, but we don't know where they are."

"Sometimes that's better than knowing," said Gavroche, who was a thinker.

"It is two hours now," continued the elder, "that we have been walking; we have been looking for things in every corner, but we can find nothing."

"I know," said Gavroche. "The dogs eat up everything."

He resumed, after a moment's silence:

"Ah! we have lost our authors. We don't know now what we have done with them. That won't do, *gamins*. It is stupid to get lost like that for people of any age. Ah, yes, we must *licher* for all that."*

Still he asked them no questions. To be without a home, what could be more natural?

Meanwhile he had stopped, and for a few minutes he had been groping and fumbling in all sorts of recesses which he had in his rags.

Finally he raised his head with an air which was only intended for one of satisfaction, but which was in reality triumphant.

"Let us compose ourselves, *momignards*. Here is enough for supper for three."

And he took a sou from one of his pockets.

Without giving the two little boys time for amazement, he pushed them both before him into the baker's shop, and laid his sou on the counter, crying:

"Boy! five centimes' worth of bread."

The man, who was the master baker himself, took a loaf and a knife.

"In three pieces, boy!" resumed Gavroche, and he added with dignity:

"There are three of us."

And seeing that the baker, after having examined the three costumes, had taken a black loaf, he thrust his finger deep into his nose with a respiration as imperious as if he had had the great Frederick's pinch of snuff at the end of his thumb, and threw full in the baker's face this indignant apostrophe:

"Whossachuav?"

Those of our readers who may be tempted to see in this summons of Gavroche to the baker a Russian or Polish word, or one of those savage cries which the Iowas and the Botocudos hurl at each other from one bank of a stream to the other in their solitudes, are informed that it is a phrase which they use every day (they, our readers), and which takes the place of this phrase: what is that you have? The baker understood perfectly well, and answered:

"Why! it is bread, very good bread of the second quality."

"You mean *larton brutal*,"† replied Gavroche, with a calm cold disdain. "White bread, boy! *larton savonné!* I am treating."

---

*Slang for "drink" (from a variant form of *lecher*, to lick).
†Black bread.

The baker could not help smiling, and while he was cutting the white bread, he looked at them in a compassionate manner which offended Gavroche.

"Come, paper cap!" said he, "what are you fathoming us like that for?"

All three placed end to end would hardly have made a fathom.

When the bread was cut, the baker put the sou in his drawer, and Gavroche said to the two children:

"*Morfilez.*"

The little boys looked at him confounded.

Gavroche began to laugh:

"Ah! stop, that is true, they don't know yet, they are so small."

And he added:

"Eat."

At the same time he handed each of them a piece of bread.

And, thinking that the elder, who appeared to him more worthy of his conversation, deserved some special encouragement and ought to be relieved of all hesitation in regard to satisfying his appetite, he added, giving him the largest piece:

"Stick that in your gun."

There was one piece smaller than the other two; he took it for himself.

The poor children were starving, Gavroche included. While they were wolfing down the bread, they encumbered the shop of the baker who, now that he had received his pay, was regarding them ill-humouredly.

"Let's go back into the street," said Gavroche.*

They went on in the direction of the Bastille.

From time to time when they were passing before a lighted shop, the smaller one stopped to look at the time by a lead watch suspended from his neck by a string.

"Here is decidedly a real ninny," said Gavroche.

Then he thoughtfully muttered between his teeth:

"It's all the same, if I had any *mômes,* I would hug them tighter than this."

Twenty years ago, there was still to be seen in the southeast corner of the Place de la Bastille, near the canal basin dug in the ancient ditch of the prison citadel, a grotesque monument which has now faded away from the memory of Parisians, and which is worthy to leave some trace, for it was an idea of the "member of the Institute, General-in-Chief of the Army of Egypt."

We say monument, although it was only a rough model. But this rough model itself, a huge plan, a vast carcass of an idea of Napoleon which two or three successive gusts of wind had carried away and thrown each time further from us, had become historical, and had acquired a definiteness which contrasted with its provisional aspect. It was an elephant, forty feet

---

*Gavroche says *rentrons dans la rue* ("let's go back inside the street") because it is literally his home.

high, constructed of framework and masonry, bearing on its back its tower, which resembled a house, formerly painted green by some house-painter, now painted black by the sun, the rain, and the weather. In that open and deserted corner of the square, the broad front of the colossus, his trunk, his tusks, his size, his enormous rump, his four feet like columns, produced at night, under the starry sky, a startling and terrible outline. One knew not what it meant. It was a sort of symbol of the force of the people. It was gloomy, enigmatic, and immense. It was a mysterious and mighty phantom, visibly standing by the side of the invisible spectre of the Bastille.

It was towards this corner of the square, dimly lighted by the reflection of a distant lamp, that the *gamin* directed the two *"mômes."*

We must be permitted to stop here long enough to declare that we are within the simple reality, and that twenty years ago the police tribunals would have had to condemn upon a complaint for vagrancy and breach of a public monument, a child who should have been caught sleeping in the interior even of the elephant of the Bastille. This fact stated, we continue.

As they came near the colossus, Gavroche comprehended the effect which the infinitely great may produce upon the infinitely small, and said:

"Brats! don't be frightened."

Then he entered through a gap in the fence into the inclosure of the elephant, and helped the *mômes* to crawl through the breach. The two children, a little frightened, followed Gavroche without saying a word, and trusted themselves to that little Providence in rags who had given them bread and promised them a lodging.

Lying by the side of the fence was a ladder, which, by day, was used by the working-men of the neighbouring wood-yard. Gavroche lifted it with singular vigour, and set it up against one of the elephant's forelegs. About the point where the ladder ended, a sort of black hole could be distinguished in the belly of the colossus.

Gavroche showed the ladder and the hole to his guests, and said to them: "Mount and enter."

The two little fellows looked at each other in terror.

"You are afraid, *mômes!*" exclaimed Gavroche.

And he added:

"You shall see."

He clasped the elephant's wrinkled foot, and in a twinkling, without deigning to make use of the ladder, he reached the crevice. He entered it as an adder glides into a hole, and disappeared, and a moment afterwards the two children saw his pallid face dimly appearing like a faded and wan form, at the edge of the hole full of darkness.

"Well," cried he, "why don't you come up, *momignards?* you'll see how nice it is! Come up," said he, to the elder, "I will give you a hand."

The little ones urged each other forward. The *gamin* made them afraid and reassured them at the same time, and then it was raining very hard. The elder ventured. The younger, seeing his brother go up, and himself left all alone between the paws of this huge beast, had a great desire to cry, but he did not dare.

The elder clambered up the rounds of the ladder. He tottered badly. Gavroche, while he was on his way, encouraged him with the exclamations of a fencing master to his scholars, or of a muleteer to his mules:

"Don't be afraid!"

"That's it!"

"Come on!"

"Put your foot there!"

"Your hand here!"

"Be brave!"

And when he came within his reach he caught him quickly and vigorously by the arm and drew him up.

"Gulped!" said he.

The *môme* had passed through the crevice.

"Now," said Gavroche, "wait for me. Monsieur, have the kindness to sit down."

And, going out by the crevice as he had entered, he let himself glide with the agility of a monkey along the elephant's leg, he dropped upon his feet in the grass, caught the little five-year-old by the waist and set him half way up the ladder, then he began to mount up behind him, crying to the elder:

"I will push him; you pull him."

In an instant the little fellow was lifted, pushed, dragged, pulled, stuffed, crammed into the hole without having had time to know what was going on. And Gavroche, entering after him, pushing back the ladder with a kick so that it fell upon the grass, began to clap his hands, and cried:

"Here we are! Hurrah for General Lafayette!"

This explosion over, he added:

"Brats, you are in my house."

Gavroche was in fact at home.

O unexpected utility of the useless! charity of great things! goodness of giants! This monstrous monument which had contained a thought of the emperor, had become the box of a *gamin*. The *môme* had been accepted and sheltered by the colossus. The bourgeois in their Sunday clothes, who passed by the elephant of the Bastille, frequently said, eyeing it scornfully with their goggle eyes: "What's the use of that?" The use of it was to save from the cold, the frost, the hail, the rain, to protect from the wintry wind, to preserve from sleeping in the mud, which breeds fever, and from sleeping in the snow, which breeds death, a little being with no father or mother, with no bread, no clothing, no asylum. The use of it was to receive the innocent whom society repulsed. The use of it was to diminish the public crime. It was a den open for him to whom all doors were closed. It seemed as if the miserable old mastodon, invaded by vermin and oblivion, covered with warts, mould, and ulcers, tottering, worm-eaten, abandoned, condemned, a sort of colossal beggar asking in vain the alms of a benevolent look in the middle of the Square, had taken pity itself on this other beggar, the poor pigmy who went with no shoes to his feet, no roof over his head, blowing his fingers, clothed in rags, fed upon what is thrown away. This was the use of the elephant of the Bastille. This idea of Napoleon, disdained by men, had been taken up by God. That which had been illustrious only, had become august. The emperor must have had, to realise what he meditated, porphyry, brass, iron, gold, marble; for God the old assemblage of boards, joists, and plaster was enough. The emperor had had a dream of genius; in this titanic elephant, armed, prodigious, brandishing his trunk, bearing his tower, and making the joyous and vivifying waters gush out on all sides about him, he desired to incarnate the people. God had done a grander thing with it, he lodged a child.

The hole by which Gavroche had entered was a break hardly visible from the outside, concealed as it was, and as we have said under the belly of the elephant, and so narrow that hardly anything but cats and *mômes* could have passed through.

"Let us begin," said Gavroche, "by telling the porter that we are not in."

And plunging into the darkness with certainty, like one who is familiar with his room, he took a board and stopped the hole.

Gavroche plunged again into the darkness. The children heard the sputtering of the taper plunged into the phosphoric bottle. The chemical taper was not yet in existence; the Fumade tinder-box represented progress at that period.

A sudden light made them wink; Gavroche had just lighted one of those bits of string soaked in resin which are called cellar-rats. The cellar-rats, which made more smoke than flame, rendered the inside of the elephant dimly visible.

Gavroche's two guests looked about them, and felt something like what one would feel who should be shut up in the great tun of Heidelberg, or better still, what Jonah must have felt in the Biblical belly of the whale. An entire gigantic skeleton appeared to them, and enveloped them. Above, a long dusky beam, from which projected at regular distances massive encircling timbers, represented the vertebral column with its ribs, stalactites of plaster hung down like the viscera, and from one side to the other huge spider-webs made dusty diaphragms. Here and there in the corners great blackish spots were seen, which had the appearance of being alive, and which changed their places rapidly with a wild and startled motion.

The debris fallen from the elephant's back upon his belly had filled up the concavity, so that they could walk upon it as upon a floor.

The smaller one hugged close to his brother and said in a low tone: "It's dark."

This word made Gavroche cry out. The petrified air of the two *mômes* rendered a shock necessary.

"What's your point?" he exclaimed. "Are we kidding around? Are we being fussy? Must you have the Tuileries? would you be fools? Say, I warn you that I do not belong to the regiment of ninnies. Are you the brats of the pope's headwaiter?"

A little roughness is good for a person who's afraid. It is reassuring. The two children came close to Gavroche.

Gavroche, paternally softened by this confidence, passed "from the grave to the gentle," and addressing himself to the smaller:

"Goosy," said he to him, accenting the insult with a caressing tone, "it is outside that it is dark. Outside it rains, here it doesn't rain; outside it is cold, here there isn't a speck of wind; outside there are heaps of folks, here there isn't anybody; outside there isn't even a moon, here there is my candle, by jinks!"

The two children began to regard the apartment with less fear; but Gavroche did not allow them much longer leisure for contemplation.

"Quick," said he.

And he pushed them towards what we are very happy to be able to call the bottom of the chamber.

His bed was there.

Gavroche's bed was complete. That is to say, there was a mattress, a covering, and an alcove with curtains.

The mattress was a straw mat, the covering a large blanket of coarse grey wool, very warm and almost new. The alcove was like this:

Three rather long laths, sunk and firmly settled into the rubbish of the floor, that is to say of the belly of the elephant, two in front and one behind, and tied together by a string at the top, so as to form a pyramidal frame. This frame supported a fine trellis of brass wire which was simply hung over it, but artistically applied and kept in place by fastenings of iron wire, in such a way that it entirely enveloped the three laths. A row of large stones fixed upon the ground all about this trellis so as to let nothing pass. This trellis was nothing more nor less than a fragment of those copper nettings which are used to cover the bird-houses in menageries. Gavroche's bed under this netting was as if in a cage. Altogether it was like an Esquimaux tent.

It was this netting which took the place of curtains.

Gavroche removed the stones a little which kept down the netting in front, and the two folds of the trellis which lay one over the other opened.

"*Mômes*, on your hands and knees!" said Gavroche.

He made his guests enter into the cage carefully, then he went in after them, creeping, pulled back the stones, and hermetically closed the opening.

They were all three stretched upon the straw.

Small as they were, none of them could have stood up in the alcove. Gavroche still held the cellar-rat in his hand.

"Now," said he, "*pioncez!* [sleep] I am going to suppress the candelabra."

"Monsieur," inquired the elder of the two brothers, of Gavroche, pointing to the netting, "what is that?"

"That," said Gavroche, "is for the rats, *pioncez!*"

The two children looked with a timid and stupefied respect upon this intrepid and inventive being, a vagabond like them, isolated like them, wretched like them, who was something wonderful and all-powerful, who seemed to them supernatural, and whose countenance was made up of all the grimaces of an old mountebank mingled with the most natural and most pleasant smile.

"Monsieur," said the elder timidly, "you are not afraid then of the sergents de ville?"

Gavroche merely answered:

"*Môme!* we don't say sergents de ville, we say *cognes.*"

The smaller boy had his eyes open, but he said nothing. As he was on
the edge of the mat, the elder being in the middle, Gavroche tucked the
blanket under him as a mother would have done, and raised the mat under
his head with some old rags in such a way as to make a pillow for the
môme. Then he turned towards the elder:

"Eh! we are pretty well off here!"

"Oh, yes," answered the elder, looking at Gavroche with the expression
of a rescued angel.

The two poor little soaked children were beginning to get warm.

"Ah, now," continued Gavroche, "what in the world were you crying
for?"

And pointing out the little one to his brother:

"A youngster like that, I don't say, but a big boy like you to cry is silly;
it makes you look like a calf."

"Well," said the child, "we had no room, no place to go."

"Brat!" replied Gavroche, "we don't say a room, we say a *piolle.*"

"And then we were afraid to be all alone like that in the night."

"We don't say night, we say *sorgue.*"

"Thank you, monsieur," said the child.

"Listen to me," continued Gavroche, "you must never whine any more
for anything. I will take care of you. You will see what fun we have. In summer we will go to the Glacière with Navet, a comrade of mine, we will go
in swimming in the Basin, we will run on the track before the Bridge of
Austerlitz all naked, that makes the washerwomen mad. They scream, they
scold, if you only knew how funny they are! We will go to see the skeleton
man. He is alive. At the Champs-Elysées. That parishioner is as thin as
anything. And then I will take you to the theatre. I will take you to see
Frederic Lemaître.* I have tickets, I know the actors, I even acted once in
a play. We were *mômes* so high, we ran about under a cloth, that made the
sea. I will have you hired at my theatre. We will go and see the savages.
They're not real, those savages. They have red tights which wrinkle, and
you can see their elbows darned with white thread. After that we will go to
the Opera. We will go in with the claqueurs. The claque at the Opera is
very select. I wouldn't go with the claque on the boulevards. At the Opera,
just think, there are some who pay twenty sous, but they are fools. They
call them dishrags. And then we will go to see the guillotining. I will show

---

*Frédéric Lemaître (1800–1876), a celebrated actor, gave rousing performances
in romantic plays. Gavroche may well have received free tickets as payment for
being part of a *claque* that would applaud vehemently—performing a function
similar to today's laugh and applause tracks on television.

you the executioner. He lives in the Rue des Marias. Monsieur Sanson. There is a letter-box on his door. Oh! we have famous fun!"

At this moment, a drop of wax fell upon Gavroche's finger, and recalled him to the realities of life.

"The deuce!" said he, "there's the match used up. Attention! I can't spend more than a sou a month for my lighting. When we go to bed, we must go to sleep. We haven't time to read the romances of Monsieur Paul de Kock. Besides the light might show through the cracks of the porte-cochère, and the *cognes* couldn't help seeing."

"And then," timidly observed the elder who alone dared to talk with Gavroche and reply to him, "a spark might fall into the straw, we must take care not to burn the house up."

"We don't say burn the house," said Gavroche, "we say *riffauder* the *bocard*."

The storm redoubled. They heard, in the intervals of the thunder, the tempest beating against the back of the colossus.

"Pour away, old rain!" said Gavroche. "It does amuse me to hear the decanter emptying along the house's legs. Winter is a fool; he throws away his goods, he loses his trouble, he can't wet us, and it makes him grumble, the old water-carrier!"

This allusion to thunder, all the consequences of which Gavroche accepted as a philosopher of the nineteenth century, was followed by a very vivid flash, so blinding that something of it entered by the crevice into the belly of the elephant. Almost at the same instant the thunder burst forth very furiously. The two little boys uttered a cry, and rose so quickly that the trellis was almost thrown out of place; but Gavroche turned his bold face towards them, and took advantage of the clap of thunder to burst into a laugh.

"Be calm, children. Don't upset the edifice. That was fine thunder; give us some more. That wasn't any fool of a flash. Bravo God! by jinks! that is most as good as it is at the theatre."

This said, he restored order in the trellis, gently pushed the two children to the head of the bed, pressed their knees to stretch them out at full length, and exclaimed:

"As God is lighting his candle, I can blow out mine. Children, we must sleep, my young humans. It is very bad not to sleep. It would make you *schlinguer* in your strainer, or, as the big bugs say, stink in your jaws. Wind yourselves up well in the peel! I'm going to extinguish. Are you all right?"

"Yes," murmured the elder, "I am right. I feel as if I had feathers under my head."

"We don't say head," cried Gavroche, "we say *tronche*."

The two children hugged close to each other. Gavroche finished arranging them upon the mat, and pulled the blanket up to their ears, then repeated for the third time the injunction in hieratic language:

"Pioncez!"

And he blew out the taper.

Hardly was the light extinguished when a singular tremor began to agitate the trellis under which the three children were lying. It was a multitude of dull rubbings, which gave a metallic sound, as if claws and teeth were grinding the copper wire. This was accompanied by all sorts of little sharp cries.

The little boy of five, hearing this tumult over his head, and shivering with fear, pushed the elder brother with his elbow, but the elder brother had already *"pioncé,"* according to Gavroche's order. Then the little boy, no longer capable of fearing him, ventured to accost Gavroche, but very low, and holding his breath:

"Monsieur?"

"Hey?" said Gavroche, who had just closed his eyes.

"What is that?"

"It is the rats," answered Gavroche.

And he laid his head again upon the mat.

The rats, in fact, which swarmed by thousands in the carcass of the elephant, and which were those living black spots of which we have spoken, had been held in awe by the flame of the candle so long as it burned, but as soon as this cavern, which was, as it were, their city, had been restored to night, smelling there what the good storyteller Perrault calls "some fresh meat," they had rushed in en masse upon Gavroche's tent, climbed to the top, and were biting its meshes as if they were seeking to get through this new-fashioned mosquito bar.

Still the little boy did not go to sleep.

"Monsieur!" he said again.

"Hey?" said Gavroche.

"What are the rats?"

"They are mice."

This explanation reassured the child a little. He had seen some white mice in the course of his life, and he was not afraid of them. However, he raised his voice again:

"Monsieur?"

"Hey?" replied Gavroche.

"Why don't you have a cat?"

"I had one," answered Gavroche, "I brought one here, but they ate her on me."

This second explanation undid the work of the first, and the little fellow again began to tremble. The dialogue between him and Gavroche was resumed for the fourth time.

"Monsieur!"

"Hey?"

"Who was it that was eaten up?"

"The cat."

"Who was it that ate the cat?"

"The rats."

"The mice?"

"Yes, the rats."

The child, dismayed by these mice who ate cats, continued:

"Monsieur, would those mice eat us?"

"Damn right!" said Gavroche.

The child's terror was complete. But Gavroche added:

"Don't be afraid! they can't get in. And when I am here. Here, take hold of my hand. Be still and *pioncez!*"

Gavroche at the same time took the little fellow's hand across his brother. The child clasped his hand against his body, and felt safe. Courage and strength have such mysterious communications. It was once more silent about them, the sound of voices had startled and driven away the rats; in a few minutes they might have returned and done their worst in vain, the three *mômes,* plunged in slumber, heard nothing more.

The hours of the night passed away. Darkness covered the immense Place de la Bastille; a wintry wind, which mingled with the rain, blew in gusts, the patrolmen ransacked the doors, alleys, yards and dark corners, and, looking for nocturnal vagabonds, passed silently by the elephant; the monster, standing, motionless, with open eyes in the darkness, appeared to be in reverie and well satisfied with his good deeds, and he sheltered from the heavens and from men the three poor sleeping children.

To understand what follows, we must remember that at that period the guard-house of the Bastille was situated at the other extremity of the Square, and that what occurred near the elephant could neither be seen nor heard by the sentinel.

Towards the end of the hour which immediately precedes daybreak, a man turned out of the Rue Saint Antoine, running, crossed the Square, turned the great inclosure of the Column of July, and glided between the palisades under the belly of the elephant. Had any light whatever shone upon this man, from his thoroughly wet clothing, one would have guessed that he had passed the night in the rain. When under the elephant he raised a grotesque call, which belongs to no human language and which a parrot alone could reproduce. He twice repeated this call, of which the following orthography gives but a very imperfect idea:

"Kirikikiou!"

At the second call, a clear, cheerful young voice answered from the belly of the elephant:

"Yes!"

Almost immediately the board which closed the hole moved away, and gave passage to a child, who descended along the elephant's leg and dropped lightly near the man. It was Gavroche. The man was Montparnasse.

As to this call, *kirikikiou,* it was undoubtedly what the child meant by, *You will ask for Monsieur Gavroche.*

On hearing it he had waked with a spring, crawled out of his "alcove," separating the netting a little, which he afterwards carefully closed again, then he had opened the trap and descended.

The man and the child recognised each other silently in the dark; Montparnasse merely said:

"We need you. Come and give us a lift."

The *gamin* did not ask any other explanation.

"I'm on hand," said he.

And they both took the direction of the Rue Saint Antoine, whence Montparnasse came, winding their way rapidly through the long file of market waggons which go down at that hour towards the market.

The market gardeners, crouching among the salads and vegetables, half asleep, buried up to the eyes in the trunks of their waggons on account of the driving rain, did not even notice these strange passengers.

3

THE FORTUNES AND MISFORTUNES OF ESCAPE

WHAT HAD TAKEN PLACE that same night at La Force was this:

An escape had been concerted between Babet, Brujon, Gueulemer, and Thénardier, although Thénardier was in solitary. Babet had done the business for himself during the day, as we have seen from the account of Montparnasse to Gavroche. Montparnasse was to help them from without.

Brujon, having spent a month in solitary, had had time, first, to twist a rope, secondly, to perfect a plan. Formerly these grim cells, in which prison discipline delivers the condemned to himself, were composed of four stone walls, a stone ceiling, a floor of paving-stones, a camp bed, a grated air-hole, a door reinforced with iron, and were called *dungeons;* but the dungeon came to be thought too horrible: today it is composed of an iron door, a grated air-hole, a camp bed, a floor of paving-stones, a stone ceiling, four stone walls, and it is called a *punitive detention cell.* There is little light in them even at noon. The disadvantage of these rooms which, as we see, are not dungeons, is that they allow beings to reflect who should be made to work.

Brujon then had reflected, and he had left his punitive detention cell with a rope. As he was reputed very dangerous in the Charlemagne Court, he was put into the Bâtiment Neuf. The first thing which he found in the Bâtiment Neuf was Gueulemer, the second was a nail; Gueulemer, that is to say crime, a nail, that is to say liberty.

Brujon, of whom it is time to give a complete idea, was, with an appearance of delicate complexion and a profoundly premeditated languor, a polished, gallant, intelligent robber, with an enticing look and a horrible smile. His look was a result of his will, and his smile of his nature. His first studies in his art were directed towards roofs; he had made a great improvement in the business of the lead strippers who strip roofing and tear off gutters by the process called: *the double membrane.*

What rendered the moment peculiarly favourable for an attempt at escape, was that some workmen were taking off and relaying, at that very time, a part of the slating of the prison. The Cour Saint Bernard was not entirely isolated from the Charlemagne Court and the Cour Saint Louis. There were scaffoldings and ladders up aloft; in other words, bridges and stairways leading towards deliverance.

Bâtiment Neuf, the most cracked and decrepit affair in the world, was the weak point of the prison. The walls were so much corroded by saltpetre that they had been obliged to put a facing of wood over the arches of the dormitories, because the stones detached themselves and fell upon the beds of the prisoners. Notwithstanding this decay, the blunder was committed of shutting up in the Bâtiment Neuf the most dangerous of the accused, of putting "the hard cases" in there, as they say in prison language.

The Bâtiment Neuf contained four dormitories one above the other and an attic which was called the Bel Air. A large chimney, probably of some ancient kitchen of the Dukes de La Force, started from the ground floor, passed through the four stories, cutting in two all the dormitories in which it appeared to be a kind of flattened pillar, and went out through the roof.

Gueulemer and Brujon were in the same dormitory. They had been put into the lower story by precaution. It happened that the heads of their beds rested against the flue of the chimney.

Thénardier was exactly above them in the attic known as the Bel Air.

The passer-by who stops in the Rue Culture Sainte Catherine beyond the barracks of the firemen, in front of the porte-cochère of the bath-house, sees a yard full of flowers and shrubs in boxes, at the further end of which is a little white rotunda with two wings enlivened by green blinds, the bucolic dream of Jean Jacques. Not more than ten years ago, above this rotunda there arose a black wall, enormous, hideous, and bare, against which it was built. This was the encircling wall of La Force.

This wall, behind this rotunda, was Milton seen behind Berquin.*

High as it was, this wall was over-topped by a still blacker roof which could be seen behind. This was the roof of the Bâtiment Neuf. You noticed in it four dormer windows with gratings; these were the windows of the Bel Air. A chimney pierced the roof, the chimney which passed through the dormitories.

The Bel Air, this attic of the Bâtiment Neuf, was a kind of large garret hall, closed with triple gratings and double sheet iron doors studded with monstrous nails. Entering at the north end, you had on your left the four

---

*Hugo contrasts the grim prison that evokes Milton's Hell with a pleasant garden that recalls the pioneering children's books by Arnaud Berquin (1741–1791), a sentimental, moralizing author.

windows, and on your right, opposite the windows, four large square cages, with spaces between, separated by narrow passages, built breast-high of masonry with bars of iron to the roof.

Thénardier had been in solitary in one of these cages since the night of the 3rd of February. Nobody has ever discovered how, or by what contrivance, he had succeeded in procuring and hiding a bottle of that wine invented, it is said, by Desrues, with which a narcotic is mixed, and which the band of the Endormeurs has rendered celebrated.

There are in many prisons treacherous employees, half jailers and half thieves, who aid in escapes, who sell a faithless service to the police, and who make much more than their salary.

On this same night, then, on which little Gavroche had picked up the two wandering children, Brujon and Gueulemer, knowing that Babet, who had escaped that very morning, was waiting for them in the street as well as Montparnasse, got up softly and began to pierce the flue of the chimney which touched their beds with the nail which Brujon had found. The fragments fell upon Brujon's bed, so that nobody heard them. The hail storm and the thunder shook the doors upon their hinges, and made a frightful and convenient uproar in the prison. Those of the prisoners who awoke made a feint of going to sleep again, and let Gueulemer and Brujon alone. Brujon was adroit; Gueulemer was vigorous. Before any sound had reached the watchman who was lying in the grated cell with a window opening into the sleeping room, the wall was pierced, the chimney scaled, the iron trellis which closed the upper orifice of the flue forced, and the two formidable bandits were upon the roof. The rain and the wind redoubled, the roof was slippery.

"What a good *sorgue* for a *crampe*,"* said Brujon.

A gulf of six feet wide and eighty feet deep separated them from the encircling wall. At the bottom of this gulf they saw a sentinel's musket gleaming in the darkness. They fastened one end of the rope which Brujon had woven in his cell, to the stumps of the bars of the chimney which they had just twisted off, threw the other end over the encircling wall, cleared the gulf at a bound, clung to the coping of the wall, bestrode it, let themselves glide one after the other down along the rope upon a little roof which adjoined the bath-house, pulled down their rope, leaped into the bath-house yard, crossed it, pushed open the porter's transom, near which hung the cord, pulled the cord, opened the porte-cochère, and were in the street.

It was not three-quarters of an hour since they had risen to their feet on their beds in the darkness, their nail in hand, their project in their heads.

A few moments afterwards they had rejoined Babet and Montparnasse, who were prowling about the neighbourhood.

In drawing down their rope, they had broken it, and there was a piece remaining fastened to the chimney on the roof. They had received no other damage than having pretty thoroughly skinned their hands.

---

*"What a good night for an escape."

That night Thénardier had received a warning, it never could be ascertained in what manner, and did not go to sleep.

About one o'clock in the morning, the night being very dark, he saw two shadows passing on the roof, in the rain and in the raging wind, before the window opposite his cage. One stopped at the window long enough for a look. It was Brujon. Thénardier recognised him, and understood. That was enough for him. Thénardier, described as an assassin, and detained under the charge of lying in wait by night with force and arms, was kept constantly in sight. A sentinel, who was relieved every two hours, marched with loaded gun before his cage. The Bel Air was lighted by a reflector. The prisoner had irons on his feet weighing fifty pounds. Every day, at four o'clock in the afternoon, a warden, escorted by two dogs—this was customary at that period—entered his cage, laid down near his bed a two pound loaf of black bread, a jug of water, and a dish full of very thin soup in which a few beans were swimming, examined his irons, and struck upon the bars. This man, with his dogs, returned twice in the night.

Thénardier had obtained permission to keep a kind of an iron spike which he used to nail his bread into a crack in the wall, "in order," said he, "to preserve it from the rats." As Thénardier was constantly in sight, they imagined no danger from this spike. However, it was remembered afterwards that a warden had said: "It would be better to let him have nothing but a wooden pike."

At two o'clock in the morning, the sentinel, who was an old soldier, was relieved, and his place was taken by a conscript. A few moments afterwards, the man with the dogs made his visit, and went away without noticing anything, except the extreme youth and the "peasant air" of the "greenhorn." Two hours afterwards, at four o'clock, when they came to relieve the conscript, they found him asleep, and lying on the ground like a log near Thénardier's cage. As to Thénardier, he was not there. His broken irons were on the floor. There was a hole in the ceiling of his cage, and above, another hole in the roof. A board had been torn from his bed, and doubtless carried away, for it was not found again. There was also seized in the cell a half empty bottle, containing the rest of the drugged wine with which the soldier had been put to sleep. The soldier's bayonet had disappeared.

At the moment of this discovery, it was supposed that Thénardier was out of all reach. The reality is, that he was no longer in the Bâtiment Neuf, but that he was still in great danger.

Thénardier on reaching the roof of the Bâtiment Neuf, found the remnant of Brujon's cord hanging to the bars of the upper trap of the chimney, but this broken end being much too short, he was unable to escape over the sentry's path as Brujon and Gueulemer had done.

On turning from the Rue des Ballets into the Rue du Roi de Sicile, on the right you meet almost immediately with a dirty recess. There was a house there in the last century, of which only the rear wall remains, a genuine ruin wall which rises to the height of the third story among the neighbouring buildings. This ruin can be recognised by two large square windows which may still be seen; the one in the middle, nearer the right gable, is crossed by a worm-eaten joist fitted like a cap-piece for a brace. Through these windows could formerly be discerned a high and dismal wall, which was a part of the encircling wall of La Force.

The void which the demolished house left upon the street is half filled by a palisade fence of rotten boards, supported by five stone posts. Hidden in this inclosure is a little shanty built against that part of the ruin which remains standing. The fence has a gate which a few years ago was fastened only by a latch.

Thénardier was upon the crest of this ruin a little after three o'clock in the morning.

How had he got there? That is what nobody has ever been able to explain or understand. The lightning must have both confused and helped him. Did he use the ladders and the scaffoldings of the slaters to get from roof to roof, from inclosure to inclosure, from compartment to compartment, to the buildings of the Charlemagne court, then the buildings of the Cour Saint Louis, the encircling wall, and from thence to the ruin on the Rue du Roi de Sicile? But there were gaps in this route which seemed to render it impossible. Did he lay down the plank from his bed as a bridge from the roof of the Bel Air to the encircling wall, and did he crawl on his belly along the coping of the wall, all round the prison as far as the ruin? But the encircling wall of La Force followed an indented and uneven line, it rose and fell, it sank down to the barracks of the firemen, it rose up to the bathing-house, it was cut by buildings, it was not of the same height on the Hotel Lamoignon as on the Rue Pavée, it had slopes and right angles everywhere; and then the sentinels would have seen the dark outline of the fugitive; on this supposition again, the route taken by Thénardier is still almost inexplicable. By either way, an impossible flight. Had Thénardier, illuminated by that fearful thirst for liberty which changes precipices into ditches, iron gratings into osier screens, a cripple into an athlete, an old gouty person into a bird, stupidity into instinct, instinct into intelligence, and intelligence into genius, had Thénardier invented and extemporised a third method? It has never been discovered.

One cannot always comprehend the marvels of escape. The man who escapes, let us repeat, is inspired; there is something of the star and the lightning in the mysterious gleam of flight; the effort towards deliverance is not less surprising than the flight towards the sublime; and we say of an escaped robber: How did he manage to scale that roof? just as it is said of Corneille: Where did he learn *that he would die?*

However this may be, dripping with sweat, soaked through by the rain, his clothes in strips, his hands skinned, his elbows bleeding, his knees torn, Thénardier had reached what children, in their figurative language, call the cutting edge of the wall of the ruin, he had stretched himself on it at full length, and there his strength failed him. A steep escarpment, three stories high, separated him from the pavement of the street.

The rope which he had was too short.

He was waiting there, pale, exhausted, having lost all the hope which he had, still covered by night, but saying to himself that day was just about to dawn, dismayed at the idea of hearing in a few moments the neighbouring clock of Saint Paul's strike four, the hour when they would come to relieve the sentinel and would find him asleep under the broken roof, gazing with a kind of stupor through the fearful depth, by the glimmer of the lamps, upon the wet and black pavement, that longed for yet terrible pavement which was death yet which was liberty.

He asked himself if his three accomplices in escape had succeeded, if they had heard him, and if they would come to his aid. He listened. Except a patrolman, nobody had passed through the street since he had been there. Nearly all the travel of the gardeners of Montreuil Charonne, Vincennes, and Bercy to the Market, is through the Rue Saint Antoine.

The clock struck four. Thénardier shuddered. A few moments afterwards, that wild and confused noise which follows upon the discovery of an escape, broke out in the prison. The sounds of doors opening and shutting, the grinding of gratings upon their hinges, the tumult in the guard-house, the harsh calls of the gate-keepers, the sound of the butts of muskets upon the pavement of the yards reached him. Lights moved up and down in the grated windows of the dormitories, a torch ran along the attic of the Bâtiment Neuf, the firemen of the barracks alongside had been called. Their caps, which the torches lighted up in the rain, were going to and fro along the roofs. At the same time Thénardier saw in the direction of the Bastille a whitish tint throwing a dismal pallor over the lower part of the sky.

He was on the top of a wall ten inches wide, stretched out beneath the storm, with two precipices, at the right and at the left, unable to stir, giddy at the prospect of falling, and horror-stricken at the certainty of arrest, and his thoughts, like the pendulum of a clock, went from one of these ideas to the other: "Dead if I fall, taken if I stay."

In this anguish, he suddenly saw, the street being still wrapped in darkness, a man who was gliding along the walls, and who came from the direction of the Rue Pavée, stop in the recess above which Thénardier was as it were suspended. This man was joined by a second, who was walking with the same precaution, then by a third, then by a fourth. When these men were together, one of them lifted the latch of the gate in the fence, and they all four entered the inclosure of the shanty. They were exactly under Thénardier. These men had evidently selected this recess so as to be able to talk without being seen by the passers-by or by the sentinel who guards the gate of La Force a few steps off. It must also be stated that the rain kept this sentinel blockaded in his sentry-box. Thénardier, not being able to distinguish their faces, listened to their words with the desperate attention of a wretch who feels that he is lost.

Something which resembled hope passed before Thénardier's eyes; these men spoke argot.

The first said, in a low voice, but distinctly:

"*Décarrons*. What is it we *maquillons icigo?*"*

---

*"Let us go. What are we doing here?"

The second answered:

"*Il lansquine* enough to put out the *riffe* of the *rabouin*. And then the *coqueurs* are going by, there is a *grivier* there who carries a *gaffe*, shall we let them *emballer* us *icicaille?*"*

These are two words, *icigo* and *icicaille*, which both mean ici [here], and which belong, the first to the argot of the Barrières, the second to the argot of the Temple, were revelations to Thénardier. By *icigo* he recognised Brujon, who was a prowler of the Barrières, and by *icicaille* Babet, who, among all his other trades, had been a second-hand dealer at the Temple.

The ancient argot of the age of Louis XIV, is now spoken only at the Temple, and Babet was the only one who spoke it quite purely. Without icicaille, Thénardier would not have recognised him, for he had entirely disguised his voice.

Meanwhile the third put in a word:

"Nothing is urgent yet, let us wait a little. How do we know that he doesn't need our help?"

By this, which was only French, Thénardier recognised Montparnasse, whose elegance consisted in understanding all argots and speaking none.

As to the fourth, he was silent, but his huge shoulders betrayed him. Thénardier had no hesitation. It was Gueulemer.

Brujon replied almost impetuously, but still in a low voice:

"What is it you *bonnez* us there? The *tapissier* couldn't draw his *crampe*. He don't know the *trus*, indeed! Bouliner his *limace* and *faucher* his *empaffes, maquiller* a *tortouse, caler boulins* in the *lourdes,* braser the *taffes, maquiller caroubles, faucher* the Bards, balance his *tortouse* outside, *panquer* himself, *camoufler* himself, one must be a *mariol?* The old man couldn't do it, he don't know how to *goupiner!*"†

Babet added, still in that prudent, classic argot which was spoken by Poulailler and Cartouche, and which is to the bold, new, strongly-coloured, and hazardous argot which Brujon used, what the language of Racine is to the language of André Chénier:

"Your *orgue tapissier* must have been made *marron* on the stairs. One must be *arcasien.* He is a *galifard.* He has been played the *harnache* by a *roussin,* perhaps even by a *roussi,* who has beaten him *comtois.* Lend your *oche,* Montparnasse, do you hear those *criblements* in the college? You have seen all those *camoufles.* He has *tombé,* come! He must be left to draw his twenty *longes.* I have no *taf,* I am no *taffeur,* that is *colombé,* but

---

*"It's raining enough to put out the devil's fire. And then the police are going by. There is a soldier there who is standing sentinel. Shall we let them arrest us here?"

†What is it you tell us there? The innkeeper couldn't escape. He don't know the trade, indeed! Tear up his shirt and cut up his bedclothes to make a rope, to make holes in the doors, to forge false papers, to make false keys, to cut his irons, to hang his rope outside, to hide himself, to disguise himself, one must be a devil! The old man couldn't do it, he don't know how to work.

there is nothing more but to make the *lezards,* or otherwise they will make us *gambiller* for it. Don't *renauder,* come with *nousiergue.* Let us go and *picter* a *rouillarde encible.*"*

"Friends are not left in difficulty," muttered Montparnasse.

"I *bonnis* you that he is *malade,*" replied Brujon. "At the hour which *toque,* the *tapissier* isn't worth a *broque!* We can do nothing here. *Décarrons.* I expect every moment that a *cogne* will *cintrer* me in *pogne!*"†

Montparnasse resisted now but feebly; the truth is, that these four men, with that faithfulness which bandits exhibit in never abandoning each other, had been prowling all night about La Force at whatever risk, in hope of seeing Thénardier rise above some wall. But the night which was becoming really too fine, it was storming enough to keep all the streets empty, the cold which was growing upon them, their soaked clothing, their wet shoes, the alarming uproar which had just broken out in the prison, the passing hours, the patrolmen they had met, hope departing, fear returning, all this impelled them to retreat. Montparnasse himself, who was, perhaps, to some slight extent a son-in-law of Thénardier, yielded. A moment more, they were gone. Thénardier gasped upon his wall like the shipwrecked sailors of the *Méduse* on their raft when they saw the ship which had appeared, vanish in the horizon.

He dared not call them, a cry overheard might destroy all; he had an idea, a final one, a flash of light; he took from his pocket the end of Brujon's rope, which he had detached from the chimney of the Bâtiment Neuf, and threw it into the inclosure.

This rope fell at their feet.

"A widow!"‡ said Babet.

"My tortouse!"§ said Brujon.

"There is the innkeeper," said Montparnasse.

They raised their eyes. Thénardier advanced his head a little.

"Quick!" said Montparnasse, "have you the other end of the rope, Brujon?"

"Yes."

"Tie the two ends together, we will throw him the rope, he will fasten it to the wall, he will have enough to get down."

---

*Your innkeeper must have been caught in the act. One must be a devil. He is an apprentice. He has been duped by a spy, perhaps even by a sheep, who made him talk. Listen, Montparnasse, do you hear those cries in the prison? You have seen all those lights. He is retaken, come! He must be left to get his twenty years. I have no fear, I am no coward, that is known; but there is nothing more to be done, or otherwise they will make us dance. Don't be angry, come with us. Let us go and drink a bottle of old wine together.

†I tell you that he is retaken. At the present time, the innkeeper isn't worth a penny. We can do nothing here. Let us go. I expect every moment that a sergent de ville will have me in his hand.

‡A rope (argot of the Temple).

§My rope (argot of the Barrières).

Thénardier ventured to speak:

"I am benumbed."

"We will warm you."

"I can't stir."

"Let yourself slip down, we will catch you."

"My hands are stiff."

"Only tie the rope to the wall."

"I can't."

"One of us must get up," said Montparnasse.

"Three stories!" said Brujon.

An old plaster flue, which had served for a stove which had formerly been in use in the shanty, crept along the wall, rising almost to the spot at which they saw Thénardier. This flue, then very much cracked and full of seams, has since fallen, but its traces can still be seen. It was very small.

"We could get up by that," said Montparnasse.

"By that flue!" exclaimed Babet, "an *orgue*,* never! it would take a *mion*."†

"It would take a *môme*,"‡ added Brujon.

"Where can we find a brat?" said Gueulemer.

"Wait," said Montparnasse, "I have the thing."

He opened the gate of the fence softly, made sure that nobody was passing in the street, went out carefully, shut the door after him, and started on a run in the direction of the Bastille.

Seven or eight minutes elapsed, eight thousand centuries to Thénardier; Babet, Brujon, and Gueulemer kept their teeth clenched; the door at last opened again, and Montparnasse appeared, out of breath, with Gavroche. The rain still kept the street entirely empty.

Little Gavroche entered the inclosure and looked upon these bandit forms with a quiet air. The water was dripping from his hair. Gueulemer addressed him:

"Brat, are you a man?"

Gavroche shrugged his shoulders and answered:

"A *môme* like *mézig* is an *orgue*, and *orgues* like *vousailles* are *mômes*."§

"How the *mion* plays with the spittoon!"‖ exclaimed Babet.

"The *môme pantinois* isn't *maquillé* of *fertille lansquinée*,"# added Brujon.

"What is it you want?" said Gavroche.

Montparnasse answered:

"To climb up by this flue."

---

*A man.

†A child (argot of the Temple).

‡A child (argot of the Barrières).

§"A child like me is a man, and men like you are children."

‖"How well the child's tongue is hung!"

#"The Parisian child isn't made of wet straw."

"With this widow,"* said Babet.

"And *ligoter* the *tortouse*,"† continued Brujon.

"To the *monté* of the *montant*,"‡ resumed Babet.

"To the *pieu* of the *vanterne*,"§ added Brujon.

"And then?" said Gavroche.

"That's it!" said Gueulemer.

The *gamin* examined the rope, the flue, the wall, the windows, and made that inexpressible and disdainful sound with the lips which signifies:

"That's all?"

"There is a man up there whom you will save," replied Montparnasse.

"Will you?" added Brujon.

"Goosy!" answered the child, as if the question appeared to him absurd; and he took off his shoes.

Gueulemer caught up Gavroche with one hand, put him on the roof of the shanty, the worm-eaten boards of which bent beneath the child's weight, and handed him the rope which Brujon had tied together during the absence of Montparnasse. The *gamin* went towards the flue, which it was easy to enter, thanks to a large hole at the roof. Just as he was about to start, Thénardier, who saw safety and life approaching, bent over the edge of the wall; the first gleam of day lighted up his forehead reeking with sweat, his livid cheeks, his thin and savage nose, his grey bristly beard, and Gavroche recognised him:

"Hold on!" said he, "it is my father!—Well, that don't hinder!"

And taking the rope in his teeth, he resolutely commenced the ascent.

He reached the top of the ruin, bestrode the old wall like a horse, and tied the rope firmly to the upper cross-bar of the window.

A moment afterwards Thénardier was in the street.

As soon as he had touched the pavement, as soon as he felt himself out of danger, he was no longer either fatigued, benumbed, or trembling; the terrible things through which he had passed vanished like a whiff of smoke, all that strange and ferocious intellect awoke, and found itself erect and free, ready to march forward. The man's first words were these:

"Now, who are we going to eat?"

It is needless to explain the meaning of this frightfully transparent word, which signifies all at once to kill, to assassinate, and to plunder. Eat, real meaning: *devour*.

"Let us hide first," said Brujon, "finish in three words and we will separate immediately. There was an affair which had a good look in the Rue Plumet, a deserted street, an isolated house, an old rusty grating upon a garden, some lone women."

"Well, why not?" inquired Thénardier.

---

*This rope.

†"Fasten the rope."

‡"To the top of the wall."

§"To the cross-bar of the window."

"Your *fée*[*] Eponine, has been to see the thing," answered Babet.

"And she brought a biscuit to Magnon," added Gueulemer, "nothing to *maquiller* there."[†]

"The *fée* isn't *loffe*,"[‡] said Thénardier. "Still we must see."

"Yes, yes," said Brujon, "we must see."

Meantime none of these men appeared longer to see Gavroche who, during this colloquy, had seated himself upon one of the stone supports of the fence; he waited a few minutes, perhaps for his father to turn towards him, then he put on his shoes, and said:

"It is over? you have no more use for me? men! you are out of your trouble. I am going. I must go and get my *mômes* up."

And he went away.

The five men went out of the inclosure one after another.

When Gavroche had disappeared at the turn of the Rue des Ballets, Babet took Thénardier aside.

"Did you notice that *mion?*" he asked him.

"What *mion?*"

"The *mion* who climbed up the wall and brought you the rope."

"Not much."

"Well, I don't know, but it seems to me that it is your son."

"Pshaw!" said Thénardier, "do you think so?"

[Book Seven "Argot (On Slang)," does not appear in this abridged edition.]

---

*Your daughter.
†"Nothing to do there."
‡Stupid.

BOOK EIGHT
ENCHANTMENT AND DESPAIR

1

SUNSHINE

THE READER HAS UNDERSTOOD that Eponine, having recognised through the grating the inhabitant of that Rue Plumet, to which Magnon had sent her, had begun by diverting the bandits from the Rue Plumet, had then conducted Marius thither, and that after several days of ecstasy before that grating, Marius, drawn by that force which pushes the iron towards the magnet and the lover towards the stones of which the house of her whom he loves is built, had finally entered Cosette's garden as Romeo did the garden of Juliet. It had even been easier for him than for Romeo; Romeo was obliged to scale a wall, Marius had only to push aside a little one of the bars of the decrepit grating, which was loosened in its rusty socket, like the teeth of old people. Marius was slender, and easily passed through.

As there was never anybody in the street, and as, moreover, Marius entered the garden only at night, he ran no risk of being seen.

From that blessed and holy hour when a kiss affianced these two souls, Marius came every evening. If, at this period of her life, Cosette had fallen into the love of a man who was unscrupulous and a libertine, she would have been ruined; for there are generous natures which give themselves, and Cosette was one. One of the magnanimities of woman is to yield. Love, at that height at which it is absolute, is associated with an inexpressibly celestial blindness of modesty. But what risks do you run, O noble souls! Often, you give the heart, we take the body. Your heart remains to you, and you look upon it in the darkness, and shudder. Love has no middle term; either it destroys, or it saves. All human destiny is this dilemma. This dilemma, destruction or salvation, no fatality proposes more inexorably than love. Love is life, if it be not death. Cradle; coffin also. The same sentiment says yes and no in the human heart. Of all the things which God has made, the human heart is that which sheds most light, and, alas! most night.

God willed that the love which Cosette met, should be one of those loves which save.*

Through all the month of May of that year 1832, there were there, every night, in that poor, wild garden, under that shrubbery each day more odourous and more dense, two beings composed of every chastity and every innocence, overflowing with all the felicities of Heaven, more nearly

---

*Whereas Cosette's mother, Fantine, met with a cruel lover who destroyed her. Hugo implies that such "permissive evil" must be part of a larger providential plan that we cannot apprehend.

archangels than men, pure, noble, intoxicated, radiant, who were resplendent to each other in the darkness. It seemed to Cosette that Marius had a crown, and to Marius that Cosette had a halo. They touched each other, they beheld each other, they clasped each other's hands, they pressed closely to each other; but there was a distance which they did not pass. Not that they respected it; they were ignorant of it. Marius felt a barrier, the purity of Cosette, and Cosette felt a support, the loyalty of Marius. The first kiss was the last also. Marius, since, had not gone beyond touching Cosette's hand, or her neckerchief, or her ringlets, with his lips. Cosette was to him a perfume, and not a woman. He breathed her. She refused nothing and he asked nothing. Cosette was happy, and Marius was satisfied. They lived in that ravishing condition which might be called the dazzling of a soul by a soul. It was that ineffable first embrace of two virginities in the ideal. Two swans meeting upon the Jungfrau.*

At that hour of love, an hour when passion is absolutely silent under the omnipotence of ecstasy, Marius, the pure and seraphic Marius, would have been capable rather of visiting a public woman than of lifting Cosette's dress to the height of her ankle. Once, on a moonlight night, Cosette stooped to pick up something from the ground, her dress loosened and displayed the rounding of her bosom. Marius turned away his eyes.

What passed between these two beings? Nothing. They were adoring each other.

At night, when they were there, this garden seemed a living and sacred place. All the flowers opened about them, and proffered them their incense; they too opened their souls and poured them forth to the flowers: the lusty and vigorous vegetation trembled full of sap and intoxication about these two innocent creatures, and they spoke words of love at which the trees thrilled.†

---

*The Jungfrau, or Virgin, is a high, snow-covered peak in the Swiss Alps. Hugo evokes a fantastic vision of white on white—absolute purity.

†In addition to being a great visionary poet and a great satiric poet, Hugo is a great love poet. See, for example, "Aurore" and "L'Âme en fleur," books I and II of *Les Contemplations* (1856).

2

THE STUPEFACTION OF
COMPLETE HAPPINESS

THEIR EXISTENCE WAS VAGUE, bewildered with happiness. They did not perceive the cholera which decimated Paris that very month [in 1832]. They had been as confidential with each other as they could be, but this had not gone very far beyond their names. Marius had told Cosette that he was an orphan, that his name was Marius Pontmercy, that he was a lawyer, that he lived by writing things for publishers, that his father was a colonel, that he was a hero, and that he, Marius, had quarrelled with his grandfather who was rich. He had also said something about being a baron; but that had produced no effect upon Cosette. Marius a baron! She did not comprehend. She did not know what that word meant. Marius was Marius. On her part she had confided to him that she had been brought up at the Convent of the Petit Picpus, that her mother was dead as well as his, that her father's name was M. Fauchelevent, that he was very kind, that he gave much to the poor, but that he was poor himself, and that he deprived himself of everything while he deprived her of nothing.

Strange to say, in the kind of symphony in which Marius had been living since he had seen Cosette, the past, even the most recent, had become so confused and distant to him that what Cosette told him satisfied him fully. He did not even think to speak to her of the night adventure at the Gorbeau tenement, the Thénardiers, the burning, and the strange attitude and the singular flight of her father. Marius had temporarily forgotten all that; he did not even know at night what he had done in the morning, nor where he had breakfasted, nor who had spoken to him; he had songs in his ear which rendered him deaf to every other thought; he existed only during the hours in which he saw Cosette. Then, as he was in Heaven, it was quite natural that he should forget the earth. They were both languorously bearing the undefinable burden of the immaterial pleasures. Thus live these somnambulists called lovers.

Alas! who has not experienced all these things? why comes there an hour when we leave this azure, and why does life continue afterwards?[2]

3

THE SHADOW GROWS

JEAN VALJEAN suspected nothing.

Cosette, a little less dreamy than Marius, was cheerful, and that was enough to make Jean Valjean happy. The thoughts of Cosette, her tender preoccupations, the image of Marius which filled her soul, detracted nothing from the incomparable purity of her beautiful, chaste, and smiling forehead. She was at the age when the maiden bears her love as the angel bears her lily. So Jean Valjean's mind was at rest. And then when two lovers have an understanding they always get along well; any third person who might disturb their love, is kept in perfect blindness by a very few precautions, always the same for all lovers. Thus never any objections from Cosette to Jean Valjean. Did he wish to take a walk? yes, my dear father. Did he wish to remain at home? very well. Would he spend the evening with Cosette? she was in raptures. As he always retired at ten o'clock, at such times Marius would not come to the garden till after that hour, when from the street he would hear Cosette open the glass-door leading out on the steps. We need not say that Marius was never met by day. Jean Valjean no longer even thought that Marius was in existence. Once, only, one morning, he happened to say to Cosette: "Why, you have something white on your back!" The evening before, Marius, in a transport, had pressed Cosette against the wall.

Old Toussaint who went to bed early, thought of nothing but going to sleep, once her work was done, and was ignorant of all, like Jean Valjean.

Never did Marius set foot into the house. When he was with Cosette they hid themselves in a recess near the steps, so that they could neither be seen nor heard from the street, and they sat there, contenting themselves often, by way of conversation, with pressing each other's hands twenty times a minute while looking into the branches of the trees. At such moments, a thunderbolt might have fallen within thirty paces of them, and they would not have suspected it, so deeply was the reverie of the one absorbed and buried in the reverie of the other.

Limpid purities. Hours all white, almost all alike. Such loves as these are a collection of lily leaves and dove-down.

The whole garden was between them and the street. Whenever Marius came in and went out, he carefully replaced the bar of the grating in such a way that no sign of tampering was visible.

Meanwhile various complications were approaching.

One evening Marius was making his way to the rendezvous by the Boulevard des Invalides; he usually walked with his head bent down; as he was just turning the corner of the Rue Plumet, he heard some one saying very near him:

"Good evening, Monsieur Marius."

He looked up, and recognised Eponine.

This produced a singular effect upon him. He had not thought even once of this girl since the day she brought him to the Rue Plumet, he had not seen her again, and she had completely gone out of his mind. He had motives of gratitude only towards her; he owed his present happiness to her, and still it was annoying to him to meet her.

It is a mistake to suppose that passion, when it is fortunate and pure, leads man to a state of perfection; it leads him simply, as we have said, to a state of forgetfulness. In this situation man forgets to be bad, but he also forgets to be good. Gratitude, duty, necessary and troublesome memories, vanish. At any other time Marius would have felt very differently towards Eponine. Absorbed in Cosette he had not even clearly in his mind that this Eponine's name was Eponine Thénardier, and that she bore a name written in his father's will, that name to which he would have been, a few months before, so ardently devoted. We show Marius just as he was. His father himself, disappeared somewhat from his soul beneath the splendour of his love.

He answered with some embarrassment:

"What! is it you, Eponine?"

"Why do you say *vous*? Have I done anything to you?"

"No," answered he.

Certainly, he had nothing against her. Far from it. Only, he felt that he could not do otherwise, now that he had whispered to Cosette, than speak coldly to Eponine.

As he was silent, she exclaimed:

"Tell me now—"

Then she stopped. It seemed as if words failed this creature, once so reckless and so bold. She attempted to smile and could not. She resumed:

"Well?—"

Then she was silent again, and stood with her eyes cast down.

"Good evening, Monsieur Marius," said she all at once abruptly, and she went away.

4

CAB ROLLS IN ENGLISH
AND YELPS IN ARGOT

THE NEXT DAY, it was the 3rd of June, the 3rd of June, 1832, a date which must be noted on account of the grave events which were at that time suspended over the horizon of Paris like thunder-clouds. Marius, at nightfall, was following the same path as the evening before, with the same rapturous thoughts in his heart, when he perceived, under the trees of the boulevard, Eponine approaching him. Two days in succession, this was too much. He turned hastily, left the boulevard, changed his route, and went to the Rue Plumet through the Rue Monsieur.

This caused Eponine to follow him to the Rue Plumet, a thing which she had not done before. She had been content until then to see him on his way through the boulevard without even seeking to meet him. The evening previous, only, had she tried to speak to him.

Eponine followed him then, without a suspicion on his part. She saw him push aside the bar of the grating, and glide into the garden.

"Why!" said she, "he is going into the house."

She approached the grating, felt of the bars one after another, and easily recognised the one which Marius had displaced.

She murmured in an undertone, with a mournful accent:

"None of that, Lisette!"

She sat down upon the sill of the grating, close beside the bar, as if she were guarding it. It was just at the point at which the grating joined the neighbouring wall. There was a dark corner there, in which Eponine was entirely hidden.

She remained thus for more than an hour, without stirring and without breathing, a prey to her own thoughts.

About ten o'clock in the evening, one of the two or three passers-by in the Rue Plumet, a belated old bourgeois who was hurrying through this deserted and ill-famed place, keeping close to the garden grating, on reaching the angle which the grating made with the wall, heard a sullen and threatening voice which said:

"I wouldn't be surprised if he came every evening!"

He cast his eyes about him, saw nobody, dared not look into that dark corner, and was very much frightened. He doubled his pace.

This person had reason to hasten, for a very few moments afterwards six men, who were walking separately and at some distance from each other along the wall, and who might have been taken for a tipsy patrol, entered the Rue Plumet.

The first to arrive at the grating of the garden stopped and waited for the others; in a second they were all six together.

These men began to talk in a low voice.

"It is *icicaille*," said one of them.

"Is there a *cab** in the garden?" asked another.

"I don't know. At all events I have *levé*† a ball of drugged bread which we will make him *morfiler*."‡

"Have you some mastic to *frangir* the *vanterne*?"§

"Yes."

"The grating is old," added a fifth, who had a voice like a ventriloquist.

"So much the better," said the second who had spoken. "It will not *criblera*‖ under the *bastringue*,# and will not be so hard to *faucher*.**

The sixth, who had not yet opened his mouth, began to examine the grating as Eponine had done an hour before, grasping each bar successively and shaking it carefully. In this way he came to the bar which Marius had loosened. Just as he was about to lay hold of this bar, a hand, starting abruptly from the shadow, fell upon his arm, he felt himself pushed sharply back by the middle of his breast, and a roughened voice said to him without crying out:

"There is a *cab*."

At the same time he saw a pale girl standing before him.

The man felt that commotion which is always given by the unexpected. He bristled up hideously; nothing is so frightful to see as ferocious beasts which are startled, their appearance when terrified is terrifying. He recoiled, and stammered:

"What is this creature?"

"Your daughter."

It was indeed Eponine who was speaking to Thénardier.

On the appearance of Eponine the five others, that is to say, Claquesous, Gueulemer, Babet, Montparnasse, and Brujon, approached without a sound, without haste, without saying a word, with the ominous slowness peculiar to these men of the night.

In their hands might be distinguished some strangely hideous tools. Gueulemer had one of those crooked crowbars which the prowlers call *fanchons*.

"Ah, there, what are you doing here? what do you want of us? are you crazy?" exclaimed Thénardier, as much as one can exclaim in a whisper. "What do you come and hinder us in our work for?"

---

*Dog.

†Brought; from the Spanish *llevar*.

‡Eat.

§To break a pane by means of a plaster of mastic, which, sticking to the window, holds the glass and prevents noise.

‖Cry.

#Saw.

**Cut.

Eponine began to laugh and sprang to his neck.

"I am here, my darling father, because I am here. Is there any law against sitting upon the stones in these days? It is you who shouldn't be here. What are you coming here for, since it is a biscuit? I told Magnon so. There is nothing to do here. But embrace me now, my dear good father! What a long time since I have seen you! You are out then?"

Thénardier tried to free himself from Eponine's arms, and muttered:

"Very well. You have embraced me. Yes, I am out. I am not in. Now, be off."

But Eponine did not loose her hold and redoubled her caresses.

"My darling father, how did you do it? You must have a good deal of wit to get out of that! Tell me about it! And my mother? where is my mother? Give me some news of mamma."

Thénardier answered:

"She is well, I don't know, let me alone, I tell you to be off."

"I don't want to go away just now," said Eponine, with the pettishness of a spoiled child, "you send me away when here it is four months that I haven't seen you, and when I have hardly had time to embrace you."

And she caught her father again by the neck.

"Ah! come now, this is foolish," said Babet.

"Let us hurry!" said Gueulemer, "the *coqueurs* may come along."

The ventriloquist sang this distich:

Nous n' sommes pas le jour de l'an,
A bécoter papa maman.*

Eponine turned towards the five bandits.

"Why, this is Monsieur Brujon. Good-day, Monsieur Babet. Good-day, Monsieur Claquesous. Don't you remember me, Monsieur Gueulemer? How goes it, Montparnasse?"

"Yes, they recognise you," said Thénardier. "But good-day, good-night, keep off! don't disturb us!"

"It is the hour for foxes, and not for pullets," said Montparnasse.

"You see well enough that we are going to *goupiner icigo*,"† added Babet.

Eponine took Montparnasse's hand.

"Take care," said he, "you will cut yourself, I have a *lingre*‡ open."

"My darling Montparnasse," answered Eponine very gently, "we must have confidence in people. I am my father's daughter, perhaps. Monsieur Babet, Monsieur Gueulemer, it is I who was charged with finding out about this affair."

It is noteworthy that Eponine was not speaking argot. Since she had known Marius, that horrid language had become impossible to her.

---

*'Tis not the first of the new year, / To hug papa and mamma dear.
†To work here.
‡Knife.

She pressed in her little hand, as bony and weak as the hand of a corpse, the great rough fingers of Gueulemer, and continued:

"You know very well that I am not a fool. Ordinarily you believe me. I have done you service on occasion. Well, I have learned all about this, you would expose yourself uselessly, do you see. I swear to you that there is nothing to be done in that house."

"There are lone women," said Gueulemer.

"No. The people have moved away."

"The candles have not, anyhow!" said Babet.

And he showed Eponine, through the top of the trees, a light which was moving about in the garret of the cottage. It was Toussaint, who had sat up to hang out her clothes to dry.

Eponine made a final effort.

"Well," said she, "they are very poor people, and it is a shanty where there isn't a sou."

"Go to the devil!" cried Thénardier. "When we have turned the house over, and when we have put the cellar at the top and the garret at the bottom, we will tell you what there is inside, and whether it is *balles, ronds*, or *broques*."*

And he pushed her to pass by.

"My good friend Monsieur Montparnasse," said Eponine, "I beg you, you who are a good boy, don't go in!"

"Take care, you will cut yourself," replied Montparnasse.

Thénardier added, with his decisive tone:

"Clear out, *fée*, and let men do their work!"

Eponine let go of Montparnasse's hand, which she had taken again, and said:

"You will go into that house then?"

"Just a little!" said the ventriloquist, with a sneer.

Then she placed her back against the grating, faced the six bandits who were armed to the teeth, and to whom the night gave faces of demons, and said in a low and firm voice:

"Well, I, I won't have it."

They stopped astounded. The ventriloquist, however, finished his sneer. She resumed.

"Friends! listen to me. That isn't the thing. Now I speak. In the first place, if you go into the garden, if you touch this grating, I shall cry out, I shall rap on doors, I shall wake everybody up, I shall have all six of you arrested, I shall call the sergents de ville."

"She would do it," said Thénardier in a low tone to Brujon and the ventriloquist.

She shook her head, and added:

"Beginning with my father!"

Thénardier approached.

---

*Francs, sous, or farthings.

"Not so near, goodman!" said she.

He drew back, muttering between his teeth: "Why, what is the matter with her?" and he added:

"Slut!"

She began to laugh in a terrible way:

"As you will, you shall not go in, I am not the daughter of a dog, for I am the daughter of a wolf. There are six of you, what is that to me? You are men. Now, I am a woman. I am not afraid of you, not a bit. I tell you that you shall not go into this house, because it does not please me. If you approach, I shall bark. I told you so, I am the *cab*, I don't care for you. Go your ways, you annoy me. Go where you like, but don't come here, I forbid it! You have knives, I have feet and hands. That makes no difference, come on now!"

She took a step towards the bandits, she was terrible, she began to laugh.

"The devil! I am not afraid. This summer, I shall be hungry; this winter, I shall be cold. Are they fools, these geese of men, to think that they can make a girl afraid! Of what! afraid? Ah, pshaw, indeed! Because you have hussies of mistresses who hide under the bed when you raise your voice, it won't do here! I, I am not afraid of anything!"

She kept her eye fixed upon Thénardier, and said:

"Not even you, father!"

Then she went on, casting her ghastly bloodshot eyes over the bandits:

"What is it to me whether somebody picks me up to-morrow on the pavement of the Rue Plumet, beaten to death with a club by my father, or whether they find me in a year in the ditches of Saint Cloud, or at the Ile de Cygnes, among the old rotten rubbish and the dead dogs?"

She was obliged to stop; a dry cough seized her, her breath came like a rattle from her narrow and feeble chest.

She resumed:

"I have but to cry out, they come, bang! You are six; but I am everybody."

Thénardier made a movement towards her.

"'Proach not!" cried she.

He stopped, and said to her mildly:

"Well, no; I will not approach, but don't speak so loud. Daughter, you want then to hinder us in our work? Still we must earn our living. Have you no love for your father now?"

"You bother me," said Eponine.

"Still we must live, we must eat——"

"Die."

Saying which, she sat down on the sill of the grating, humming:

Mon bras si dodu,
Ma jambe bien faite,
Et le temps perdu.*

---

*So plump is my arm, / My leg so well formed, / Yet my time has no charm.

She had her elbow on her knee and her chin in her hand, and she was swinging her foot with an air of indifference. Her dress was full of holes, and showed her sharp shoulder-blades. The neighbouring lamp lit up her profile and her attitude. Nothing could be more resolute or more surprising.

The six assassins, sullen and abashed at being held in check by a girl, went under the protecting shade of the lantern and held counsel, with humiliated and furious shrugs of their shoulders.

She watched them the while with a quiet yet indomitable air.

"Something is the matter with her," said Babet. "Some reason. Is she in love with the *cab?* But it is a pity to lose it. Two women, an old fellow who lodges in a back-yard, there are pretty good curtains at the windows. The old fellow must be a *guinal.** I think it is a good thing."

"Well, go in the rest of you," exclaimed Montparnasse. "Do the thing. I will stay here with the girl, and if she budges——"

He made the open knife which he had in his hand gleam in the light of the lantern.

Thénardier said not a word and seemed ready for anything.[†]

Brujon, who was something of an oracle, and who had, as we know, "got up the thing," had not yet spoken. He appeared thoughtful. He had a reputation for recoiling from nothing, and they knew that he had plundered, from sheer bravado, a police station. Moreover he made verses and songs, which gave him a great authority.

Babet questioned him.

"You don't say anything, Brujon?"

Brujon remained silent a minute longer, then he shook his head in several different ways, and at last decided to speak.

"Here: I met two sparrows fighting this morning; to-night, I run against a woman quarrelling. All this is bad. Let us go away."

They went away.

As they went, Montparnasse murmured:

"No matter, if they had said so, I would have finished her off."

Babet answered:

"Not I. I don't strike a lady."

At the corner of the street, they stopped and exchanged this enigmatic dialogue in a smothered voice:

"Where are we going to sleep to-night?"

"Under *Patin.*"[‡]

"Have you the key of the grating with you, Thénardier?"

"Humph."

Eponine, who had not taken her eyes off from them, saw them turn

---

*A Jew.

†Thénardier, who has become a complete monster, is ready to see his daughter murdered without blinking an eye.

‡Pantin, Paris.

back the way they had come. She rose and began to creep along the walls and houses behind them. She followed them as far as the boulevard. There, they separated, and she saw these men sink away in the darkness into which they seemed to melt.

5 (6)

MARIUS BECOMES SO REAL AS TO
GIVE COSETTE HIS ADDRESS

WHILE THIS SPECIES of dog in human form was mounting guard over the grating, and the six bandits were slinking away before a girl, Marius was with Cosette.

Never had the sky been more studded with stars, or more charming, the trees more tremulous, the odour of the shrubs more penetrating; never had the birds gone to sleep in the leaves with a softer sound; never had all the harmonies of the universal serenity better responded to the interior music of love; never had Marius been more enamoured, more happy, more in ecstasy. But he had found Cosette sad. Cosette had been weeping. Her eyes were red.

It was the first cloud in this wonderful dream.

Marius' first word was:

"What is the matter?"

"See."

Then she sat down on the bench near the stairs, and as he took his place all trembling beside her, she continued:

"My father told me this morning to hold myself in readiness, that he had business, and that perhaps we should go away."

Marius shuddered from head to foot.

When we are at the end of life, to die means to go away; when we are at the beginning, to go away means to die.

For six weeks Marius, gradually, slowly, by degrees, had been each day taking possession of Cosette. A possession entirely ideal, but thorough. Marius felt Cosette living within him. To have Cosette, to possess Cosette, this to him was not separable from breathing. Into the midst of this faith, of this intoxication, of this virginal possession, marvellous and absolute, of this sovereignty, these words: "We are going away," fell all at once, and the sharp voice of reality cried to him: "Cosette is not yours!"

Marius awoke. For six weeks Marius had lived, as we have said, outside of life; this word, going away, brought him roughly back to it.

He could not find a word. She said to him in her turn:

"What is the matter?"

He answered so low that Cosette hardly heard him:

"I don't understand what you have said."

She resumed:

"This morning my father told me to arrange all my little affairs and to be ready, that he would give me his clothes to pack, that he was obliged to take a journey, that we were going away, that we must have a large trunk for me and a small one for him, to get all that ready within a week from now, and that we should go perhaps to England."

"But it is monstrous!" exclaimed Marius.

It is certain that at that moment, in Marius' mind, no abuse of power, no violence, no abomination of the most cruel tyrants, no action of Busiris, Tiberius, or Henry VIII, was equal in ferocity to this: M. Fauchelevent taking his daughter to England because he has business.

He asked in a feeble voice:

"And when would you start?"

"He didn't say when."

"And when should you return?"

"He didn't say when."

Marius arose, and said coldly:

"Cosette, shall you go?"

Cosette turned upon him her beautiful eyes full of anguish and answered with a sort of bewilderment:

"Where?"

"To England? shall you go?"

"Why do you speak so to me?"

"I ask you if you shall go?"

"What would you have me do?" said she, clasping her hands.

"So, you will go?"

"If my father goes."

"So, you will go?"

Cosette took Marius' hand and pressed it without answering.

"Very well," said Marius. "Then I shall go elsewhere."

Cosette felt the meaning of this word still more than she understood it. She turned so pale that her face became white in the darkness. She stammered:

"What do you mean?"

Marius looked at her, then slowly raised his eyes towards heaven and answered:

"Nothing."

When his eyes were lowered, he saw Cosette smiling upon him. The smile of the woman whom we love has a brilliancy which we can see by night.

"How stupid we are! Marius, I have an idea."

"What?"

"Go if we go! I will tell you where! Come and join me where I am!"

Marius was now a man entirely awakened. He had fallen back into
reality. He cried to Cosette:

"Go with you? are you mad? But it takes money, and I have none! Go
to England? Why I owe now, I don't know, more than ten louis to Courfeyrac, one of my friends whom you do not know! Why I have an old hat
which is not worth three francs, I have a coat from which some of the buttons are gone in front, my shirt is all torn, my elbows are out, my boots let
in the water; for six weeks I have not thought of it, and I have not told you
about it. Cosette! I am a miserable wretch. You only see me at night, and
you give me your love; if you should see me by day, you would give me a
sou! Go to England? Ah! I have not the means to pay for a passport!"

He threw himself against a tree which was near by, standing with his
arms above his head, his forehead against the bark, feeling neither the tree
which was chafing his skin, nor the fever which was hammering his temples, motionless, and ready to fall, like a statue of Despair.

He was a long time thus. One might remain through eternity in such
abysses. At last he turned. He heard behind him a little stifled sound, soft
and sad.

It was Cosette sobbing.

She had been weeping more than two hours while Marius had been
thinking.

He came to her, fell on his knees, and, prostrating himself slowly, he
took the tip of her foot which peeped from under her dress and kissed it.

She allowed it in silence. There are moments when woman accepts, like
a goddess sombre and resigned, the religion of love.

"Do not weep," said he.

She murmured:

"Because I am perhaps going away, and you cannot come!"

He continued:

"Do you love me?"

She answered him by sobbing out that word of Paradise which is never
more enrapturing than when it comes through tears:

"I adore you."

He continued with a tone of voice which was an inexpressible caress:

"Do not weep. Tell me, will you do this for me, not to weep?"

"Do you love me, too?" said she.

He caught her hand.

"Cosette, I have never given my word of honour to anybody, because I
stand in awe of my word of honour. I feel that my father is at my side. Now,
I give you my most sacred word of honour that, if you go away, I shall die."

There was in the tone with which he pronounced these words a melancholy so solemn and so quiet, that Cosette trembled. She felt that chill
which is given by a stern and true fact passing over us. From the shock she
ceased weeping.

"Now listen," said he, "do not expect me to-morrow."

"Why not?"

"Do not expect me till the day after to-morrow!"

"Oh! why not?"

"You will see."

"A day without seeing you! Why, that is impossible."

"Let us sacrifice one day to gain perhaps a whole life."

And Marius added in an under-tone, and aside:

"He is a man who changes none of his habits, and he has never received anybody till evening."

"What man are you speaking of?" inquired Cosette.

"Me? I said nothing."

"What is it you hope for, then?"

"Wait till day after to-morrow."

"You wish it?"

"Yes, Cosette."

She took his head in both her hands, rising on tiptoe to reach his height, and striving to see his hope in his eyes.

Marius continued:

"It occurs to me, you must know my address, something may happen, we don't know; I live with that friend named Courfeyrac, Rue de la Verrerie, number 16."

He put his hand in his pocket, took out a penknife, and wrote with the blade upon the plastering of the wall:

16, *Rue de la Verrerie.*

Cosette, meanwhile, began to look into his eyes again.

"Tell me your idea. Marius, you have an idea. Tell me. Oh! tell me, so that I may pass a good night!"

"My idea is this: that it is impossible that God should wish to separate us. Expect me day after to-morrow."

"What shall I do till then?" said Cosette. "You, you are out doors, you go, you come! How happy men are. I have to stay alone. Oh! how sad I shall be! What is it you are going to do to-morrow evening, tell me?"

"I shall try a plan."

"Then I will pray God, and I will think of you from now till then, that you may succeed. I will not ask any more questions, since you wish me not to. You are my master. I shall spend my evening to-morrow singing that music of Euryanthe which you love, and which you came to hear one evening behind my shutter. But day after to-morrow you will come early; I shall expect you at night, at nine o'clock precisely. I forewarn you. Oh, dear! how sad it is that the days are long! You understand;—when the clock strikes nine, I shall be in the garden."

"And I too."

And without saying it, moved by the same thought, drawn on by those electric currents which put two lovers in continual communication, both intoxicated with pleasure even in their grief, they fell into each other's arms, without perceiving that their lips were joined, while their uplifted eyes, overflowing with ecstasy and full of tears, were fixed upon the stars.

When Marius went out, the street was empty. It was the moment when Eponine was following the bandits to the boulevard.

While Marius was thinking with his head against the tree, an idea had passed through his mind; an idea, alas! which he himself deemed senseless and impossible. He had formed a desperate resolution.

6 (7)

THE OLD HEART AND YOUNG HEART IN PRESENCE

GRANDFATHER GILLENORMAND had, at this period, fully completed his ninety-first year. He still lived with Mademoiselle Gillenormand, Rue des Filles du Calvaire, No. 6, in that old house which belonged to him. He was, as we remember, one of those antique old men who await death still erect, whom age loads without making them stoop, and whom grief itself does not bend.

Still, for some time, his daughter had said: "My father is failing." He no longer beat the servants; he struck his cane with less animation on the landing of the stairs, when Basque was slow in opening the door. The revolution of July had hardly exasperated him for six months. He had seen almost tranquilly in the *Moniteur* this coupling of words: M. Humblot Conté, peer of France. The fact is, that the old man was filled with dejection. He did not bend, he did not yield; that was no more a part of his physical than of his moral nature; but he felt himself interiorly failing. Four years he had been waiting for Marius, with resolve, that is just the word, in the conviction that that naughty little scapegrace would ring at his door some day or other: now he had come, in certain gloomy hours, to say to himself that even if Marius should delay, but little longer—It was not death that was unbearable to him; it was the idea that perhaps he should never see Marius again. Never see Marius again,—that had not, even for an instant, entered into his thought until this day; now this idea began to appear to him, and it chilled him. Absence, as always happens when feelings are natural and true, had only increased his grandfather's love for the ungrateful child who had gone away like that. It is on December nights, with the thermometer at zero, that we think most of the sun. M. Gillenormand was, or thought himself, in any event, incapable of taking a step, he the grandfather, towards his grandson; "I would die first," said he. He acknowledged no fault on his part; but he thought of Marius only with a deep tenderness and the mute despair of an old goodman who is going away into the darkness.

He was beginning to lose his teeth, which added to his sadness.

M. Gillenormand, without however acknowledging it to himself for he would have been furious and ashamed at it, had never loved a mistress as he loved Marius.

He had had hung in his room, at the foot of his bed, as the first thing which he wished to see on awaking, an old portrait of his other daughter, she who was dead, Madame Pontmercy, a portrait taken when she was eighteen years old. He looked at this portrait incessantly. He happened one day to say, while looking at it:

"I think it looks like the child."

"Like my sister?" replied Mademoiselle Gillenormand. "Why yes."

The old man added:

"And like him also."

Once, as he was sitting, his knees pressed together, and his eyes almost closed, in a posture of dejection, his daughter ventured to say to him:

"Father, are you still so angry with him?"

She stopped, not daring to go further.

"With whom?" asked he.

"With that poor Marius?"

He raised his old head, laid his thin and wrinkled fist upon the table, and cried in his most irritated and quivering tone:

"Poor Marius, you say? That gentleman is a rascal, a worthless knave, a little ungrateful vanity, with no heart, no soul, a proud, a wicked man!"

And he turned away that his daughter might not see the tear he had in his eyes.

Three days later, after a silence which had lasted for four hours, he said to his daughter snappishly:

"I have had the honour to beg Mademoiselle Gillenormand never to speak to me of him."

Aunt Gillenormand gave up all attempts and came to this profound diagnosis: "My father never loved my sister very much after her folly. It is clear that he detests Marius."

"After her folly" meant: after she married the colonel.

Still, as may have been conjectured, Mademoiselle Gillenormand had failed in her attempt to substitute her favourite, the officer of lancers, for Marius. The supplanter Théodule had not succeeded. Monsieur Gillenormand had not accepted the *quid pro quo*. The void in the heart does not accommodate itself to a proxy. Théodule, for his part, even while scenting the inheritance, revolted at the drudgery of pleasing. The goodman wearied the lancer, and the lancer shocked the goodman. Lieutenant Théodule was lively doubtless, but a babbler; frivolous, but vulgar; a good liver, but of bad company; he had mistresses, it is true, and he talked about them a good deal, that is also true; but he talked about them badly. All his qualities had a defect. Monsieur Gillenormand was wearied out with hearing him tell of all the favours that he had won in the neighbourhood of his barracks, Rue de Babylone. And then Lieutenant Théodule sometimes came in his uniform with the tricolour cockade. This rendered him altogether unbearable.* Grandfather Gillenormand, at last, said to his daughter: "I have had enough of him, your Théodule. I have little taste for warriors in time of peace. Entertain him yourself, if you like. I am not sure, but I like the sabrers even better than the trailers of the sabre. The clashing of blades in battle is not so wretched, after all, as the rattling of the sheaths on the pavement. And then, to harness himself like a bully, and to strap himself up like a flirt, to wear a corset under a cuirass, is to be ridiculous twice over. A genuine man keeps himself at an equal distance from swagger and roguery. Neither hector, nor heartless. Keep your Théodule for yourself."

It was of no use for his daughter to say: "Still he is your grandnephew," it turned out that Monsieur Gillenormand, who was grandfather to the ends of his nails, was not grand-uncle at all.

In reality, as he had good judgment and made the comparison, Théodule only served to increase his regret for Marius.

One evening, it was the 4th of June, which did not prevent Monsieur Gillenormand from having a blazing fire in his fireplace, he had said good-night to his daughter who was sewing in the adjoining room. He was alone in his room with the rural scenery, his feet upon the andirons, half enveloped in his vast coromandel screen with nine folds, leaning upon his table on which two candles were burning under a green shade, buried in his tapes-tried armchair, a book in his hand, but not reading. He was dressed, accord-ing to his custom, *en incroyable,* and resembled an antique portrait of Garat. This would have caused him to be followed in the streets, but his daughter always covered him when he went out, with a huge bishop's dou-blet, which hid his dress. At home, except in getting up and going to bed, he never wore a dressing-gown. *"It gives an old look,"* said he.

Monsieur Gillenormand thought of Marius lovingly and bitterly; and, as usual, the bitterness predominated. An increase of tenderness always ended by boiling over and turning into indignation. He was at that point where we seek to adopt a course, and to accept what rends us. He was just explaining to himself that there was now no longer any reason for Marius to return, that if he had been going to return, he would have done so already, that he must give him up. He endeavoured to bring himself to the idea that it was over with and that he would die without seeing "that gen-tleman" again. But his whole nature revolted; his old paternity could not consent to it. "What?" said he, this was his sorrowful refrain, "he will not come back!" His bald head had fallen upon his breast, and he was vaguely fixing a lamentable and irritated look upon the embers on his hearth.

In the deepest of this reverie, his old domestic, Basque, came in and asked:

"Can monsieur receive Monsieur Marius?"

---

*Théodule is "unbearable" because the three-colored cockade on his uniform, symbol of the constitutional compromise between the king (white) and the peo-ple (blue and red are the colors of Paris) offends M. Gillenormand, a conserva-tive royalist.

The old man straightened up, pallid and like a corpse which rises under a galvanic shock. All his blood had flown back to his heart. He faltered:

"Monsieur Marius what?"

"I don't know," answered Basque, intimidated and thrown out of countenance by his master's appearance. "I have not seen him. Nicolette just told me: There is a young man here, say that it is Monsieur Marius."

M. Gillenormand stammered out in a whisper:

"Show him in."

And he remained in the same attitude, his head shaking, his eyes fixed on the door. It opened. A young man entered. It was Marius.

Marius stopped at the door, as if waiting to be asked to come in.

His almost wretched dress was not perceived in the darkness produced by the green shade. Only his face, calm and grave, but strangely sad, could be distinguished.

M. Gillenormand, as if congested with astonishment and joy, sat for some moments without seeing anything but a light, as when one is in the presence of an apparition. He was almost fainting; he perceived Marius through a blinding haze. It was indeed he, it was indeed Marius!

At last! after four years! He seized him, so to speak, all over at a glance. He thought him beautiful, noble, striking, adult, a complete man, with graceful attitude and pleasing air. He would gladly have opened his arms, called him, rushed upon him, his heart melted in rapture, affectionate words welled and overflowed in his breast; indeed, all his tenderness started up and came to his lips, and, through the contrast which was the groundwork of his nature, there came forth a harsh word. He said abruptly:

"What is it you come here for?"

Marius answered with embarrassment:

"Monsieur——"

M. Gillenormand would have had Marius throw himself into his arms. He was displeased with Marius and with himself. He felt that he was rough, and that Marius was cold. It was to the goodman an unbearable and irritating anguish, to feel himself so tender and so much in tears within, while he could only be harsh without. The bitterness returned. He interrupted Marius with a sharp tone:

"Then what do you come for?"

This then signified: *If you don't come to embrace me*. Marius looked at his grandfather, whose pallor had changed to marble.

"Monsieur——"

The old man continued, in a stern voice:

"Do you come to ask my pardon? have you seen your fault?"

He thought to put Marius on the track, and that "the child" was going to bend. Marius shuddered; it was the disavowal of his father which was asked of him; he cast down his eyes and answered:

"No, monsieur."

"And then," exclaimed the old man impetuously, with a grief which was bitter and full of anger, "what do you want with me?"

Marius clasped his hands, took a step, and said in a feeble and trembling voice:

"Monsieur, have pity on me."

This word moved M. Gillenormand; spoken sooner, it would have softened him, but it came too late. The grandfather arose; he supported himself upon his cane with both hands, his lips were white, his forehead quivered, but his tall stature commanded the stooping Marius.

"Pity on you, monsieur! The youth asks pity from the old man of ninety-one! You are entering life, I am leaving it; you go to the theatre, the ball, the café, the billiard-room; you have wit, you please the women, you are a handsome fellow, while I cannot leave my chimney corner in midsummer; you are rich, with the only riches there are, while I have all the poverties of old age; infirmity, isolation. You have your thirty-two teeth, a good stomach, a keen eye, strength, appetite, health, cheerfulness, a forest of black hair, while I have not even white hair left; I have lost my teeth, I am losing my legs, I am losing my memory, there are three names of streets which I am always confounding, the Rue Charlot, the Rue du Chaume, and the Rue Saint Claude, there is where I am; you have the whole future before you full of sunshine, while I am beginning not to see another drop of it, so deep am I getting into the night; you are in love, of course, I am not loved by anybody in the world; and you ask pity of me. Zounds, Molière forgot this. If that is the way you jest at the Palais, Messieurs Lawyers, I offer you my sincere compliments. You are funny fellows."

And the old man resumed in an angry and stern voice:

"Come now, what do you want of me?"

"Monsieur," said Marius, "I know that my presence is displeasing to you, but I come only to ask one thing of you, and then I will go away immediately."

"You are a fool!" said the old man. "Who's telling you to go away?"

This was the translation of those loving words which he had deep in his heart: *Come, ask my pardon now! Throw yourself on my neck!* M. Gillenormand felt that Marius was going to leave him in a few moments, that his unkind reception repelled him, that his harshness was driving him away; he said all this to himself, and his anguish increased; and as his anguish immediately turned into anger, his harshness augmented. He would have had Marius comprehend, and Marius did not comprehend; which rendered the goodman furious. He continued:

"What! you have left me! me, your grandfather, you have left my house to go nobody knows where; you have afflicted your aunt, you have been, that is clear, it is more pleasant, leading the life of a bachelor, playing the elegant, going home at all hours, amusing yourself; you have not given me a sign of life; you have contracted debts without even telling me to pay them; you have made yourself a breaker of windows and a rioter, and, at the end of four years, you come to my house, and have nothing to say but that!"

This violent method of pushing the grandson to tenderness produced only silence on the part of Marius. M. Gillenormand folded his arms, a posture which with him was particularly imperious, and apostrophised Marius bitterly.

"Let us make an end of it. You have come to ask something of me, say you? Well what? what is it? speak!"

"Monsieur," said Marius, with the look of a man who feels that he is about to fall into an abyss, "I come to ask your permission to marry."

M. Gillenormand rang. Basque half opened the door.

"Send my daughter in."

A second later—the door opened again. Mademoiselle Gillenormand did not come in, but showed herself. Marius was standing mute, his arms hanging down, with the look of a criminal. M. Gillenormand was coming and going up and down the room. He turned towards his daughter and said to her:

"Nothing. It is Monsieur Marius. Bid him good evening. Monsieur wishes to marry. That is all. Go."

The crisp, harsh tones of the old man's voice announced a strange fulness of feeling. The aunt looked at Marius with a bewildered air, appeared hardly to recognise him, allowed neither a motion nor a syllable to escape her, and disappeared at a breath from her father, quicker than a dry leaf before a hurricane.

Meanwhile Grandfather Gillenormand had returned and stood with his back to the fireplace.

"You marry! at twenty-one! You have arranged that! You have nothing but a permission to ask! a formality. Sit down, monsieur. Well, you have had a revolution since I had the honour to see you. The Jacobins have had the upper hand. You ought to be satisfied. You are a republican, are you not, since you are a baron? You arrange that. The republic is sauce to the barony. Are you decorated by July?—did you take a bit of the Louvre, monsieur? There is close by here, in the Rue Saint Antoine, opposite the Rue des Nonaindières, a cannonball embedded in the wall of the fourth story of a house with this inscription: July 28th, 1830. Go and see that. That produces a good effect. Ah! Pretty things those friends of yours do. By the way, are they not making a fountain in the square of the monument of M. the Duke de Berry? So you want to marry? Whom? can the question be asked without indiscretion?"

He stopped, and, before Marius had had time to answer, he added violently:

"Come now, you have a business? your fortune made? how much do you earn at your lawyer's trade?"

"Nothing," said Marius, with a firmness and resolution which were almost savage.

"Nothing? you have nothing to live on but the twelve hundred livres which I send you?"

Marius made no answer. M. Gillenormand continued:

"Then I understand the girl is rich?"

"As I am."

"What! no dowry?"

"No."

"Some expectations?"

"I believe not."

"With nothing to her back! and what is the father?"

"I do not know."

"What is her name?"

"Mademoiselle Fauchelevent."

"Fauchewhat?"

"Fauchelevent."

"Pttt!" said the old man.

"Monsieur!" exclaimed Marius.

M. Gillenormand interrupted him with the tone of a man who is talking to himself.

"That is it, twenty-one, no business, twelve hundred livres a year, Madame the Baroness Pontmercy will go to the market to buy two sous' worth of parsley."

"Monsieur," said Marius, in the desperation of the last vanishing hope, "I supplicate you! I conjure you, in the name of heaven, with clasped hands, monsieur, I throw myself at your feet, allow me to marry her!"

The old man burst into a shrill, dreary laugh, through which he coughed and spoke.

"Ha, ha, ha! you said to yourself, 'The devil! I will go and find that old wig, that silly dolt! What a pity that I am not twenty-five! how I would toss him a good respectful notice! how I would give him the go-by. Never mind, I will say to him: Old idiot, you are too happy to see me, I desire to marry, I desire to espouse mamselle no matter whom, daughter of monsieur no matter what, I have no shoes, she has no chemise, all right; I desire to throw to the dogs my career, my future, my youth, my life; I desire to make a plunge into misery with a wife at my neck, that is my idea, you must consent to it! and the old fossil will consent.' Go, my boy, as you like, tie your stone to yourself, espouse your Pousselevent, your Couplevent—Never, monsieur! never!"

"Father!"

"Never!"

At the tone in which this "never" was pronounced Marius lost all hope. He walked the room with slow steps, his head bowed down, tottering, more like a man who is dying than like one who is going away. M. Gillenormand followed him with his eyes, and, at the moment the door opened and Marius was going out, he took four steps with the senile vivacity of impetuous and self-willed old men, seized Marius by the collar, drew him back forcibly into the room, threw him into an armchair, and said to him:

"Tell me about it!"

It was that single word, *father,* dropped by Marius, which had caused this revolution.

Marius looked at him in bewilderment. The changing countenance of M. Gillenormand expressed nothing now but a rough and ineffable good-nature. The guardian had given place to the grandfather.

"Come, let us see, speak, tell me about your love scrapes, jabber, tell me all! Lord! how foolish these young folks are!"

"Father," resumed Marius——

The old man's whole face shone with an unspeakable radiance.

"Yes! that is it! call me father, and you shall see!"

There was now something so kind, so sweet, so open, so paternal in this abruptness, that Marius, in this sudden passage from discouragement to hope, was, as it were, intoxicated, stupefied. He was sitting near the tables, the light of the candle made the wretchedness of his dress apparent, and the grandfather gazed at it in astonishment.

"Well, father," said Marius——

"Come now," interrupted M. Gillenormand, "then you really haven't a sou? you are dressed like a robber."

He fumbled in a drawer and took out a purse, which he laid upon the table:

"Here, there is a hundred louis, buy yourself a hat."

"Father," pursued Marius, "my good father, if you knew. I love her. You don't realise it; the first time that I saw her was at the Luxembourg Gardens, she came there; in the beginning I did not pay much attention to her, and then I do not know how it came about, I fell in love with her. Oh! how wretched it has made me! Now at last I see her every day, at her own house, her father does not know it, only think that they are going away, we see each other in the garden in the evening, her father wants to take her to England, then I said to myself: I will go and see my grandfather and tell him about it. I should go crazy in the first place, I should die, I should make myself sick, I should throw myself into the river. I must marry her because I should go crazy. Now, that is the whole truth, I do not believe that I have forgotten anything. She lives in a garden where there is a railing, in the Rue Plumet. It is near the Invalides."

Grandfather Gillenormand, radiant with joy, had sat down by Marius' side. While listening to him and enjoying the sound of his voice, he enjoyed at the same time a long pinch of snuff. At that word, Rue Plumet, he checked his inspiration and let the rest of his snuff fall on his knees.

"Rue Plumet!—you say Rue Plumet?—Let us see now!—Are there not some barracks down there? Why yes, that is it. Your cousin Théodule has told me about her. The lancer, the officer.—A lassie, my good friend, a lassie!—Lord yes, Rue Plumet. That is what used to be called Rue Blomet. It comes back to me now. I have heard tell about this little girl of the grating in the Rue Plumet. In a garden, a Pamela. Your taste is not bad. They say she is nice. Between ourselves, I believe that ninny of a lancer has paid his court to her a little. I do not know how far it went. After all that does not amount to anything. And then, we must not believe him. He is a boaster. Marius! I think it is very well for a young man like you to be in love. It belongs to your age. I like you better in love than as a Jacobin. I like you better taken by a petticoat, Lord! by twenty petticoats, than by Monsieur de Robespierre. For my part, I do myself this justice that in the matter of *sansculottes,* I have never liked anything but women. Pretty women are pretty women, the devil! there is no objection to that. As to the little girl, she receives you unknown to papa. That is all right. I have had adventures like that myself. More than one. Do you know how we do? we don't take the thing ferociously; we don't rush into the tragic; we don't conclude with marriage and with Monsieur the Mayor and his scarf. We are altogether a shrewd fellow. We have good sense. Glide over it, mortals, don't marry. We come and find grandfather who is a goodman at heart, and who almost always has a few rolls of louis in an old drawer; we say to him: 'Grandfather, that's how it is.' And grandfather says: 'That is all natural. Youth must fare and old age must wear. I have been young, you will be old. Go on, my boy, you will repay this to your grandson. There are two hundred pistoles. Amuse yourself, roundly! Nothing better! that is the way the thing should be done. We don't marry, but that doesn't hinder.' You understand me?"

Marius, petrified and unable to articulate a word, shook his head.

The goodman burst into a laugh, winked his old eye, gave him a tap on the knee, looked straight into his eyes with a significant and sparkling expression, and said to him with the most amorous shrug of the shoulders:

"Stupid! make her your mistress."

Marius turned pale. He had understood nothing of all that his grandfather had been saying. This rigmarole of Rue Blomet, of Pamela, of barracks, of a lancer, had passed before Marius like a phantasmagoria. Nothing of all could relate to Cosette, who was a lily. The goodman was wandering. But this wandering had terminated in a word which Marius did understand, and which was a deadly insult to Cosette. That phrase, *make her your mistress,* entered the heart of the chaste young man like a sword.

He rose, picked up his hat which was on the floor, and walked towards the door with a firm and assured step. There he turned, bowed profoundly before his grandfather, raised his head again and said:

"Five years ago you outraged my father; to-day you have outraged my wife. I ask nothing more of you, monsieur. Adieu."

Grandfather Gillenormand, astounded, opened his mouth, stretched out his arms, attempted to rise, but before he could utter a word, the door closed and Marius had disappeared.

The old man was for a few moments motionless, and as it were thunderstricken, unable to speak or breathe, as if a hand were clutching his throat. At last he tore himself from his chair, ran to the door as fast as a man who is ninety-one can run, opened it and cried:

"Help! help!"

His daughter appeared, then the servants. He continued with a pitiful rattle in his voice:

"Run after him! catch him! what have I done to him! he is mad! he is going away! Oh! my God! oh! my God!—this time he will not come back!"

He went to the window which looked upon the street, opened it with his tremulous old hands, hung more than half his body, outside, while Basque and Nicolette held him from behind, and cried:

"Marius! Marius! Marius! Marius!"

But Marius was already out of hearing, and was at that very moment turning the corner of the Rue Saint Louis.

The old man carried his hands to his temples two or three times, with an expression of anguish, drew back tottering, and sank into an armchair, pulseless, voiceless, tearless, shaking his head, and moving his lips with a stupid air, having now nothing in his eyes or in his heart but something deep and mournful, which resembled night.

BOOK NINE
WHERE ARE THEY GOING?

1

JEAN VALJEAN

THAT VERY DAY, towards four o'clock in the afternoon, Jean Valjean was sitting alone upon the reverse of one of the most solitary embankments of the Champ de Mars. Whether from prudence, or from a desire for meditation, or simply as a result of one of those insensible changes of habits which creep little by little into all lives, he now rarely went out with Cosette. He wore his working-man's waistcoat, brown linen trousers, and his cap with the long visor hid his face. He was now calm and happy in regard to Cosette; what had for some time alarmed and disturbed him was dissipated; but within a week or two anxieties of a different nature had come upon him. One day, when walking on the boulevard, he had seen Thénardier; thanks to his disguise, Thénardier had not recognised him; but since then Jean Valjean had seen him again several times, and he was now certain that Thénardier was prowling about the neighbourhood. This was sufficient to make him take a serious step. Thénardier there! this was all dangers at once. Moreover, Paris was not quiet: the political troubles had this inconvenience for him who had anything in his life to conceal, that the police had become very active, and very secret, and that in seeking to track out a man like Pépin or Morey, they would be very likely to discover a man like Jean Valjean. Jean Valjean had decided to leave Paris, and even France, and to pass over to England. He had told Cosette. In less than a week he wished to be gone. He was sitting on the embankment in the Champ de Mars, revolving all manner of thoughts in his mind, Thénardier, the police, the journey, and the difficulty of procuring a passport.

On all these points he was anxious.

Finally, an inexplicable circumstance which had just burst upon him, and with which he was still warm, had added to his alarm. On the morning of that very day, being the only one up in the house, and walking in the garden before Cosette's shutters were open, he had suddenly come upon this line scratched upon the wall, probably with a nail.

16, *Rue de la Verrerie.*

It was quite recent, the lines were white in the old black mortar, a tuft of nettles at the foot of the wall was powdered with fresh fine plaster. It had probably been written during the night. What was it? an address? a signal for others? a warning for him? At all events, it was evident that the garden had been violated, and that some persons unknown had penetrated into it. He recalled the strange incidents which had already alarmed the house. His mind worked upon this canvass. He took good care not to speak to Cosette of the line written on the wall, for fear of frightening her.

In the midst of these meditations, he perceived, by a shadow which the sun had projected, that somebody had just stopped upon the crest of the embankment immediately behind him. He was about to turn round, when a folded paper fell upon his knees, as if a hand had dropped it from above his head. He took the paper, unfolded it, and read on it this word, written in large letters with a pencil:

MOVE OUT.

Jean Valjean rose hastily, there was no longer anybody on the embankment; he looked about him, and perceived a species of being larger than a child, smaller than a man, dressed in a grey smock and trousers of dirt-coloured cotton velvet, which jumped over the parapet and let itself slide into the ditch of the Champ de Mars.

Jean Valjean returned home immediately, full of thought.

2

MARIUS

MARIUS HAD LEFT M. Gillenormand's desolate. He had entered with a very small hope; he came out with an immense despair.

He began to walk the streets, the resource of those who suffer. He thought of nothing which he could ever remember. At two o'clock in the morning he returned to Courfeyrac's, and threw himself, dressed as he was, upon his mattress. It was broad sunlight when he fell asleep, with that frightful, heavy slumber in which the ideas come and go in the brain. When he awoke, he saw standing in the room, their hats upon their heads, all ready to go out, very busy, Courfeyrac, Enjolras, Feuilly, and Combeferre.

Courfeyrac said to him:

"Are you going to the funeral of General Lamarque?"

It seemed to him that Courfeyrac was speaking Chinese.

He went out some time after them. He put into his pocket the pistols which Javert had confided to him at the time of the adventure of the 3rd of February, and which had remained in his hands. These pistols were still loaded. It would be difficult to say what dark thought he had in his mind in taking them with him.

He rambled about all day without knowing where; it rained at intervals, he did not perceive it; for his dinner he bought a penny roll at a baker's, put it in his pocket, and forgot it. It would appear that he took a bath in the Seine without being conscious of it. There are moments when a man has a furnace in his brain. Marius was in one of those moments. He hoped nothing more, he feared nothing more; he had reached this condition since the evening before. He waited for night with feverish impatience, he had but one clear idea; that was, that at nine o'clock he should see Cosette. This last happiness was now his whole future; afterwards, darkness. At intervals, while walking along the most deserted boulevards, he seemed to hear strange sounds in Paris. He roused himself from his reverie, and said: "Are they fighting?"

At nightfall, at precisely nine o'clock, as he had promised Cosette, he was in the Rue Plumet. When he approached the grating he forgot everything else. It was forty-eight hours since he had seen Cosette, he was going to see her again, every other thought faded away, and he felt now only a deep and wonderful joy. Those minutes in which we live centuries always have this sovereign and wonderful peculiarity, that for the moment while they are passing, they entirely fill the heart.

Marius displaced the grating, and sprang into the garden. Cosette was not at the place where she usually waited for him. He crossed the thicket and went to the recess near the steps. "She is waiting for me there," said he. Cosette was not there. He raised his eyes, and saw the shutters of the house were closed. He took a turn around the garden, the garden was deserted. Then he returned to the house, and, mad with love, intoxicated, dismayed, exasperated with grief and anxiety, like a master who returns home in an untoward hour, he rapped on the shutters. He rapped, he rapped again, at the risk of seeing the window open and the forbidding face of the father appear and ask him: "What do you want?" This was nothing compared with what he now began to see. When he had rapped, he raised his voice and called Cosette. "Cosette!" cried he. "Cosette!" repeated he imperiously. There was no answer. It was settled. Nobody in the garden; nobody in the house.

Marius fixed his despairing eyes upon that dismal house, as black, as silent, and more empty than a tomb. He looked at the stone bench where he had passed so many adorable hours with Cosette. Then he sat down upon the steps, his heart full of tenderness and resolution, he blessed his love in the depths of his thought, and he said to himself that since Cosette was gone, there was nothing more for him but to die.

Suddenly he heard a voice which appeared to come from the street, and which cried through the trees:

"Monsieur Marius!"

He arose.

"Hey?" said he.

"Monsieur Marius, is it you?"

"Yes."

"Monsieur Marius," added the voice, "your friends are expecting you at the barricade, in the Rue de la Chanvrerie."

This voice was not entirely unknown to him. It resembled the harsh and roughened voice of Eponine. Marius ran to the grating, pushed aside the movable bar, passed his head through, and saw somebody who appeared to him to be a young man rapidly disappearing in the twilight.

[Book Ten "June 5th, 1832," does not appear in this abridged edition.]

BOOK ELEVEN
THE ATOM FRATERNISES
WITH THE HURRICANE

1 (6)

RECRUITS

THE BAND INCREASED at every moment. Towards the Rue des Billettes a man of tall stature, who was turning grey, whose rough and bold mien Courfeyrac, Enjolras, and Combeferre noticed, but whom none of them knew, joined them. Gavroche, busy singing, whistling, humming, going forward and rapping on the shutters of the shops with the butt of his hammerless pistol, paid no attention to this man.

It happened that, in the Rue de la Verrerie, they passed by Courfeyrac's door.

"That is lucky," said Courfeyrac, "I have forgotten my purse and I have lost my hat." He left the company and went up to his room, four stairs at a time. He took an old hat and his purse. He took also a large square box, of the size of a big valise, which was hidden among his dirty clothes. As he was running down again, the portress hailed him:

"Monsieur de Courfeyrac?"

"Portress, what is your name?" responded Courfeyrac.

The portress stood aghast.

"Why, you know it very well; I am the portress, my name is Mother Veuvain."

"Well, if you call me Monsieur de Courfeyrac again, I shall call you Mother de Veuvain. Now, speak, what is it? What do you want?"

"There is somebody who wishes to speak to you."

"Who is it?"

"I don't know."

"Where is he?"

"In my lodge."

"The devil!" said Courfeyrac.

"But he has been waiting more than an hour for you to come home!" replied the portress.

At the same time, a sort of young working-man, thin, pale, small, freckled, dressed in a torn smock and patched trousers of ribbed velvet, and who had rather the appearance of a girl in boy's clothes than of a man, came out of the lodge and said to Courfeyrac in a voice which, to be sure, was not the least in the world like a woman's voice.

"Monsieur Marius, if you please?"

"He is not in."

"Will he be in this evening?"

"I don't know anything about it."

And Courfeyrac added: "As for myself, I shall not be in."

The young man looked fixedly at him, and asked him:

"Why so?"

"Because."

"Where are you going then?"

"What is that to you?"

"Do you want me to carry your box?"

"I am going to the barricades."

"Do you want me to go with you?"

"If you like," answered Courfeyrac. "The road is free; the streets belong to everybody."

And he ran off to rejoin his friends. When he had rejoined them, he gave the box to one of them to carry. It was not until a quarter of an hour afterwards that he perceived that the young man had in fact followed them.

A mob does not go precisely where it wishes. We have explained that a gust of wind carries it along. They went beyond Saint Merry and found themselves, without really knowing how, in the Rue Saint-Denis.

BOOK TWELVE
CORINTH

1

HISTORY OF CORINTH FROM ITS
FOUNDATION

THE PARISIANS who, to-day, upon entering the Rue Rambuteau from the side of the markets, notice on their right, opposite the Rue Mondétour, a basket-maker's shop, with a basket for a sign, in the shape of the Emperor Napoleon the Great, with this inscription:

NAPOLÉON EST FAIT
TOUT EN OSIER,*

do not suspect the terrible scenes which this very place saw thirty years ago.

Here were the Rue de la Chanvrerie, which the old signs spelled Chanverrerie, and the celebrated tavern called Corinth.

The reader will remember all that has been said about the barricade erected on this spot and eclipsed elsewhere by the barricade of Saint Merry. Upon this famous barricade of the Rue de la Chanvrerie, now fallen into deep obscurity, we are about to throw some little light.

Permit us to resort, for the sake of clearness, to the simple means already employed by us for Waterloo. Those who would picture to themselves with sufficient exactness the confused blocks of houses which stood at that period near the Pointe Saint Eustache, at the northeast corner of the markets of Paris, where is now the mouth of the Rue Rambuteau, have only to figure to themselves, touching the Rue Saint-Denis at its summit, and the markets at its base, an N, of which the two vertical strokes would be the Rue de la Grande Truanderie and the Rue de la Chanvrerie, and the Rue de la Petite Truanderie would make the transverse stroke. The old Rue Mondétour cut the three strokes at the most awkward angles. So that the labyrinthine entanglement of these four streets sufficed to make, in a space of four hundred square yards, between the markets and the Rue Saint-Denis, in one direction, and between the Rue du Cygne and the Rue des Prêcheurs in the other direction, seven islets of houses, oddly intersecting, of various sizes, placed crosswise and as if by chance, and separated but slightly, like blocks of stone in a stone yard, by narrow crevices.

We say narrow crevices, and we cannot give a more just idea of those dark, contracted, angular lanes, bordered by ruins eight stories high. These houses were so dilapidated, that in the Rues de la Chanvrerie and de la Petite Truanderie, the fronts were shored up with beams, reaching from

---

*Napoléon is made, / All of willow braid.

one house to another. The street was narrow and the gutter wide, the passer-by walked along a pavement which was always wet, beside shops that were like cellars, great stone blocks encircled with iron, immense garbage heaps, and alley gates armed with enormous and venerable gratings. The Rue Rambuteau has devastated all this.

The name Mondétour pictures marvellously well the windings of all this route. A little further along you found them still better expressed by the *Rue Pirouette,* which ran into the Rue Mondétour.

The pedestrian who came from the Rue Saint-Denis into the Rue de la Chanvrerie saw it gradually narrow away before him as if he had entered an elongated funnel. At the end of the street, which was very short, he found the passage barred on the market side, and he would have thought himself in a cul-de-sac, if he had not perceived on the right and on the left two black openings by which he could escape. These were the Rue Mondétour, which communicated on the one side with the Rue des Prêcheurs, on the other with the Rues du Cygne and Petite Truanderie. At the end of this sort of cul-de-sac, at the corner of the opening on the right, might be seen a house lower than the rest, and forming a kind of cape on the street.

In this house, only three stories high, had been festively installed for three hundred years an illustrious tavern. The location was good. The proprietorship descended from father to son.

As we have said, Corinth was one of the meeting, if not rallying places, of Courfeyrac and his friends. It was Grantaire who had discovered Corinth. He had entered on account of *Carpe Horas,* and he returned on account of *Carpes au Gras.* They drank there, they ate there, they shouted there; they paid little, they paid poorly, they did not pay at all, they were always welcome. Father Hucheloup was a goodman.

Hugo characterizes Corinth, its proprietors—the late Father Hucheloup and the Widow Hucheloup, and its two waitresses "Chowder and Fricassee." At nine in the morning of the day the revolutionary barricade will be erected, the friends Joly, Laigle de Meaux ("Bossuet"), and Grantaire gather there. They become very drunk. Grantaire, who loves and admires Enjolras, laments that the latter—the fiery revolutionary heart of their conspiratorial group—despises him.

Bossuet, very drunk, had preserved his calm.

He sat in the open window, wetting his back with the falling rain, and gazed at his two friends.

Suddenly he heard a tumult behind him, hurried steps, cries to arms! He turned, and saw in the Rue Saint-Denis, at the end of the Rue de la Chanvrerie, Enjolras passing, carbine in hand, and Gavroche with his pistol, Feuilly with his sabre, Courfeyrac with his sword, Jean Prouvaire with his musketoon, Combeferre with his musket, Bahorel with his musket, and all the armed and stormy gathering which followed them.

The Rue de la Chanvrerie was hardly as long as the range of a carbine. Bossuet improvised a speaking trumpet with his two hands, and shouted:

"Courfeyrac! Courfeyrac! ahoy!"

Courfeyrac heard the call, perceived Bossuet, and came a few steps into the Rue de la Chanvrerie, crying a "what do you want?" which was met on the way by a "where are you going?"

"To make a barricade," answered Courfeyrac.

"Well, here! This is a good place! make it here!"

"That is true, Eagle," said Courfeyrac.

And at a sign from Courfeyrac, the band rushed into the Rue de la Chanvrerie.

2 (3)

NIGHT BEGINS TO GATHER
OVER GRANTAIRE

THE PLACE WAS indeed admirably chosen, the entrance of the street wide, the further end contracted and like a cul-de-sac, Corinth throttling it, Rue Mondétour easy to bar at the right and left, no attack possible except from the Rue Saint-Denis, that is from the front, and without cover. Bossuet tipsy had the *coup d'œil* of Hannibal fasting.

At the irruption of the mob, dismay seized the whole street, not a passer-by but had gone into eclipse. In a flash, at the end, on the right, on the left, shops, stalls, alley gates, windows, blinds, dormer-windows, shutters of every size, were closed from the ground to the roofs. One frightened old woman had fixed a mattress before her window on two clothes poles, as a shield against the musketry. The tavern was the only house which remained open; and that for a good reason, because the band had rushed into it. "Oh my God! Oh my God!" sighed Ma'am Hucheloup.

Bossuet had gone down to meet Courfeyrac.

Joly, who had come to the window, cried:

"Courfeyrac, you bust take ad ubbrella. You will catch cold."

Meanwhile, in a few minutes, twenty iron bars had been wrested from the grated front of the tavern, twenty yards of pavement had been torn up, Gavroche and Bahorel had seized on its passage and tipped over the dray of a lime merchant named Anceau, this dray contained three barrels full of lime, which they had placed under the piles of paving-stones; Enjolras had opened the trap-door of the cellar and all the widow Hucheloup's empty casks had gone to flank the lime barrels; Feuilly, with his fingers accustomed to colour the delicate folds of fans, had buttressed the barrels and the dray with two massive heaps of stones. Stones improvised like the rest, and obtained nobody knows where. Some shoring-timbers had been pulled down from the front of a neighbouring house and laid upon the casks. When Bossuet and Courfeyrac turned round, half the street was already barred by a rampart higher than a man. There is nothing like the popular hand to build whatever can be built by demolishing.

Chowder and Fricassee had joined the labourers. Fricassee went back and forth loaded with rubbish. Her weariness contributed to the barricade. She served paving-stones, as she would have served wine, with a sleepy air.

An omnibus with two white horses passed at the end of the street.

Bossuet sprang over the pavement, ran, stopped the driver, made the passengers get down, gave his hand "to the ladies," dismissed the conductor, and came back with the vehicle, leading the horses by the bridle.

"An omnibus," said he, "doesn't pass by Corinth. *Non licet omnibus adire Corinthum.*"

A moment later the horses were unhitched and going off at will through the Rue Mondétour, and the omnibus, lying on its side, completed the barring of the street.

Ma'am Hucheloup, completely upset, had taken refuge in the second story.

Her eyes were wandering, and she looked without seeing, crying in a whisper. Her cries were dismayed and dared not come out of her throat.

"It is the end of the world," she murmured.

Joly deposited a kiss upon Ma'am Hucheloup's coarse, red, and wrinkled neck, and said to Grantaire: "My dear fellow, I have always considered a woman's neck an infinitely delicate thing."

But Grantaire was attaining the highest regions of dithyramb. Chowder having come up to the second floor, Grantaire seized her by the waist and pulled her towards the window with long bursts of laughter.

"Chowder is ugly!" cried he; "Chowder is the dream of ugliness! Chowder is a chimera. Listen to the secret of her birth: a Gothic Pygmalion who was making cathedral waterspouts, fell in love with one of them one fine morning, the most horrible of all. He implored Love to animate her, and that made Chowder. Behold her, citizens! her hair is the colour of chromate of lead, like that of Titian's mistress, and she is a good girl. I warrant you that she will fight well. Every good girl contains a hero. As for Mother Hucheloup, she is an old soldier. Look at her moustaches! she inherited them from her husband. A hussaress, indeed, she will fight too. They two by themselves will frighten the banlieue. Comrades, we will overturn the government, as true as there are fifteen acids intermediate between margaric acid and formic acid; besides, I don't care. Messieurs, my father always detested me because I could not understand mathematics. I only understand love and liberty. I am Grantaire, a good boy. Never having had any money, I have never got used to it, and by that means I have never felt the need of it, but if I had been rich, there would have been no more poor! you should have seen. Oh! if the good hearts had the fat purses, how much better everything would go! I imagine Jesus Christ with Rothschild's fortune! How much good he would have done! Chowder, embrace me! you are voluptuous and timid! you have cheeks which call for the kiss of a sister, and lips which demand the kiss of a lover."

"Be still, wine-cask!" said Courfeyrac.

Grantaire answered:

"I am Capitoul and Master of Floral Games!"

Enjolras, who was standing on the crest of the barricade, musket in hand, raised his fine austere face. Enjolras, we know, had something of the Spartan and of the Puritan. He would have died at Thermopylæ with Leonidas, and would have burned Drogheda with Cromwell.

"Grantaire," cried he, "go sleep yourself sober away from here. This is the place for intoxication and not for drunkenness. Do not dishonour the barricade!"

This angry speech produced upon Grantaire a singular effect. One would have said that he had received a glass of cold water in his face. He appeared suddenly sobered. He sat down, leaned upon a table near the window, looked at Enjolras with an inexpressible gentleness, and said to him:

"Let me sleep here."

"Go sleep elsewhere," cried Enjolras.

But Grantaire, keeping his tender and troubled eyes fixed upon him, answered:

"Let me sleep here—until I die here."

Enjolras regarded him with a disdainful eye:

"Grantaire, you are incapable of belief, of thought, of will, of life, and of death."

Grantaire answered gravely: "You'll see."

He stammered out a few more unintelligible words, then his head fell heavily upon the table, and, a common effect of the second stage of inebriety into which Enjolras had roughly and suddenly pushed him, a moment later he was asleep.

3 (4)

ATTEMPT TO CONSOLE THE WIDOW HUCHELOUP

Bahorel, in ecstasies over the barricade, cried:

"There is the street in a low neck, how well it looks!"

Courfeyrac, even while helping to demolish the tavern, sought to console the widowed landlady.

"Mother Hucheloup, were you not complaining the other day that you had been summoned and fined because Fricassee had shaken a rug out of your window?"

"Yes, my good Monsieur Courfeyrac. Oh! my God! are you going to put that table also into your horror? And besides that, for the rug, and also for a flower-pot which fell from the attic into the street, the government fined me a hundred francs. If that isn't an abomination!"

"Well, Mother Hucheloup, we are avenging you."

Mother Hucheloup, in this reparation which they were making her, did not seem to understand her advantage very well. She was satisfied after the manner of that Arab woman who, having received a blow from her husband, went to complain to her father, crying for vengeance and saying: "Father, you owe my husband affront for affront." The father asked: "Upon which cheek did you receive the blow?" "Upon the left cheek." The father struck the right cheek, and said: "Now you are satisfied. Go and tell your husband that he has struck my daughter, but that I have struck his wife."

The rain had ceased. Recruits had arrived. Some working-men had brought under their smocks a keg of powder, a hamper containing bottles of vitriol, two or three carnival torches, and a basket full of lamps, "relics of the king's fête," which fête was quite recent, having taken place the 1st of May. It was said that these supplies came from a grocer of the Faubourg Saint Antoine, named Pépin. They broke the only lamp in the Rue de la Chanvrerie, the lamp opposite the Rue Saint-Denis, and all the lamps in the surrounding streets, Mondétour, du Cygne, des Prêcheurs, and de la Grande and de la Petite Truanderie.

Enjolras, Combeferre, and Courfeyrac, directed everything. Two barricades were now building at the same time, both resting on the house of Corinth and making a right angle; the larger one closed the Rue de la Chanvrerie, the other closed the Rue Mondétour in the direction of the Rue du Cygne. This last barricade, very narrow, was constructed only of casks and paving-stones. There were about fifty labourers there, some thirty armed with muskets, for, on their way, they had taken out a wholesale loan from an armourer's shop.

Nothing could be more fantastic and more motley than this band. One had a short jacket, a cavalry sabre, and two horse-pistols; another was in shirt sleeves, with a round hat, and a powder-horn hung at his side; a third had a breast-plate of nine sheets of brown paper, and was armed with a saddler's awl. There was one of them who cried: *"Let us exterminate to the last man, and die on the point of our bayonets!"* This man had no bayonet. Another displayed over his coat a cross-belt and cartridge-box of the National Guard, with the box cover adorned with this inscription in red cloth: *Public Order*. Many muskets bearing the numbers of their legions, few hats, no cravats, many bare arms, some pikes. Add to this all ages, all faces, small pale young men, bronzed longshoremen. All were hurrying, and, while helping each other, they talked about the possible chances—that they would have help by three o'clock in the morning—that they were sure of one regiment—that Paris would rise. Terrible subjects, with which were mingled a sort of cordial joviality. One would have said they were brothers, they did not know each other's names. Great perils have this beauty, that they bring to light the fraternity of strangers.

A fire had been kindled in the kitchen, and they were melting pitchers, dishes, forks, all the pewter ware of the tavern into bullets. They drank through it all. Percussion-caps and buck-shot rolled pell-mell upon the tables with glasses of wine. In the billiard-room, Ma'am Hucheloup, Chowder, and Fricassee, variously modified by terror, one being stupefied, another breathless, the third alert, were tearing up old linen and making lint; three insurgents assisted them, three long-haired, bearded, and mous-tached wags who tore up the cloth with the fingers of a laundress, and who made them tremble.

The man of tall stature whom Courfeyrac, Combeferre, and Enjolras had noticed, at the moment he joined the company at the corner of the Rue des Billettes, was working on the little barricade, and making himself useful there. Gavroche worked on the large one. As for the young man who had waited for Courfeyrac at his house, and had asked him for Mon-sieur Marius, he had disappeared very nearly at the moment the omnibus was overturned.

Gavroche, completely carried away and radiant, had charged himself with making all ready. He went, came, mounted, descended, remounted, bustled, sparkled. He seemed to be there for the encouragement of all. Had he a spur? yes, certainly, his misery; had he wings? yes, certainly, his joy. Gavroche was a whirlwind. They saw him incessantly, they heard him constantly. He filled the air, being everywhere at once. He was a kind of stimulating ubiquity; no stop possible with him. The enormous barricade felt him on its back. He vexed the loungers, he urged on the idle, he reani-mated the weary, he provoked the thoughtful, kept some in cheerfulness, others in breath, others in anger, all in motion, piqued a student, was biting to a working-man; took position, stopped, started on, flitted above the tumult and the effort, leaped from these to those, murmured, hummed, and stirred up the whole train; the fly of the revolutionary coach.*

Perpetual motion was in his little arms, and perpetual clamour in his lit-tle lungs.

"Go to it! more paving stones! more barrels! more gizmos! where are they? A basket of plaster, to stop that hole. It is too small, your barricade. It must go higher. Pile on everything, brace it with everything. Break up the house. A barricade is Mother Gibou's tea-party. Hold on, there is a glass-door."

This made the labourers exclaim:

"A glass-door? what do you want us to do with a glass-door, you little wart?"

---

*Evokes a well-known fable by Jean de La Fontaine, in which a buzzing, pesky fly takes credit for having gotten a team of horses to haul a heavy coach uphill; Gavroche acts like that fly (but more effectively).

"Wart yourselves," retorted Gavroche. "A glass-door in a barricade is excellent. It doesn't prevent attacking it, but it bothers them in taking it. Then you have never snitched apples over a wall with broken bottles on it? A glass-door will cut the corns of the National Guards, when they try to climb over the barricade. Golly! glass is the devil. Ah, now, you haven't an unbridled imagination, my comrades."

Still, he was furious at his pistol without a hammer. He went from one to another, demanding: "A musket? I want a musket! Why don't you give me a musket?"

"A musket for you?" said Combeferre.

"Well?" replied Gavroche, "why not? I had one in 1830, when we had a disagreement with Charles X."

Enjolras shrugged his shoulders.

"When there are enough for the men, we will give them to the children."

Gavroche turned fiercely, and answered him:

"If you are killed before me, I will take yours."

"Gamin!" said Enjolras.

"Novice!" said Gavroche.

A stray dandy who was lounging at the end of the street made a diversion. Gavroche cried to him:

"Come with us, young man? Well, this poor old country, you won't do anything for her then?"

The dandy fled.

4 (5)

THE PREPARATIONS

THE JOURNALS OF THE TIME which said that the barricade of the Rue de la Chanvrerie, that *almost inexpugnable construction*, as they call it, attained the level of a second story, were mistaken. The fact is, that it did not exceed an average height of six or seven feet. It was built in such a manner that the combatants could, at will, either disappear behind the wall, or look over it, and even scale the crest of it by means of a quadruple range of paving-stones superposed and arranged like steps on the inner side. The front of the barricade on the outside, composed of piles of paving-stones and of barrels bound together by timbers and boards which were inter-locked in the wheels of the Anceau cart and the overturned omnibus, had a bristling and inextricable aspect.

An opening sufficient for a man to pass through had been left between the wall of the houses and the extremity of the barricade furthest from the tavern; so that a sortie was possible. The pole of the omnibus was turned directly up and held with ropes, and a red flag fixed to this pole floated over the barricade.

The little Mondétour barricade, hidden behind the tavern, was not visible. The two barricades united formed a staunch redoubt. Enjolras and Courfeyrac had not thought proper to barricade the other end of the Rue Mondétour which opens a passage to the markets through the Rue des Prêcheurs, wishing doubtless to preserve a possible communication with the outside, and having little dread of being attacked from the dangerous and difficult alley des Prêcheurs.

Except this passage remaining free, which constituted what Folard, in his strategic style, would have called a branch-trench, and bearing in mind also the narrow opening arranged on the Rue de la Chanvrerie, the interior of the barricade, where the tavern made a salient angle, presented an irregular quadrilateral closed on all sides. There was an interval of about twenty yards between the great barricade and the tall houses which formed the end of the street, so that we might say that the barricade leaned against these houses all inhabited, but closed from top to bottom.

All this labour was accomplished without hindrance in less than an hour, and without this handful of bold men seeing a bearskin-cap or a bayonet arise. The few bourgeois who still ventured at that period of the émeute into the Rue Saint-Denis cast a glance down the Rue de la Chanvrerie, perceived the barricade, and redoubled their pace.

The two barricades finished, the flag run up, a table was dragged out of the tavern; and Courfeyrac mounted upon the table. Enjolras brought the square box and Courfeyrac opened it. This box was filled with cartridges. When they saw the cartridges, there was a shudder among the bravest, and a moment of silence.

Courfeyrac distributed them with a smile.

Each one received thirty cartridges. Many had powder and set about making others with the balls which they were moulding. As for the keg of powder, it was on a table by itself near the door, and it was reserved.

The call to arms which was resounding throughout Paris was not discontinued, but it had got to be only a monotonous sound to which they paid no more attention, with melancholy undulations.

They loaded their muskets and their carbines all together, without precipitation, with a solemn gravity. Enjolras placed three sentinels outside the barricades, one in the Rue de la Chanvrerie, the second in the Rue des Prêcheurs, the third at the corner of la Petite Truanderie.

Then, the barricades built, the posts assigned, the muskets loaded, the sentinels posted, alone in these fearful streets in which there were now no passers-by, surrounded by these dumb, and as it were dead houses, which throbbed with no human motion, enwrapped by the deepening shadows of the twilight, which was beginning to fall, in the midst of this darkness and this silence, through which they felt the advance of something inexpressibly tragical and terrifying, isolated, armed, determined, tranquil, they waited.

THE MAN RECRUITED IN
THE RUE DES BILLETTES

IT WAS NOW QUITE DARK, nothing came. There were only faint sounds, and at intervals volleys of musketry; but infrequent, scattered, and distant. This respite, which was thus prolonged, was a sign that the government was taking its time, and massing its forces. These fifty men were awaiting sixty thousand.

Enjolras felt himself possessed by that impatience which seizes strong souls on the threshold of formidable events. He went to find Gavroche who had set himself to making cartridges in the basement room by the uncertain light of two candles placed upon the counter through precaution on account of the powder scattered over the tables. These two candles threw no rays outside. The insurgents moreover had taken care not to have any lights in the upper stories.

Gavroche at this moment was very much engaged, not exactly with his cartridges.

The man from the Rue des Billettes had just entered the basement room and had taken a seat at the table which was least lighted. An infantry musket of large model had fallen to his lot, and he held it between his knees. Gavroche hitherto, distracted by a hundred "amusing" things, had not even seen this man.

When he came in, Gavroche mechanically followed him with his eyes, admiring his musket, then, suddenly, when the man had sat down, the *gamin* arose. Had any one watched this man up to this time, he would have seen him observe everything in the barricade and in the band of insurgents with a singular attention; but since he had come into the room, he had fallen into a kind of meditation and appeared to see nothing more of what was going on. The *gamin* approached this thoughtful personage, and began to turn about him on the points of his toes as one walks when near somebody whom he fears to awake. At the same time, over his childish face, at once so saucy and so serious, so flighty and so profound, so cheerful and so touching, there passed all those grimaces of the old which signify: "Oh, bah! impossible! I'm seeing things! I am dreaming! can it be? no, it isn't! why yes! why no!" etc. Gavroche swayed upon his heels, clenched both fists in his pockets, twisted his neck like a bird, expended in one measureless pout all the sagacity of his lower lip. He was stupefied, uncertain, credulous, convinced, bewildered. He had the appearance of the chief of the eunuchs in the slave market discovering a Venus among fatties, and the air of an amateur recognising a Raphael in a heap of daubs. Everything in him was at work, the instinct which scents and the intellect which combines. It was evident that an event had occurred with Gavroche.

It was in the deepest of this meditation that Enjolras accosted him.

"You are small," said Enjolras, "nobody will see you. Go out of the barricades, glide along by the houses, look about the streets a little, and come and tell me what is going on."

Gavroche straightened himself up.

"Little folks are good for something then! that is very lucky! I will go! meantime, trust the little folks, distrust the big——" And Gavroche, raising his head and lowering his voice, added, pointing to the man of the Rue des Billettes:

"You see that big fellow there?"

"Well?"

"He is a spy."

"You are sure?"

"It isn't a fortnight since he pulled me by the ear off the cornice of the Pont Royal where I was taking the air."

Enjolras hastily left the *gamin,* and murmured a few words very low to a working-man from the wine docks who was there. The working-man went out of the room and returned almost immediately, accompanied by three others. The four men, four broad-shouldered porters, placed themselves, without doing anything which could attract his attention, behind the table on which the man of the Rue des Billettes was leaning. They were evidently ready to throw themselves upon him.

Then Enjolras approached the man and asked him:

"Who are you?"

At this abrupt question, the man gave a start. He looked straight to the bottom of Enjolras' frank eye and appeared to catch his thought. He smiled with a smile which, of all things in the world, was the most disdainful, the most energetic, and the most resolute, and answered with a haughty gravity:

"I see how it is——Well, yes!"

"You are a spy?"

"I am an officer of the government."

"Your name is?"

"Javert."

Enjolras made a sign to the four men. In a twinkling, before Javert had had time to turn around, he was collared, thrown down, bound, searched.

They found upon him a little round card framed between two glasses, and bearing on one side the arms of France, engraved with this legend: *Surveillance et vigilance,* and on the other side this endorsement: JAVERT, inspector of police, aged fifty-two, and the signature of the prefect of police of the time, M. Gisquet.

He had besides his watch and his purse, which contained a few gold coins. They left him his purse and his watch. Under the watch, at the bottom of his fob, they felt and seized a paper in an envelope, which Enjolras opened, and on which he read these six lines, written by the prefect's own hand.

"As soon as his political mission is fulfilled, Inspector Javert will ascertain, by a special examination, whether it be true that malefactors have hideouts on the slope of the right bank of the Seine, near the bridge of Jena."

The search finished, they raised Javert, tied his arms behind his back, fastened him in the middle of the basement-room to that celebrated post which had formerly given its name to the tavern.

Gavroche, who had witnessed the whole scene and approved the whole by silent nods of his head, approached Javert and said to him:

"The mouse has caught the cat."

All this was executed so rapidly that it was finished as soon as it was perceived about the tavern. Javert had not uttered a cry. Seeing Javert tied to the post, Courfeyrac, Bossuet, Joly, Combeferre, and the men scattered about the two barricades, ran in.

Javert, backed up against the post, and so surrounded with ropes that he could make no movement, held up his head with the intrepid serenity of the man who has never lied.

"It is a spy," said Enjolras.

And turning towards Javert:

"You will be shot ten minutes before the barricade is taken."

Javert replied in his most imperious tone:

"Why not immediately?"

"We are economising powder."

"Then do it with a knife."

"Spy," said the handsome Enjolras, "we are judges, not assassins."

Then he called Gavroche.

"You! go about your business! Do what I told you."

"I am going," cried Gavroche.

And stopping just as he was starting:

"By the way, you will give me his musket!" And he added: "I leave you the musician, but I want the clarionet."

The *gamin* made a military salute, and sprang gaily through the opening in the large barricade.

BOOK THIRTEEN
MARIUS ENTERS THE SHADOW

1

FROM THE RUE PLUMET TO
THE QUARTIER SAINT-DENIS

THAT VOICE WHICH through the twilight had called Marius to the barricade of the Rue de la Chanvrerie, sounded to him like the voice of destiny. He wished to die, the opportunity presented itself; he was knocking at the door of the tomb, a hand in the shadow held out the key. These dreary clefts in the darkness before despair are tempting. Marius pushed aside the bar which had let him pass so many times, came out of the garden, and said: "Let us go!"

Mad with grief, feeling no longer anything fixed or solid in his brain, incapable of accepting anything henceforth from fate, after these two months passed in the intoxications of youth and of love, overwhelmed by all the reveries of despair, he had now but one desire: to make an end of it very quickly.

He began to walk rapidly. It happened that he was armed, having Javert's pistols with him.

2 (3)

THE EXTREME LIMIT

MARIUS HAD reached the markets.

There all was more calm, more dark, and more motionless still than in the neighbouring streets. One would have said that the icy peace of the grave had come forth from the earth and spread over the sky.

A red glare, however, cut out upon this dark background the high roofs of the houses which barred the Rue de la Chanvrerie on the side towards Saint Eustache. It was the reflection of the torch which was blazing in the barricade of Corinth. Marius directed his steps towards this glare. It led him to the Beet Market, and he dimly saw the dark mouth of the Rue des Prêcheurs. He entered it. The sentinel of the insurgents who was on guard at the other end did not perceive him. He felt that he was very near what he had come to seek, and he walked upon tiptoe. He reached in this way the elbow of that short end of the Rue Mondétour, which was, as we remember, the only communication preserved by Enjolras with the outside. Round the corner of the last house on his left, cautiously advancing his head, he looked into this end of the Rue Mondétour.

A little beyond the black corner of the alley and the Rue de la Chanvrerie, which threw a broad shadow, in which he was himself buried, he perceived a light upon the pavement, a portion of the tavern, and behind, a lamp twinkling in a kind of shapeless wall, and men crouching down with muskets on their knees. All this was within twenty yards of him. It was the interior of the barricade.

The houses on the right of the alley hid from him the rest of the tavern, the great barricade, and the flag.

Marius had but one step more to take.

Then the unhappy young man sat down upon a stone, folded his arms, and thought of his father.

He thought of that heroic Colonel Pontmercy who had been so brave a soldier, who had defended the frontier of France under the republic, and reached the frontier of Asia under the emperor, who had seen Genoa, Alessandria, Milan, Turin, Madrid, Vienna, Dresden, Berlin, Moscow, who had left upon every field of victory in Europe drops of that same blood which he, Marius, had in his veins, who had grown grey before his time in discipline and in command, who had lived with his sword-belt buckled, his epaulets falling on his breast, his cockade blackened by powder, his forehead wrinkled by the cap, in the barracks, in the camp, in the bivouac, in the ambulance, and who after twenty years had returned from the great wars with his cheek scarred, his face smiling, simple, tranquil, admirable, pure as a child, having done everything for France and nothing against her.

He said to himself that his day had come to him also, that his hour had at last struck, that after his father, he also was to be brave, intrepid, bold, to run amidst bullets, to bare his breast to the bayonets, to pour out his blood, to seek the enemy, to seek death, that he was to wage war in his turn and to enter upon the field of battle, and that that field of battle upon which he was about to enter, was the street, and that war which he was about to wage, was civil war!

He saw civil war yawning like an abyss before him, and that in it he was to fall.

And then he began to weep bitterly.

It was horrible. But what could he do? Live without Cosette, he could not. Since she had gone away, he must surely die. Had he not given her his word of honour that he should die? She had gone away knowing that; therefore it pleased her that Marius should die. And then it was clear that she no longer loved him, since she had gone away thus, without notifying him, without a word, without a letter, and she knew his address! What use in life and why live longer? And then, indeed! to have come so far, and to recoil! to have approached the danger, and to flee! to have come and looked into the barricade, and to slink away! to slink away all trembling, saying: "in fact, I have had enough of this, I have seen, that is sufficient, it is civil war, I am going away!" To abandon his friends who were expecting him! who perhaps had need of him! who were a handful against an army! To fail in all things at the same time, in his love, his friendship, his word! To give his poltroonery the pretext of patriotism! But this was impossible, and if his father's ghost were there in the shadow and saw him recoil, he would strike him with the flat of his sword and cry to him: "Advance, coward!"

A prey to the swaying of his thoughts, he bowed his head.

Suddenly he straightened up. A sort of splendid rectification was wrought in his spirit. There was an expansion of thought fitted to the confinity of the tomb; to be near death makes us see the truth. The vision of the act upon which he felt himself, perhaps on the point of entering, appeared to him no longer lamentable, but superb. The war of the street was suddenly transfigured by some indescribable interior travail of the soul, before the eye of his mind. All the tumultuous interrogation points of his reverie thronged upon him, but without troubling him. He left none without an answer.[*]

Let us see, why should his father be indignant? are there not cases when insurrection rises to the dignity of duty? what would there be then belittling to the son of Colonel Pontmercy in the impending combat? It is no longer Montmirail or Champaubert; it is something else. It is no longer a question of a sacred territory, but of a holy idea. The country laments, so be it; but humanity applauds. Besides is it true that the country mourns? France bleeds, but liberty smiles; and before the smile of liberty, France forgets her wound. And then, looking at the matter from a still higher stand, why do men talk of civil war?

Civil war? What does this mean? Is there any foreign war? Is not every war between men, war between brothers? War is modified only by its aim. There is neither foreign war, nor civil war; there is only unjust war and just war. Until the day when the great human concordat shall be concluded, war, that at least which is the struggle of the hurrying future against the lingering past, may be necessary. What reproach can be brought against such war! War becomes shame, the sword becomes a dagger, only when it assassinates right, progress, reason, civilisation, truth. Then, civil war or foreign war, it is iniquitous; its name is crime. When the master falls in France, he falls everywhere. In short, to re-establish social truth, to give back to liberty her throne, to give back the people to the people, to give back sovereignty to man, to replace the purple upon the head of France, to restore in their fulness reason and equity, to suppress every germ of antagonism by restoring every man to himself, to abolish the obstacle which royalty opposes to the immense universal concord, to replace the human race on a level with right, what cause more just, and, consequently, what war more grand? These wars construct peace. An enormous fortress of prejudices, of privileges, of superstitions, of lies, of exactions, of abuses, of violence, of iniquity,

---

[*]In a privileged moment of moral and political insight, Marius understands the dignity and necessity of his participation in the uprising of 1832. The next two paragraphs represent his thoughts in free indirect discourse.

of darkness, is still standing upon the world with its towers of hatred. It must be thrown down. This monstrous pile must be made to fall. To conquer at Austerlitz is grand; to take the Bastille is immense.*

Even while thinking thus, overwhelmed but resolute, hesitating, however, and, indeed, shuddering in view of what he was about to do, his gaze wandered into the interior of the barricade. The insurgents were chatting in undertone, without moving about; and that quasi-silence was felt which marks the last phase of delay.

---

*Napoléon's victory there was grand, because many soldiers were involved; to capture the Bastille (where the defenders surrendered, and which at the time contained only three prisoners) was "immense" owing to its symbolic importance.

Book Fourteen
THE GRANDEUR OF DESPAIR

1

THE FLAG: FIRST ACT

A HEADLONG RUN startled the empty street; they saw a creature nimbler than a clown climb over the omnibus, and Gavroche bounded into the barricade all breathless, saying:

"My musket! Here they are."

An electric thrill ran through the whole barricade, and a moving of hands was heard, feeling for their muskets.

"Do you want my carbine?" said Enjolras to the *gamin*.

"I want the big musket," answered Gavroche.

And he took Javert's musket.

Two sentinels had been driven back, and had come in almost at the same time as Gavroche. They were the sentinel from the end of the street, and the sentinel from de la Petite Truanderie. The sentinel in the little Rue des Prêcheurs remained at his post, which indicated that nothing was coming from the direction of the bridges and the markets.

Every man had taken his post for the combat.

Forty-three insurgents, among them Enjolras, Combeferre, Courfeyrac, Bossuet, Joly, Bahorel, and Gavroche, were on their knees in the great barricade, their heads even with the crest of the wall, the barrels of their muskets and their carbines pointed over the paving-stones as through loopholes, watchful, silent, ready to fire. Six, commanded by Feuilly, were stationed with their muskets at their shoulders, in the windows of the two upper stories of Corinth.

A few moments more elapsed, then a sound of steps, measured, heavy, numerous, was distinctly heard from the direction of Saint Leu. This sound, at first faint, then distinct, then heavy and sonorous, approached slowly, without halt, without interruption, with a tranquil and terrible continuity. Nothing but this could be heard. It was at once the silence and the sound of the statue of the Commander, but this stony tread was so indescribably enormous and so multiplex, that it called up at the same time the idea of a throng and of a spectre. You would have thought you heard the stride of the fearful statue Legion. This tread approached; it approached still nearer, and stopped. They seemed to hear at the end of the street the breathing of many men. They saw nothing, however, only they discovered at the very end, in that dense darkness, a multitude of metallic threads, as fine as needles and almost imperceptible, which moved about like those indescribable phosphoric networks which we perceive under our closed eyelids at the moment of going to sleep, in the first mists of slumber. They were bayonets and musket barrels dimly lighted up by the distant reflection of the torch.

There was still a pause, as if on both sides they were awaiting. Suddenly, from the depth of that shadow, a voice, so much the more ominous, because nobody could be seen, and because it seemed as if it were the darkness itself which was speaking, cried:

"Who goes there?"

At the same time they heard the click of the levelled muskets.

Enjolras answered in a lofty and ringing tone:

"French Revolution!"

"Fire!" said the voice.

A flash empurpled all the façades on the street, as if the door of a furnace were opened and suddenly closed.

A fearful explosion burst over the barricade. The red flag fell. The volley had been so heavy and so dense that it had cut the staff, that is to say, the very point of the pole of the omnibus. Some balls, which ricocheted from the cornices of the houses, entered the barricade and wounded several men.

The impression produced by this first charge was freezing. The attack was impetuous, and such as to make the boldest ponder. It was evident that they had to do with a whole regiment at least.

"Comrades," cried Courfeyrac, "don't waste the powder. Let us wait to reply till they come into the street."

During this time little Gavroche, who alone had not left his post and had remained on the watch, thought he saw some men approaching the barricade with a stealthy step. Suddenly he cried:

"Take care!"

Courfeyrac, Enjolras, Jean Prouvaire, Combeferre, Joly, Bahorel, Bossuet, all sprang tumultuously from the tavern. There was hardly a moment to spare. They perceived a sparkling breadth of bayonets undulating above the barricade. Municipal Guards of tall stature were penetrating, some by climbing over the omnibus, others by the opening, pushing before them the *gamin,* who fell back, but did not fly.

The moment was critical. It was that first fearful instant of the inundation, when the stream rises to the level of the bank and when the water begins to infiltrate through the fissures in the dyke. A second more, and the barricade had been taken.

Bahorel sprang upon the first Municipal Guard who entered, and killed him at the very muzzle of his carbine; the second killed Bahorel with his bayonet. Another had already prostrated Courfeyrac, who was crying "Help!" The largest of all, a kind of colossus, marched upon Gavroche with fixed bayonet. The *gamin* took Javert's enormous musket in his little arms, aimed it resolutely at the giant, and pulled the trigger. Nothing went off. Javert had not loaded his musket. The Municipal Guard burst into a laugh and raised his bayonet over the child.

Before the bayonet touched Gavroche the musket dropped from the soldier's hands, a ball had struck the Municipal Guard in the middle of the forehead, and he fell on his back. A second ball struck the other Guard, who had assailed Courfeyrac, full in the breast, and threw him upon the pavement.

It was Marius who had just entered the barricade.

2 (4)

THE KEG OF POWDER

MARIUS, still hidden in the corner of the Rue Mondétour, had watched the first phase of the combat, irresolute and shuddering. However, he was not able long to resist that mysterious and sovereign infatuation which we may call the appeal of the abyss. Before the imminence of the danger, before Bahorel slain, Courfeyrac crying "Help!" that child threatened, his friends to succour or to avenge, all hesitation had vanished, and he had rushed into the conflict, his two pistols in his hands. By the first shot he had saved Gavroche and by the second delivered Courfeyrac.

At the shots, at the cries of the wounded Guards, the assailants had scaled the intrenchment, upon the summit of which could now be seen thronging Municipal Guards, soldiers of the Line, National Guards of the banlieue, musket in hand. They already covered more than two-thirds of the wall, but they did not leap into the inclosure; they seemed to hesitate, fearing some snare. They looked into the dark barricade as one would look into a den of lions. The light of the torch only lighted up their bayonets, their bearskin caps, and the upper part of their anxious and angry faces.

Marius had now no arms, he had thrown away his discharged pistols, but he had noticed the keg of powder in the basement-room near the door.

As he turned half round, looking in that direction, a soldier aimed at him. At the moment the soldier aimed at Marius, a hand was laid upon the muzzle of the musket, and stopped it. It was somebody who had sprung forward, the young working-man with velvet trousers. The shot went off, passed through the hand, and perhaps also through the working-man, for he fell, but the ball did not reach Marius. All this in the smoke, rather guessed than seen. Marius, who was entering the basement-room, hardly noticed it. Still he had caught a dim glimpse of that musket directed at him, and that hand which had stopped it, and he had heard the shot: But in moments like that the things which we see, waver and rush headlong, and we stop for nothing. We feel ourselves vaguely pushed towards still deeper shadow, and all is cloud.

The insurgents, surprised, but not dismayed, had rallied. Enjolras had cried: "Wait! don't fire at random!" In the first confusion, in fact, they might hit one another. Most of them had gone up to the window of the second story and to the dormer-windows, whence they commanded the assailants. The most determined, with Enjolras, Courfeyrac, Jean Prouvaire, and Combeferre, had haughtily placed their backs to the houses in the rear, openly facing the ranks of soldiers and guards which crowded the barricade.

All this was accomplished without precipitation, with that strange and threatening gravity which precedes mêlées. On both sides they were taking aim, the muzzles of the guns almost touching; they were so near that they could talk with each other in an ordinary tone. Just as the spark was about to fly, an officer in a gorget and with huge epaulets, extended his sword and said:

"Take aim!"

"Fire!" said Enjolras.

The two explosions were simultaneous, and everything disappeared in the smoke.

A stinging and stifling smoke amid which writhed, with dull and feeble groans, the wounded and the dying.

When the smoke cleared away, on both sides the combatants were seen, thinned out, but still in the same places, and reloading their pieces in silence.

Suddenly, a thundering voice was heard, crying:

"Clear out, or I'll blow up the barricade!"

All turned in the direction whence the voice came.

Marius had entered the basement room, and had taken the keg of powder, then he had profited by the smoke and the kind of dark fog which filled the intrenched inclosure, to glide along the barricade as far as that cage of paving-stones in which the torch was fixed. To pull out the torch, to put the keg of powder in its place, to push the pile of paving-stones upon the keg, which stove it in, with a sort of terrible self-control—all this had been for Marius the work of stooping down and rising up; and now all, National Guards, Municipal Guards, officers, soldiers, grouped at the other extremity of the barricade, beheld him with horror, his foot upon the stones, the torch in his hand, his stern face lighted by a deadly resolution, bending the flame of the torch towards that formidable pile in which they discerned the broken barrel of powder, and uttering that terrific cry:

"Clear out, or I'll blow up the barricade!"

Marius upon this barricade, after the octogenarian, was the vision of the young revolution after the apparition of the old.

"Blow up the barricade!" said a sergeant, "and yourself also!"

Marius answered:

"And myself also."

And he brought the torch closer to the keg of powder.

But there was no longer anybody on the wall. The assailants, leaving their dead and wounded, fled pell-mell and in disorder towards the extremity of the street, and were again lost in the night. It was a rout.

The barricade was redeemed.

3 (5)

END OF JEAN PROUVAIRE'S RHYME

ALL FLOCKED round Marius. Courfeyrac sprang to his neck.

"You here!"

"How fortunate!" said Combeferre.

"You came in good time!" said Bossuet.

"Without you I should have been dead!" continued Courfeyrac.

"Without you I'd been gobbled!" added Gavroche.

Marius inquired:

"Where is the chief?"

"You are the chief," said Enjolras.

Marius had all day had a furnace in his brain, now it was a whirlwind. This whirlwind which was within him, affected him as if it were without, and were sweeping him along. It seemed to him that he was already at an immense distance from life. His two luminous months of joy and of love, terminating abruptly upon this frightful precipice, Cosette lost to him, this barricade, himself a chief of insurgents, all these things appeared a monstrous nightmare. He was obliged to make a mental effort to assure himself that all this which surrounded him was real. Marius had lived too little as yet to know that nothing is more imminent than the impossible, and that what we must always foresee is the unforeseen. He was a spectator of his own drama, as of a play which one does not comprehend.

In this mist in which his mind was struggling, he did not recognise Javert who, bound to his post, had not moved his head during the attack upon the barricade, and who beheld the revolt going on about him with the resignation of a martyr and the majesty of a judge. Marius did not even perceive him.

Meanwhile the assailants made no movement, they were heard marching and swarming at the end of the street, but they did not venture forward, either that they were awaiting orders, or that before rushing anew upon that impregnable redoubt, they were awaiting reinforcements. The insurgents had posted sentinels, and some who were students in medicine had set about dressing the wounded.

A bitter emotion came to darken their joy over the redeemed barricade. They called the roll. One of the insurgents was missing. And who? One of the dearest. One of the most valiant, Jean Prouvaire. They sought him among the wounded, he was not there. They sought him among the dead, he was not there. He was evidently a prisoner.

Combeferre said to Enjolras:

"They have our friend; we have their officer. Have you set your heart on the death of this spy?"

"Yes," said Enjolras; "but less than on the life of Jean Prouvaire."

This passed in the basement-room near Javert's post.

"Well," replied Combeferre, "I am going to tie my handkerchief to my cane, and go with a flag of truce to offer to give them their man for ours."

"Listen," said Enjolras, laying his hand on Combeferre's arm.

There was a significant clicking of arms at the end of the street.

They heard a manly voice cry:

"Vive la France! Vive l'avenir!"

They recognised Prouvaire's voice.

There was a flash and an explosion.

Silence reigned again.

"They have killed him," exclaimed Combeferre.

Enjolras looked at Javert and said to him:

"Your friends have just shot you."

4 (6)

THE AGONY OF DEATH AFTER
THE AGONY OF LIFE

A PECULIARITY OF THIS KIND of war is that the attack on the barricades is almost always made in front, and that in general the assailants abstain from turning the positions, whether it be that they dread ambush, or that they fear to become entangled in the crooked streets. The whole attention of the insurgents therefore was directed to the great barricade, which was evidently the point still threatened, and where the struggle must infallibly recommence. Marius, however, thought of the little barricade and went to it. It was deserted, and was guarded only by the lamp which flickered between the stones. The little Rue Mondétour, moreover, and the branch streets de la Petite Truanderie and du Cygne, were perfectly quiet.

As Marius, the inspection made, was retiring, he heard his name faintly pronounced in the darkness:

"Monsieur Marius!"

He shuddered, for he recognised the voice which had called him two hours before, through the grating in the Rue Plumet.

Only this voice now seemed to be but a breath.

He looked about him and saw nobody.

Marius thought he was deceived, and that it was an illusion added by his mind to the extraordinary realities which were thronging about him. He started to leave the retired recess in which the barricade was situated.

"Monsieur Marius!" repeated the voice.

This time he could not doubt, he had heard distinctly; he looked, and saw nothing.

"At your feet," said the voice.

He stooped and saw a form in the shadow, which was dragging itself towards him. It was crawling along the pavement. It was this that had spoken to him.

The lamp enabled him to distinguish a smock, a pair of torn trousers of coarse velvet, bare feet, and something which resembled a pool of blood. Marius caught a glimpse of a pale face which rose towards him and said to him:

"You do not know me?"

"No."

"Eponine."

Marius bent down quickly. It was indeed that unhappy child. She was dressed as a man.

"How came you here? what are you doing there?"

"I am dying," said she.

There are words and incidents which rouse beings who are crushed. Marius exclaimed, with a start:

"You are wounded! Wait, I will carry you into the room! They will dress your wounds! Is it serious? how shall I take you up so as not to hurt you? Where are you hurt? Help! my God! But what did you come here for?"

And he tried to pass his arm under her to lift her.

In lifting her he touched her hand.

She uttered a feeble cry.

"Have I hurt you?" asked Marius.

"A little."

"But I have only touched your hand."

She raised her hand into Marius' sight, and Marius saw in the centre of that hand a black hole.

"What is the matter with your hand?" said he.

"It is pierced."

"Pierced?"

"Yes."

"By what?"

"By a ball."

"How?"

"Did you see a musket aimed at you?"

"Yes, and a hand which stopped it."

"That was mine."

Marius shuddered.

"What madness! Poor child! But that is not so bad, if that is all, it is nothing, let me carry you to a bed. They will care for you, people don't die from a shot in the hand."

She murmured:

"The ball passed through my hand, but it went out through my back. It is useless to take me from here. I will tell you how you can care for me, better than a surgeon. Sit down by me on that stone."

He obeyed; she laid her head on Marius' knees, and without looking at him, she said:

"Oh! how good it is! How kind he is! That is it! I don't suffer any more!"

She remained a moment in silence, then she turned her head with effort and looked at Marius.

"Do you know, Monsieur Marius? It worried me that you should go into that garden, it was silly, since it was I who had shown you the house, and then indeed I ought surely to have known that a young man like you—"

She stopped, and, leaping over the gloomy transitions which were doubtless in her mind, she added with a heartrending smile:

"You thought me ugly, didn't you?"

She continued:

"See, you are lost! Nobody will get out of the barricade, now. It was I who led you into this, it was! You are going to die, I am sure. And still when I saw him aiming at you, I put up my hand upon the muzzle of the musket. How droll it is! But it was because I wanted to die before you. When I got this ball, I dragged myself here, nobody saw me, nobody picked me up. I waited for you, I said: He will not come then? Oh! if you knew, I bit my smock, I suffered so much! Now I am well. Do you remember the day when I came into your room, and when I looked at myself in your mirror, and the day when I met you on the boulevard near some work-women? How the birds sang! It was not very long ago. You gave me a hundred sous, and I said to you: I don't want your money. Did you pick up your coin? You are not rich. I didn't think to tell you to pick it up. The sun shone bright, I was not cold. Do you remember, Monsieur Marius? Oh! I am happy! We are all going to die."

She had a wandering, grave, and touching air. Her torn smock showed her bare throat. While she was talking she rested her wounded hand upon her breast where there was another hole, from which there came with each pulsation a flow of blood like a jet of wine from an open bung.

Marius gazed upon this unfortunate creature with profound compassion.

"Oh!" she exclaimed suddenly, "it is coming back. I am stifling!"

She seized her smock and bit it, and her legs writhed upon the pavement.

She was sitting almost upright, but her voice was very low and broken by hiccoughs. At intervals the death-rattle interrupted her. She approached her face as near as she could to Marius' face. She added with a strange expression:

"Listen, I don't want to deceive you. I have a letter in my pocket for you. Since yesterday. I was told to put it in the post. I kept it. I didn't want it to reach you. But you would not like it of me perhaps when we meet again so soon. We do meet again, don't we? Take your letter."

She grasped Marius' hand convulsively with her wounded hand, but she seemed no longer to feel the pain. She put Marius' hand into the pocket of her smock. Marius really felt a paper there.

"Take it," said she.

Marius took the letter.

She made a sign of satisfaction and of consent.

"Now for my pains, promise me——"

And she hesitated.

"What?" asked Marius.

"Promise me!"

"I promise you."

"Promise to kiss me on the forehead when I am dead. I shall feel it."

She let her head fall back upon Marius' knees and her eyelids closed. He thought that poor soul had gone. Eponine lay motionless; but just when Marius supposed her for ever asleep, she slowly opened her eyes in which the gloomy deepness of death appeared, and said to him with an accent the sweetness of which already seemed to come from another world:

"And then, do you know, Monsieur Marius, I believe I was a little in love with you."

She essayed to smile again and expired.

5 (7)

GAVROCHE A PROFOUND CALCULATOR OF DISTANCES

MARIUS KEPT his promise. He kissed that livid forehead from which oozed an icy sweat. This was not infidelity to Cosette; it was a thoughtful and gentle farewell to an unhappy soul.

He had not taken the letter which Eponine had given him without a thrill. He had felt at once the presence of an event. He was impatient to read it. The heart of man is thus made; the unfortunate child had hardly closed her eyes when Marius thought to unfold this paper. He laid her gently upon the ground, and went away. Something told him that he could not read that letter in sight of this corpse.

He went to a candle in the basement-room. It was a little note, folded and sealed with the elegant care of a woman. The address was in a woman's hand, and ran:

"To Monsieur, Monsieur Marius Pontmercy, at M. Courfeyrac's, Rue de la Verrerie, No. 16."

He broke the seal and read:

"My beloved, alas! my father wishes to start immediately. We shall be to-night in the Rue de l'Homme Armé, No. 7. In a week we shall be in England. COSETTE June 4th."

Such was the innocence of this love that Marius did not even know Cosette's handwriting.

What happened may be told in a few words. Eponine had done it all. After the evening of the 3rd of June, she had had a double thought, to thwart the projects of her father and the bandits upon the house in the Rue Plumet, and to separate Marius from Cosette. She had changed rags with the first young rogue who thought it amusing to dress as a woman while Eponine disguised herself as a man. It was she who, in the Champ de Mars, had given Jean Valjean the expressive warning: *Move out*. Jean Valjean returned home, and said to Cosette: *we start to-night, and we are going to the Rue de l'Homme Armé with Toussaint. Next week we shall be in London.* Cosette, prostrated by this unexpected blow, had hastily written two lines to Marius. But how should she get the letter to the post? She did not go out alone, and Toussaint, surprised at such an errand, would surely show the letter to M. Fauchelevent. In this anxiety, Cosette saw, through the grating, Eponine in men's clothes, who was now prowling continually about the garden. Cosette called "this young working-man" and handed him five francs and the letter, saying to him: "carry this letter to its address right away." Eponine put the letter in her pocket. The next day, June 5th, she went to Courfeyrac's to ask for Marius, not to give him the letter, but, a thing which every jealous and loving soul will understand, "to see." There she waited for Marius, or, at least, for Courfeyrac—still to see. When Courfeyrac said to her: we are going to the barricades, an idea flashed across her mind. To throw herself into that death as she would have thrown herself into any other, and to push Marius into it. She followed Courfeyrac, made sure of the post where they were building the barricade; and very sure, since Marius had received no notice, and she had intercepted the letter, that he would at nightfall be at his usual evening rendezvous, she went to the Rue Plumet, waited there for Marius, and sent him, in the name of his friends, that appeal which must, she thought, lead him to the barricade. She counted upon Marius' despair when he should not find Cosette; she was not mistaken. She returned herself to the Rue de la Chanvrerie. We have seen what she did there. She died with that tragic joy of jealous hearts which drag the being they love into death with them, saying: nobody shall have him!

Marius covered Cosette's letter with kisses. She loved him then? He had for a moment the idea that now he need not die. Then he said to himself: "She is going away. Her father takes her to England and my grandfather refuses to consent to the marriage. Nothing is changed in our fate." Dreamers, like Marius, have these supreme depressions, and paths hence are chosen in despair. The fatigue of life is unbearable; death is sooner over. Then he thought that there were two duties remaining for him to fulfil: to inform Cosette of his death and to send her a last farewell, and to save from the imminent catastrophe which was approaching, this poor child, Eponine's brother and Thénardier's son.

He had a pocket-book with him; the same that had contained the pages upon which he had written so many thoughts of love for Cosette. He tore out a leaf and wrote with a pencil these few lines:

"Our marriage was impossible. I have asked my grandfather, he has refused; I am without fortune, and you also. I ran to your house, I did not find you, you know the promise that I gave you? I keep it, I die, I love you. When you read this, my soul will be near you, and will smile upon you."

Having nothing to seal this letter with, he merely folded the paper, and wrote upon it this address:

"To Mademoiselle Cosette Fauchelevent, at M. Fauchelevent's, Rue de l'Homme Armé, No. 7."

The letter folded, he remained a moment in thought, took his pocketbook again, opened it, and wrote these four lines on the first page with the same pencil:

"My name is Marius Pontmercy. Carry my corpse to my grandfather's, M. Gillenormand, Rue des Filles du Calvaire, No. 6, in the Marais."

He put the book into his coat-pocket, then he called Gavroche. The *gamin,* at the sound of Marius' voice, ran up with his joyous and devoted face:

"Will you do something for me?"

"Anything," said Gavroche. "God of the good God! without you I should have been cooked, sure."

"You see this letter?"

"Yes."

"Take it. Go out of the barricade immediately (Gavroche, disturbed, began to scratch his ear), and to-morrow morning you will carry it to its address, to Mademoiselle Cosette, at M. Fauchelevent's, Rue de l'Homme Armé, No. 7."

The heroic boy answered:

"Ah, well, but in that time they'll take the barricade, and I shan't be here."

"The barricade will not be attacked again before daybreak, according to all appearance, and will not be taken before to-morrow noon."

The new respite which the assailants allowed the barricade was, in fact, prolonged. It was one of those intermissions, frequent in night combats, which are always followed by a redoubled fury.

"Well," said Gavroche, "suppose I go and carry your letter in the morning?"

"It will be too late. The barricade will probably be blockaded; all the streets will be guarded, and you could not get out. Go, right away!"

Gavroche had nothing more to say; he stood there, undecided, and sadly scratching his ear. Suddenly, with one of his birdlike motions, he took the letter:

"All right," said he.

And he started off on a run by the little Rue Mondétour.

Gavroche had an idea which decided him, but which he did not tell, for fear Marius would make some objection to it.

That idea was this:

"It is hardly midnight, the Rue de l'Homme Armé is not far, I will carry the letter right away, and I shall get back in time."

BOOK FIFTEEN
THE RUE DE L'HOMME ARMÉ

1

BLOTTER, BLABBER

WHAT ARE THE CONVULSIONS of a city compared with the riots of the soul? Man is deeper still than the people. Jean Valjean, at that very moment, was a prey to a frightful uprising. Every abyss of rage and despair was gaping once again within him. He also, like Paris, was shuddering on the threshold of a formidable and dark revolution. A few hours had sufficed. His destiny and his conscience were suddenly covered with shadow. Of him also, as of Paris, we might say: the two principles are face to face. The angel of light and the angel of darkness are to wrestle on the bridge of the abyss. Which of the two shall hurl down the other? which shall triumph?

On the eve of that same day, June 5th, Jean Valjean, accompanied by Cosette and Toussaint, had installed himself in the Rue de l'Homme Armé. A sudden turn of fortune awaited him there.

Cosette had not left the Rue Plumet without an attempt at resistance. For the first time since they had lived together, Cosette's will and Jean Valjean's will had shown themselves distinct, and had been, if not conflicting, at least contradictory. There was objection on one side and inflexibility on the other. The abrupt advice: *move out,* thrown to Jean Valjean by an unknown hand, had so far alarmed him as to render him absolute. He believed himself tracked down and pursued. Cosette had to yield.

They both arrived in the Rue de l'Homme Armé without opening their mouths or saying a word, absorbed in their personal meditations; Jean Valjean so anxious that he did not perceive Cosette's sadness, Cosette so sad that she did not perceive Jean Valjean's anxiety.

Jean Valjean had brought Toussaint, which he had never done in his preceding absences. He saw that possibly he should not return to the Rue Plumet, and he could neither leave Toussaint behind, nor tell her his secret. Besides he felt that she was devoted and safe. Between domestic and master, treason begins with curiosity. But Toussaint, as if she had been predestined to be the servant of Jean Valjean, was not curious. She said through her stuttering, in her Barneville peasant's speech: "I am from same to same; I thing my act; the remainder is not my labour." (I am so; I do my work! the rest is not my affair.)

In this departure from the Rue Plumet, which was almost a flight, Jean Valjean carried nothing but the little fragrant valise christened by Cosette the *inseparable.* Full trunks would have required porters, and porters are witnesses. They had a coach come to the door on the Rue de Babylone, and they went away.

It was with great difficulty that Toussaint obtained permission to pack up a little linen and clothing and a few toilet articles. Cosette herself carried only her writing-desk and her blotter.

Jean Valjean, to increase the solitude and mystery of this disappearance, had arranged so as not to leave the cottage on the Rue Plumet till the close of the day, which left Cosette time to write her note to Marius. They arrived in the Rue de l'Homme Armé after nightfall.

They went silently to bed.

The lodging in the Rue de l'Homme Armé was situated in a rear court, on the third story, and consisted of two bedrooms, a dining-room, and a kitchen adjoining the dining-room, with a loft where there was a cot which fell to Toussaint. The dining-room was at the same time the antechamber, and separated the two bedrooms. The apartment contained the necessary kitchen ware.

We are reassured almost as foolishly as we are alarmed; human nature is so constituted. Hardly was Jean Valjean in the Rue de l'Homme Armé before his anxiety grew less, and by degrees dissipated. There are quieting spots which somehow act mechanically upon the mind. Dim street, peaceful inhabitants. Jean Valjean felt some strange contagion of tranquillity in that lane of the old Paris, so narrow that it was barred to carriages by a beam laid upon two posts, dumb and deaf in the midst of the noisy city, twilight in broad day, and so to speak, incapable of emotions between its two rows of lofty, century-old houses which are silent like the patriarchs that they are. There is stagnant oblivion in this street. Jean Valjean breathed freely there. By what means could anybody find him there?

His first care was to place the *inseparable* by his side.

He slept well. Night counsels; we may add: night calms. Next morning he awoke almost cheerful. He thought the dining-room charming, although it was hideous, furnished with an old round table, a low sideboard surmounted by a cracked mirror, a worm-eaten armchair, and a few other chairs loaded down with Toussaint's bundles. Through an opening in one of these bundles, Jean Valjean's National Guard uniform could be seen.

As for Cosette, she had Toussaint bring a bowl of soup to her room, and did not make her appearance till evening.

About five o'clock, Toussaint, who was coming and going, very busy with this little move, set a cold fowl on the dining-room table, which Cosette, out of deference to her father, consented to look at.

This done, Cosette, upon pretext of a severe headache, said good-night to Jean Valjean, and shut herself in her bedroom. Jean Valjean ate a chicken's wing with a good appetite, and, leaning on the table, clearing his brow little by little, was regaining his sense of security.

While he ate this frugal dinner, he became confusedly aware, on two or three occasions, of the stammering of Toussaint, who said to him: "Monsieur, there is a row; they are fighting in Paris." But, absorbed in a multitude of plans, he paid no attention. To tell the truth, he had not heard.

He arose and began to walk from the window to the door, and from the door to the window, growing calmer and calmer.

With calmness, Cosette, his single engrossing care, returned to his thoughts. Not that he was troubled about this headache, a petty disturbance of the nerves, a young girl's pouting, the cloud of a moment, in a day or two it would be gone; but he thought of the future, and, as usual, he thought of it pleasantly. After all, he saw no obstacle to their happy life resuming its course. At certain hours, everything seems impossible; at other hours, everything appears easy; Jean Valjean was in one of those happy hours. To have left the Rue Plumet without complication and without accident, was already a piece of good fortune. Perhaps it would be prudent to leave the country, were it only for a few months, and go to London. Well, they would go. To be in France, to be in England, what did that matter, if he had Cosette with him? Cosette was his nation. Cosette sufficed for his happiness; the idea that perhaps he did not suffice for Cosette's happiness, this idea, which formerly had caused him insomnia, did not even present itself to his mind. All his past griefs had disappeared, and he was in full tide of optimism. Cosette, being near him, seemed to belong to him; an optical effect which everybody has experienced. He arranged in his own mind and with every possible facility, the departure for England with Cosette, and he saw his happiness reconstructed, no matter where, in the perspective of his reverie.

While yet walking up and down, with slow steps, his eye suddenly met something strange.

He perceived facing him, in the tilted mirror above the sideboard, and distinctly read these lines:

"My beloved, alas! my father wishes to leave immediately. We shall be to-night in the Rue de l'Homme Armé, No. 7. In a week we shall be in London. COSETTE. June 4th."

Jean Valjean stood aghast.

Cosette, on arriving, had laid her blotter on the sideboard before the mirror, and, wholly absorbed in her sorrowful anguish, had forgotten it there, without even noticing that she left it wide open, and open exactly at the page upon which she had dried the five lines written by her, and which she had given to the young workman passing through the Rue Plumet. The writing was imprinted upon the blotter.

The mirror reflected the writing.

It was simple and withering.

Jean Valjean went to the mirror. He read the five lines again, but he did not believe it. They produced upon him the effect of an apparition in a flash of lightning. It was a hallucination. It was impossible. It was not.

Little by little his perception became more precise; he looked at Cosette's blotter, and the consciousness of the real fact returned to him. He took the blotter and said: "It comes from that." He feverishly examined the five lines imprinted on the blotter, the reversal of the letters made a fantastic scrawl of them, and he saw no sense in them. Then he said to himself: "But that does not mean anything, there is nothing written there." And he drew a long breath, with an inexpressible sense of relief. Who has not felt these silly joys in moments of horror? The soul does not give itself up to despair until it has exhausted all illusions.

He held the blotter in his hand and gazed at it, stupidly happy, almost laughing at the hallucination of which he had been the dupe. All at once his eyes fell upon the mirror, and he saw the vision again. This time it was not a mirage. The second sight of a vision is a reality, it was palpable, it was the writing restored by the mirror. He understood.

Jean Valjean tottered, let the blotter fall, and sank down into the old armchair by the sideboard, his head drooping, his eyes glassy, bewildered. He said to himself that it was clear, and that the light of the world was for ever eclipsed, and that Cosette had written that to somebody. Then he heard his soul, again become terrible, give a sullen roar in the darkness.

A circumstance strange and sad, Marius at that moment had not yet Cosette's letter; chance had brought it, like a traitor, to Jean Valjean before delivering it to Marius.

Jean Valjean till this day had never been vanquished when put to the test. He had been subjected to fearful trials; no violence of ill fortune had been spared him; the ferocity of fate, armed with every vengeance and with every scorn of society, had taken him for a subject and had greedily pursued him. He had neither recoiled nor flinched before anything. He had accepted, when he must, every extremity; he had sacrificed his reconquered inviolability, sacrificed his liberty, risked his head, lost all, suffered all, and he had remained so disinterested and stoical that at times one might have believed him selfless, like a martyr. His conscience, inured to all possible assaults of adversity, might seem for ever impregnable. Well, whoever could have seen his inner soul would have been compelled to admit that at this hour it was growing weak.

For, of all the tortures which he had undergone in that prolonged inquisition of destiny, this was the most fearsome. Never had such pincers seized him. He felt the mysterious quiver of every latent sensibility. Alas, the supreme ordeal, let us say rather, the only ordeal, is the loss of the beloved being.

Poor old Jean Valjean did not, certainly, love Cosette otherwise than as a father; but, as we have already mentioned, into this paternity the very bereavement of his life had introduced every love; he loved Cosette as his daughter, and he loved her as his mother, and he loved her as his sister; and, as he had never had either sweetheart or wife, as nature is a creditor who accepts no bounced checks, that sentiment, also, the most indestructible of all, was mingled with the others, vague, ignorant, pure with the purity of blindness, unconscious, celestial, angelic, divine; less like a sentiment than like an instinct, less like an instinct than like an attraction, imperceptible and invisible, but real; and love, properly speaking, existed in his enormous tenderness for Cosette as does the vein of gold in the mountain, dark and virgin.

So, when he saw that it was positively ended, that she escaped him, that she glided from his hands, that she eluded him, that it was cloud, that it was water, when he had before his eyes this crushing evidence; another is the aim of her heart, another is the desire of her life, there is a beloved; I am only the father; I no longer exist; when he could no more doubt when he said to himself: "She is going away out of me!" the grief which he felt surpassed the possible. To have done all that he had done to come to this! and, what! to be nothing! Then, as we have just said, he felt from head to foot a shudder of revolt. He felt even to the roots of his hair the immense awakening of selfishness, and the Me howled in the abyss of his soul.

His instinct did not hesitate. He put together certain circumstances, certain dates, certain blushes, and certain pallors of Cosette, and he said to himself: "It is he." The intuition of despair is a sort of mysterious bow which never misses its aim. With his first conjecture, he hit Marius. He did not know the name, but he found the man at once. He perceived distinctly, at the bottom of the implacable evocation of memory, the unknown prowler of the Luxembourg Gardens, that wretched seeker of amours, that romantic idler, that imbecile, that coward, for it is cowardice to come and make sweet eyes at girls who are beside their father who loves them.

After he had fully determined that that young man was at the bottom of this state of affairs, and that it all came from him, he, Jean Valjean, the regenerated man, the man who had laboured so much upon his soul, the man who had made so many efforts to resolve all life, all misery, and all misfortune into love; he looked within himself, and there he saw a spectre, Hatred.

While he was thinking, Toussaint entered. Jean Valjean arose, and asked her:

"In what direction is it? Do you know?"

Toussaint, astonished, could only answer:

"If you please?"

Jean Valjean resumed:

"Didn't you tell me just now that they were fighting?"

"Oh! yes, monsieur," answered Toussaint. "It is over by Saint Merry."

There are some mechanical impulses which come to us, without our knowledge even, from our deepest thoughts. It was doubtless under the influence of an impulse of this kind, and of which he was hardly conscious, that Jean Valjean five minutes afterwards found himself in the street.

He was bare-headed, seated upon the stone block by the door of his house. He seemed to be listening.

The night had come.

2

THE GAMIN AN ENEMY OF LIGHT

SUDDENLY he raised his eyes, somebody was walking in the street, he heard steps near him, he looked, and, by the light of the lamp, in the direction of the Archives, he perceived a livid face, young and radiant.

Gavroche had just arrived in the Rue de l'Homme Armé.

Gavroche was looking in the air, and appeared to be searching for something. He saw Jean Valjean perfectly, but he took no notice of him.

Gavroche, after looking into the air, looked on the ground; he raised himself on tiptoe and felt of the doors and windows of the ground floors; they were all closed, bolted, and chained. After having found five or six houses barricaded in this way, the *gamin* shrugged his shoulders, and took counsel with himself in these terms:

"Golly!"

Then he began to look into the air again.

Jean Valjean, who, the instant before, in the state of mind in which he was, would not have spoken nor even replied to anybody, felt irresistibly impelled to address a word to this child.

"Little boy," said he, "what is the matter with you?"

"The matter is that I am hungry," answered Gavroche tartly. And he added: "Little yourself."

Jean Valjean felt in his pocket and took out a five-franc coin.

But Gavroche, who was of the wagtail species, and who passed quickly from one action to another, had picked up a stone. He had noticed a lamp.

"Hold on," said he, "you have your lamps here still. You are not regular, my friends. It is disorderly. Break that for me."

And he threw the stone into the lamp, the glass from which fell with such a clatter that some bourgeois, hid behind their curtains in the opposite house, cried: "There is 'Ninety-three!"

The lamp swung violently and went out. The street became suddenly dark.

"That's it, old street," said Gavroche, "put on your nightcap."

Jean Valjean approached Gavroche.

"Poor creature," said he, in an undertone, and speaking to himself, "he is hungry."

And he put the hundred-sous coin into his hand.

Gavroche cocked up his nose, astonished at the size of this big sou; he looked at it in the dark, and the whiteness of the big sou dazzled him. He knew five-franc coins by hearsay; their reputation was agreeable to him; he was delighted to see one so near. He said: "let us contemplate the tiger."

He gazed at it for a few moments in ecstasy; then, turning towards Jean Valjean, he handed him the coin, and said majestically:

"Bourgeois, I prefer to break lamps. Take back your wild beast. You don't corrupt me. It has five claws; but it don't scratch me."

"Have you a mother?" inquired Jean Valjean.

Gavroche answered:

"Perhaps more than you have."

"Well," replied Jean Valjean, "keep this money for your mother."

Gavroche felt softened. Besides he had just noticed that the man who was talking to him, had no hat, and that inspired him with confidence.

"Really," said he, "it isn't to prevent my breaking the lamps?"

"Break all you like."

"You are a fine fellow," said Gavroche.

And he put the five-franc coin into one of his pockets.

His confidence increasing, he added:

"Do you live here?"

"Yes; why?"

"Could you show me number seven?"

"What do you want with number seven?"

Here the boy stopped; he feared that he had said too much; he plunged his nails vigorously into his hair, and merely answered:

"Ah! that's it."

An idea flashed across Jean Valjean's mind. Anguish has such lucidities. He said to the child:

"Have you brought the letter I am waiting for?"

"You?" said Gavroche. "You are not a woman."

"The letter is for Mademoiselle Cosette; isn't it?"

"Cosette?" muttered Gavroche, "yes, I believe it is that funny name."

"Well," resumed Jean Valjean, "I am to deliver the letter to her. Give it to me."

"In that case you must know that I am sent from the barricade?"

"Of course," said Jean Valjean.

Gavroche thrust his hand into another of his pockets, and drew out a folded paper.

Then he gave a military salute.

"Respect for the despatch," said he. "It comes from the provisional government."

And he handed the paper to Jean Valjean.

"And hurry yourself, Monsieur What's-your-name, for Mamselle What's-her-name is waiting."

Gavroche was proud of having produced this witticism.

Jean Valjean asked:

"Is it to Saint Merry that the answer is to be sent?"

"In that case," exclaimed Gavroche, "you would be making one of those pastries commonly called blunders [brioches]. That letter comes from the barricade in the Rue de la Chanvrerie, and I am going back there. Good night, citizen."

This said, Gavroche went away, or rather, resumed his flight like an escaped bird towards the spot whence he came. He plunged back into the darkness as if he made a hole in it, with the rapidity and precision of a projectile; the little Rue de l'Homme Armé again became silent and solitary; in a twinkling, this strange child, who had within him shadow and dream, was buried in the dusk of those rows of black houses, and was lost therein like smoke in the darkness; and one might have thought him dissipated and vanished, if, a few minutes after his disappearance, a loud crashing of glass and the splendid patatras of a lamp falling upon the pavement had not abruptly reawakened the indignant bourgeois. It was Gavroche passing along the Rue du Chaume.

3

WHILE COSSETE AND TOUSSAINT SLEEP

JEAN VALJEAN WENT inside with Marius' letter.

He groped his way upstairs, pleased with the darkness like an owl which holds his prey, opened and softly closed the door, listened to see if he heard any sound, decided that, according to all appearances, Cosette and Toussaint were asleep, plunged three or four matches into the bottle of the Fumade tinder-box before he could raise a spark, his hand trembled so much; there was theft in what he was about to do. At last, his candle was lighted, he leaned his elbows on the table, unfolded the paper, and read.

In violent emotions, we do not read, we wrestle down the paper which we hold, so to speak, we strangle it like a victim, we crush the paper, we bury the nails of our wrath or of our delight in it; we run to the end, we leap to the beginning; the attention has a fever; it comprehends by wholesale, almost, the essential; it seizes a point, and all the rest disappears. In Marius' note to Cosette, Jean Valjean saw only these words.

"——I die. When you read this, my soul will be near you."

Before these two lines, he was horribly dazzled; he sat a moment as if crushed by the change of emotion which was wrought within him, he looked at Marius' note with a sort of drunken astonishment; he had before his eyes that splendour, the death of the hated being.

He uttered a hideous cry of inward joy. So, it was finished. The end came sooner than he had dared to hope. The being who encumbered his destiny was disappearing. He was going away of himself, freely, of his own accord. Without any intervention on his, Jean Valjean's part, without any fault of his, "that man" was about to die. Perhaps even he was already dead.—Here his fever began to calculate.—No. He is not dead yet. The letter was evidently written to be read by Cosette in the morning; since those two discharges which were heard between eleven o'clock and midnight, there had been nothing; the barricade will not be seriously attacked till daybreak; but it is all the same, for the moment "that man" meddled with this war, he was lost; he is caught in the net. Jean Valjean felt that he was delivered. He would then find himself once more alone with Cosette. Rivalry ceased; the future began again. He had only to keep the note in his pocket. Cosette would never know what had become of "that man." "I have only to let things take their course. That man cannot escape. If he is not dead yet, it is certain that he will die. What happiness!"

All this said within himself, he became gloomy.*

Then he went down and waked the porter.

About an hour afterwards, Jean Valjean went out in the full dress of a National Guard, and armed. The porter had easily found in the neighbourhood what was necessary to complete his equipment. He had a loaded musket and a cartridge-box full of cartridges. He went in the direction of the markets.

---

*As in the Champmathieu affair, despite the strong temptation, Jean Valjean cannot allow another person to die to ensure his own happiness. He sadly recognizes his painful moral duty to do everything possible to save Marius.

JEAN VALJEAN

BOOK ONE
WAR BETWEEN FOUR WALLS

1 (2)

WHAT CAN BE DONE IN THE ABYSS
BUT TO TALK

THE INSURGENTS, under the eye of Enjolras, for Marius no longer looked to anything, turned the night to advantage. The barricade was not only repaired, but made larger. They raised it two feet. Iron bars planted in the paving-stones resembled lances in rest. All sorts of rubbish added, and brought from all sides, increased the exterior intricacy. The redoubt was skilfully made over into a wall within and a thicket without.

They rebuilt the stairway of paving-stones, which permitted ascent, as upon a citadel wall.

They put the barricade in order, cleared up the basement room, took the kitchen for a hospital, completed the dressing of the wounds; gathered up the powder scattered over the floor and the tables, cast bullets, made cartridges, scraped lint, distributed the arms of the fallen, cleaned the interior of the redoubt, picked up the fragments, carried away the corpses.

They deposited the dead in a heap in the little Rue Mondétour, of which they were still masters. The pavement was red for a long time at that spot. Among the dead were four National Guards of the banlieue. Enjolras had their uniforms laid aside.

No meals could now be had. There was neither bread nor meat. The fifty men of the barricade, in the sixteen hours that they had been there, had very soon exhausted the meagre provisions of the tavern. In a given time, every barricade which holds out, inevitably becomes the raft of le Méduse. They must resign themselves to famine. They were in the early hours of that Spartan day of the 6th of June, when, in the barricade Saint Merry, Jeanne, surrounded by insurgents who were asking for bread, to all those warriors, crying: "Something to eat!" answered: "What for? it is three o'clock. At four o'clock we shall be dead."

About two o'clock in the morning, they took a count. There were thirty-seven of them left.

2 (3)

LIGHT DAWNS AND DARKENS

ENJOLRAS had gone to make a reconnaissance. He went out by the Little Rue Mondétour, creeping along by the houses.

The insurgents, we must say, were full of hope. The manner in which they had repelled the attack during the night, had led them almost to contempt in advance for the attack at daybreak. They awaited it, and smiled at it. They had no more doubt of their success than of their cause. Moreover, help was evidently about to come. They counted on it. With that facility for triumphant prophecy which is a part of the strength of the fighting Frenchman, they divided into three distinct phases the day which was opening: at six o'clock in the morning a regiment, "which had been worked on," would come over to their side. At noon, insurrection of all Paris; at sundown, revolution.

They heard the alarm bell of Saint Merry, which had not been silent a moment since the evening; a proof that the other barricade, the great one, that of Jeanne, still held out.

All these hopes were communicated from one to another in a sort of cheerful yet terrible whisper, which resembled the buzz of a hive of bees at war.

Enjolras reappeared. He returned from his gloomy eagle's walk in the darkness without. He listened for a moment to all this joy with folded arms, one hand over his mouth. Then, fresh and rosy in the growing whiteness of the morning, he said:

"The whole army of Paris is fighting. A third of that army is pressing upon the barricade in which you are. Besides the National Guard, I distinguished the shakos of the Fifth of the line and the colours of the Sixth Legion. You will be attacked in an hour. As for the people, they were boiling yesterday, but this morning they do not stir. Nothing to expect, nothing to hope. No more from a suburb than from a regiment. You have been abandoned."

These words fell upon the buzzing of the groups, and wrought the effect which the first drops of the tempest produce upon the swarm. All were dumb. There was a moment of inexpressible silence, when you might have heard the flight of death.

This moment was short.

A voice, from the most dark depths of the groups, cried to Enjolras:

"So be it. Let us make the barricade twenty feet high, and let us all stand by it. Citizens, let us offer the protest of corpses. Let us show that, if the people abandon the republicans, the republicans do not abandon the people."

3 (4)

FIVE LESS, ONE MORE

AFTER THE MAN of the people, who decreed "the protest of corpses," had spoken and given the formula of the common soul, from all lips arose a strangely satisfied and terrible cry, funereal in meaning and triumphant in tone:

"Long live death! Let us all stay!"

"Why all?" said Enjolras.

"All! all!"

Enjolras resumed:

"The position is good, the barricade is fine. Thirty men are enough. Why sacrifice forty?"

They replied:

"Because nobody wants to leave."

"Citizens," cried Enjolras, and there was in his voice almost an angry tremor, "the republic is not rich enough in men to incur useless expenditures. Vainglory is a squandering. If it is the duty of some to go away, that duty should be performed as well as any other."

Enjolras, the man of principle, had over his co-religionists that sort of omnipotence which emanates from the absolute. Still, notwithstanding this omnipotence, there was a murmur.

Chief to his finger-ends, Enjolras, seeing that they murmured, insisted. He resumed haughtily:

"Let those who fear to be one of but thirty, say so."

The murmurs redoubled.

"Besides," observed a voice from one of the groups, "to go away is easily said. The barricade is hemmed in."

"Not towards the markets," said Enjolras. "The Rue Mondétour is open, and by the Rue des Prêcheurs one can reach the Marché des Innocents."

"And there," put in another voice from the group, "he will be taken. He will fall upon some grand guard of the line or the banlieue. They will see a man going by in cap and smock. 'Where do you come from, fellow? you belong to the barricade, don't you?' And they look at your hands. You smell of powder. Shot."

Enjolras, without answering, touched Combeferre's shoulder, and they both went into the basement room.

They came back a moment afterwards. Enjolras held out in his hands the four uniforms which he had reserved. Combeferre followed him, bringing the cross belts and shakos.

"With this uniform," said Enjolras, "you can mingle with the ranks and escape. Here are enough for four."

And he threw the four uniforms upon the unpaved ground.

No wavering in the stoical auditory. Combeferre spoke:

"Come," said he, "we must have a little pity. Do you know what the question is now? It is a question of women. Let us see. Are there any wives, yes or no? are there any children, yes or no? Are there, yes or no, any mothers, who rock the cradle with their foot and who have heaps of little ones about them? Let him among you who have never seen the breast of a nursing-woman hold up his hand. Ah! you wish to die, I wish it also, I, who am speaking to you, but I do not wish to feel the ghosts of women wringing their hands about me. Die, so be it, but do not make others die. Suicides like those which will be accomplished here are sublime; but suicide is strict, and can have no extension; and as soon as it touches those next you, the name of suicide is murder. Think of the little flaxen heads, and think of the white hairs. We know very well what you are; we know very well that you are all brave, good heavens! we know very well that your souls are filled with joy and glory at giving your life for the great cause; we know very well that you feel that you are elected to die usefully and magnificently, and that each of you clings to his share of the triumph. Well and good. But you are not alone in this world. There are other beings of whom we must think. We must not be selfish."

All bowed their heads with a gloomy air.

Strange contradictions of the human heart in its most sublime moments! Combeferre, who spoke thus, was not an orphan. He remembered the mothers of others, and he forgot his own. He was going to be killed. He was "selfish."

Marius, fasting, feverish, successively driven from every hope, stranded upon grief, most dismal of shipwrecks, saturated with violent emotions and feeling the end approach, was sinking deeper and deeper into that visionary stupor which always precedes the fatal hour when voluntarily accepted.

Still this moved him. There was one point in this scene which pierced through to him, and which woke him. He had now but one idea, to die, and he would not be diverted from it; but he thought, in his funereal somnambulism, that while destroying oneself it is not forbidden to save another.

He raised his voice:

"Enjolras and Combeferre are right," said he; "no useless sacrifice. I add my voice to theirs, and we must hasten. Combeferre has given the criteria. There are among you some who have families, mothers, sisters, wives, children. Let those leave the ranks."

Nobody stirred.

"Married men and supporters of families, out of the ranks!" repeated Marius.

His authority was great. Enjolras was indeed the chief of the barricade, but Marius was its saviour.

"I order it," cried Enjolras.

"I beseech you," said Marius.

Then, roused by the words of Combeferre, shaken by the order of Enjolras, moved by the prayer of Marius, those heroic men began to inform against each other. "That is true," said a young man to a middle-aged man. "You are the father of a family. Go away." "It is you rather," answered the man, "you have two sisters whom you support." And an unparalleled conflict broke out. It was as to which should not allow himself to be laid at the door of the tomb.

"Make haste," said Courfeyrac, "in a quarter of an hour it will be too late."

"Citizens," continued Enjolras, "this is the republic, and universal suffrage reigns. Designate yourselves those who ought to go."

They obeyed. In a few minutes five were unanimously designated and left the ranks.

"There are five!" exclaimed Marius.

There were only four uniforms.

"Well," resumed the five, "one must stay."

And it was who should stay, and who should find reasons why the others should not stay. The generous quarrel recommenced.

"You, you have a wife who loves you." "As for you, you have your old mother." "You have neither father nor mother, what will become of your three little brothers?" "You are the father of five children." "You have a right to live, you are seventeen, it is too soon."

These grand revolutionary barricades were rendezvous of heroisms. The improbable there was natural. These men were not astonished at each other.

"Be quick," repeated Courfeyrac.

Somebody cried out from the group, to Marius:

"Designate yourself, which must stay."

"Yes," said the five, "choose. We will obey you."

Marius now believed no emotion possible. Still at this idea: to select a man for death, all his blood flowed back towards his heart. He would have turned pale if he could have been paler.

He advanced towards the five, who smiled upon him, and each, his eye full of that grand flame which we see in the depth of history over the Thermopylæ, cried to him:

"Me! me! me!"

And Marius, in a stupor, counted them; there were still five! Then his eyes fell upon the four uniforms.

At this moment a fifth uniform dropped, as if from heaven, upon the four others.

The fifth man was saved.

Marius raised his eyes and saw M. Fauchelevent.

Jean Valjean had just entered the barricade.

Whether by information obtained, or by instinct, or by chance, he came by the little Rue Mondétour. Thanks to his National Guard dress, he had passed easily.

The sentry placed by the insurgents in the Rue Mondétour, had not given the signal of alarm for a single National Guard. He permitted him to get into the street, saying to himself: "he is a reinforcement, probably, and at the very worst a prisoner." The moment was too serious for the sentinel to be diverted from his duty and his post of observation.

At the moment Jean Valjean entered the redoubt, nobody had noticed him, all eyes being fixed upon the five chosen ones and upon the four uniforms. Jean Valjean, himself, saw and understood, and silently, he stripped off his coat, and threw it upon the pile with the others.

The commotion was indescribable.

"Who is this man?" asked Bossuet.

"He is," answered Combeferre, "a man who saves others."

Marius added in a grave voice:

"I know him."

This assurance was enough for all.

Enjolras turned towards Jean Valjean:

"Citizen, you are welcome."

And he added:

"You know that we are going to die."

Jean Valjean, without answering, helped the insurgent whom he saved to put on his uniform.

4 (5)

WHAT HORIZON IS VISIBLE FROM THE TOP OF THE BARRICADE

ENJOLRAS WAS STANDING on the paving-stone steps, his elbow upon the muzzle of his carbine. He was thinking; he started, as at the passing of a gust; places where death is have such tripodal effects. There came from his eyes, full of the interior sight, a kind of stifled fire. Suddenly he raised his head, his fair hair waved backwards like that of the angel upon his sombre car of stars, it was the mane of a startled lion flaming with a halo, and Enjolras exclaimed:

"Citizens, do you picture to yourselves the future? The streets of the cities flooded with light, green branches upon the thresholds, the nations sisters, men just, the old men blessing the children, the past loving the present, thinkers in full liberty, believers in full equality, for religion the heavens; the priesthood of every believer, human conscience become the altar, no more hatred, the fraternity of the workshop and the school, for reward and for penalty notoriety, to all, labour, for all, law, over all, peace, no more bloodshed, no more war, mothers happy! To subdue matter is the first step; to realise the ideal is the second. We are tending towards the union of the peoples; we are tending towards the unity of man. No more fictions; no more parasites. The real governed by the true, such is the aim. Civilisation will hold its courts on the summit of Europe, and later at the centre of the continents, in a grand parliament of intelligence. Citizens, whatever may happen to-day, through our defeat as well as through our victory, we are going to effect a revolution. Just as conflagrations light up the whole city, revolutions light up the whole human race. And what revolution shall we effect? I have just said, the revolution of the True. From the political point of view, there is but one single principle: the sovereignty of man over himself. This sovereignty of myself over myself is called Liberty. Where two or several of these sovereignties associate the state begins. But in this association there is no abdication. Each sovereignty gives up a certain portion of itself to form the common right. That portion is the same for all. This identity of concession which each makes to all, is Equality. The common right is nothing more or less than the protection of all radiating upon the right of each. This protection of all over each is called Fraternity. The point of intersection of all these aggregated sovereignties is called Society. This intersection being a junction, this point is a knot. Hence what is called the social tie. Some say social contract; which is the same thing, the word contract being etymologically formed with the idea of tie. Let us understand each other in regard to equality; for, if liberty is the summit, equality is the base. Equality, citizens, is not all vegetation on a level, a society of big spears of grass and little oaks; a neighbourhood of jealousies emasculating each other; it is, civilly, all aptitudes having equal opportunity; politically, all votes having equal weight; religiously, all consciences having equal rights. Equality has an organ: gratuitous and obligatory instruction. The right to the alphabet, we must begin by that. The primary school obligatory upon all the higher school offered to all, such is the law. From the identical school springs equal society. Yes, instruction! Light! Light! all comes from light, and all returns to it. Citizens, the nineteenth century is grand, but the twentieth century will be happy. Then there will be nothing more like old history. Men will no longer have to fear, as now, a conquest, an invasion, a usurpation, a rivalry of nations with the armed hand, an interruption of civilisation depending on a marriage of kings, a birth in the hereditary tyrannies, a partition of the peoples by a Congress, a dismemberment by the downfall of a dynasty, a combat of two religions meeting head to head, like two goats of darkness, upon the bridge of the infinite; they will no longer have to fear famine, speculation, prostitution from distress, misery from lack of work, and the scaffold, and the sword, and the battle, and all the brigandages of chance in the forest of events. We might almost say: there will be no more events. Men will be happy. The human race will fulfil its law as the terrestrial globe fulfils its; harmony will be re-established between the soul and the star; the soul will gravitate about the truth like the star about the light. Friends, the hour in which we live, and in which I speak to you, is a gloomy hour, but of such is the terrible price of the future. A revolution is a toll-gate. Oh! the human race shall be delivered, uplifted, and consoled! We affirm it on this barricade. Whence shall arise the shout of love, if it be not from the summit of sacrifice? O my brothers, here is the junction between those who think and those who suffer; this barricade is made neither of paving-stones, nor of timbers, nor of iron; it is made of two mounds, a mound of ideas and a mound of sorrows. Misery here encounters the ideal. Here day embraces night, and says: I will die with thee and thou shalt be born again with me. From the pressure of all desolations faith gushes forth. Sufferings bring their agony here, and ideas their immortality. This agony and this immortality are to mingle and compose our death. Brothers, he who dies here dies in the radiance of the future, and we are entering a grave illuminated by the dawn."

Enjolras broke off rather than ceased, his lips moved noiselessly, as if he were continuing to speak to himself, and they looked at him with attention, endeavouring still to hear. There was no applause; but they whispered for a long time. Speech being breath, the rustling of intellects resembles the rustling of leaves.

5 (6)

MARIUS HAGGARD, JAVERT LACONIC

THE FIVE MEN designated went out of the barricade by the little Rue Mondétour; they resembled National Guards perfectly; one of them went away weeping. Before starting, they embraced those who remained.

When the five men sent away into life had gone, Enjolras thought of the one condemned to death. He went into the basement room. Javert, tied to the pillar, was thinking.

"Do you need anything?" Enjolras asked him.

Javert answered:

"When shall you kill me?"

"Wait. We need all our cartridges at present."

"Then, give me a drink," said Javert.

Enjolras presented him with a glass of water himself, and, as Javert was bound, he helped him to drink.

"Is that all?" resumed Enjolras.

"I am uncomfortable at this post," answered Javert. "It was not affectionate to leave me to pass the night here. Tie me as you please, but you can surely lay me on a table."

There was, it will be remembered, at the back of the room, a long wide table, upon which they had cast balls and made cartridges. All the cartridges being made and all the powder used up, this table was free.

At Enjolras' order, four insurgents untied Javert from the post. While they were untying him, a fifth held a bayonet to his breast. They left his hands tied behind his back, they put a small yet strong whipcord about his feet, which permitted him to take fifteen-inch steps like those who are mounting the scaffold, and they made him walk to the table at the back of the room, on which they extended him, tightly bound by the middle of his body.

For greater security, by means of a rope fixed to his neck, they added to the system of bonds which rendered all escape impossible, that species of ligature, called in the prisons a martingale, which, starting from the back of the neck, divides over the stomach, and is fastened to the hands after passing between the legs.

While they were binding Javert, a man, on the threshold of the door, gazed at him with singular attention. The shade which this man produced made Javert turn his head. He raised his eyes and recognised Jean Valjean. He did not even start, he haughtily dropped his eyelids, and merely said: "It is very natural."

6 (7)

THE SITUATION GROWS SERIOUS

IT WAS GROWING light rapidly. But not a window was opened, not a door stood ajar; it was the dawn, not the hour of awakening. The extremity of the Rue de la Chanvrerie opposite the barricade had been evacuated by the troops, as we have said; it seemed free, and lay open for wayfarers with an ominous tranquillity. The Rue Saint Denis was as silent as the avenue of the Sphinxes at Thebes. Not a living being at the corners, which were whitening in a reflection of the sun. Nothing is so dismal as this brightness of deserted streets.

They saw nothing, but they heard. A mysterious movement was taking place at some distance. It was evident that the critical moment was at hand. As in the evening the sentries were driven in; but this time all.

The barricade was stronger than at the time of the first attack. Since the departure of the five, it had been raised still higher.

On the report of the sentry who had been observing the region of the markets, Enjolras, for fear of a surprise from the rear, formed an important resolution. He had barricaded the little passage of the Rue Mondétour, which till then had been open. For this purpose they unpaved the length of a few more houses. In this way, the barricade, walled in upon three streets, in front upon the Rue de la Chanvrerie, at the left upon the Rue du Cygne and la Petite Truanderie, at the right upon the Rue Mondétour, was really almost impregnable; it is true that they were fatally shut in. It had three fronts, but no longer an outlet. "A fortress, but mousetrap," said Courfeyrac with a laugh.

The silence was now so profound on the side from which the attack must come, that Enjolras made each man resume his post for combat.

A ration of brandy was distributed to all.

As soon as Enjolras had taken his double-barrelled carbine, and placed himself on a kind of battlement which he had reserved, all were silent. A little dry snapping sound was heard confusedly along the wall of paving-stones. They were cocking their muskets.

Moreover, their bearing was firmer and more confident than ever; excess of sacrifice is a support; they had hope no longer, but they had despair. Despair, that ultimate weapon, which sometimes gives victory; Virgil has said so. Supreme resources spring from extreme resolutions.

They had not long to wait. Activity distinctly recommenced in the direction Saint Leu, but it did not resemble the movement of the first attack. A rattle of chains, the menacing jolt of a mass, a clicking of brass bounding over the pavement, a sort of solemn uproar, announced that an ominous body of iron was approaching. There was a shudder in the midst of those peaceful old streets, cut through and built up for the fruitful circulation of interests and ideas, and which were not made for the monstrous rumbling of the wheels of war.

The stare of all the combatants upon the extremity of the street became wild.

An artillery piece appeared.

The gunners pushed the cannon forward; it was all ready to be loaded; the forewheels had been removed; two supported the carriage, four were at the wheels, others followed with the caisson. The smoke of the burning match was seen.

"Fire!" cried Enjolras.

The whole barricade flashed fire, the explosion was terrible; an avalanche of smoke covered and effaced the gun and the men; in a few seconds the cloud dissipated, and the cannon and the men reappeared; those in charge of the piece placed it in position in front of the barricade, slowly, correctly, and without haste. Not a man had been touched. Then the gunner, bearing his weight on the breech, to elevate the range, began to point the cannon with the gravity of an astronomer adjusting a telescope.

"Bravo for the gunners!" cried Bossuet.

And the whole barricade clapped hands.

A moment afterwards, placed squarely in the very middle of the street, astride of the gutter, the gun was in battery. A formidable mouth was opened upon the barricade.

"Come, be lively!" said Courfeyrac. "There is the brute. After the fillip, the knock-down. The army stretches out its big paw to us. The barricade is going to be seriously shaken. The musketry feels, the artillery takes."

"Reload arms," said Enjolras.

How was the facing of the barricade going to behave under fire? would the shot make a breach? That was the question. While the insurgents were reloading their muskets, the gunners loaded the cannon.

There was intense anxiety in the redoubt.

The gun went off; the detonation burst upon them.

"Present!" cried a cheerful voice.

And at the same time with the ball, Gavroche tumbled into the barricade.

He came by way of the Rue du Cygne, and he had nimbly clambered over the minor barricade, which fronted upon the labyrinth of the Petite Truanderie.

Gavroche produced more effect in the barricade than the ball.

The ball lost itself in the jumble of the rubbish. At the very utmost it broke a wheel of the omnibus, and finished the old Anceau cart. Seeing which, the barricade began to laugh.

"Proceed," cried Bossuet to the gunners.

7 (8)

THE GUNNERS PRODUCE
A SERIOUS IMPRESSION

THEY surrounded Gavroche.

But he had no time to tell anything. Marius, shuddering, took him aside.

"What have you come here for?"

"Hold on!" said the boy. "What have you come for?"

And he looked straight at Marius with his epic effrontery. His eyes grew large with the proud light which was in them.

Marius continued, in a stern tone:

"Who told you to come back? At least you carried my letter to its address?"

Gavroche had some little remorse in relation to that letter. In his haste to return to the barricade, he had got rid of it rather than delivered it. He was compelled to acknowledge to himself that he had intrusted it rather rashly to that stranger, whose face even he could not distinguish. True, this man was bareheaded, but that was not enough. On the whole, he had some little interior remonstrances on this subject, and he feared Marius' reproaches. He took, to get out of the trouble, the simplest course; he lied abominably.

"Citizen, I carried the letter to the porter. The lady was asleep. She will get the letter when she wakes up."

Marius, in sending this letter, had two objects: to say farewell to Cosette, and to save Gavroche. He was obliged to be content with the half of what he intended.

The sending of his letter, and the presence of M. Fauchelevent in the barricade, this coincidence occurred to his mind. He pointed out M. Fauchelevent to Gavroche.

"Do you know that man?"

"No," said Gavroche.

Gavroche, in fact, as we have just mentioned, had only seen Jean Valjean in the night.

The troubled and sickly conjectures which had arisen in Marius' mind were dissipated. Did he know M. Fauchelevent's opinions? M. Fauchelevent was a republican, perhaps. Hence his very natural presence in this conflict.

Meanwhile Gavroche was already at the other end of the barricade, crying: "My musket!"

Courfeyrac ordered it to be given him.

Gavroche warned his "comrades," as he called them, that the barricade was surrounded. He had had great difficulty in getting through. A battalion of the line whose muskets were stacked in la Petite Truanderie, were observing the side on the Rue du Cygne; on the opposite side the municipal guard occupied the Rue des Prêcheurs. In front, they had the bulk of the army.

Meanwhile Enjolras, on his battlement, was watching, listening with intense attention.

The assailants, dissatisfied doubtless with the effect of their fire, had not repeated it.

A company of infantry of the line had come in and occupied the extremity of the street, in the rear of the gun. The soldiers tore up the pavement, and with the stones constructed a little low wall, a sort of breastwork, which was hardly more than eighteen inches high, and which fronted the barricade. At the corner on the left of this breastwork, they saw the head of the column of a battalion of the banlieue massed in the Rue St.-Denis.

Enjolras, on the watch, thought he distinguished the peculiar sound which is made when canisters of grapeshot are taken from the caisson, and he saw the gunner change the aim and incline the piece slightly to the left. Then the cannoneers began to load. The gunner seized the linstock himself and brought it near the touch-hole.

"Heads down, keep close to the wall!" cried Enjolras, "and all on your knees along the barricade!"

The insurgents, who were scattered in front of the tavern, and who had left their posts of combat on Gavroche's arrival, rushed pell-mell towards the barricade; but before Enjolras' order was executed, the discharge took place with the fearful rattle of grapeshot. It was so in fact.

The charge was directed at the opening of the redoubt, it ricocheted upon the wall, and this terrible ricochet killed two men and wounded three.

If that continued, the barricade was no longer tenable. It was not proof against grapeshot.

There was a sound of consternation.

"Let us prevent the second shot, at any rate," said Enjolras.

And, lowering his carbine, he aimed at the gunner, who, at that moment, bending over the breech of the gun, was correcting and finally adjusting the aim.

This gunner was a fine-looking sergeant of artillery, quite young, of fair complexion, with a very mild face, and the intelligent air peculiar to that predestined and formidable arm which, by perfecting itself in horror, must end in killing war.

Combeferre, standing near Enjolras, looked at this young man.

"What a pity!" said Combeferre. "What a hideous thing these butcheries are! Come, when there are no more kings, there will be no more war. Enjolras, you are aiming at that sergeant, you are not looking at him. Just think that he is a charming young man; he is intrepid; you see that he is a thinker; these young artillery-men are well educated; he has a father, a mother, a family; he is in love probably; he is at most twenty-five years old; he might be your brother."

"He is," said Enjolras.

"Yes," said Combeferre, "and mine also. Well, don't let us kill him."

"Let me alone. We must do what we must."

And a tear rolled slowly down Enjolras' marble cheek.

At the same time he pressed the trigger of his carbine. The flash leaped forth. The artillery-man turned twice round, his arms stretched out before him, and his head raised as if to drink the air, then he fell over on his side upon the gun, and lay there motionless. His back could be seen, from the centre of which a stream of blood gushed upwards. The ball had entered his breast and passed through his body. He was dead.

It was necessary to carry him away and to replace him. It was indeed some minutes gained.

8 (9)

USE OF THAT OLD POACHER'S SKILL, AND THAT INFALLIBLE AIM WHICH INFLUENCED THE CONVICTION OF 1796

THERE WAS confusion in the counsel of the barricade. The gun was about to be fired again. They could not hold out a quarter of an hour in that storm of grapeshot. It was absolutely necessary to deaden the blows.

Enjolras threw out his command:

"We must put a mattress there."

"We have none," said Combeferre, "the wounded are on them."

Jean Valjean, seated apart on a block, at the corner of the tavern, his musket between his knees, had, up to this moment, taken no part in what was going on. He seemed not to hear the combatants about him say: "There is a musket which is doing nothing."

At the order given by Enjolras, he got up.

It will be remembered that on the arrival of the company in the Rue de la Chanvrerie, an old woman, foreseeing bullets, had put her mattress before her window. This window, a garret window, was on the roof of a house of seven stories standing a little outside of the barricade. The mattress, placed crosswise, rested at the bottom upon two clothes-poles, and was sustained above by two ropes which, in the distance, seemed like threads, and which were fastened to nails driven into the window casing. These two ropes could be seen distinctly against the sky like hairs.

"Can somebody lend me a double-barrelled carbine?" said Jean Valjean.

Enjolras, who had just reloaded his, handed it to him.

Jean Valjean aimed at the window and fired.

One of the two ropes of the mattress was cut.

The mattress now hung only by one thread.

Jean Valjean fired the second barrel. The second rope struck the glass of the window. The mattress slid down between the two poles and fell into the street.

The barricade applauded.

All cried:

"There is a mattress."

"Yes," said Combeferre, "but who will go after it?"

The mattress had, in fact, fallen outside of the barricade, between the besieged and the besiegers. Now, the death of the gunner having exasperated the troops, the soldiers, for some moments, had been lying on their faces behind the line of paving-stones which they had raised, and, to make up for the compulsory silence of the gun, which was quiet while its service was being reorganised, they had opened fire on the barricade. The insurgents made no response to this musketry, to spare their ammunition. The fusilade was broken against the barricade; but the street, which it filled with balls, was terrible.

Jean Valjean went out at the opening, entered the street, passed through the storm of balls, went to the mattress, picked it up, put it on his back, and returned to the barricade.

He put the mattress into the opening himself. He fixed it against the wall in such a way that the artillerymen did not see it.

This done, they awaited the charge of grapeshot.

They had not long to wait.

The cannon vomited its package of shot with a roar. But there was no ricochet. The grapeshot miscarried upon the mattress. The desired effect was obtained. The barricade was preserved.

"Citizen," said Enjolras to Jean Valjean, "the republic thanks you."

Bossuet admired and laughed. He exclaimed:

"It is immoral that a mattress should have so much power. Triumph of that which yields over that which thunders. But it is all the same; glory to the mattress which nullifies a cannon."

9 (10)

DAWN

AT THAT MOMENT Cosette awoke.

Her room was small, neat, retired, with a long window to the east, looking upon the back-yard of the house.

Cosette knew nothing of what was going on in Paris. She had not been out of her room in the evening, and she had already withdrawn to it when Toussaint said: "It appears that there is a row."

Cosette had slept few hours, but well. She had had sweet dreams which was partly owing perhaps to her little bed being very white. Somebody who was Marius had appeared to her surrounded by a halo. She awoke with the sun in her eyes, which at first produced the effect of a continuation of her dream.

Her first emotion, on coming out of this dream, was joyous. Cosette felt entirely reassured. She was passing through, as Jean Valjean had done a few hours before, that reaction of the soul which absolutely refuses woe. She began to hope with all her might without knowing why. Then came an oppression of the heart. Here were three days now that she had not seen

Marius. But she said to herself that he must have received her letter, that he knew where she was, and that he was so clever, that he would find means to reach her. And that certainly to-day, and perhaps this very morning. It was broad day, but the rays of light were very horizontal, she thought it was very early; that she must get up, however, to receive Marius.

She felt that she could not live without Marius, and that consequently, that was enough, and that Marius would come. No objection was admissible. All that was certain. It was monstrous enough already to have suffered three days. Marius absent three days, it was horrible in the eyes of the good Lord. Now this cruel teasing of Heaven was an ordeal that was over. Marius was coming, and would bring good news. Thus is youth constituted; it quickly wipes its eyes; it believes sorrow useless and does not accept it. Youth is the smile of the future before an unknown being which is itself. It is natural for it to be happy. It seems as though it breathed hope.

Besides, Cosette could not succeed in recalling what Marius had said to her on the subject of this absence which was to last but one day, or what explanation he had given her about it.

Cosette dressed herself very quickly, combed and arranged her hair, which was a very simple thing at that time, when women did not puff out their ringlets and plaits with cushions and rolls, and did not put crinoline in their hair. Then she opened the window and looked all about, hoping to discover something of the street, a corner of a house, a patch of pavement, and to be able to watch for Marius there. But she could see nothing of the street. The back-yard was surrounded with high walls, and a few gardens only were in view. Cosette pronounced these gardens hideous; for the first time in her life she found flowers ugly. The least bit of a street gutter would have been more to her mind. She finally began to look at the sky, as if she thought that Marius might come that way also.

Suddenly, she melted into tears. Not that it was fickleness of soul; but, hopes cut off by faintness of heart, such was her situation. She vaguely felt some indefinable horror. Things float in the air in fact. She said to herself that she was not sure of anything; that to lose from sight, was to lose; and the idea that Marius might indeed return to her from the sky, appeared no longer charming, but dismal.

Then, such are these clouds, calmness returned to her, and hope, and a sort of smile, unconscious, but trusting in God.

Everybody was still in bed in the house. A rural silence reigned. No shutter had been opened. The porter's box was closed. Toussaint was not up, and Cosette very naturally thought that her father was asleep. She must have suffered indeed, and she must have been still suffering, for she said to herself that her father had been unkind; but she counted on Marius. The eclipse of such a light was entirely impossible. At intervals she heard at some distance a kind of sullen jar, and she said: "It is singular that people are opening and shutting porte-cochères so early." It was the cannon battering the barricade.

10 (11)

THE SHOT WHICH MISSES NOTHING
AND KILLS NOBODY

THE FIRE of the assailants continued. The musketry and the grapeshot alternated, without much damage indeed. The top of the façade of Corinth alone suffered; the window of the second story and the dormer windows on the roof, riddled with shot and ball, were slowly demolished. The combatants who were posted there, had to withdraw. Besides, this is the art of attacking barricades; to tease for a long time, in order to exhaust the ammunition of the insurgents if they commit the blunder of replying. When it is perceived, from the slackening of their fire, that they have no longer either balls or powder, the assault is made. Enjolras did not fall into this snare; the barricade did not reply.

At each platoon fire, Gavroche thrust out his cheek with his tongue, a mark of lofty disdain:

"That's right," said he, "tear up the cloth. We want lint."

Courfeyrac jested with the grapeshot about its lack of effect, and said to the cannon:

"You are getting diffuse, my goodman."

In a battle people force themselves upon acquaintance, as at a ball. It is probable that this silence of the redoubt began to perplex the besiegers, and make them fear some unlooked-for accident, and that they felt the need of seeing through that heap of paving-stones and knowing what was going on behind that impassable wall, which was receiving their fire without answering it. The insurgents suddenly perceived a helmet shining in the sun upon a neighbouring roof. An army engineer was backed up against a tall chimney, and seemed to be there as a sentinel. He looked directly into the barricade.

"There is a troublesome observer," said Enjolras.

Jean Valjean had returned his carbine to Enjolras, but he had his musket.

Without saying a word, he aimed at the engineer, and, a second afterwards, the helmet, struck by a ball, fell noisily into the street. The startled soldier hastened to disappear.

A second observer took his place. This was an officer. Jean Valjean, who had reloaded his musket, aimed at the new-comer, and sent the officer's helmet to keep company with the soldier's. The officer was not obstinate, and withdrew very quickly. This time the warning was understood. Nobody appeared upon the roof again, and they gave up watching the barricade.

"Why didn't you kill the man?" asked Bossuet of Jean Valjean.

Jean Valjean did not answer.

11 (13)

PASSING GLEAMS

IN THE CHAOS of sentiments and passions which defend a barricade, there is something of everything; there is bravery, youth, honour, enthusiasm, the ideal, conviction, the eager fury of the gamester, and above all, intervals of hope.

One of those intervals, one of those vague thrills of hope, suddenly crossed, at the most unexpected moment, the barricade of the Rue de la Chanvrerie.

"Hark!" abruptly exclaimed Enjolras, who was constantly on the alert, "it seems to me that Paris is waking."

It is certain that on the morning of the 6th of June the insurrection had, for an hour or two, a certain recrudescence. The obstinacy of the tocsin of Saint Merry reanimated some dull hopes. In the Rue du Poirier, in the Rue des Gravilliers, barricades were planned out. In front of the Porte Saint Martin, a young man, armed with a carbine, attacked singly a squadron of cavalry. Without any shelter, in the open boulevard, he dropped on one knee, raised his weapon to his shoulder, fired, killed the chief of the squadron, and turned round saying: *"There is another who will do us no more harm."* He was sabred. In the Rue Saint-Denis, a woman fired upon the Municipal Guard from behind a Venetian blind. The slats of the blind were seen to tremble at each report. A boy of fourteen was arrested in the Rue de la Cossonerie with his pockets full of cartridges. Several posts were attacked. At the entrance of the Rue Bertin Poiree, a very sharp and entirely unexpected fusilade greeted a regiment of cuirassiers, at the head of which marched General Cavaignac de Baragne. In the Rue Planche Mibray they threw upon the troops, from the roofs, old fragments of household vessels and utensils; a bad sign; and when this fact was reported to Marshal Soult, the old lieutenant of Napoleon grew thoughtful, remembering the saying of Suchet at Saragossa: *"We are lost when the old women empty their pots upon our heads."*

These general symptoms which were manifested just when it was supposed the émeute was localised, this fever of wrath which was regaining the upper hand, these sparks which flew here and there above those deep masses of combustible material which are called the Faubourgs of Paris, all taken together rendered the military chiefs anxious. They hastened to extinguish these beginnings of conflagration. They delayed, until these sparks should be quenched, the attack on the barricades Maubuée, de la Chanvrerie, and Saint Merry, that they might have them only to deal with, and might be able to finish all at one blow. Columns were thrown into the streets in fermentation, sweeping the large ones, probing the small on the right, on the left, sometimes slowly and with precaution, sometimes at a double quick step. The troops beat in the doors of the houses from which there had been firing; at the same time manœuvres of cavalry dispersed the groups on the boulevards. This repression was not accomplished without noise, nor without that tumultuous uproar peculiar to shocks between the army and the people. This was what Enjolras caught, in the intervals of the cannonade and the musketry. Besides, he had seen some wounded passing at the end of the street upon litters, and said to Courfeyrac: "Those wounded do not come from our fire."

The hope did not last long; the gleam was soon eclipsed. In less than half an hour that which was in the air vanished; it was like heat lightning, and the insurgents felt that kind of leaden pall fall upon them which the indifference of the people casts over the wilful when abandoned.

The general movement, which seemed to have been vaguely projected, had miscarried; and the attention of the Minister of War and the strategy of the generals could now be concentrated upon the three or four barricades remaining standing.

The sun rose above the horizon.

An insurgent called to Enjolras:

"We are hungry here. Are we really going to die like this without eating?"

Enjolras, still leaning upon his battlement, without taking his eyes off the end of the street, nodded his head.

12 (14)

IN WHICH WILL BE FOUND THE NAME OF ENJOLRAS' MISTRESS

"I ADMIRE ENJOLRAS," said Bossuet. "His impassive boldness astonishes me. He lives alone, which renders him perhaps a little sad. Enjolras suffers for his greatness, which binds him to widowhood. The rest of us have all, more or less, mistresses who make fools of us, that is to say braves. When we are as amorous as a tiger the least we can do is to fight like a lion. It is a way of avenging ourselves for the tricks which Mesdames our grisettes play us. Roland gets himself killed to spite Angelica; all our heroisms come from our women. A man without a woman, is a pistol without a hammer; it is the woman who makes the man go off. Now, Enjolras has no woman. He is not in love, and he finds a way to be intrepid. It is a marvellous thing that a man can be as cold as ice and as bold as fire."

Enjolras did not appear to listen, but had anybody been near him he would have heard him murmur in an undertone, *"Patria."**

Bossuet was laughing still when Courfeyrac exclaimed:

"Something new!"

And, assuming the manner of an usher announcing an arrival, he added: "My name is Eight-Pounder."

In fact, a new personage had just entered upon the scene. It was a second piece of ordnance.

The artillerymen quickly executed the manœuvres, and placed this second piece in battery near the first.

This suggested the conclusion.

A few moments afterwards, the two pieces, rapidly served, opened directly upon the redoubt; the platoon firing of the line and the banlieue supported the artillery.

Another cannonade was heard at some distance. At the same time that two cannon were raging against the redoubt in the Rue de la Chanvrerie, two other pieces of ordnance, pointed, one on the Rue Saint-Denis, the other on the Rue Aubry le Boucher, were riddling the barricade St. Merry. The four cannon made dreary echo to one another.

The bayings of the dismal dogs of war answered each other.

Of the two pieces which were now battering the barricade in the Rue de la Chanvrerie, one fired grapeshot, the other ball.

The gun which threw balls was elevated a little, and the range was calculated so that the ball struck the extreme edge of the upper ridge of the barricade, dismantled it, and crumbled the paving-stones over the insurgents in showers.

This peculiar aim was intended to drive the combatants from the summit of the redoubt, and to force them to crowd together in the interior, that is, it announced the assault.

The combatants once driven from the top of the barricade by the balls and from the windows of the tavern by the grapeshot, the attacking columns could venture into the street without being watched, perhaps even without being under fire, suddenly scale the redoubt, as on the evening before, and, who knows? take it by surprise.

"We must at all events diminish the inconvenience of those pieces," said Enjolras, and he cried: "fire upon the cannoneers!"

All were ready. The barricade, which had been silent for a long time, opened fire desperately; seven or eight discharges succeeded each other with a sort of rage and joy; the street was filled with a blinding smoke, and after a few minutes, through this haze pierced by flame, they could confusedly make out two thirds of the cannoneers lying under the wheels of the

---

*The Mother Country.

guns. Those who remained standing continued to serve the pieces with rigid composure, but the fire was slackened.

"This goes well," said Bossuet to Enjolras. "Success."

Enjolras shook his head and answered:

"A quarter of an hour more of this success, and there will not be ten cartridges in the barricade."

It would seem that Gavroche heard this remark.

13 (15)

GAVROCHE OUTSIDE

COURFEYRAC suddenly perceived somebody at the foot of the barricade, outside in the street, under the balls.

Gavroche had taken a basket from the tavern, had gone out by the opening, and was quietly occupied in emptying into his basket the full cartridge-boxes of the National Guards who had been killed on the slope of the redoubt.

"What are you doing there?" said Courfeyrac.

Gavroche cocked up his nose.

"Citizen, I am filling my basket."

"Why, don't you see the grapeshot?"

Gavroche answered:

"Well, it rains. What then?"

Courfeyrac cried:

"Come back!"

"Directly," said Gavroche.

And with a bound, he sprang into the street.

It will be remembered that the Fannicot company, on retiring, had left behind them a trail of corpses.

Some twenty dead lay scattered along the whole length of the street on the pavement. Twenty cartridge-boxes for Gavroche, a supply of cartridges for the barricade.

The smoke in the street was like a fog. Whoever has seen a cloud fall into a mountain gorge between two steep slopes can imagine this smoke crowded and as if thickened by two gloomy lines of tall houses. It rose slowly and was constantly renewed; hence a gradual darkening which even rendered broad day pallid. The combatants could hardly perceive each other from end to end of the street, although it was very short.

This darkness, probably desired and calculated upon by the leaders who were to direct the assault upon the barricade, was of use to Gavroche.

Under the folds of this veil of smoke, and thanks to his small size, he could advance far into the street without being seen. He emptied the first seven or eight cartridge-boxes without much danger.

He crawled on his belly, ran on his hands and feet, took his basket in his teeth, twisted, glided, writhed, wormed his way from one body to another, and emptied a cartridge-box as a monkey opens a nut.

From the barricade, of which he was still within hearing, they dared not call to him to return, for fear of attracting attention to him.

On one corpse, that of a corporal, he found a powder-flask.

"In case of thirst," said he as he put it into his pocket.

By successive advances, he reached a point where the fog from the firing became transparent.

So that the sharp-shooters of the line drawn up and on the alert behind their wall of paving-stones, and the sharp-shooters of the banlieue massed at the corner of the street, suddenly discovered something moving in the smoke.

Just as Gavroche was relieving a sergeant who lay near a stone-block of his cartridges, a ball struck the body.

"The deuce!" said Gavroche. "So they are killing my dead for me."

A second ball splintered the pavement beside him. A third upset his basket.

Gavroche looked and saw that it came from the banlieue.

He rose up straight, on his feet, his hair in the wind, his hands upon his hips, his eye fixed upon the National Guards who were firing, and he sang:

> On est laid à Nanterre
> C'est la faute à Voltaire,
> Et bête à Palaiseau,
> C'est la faute à Rousseau.[1]

Then he picked up his basket, put into it the cartridge which had fallen out, without losing a single one, and, advancing towards the fusilade, began to empty another cartridge-box. There a fourth ball just missed him again. Gavroche sang:

> Je ne suis pas notaire,
> C'est la faute à Voltaire;
> Je suis petit oiseau,
> C'est la faute à Rousseau.

A fifth ball succeeded only in drawing a third couplet from him.

> Joie est mon caractère,
> C'est la faute à Voltaire;

> Misère est mon trousseau,
> C'est la faute à Rousseau.

This continued thus for some time.

The sight was appalling and fascinating. Gavroche, fired at, mocked the firing. He appeared to be very much amused. It was the sparrow pecking at the hunters. He replied to each discharge by a couplet. They aimed at him incessantly, they always missed him. The National Guards and the soldiers laughed as they aimed at him. He lay down, then rose up, hid himself in a doorway, then sprang out, disappeared, reappeared, escaped, returned, retorted upon the volleys by wry faces, and meanwhile pillaged cartridges, emptied cartridge-boxes, and filled his basket. The insurgents, breathless with anxiety, followed him with their eyes. The barricade was trembling; he was singing. It was not a child; it was not a man; it was a strange fairy *gamin*. One would have said the invulnerable dwarf of the mêlée. The bullets ran after him, he was more nimble than they. He was playing an indescribably terrible game of hide-and-seek with death; every time the flat-nosed face of the spectre approached, the *gamin* snapped his fingers.

One bullet, however, better aimed or more treacherous than the others, reached the Will-o'-the-wisp child. They saw Gavroche totter, then he fell. The whole barricade gave a cry; but there was an Antæus in this pigmy; for the *gamin* to touch the pavement is like the giant touching the earth; Gavroche had fallen only to rise again; he sat up, a long stream of blood rolled down his face, he raised both arms in air, looked in the direction whence the shot came, and began to sing:

> Je suis tombé par terre,
> C'est la faute à Voltaire,
> La nez dans le ruisseau,
> C'est la faute à——

He did not finish. A second ball from the same marksman cut him short. This time he fell with his face upon the pavement, and did not stir again. That great little soul had taken flight.

14 (16)

HOW BROTHER BECOMES FATHER

THERE WERE at that very moment in the garden of the Luxembourg—for the eye of the drama should be everywhere present—two children holding each other by the hand.[*] One might have been seven years old, the other five. Having been soaked in the rain, they were walking in the paths on the sunny side; the elder was leading the little one; they were pale and in rags; they looked like wild birds. The smaller said: "I want something to eat."

The elder, already something of a protector, led his brother with his left hand and had a stick in his right hand.

They were alone in the garden. The garden was empty, the gates being closed by order of the police on account of the insurrection. The troops which had bivouacked there had been called away by the necessities of the combat.

These two children were the very same about whom Gavroche had been in trouble, and whom the reader remembers. Children of the Thénardiers, rented out to Magnon, attributed to M. Gillenormand, and now leaves fallen from all these rootless branches, and whirled over the ground by the wind.

Their clothing, neat in Magnon's time, and which served her as a prospectus in the sight of M. Gillenormand, had become tatters.

These creatures belonged henceforth to the statistics of "abandoned children," whom the police report, collect, scatter, and find again on the streets of Paris.

It required the commotion of such a day for these little outcasts to be in this garden. If the officers had noticed them, they would have driven away these rags. Poor children cannot enter the public gardens; still one would think that, as children, they had a right in the flowers.

The two little abandoned creatures were near the great basin, and slightly disturbed by all this light, they endeavoured to hide, an instinct of the poor and feeble before magnificence, even impersonal, and they kept behind the shelter for the swans.

Here and there, at intervals, when the wind fell, they faintly heard cries, a hum, a kind of tumultuous rattle, which was the musketry, and dull blows, which were reports of cannon. There was smoke above the roofs in the direction of the markets. A bell, which appeared to be calling, sounded in the distance.

---

[*]Nearly every time Hugo mentions children in this novel, he implicitly advocates for more public aid for those orphaned and abandoned.

These children did not seem to notice these sounds. The smaller one repeated from time to time in an undertone: "I want something to eat."

Almost at the same time with the two children, another couple approached the great basin. This was a goodman of fifty, who was leading by the hand a goodman of six. Doubtless a father with his son. The goodman of six had a big bun in his hand.

At that period, certain adjoining houses, in the Rue Madame and the Rue d'Enfer, had keys to the Luxembourg Gardens which the occupants used when the gates were closed, a favour since suppressed. This father and this son probably came from one of those houses.

The two poor little fellows saw "this Monsieur" coming, and hid themselves a little more closely.

He was a bourgeois. The same, perhaps, whom one day Marius, in spite of his love fever, had heard, near this same great basin, counselling his son "to beware of extremes." He had an affable and lofty manner, and a mouth which, never closing, was always smiling. This mechanical smile, produced by too much jaw and too little skin, shows the teeth rather than the soul. The child, with his bitten bun, which he did not finish, seemed stuffed. The boy was dressed as a National Guard, on account of the émeute, and the father remained in citizen's clothes for the sake of prudence.

The father and son stopped near the basin in which the two swans were sporting. This bourgeois appeared to have a special admiration for the swans. He resembled them in this respect, that he walked like them.

For the moment, the swans were swimming, which is their principal talent, and they were superb.

If the two poor little fellows had listened, and had been of an age to understand, they might have gathered up the words of a grave man. The father said to the son:

"The sage lives content with little. Behold me, my son. I do not love pomp. Never am I seen with coats bedizened with gold and gems; I leave this false splendour to badly organised minds."

Here the deep sounds, which came from the direction of the markets, broke out with a redoubling of bell and of uproar.

"What is that?" inquired the child.

The father answered:

"They are saturnalia."

Just then he noticed the two little ragged fellows standing motionless behind the green cottage of the swans.

"There is the beginning," said he.

And after a moment, he added:

"Anarchy is entering this garden."

Meanwhile the son bit the bun, spit it out, and suddenly began to cry.

"What are you crying for?" asked the father.

"I am not hungry any more," said the child.

The father's smile grew broad.

"You don't need to be hungry, to eat a cake."

"I am sick of my cake. It is stale."

"You don't want any more of it?"

"No."

The father showed him the swans.

"Throw it to those palmipeds."

The child hesitated. Not to want any more of one's cake, is no reason for giving it away.

The father continued.

"Be humane. We must take pity on the animals."

And, taking the cake from his son, he threw it into the basin.

The cake fell near the edge.

The swans were at a distance, in the centre of the basin, and busy with some prey. They saw neither the bourgeois nor the bun.

The bourgeois, feeling that the cake was in danger of being lost, and aroused by this useless shipwreck, devoted himself to a telegraphic agitation which finally attracted the attention of the swans.

They perceived something floating, veered about like the ships they are, and directed themselves slowly towards the bun with that serene majesty which is fitting to white animals.

"*Cygnes* [swans] understand *signes* [signs]," said the bourgeois, delighted at his wit.

Just then the distant tumult in the city suddenly increased again. This time it was ominous. There are some gusts of wind that speak more distinctly than others. That which blew at that moment brought clearly the rolls of drums, shouts, platoon firing, and the dismal replies of the tocsin and the cannon. This was coincident with a black cloud which abruptly shut out the sun.

The swans had not yet reached the bun.

"Come home," said the father, "they are attacking the Tuileries."

He seized his son's hand again. Then he continued:

"From the Tuileries to the Luxembourg, there is only the distance which separates royalty from the peerage; it is not far. It is going to rain musket-balls."

He looked at the cloud.

"And perhaps also the rain itself is going to rain; the heavens are joining in; the younger branch is condemned. Come home, quick."

"I should like to see the swans eat the bun," said the child.

The father answered:

"That would be an imprudence."

And he led away his little bourgeois.

The son, regretting the swans, turned his head towards the basin, until a turn in the rows of trees hid it from him.

Meanwhile, at the same time with the swans, the two little wanderers had approached the bun. It was floating on the water. The smaller was looking at the cake, the larger was looking at the bourgeois who was going away.

The father and the son entered the labyrinth of walks which leads to the grand stairway of the cluster of trees on the side towards the Rue Madame.

As soon as they were out of sight, the elder quickly lay down with his face over the rounded edge of the basin, and, holding by it with his left hand, hanging over the water, almost falling in, with his right hand reached his stick towards the cake. The swans, seeing the enemy, made haste, and in making haste produced an effect with their breasts which was useful to the little fisher; the water flowed back before the swans, and one of those smooth concentric waves pushed the bun gently towards the child's stick. As the swans came up, the stick touched the cake. The child made a quick movement, drew in the bun, frightened the swans, seized the cake, and got up. The cake was soaked; but they were hungry and thirsty. The eldest broke the bun into two pieces, one large and one small, took the small one for himself, gave the large one to his little brother, and said to him:

"Stick that in your gun."

15 (17)

MORTUUS PATER FILIUM MORITURUM EXPECTAT

MARIUS had sprung out of the barricade. Combeferre had followed him. But it was too late. Gavroche was dead. Combeferre brought back the basket of cartridges; Marius brought back the child.

"Alas!" thought he, "what the father had done for his father he was returning to the son; only Thénardier had brought back his father living, while he brought back the child dead."

When Marius re-entered the redoubt with Gavroche in his arms, his face, like the child's, was covered with blood.

Just as he had stooped down to pick up Gavroche, a ball grazed his skull; he did not perceive it.

Courfeyrac took off his cravat and bound up Marius' forehead.

Combeferre distributed the cartridges from the basket which he had brought back.

This gave each man fifteen shots.

Jean Valjean was still at the same place, motionless upon his block. When Combeferre presented him his fifteen cartridges, he shook his head.

"There is a rare eccentric," said Combeferre in a low tone to Enjolras. "He finds means not to fight in this barricade."

"Which does not prevent him from defending it," answered Enjolras.

"Heroism has its originals," replied Combeferre.

Suddenly between two discharges they heard the distant sound of a clock striking.

"It is noon," said Combeferre.

The twelve strokes had not sounded when Enjolras sprang to his feet, and flung down from the top of the barricade this thundering shout:

"Carry some paving-stones into the house. Fortify the windows with them. Half the men to the muskets, the other half to the stones. Not a minute to lose."

A platoon of sappers, their axes on their shoulders, had just appeared in order of battle at the end of the street.

This could only be the head of a column; and of what column? The column of attack, evidently. The sappers, whose duty it is to demolish the barricade, must always precede the soldiers whose duty it is to scale it.

Enjolras' order was executed with the correct haste peculiar to ships and barricades, the only places of combat whence escape is impossible. In less than a minute, two-thirds of the paving-stones which Enjolras had had piled up at the door of Corinth were carried up to the first story and to the garret; and before a second minute had elapsed, these stones, artistically laid one upon another, walled up half the height of the window on the first story and the dormer windows of the attic. A few openings, carefully arranged by Feuilly, chief builder, allowed musket barrels to pass through. This armament of the windows could be performed the more easily since the grapeshot had ceased. The two pieces were now firing balls upon the centre of the wall, in order to make a hole, and if it were possible, a breach for the assault.

Then they barricaded the basement window, and they held in readiness the iron cross-pieces which served to bar the door of the tavern on the inside at night.

The fortress was complete. The barricade was the rampart, the tavern was the donjon.

With the paving-stones which remained, they closed up the opening beside the barricade.

As the defenders of a barricade are always obliged to husband their ammunition, and as the besiegers know it, the besiegers perfect their arrangements with a sort of provoking leisure, expose themselves to fire before the time, but in appearance more than in reality, and take their ease. The preparations for attack are always made with a certain methodical slowness, after which, the thunderbolt.

This slowness allowed Enjolras to look over the whole, and to perfect the whole. He felt that since such men were to die, their death should be a masterpiece.

He said to Marius: "We are the two chiefs; I will give the last orders within. You stay outside and watch."

Marius posted himself for observation upon the crest of the barricade.

Enjolras had the door of the kitchen, which, we remember, was the hospital, nailed up.

"No spattering on the wounded," said he.

He gave his last instructions in the basement-room in a quick, but deep and calm voice; Feuilly listened, and answered in the name of all.

"Second story, hold your axes ready to cut the staircase. You have them?"

"Yes," said Feuilly.

"How many?"

"Two axes and a pole-axe."

"Very well. There are twenty-six effective men left."

"How many muskets are there?"

"Thirty-four."

"Eight too many. Keep these eight muskets loaded like the rest, and at hand. Swords and pistols in your belts. Twenty men to the barricade. Six in ambush at the dormer windows and at the window on the second story to fire upon the assailants through the loopholes in the paving-stones. Let there be no useless labourer here. Immediately, when the drum beats the charge, let the twenty from below rush to the barricade. The first there will get the best places."

These dispositions made, he turned towards Javert, and said to him:

"I won't forget you."

And, laying a pistol on the table, he added:

"The last man to leave this room will blow out the spy's brains!"

"Here?" inquired a voice.

"No, do not leave this corpse with ours. You can climb over the little barricade on the Rue Mondétour. It is only four feet high. The man is well tied. You will take him there, and execute him there."

There was one man, at that moment, who was more impassible than Enjolras; it was Javert.

Here Jean Valjean appeared.

He was in the throng of insurgents. He stepped forward, and said to Enjolras:

"You are the commander?"

"Yes."

"You thanked me just now."

"In the name of the republic. The barricade has two saviours, Marius Pontmercy and you."

"Do you think that I deserve a reward?"

"Certainly."

"Well, I ask one."

"What?"

"To blow out that man's brains myself."

Javert raised his head, saw Jean Valjean, made an imperceptible movement, and said:

"That is appropriate."

As for Enjolras, he had begun to reload his carbine; he cast his eyes about him:

"No objection."

And turning towards Jean Valjean: "Take the spy."

Jean Valjean, in fact, took possession of Javert by sitting down on the end of the table. He caught up the pistol, and a slight click announced that he had cocked it.

Almost at the same moment, they heard a flourish of trumpets.

"Come on!" cried Marius, from the top of the barricade.

Javert began to laugh with that noiseless laugh which was peculiar to him, and, looking fixedly upon the insurgents, said to them:

"Your health is hardly better than mine."

"All outside?" cried Enjolras.

The insurgents sprang forward in a tumult, and, as they went out, they received in the back, allow us the expression, this speech from Javert:

"Farewell till immediately!"

16 (19)

JEAN VALJEAN TAKES HIS REVENGE

WHEN Jean Valjean was alone with Javert, he untied the rope that held the prisoner by the middle of the body, the knot of which was under the table. Then he motioned to him to get up.

Javert obeyed, with that undefinable smile into which the supremacy of enchained authority is condensed.

Jean Valjean took Javert by the martingale as you would take a beast of burden by a strap, and, drawing him after him, went out of the tavern slowly, for Javert, with his legs fettered, could take only very short steps.

Jean Valjean had the pistol in his hand.

They crossed thus the interior trapezium of the barricade. The insurgents, intent upon the imminent attack, were looking the other way.

Marius, alone, placed towards the left extremity of the wall, saw them pass. This group of the victim and the executioner borrowed a light from the sepulchral gleam which he had in his soul.

Jean Valjean, with some difficulty, bound as Javert was, but without letting go of him for a single instant, made him scale the little intrenchment on the Rue Mondétour.

When they had climbed over this wall, they found themselves alone in the little street. Nobody saw them now. The corner of the house hid them from insurgents. The corpses carried out from the barricades made a terrible mound a few steps off.

They distinguished in a heap of dead, a livid face, a flowing head of hair, a wounded hand, and a woman's breast half naked. It was Eponine.

Javert looked aside at this dead body, and, perfectly calm, said in an undertone:

"It seems to me that I know that girl."

Then he turned towards Jean Valjean.

Jean Valjean put the pistol under his arm, and fixed upon Javert a look which had no need of words to say: "Javert, it is I."

Javert answered.

"Take your revenge."

Jean Valjean took a knife out of his pocket, and opened it.

"A *surin!*" exclaimed Javert. "You are right. That suits you better."

Jean Valjean cut the martingale which Javert had about his neck, then he cut the ropes which he had on his wrists, then, stooping down, he cut the cord which he had on his feet; and, rising, he said to him:

"You are free."

Javert was not easily astonished. Still, complete master as he was of himself, he could not escape an emotion. He stood aghast and motionless.

Jean Valjean continued:

"I don't expect to leave this place. Still, if by chance I should, I live, under the name of Fauchelevent, in the Rue de l'Homme Armé, Number Seven."

Javert had the scowl of a tiger half opening the corner of his mouth, and he muttered between his teeth:

"Take care."

"Go," said Jean Valjean.

Javert resumed:

"You said Fauchelevent, Rue de l'Homme Armé?"

"Number Seven."

Javert repeated in an undertone: "Number seven." He buttoned his coat, restored the military stiffness between his shoulders, turned half round, folded his arms, supporting his chin with one hand, and walked off in the direction of the markets. Jean Valjean followed him with his eyes. After a few steps, Javert turned back, and cried to Jean Valjean:

"You annoy me. Kill me rather."

Javert did not notice that his tone was more respectful towards Jean Valjean.

"Go away," said Jean Valjean.

Javert receded with slow steps. A moment afterwards, he turned the corner of the Rue des Prêcheurs.

When Javert was gone, Jean Valjean fired the pistol in the air.

Then he reentered the barricade and said: "It is done."

Meanwhile what had taken place is this:

Marius, busy rather with the street than the tavern, had not until then looked attentively at the spy who was bound in the dusky rear of the basement-room.

When he saw him in broad day clambering over the barricade on his way to die, he recognised him. A sudden reminiscence came into his mind. He remembered the inspector of the Rue de Pontoise, and the two pistols which he had handed him and which he had used, he, Marius, in this very barricade; and not only did he recollect the face, but he recalled the name.

This reminiscence, however, was misty and indistinct, like all his ideas.

It was not an affirmation which he made to himself, it was a question which he put: "Is not this that inspector of police who told me his name was Javert?"

Perhaps there was still time to interfere for this man? But he must first know if it were indeed that Javert.

Marius called to Enjolras, who had just taken his place at the other end of the barricade.

"Enjolras!"

"What?"

"What is that man's name?"

"Who?"

"The police officer. Do you know his name?"

"Of course. He told us."

"What is his name?"

"Javert."

Marius sprang up.

At that moment they heard the pistol-shot.

Jean Valjean reappeared and cried: "It is done."

A dreary chill passed through the heart of Marius.

17 (20)

THE DEAD ARE RIGHT AND THE LIVING ARE NOT WRONG

THE DEATH-AGONY of the barricade was approaching. When the condition of affairs was not ripe, when the insurrection was not decidedly acceptable, when the mass disavowed the movement, it was all over with the combatants, the city changed into a desert about the revolt, souls were chilled, asylums were walled up, and the street became a defile to aid the army in taking the barricade.

A people cannot be surprised into a more rapid progress than it wills. Woe to him who attempts to force its hand! A people does not allow itself to be used. Then it abandons the insurrection to itself. The insurgents become pestiferous. A house is an escarpment, a door is a refusal, a façade is a wall. This wall sees, hears, and will not. It might open and save you. No. This wall is a judge. It looks upon you and condemns you. How gloomy are these closed houses! They seem dead, they are living. Life, which is as it were suspended in them, still exists. Nobody has come out of them for twenty-four hours, but nobody is missing. In the interior of this rock, people go and come, they lie down, they get up; they are at home there; they drink and eat; they are afraid there, a fearful thing! Fear excuses this terrible inhospitality; it tempers it with timidity, a mitigating circumstance. Sometimes even, and this has been seen, fear becomes passion; fright may change into fury, as prudence into rage; hence this saying so profound: *The madmen of moderation.* There are flamings of supreme dismay from which rage springs like a dismal smoke. "What do these people want? They are never contented. They compromise peaceable men as if we had not had revolution enough like this! What do they come here for? Let them get out of it themselves. So much the worse for them. It is their own fault. They have only got what they deserve. It doesn't concern us. Here is our poor street riddled with balls. They are a parcel of scamps. Above all, don't open the door." And the house puts on the semblance of a tomb. The insurgent before that door is in his last agony; he sees the grapeshot and the drawn sabres coming; if he calls, he knows that they hear him, but that they will not come; there are walls which might protect him, there are men who might save him; and those walls have ears of flesh, and those men have bowels of stone.

Let us acknowledge it without bitterness, the individual has his distinct interest, and may without offence set up that interest and defend it: the present has its excusable quantum of selfishness; the life of the moment has its rights, and is not bound to sacrifice itself continually to the future. The generation which has now its turn of passing over the earth is not compelled to abridge it for the generations, its equals, after all, which are to have their turn afterwards. "I exist," murmurs that somebody whose name is All. "I am young and I am in love, I am old and I want to rest, I am the father of a family, I am working, I am prospering, I am doing a good business, I have houses to rent, I have money in the government, I am happy. I have a wife and children, I love all this, I desire to live, let me alone." Hence, at certain periods, a deep chill upon the magnanimous vanguard of the human race.

Utopia, moreover, we must admit, departs from its radiant sphere in making war. The truth of to-morrow, she borrows her process, battle, from the lie of yesterday. She, the future, acts like the past. She, the pure idea, becomes an act of force. She compromises her heroism by a violence for which it is just that she should answer; a violence of opportunity and of expediency, contrary to principles, and for which she is fatally punished. Utopia as insurrection fights, the old military code in her hand; she shoots spies, she executes traitors, she suppresses living beings and casts them into the unknown dark. She uses death, a solemn thing. It seems as though Utopia had lost faith in the radiation of light, her irresistible and incorruptible strength. She strikes with the sword. Now, no sword is simple. Every blade has two edges; he who wounds with one wounds himself with the other.

To go to war upon every summons and whenever Utopia desires it, is not the part of the people. The nations have not always and at every hour the temperament of heroes and of martyrs.

They are positive. A priori, insurrection repels them; first, because it often results in disaster, secondly, because it always has an abstraction for its point of departure.

For, and this is beautiful, it is always for the ideal, and for the ideal alone, that those devote themselves who do devote themselves. An insurrection is an enthusiasm. Enthusiasm may work itself into anger; hence the resort to arms. But every insurrection which is directed against a government or a régime aims still higher. Thus, for instance, let us repeat what the chiefs of the insurrection of 1832, and in particular the young enthusiasts of the Rue de la Chanvrerie, fought against, was not exactly Louis-Philippe. Most of them, speaking frankly, rendered justice to the qualities of this king, midway between the monarchy and the revolution; none hated him. But they attacked the younger branch of divine right in Louis-Philippe as they had attacked the elder branch in Charles X; and what they desired to overthrow in overthrowing royalty in France as we have explained, was the usurpation of man over man, and of privilege over right, in the whole world. Paris without a king has, as a consequence, the world without despots. They reasoned in this way. Their aim was distant doubtless, vague perhaps, and receding despite their effort, but great.

Thus it is. And men sacrifice themselves for these visions, which, to the sacrificed, are illusions almost always, but illusions with which, upon the whole, all human certainty is mingled. The insurgent poetises and gilds the insurrection. He throws himself into these tragic things, intoxicated with what he is going to do. Who knows? they will succeed perhaps. They are but few; they have against them a whole army; but they defend right, natural law, that sovereignty of each over himself, of which there is no abdication possible, justice, truth.

A word more before returning to the conflict.

A battle like this which we are now describing is nothing but a convulsive movement towards the ideal. Enfettered progress is sickly, and it has these tragic epilepsies. This disease of progress, civil war, we have had to encounter upon our passage. It is one of the fatal phases, at once act and interlude, of this drama, the pivot of which is a social outcast, and the true title of which is: *Progress*.

Progress!

This cry which we often raise, is our whole thought; and, at the present point of this drama, the idea that it contains having still more than one ordeal to undergo, it is permitted us perhaps, if not to lift the veil from it, at least to let the light shine clearly through.

The book which the reader has now before his eyes is, from one end to the other, in its whole and in its details, whatever may be the intermissions, the exceptions, or the defaults, the march from evil to good, from injustice to justice, from the false to the true, from night to day, from appetite to conscience, from rottenness to life, from brutality to duty, from Hell to Heaven, from nothingness to God. Starting point: matter; goal: the soul. Hydra at the beginning, angel at the end.*

---

*This paragraph encapsulates Hugo's vision of spiritual progress for all humanity.

18 (21)

THE HEROES

SUDDENLY the drum beat the charge.

The attack was a hurricane. In the evening, in the darkness, the barricade had been approached silently as if by a boa. Now, in broad day, in this open street, surprise was entirely impossible; the strong hand, moreover, was unmasked, the cannon had commenced the roar, the army rushed upon the barricade. Fury was now skill. A powerful column of infantry of the line, intersected at equal intervals by National Guards and Municipal Guards on foot, and supported by deep masses heard but unseen, turned into the street at a quick step, drums beating, trumpets sounding, bayonets fixed, sappers at their head, and, unswerving under the projectiles, came straight upon the barricade with the weight of a bronze column upon a wall.

The wall held.

The insurgents fired impetuously. The barricade scaled was like a mane of flashes. The assault was so sudden that for a moment it was overflowed by assailants; but it shook off the soldiers as the lion does the dogs, and it was covered with besiegers only as a cliff is with foam, to reappear, a moment afterwards, steep, black, and formidable.

The column, compelled to fall back, remained massed in the street, unsheltered, but terrible, and replied to the redoubt by a fearful fusilade. Whoever has seen fireworks remembers that sheaf made by a crossing of flashes which is called the bouquet. Imagine the bouquet, not now vertical, but horizontal, bearing a ball, a buckshot, or a bullet, at the point of each of its jets of fire, and scattering death in its clusters of thunder. The barricade was beneath it.

On both sides equal resolution. Bravery there was almost barbaric, and was mingled with a sort of heroic ferocity which began with the sacrifice of itself. Those were the days when a National Guard fought like a Zouave. The troops desired to make an end of it; the insurrection desired to struggle. The acceptance of death in full youth and in full health makes a frenzy of intrepidity. Every man in this mêlée felt the aggrandisement given by the supreme hour. The street was covered with dead.

Enjolras was at one end of the barricade, and Marius at the other. Enjolras, who carried the whole barricade in his head, reserved and sheltered himself; three soldiers fell one after the other under his battlement, without even having perceived him; Marius fought without shelter. He took no aim. He stood with more than half his body above the summit of the redoubt. There is no wilder prodigal than a miser who takes the bit in his teeth; there is no man more fearful in action than a dreamer. Marius was terrible and pensive. He was in the battle as in a dream. One would have said a phantom firing a musket.

The interior of the barricade was so strewn with torn cartridges that one would have said it had been snowing.

The assailants had the numbers; the insurgents the position. They were on the top of a wall, and they shot down the soldiers at the muzzles of their muskets, as they stumbled over the dead and wounded and became entangled in the escarpment. This barricade, built as it was, and admirably supported, was really one of those positions in which a handful of men hold a legion in check. Still, constantly reinforced and increasing under the shower of balls, the attacking column inexorably approached, and now, little by little, step by step, but with certainty, the army hugged the barricade as the screw hugs the wine press.

There was assault after assault. The horror continued to increase.

Then resounded over this pile of paving-stones, in this Rue de la Chanvrerie, a struggle worthy of the walls of Troy. These men, wan, tattered, and exhausted, who had not eaten for twenty-four hours, who had not slept, who had but a few more shots to fire, who felt their pockets empty of cartridges, nearly all wounded, their heads or arms bound with a smutty and blackened cloth, with holes in their coats whence the blood was flowing, scarcely armed with worthless muskets and with old notched swords, became Titans. The barricade was ten times approached, assaulted, scaled, and never taken.

They fought breast to breast, foot to foot, with pistols, with sabres, with fists, at a distance, close at hand, from above, from below, from everywhere, from the roofs of the house, from the windows of the tavern, from the gratings of the cellars into which some had slipped. They were one against sixty. The façade of Corinth, half demolished, was hideous. The window, riddled with grapeshot, had lost glass and sash, and was now nothing but a shapeless hole, confusedly blocked with paving-stones. Bossuet was killed; Feuilly was killed; Courfeyrac was killed; Joly was killed; Combeferre, pierced by three bayonet-thrusts in the breast, just as he was lifting a wounded soldier, had only time to look to heaven, and expired.

Marius, still fighting, was so hacked with wounds, particularly about his head, that the countenance was lost in blood, and you would have said that he had his face covered with a red handkerchief.

Enjolras alone was untouched. When his weapon failed, he reached his hand to right or left, and an insurgent put whatever weapon he could in his grasp. Of four swords, one more than Francis I at Marignan, he now had but one stump remaining.

19 (22)

FOOT TO FOOT

WHEN there were none of the chiefs alive save Enjolras and Marius, who were at the opposite ends of the barricade, the centre, which Courfeyrac, Joly, Bossuet, Feuilly, and Combeferre had so long sustained, gave way. The artillery, without making a practicable breach, had deeply indented the centre of the redoubt; there, the summit of the wall had disappeared under the balls, and had tumbled down; and the rubbish which had fallen, sometimes on the interior, sometimes on the exterior, had finally made, as it was heaped up, on either side of the wall, a kind of talus, both on the inside, and on the outside. The exterior talus offered an inclined plane for attack.

A final assault was now attempted, and this assault succeeded. The mass bristling with bayonets and hurled at a double-quick step, came on irresistible, and the dense battle-front of the attacking column appeared in the smoke at the top of the escarpment. This time, it was finished. The group of insurgents who defended the centre fell back pell-mell.

Then grim love of life was roused in some. Covered by the aim of that forest of muskets, several were now unwilling to die. This is a moment when the instinct of self-preservation raises a howl, and the animal reappears in the man. They were pushed back to the high seven-story house which formed the rear of the redoubt. This house might be safety. This house was barricaded, and, as it were, walled in from top to bottom. Before the troops of the line would be in the interior of the redoubt, there was time for a door to open and shut, a flash was enough for that, and the door of this house, suddenly half opened and closed again immediately, to these despairing men was life. In the rear of this house, there were streets, possible flight, space. They began to strike this door with the butts of their muskets, and with kicks, calling, shouting, begging, wringing their hands. Nobody opened. From the window on the fourth story, the death's head looked at them.

But Enjolras and Marius, with seven or eight who had been rallied about them, sprang forward and protected them. Enjolras cried to the soldiers: "Keep back!" and an officer not obeying, Enjolras killed the officer. He was now in the little interior court of the redoubt, with his back to the house of Corinth, his sword in one hand, his carbine in the other, keeping the door of the tavern open while he barred it against the assailants. He cried to the despairing: "There is but one door open. This one." And, covering them with his body, alone facing a battalion, he made them pass in behind him. All rushed in, Enjolras executing with his carbine, which he now used as a cane, what cudgel-players call *la rose couverte* beat down the bayonets about him and before him, and entered last of all; and for an instant it was horrible, the soldiers struggling to get in, the insurgents to close the door. The door was closed with such violence that, in shutting into its frame, it exposed, cut off, and glued to the casement, the thumb and fingers of a soldier who had caught hold of it.

Marius remained without. A ball had broken his shoulder-blade; he felt that he was fainting, and that he was falling. At that moment his eyes already closed, he experienced the shock of a vigorous hand seizing him, and his fainting fit, in which he lost consciousness, left him hardly time for this thought, mingled with the last memory of Cosette: "I am taken prisoner. I shall be shot."

Enjolras, not seeing Marius among those who had taken refuge in the tavern, had the same idea. But they had reached that moment when each has only time to think of his own death. Enjolras fixed the bar of the door and bolted it, and fastened it with a double turn of lock and padlock, while they were beating furiously on the outside, the soldiers with the butts of their muskets, the sappers with their axes. The assailants were massed upon this door. The siege of the tavern was now beginning.

The soldiers, we must say, were greatly irritated.

The death of the sergeant of artillery had angered them; and then, a more deadly thing, during the few hours which preceded the attack, it had been told among them that the insurgents mutilated prisoners, and that there was in the tavern the body of a soldier headless. This sort of unfortunate rumour is the ordinary accompaniment of civil wars, and it was a false report of this kind which, at a later day, caused the catastrophe of the Rue Transnonain.*

When the door was barricaded, Enjolras said to the rest:

"Let us sell ourselves dearly."

We must be brief. The barricade had struggled like a gate of Thebes; the tavern struggled like a house of Saragossa. Such resistances are dogged. No quarter. No parley possible. They are willing to die provided they kill. When Suchet says: "Capitulate," Palafox answers: "After the war with cannon, war with the knife." Nothing was wanting to the storming of the Hucheloup tavern: neither the paving-stones raining from the window and the roof upon the besiegers, and exasperating the soldiers by their horrible mangling, nor the shots from the cellars and the garret windows, nor fury of attack, nor rage of defence; nor, finally, when the door yielded, the frenzied madness of the extermination. The assailants, on rushing into the tavern, their feet entangled in the panels of the door, which were beaten in and scattered over the floor, found no combatant there. The spiral stairway, which had been cut down with the axe, lay in the middle of the basement room, a few wounded had just expired, all who were not killed were in the second story, and there,

---

*On April 15, 1834, government agents mistakenly murdered an innocent working man and his family in a poor neighborhood of Paris, on suspicion of subversive activities. Honoré Daumier protested with a famous lithograph.

through the hole in the ceiling, which had been the entrance for the stairway, a terrific firing broke out. It was the last of the cartridges. When they were gone, when these terrible men in their death-agony had no longer either powder or ball, each took two of those bottles reserved by Enjolras, of which we have spoken, and they defended the ascent with these frightfully fragile clubs. They were bottles of aquafortis. We describe these gloomy facts of the carnage as they are. The besieged, alas, make a weapon of everything. Greek fire did not dishonour Archimedes, boiling pitch did not dishonour Bayard. All war is appalling, and there is nothing to choose in it. The fire of the besiegers, although difficult and from below upwards, was murderous. The edge of the hole in the ceiling was very soon surrounded with the heads of the dead, from which flowed long red and reeking lines. The uproar was inexpressible; a stifled and burning smoke made night almost over this combat. Words fail to express horror when it reaches this degree. There were men no longer in this now infernal conflict. They were no longer giants against colossi. It resembled Milton and Dante rather than Homer. Demons attacked, spectres resisted.

It was the heroism of monsters.

20 (23)

ORESTES FASTING AND PYLADES DRUNK

AT LAST, mounting on each other's shoulders, helping themselves by the skeleton of the staircase, climbing up the walls, hanging to the ceiling, cutting to pieces, at the very edge of the hatchway, the last to resist, some twenty of the besiegers, soldiers, National Guards, Municipal Guards, pell-mell, most disfigured by wounds in the face of this terrible ascent, blinded with blood, furious, become savages, burst into the room of the second story. There was now but a single man there on his feet, Enjolras. Without cartridges, without a sword, he had now in his hand only the barrel of his carbine, the stock of which he had broken over the heads of those who were entering. He had put the billiard table between the assailants and himself; he had retreated to the corner of the room, and there, with proud eye, haughty head, and that stump of a weapon in his grasp, he was still so formidable that a large space was left about him. A cry arose:

"This is the chief. It is he who killed the artilleryman. As he has put himself there, it is a good place. Let him stay. Let us shoot him on the spot."

"Shoot me," said Enjolras.

And, throwing away the stump of his carbine, and folding his arms, he presented his breast.

The boldness that dies well always moves men. As soon as Enjolras had folded his arms, accepting the end, the uproar of the conflict ceased in the room, and that chaos suddenly hushed into a sort of sepulchral solemnity. It seemed as if the menacing majesty of Enjolras, disarmed and motionless, weighed upon that tumult, and as if, merely by the authority of his tranquil eye, this young man, who alone had no wound, superb, bloody, fascinating, indifferent as if he were invulnerable, compelled that sinister mob to kill him respectfully. His beauty, at that moment, augmented by his dignity, was a resplendence, and, as if he could no more be fatigued than wounded, after the terrible twenty-four hours which had just elapsed, he was fresh and rosy. It was of him perhaps that the witness spoke who said afterwards before the court-martial: "There was one insurgent whom I heard called Apollo." A National Guard who was aiming at Enjolras, dropped his weapon, saying: "It seems to me that I am shooting a flower."

Twelve men formed in platoon in the corner opposite Enjolras and made their muskets ready in silence.

Then a sergeant cried: "Take aim!"

An officer intervened.

"Wait."

And addressing Enjolras:

"Do you wish your eyes bandaged?"

"No."

"Was it really you who killed the sergeant of artillery?"

"Yes."

Within a few seconds Grantaire had awakened.

Grantaire, it will be remembered, had been asleep since the day previous in the upper room of the tavern sitting in a chair, leaning heavily forward on a table.

He realised, in all its energy, strength, the old metaphor: dead drunk. The hideous potion, the absinthe-stout-alcohol, had thrown him into a lethargy. His table being small, and of no use in the barricade, they had left it to him. He had continued in the same posture, his breast doubled over the table, his head lying flat upon his arms, surrounded by glasses, jugs, and bottles. He slept with that crushing sleep of the torpid bear and the overfed leech. Nothing had affected him, neither the musketry, nor the balls, nor the grapeshot which penetrated through the casement into the room in which he was. Nor the prodigious uproar of the assault. Only, he responded sometimes to the cannon with a snore. He seemed waiting there for a ball to come and save him the trouble of awaking. Several corpses lay about him; and, at the first glance, nothing distinguished him from those deep sleepers of death.

Noise does not waken a drunkard; silence wakens him. This peculiarity has been observed more than once. The fall of everything about him augmented Grantaire's oblivion; destruction was a lullaby to him. The kind of halt in the tumult before Enjolras was a shock to his heavy sleep. It was the effect of a waggon at a gallop stopping short. The sleepers are roused by it. Grantaire rose up with a start, stretched his arms, rubbed his eyes, looked, gaped, and understood.

Drunkenness ending is like a curtain torn away. We see altogether, and at a single glance, all that is concealed. Everything is suddenly presented to the memory; and the drunkard who knows nothing of what has taken place for twenty-four hours, has no sooner opened his eyes than he is aware of all that has happened. His ideas come back to him with an abrupt lucidity; the effacement of drunkenness, a sort of lye-wash which blinds the brain, dissipates, and give place to clear and precise impressions of the reality.

Retired as he was in a corner and as it were sheltered behind the billiard-table, the soldiers, their eyes fixed upon Enjolras, had not even noticed Grantaire, and the sergeant was preparing to repeat the order: "Take aim!" when suddenly they heard a powerful voice cry out beside them:

"*Vive la République!* I belong to it."

Grantaire had arisen.

The immense glare of the whole combat which he had missed and in which he had not been, appeared in the flashing eye of the transfigured drunkard.

He repeated: "*Vive la République!*" crossed the room with a firm step, and took his place before the muskets beside Enjolras.

"Two at one shot," said he.

And, turning towards Enjolras gently, he said to him:

"Will you permit it?"

Enjolras grasped his hand with a smile.

The smile was not finished when the report was heard.

Enjolras, pierced by eight balls, remained backed against the wall as if the balls had nailed him there. Only he bowed his head.

Grantaire, stricken down, fell at his feet.

A few moments afterwards, the soldiers dislodged the last insurgents who had taken refuge in the top of the house. They fired through a wooden lattice into the garret. They fought in the attics. They threw the bodies out of the windows, some living. Two voltigeurs, who were trying to raise the shattered omnibus, were killed by two shots from a carbine fired from the dormer-windows. A man in a smock was pitched out headlong, with a bayonet thrust in his belly, and his death-rattle was finished upon the ground. A soldier and an insurgent slipped together on the slope of the tiled roof, and would not let go of each other, and fell, clasped in a wild embrace. Similar struggle in the cellar. Cries, shots, savage stamping. Then silence. The barricade was taken.

The soldiers commenced the search of the houses round about and the pursuit of the fugitives.

21 (24)

PRISONER

MARIUS was in fact a prisoner. Prisoner of Jean Valjean.

The hand which had seized him from behind at the moment he was falling, and the grasp of which he had felt in losing consciousness, was the hand of Jean Valjean.

Jean Valjean had taken no other part in the combat than to expose himself. Save for him, in that supreme phase of the death-struggle, nobody would have thought of the wounded. Thanks to him, everywhere present in the carnage like a providence, those who fell were taken up, carried into the basement-room, and their wounds dressed. In the intervals, he repaired the barricade. But nothing which could resemble a blow, an attack, or even a personal defence came from his hands. He was silent, and gave aid. Moreover, he had only a few scratches. The balls refused him. If suicide were a part of what had occurred to him in coming to this sepulchre, in that respect he had not succeeded. But we doubt whether he had thought of suicide, an irreligious act.

Jean Valjean, in the thick cloud of the combat, did not appear to see Marius; the fact is, that he did not take his eyes from him. When a shot struck down Marius, Jean Valjean bounded with the agility of a tiger, dropped upon him as upon a prey, and carried him away.

The whirlwind of the attack at that instant concentrated so fiercely upon Enjolras and the door of the tavern, that nobody saw Jean Valjean cross the unpaved field of the barricade, holding the senseless Marius in his arms, and disappear behind the corner of the house of Corinth.

It will be remembered that this corner was a sort of cape on the street; it sheltered from balls and grapeshot, and from sight also, a few square feet of ground. Thus, there is sometimes in conflagrations a room which does not burn; and in the most furious seas, beyond a promontory or at the end of a cul-de-sac of shoals, a placid little haven. It was in this recess of the interior trapezium of the barricade that Eponine had died.

There Jean Valjean stopped; he let Marius slide to the ground, set his back to the wall, and cast his eyes about him.

The situation was appalling.

For the moment, for two or three minutes, perhaps, this skirt of wall was a shelter; but how escape from this massacre? He remembered the anguish in which he was in the Rue Polonceau, eight years before, and how he had succeeded in escaping; that was difficult then, to-day it was impossible. Before him he had that deaf and implacable house of seven stories, which seemed inhabited only by the dead man, leaning over his window; on his right he had the low barricade, which closed the Petite Truanderie; to clamber over this obstacle appeared easy, but above the crest of the wall a range of bayonet-points could be seen. A company of the line was posted beyond this barricade, on the watch. It was evident that to cross the barricade was to meet the fire of a platoon, and that every head which should venture to rise above the top of the wall of paving-stones would serve as a target for sixty muskets. At his left he had the field of combat. Death was behind the corner of the wall.

What should he do?

A bird alone could have extricated himself from that place.

And he must decide upon the spot, find an expedient, adopt his course. They were fighting a few steps from him; by good luck all were fiercely intent upon a single point, the door of the tavern; but let one soldier, a single one, conceive the idea of turning the house, of attacking it in flank, and all was over.

Jean Valjean looked at the house in front of him, he looked at the barricade by the side of him, then he looked upon the ground, with the violence of the last extremity, in desperation, and as if he would have made a hole in it with his eyes.

Beneath his persistent look, something vaguely tangible in such an agony outlined itself and took form at his feet, as if there were a power in the eye to develop the thing desired. He perceived a few steps from him, at the foot of the little wall so pitilessly watched and guarded on the outside, under some fallen paving-stones which partly hid it, an iron grating laid flat and level with the ground. This grating, made of strong transverse bars, was about two feet square. The stone frame which held it had been torn up, and it was as it were unset. Through the bars a glimpse could be caught of a dark opening, something like the flue of a chimney or the main of a cistern. Jean Valjean sprang forward. His old science of escape mounted to his brain like a flash. To remove the stones, to lift the grating, to load Marius, who was as inert as a dead body, upon his shoulders, to descend, with that burden upon his back, by the aid of his elbows and knees, into this kind of well, fortunately not very deep, to let fall over his head the heavy iron trapdoor upon which the stones were shaken back again, to find a foothold upon a flagged surface ten feet below the ground, this was executed like what is done in delirium, with the strength of a giant and the rapidity of an eagle; it required but very few moments.

Jean Valjean found himself, with Marius still senseless, in a sort of long underground passage.

There, deep peace, absolute silence, night.

The impression which he had formerly felt in falling from the street into the convent came back to him. Only, what he was now carrying away was not Cosette; it was Marius.

He could now hardly hear above him, like a vague murmur, the fearful tumult of the tavern taken by assault.

[Book Two, "The Leviathan's Bowels," does not appear in this abridged edition.]

BOOK THREE
MIRE, BUT SOUL

1

THE CLOACA AND ITS SURPRISES

IT WAS in the sewer of Paris that Jean Valjean found himself.

The transition was marvellous. From the very centre of the city, Jean Valjean had gone out of the city, and, in the twinkling of an eye, the time of lifting a cover and closing it again, he had passed from broad day to complete darkness, from noon to midnight, from uproar to silence, from the whirl of the thunder to the stagnation of the tomb, and, by a mutation much more prodigious still than that of the Rue Polonceau, from the most extreme peril to the most absolute security.

Only, the wounded man did not stir, and Jean Valjean did not know whether what he was carrying away in this grave were alive or dead.

His first sensation was blindness. Suddenly he saw nothing more. It seemed to him also that in one minute he had become deaf. He heard nothing more. The frenzied storm of murder which was raging a few feet above him only reached him, as we have said, thanks to the thickness of the earth which separated him from it, stifled and indistinct, and like a rumbling at a great depth. He felt that it was solid under his feet; that was all; but that was enough. He reached out one hand, then the other, and touched the wall on both sides, and realised that the passage was narrow; he slipped, and realised that the pavement was wet. He advanced one foot with precaution, fearing a hole, a pit, some gulf; he made sure that the pavement continued. A whiff of fetidness informed him where he was.

After a few moments, he ceased to be blind. A little light fell from the air-hole through which he had slipped in, and his eye became accustomed to this cave. He began to distinguish something. The passage in which he had gone to ground, no other word better expresses the condition, was walled up behind him. It was one of those cul-de-sacs technically called branchments. Before him, there was another wall, a wall of night. The light from the air-hole died out ten or twelve paces from the point at which Jean Valjean stood, and scarcely produced a pallid whiteness over a few yards of the damp wall of the sewer. Beyond, the opaqueness was massive; to penetrate it appeared horrible, and to enter it seemed like being engulfed. He could, however, force his way into that wall of mist, and he must do it. He must even hasten. Jean Valjean thought that that grating, noticed by him under the paving-stones, might also be noticed by the soldiers, and that all depended upon that chance. They also could descend into the well and explore it. There was not a minute to be lost. He had laid Marius upon the ground, he gathered him up, this is again the right word, replaced him upon his shoulders, and began his journey. He resolutely entered that darkness.

The truth is, that they were not so safe as Jean Valjean supposed. Perils of another kind, and not less great, awaited them perhaps. After the flashing whirl of the combat, the cavern of miasmas and pitfalls; after chaos, the cloaca. Jean Valjean had fallen from one circle of Hell to another.[*]

At the end of fifty paces he was obliged to stop. A question presented itself. The passage terminated in another which it met transversely. These two roads were offered. Which should he take? should he turn to the left or to the right? How guide himself in this black labyrinth? This labyrinth, as we have remarked, has a clue: its descent. To follow the descent is to go to the river.

Jean Valjean understood this at once.

He said to himself that he was probably in the sewer of the markets; that, if he should choose the left and follow the descent, he would come in less than a quarter of an hour to some mouth upon the Seine between the Pont au Change and the Pont Neuf, that is to say, he would reappear in broad day in the most populous portion of Paris. He might come out in some gathering of corner idlers. Amazement of the passers-by at seeing two bloody men come out of the ground under their feet. Arrival of sergent de ville, call to arms in the next guard-house. He would be seized before getting out. It was better to plunge into the labyrinth, to trust to this darkness, and to rely on Providence for the outcome.

He chose the right, and went up the ascent.

When he had turned the corner of the gallery, the distant gleam of the air-hole disappeared, the curtain of darkness fell back over him, and he again became blind. He went forward none the less, and as rapidly as he could. Marius' arms were passed about his neck, and his feet hung behind him. He held both arms with one hand, and groped for the wall with the other. Marius' cheek touched his and stuck to it, being bloody. He felt a warm stream, which came from Marius, flow over him and penetrate his clothing. Still, a moist warmth at his ear, which touched the wounded man's mouth, indicated respiration, and consequently life. The passage through which Jean Valjean was now moving was not so narrow as the first. Jean Valjean walked in it with difficulty. The rains of the previous day had not yet run off, and made a little stream in the centre of the floor, and he was compelled to hug the wall, to keep his feet out of the water. Thus he went on in midnight. He resembled the creatures of night groping in the invisible, and lost underground in the veins of the darkness.

However, little by little, whether some distant air-holes sent a little floating light into this opaque mist, or that his eyes became accustomed to the dark, some dim vision came back to him, and he again began to receive a confused perception, now of the wall which he was touching, and now of the arch under which he was passing. The pupil dilates in the night, and at last finds day in it, even as the soul dilates in misfortune, and at last finds God in it.

To find his way was difficult.

---

[*]Another allusion to Dante's *Inferno*, with the implication that Jean Valjean's horrible struggles will ultimately prove redemptive.

He went forward, anxious but calm, seeing nothing, knowing nothing, plunged into chance, that is to say, swallowed up in Providence.

By degrees, we must say, some horror penetrated him. The shadow which enveloped him entered his mind. He was walking in an enigma. This aqueduct of the cloaca is formidable; it is dizzily intertangled. It is a dreary thing to be caught in this Paris of darkness. Jean Valjean was obliged to find and almost to invent his route without seeing it. In that unknown region, each step which he ventured might be the last. How should he get out? Should he find an outlet? Should he find it in time? Would this colossal subterranean sponge with cells of stone admit of being penetrated and pierced? Would he meet with some unlooked-for knot of obscurity? Would he encounter the inextricable and the insurmountable? Would Marius die of hæmorrhage, and he of hunger? Would they both perish there at last, and make two skeletons in some niche of that night? He did not know. He asked himself all this, and he could not answer. The intestine of Paris is an abyss. Like the prophet, he was in the belly of the monster.

Suddenly he was surprised. At the most unexpected moment, and without having diverged from a straight line, he discovered that he was no longer rising; the water of the brook struck coming against his heels instead of upon the top of his feet. The sewer now descended. Why? would he then soon reach the Seine? This danger was great, but the peril of retreat was still greater. He continued to advance.

He had been walking for about half an hour, at least by his own calculation, and had not yet thought of resting; only he had changed the hand which supported Marius. The darkness was deeper than ever, but this depth reassured him.

All at once he saw his shadow before him. It was marked out on a feeble ruddiness almost indistinct, which vaguely empurpled the floor at his feet, and the arch over his head, and which glided along at his right and his left on the two slimy walls of the corridor. In amazement he turned round.

Behind him, in the portion of the passage through which he had passed, at a distance which appeared to him immense, flamed, throwing its rays into the dense darkness, a sort of horrible star which appeared to be looking at him.

It was the gloomy star of the police which was rising in the sewer.

Behind this star were moving without order eight or ten black forms, straight, indistinct, terrible.

2

EXPLANATION

DURING the day of the 6th of June, a thorough search of the sewers had been ordered. It was feared that they would be taken as a refuge by the vanquished, and prefect Gisquet was to ransack the occult Paris, while General Bugeaud was sweeping the public Paris; a connected double operation which demanded a double strategy of the public power, represented above by the army and below by the police. Three platoons of officers and sewermen explored the subterranean streets of Paris, the first, the right bank, the second, the left bank, the third, in the City.*

The officers were armed with carbines, clubs, swords, and daggers.

That which was at this moment directed upon Jean Valjean, was the lantern of the patrol of the right bank.

This patrol had just searched the crooked gallery and the three blind alleys which are beneath the Rue du Cadran. While they were taking their candle to the bottom of these blind alleys, Jean Valjean had come to the entrance of the gallery upon his way, had found it narrower than the principal passage, and had not entered it. He had passed beyond. The policemen, on coming out from the Cadran gallery, had thought they heard the sound of steps in the direction of the belt sewer. It was in fact Jean Valjean's steps. The sergeant in command of the patrol lifted his lantern, and the squad began to look into the mist in the direction whence the sound came.

This was to Jean Valjean an indescribable moment.

Luckily, if he saw the lantern well, the lantern saw him badly. It was light and he was shadow. He was far off, and merged in the blackness of the place. He drew close to the side of the wall, and stopped.

Still, he formed no idea of what was moving there behind him. Lack of sleep, want of food, emotions, had thrown him also into the visionary state. He saw a flaring flame, and about that flame, goblins. What was it? He did not understand.

Jean Valjean having stopped, the noise ceased.

The men of the patrol listened and heard nothing, they looked and saw nothing. They consulted.

Jean Valjean saw these goblins form a kind of circle. These mastiffs' heads drew near each other and whispered.

The result of this council held by the watch-dogs was that they had been mistaken, that there had been no noise, that there was nobody there, that it was needless to trouble themselves with the belt sewer, that that

---

*"The City" includes l'Île de la Cité and l'Île Saint-Louis in the Seine.

would be time lost, but that they must hasten towards Saint Merry, that if there were anything to do and any "bousingot" [rabble-rouser] to track down, it was in that quarter.

The sergeant gave the order to file left towards the descent to the Seine. If they had conceived the idea of dividing into two squads and going in both directions, Jean Valjean would have been caught. That hung by this thread. It is probable that the instructions from the prefecture, foreseeing the possibility of a combat and that the insurgents might be numerous, forbade the patrol to separate. The patrol resumed its march, leaving Jean Valjean behind. Of all these movements, Jean Valjean perceived nothing except the eclipse of the lantern, which suddenly turned back.

Before going away, the sergeant, to ease the police conscience, discharged his carbine in the direction they were abandoning, towards Jean Valjean. The detonation rolled from echo to echo in the vault like the rumbling of this titanic bowel. Some plastering which fell into the stream and spattered the water a few steps from Jean Valjean made him aware that the ball had struck the arch above his head.

Slow and measured steps resounded upon the floor for some time, more and more deadened by the progressive increase of the distance, the group of black forms sank away, a glimmer oscillated and floated, making a ruddy circle in the vault, which decreased, then disappeared, the silence became deep again, the darkness became again complete, blindness and deafness resumed possession of the darkness; and Jean Valjean, not yet daring to stir, stood for a long time with his back to the wall, his ear intent and eye dilated, watching the vanishing of that phantom patrol.

3

THE MAN TAILED

WE MUST do the police of that period this justice that, even in the gravest public conjunctures, it imperturbably performed its duties of surveillance and regulating traffic. A riot was not in its eyes a pretext for giving malefactors a loose rein, and for neglecting society because the government was in peril. The ordinary duty was performed correctly in addition to the extraordinary duty, and was not disturbed by it. In the midst of the beginning of an incalculable political event, under the pressure of a possible revolution, without allowing himself to be diverted by the insurrection and the barricade, an officer would "tail" a thief.

Something precisely like this occurred in the afternoon of the 6th of June at the brink of the Seine, on the walkway along the right bank, a little beyond the Pont des Invalides.

There is no walkway there now. The appearance of the place has changed. On this quai, two men some distance apart seemed to be observing each other, one avoiding the other. The one who was going before was endeavouring to increase the distance, the one who came behind to lessen it.

It was like a game of chess played from a distance and silently. Neither seemed to hurry, and both walked slowly, as if either feared that by too much haste he would double the pace of his partner.

One would have said it was an appetite following a prey, without appearing to do it on purpose. The prey was crafty, and kept on its guard.

The requisite proportions between the tracked marten and the tracking hound were observed. He who was trying to escape had a feeble frame and a sorry mien; he who was trying to seize, a fellow of tall stature, was rough in aspect, and promised to be rough in encounter.

The first, feeling himself the weaker, was avoiding the second; he avoided him in a very furious way; he who could have observed him would have seen in his eyes the gloomy hostility of flight, and all the menace which there is in fear.

The way was solitary; there were no passers-by; not even a boatman nor a longshoreman on the barges moored here and there.

These two men could not have been easily seen, except from the quai in front, and to him who might have examined them from that distance, the man who was going forward would have appeared like a bristly creature, tattered and skulking, restless and shivering under a ragged smock, and the other, like a classic and official person, wearing the overcoat of authority buttoned to the chin.

If the other was allowing him to go on and did not yet seize him, it was, according to all appearance, in the hope of seeing him bring up at some significant rendezvous, some group of good prizes. This delicate operation is called "spinning."

What renders this conjecture the more probable is, that the closely buttoned man, perceiving from the shore a fiacre which was passing on the quai empty, beckoned to the driver; the driver understood, evidently recognised with whom he had to deal, turned his horse, and began to follow the two men on the upper part of the quai at a walk. This was not noticed by the equivocal and ragged personage who was in front.

One of the secret instructions of the police to officers contains this article: "Always have a vehicle within call, in case of need."

While manœuvring, each on his side, with an irreproachable strategy, these two men approached a ramp of the quai descending to the water's edge, which, at that time, allowed the coach-drivers coming from Passy to go to the river to water their horses. This ramp has since been removed, for the sake of symmetry; the horses perish with thirst, but the eye is satisfied.

It seemed probable that the man in the smock would go up by this ramp in order to attempt escape into the Champs-Elysées, a place ornamented with trees, but on the other hand thickly dotted with officers, and where his pursuer would have easily seized him with a strong hand.

To the great surprise of his observer, the man pursued did not ascend the ramp from the watering-place. He continued to advance on the beach along the quai.

His position was visibly becoming critical.

If not to throw himself into the Seine, what was he going to do?

No means henceforth of getting up to the quai; no other slope, and no staircase; and they were very near the spot, marked by the turn of the Seine towards the Pont d'Iéna, where the walkway, narrowing more and more, terminates in a slender tongue, and vanishes beneath the water. There he would inevitably find himself blockaded between the steep wall on his right, the river on the left and in front, and authority upon his heels.

It is true that this end of the quai was hidden by a mound of rubbish from six to seven feet high, the product of some demolition. But did this man hope to hide with any effect behind this heap of fragments, which the other had only to walk around. The expedient would have been puerile. He certainly did not dream of it. The innocence of robbers does not reach this extent.

The heap of rubbish made a sort of hillock at the edge of the water, and extended like a promontory, as far as the wall of the quai.

The man pursued reached this little hill and walked around it, so that he ceased to be seen by the other.

The latter, not seeing, was not seen; he took advantage of this to abandon all dissimulation, and to walk very rapidly. In a few seconds he came to the mound of rubbish, and went around. There, he stopped in amazement. The man whom he was hunting was gone.

The fugitive could not have thrown himself into the Seine nor scaled the quai without being seen by him who was following him. What had become of him?

The man in the closely buttoned coat walked to the end of the quai, and stopped there a moment thoughtful, his fists convulsive, his eyes ferreting. Suddenly he slapped his forehead. He had noticed, at the point where the land and the water began, an iron grating broad and low, arched, with a heavy lock and three massive hinges. This grating, a sort of door cut into the bottom of the quai, opened upon the river as much as upon the beach. A blackish stream flowed from beneath it. This stream emptied into the Seine.

Beyond its heavy rusty bars could be distinguished a sort of corridor arched and dark.

The man folded his arms and looked at the grating reproachfully.

This look not sufficing, he tried to push it; he shook it, it resisted firmly. It was probable that it had just been opened, although no sound had been heard, a singular circumstance with a grating so rusty; but it was certain that it had been closed again. That indicated that he before whom this door had just turned, had not a hook but a key.

This evident fact burst immediately upon the mind of the man who was exerting himself to shake the grating, and forced from him this indignant epiphonema:[*]

"This is fine! a government key!"

4

HE ALSO BEARS HIS CROSS[†]

JEAN VALJEAN had resumed his advance, and had not stopped again.

This advance became more and more laborious. The level of these arches varies; the medium height is about five feet six inches, and was calculated for the stature of a man; Jean Valjean was compelled to bend so, as not to hit Marius against the arch; he had to stoop every second, then rise up, to grope incessantly for the wall. The moisture of the stones and the sliminess of the floor made them bad points of support, whether for the hand or the foot. He was wading in the hideous muck of the city. The occasional gleams from the air-holes appeared only at long intervals, and so

---

[*]A rhetorical term for a pithy concluding exclamation, here used whimsically to create a mock-heroic style.

[†]Not only is Marius' body heavy to carry, but Marius also represents a figurative cross to bear because he makes Jean Valjean suffer jealousy, rage, and the fear of losing Cosette.

ghastly were they that the noonday seemed but moonlight; all the rest was mist, miasma, opacity, blackness. Jean Valjean was hungry and thirsty; thirsty especially; and this place, like the sea, is one full of water where you cannot drink. His strength, which was prodigious, and very little diminished by age, thanks to his chaste and sober life, began to give way notwithstanding. Fatigue grew upon him, and as his strength diminished the weight of his load increased. Marius, dead perhaps, weighed heavily upon him as inert bodies do. Jean Valjean supported him in such a way that his breast was not compressed and his breathing could always be as free as possible. He felt the rapid gliding of the rats between his legs. One of them was so frightened as to bite him. There came to him from time to time through the aprons of the mouths of the sewer a breath of fresh air which revived him.

It might have been three o'clock in the afternoon when he arrived at the belt sewer.

He was first astonished at this sudden enlargement. He abruptly found himself in the gallery where his outstretched hands did not reach the two walls, and under an arch which his head did not touch. The Grand Sewer indeed is eight feet wide and seven high.

At the point where the Montmartre sewer joins the Grand Sewer, two other subterranean galleries, that of the Rue de Provence and that of the Abattoir, coming in, make a square. Between these four ways a less sagacious man would have been undecided. Jean Valjean took the widest, that is to say, the belt sewer. But there the question returned: to descend, or to ascend? He thought that the condition of affairs was urgent, and that he must, at whatever risk, now reach the Seine. In other words, descend. He turned to the left.

His instinct served him well. To descend was, in fact, possible safety.

He left on his right the two passages which ramify in the form of a claw under the Rue Lafitte and the Rue Saint Georges, and the long forked corridor of the Chaussée d'Antin.

A little beyond an affluent which was probably the branching of the Madeleine, he stopped. He was very tired. A large air-hole, probably the vista on the Rue d'Anjou, produced an almost vivid light. Jean Valjean, with the gentleness of movement of a brother for his wounded brother, laid Marius upon the side bank of the sewer. Marius' bloody face appeared, under the white gleam from the air-hole, as if at the bottom of a tomb. His eyes were closed, his hair adhered to his temples like brushes dried in red paint, his hands dropped down lifeless, his limbs were cold, there was coagulated blood at the corners of his mouth. A clot of blood had gathered in the tie of his cravat; his shirt was bedded in the wounds, the cloth of his coat chafed the gaping gashes in the living flesh. Jean Valjean, removing the garments with the ends of his fingers, laid his hand upon his breast; the heart still beat. Jean Valjean tore up his shirt, bandaged the wounds as well as he could, and staunched the flowing blood; then, bending in the twilight over Marius, who was still unconscious and almost lifeless, he looked at him with an inexpressible hatred.

In opening Marius' clothes, he had found two things in his pockets, the bread which had been forgotten there since the day previous, and Marius' pocket-book. He ate the bread and opened the pocket-book. On the first page he found the four lines written by Marius. They will be remembered.

"My name is Marius Pontmercy. Carry my corpse to my grandfather's, M. Gillenormand, Rue des Filles du Calvaire, No. 6, in the Marais."

By the light of the air-hole, Jean Valjean read these four lines, and stopped a moment as if absorbed in himself, repeating in an undertone: "Rue des Filles du Calvaire, Number Six, Monsieur Gillenormand." He replaced the pocket-book in Marius' pocket. He had eaten, strength had returned to him: he took Marius on his back again, laid his head carefully upon his right shoulder, and began to descend the sewer.

Nothing told him what zone of the city he was passing through, nor what route he had followed. Only the growing pallor of the gleams of light which he saw from time to time, indicated that the sun was withdrawing from the pavement and that the day would soon be gone; and the rumblings of the waggons above his head, from continuous having become intermittent, then having almost ceased, he concluded that he was under central Paris no longer, and that he was approaching some solitary region, in the vicinity of the outer boulevards or the furthest quais. Where there are fewer houses and fewer streets, the sewer has fewer air-holes. The darkness thickened about Jean Valjean. He none the less continued to advance, groping in the darkness.

This darkness suddenly became terrible.

5

FOR SAND AS WELL AS WOMAN THERE IS A FINESSE WHICH IS PERFIDY

HE FELT that he was entering the water, and that he had under his feet, pavement no longer, but mud.

6

THE FONTIS

JEAN VALJEAN found himself in the presence of a fontis. The fontis which Jean Valjean fell upon was caused by the showers of the previous day. A yielding of the pavement, imperfectly upheld by the underlying sand, had occasioned a damming of the rain-water. Infiltration having taken place, sinking had followed. The floor, broken up, had disappeared in the mire. For what distance? Impossible to say. The darkness was deeper than anywhere else. It was a mudhole in the cavern of night.

Jean Valjean felt the pavement slipping away under him. He entered into this slime. It was water on the surface, mire at the bottom. He must surely pass through. To retrace his steps was impossible. Marius was expiring, and Jean Valjean exhausted. Where else could he go? Jean Valjean advanced. Moreover, the quagmire appeared not very deep for a few steps. But in proportion as he advanced, his feet sank in. He very soon had the mire half-knee deep and water above his knees. He walked on, holding Marius with both arms as high above the water as he could. The mud now came up to his knees, and the water to his waist. He could no longer turn back. He sank in deeper and deeper. This mire, dense enough for one man's weight, evidently could not bear two. Marius and Jean Valjean would have had a chance of escape separately. Jean Valjean continued to advance, supporting this dying man, who was perhaps a corpse.

The water came up to his armpits; he felt that he was foundering; it was with difficulty that he could move in the depth of mire in which he was. The density, which was the support, was also the obstacle. He still held Marius up, and, with an unparalleled outlay of strength, he advanced; but he sank deeper. He now had only his head out of the water, and his arms supporting Marius. There is in the old pictures of the deluge, a mother doing thus with her child.

He sank still deeper, he threw his face back to escape the water, and to be able to breathe; he who should have seen him in this darkness would have thought he saw a mask floating upon the darkness; he dimly perceived Marius' drooping head and livid face above him; he made a desperate effort, and thrust his foot forward; his foot struck something solid; a support. It was time.

He rose and writhed and rooted himself upon this support with a sort of fury. It produced the effect upon him of the first step of a staircase reascending towards life.

This support, discovered in the mire at the last moment, was the beginning of the other slope of the floor, which had bent without breaking, and had curved beneath the water like a board, and in a single piece. A well-constructed paving forms an arch, and has this firmness. This fragment of the floor, partly submerged, but solid, was a real slope, and, once upon this slope, they were saved. Jean Valjean ascended this inclined plane, and reached the other side of the quagmire.

On coming out of the water, he struck against a stone, and fell upon his knees. This seemed to him fitting, and he remained thus for some time, his soul lost in unspoken prayer to God.

He rose, shivering, chilled, reeking, bending beneath this dying man, whom he was dragging on, all dripping with slime, his soul filled with a strange light.

7

EXTREMITIES

HE SET OFF once more.

However, if he had not left his life in the fontis, he seemed to have left his strength. This supreme effort had exhausted him. His exhaustion was so great, that every three or four steps he was obliged to take breath, and leaned against the wall. Once he had to sit down upon the curb to change Marius' position and he thought he should stay there. But if his vigour were dead his energy was not. He rose again. He walked with desperation, almost with rapidity, for a hundred paces, without raising his head, almost without breathing, and suddenly struck against the wall. He had reached an angle of the sewer, and, arriving at the turn with his head down, he had encountered the wall. He raised his eyes, and at the extremity of the passage, down there before him, far, very far away, he perceived a light. This time, it was not the terrible light; it was the good and white light. It was the light of day.

Jean Valjean saw the outlet.

A condemned soul who, from the midst of the furnace, should suddenly perceive an exit from Gehenna, would feel what Jean Valjean felt. It would fly frantically with the stumps of its burned wings towards the radiant door. Jean Valjean felt exhaustion no more, he felt Marius' weight no longer, he found again his knees of steel, he ran rather than walked. As he approached, the outlet assumed a more and more distinct outline. It was a circular arch, not so high as the vault which sank down by degrees, and not so wide as the gallery which narrowed as the top grew lower. The tunnel ended on the inside in the form of a funnel; an ill-advised contraction, copied from the wickets of houses of detention, logical in a prison, illogical in a sewer, and which has since been corrected.

Jean Valjean reached the outlet.

There he stopped.

It was indeed the outlet, but it did not let him out.

The arch was closed by a strong grating, and the grating which, according to all appearance, rarely turned upon its rusty hinges, was held in its stone frame by a stout lock which, red with rust, seemed an enormous brick. He could see the keyhole, and the strong bolt deeply plunged into the iron staple. The lock was plainly a double-lock. It was one of those fortress locks of which the old Paris was so lavish.

Beyond the grating, the open air, the river, the daylight, the quai, very narrow, but sufficient to get away. The distant quai, Paris, that gulf in which one is so easily lost, the wide horizon, liberty. He distinguished at his right, below him, the Pont d'Iéna, and at his left, above, the Pont des Invalides; the spot would have been propitious for awaiting night and escaping. It was one of the most solitary points in Paris; the embankment which fronts on the Gros Caillou. The flies came in and went out through the bars of the grating.

It might have been half-past eight o'clock in the evening. The day was declining.

Jean Valjean laid Marius along the wall on the dry part of the floor, then walked to the grating and clenched the bars with both hands; the shaking was frenzied, the shock nothing. The grating did not stir. Jean Valjean seized the bars one after another, hoping to be able to tear out the least solid one, and to make a lever of it to lift the door or break the lock. Not a bar yielded. A tiger's teeth are not more solid in their sockets. No lever; no possible purchase. The obstacle was invincible. No means of opening the door.

Must he then perish there? What should he do? what would become of them? go back; recommence the terrible road which he had already traversed; he had not the strength. Besides, how cross that quagmire again, from which he had escaped only by a miracle? And after the quagmire, was there not that police patrol from which, certainly, one would not escape twice? And then where should he go? what direction take? to follow the descent was not to reach the goal. Should he come to another outlet, he would find it obstructed by a door or a grating. All the outlets were undoubtedly closed in this way. Chance had unsealed the grating by which they had entered, but evidently all the other mouths of the sewer were fastened. He had only succeeded in escaping into a prison.

It was over. All that Jean Valjean had done was useless. God was denying him.

They were both caught in the gloomy and immense web of death, and Jean Valjean felt running over those black threads trembling in the darkness, the appalling spider.[*]

He turned his back to the grating, and dropped upon the pavement,

---

[*]A universal symbol of evil and entrapment, often used by Hugo.

rather prostrated than sitting, beside the yet motionless Marius, and his head sank between his knees. No exit. This was the last drop of anguish.*

Of whom did he think in this overwhelming dejection? Neither of himself nor of Marius. He thought of Cosette.

8

THE TORN COAT-TAIL

IN THE MIDST of this annihilation, a hand was laid upon his shoulder, and a voice which spoke low, said to him:

"Go halves."

Somebody in that darkness? Nothing is so like a dream as despair, Jean Valjean thought he was dreaming. He had heard no steps. Was it possible? he raised his eyes.

A man was before him.

This man was dressed in a smock; he was barefooted; he held his shoes in his left hand; he had evidently taken them off to be able to reach Jean Valjean without being heard.

Jean Valjean had not a moment's hesitation. Unforeseen as was the encounter, this man was known to him. This man was Thénardier.

Although wakened, so to speak, with a start, Jean Valjean, accustomed to be on the alert and on the watch for unexpected blows which he must quickly parry, instantly regained possession of all his presence of mind. Besides, the condition of affairs could not be worse, a certain degree of distress is no longer capable of crescendo, and Thénardier himself could not add to the blackness of this night.

There was a moment of delay.

Thénardier, lifting his right hand to the height of his forehead, shaded his eyes with it, then brought his brows together while he winked his eyes, which, with a slight pursing of the mouth, characterises the sagacious attention of a man who is seeking to recognise another. He did not succeed. Jean Valjean, we have just said, turned his back to the light, and was moreover so disfigured, so muddy and so blood-stained, that in full noon he would have been unrecognisable. On the other hand, with the light from the grating shining in his face, a cellar light, it is true, livid, but precise in its lividness,

---

*Refers to the figurative chalice of suffering that Christ, foreseeing his crucifixion, had to accept at Gethsemane and drain to the bottom.

Thénardier, as the energetic, trite metaphor expresses it, struck Jean Valjean at once. This inequality of conditions was enough to insure Jean Valjean some advantage in this mysterious duel which was about to open between the two conditions and the two men. The encounter took place between Jean Valjean veiled and Thénardier unmasked.

Jean Valjean perceived immediately that Thénardier did not recognise him.

They gazed at each other for a moment in this penumbra, as if they were taking each other's measure. Thénardier was first to break the silence.

"How are you going to manage to get out?"

Jean Valjean did not answer.

Thénardier continued:

"Impossible to pick the lock. Still you must get away from here."

"That is true," said Jean Valjean.

"Well, go halves."

"What do you mean?"

"You have killed the man; very well. Me, I have the key."

Thénardier pointed to Marius. He went on:

"I don't know you, but I would like to help you. You must be a friend."

Jean Valjean began to understand. Thénardier took him for an assassin.

Thénardier resumed:

"Listen, comrade. You haven't killed that man without looking to what he had in his pockets. Give me my half. I will open the door for you."

And, drawing a big key half out from under his smock, which was full of holes, he added:

"Would you like to see what freedom looks like?* There it is."

Jean Valjean "remained stupid," the expression is the elder Corneille's, so far as to doubt whether what he saw was real. It was Providence appearing in a guise of horror, and the good angel springing out of the ground under the form of Thénardier.

Thénardier plunged his fist into a huge pocket hidden under his smock, pulled out a rope, and handed it to Jean Valjean.

"Here," said he, "I'll give you the rope to boot."

"A rope, what for?"

"You want a stone too, but you'll find one outside. There is a heap of rubbish there."

"A stone, what for?"

"Fool, as you are going to throw the stiff into the river, you want a stone and a rope; without them it would float on the water."

Jean Valjean took the rope. Everybody has accepted things thus mechanically.

Thénardier snapped his fingers as over the arrival of a sudden idea:

"Ah now, comrade, how did you manage to get out of the quagmire

---

*Thénardier puns by using the French idiom for "liberty"—*la clé des champs* ("the key to the fields").

yonder? I haven't dared to risk myself there. Peugh! you don't smell good."

After a pause, he added:

"I ask you questions, but you are right in not answering them. That is an apprenticeship for the examining judge's cursed quarter of an hour. And then by not speaking at all, you run no risk of speaking too loud. It is all the same, because I don't see your face, and because I don't know your name, you would do wrong to suppose that I don't know who you are and what you want. Understood. You have smashed this gentleman a little; now you want to stow him somewhere. You need the river, the great hide-folly. I am going to get you out of the scrape. To help a good fellow in trouble, that's what I like."*

While approving Jean Valjean for keeping silence, he was evidently seeking to make him speak. He pushed his shoulders, so as to endeavour to see his profile, and exclaimed, without however rising above a moderate tone:

"Speaking of the quagmire, you are a proud animal. Why didn't you throw the man in there?"

Jean Valjean preserved silence.

Thénardier resumed, raising the rag which served him as a cravat up to his Adam's apple, a gesture which completes the air of sagacity of a serious man:

"Indeed, perhaps you have acted prudently. The workmen when they come to-morrow to stop the hole, would certainly have found the dummy forgotten there, and they would have been able, thread by thread, straw by straw, to find the trace, and to get to you. Something has passed through the sewer? Who? Where did he come out? Did anybody see him come out? The police has plenty of brains. The sewer is treacherous and informs against you. Such a discovery is a rarity, it attracts attention, few people use the sewer in their business while the river is at everybody's service. The river is the true grave. At the month's end, they fish you up the man at the nets of Saint Cloud. Well, what does that amount to? It is a carcass, indeed! Who killed this man? Paris. And justice don't even inquire into it. You have done right."

The more loquacious Thénardier was, the more dumb was Jean Valjean. Thénardier pushed his shoulder anew.

"Now, let us finish the business. Let us divide. You have seen my key, show me your money."

Thénardier was haggard, savage, shady, a little threatening, nevertheless friendly.

There was one strange circumstance; Thénardier's manner was not natural; he did not appear entirely at his ease; while he did not affect an air of mystery, he talked low; from time to time he laid his finger on his mouth,

---

*Thénardier uses the idiomatic expression *ça me botte*—"that puts boots on my feet" (in a day when many had to go barefoot).

and muttered: "Hush!" It was difficult to guess why. There was nobody there but them. Jean Valjean thought that perhaps some other bandits were hidden in some recess not far off, and that Thénardier did not care to share with them.

Thénardier resumed:

"Let us finish. How much did the stiff have in his deeps?"

Jean Valjean felt in his pockets.

It was, as will be remembered, his custom always to have money about him. The gloomy life of expedients to which he was condemned, made this a law to him. This time, however, he was caught unprepared. On putting on his National Guard's uniform, the evening before, he had forgotten, gloomily absorbed as he was, to take his pocket-book with him. He had only some coins in his waistcoat pocket. He turned out his pocket, all soaked with filth, and displayed upon the curb of the sewer a louis d'or, two five-franc coins, and five or six big sous.

Thénardier thrust out his under lip with a significant twist of the neck.

"You didn't kill him very dear," said he.

He began to handle, in all familiarity, the pockets of Jean Valjean and Marius. Jean Valjean, principally concerned in keeping his back to the light, did not interfere with him. While he was feeling of Marius' coat, Thénardier, with the dexterity of a juggler, found means, without attracting Jean Valjean's attention, to tear off a strip, which he hid under his smock, probably thinking that this scrap of cloth might assist him afterwards to identify the assassinated man and the assassin. He found, however, nothing more than the thirty francs.

"It is true," said he, "both together, you have no more than that."

And, forgetting his words, *go halves,* he took the whole.

He hesitated a little before the big sous. Upon reflection, he took them also, mumbling:

"No matter! this is sticking people too cheap."

This said, he took the key from under his smock anew.

"Now, friend, you must go out. This is like the fair, you pay on going out. You have paid, go out."

And he began to laugh.

That he had, in extending to an unknown man the help of this key, and in causing another man than himself to go out by this door, the pure and disinterested intention of saving an assassin, is something which it is permissible to doubt.

Thénardier helped Jean Valjean to replace Marius upon his shoulders; then he went towards the grating upon the points of his bare feet, beckoning to Jean Valjean to follow him, he looked outside, laid his finger on his mouth, and stood a few seconds as if in suspense; the inspection over, he put the key into the lock. The bolt slid and the door turned. There was neither snapping nor grinding. It was done very quietly. It was plain that this grating and its hinges, oiled with care, were opened oftener than would have been guessed. This quiet was ominous; you felt in it the furtive goings and comings, the silent entrances and exits of the men of the night, and the wolf-like tread of crime. The sewer was evidently in complicity with some mysterious band. This taciturn grating harboured fugitives from justice.*

Thénardier half opened the door, left just enough room for Jean Valjean, closed the grating again, turned the key twice in the lock, and plunged back into the darkness, without making more noise than a breath. He seemed to walk with the velvet paws of a tiger. A moment afterwards, this hideous providence had entered again into the invisible.

Jean Valjean found himself outside.

9

MARIUS SEEMS TO BE DEAD TO ONE WHO IS A GOOD JUDGE

HE LET Marius slide down upon the quai.

They were outside!

The miasmas, the darkness, the horror were behind him. The balmy air, pure, living, joyful, freely respirable, flowed around him. Everywhere about him silence, but the charming silence of a sunset in a clear sky. Twilight had fallen; night was coming, the great liberator, the friend of all those who need a mantle of darkness to escape from an anguish. The sky extended on every side like an enormous calm. The river came to his feet with the sound of a kiss. He heard the airy dialogues of the nests bidding each other good night in the elms of the Champs-Elysées. A few stars, faintly piercing the pale blue of the zenith, and visible to reverie alone, produced their imperceptible little resplendencies in the immensity. Evening was unfolding over Jean Valjean's head all the caresses of the infinite.

It was the undecided and exquisite hour which says neither yes nor no. There was already night enough for one to be lost in it at a little distance, and still day enough for one to be recognised near at hand.

Jean Valjean was for a few seconds irresistibly overcome by all this august and caressing serenity; there are such moments of forgetfulness; suffering refuses to harass the wretched; all is eclipsed in thought; peace covers the dreamer like a night; and, under the twilight which is flinging forth its rays, and in imitation of the sky which is lighting up, the soul

---

*The French term used is *le recel,* which refers to the felonies of receiving stolen goods or hiding persons wanted by the police.

becomes starry. Jean Valjean could not but gaze at that vast clear shadow which was above him; pensive, in the majestic silence of the eternal heavens, he took a bath of ecstasy and prayer. Then, hastily, as if a feeling of duty came back to him, he bent over Marius, and, dipping up some water in the hollow of his hand, he threw a few drops gently into his face. Marius' eyelids did not part; but his half-open mouth breathed.

Jean Valjean was plunging his hand into the river again, when suddenly he felt an indescribable uneasiness, such as we feel when we have somebody behind us, without seeing him.

We have already referred elsewhere to this impression, with which everybody is acquainted.

He turned round.

As just a few minutes earlier, somebody was indeed behind him.

A man of tall stature, wrapped in a long overcoat, with folded arms, and holding in his right hand a club, the leaden knob of which could be seen, stood erect a few steps in the rear of Jean Valjean, who was stooping over Marius.

It was, with the aid of the shadow, a sort of apparition. A simple-minded man would have been afraid on account of the twilight, and a reflective man on account of the club.

Jean Valjean recognised Javert.

The reader has doubtless guessed that Thénardier's pursuer was none other than Javert. Javert, after his unhoped-for departure from the barricade, had gone to the prefecture of police, had given an account verbally to the prefect in person in a short audience, had then immediately returned to his duty, which implied—the note found upon him will be remembered—a certain surveillance of the shore on the right bank near the Champs-Elysées, which for some time had attracted the attention of the police. There he had seen Thénardier, and had followed him. The rest is known.

It is understood also that the opening of that grating so obligingly before Jean Valjean was a piece of shrewdness on the part of Thénardier. Thénardier felt that Javert was still there; the man who is watched has a scent which does not deceive him; a bone must be thrown to this hound. An assassin, what a godsend! It was the scapegoat, which must never be refused. Thénardier, by putting Jean Valjean out in his place, gave a victim to the police, threw them off his own track, caused himself to be forgotten in a larger matter, rewarded Javert for his delay, which always flatters a spy, gained thirty francs, and counted surely, as for himself, upon escaping by the aid of this diversion.

Jean Valjean had passed from one shoal to another.

These two encounters, blow on blow, to fall from Thénardier upon Javert, it was hard.

Javert did not recognise Jean Valjean, who, as we have said, no longer resembled himself. He did not unfold his arms, he secured his club in his grasp by an imperceptible movement, and said in a clipped, calm voice:

"Who are you?"

"I."

"What you?"

"Jean Valjean."

Javert put the club between his teeth, bent his knees, inclined his body, laid his two powerful hands upon Jean Valjean's shoulders, which they clamped like two vices, examined him, and recognised him. Their faces almost touched. Javert's look was terrible.

Jean Valjean stood inert under the grasp of Javert like a lion who should submit to the claw of a lynx.

"Inspector Javert," said he, "you have got me. Besides, since this morning, I have considered myself your prisoner. I did not give you my address to try to escape you. Take me. Only grant me one thing."

Javert seemed not to hear. He rested his fixed eye upon Jean Valjean. His rising chin pushed his lips towards his nose, a sign of savage musing. At last, he let go of Jean Valjean, rose up as straight as a stick, took his club firmly in his grasp, and, as if in a dream, murmured rather than pronounced this question:

"What are you doing here? and who is this man?"

Jean Valjean answered, and the sound of his voice appeared to awaken Javert:

"It is precisely of him that I wished to speak. Dispose of me as you please; but help me first to carry him home. I ask only that of you."

Javert's face contracted, as it happened to him whenever anybody seemed to consider him capable of a concession. Still he did not say no.

He stooped down again, took a handkerchief from his pocket, which he dipped in the water, and wiped Marius' blood-stained forehead.

"This man was in the barricade," said he in an undertone, and as if speaking to himself. "This is he whom they called Marius."

A spy of the first quality, who had observed everything, listened to everything, heard everything, and recollected everything, believing he was about to die; who spied even in his death-agony, and who, leaning upon the first step of the grave, had taken notes.

He seized Marius' hand, seeking for his pulse.

"He is wounded," said Jean Valjean.

"He is dead," said Javert.

Jean Valjean answered:

"No. Not yet."

"You have brought him, then, from the barricade here?" observed Javert.

His preoccupation must have been deep, as he did not dwell longer upon this perplexing escape through the sewer, and did not even notice Jean Valjean's silence after his question.

Jean Valjean, for his part, seemed to have but one idea. He resumed:

"He lives in the Marais, Rue des Filles du Calvaire, at his grandfather's—I forget the name."

Jean Valjean felt in Marius' coat, took out the pocket-book, opened it at the page pencilled by Marius, and handed it to Javert.

There was still enough light floating in the air to enable one to read. Javert, moreover, had in his eye the feline phosphorescence of the birds of the night. He deciphered the few lines written by Marius, and muttered: "Gillenormand, Rue des Filles du Calvaire, No. 6."

Then he cried: "Driver?"

The reader will remember the fiacre which was waiting, in case of need. Javert kept Marius' pocket-book.

A moment later, the carriage, descending by the slope of the watering-place, was on the quai. Marius was laid upon the back seat, and Javert sat down by the side of Jean Valjean on the front seat.

When the door was shut, the fiacre moved rapidly off, going up the quai in the direction of the Bastille.

They left the quai and entered the streets. The driver, a black silhouette upon his box, whipped up his bony horses. Icy silence in the coach. Marius, motionless, his body braced in the corner of the carriage, his head dropping down upon his breast, his arms hanging, his legs rigid, appeared to await nothing now but a coffin; Jean Valjean seemed made of shadow, and Javert of stone; and in that carriage full of night, the interior of which, whenever it passed before a lamp, appeared to turn lividly pale, as if from an intermittent flash, chance grouped together, and seemed dismally to confront the three tragic immobilities, the corpse, the spectre, and the statue.

10

RETURN OF THE PRODIGAL
SON—OF HIS LIFE

AT EVERY JOLT over the pavement, a drop of blood fell from Marius' hair.

It was after nightfall when the fiacre arrived at No. 6, in the Rue des Filles du Calvaire.

Javert first set foot on the ground, verified at a glance the number above the porte-cochère, and, lifting the heavy wrought-iron knocker, embellished in the old fashion, with a goat and a satyr defying each other, struck a violent blow. The panel of the door partly opened, and Javert pushed it. The porter showed himself, gaping and half-awake, a candle in his hand.

Everybody in the house was asleep. People go to bed early in the Marais, especially on days of riot. That good old neighbourhood, startled by the Revolution, takes refuge in slumber, as children, when they hear Bugaboo coming, hide their heads very quickly under their coverlets.

Meanwhile Jean Valjean and the driver lifted Marius out of the coach, Jean Valjean supporting him by the armpits, and the coachman by the knees.

While he was carrying Marius in this way, Jean Valjean slipped his hand under his clothes, which were much torn, felt his breast, and assured himself that the heart still beat. It beat even a little less feebly, as if the motion of the carriage had determined a certain renewal of life.

Javert called out to the porter in the tone which befits the government, in presence of the porter of an insurrectionist.

"Somebody whose name is Gillenormand?"

"It is here. What do you want with him?"

"We've brought his son home."

"His son?" said the porter with amazement.

"He is dead."

Jean Valjean, who came ragged and dirty, behind Javert, and whom the porter beheld with some horror, motioned to him with his head that he was not.

The porter did not appear to understand either Javert's words, or Jean Valjean's signs.

Javert continued:

"He has been to the barricade, and here he is."

"To the barricade!" exclaimed the porter.

"He has got himself killed. Go and wake his father."

The porter did not stir.

"Get to it!" repeated Javert.

The porter merely woke Basque. Basque woke Nicolette; Nicolette woke Aunt Gillenormand. As to the grandfather, they let him sleep, thinking that he would know it soon enough at all events.

They carried Marius up to the second story, without anybody, moreover, perceiving it in the other portions of the house, and they laid him on an old couch in M. Gillenormand's ante-chamber; and, while Basque went for a doctor and Nicolette was opening the linen closets, Jean Valjean felt Javert touch him on the shoulder. He understood, and went down stairs, having behind him Javert's following steps.

The porter saw them depart as he had seen them arrive, with drowsy dismay.

They got into the fiacre again, and the driver mounted upon his box.

"Inspector Javert," said Jean Valjean, "grant me one thing more."

"What?" asked Javert roughly.

"Let me go home a moment. Then you shall do with me what you will."

Javert remained silent for a few seconds, his chin drawn back into the collar of his overcoat, then he let down the window in front.

"Driver," said he, "Rue de l'Homme Armé, No. 7."

11

COMMOTION IN THE ABSOLUTE

THEY DID NOT open their mouths again for the whole distance.

What did Jean Valjean desire? To finish what he had begun; to inform Cosette, to tell her where Marius was, to give her perhaps some other useful information, to make, if he could, certain final dispositions. As to himself, as to what concerned him personally, it was all over; he had been seized by Javert and did not resist; another than he, in such a condition, would perhaps have thought vaguely of that rope which Thénardier had given him and of the bars of the first cell which he should enter; but, since the bishop, there had been in Jean Valjean, in view of any violent attempt, were it even upon his own life, let us repeat, a deep religious hesitation.

Suicide, that mysterious assault upon the unknown, which may contain, in a certain measure, the death of the soul, was impossible to Jean Valjean.

At the entrance of the Rue de l'Homme Armé, the fiacre stopped, this street being too narrow for carriages to enter. Javert and Jean Valjean got out.

The driver humbly represented to monsieur the inspector that the Utrecht velvet of his carriage was all stained with the blood of the assassinated man and with the mud of the assassin. That was what he had understood. He added that an indemnity was due him. At the same time, taking his little book from his pocket, he begged monsieur the inspector to have the goodness to write him "a little scrap of certificate as to what."

Javert pushed back the little book which the driver handed him, and said:

"How much must you have, including your stop and your trip?"

"It is seven hours and a quarter," answered the driver, "and my velvet was brand new. Eighty francs, monsieur the inspector."

Javert took four napoleons from his pocket and dismissed the fiacre.

Jean Valjean thought that Javert's intention was to take him on foot to the post of the Blancs-Manteaux or to the post of the Archives which are quite near by.

They entered the street. It was, as usual, empty. Javert followed Jean Valjean. They reached No. 7. Jean Valjean rapped. The door opened.

"Very well," said Javert. "Go up."

He added with a strange expression and as if he were making an effort in speaking in such a way:

"I will wait here for you."

Jean Valjean looked at Javert. This manner of proceeding was little in accordance with Javert's habits. Still, that Javert should now have a sort of haughty confidence in him, the confidence of the cat which grants the mouse the liberty of the length of her claw, resolved as Jean Valjean was to deliver himself up and make an end of it, could not surprise him very much. He opened the door, went into the house, cried to the porter who was in bed and who had drawn the bolt without getting up: "It is I!" and mounted the stairs.

On reaching the second story, he paused. All painful paths have their halting-places. The window on the landing, which was a sliding window, was open. As in many old houses, the stairway admitted the light, and had a view upon the street. The street lamp, which stood exactly opposite, threw some rays upon the stairs, which produced an economy in light.

Jean Valjean, either to take breath or mechanically, looked out of this window. He leaned over the street. It is short, and the lamp lighted it from one end to the other. Jean Valjean was bewildered with amazement; there was nobody there.

Javert had gone.

12

THE ANCESTOR

ON THE DOCTOR'S ORDER, a cot had been set up near the couch. The doctor examined Marius, and, after having determined that the pulse still beat, that the sufferer had no wound penetrating his breast, and that the blood at the corners of his mouth came from the nasal cavities, he had him laid flat upon the bed, without a pillow, his head on a level with his body, and even a little lower with his chest bare, in order to facilitate respiration. Mademoiselle Gillenormand, seeing that they were taking off Marius' clothes, withdrew. She began to say the rosary in her room.

The body had not received any interior lesion; a ball, deadened by the wallet, had turned aside, and made the tour of the ribs with a hideous gash, but not deep, and consequently not dangerous. The long walk underground had completed the dislocation of the broken shoulder-blade, and there were serious difficulties there. There were sword cuts on the arms. No scar disfigured his face; the head, however, was as it were covered with hacks; what would be the result of these wounds on the head? did they stop at the scalp? did they affect the skull? That could not yet be told. A serious symptom was, that they had caused the fainting, and men do not always wake from such faintings. The hæmorrhage, moreover, had exhausted the wounded man. From the waist down, the body had been protected by the barricade.

Basque and Nicolette tore up linen and made bandages; Nicolette sewed them, Basque folded them. There being no lint, the doctor stopped the flow of blood from the wounds temporarily with rolls of wadding. By the side of the bed, three candles were burning on a table upon which the surgical instruments were spread out. The doctor washed Marius' face and hair with cold water. A bucketful was red in a moment. The porter, candle in hand, stood by.

The physician seemed reflecting sadly. From time to time he shook his head, as if he were answering some question which he had put to himself internally. A bad sign for the patient, these mysterious dialogues of the physician with himself.

At the moment the doctor was wiping the face and touching the still closed eyelids lightly with his finger, a door opened at the rear end of the parlour, and a long, pale figure approached.

It was the grandfather.

The émeute, for two days, had very much agitated, exasperated, and absorbed M. Gillenormand. He had not slept during the preceding night, and he had had a fever all day. At night, he had gone to bed very early, recommending that everything in the house be bolted; and, from fatigue, he had fallen asleep.

The slumbers of old men are easily broken; M. Gillenormand's room was next the parlour, and, in spite of the precautions they had taken, the noise had awakened him. Surprised by the light which he saw at the crack of his door, he had got out of bed, and groped his way along.

He was on the threshold, one hand on the knob of the half-opened door, his head bent a little forward and shaking, his body wrapped in a white nightgown, straight and without folds like a shroud; he was astounded; and he had the appearance of a phantom who is looking into a tomb.

He perceived the bed, and on the mattress that bleeding young man, white with a waxy whiteness, his eyes closed, his mouth open, his lips pallid, naked to the waist, gashed everywhere with red wounds, motionless, brightly lighted.

The grandfather had, from head to foot, as much of a shiver as ossified limbs can have; his eyes, the cornea of which had become yellow from his great age, were veiled with a sort of glassy haze; his whole face assumed in an instant the cadaverous angles of a skull, his arms fell and hung as if a spring were broken in them, and his stupefied astonishment was expressed by the separation of the fingers of his aged, tremulous hands; his knees bent forward, showing through the opening of his nightgown his poor naked legs bristling with white hairs, and he murmured:

"Marius!"

"Monsieur," said Basque, "monsieur has just been brought home. He has been to the barricade, and——"

"He is dead!" cried the old man in a terrible voice. "Oh! the brigand."

Then a sort of sepulchral transfiguration made this centenarian as straight as a young man.

"Monsieur," said he, "you are the doctor. Come, tell me one thing. He is dead, isn't he?"

The physician, in the height of anxiety, kept silence.

M. Gillenormand wrung his hands with a terrifying burst of laughter.

"He is dead! he is dead! He has got killed at the barricade! in hatred of me! It is against me that he did this! Ah, the blood-drinker! This is the way he comes back to me! Misery of my life, he is dead!"

He went to a window, opened it wide as if he were stifling, and, standing before the shadow, he began to talk into the street to the night:

"Pierced, sabred, slaughtered, exterminated, slashed, cut in pieces! do you see that, the vagabond! He knew very well that I was waiting for him and that I had had his room arranged for him, and that I had had his portrait of the time when he was a little boy hung at the head of my bed! He knew very well that he had only to come back, and that for years I had been calling him, and that I sat at night in my chimney corner, with my hands on my knees, not knowing what to do, and that I was a fool for his sake! You knew it very well, that you had only to come in and say: 'It is I,' and that you would be the master of the house, and that I would obey you, and that you would do whatever you liked with your old booby of a grandfather. You knew it very well, and you said: 'No, he is a royalist; I won't go!' And you went to the barricades, and you got yourself killed, out of spite! to revenge yourself for what I said to you about Monsieur the Duke de Berry! That is infamous! Go to bed, then, and sleep quietly! He is dead! That is my waking."

The physician, who began to be anxious on two accounts, left Marius a moment, and went to M. Gillenormand and took his arm. The grandfather turned round, looked at him with eyes which seemed swollen and bloody, and said quietly:

"Monsieur, I thank you. I am calm, I am a man, I saw the death of Louis XVI, I know how to bear up under events. There is one thing which is terrible, to think that it is your newspapers that do all the harm. You will have scribblers, talkers, lawyers, orators, tribunes, discussions, progress, lights, rights of man, freedom of the press, and this is the way they bring home your children for you. Oh! Marius! it is abominable! Killed! dead before me! A barricade! Oh! the bandit! Doctor, you live in the neighborhood, I believe? Oh! I know you well. I see your carriage pass from my window. I am going to tell you. You would be wrong to think I am angry. We don't get angry with a dead man; that would be stupid. That is a child I brought up. I was an old man when he was yet quite small. He played at the Tuileries with his little spade and his little chair, and, so that the keeper should not scold, with my cane I filled up the holes in the ground that he made with his spade. One day he cried: 'Down with Louis XVIII!' and went away. It is not my fault. He was all rosy and fair. His mother is dead. Have you noticed that all little children are fair? What is the reason of it? He is the son of one of those brigands of the Loire; but children are innocent of the crimes of their fathers. I remember when he was as high as this. He could not pronounce the *d*'s. His talk was so soft and so faint that you would have thought it was a bird. I recollect that once, before the Farnese

Hercules, they made a circle to admire and wonder at him, that child was so beautiful! It was such a head as you see in pictures. I spoke to him in my gruff voice, I frightened him with my cane, but he knew very well it was for fun. In the morning, when he came into my room, I scolded, but it seemed like sunshine to me. You can't defend yourself against these brats. They take you, they hold on to you, they never let go of you. The truth is, that there was never such a love as that child. Now, what do you say of your Lafayette, your Benjamin Constant, and of your Tirecuir de Corcelles, who kill him for me! It can't go on like this."

He approached Marius, who was still livid and motionless, and to whom the physician had returned, and he began to wring his hands. The old man's white lips moved as if mechanically, and made way for almost indistinct words, like whispers in a death-rattle, which could scarcely be heard: "Oh! heartless! Oh! conspirator! Oh! scoundrel! Oh! Septembrist!" Reproaches whispered by a dying man to a corpse.

Little by little, as internal eruptions must always make their way out, the connection of his words returned, but the grandfather appeared to have lost the strength to utter them, his voice was so dull and faint that it seemed to come from the other side of an abyss:

"It is all the same to me, I am going to die too, myself. And to say that there is no little creature in Paris who would have been glad to make the wretch happy! A rascal who, instead of amusing himself and enjoying life, went to fight and got himself riddled like a brute! And for whom? for what? For the republic! Instead of going to dance at the Chaumière, as young people should! What's the good of being twenty years old. The republic, a deuced fine folly. Poor mothers, raise your pretty boys then. Come, he is dead. That will make two funerals under the porte-cochère. Then you fixed yourself out like that for the sake of General Lamarque! What had he done for you, this General Lamarque? A sabrer! a babbler! To get killed for a dead man! If it isn't enough to make a man crazy! Think of it! At twenty! And without turning his head to see if he was not leaving somebody behind him! Here now are the poor old goodmen who must die alone. Perish in your corner, owl! Well, indeed, so much the better, it is what I was hoping, it is going to kill me dead. I am too old, I am a hundred, I am a hundred thousand; it is a long time since I have had a right to be dead. With this blow, it is done. It is all over then, how lucky! What is the use of making him breathe smelling salts and all this heap of drugs? You are losing your pains, dolt of a doctor! Go along, he is dead, stone dead. I understand it, I, who am dead also. He hasn't done the thing half way. Yes, these times are infamous, infamous, infamous, and that is what I think of you, of your ideas, of your systems, of your masters, of your oracles, of your doctors, of your scamps of writers, of your beggars of philosophers, and of all the revolutions which for sixty years have frightened the flocks of crows in the Tuileries! And as you had no pity in getting yourself killed like that, I shall not have even any grief for your death, do you understand, assassin?"

At this moment, Marius slowly raised his lids, and his gaze, still veiled in the astonishment of lethargy, rested upon M. Gillenormand.

"Marius!" cried the old man. "Marius! my darling Marius! my child! my dear son! You are opening your eyes, you are looking at me, you are alive, thanks!"

And he fell, unconscious.

BOOK FOUR
JAVERT DERAILED

1

JAVERT DERAILED

JAVERT made his way with slow steps from the Rue de l'Homme Armé.

He walked with his head down, for the first time in his life, and, for the first time in his life as well, with his hands behind his back.

Until that day, Javert had taken, from Napoleon's two postures, only that which expresses resolution, the arms folded upon the breast; that which expresses uncertainty, the hands behind the back, was unknown to him. Now, a change had taken place; his whole person, slow and gloomy, bore the impress of anxiety.

He plunged into the silent streets.

Still he followed one direction.

He took the shortest route towards the Seine, reached the Quai des Ormes, went along the quai, passed the Grève, and stopped, at a little distance from the Police Station of the Place du Châtelet, at the corner of the Pont Notre Dame. The Seine there forms between the Pont Notre Dame and the Pont au Change in one direction, and in the other between the Quai de la Mégisserie and the Quai aux Fleurs, a sort of square lake crossed by a rapid.

This point of the Seine is dreaded by mariners. Nothing is more dangerous than this rapid, narrowed at that period and intensified by the pilings of the mill on the bridge, since removed. The two bridges, so near each other, increase the danger, the water hurrying fearfully under the arches. It rolls on with broad, terrible folds; it gathers and heaps up; the flood strains at the supports of the bridge as if to tear them out with huge liquid ropes. Men who fall in there, one never sees again; the best swimmers are drowned.

Javert leaned both elbows on the parapet, with his chin in his hands, and while his fingers were clenched mechanically in the thickest of his whiskers, he reflected.

There had been a new thing, a revolution, a catastrophe in the depths of his being; and there was matter for self-examination.

Javert was suffering frightfully.

For some hours Javert had ceased to be natural. He was troubled; this brain, so limpid in its blindness, had lost its transparency; there was a cloud in this crystal. Javert felt that duty was growing weaker in his conscience, and he could not hide it from himself. When he had so unexpectedly met Jean Valjean upon the quai of the Seine, there had been in him something of the wolf, which seizes his prey again, and of the dog, which again finds his master.

He saw before him two roads, both equally straight; but he saw two;

and that terrified him—him, who had never in his life known but one straight line. And, bitter anguish, these two roads were contradictory. One of these two straight lines excluded the other. Which of the two was the true one?

His condition was inexpressible.

To owe life to a malefactor, to accept that debt and to pay it, to be, in spite of himself, on a level with a fugitive from justice, and to pay him for one service with another service; to allow him to say: "Go away," and to say to him in turn: "Be free;" to sacrifice duty, that general obligation, to personal motives, and to feel in these personal motives something general also, and perhaps superior; to betray society in order to be true to his own conscience; that all these absurdities should be realised and that they should be accumulated upon himself, this it was by which he was prostrated.

One thing had astonished him, that Jean Valjean had spared him, and one thing had petrified him, that he, Javert, had spared Jean Valjean.

Where was he? He sought himself and found himself no longer.

What should he do now? Surrender Jean Valjean to justice, that was wrong; leave Jean Valjean free, that was wrong. In the first case, the man of authority would fall lower than the man of the galley; in the second, a convict rose higher than the law and set his foot upon it. In both cases, dishonour to him, Javert. In every course which was open to him, there was a fall. Destiny has certain extremities that drop off like cliffs upon the impossible, and beyond which life is no more than an abyss. Javert was at one of these extremities.

Jean Valjean confounded him. All the axioms which had been the supports of his whole life crumbled away before this man. Jean Valjean's generosity towards him, Javert, overwhelmed him. Other acts, which he remembered and which he had hitherto treated as lies and follies, returned to him now as realities. M. Madeleine reappeared behind Jean Valjean, and the two figures overlaid each other so as to make but one, which was venerable. Javert felt that something horrible was penetrating his soul, admiration for a convict. Respect for a galley-slave, can that be possible? He shuddered at it, yet could not shake it off. It was useless to struggle, he was reduced to confess before his own inner tribunal the sublimity of this wretch. That was hateful.

A beneficent malefactor, a compassionate convict, kind, helpful, clement, returning good for evil, returning pardon for hatred, loving pity rather than vengeance, preferring to destroy himself rather than to destroy his enemy, saving him who had stricken him, kneeling upon the height of virtue, nearer the angels than men. Javert was compelled to acknowledge that this monster existed.

This could not last.

Certainly, and we repeat it, he had not given himself up without resistance to this monster, this infamous angel, this hideous hero, at whom he was almost as indignant as he was astounded. Twenty times, while he was in that carriage face to face with Jean Valjean, the legal tiger had roared within him. Twenty times he had been tempted to throw himself upon Jean

Valjean, to seize him and to devour him, that is to say, to arrest him. What more simple, indeed? To cry at the first post in front of which they passed: "Here is a fugitive from justice!" to call the gendarmes and say to them: "This man is yours!" then to go away, to leave this condemned man there, to ignore the rest, and to have nothing more to do with it.

Since he had been of the age of a man, and an official, he had put almost all his religion in the police. Being, and we employ the words here without the slightest irony and in their most serious meaning, being, we have said, a spy as men are priests. He had a superior, M. Gisquet; he had scarcely thought, until today, of that other superior, God.

This new chief, God, he felt unawares, and was perplexed thereat.

He had lost his bearings in this unexpected presence; he did not know what to do with this superior; he who was not ignorant that the subordinate is bound always to yield, that he ought neither to disobey, nor to blame, nor to argue, and that, in presence of a superior who astonishes him too much, the inferior has no resource but resignation.

But how manage to send in his resignation to God?

He had lived up to this moment by that blind faith which a dark probity engenders. This faith was leaving him, this probity was failing him. All that he had believed was dissipated. Truths which he had no wish for inexorably besieged him. He must henceforth be another man. He suffered the strange pangs of a conscience suddenly operated upon for the cataract. He saw what he revolted at seeing. He felt that he was emptied, useless, broken off from his past life, destitute, dissolved. Authority was dead in him. He had no further reason for existence.

The darkness was complete. It was the sepulchral moment which follows midnight. A ceiling of clouds concealed the stars. The sky was only an ominous depth. The houses in the city no longer showed a single light; nobody was passing; all that he could see of the streets and the quai was deserted; Notre Dame and the towers of the Palais de Justice seemed like features of the night. A lamp reddened the curb of the quai. The silhouettes of the bridges were distorted in the mist, one behind the other. The rains had swelled the river.

The place where Javert was leaning was, it will be remembered, situated exactly over the rapids of the Seine, perpendicularly over that formidable whirlpool which knots and unknots itself like an endless screw.

Javert bent his head and looked. All was black. He could distinguish nothing. He heard a frothing sound; but he did not see the river. At intervals, in that giddy depth, a gleam appeared in dim serpentine contortions, the water having this power, in the most complete night, of taking light, nobody knows whence, and changing it into an adder. The gleam vanished, and all became again indistinct. Immensity seemed open there. What was beneath was not water, it was chasm. The wall of the quai, abrupt, confused, mingled with vapour, suddenly lost to sight, seemed like an escarpment of the infinite.

He saw nothing, but he perceived the hostile chill of the water, and the insipid odour of the moist stones. A fierce breath rose from that abyss. The swollen river guessed at rather than perceived, the tragical whispering of the flood, the dismal vastness of the arches of the bridge, the imaginable fall into that gloomy void, all that shadow was full of horror.

Javert remained for some minutes motionless, gazing into that opening of darkness; he contemplated the invisible with a fixedness which resembled attention. The water gurgled. Suddenly he took off his hat and laid it on the edge of the quai. A moment afterwards, a tall and black form, which from the distance some belated passer-by might have taken for a phantom, appeared standing on the parapet, bent towards the Seine, then sprang up, and fell straight into the darkness; there was a dull splash; and the shadow alone was in the secret of the convulsions of that dark form which had disappeared under the water.

BOOK FIVE
THE GRANDSON AND
THE GRANDFATHER

1 (2)

MARIUS, ESCAPING FROM CIVIL WAR, PREPARES FOR DOMESTIC WAR

MARIUS was for a long time neither dead nor alive. He had for several weeks a fever accompanied with delirium, and serious cerebral symptoms resulting rather from the concussion produced by the wounds in the head than from the wounds themselves.

He repeated the name of Cosette during entire nights in the dismal loquacity of fever and with the gloomy obstinacy of agony. The size of certain gashes was a serious danger, the suppuration of large wounds always being liable to reabsorption, and consequently to kill the patient, under certain atmospheric influences; at every change in the weather, at the slightest storm, the physician was anxious. "Above all, let the wounded man have no excitement," he repeated. The dressings were complicated and difficult, the fastening of cloths and bandages with adhesive tape not being invented at that period. Nicolette used for lint a sheet "as big as a ceiling," said she. It was not without difficulty that the chlorinated salves and the tincture of silver nitrate brought the gangrene to an end. As long as there was danger, M. Gillenormand, in despair at the bedside of his grandson was, like Marius, neither dead nor alive.

Every day, and sometimes twice a day, a very well-dressed gentleman with white hair, such was the description given by the porter, came to inquire after the wounded man, and left a large package of lint for the dressings.

At last, on the 7th of September, four months, to a day, after the sorrowful night when they had brought him home dying to his grandfather, the physician declared him out of danger. Convalescence began. Marius was, however, obliged still to remain for more than two months stretched on a long chair, on account of the accidents resulting from the fracture of the shoulder-blade. There is always a last wound like this which will not close, and which prolongs the dressings, to the great disgust of the patient.

However, this long sickness and this long convalescence saved him from pursuit. In France, there is no anger, even governmental, which six months does not extinguish. Émeutes, in the present state of society, are so much the fault of everybody that they are followed by a certain necessity of closing the eyes.

Let us add that the infamous Gisquet order, which enjoined physicians to inform against the wounded, having outraged public opinion, and not only public opinion, but the king first of all, the wounded were shielded and protected by this indignation; and, with the exception of those who had been taken prisoners in actual combat, the courts-martial dared not disturb any. Marius was therefore left in peace.

M. Gillenormand passed first through every anguish, and then every ecstasy. They had great difficulty in preventing him from passing every night with the wounded man; he had his large armchair brought to the side of Marius' bed; he insisted that his daughter should take the finest linen in the house for compresses and bandages.

On the day the physician announced to him that Marius was out of danger, the goodman was in delirium.

Then he knelt upon a chair, and Basque, who watched him through the half-open door, was certain that he was praying.

Hitherto, he had hardly believed in God.

As for Marius, while he let them dress his wounds and care for him, he had one fixed idea: Cosette.

Since the fever and the delirium had left him, he had not uttered that name, and they might have supposed that he no longer thought of it. He held his peace, precisely because his soul was in it.

He did not know what had become of Cosette; the whole affair of the Rue de la Chanvrerie was like a cloud in his memory; shadows, almost indistinct, were floating in his mind, Eponine, Gavroche, Mabeuf, the Thénardiers, all his friends mingled drearily with the smoke of the barricade; the strange passage of M. Fauchelevent in that bloody drama produced upon him the effect of an enigma in a tempest; he understood nothing in regard to his own life; he neither knew how, nor by whom, he had been saved, and nobody about him knew; all that they could tell him was that he had been brought to the Rue des Filles du Calvaire in a fiacre by night; past, present, future, all was now to him but the mist of a vague idea; but there was within this mist an immovable point, one clear and precise feature, something which was granite, a resolution, a will: to find Cosette again. To him the idea of life was not distinct from the idea of Cosette; he had decreed in his heart that he would not accept the one without the other, and he was unalterably determined to demand from anybody, no matter whom, who should wish to compel him to live, from his grandfather, from Fate, from Hell, the restitution of his vanished Eden.

He did not hide the obstacles from himself.

Let us emphasise one point here: he was not won over, and was little softened by all the solicitude and all the tenderness of his grandfather. In the first place, he was not in the secret of it all; then, in his sick man's reveries, still feverish perhaps, he distrusted this gentleness as a new and strange thing, the object of which was to subdue him. He remained cold. The grandfather expended his poor old smile for nothing. Marius said to himself it was well so long as he, Marius, did not speak and offered no resistance; but that, when the question of Cosette was raised, he would find another face, and his grandfather's real attitude would be unmasked. Then it would be harsh recrudescence of family questions, every sarcasm and every objection at once: Fauchelevent, Coupelevent, fortune, poverty, misery, the millstone around the neck, the future. Violent opposition; conclusion, refusal. Marius was bracing himself in advance.

And then, in proportion as he took new hold of life, his former griefs reappeared, the old ulcers of his memory reopened, he thought once more of the past. Colonel Pontmercy appeared again between M. Gillenormand and him, Marius; he said to himself that there was no real goodness to be hoped for from him who had been so unjust and so hard to his father. And with health, there returned to him a sort of harshness towards his grandfather. The old man suffered from it, but with gentleness.

M. Gillenormand, without manifesting it in any way, noticed that Marius, since he had been brought home and restored to consciousness, had not once said to him "father." He did not say monsieur, it is true; but he found means to say neither the one nor the other, by a certain manner of turning his sentences.

A crisis was evidently approaching.

As it almost always happens in similar cases, Marius, in order to try himself, skirmished before offering battle. This is called feeling the ground. One morning it happened that M. Gillenormand, over a newspaper which had fallen into his hands, spoke lightly of the Convention and discharged a royalist epiphonema upon Danton, Saint Just, and Robespierre. "The men of '93 were giants," said Marius, sternly. The old man was silent, and did not whisper for the rest of the day.

Marius, who had always present to his mind the inflexible grandfather of his early years, saw in this silence an intense concentration of anger, augured from it a sharp conflict, and increased his preparations for combat in the inner recesses of his thought.

He determined that in case of refusal he would tear off his bandages, dislocate his shoulder, lay bare and open his remaining wounds, and refuse all nourishment. His wounds were his ammunition. To have Cosette or to die.

He waited for the favourable moment with the crafty patience of the sick.

That moment came.

2 (3)

MARIUS ATTACKS

ONE DAY M. Gillenormand, while his daughter was putting in order the vials and the cups upon the marble top of the bureau, bent over Marius and said to him in his most tender tone:

"Do you see, my darling Marius, in your place I would eat meat now rather than fish. A fried sole is excellent to begin a convalescence, but, to put the sick man on his legs, it takes a good cutlet."

Marius, nearly all whose strength had returned, gathered it together, sat up in bed, rested his clenched hands on the sheets, looked his grandfather in the face, assumed a terrible air, and said:

"This leads me to say something to you."

"What is it?"

"It is that I wish to marry."

"Foreseen," said the grandfather. And he burst out laughing.

"How foreseen?"

"Yes, foreseen. You shall have her, your lassie."

Marius, astounded, and overwhelmed by the dazzling burst of happiness, trembled in every limb.

M. Gillenormand continued:

"Yes, you shall have her, your handsome, pretty little girl. She comes every day in the shape of an old gentleman to inquire after you. Since you were wounded, she has passed her time in weeping and making lint. I have made inquiry. She lives in the Rue de l'Homme Armé, Number Seven. Ah, we are ready! Ah! you want her! Well, you shall have her. That catches you. You had arranged your little plot; you said to yourself: I am going to make it known bluntly to that grandfather, to that mummy of the Regency and of the Directory, to that old beau, to that Dorante become a Géronte; he has had his levities too, himself, and his amours, and his grisettes, and his Cosettes; he has had his skirts, he has had his wings, he has eaten his spring bread; he must remember it well. We shall see. Battle. Ah! you take the bull by the horns. That is good. I propose a cutlet, and you answer: 'A propos, I wish to marry.' That is what I call a transition. Ah! you had reckoned upon some bickering. You didn't know that I was an old coward. What do you say to that? You are spited. To find your grandfather still more stupid than yourself, you didn't expect that, you lose the argument which you were to have made to me, monsieur advocate; it is provoking. Well, it is all the same, rage. I do what you wish, that shuts you up, idiot. Listen. I have made inquiries, I am sly too; she is charming, she is modest, the lancer is not true, she has made heaps of lint, she is a jewel, she worships you; if you had died, there would have been three of us; her bier would have accompanied mine. I had a strong notion, as soon as you were better, to plunk her right at your bedside, but it is only in romances that they introduce young girls unceremoniously to the side of the couch of the pretty wounded men who interest them. That does not do. What would your aunt have said? You have been quite naked three-quarters of the time, my goodman. Ask Nicolette, who has not left you a minute, if it was possible for a woman to be here. And then what would the doctor have said? That doesn't cure a fever, a pretty girl. Finally, it is all right; don't let us talk any more about it, it is said, it is done, it is fixed; take her. Such is my ferocity. Do you see, I saw that you did not love me; I said: What is there that I can do, then, to make this animal love me? I said: Hold on! I have my little Cosette under my hand; I will give her to him, he must surely love a little then, or let him tell why. Ah! you thought that the old fellow was going to storm, to make a gruff voice, to cry No, and to lift his cane upon all this dawn. Not at all. Cosette, so be it; Love, so be it; I ask nothing better. Monsieur, take the trouble to marry. Be happy, my dear child."

This said, the old man burst into sobs.

And he took Marius' head, and he hugged it in both arms against his old breast, and they both began to weep. That is one of the forms of supreme happiness.

"Father!" exclaimed Marius.

"Ah! you love me then!" said the old man.

There was an ineffable moment. They choked and could not speak.

At last the old man stammered:

"Come! the ice is broken. He has called me 'Father.'"

Marius released his head from his grandfather's arms, and said softly:

"But, father, now that I am well, it seems to me that I could see her."

"Foreseen again, you shall see her to-morrow."

"Father!"

"What?"

"Why not to-day?"

"Well, to-day. Here goes for to-day. You have called me 'Father,' three times, it is well worth that. I will see to it. She shall be brought to you. Foreseen, I tell you. This has already been put into verse."

3 (4)

MADEMOISELLE GILLENORMAND
AT LAST THINKS IT NOT IMPROPER
THAT MONSIEUR FAUCHELEVENT
SHOULD COME IN WITH SOMETHING
UNDER HIS ARM

COSETTE and Marius saw each other again.

What the interview was, we will not attempt to tell. There are things which we should not undertake to paint; the sun is of the number.

The whole family, including Basque and Nicolette, were assembled in Marius' room when Cosette entered.

She appeared on the threshold; it seemed as if she were in a cloud.

Just at that instant the grandfather was about to blow his nose; he stopped short, holding his nose in his handkerchief, and looking at Cosette above it:

"Adorable!" he exclaimed.

Then he blew his nose with a loud noise.

Cosette was intoxicated, enraptured, startled, in Heaven. She was as frightened as one can be by happiness. She stammered, quite pale, quite red, wishing to throw herself into Marius' arms, and not daring to. Ashamed to show her love before all those people. We are pitiless towards happy lovers; we stay there when they have the strongest desire to be alone. They, however, have no need at all of society.

With Cosette and behind her had entered a man with white hair, grave, smiling nevertheless, but with a vague and poignant smile. This was "Monsieur Fauchelevent;" this was Jean Valjean.

He was *very well dressed,* as the porter had said, in a new black suit, with a white cravat.

The porter was a thousand miles from recognising in this correct bourgeois, in this probable notary, the frightful corpse-bearer who had landed at his door on the night of the 7th of June, ragged, muddy, hideous, haggard, his face masked by blood and dirt, supporting the fainting Marius in his arms; still his porter's scent was awakened. When M. Fauchelevent had arrived with Cosette, the porter could not help confiding this remark to his wife: "I don't know why I always imagine that I have seen that face somewhere."

Monsieur Fauchelevent, in Marius' room, stayed near the door, as if apart. He had under his arm a package similar in appearance to an octavo volume, wrapped in paper. The paper of the envelope was greenish, and seemed mouldy.

"Does this gentleman always have books under his arm like that?" asked Mademoiselle Gillenormand, who did not like books, in a low voice of Nicolette.

"Well," answered M. Gillenormand, who had heard her, in the same tone, "he is a scholar. What then? is it his fault? Monsieur Boulard, whom I knew, never went out without a book, he neither, and always had an old volume against his heart, like that."

And bowing, he said, in a loud voice:

"Monsieur Tranchelevent——"

Father Gillenormand did not do this on purpose, but inattention to proper names was an aristocratic way he had.

"Monsieur Tranchelevent, I have the honour of asking of you for my grandson, Monsieur the Baron Marius Pontmercy, the hand of mademoiselle."

Monsieur Tranchelevent bowed.

"It is done," said the grandfather.

And, turning towards Marius and Cosette, with arms extended in blessing, he cried:

"Permission to adore each other."

They did not make him say it twice. It was all the same! The cooing began. They talked low, Marius leaning on his long chair, Cosette standing near him. "Oh, my God!" murmured Cosette, "I see you again! It is you! it is you! To have gone to fight like that! But why? It is horrible. For four months I have been dead. Oh, how naughty it is to have been in that battle!

What had I done to you? I pardon you, but you won't do it again. Just now, when they came to tell us to come, I thought again I should die, but it was of joy. I was so sad! I did not take time to dress myself; I must look like a fright. What will your relatives say of me, to see me with a collar all wrinkled? But speak now! You let me do all the talking. We are still in the Rue de l'Homme Armé. Your shoulder, that was terrible. They told me they could put their fist into it. And then they have cut your flesh with scissors. That is frightful. I have cried; I have no eyes left. It is strange that anybody can suffer like that. Your grandfather has a very kind appearance. Don't disturb yourself; don't rest on your elbow; take care, you will hurt yourself. Oh, how happy I am! So our trouble is all over! I am very silly. I wanted to say something to you that I have forgotten completely. Do you love me still? We live in the Rue de l'Homme Armé. There is no garden. I have been making lint all the time. Here, monsieur, look, it is your fault, my fingers are callous."

"Angel!" said Marius.

Angel is the only word in the language which cannot be worn out. No other word would resist the pitiless use which lovers make of it.

Then, as there were spectators, they stopped, and did not say another word, contenting themselves with touching each other's hands very gently.

M. Gillenormand turned towards all those who were in the room and cried:

"Why don't you talk loud, the rest of you? Make a noise, behind the scenes. Come, a little uproar, the devil! so that these children can chatter at their ease."

And, approaching Marius and Cosette, he said to them very low:

"Say *tu*. Don't let us bother you."

Aunt Gillenormand witnessed with amazement this irruption of light into her aged interior. This amazement was not at all aggressive; it was not the least in the world the scandalised and envious look of an owl upon two ringdoves; it was the dull eye of a poor innocent girl of fifty-seven; it was incomplete life beholding that triumph, love.

"Mademoiselle Gillenormand the elder," said her father to her, "I told you plainly that this would happen."

He remained silent a moment and added:

"Behold the happiness of others."

Then he turned towards Cosette:

"How pretty she is! how pretty she is! She is a Greuze.* You are going to have her all alone to yourself then, rascal! Ah! my rogue, you have a narrow escape from me, you are lucky, if I were not fifteen years too old, we would cross swords for who should have her.

"She is exquisite, this darling. She is a masterpiece, this Cosette. She is a very little girl and a very great lady. She will be only a baroness, that is stoop-

---

*Jean-Baptiste Greuze (1725–1805) was a prominent painter of maudlin, moralizing subjects, and cloyingly cute children and girls.

ing; she was born a marchioness. Hasn't she lashes for you? My children, fix it well in your noddles that you are in the right of it. Love one another. Be foolish about it. Love is the foolishness of men, and the wisdom of God. Adore each other. Only," added he, suddenly darkening, "what a misfortune! This is what I am thinking of! More than half of what I have is in annuity; as long as I live, it's all well enough, but after my death, twenty years from now, ah! my poor children, you will not have a sou. Your beautiful white hands, Madame the Baroness, will do the devil the honour to pull him by the tail."*

"Mademoiselle Euphrasie Fauchelevent has six hundred thousand francs."

It was Jean Valjean's voice.

He had not yet uttered a word, nobody seemed even to remember that he was there, and he stood erect and motionless behind all these happy people.

"How is Mademoiselle Euphrasie in question?" asked the grandfather, startled.

"That is me," answered Cosette.

"Six hundred thousand francs!" resumed M. Gillenormand.

"Less fourteen or fifteen thousand francs, perhaps," said Jean Valjean.

And he laid on the table the package which Aunt Gillenormand had taken for a book.

Jean Valjean opened the package himself; it was a bundle of banknotes. They ran through them, and they counted them. There were five hundred bills of a thousand francs, and a hundred and sixty-eight of five hundred. In all, five hundred and eighty-four thousand francs.

"That is a good book," said M. Gillenormand.

"Five hundred and eighty-four thousand francs!" murmured the aunt.

"This arranges things very well, does it not, Mademoiselle Gillenormand the elder?" resumed the grandfather. "This devil of a Marius, he has found you a grisette millionaire on the tree of dreams! Then trust in the love-making of young folks nowadays! Students find studentesses with six hundred thousand francs. Chérubin works better than Rothschild."

"Five hundred and eighty-four thousand francs!" repeated Mademoiselle Gillenormand in an undertone. "Five hundred and eighty-four! you might call it six hundred thousand, indeed!"

As for Marius and Cosette, they were looking at each other during this time; they paid little attention to this incident.

---

*"To pull the Devil by the tail" is a French idiom for "to have trouble making ends meet."

4 (5)

DEPOSIT YOUR MONEY RATHER IN SOME FOREST THAN WITH SOME LAWYER*

THE READER has doubtless understood, without it being necessary to explain at length, that Jean Valjean, after the Champmathieu affair, had been able, thanks to his first escape for a few days to come to Paris, and to withdraw the sum made by him, under the name of Monsieur Madeleine, at M—— sur M——, from Laffitte's in time; and that, in the fear of being recaptured, which happened to him, in fact, a short time after, he had concealed and buried that sum in the forest of Montfermeil, in the place called the Blaru grounds. The sum, six hundred and thirty thousand francs, all in bank-notes, was of small bulk, and was contained in a box; but to preserve the box from moisture he had placed it in an oaken chest, full of chestnut shavings. In the same chest, he had put his other treasure, the bishop's candlesticks. It will be remembered that he carried away these candlesticks when he escaped from M—— sur M——. The man perceived one evening, for the first time, by Boulatruelle, was Jean Valjean.—— Afterwards, whenever Jean Valjean was in need of money, he went to the Blaru glade for it. Hence the absences of which we have spoken. He had a pickaxe somewhere in the bushes, in a hiding-place known only to himself. When he saw Marius convalescent, feeling that the hour was approaching when this money might be useful, he had gone after it; and it was he again whom Boulatruelle saw in the wood, but this time in the morning, and not at night. Boulatruelle inherited the pickaxe.

The real sum was five hundred and eighty-four thousand five hundred francs. Jean Valjean took out five hundred francs for himself. "We will see afterwards," thought he.

The difference between this sum and the six hundred and thirty thousand francs withdrawn from Laffitte's represented the expenses of ten years, from 1823 to 1833. The five years spent in the convent had cost only five thousand francs.

Jean Valjean put the two silver candlesticks upon the mantel, where they shone, to Toussaint's great admiration.

Moreover, Jean Valjean knew that he was delivered from Javert. It had been mentioned in his presence, and he had verified the fact in the *Moniteur,* which published it, that an inspector of police, named Javert, had been found drowned under a washerwoman's boat between the Pont au Change

---

*French lawyers often served as investment managers for individuals and were notorious for absconding with their clients' funds. See Flaubert's "Un coeur simple."

and Pont Neuf, and that a paper left by this man, otherwise irreproachable and highly esteemed by his chiefs, led to a belief that he had committed suicide during a fit of mental aberration. "In fact," thought Jean Valjean, "since having me in his power, he let me go, he must already have been crazy."

5 (6)

THE TWO OLD MEN DO EVERYTHING, EACH IN HIS OWN WAY, THAT COSETTE MAY BE HAPPY

ALL the preparations were made for the marriage. The physician being consulted said that it might take place in February. This was in December. Some ravishing weeks of perfect happiness rolled away.

The least happy, was not the grandfather. He would remain for a quarter of an hour at a time gazing at Cosette.

"The wonderful pretty girl!" he exclaimed. "And her manners are so sweet and so good. It is of no use to say my love my heart, she is the most charming girl that I have ever seen in my life. Besides, she will have virtues for you sweet as violets. She is a grace, indeed! You can but live nobly with such a creature. Marius, my boy, you are a baron, you are rich, don't pettifog, I beg of you."

Cosette and Marius had passed abruptly from the grave to paradise. There had been but little caution in the transition, and they would have been stunned if they had not been dazzled.

"Do you understand anything about it?" said Marius to Cosette.

"No," answered Cosette, "but it seems to me that the good God is caring for us."

Jean Valjean did all, smoothed all, conciliated all, made all easy. He hastened towards Cosette's happiness with as much eagerness, and apparently as much joy, as Cosette herself.

As he had been a mayor, he knew how to solve a delicate problem, in the secret of which he was alone: Cosette's civil state. To bluntly give her origin, who knows? that might prevent the marriage. He drew Cosette out of all difficulty. He arranged a family of dead people for her, a sure means of incurring no objection. Cosette was what remained of an extinct family; Cosette was not his daughter, but the daughter of another Fauchelevent. Two brothers Fauchelevent had been gardeners at the convent of the Petit Picpus. They went to this convent, the best recommendations and the most respectable testimonials abounded; the good nuns, little apt and little inclined to fathom questions of paternity, and understanding no malice, had never known very exactly of which of the two Fauchelevents little Cosette was the daughter. They said what was wanted of them, and said it with zeal. A notary's act was drawn up. Cosette became before the law Mademoiselle Euphrasie Fauchelevent. She was declared an orphan. Jean Valjean arranged matters in such a way as to be designated, under the name of Fauchelevent, as Cosette's guardian, with M. Gillenormand as overseeing guardian.

As for the five hundred and eighty-four thousand francs, that was a legacy left to Cosette by a dead person who desired to remain unknown. The original legacy had been five hundred and ninety-four thousand francs; but ten thousand francs had been expended for Mademoiselle Euphrasie's education, of which five thousand francs were paid to the convent itself. This legacy, deposited in the hands of a third party, was to be given up to Cosette at her majority or at the time of her marriage. Altogether this was very acceptable, as we see, especially with a basis of more than half a million. There were indeed a few singularities here and there, but nobody saw them; one of those interested had his eyes bandaged by love, the other by the six hundred thousand francs.

Cosette learned that she was not the daughter of that old man whom she had so long called father. He was only a relative; another Fauchelevent was her real father. At any other time, this would have broken her heart. But at this ineffable hour, it was only a little shadow, a darkening, and she had so much joy that this cloud was of short duration. She had Marius. The young man came, the goodman faded away, such is life.

And then, Cosette had been accustomed for long years to see enigmas about her: everybody who has had a mysterious childhood is always ready for certain renunciations.

She continued, however, to say "Father" to Jean Valjean.

Cosette, in raptures, was enthusiastic about Grandfather Gillenormand. It is true that he loaded her with madrigals and with presents. While Jean Valjean was building a normal condition in society for Cosette, and a possession of an unimpeachable state, M. Gillenormand was watching over the wedding basket. Nothing amused him so much as being magnificent. He had given Cosette a dress of Binche guipure which had come down to him from his own grandmother. "These fashions have come round again," said he, "old things are the rage, and the young women of my old age dress like the old women of my childhood."

It was arranged that the couple should live with the grandfather. M. Gillenormand absolutely insisted upon giving them his room, the finest in the house. *"It will rejuvenate me,"* he declared. *"It is an old project. I always had the idea of having a wedding party in my room."** He filled this room with a profusion of gay old furniture. He hung the walls and the ceiling with

---

*The French *faire la noce* is a pun also meaning "have an orgy." Thénardier, disguised as a Spaniard in the Mardi Gras procession, makes the same pun when he sees Cosette and Marius' wedding carriage pass: *"We're the *real* 'noce.' "*

an extraordinary stuff which he had in a bolt, and which he believed to be from Utrecht, a satin background with golden immortelles, and velvet auriculas. "With this stuff," said he, "the Duchess d'Anville's bed was draped at La Roche Guyon." He put a little Saxony figure on the mantel, holding a muff over her naked belly.

M. Gillenormand's library became the attorney's office which Marius required; an office, it will be remembered, being rendered necessary by the rules of the order.

6 (7)

THE EFFECTS OF DREAM MINGLED WITH HAPPINESS

THE LOVERS saw each other every day. Cosette came with M. Fauchelevent. "It is reversing the order of things," said Mademoiselle Gillenormand, "that the intended should come to the house to be courted like this." But Marius' convalescence had led to the habit; and the armchairs in the Rue des Filles du Calvaire, better for long talks than the straw chairs of the Rue de l'Homme Armé, had rooted it. Marius and M. Fauchelevent saw one another, but did not speak to each other. That seemed to be understood. Every girl needs a chaperon. Cosette could not have come without M. Fauchelevent. To Marius, M. Fauchelevent was the condition of Cosette. He accepted it. In bringing upon the carpet, vaguely and generally, matters of policy, from the point of view of the general amelioration of the lot of all, they succeeded in saying a little more than yes and no to each other. Once, on the subject of education, which Marius wished gratuitous and obligatory, multiplied under all forms, lavished upon all like the air and the sunshine, in one word, respirable by the entire people, they fell into unison and almost into a conversation. Marius remarked on this occasion that M. Fauchelevent talked well, and even with a certain elevation of language. There was, however, something wanting. M. Fauchelevent had something less than a man of the world, and something more.

Marius, inwardly and in the depth of his thought, surrounded this M. Fauchelevent, who was to him simply benevolent and cold, with all sorts of silent questions. There came to him at intervals doubts about his own recollections. In his memory there was a hole, a black place, an abyss scooped out by four months of agony. Many things were lost in it. He was led to ask himself if it were really true that he had seen M. Fauchelevent, such a man, so serious and so calm, in the barricade.

And himself, was he really the same man? He, the poor, he was rich; he, the abandoned, he had a family; he, the despairing, he was marrying Cosette. It seemed to him that he had passed through a tomb, and that he had gone in black, and that he had come out white. And in this tomb, the others had remained. At certain moments, all these beings of the past, returned and present, formed a circle about him and rendered him gloomy; then he thought of Cosette, and again became serene; but it required nothing less than this felicity to efface this catastrophe.

M. Fauchelevent almost had a place among these vanished beings. Marius hesitated to believe that the Fauchelevent of the barricade was the same as this Fauchelevent in flesh and blood, so gravely seated near Cosette. The first was probably one of those nightmares coming and going with his hours of delirium. Moreover, their two natures showing a steep front to each other, no question was possible from Marius to M. Fauchelevent. The idea of it did not even occur to him. We have already indicated this characteristic circumstance.

Two men who have a common secret, and who, by a sort of tacit agreement, do not exchange a word upon the subject, such a thing is less rare than one would think.

Once only, Marius made an attempt. He brought the Rue de la Chanvrerie into the conversation, and, turning towards M. Fauchelevent, he said to him:

"You are well acquainted with that street?"

"What street?"

"The Rue de la Chanvrerie."

"I have no idea of the name of that street," answered M. Fauchelevent in the most natural tone in the world.

The answer, which bore upon the name of the street, and not upon the street itself, appeared to Marius more conclusive than it was.

"Decidedly," thought he, "I have been dreaming. I have had a hallucination. It was somebody who resembled him. M. Fauchelevent was not there."

7 (8)

TWO MEN IMPOSSIBLE TO FIND

THE ENCHANTMENT, great as it was, did not efface other preoccupations from Marius' mind.

During the preparations for the marriage, and while waiting for the time fixed upon, he had some difficult and careful retrospective researches made.

He owed gratitude on several sides, he owed some on his father's account, he owed some on his own.

There was Thénardier; there was the unknown man who had brought him, Marius, to M. Gillenormand's.

Marius persisted in trying to find these two men, not intending to marry, to be happy, and to forget them, and fearing lest these debts of duty unpaid might cast a shadow over his life, so luminous henceforth. It was impossible for him to leave all these arrears unsettled behind him; and he wished, before entering joyously into the future, to have a quittance from the past.

That Thénardier was a scoundrel, took away nothing from this fact that he had saved Colonel Pontmercy. Thénardier was a bandit to everybody except Marius.

And Marius, ignorant of the real scene of the battle-field of Waterloo, did not know this peculiarity, that his father was, with reference to Thénardier, in this singular situation, that he owed his life to him without owing him any thanks.

None of the various agents whom Marius employed succeeded in finding Thénardier's track. Effacement seemed complete on that side. The Thénardiess had died in prison pending the examination on the charge. Thénardier and his daughter Azelma, the two who alone remained of that woeful group, had plunged back into the shadow. The gulf of the social Unknown had silently closed over these beings. There could no longer even be seen on the surface that quivering, that trembling, those dark concentric circles which announce that something has fallen there, and that we might drag the bottom.

As for the other, as for the unknown man who had saved Marius, the researches at first had some result, then stopped short. They succeeded in finding the fiacre which had brought Marius to the Rue des Filles du Calvaire on the evening of the 6th of June. The driver declared that on the 6th of June, by order of a police officer, he had been "stationed," from three o'clock in the afternoon until night, on the quai of the Champs-Elysées, above the outlet of the Grand Sewer; that, about nine o'clock in the evening, the grating of the sewer, which overlooks the river beach, was opened; that a man came out, carrying another man on his shoulders, who seemed to be dead; that the officer, who was watching at that point, arrested the living man, and seized the dead man; that, on the order of the officer, he, the driver, received "all those people" into the fiacre; that they went first to the Rue des Filles du Calvaire; that they left the dead man there; that the dead man was Monsieur Marius, and that he, the driver, recognised him plainly, although he was alive "this time"; that they then got into his carriage again; that he whipped up his horses; that, within a few steps of the door of the Archives, he had been called to stop; that there, in the street, he had been paid and left, and that the officer took away the other man; that he knew nothing more, that the night was very dark.

Marius, we have said, recollected nothing. He merely remembered having been seized from behind by a vigorous hand at the moment he fell backwards into the barricades, then all became a blank to him. He had recovered consciousness only at M. Gillenormand's.

He was lost in conjectures.

He could not doubt his own identity. How did it come about, however, that, falling in the Rue de la Chanvrerie, he had been picked up by the police officer on the banks of the Seine, near the Pont des Invalides? Somebody had carried him from the neighborhood of the markets to the Champs-Elysées. And how? By the sewer. Unparalleled devotion!

Somebody? who?

It was this man whom Marius sought.

Of this man, who was his saviour, nothing; no trace; not the least indication.

Marius, although compelled to great reserve in this respect, pushed his researches as far as the prefecture of police. There, no more than elsewhere, did the information obtained lead to any eclaircissement. The prefecture knew less than the driver of the fiacre. They had no knowledge of any arrest made on the 6th of June at the grating of the Grand Sewer; they had received no officer's report upon that fact, which, at the prefecture, was regarded as a fable. They attributed the invention of this fable to the driver. A driver who wants drink-money is capable of anything, even of imagination. The thing was certain, for all that, and Marius could not doubt it, unless by doubting his own identity, as we have just said.

Everything, in this strange enigma, was inexplicable.

This man, this mysterious man, whom the driver had seen come out of the grating of the Grand Sewer bearing Marius senseless upon his back, and whom the police officer on the watch had arrested in the very act of saving an insurgent, what had become of him? what had become of the officer himself? Why had this officer kept silence? had the man succeeded in escaping? had he bribed the officer? Why did this man give no sign of life to Marius, who owed everything to him? His disinterestedness was not less wonderful than his devotion. Why did not this man reappear? Perhaps he was above recompense, but nobody is above gratitude. Was he dead? what kind of a man was this? how did he look? Nobody could tell. The driver answered: "The night was very dark." Basque and Nicolette, in their amazement, had only looked at their young master covered with blood. The porter, whose candle had lighted the tragic arrival of Marius, alone had noticed the man in question, and this is the description which he gave of him: "This man was horrible."

In the hope of deriving aid in his researches from them, Marius had had preserved the bloody clothes which he wore when he was brought back to his grandfather's. On examining the coat, it was noticed that one tail was oddly torn. A piece was missing.

One evening, Marius spoke, before Cosette and Jean Valjean, of all this singular adventure, of the numberless inquiries which he had made, and of the uselessness of his efforts. The cold countenance of "Monsieur Fauchelevent" made him impatient. He exclaimed with a vivacity which had almost the vibration of anger:

"Yes, that man, whoever he may be, was sublime. Do you know what he did, monsieur? He intervened like the archangel. He must have thrown himself into the midst of the combat, have snatched me out of it, have opened the sewer, have drawn me into it, have borne me through it! He must have made his way for more than four miles through hideous subterranean galleries, bent, stooping, in the darkness, in the cloaca, more than four miles, monsieur, with a corpse upon his back! And with what object? With the single object of saving that corpse. And that corpse was I. He said to himself: 'There is perhaps a glimmer of life still there; I will risk my own life for that miserable spark!' And his life, he did not risk it once, but twenty times! And each step was a danger. The proof is, that on coming out of the sewer he was arrested. Do you know, monsieur, that that man did all that? And he could expect no recompense. What was I? An insurgent. What was I? A vanquished man. Oh! if Cosette's six hundred thousand francs were mine—"

"They are yours," interrupted Jean Valjean.

"Well," resumed Marius, "I would give them to find that man!"

Jean Valjean kept silence.

BOOK SIX
THE SLEEPLESS NIGHT

1 (2)

JEAN VALJEAN STILL HAS HIS ARM IN A SLING

To REALISE his dream. To whom is that given? There must be elections for that in heaven; we are all unconscious candidates; the angels vote. Cosette and Marius had been elected.

Cosette, at the mairie and in the church, was brilliant and touching. Toussaint, aided by Nicolette, had dressed her.

Cosette wore her dress of Binche guipure over a skirt of white taffetas, a veil of English point, a necklace of fine pearls, a crown of orange flowers; all this was white, and, in this whiteness, she was radiant. It was an exquisite candour, dilating and transfiguring itself into luminousness. One would have said she was a virgin in process of becoming a goddess.

Marius' beautiful hair was perfumed and lustrous; here and there might be discerned, under the thickness of the locks, pallid lines, which were the scars of the barricade.

The grandfather, superb, his head held high, uniting more than ever in his toilet and manners all the elegances of the time of Barras, conducted Cosette. He took the place of Jean Valjean, who, as his arm was in a sling, could not give his hand to the bride.

Jean Valjean, in black, followed and smiled.

When, at the completion of all the ceremonies, after having pronounced before the mayor and the priest every possible yes, after having signed the registers at the municipality and at the sacristy, after having exchanged their rings, after having been on their knees elbow to elbow under the canopy of white moire in the smoke of the censer, hand in hand, admired and envied by all, Marius in black, she in white, preceded by the usher in colonel's epaulettes, striking the pavement with his halberd, between two hedges of marvelling spectators, they arrived under the portal of the church where the folding-doors were both open, ready to get into the carriage again, and all was over, Cosette could not yet believe it. She looked at Marius, she looked at the throng, she looked at the sky; it seemed as if she were afraid of awaking. Her astonished and bewildered air rendered her unspeakably bewitching. To return, they got into the same carriage, Marius by Cosette's side; M. Gillenormand and Jean Valjean sat opposite. Aunt Gillenormand had drawn back one degree, and was in the second carriage. "My children," said the grandfather, "here you are Monsieur the Baron and Madame the Baroness, with thirty thousand francs a year." And Cosette, leaning close up to Marius, caressed his ear with this angelic whisper: "It is true, then. My name is Marius. I am Madame You."

To have suffered, how good it is! Their grief made a halo about their happiness. The long agony of their love terminated in an ascension.

There was in these two souls the same enchantment, shaded with anticipation in Marius and with modesty in Cosette. They said to each other in a whisper: "We will go and see our little garden in the Rue Plumet again." The folds of Cosette's dress were over Marius.

Then they returned to the Rue des Filles du Calvaire, to their home. Marius, side by side with Cosette, ascended, triumphant and radiant, that staircase up which he had been carried dying. The poor gathered before the door, and, sharing their purses, they blessed them. There were flowers everywhere. The house was not less perfumed than the church; after incense, roses. They thought they heard voices singing in the infinite; they had God in their hearts; destiny appeared to them like a ceiling of stars; they saw above their heads a gleam of sunrise. Suddenly the clock struck. Marius looked at Cosette's bewitching bare arm and the rosy things which he dimly perceived through the lace of her corsage, and Cosette, seeing Marius look, began to blush even to the tips of her ears.

A banquet had been prepared in the dining-room.

Two large arm-chairs were placed, on the right and on the left of the bride, the first for M. Gillenormand, the second for Jean Valjean. M. Gillenormand took his seat. The other arm-chair remained empty.

All eyes sought "Monsieur Fauchelevent."

He was not there.

M. Gillenormand called Basque.

"Do you know where Monsieur Fauchelevent is?"

"Monsieur," answered Basque. "Exactly. Monsieur Fauchelevent told me to say to monsieur that he was suffering a little from his sore hand, and could not dine with Monsieur the Baron and Madame the Baroness. That he begged they would excuse him, that he would come to-morrow morning. He has just gone away."

This empty arm-chair chilled for a moment the effusion of the nuptial repast. But, M. Fauchelevent absent, M. Gillenormand was there, and the grandfather was brilliant enough for two. He declared that M. Fauchelevent did well to go to bed early, if he was suffering, but that it was only a "scratch." This declaration was enough. Besides, what is one dark corner in such a deluge of joy? Cosette and Marius were in one of those selfish and blessed moments when we have no faculty save for the perception of happiness. And then, M. Gillenormand had an idea. "By Jove, this arm-chair is empty. Come here, Marius. Your aunt, although she has a right to you, will allow it. This arm-chair is for you. It is legal, and it is proper. 'Fortunatus beside Fortunata.'" Applause from the whole table. Marius took Jean Valjean's place at Cosette's side; and things arranged themselves in such a way that Cosette, at first saddened by Jean Valjean's absence, was finally satisfied with it. From the moment that Marius was the substitute, Cosette would not have regretted God. She put her soft little foot encased in white satin upon Marius' foot.

The arm-chair occupied, M. Fauchelevent was effaced; and nothing was missed. And, five minutes later, the whole table was laughing from one end to the other with all the spirit of forgetfulness.

The evening was lively, gay, delightful. The sovereign good-humour of the grandfather gave the key-note to the whole festival, and everybody regulated himself by this almost centenarian cordiality. They danced a little, they laughed much; it was a good childlike wedding. Yesteryear they might have invited the goodman. Indeed, he was there in the person of Grandfather Gillenormand.

There was tumult, then silence.

The bride and groom disappeared.

A little after midnight the Gillenormand house became a temple.

If, at that supreme hour, the wedded pair, bewildered with pleasure, and believing themselves alone, were to listen, they would hear in their chamber a rustling of confused wings. Perfect happiness implies the solidarity of the angels. That little dark alcove has for its ceiling the whole heavens. When two mouths, made sacred by love, draw near each other to create, it is impossible that above that ineffable kiss there should not be a thrill in the immense mystery of the stars.

These are the true felicities. No joy beyond these joys. Love is the only ecstasy, everything else weeps.

To love or to have loved, that is enough. Ask nothing further. There is no other pearl to be found in the dark folds of life. To love is a consummation.

2 (3)

THE INSEPARABLE

WHAT had become of Jean Valjean?

Immediately after having laughed, upon Cosette's playful injunction, nobody observing him, Jean Valjean had left his seat, got up, and, unperceived, had reached the antechamber. It was that same room which eight months before he had entered, black with mire, blood, and powder, bringing the grandson home to the grandfather. The old woodwork was garlanded with leaves and flowers; the musicians were seated on the couch upon which they had placed Marius. Basque, in a black coat, short breeches, white stockings, and white gloves, was arranging crowns of roses about each of the dishes which was to be served up. Jean Valjean had shown him his arm in a sling, charged him to explain his absence, and gone away.

The windows of the dining-room looked upon the street. Jean Valjean stood for some minutes motionless in the darkness under those radiant windows. He listened. The confused sounds of the banquet reached him. He heard the loud and authoritative words of the grandfather, the violins, the clatter of the plates and glasses, the bursts of laughter, and through all that gay uproar he distinguished Cosette's sweet joyous voice.

He left the Rue des Filles du Calvaire and returned to the Rue de l'Homme Armé.

Jean Valjean returned home. He lighted his candle and went upstairs. The apartment was empty. Toussaint herself was no longer there. Jean Valjean's step made more noise than usual in the rooms. All the closets were open. He went into Cosette's room. There were no sheets on the bed. The pillow, without a pillow-case and without laces, was laid upon the coverlets folded at the foot of the mattress of which the ticking was to be seen and on which nobody should sleep henceforth. All the little feminine objects to which Cosette clung had been carried away; there remained only the heavy furniture and the four walls. Toussaint's bed was also stripped. A single bed was made and seemed waiting for somebody, that was Jean Valjean's.

Jean Valjean looked at the walls, shut some closet doors, went and came from one room to the other.

Then he found himself again in his own room, and he put his candle on the table.

He had released his arm from the sling, and he helped himself with his right hand as if he did not suffer from it.

He approached his bed, and his eye fell, was it by chance? was it with intention? upon the *inseparable,* of which Cosette had been jealous, upon the little trunk which never left him. On the 4th of June, on arriving in the Rue de l'Homme Armé, he had placed it upon a candle-stand at the head of his bed. He went to this stand with a sort of vivacity, took a key from his pocket, and opened the valise.

He took out slowly the garments in which, ten years before, Cosette had left Montfermeil, first the little dress, then the black scarf, then the great heavy child's shoes which Cosette could have almost put on still, so small a foot she had, then the bodice of very thick fustian, then the knit-skirt, then the apron with pockets, then the woollen stockings. Those stockings, on which the shape of a little leg was still gracefully marked, were hardly longer than Jean Valjean's hand. These were all black. He had carried these garments for her to Montfermeil. As he took them out of the valise, he laid them on the bed. He was thinking. He remembered. It was in winter, a very cold December, she shivered half-naked in rags, her poor little feet all red in her wooden shoes. He, Jean Valjean, he had taken her away from those rags to clothe her in this mourning garb. The mother must have been pleased in her tomb to see her daughter wear mourning for her, and especially to see that she was clad, and that she was warm. He thought of that forest of Montfermeil; they had crossed it together, Cosette and he; he thought of the weather, of the trees without leaves, of the forest without birds, of the sky without sun; it is all the same, it was charming. He arranged the little things upon the bed, the scarf next the skirt, the stockings beside the shoes, the bodice beside the dress, and he looked at them one after another. She was no higher than that, she had her great doll in her arms, she had put her louis d'or in the pocket of this apron, she laughed, they walked holding each other by the hand, she had nobody but him in the world.

Then his venerable white head fell upon the bed, this old stoical heart broke, his face was swallowed up, so to speak, in Cosette's garments, and anybody who had passed along the staircase at that moment, would have heard fearful sobs.

3 (4)

UNDYING FAITH

THE FORMIDABLE old struggle, several phases of which we have already seen, recommenced.

Jacob wrestled with the angel but one night. Alas! how many times have we seen Jean Valjean clenched, body to body, in the darkness with his conscience, and wrestling desperately against it.

He had reached the last crossing of good and evil. He had that dark intersection before his eyes. This time again, as it had already happened to him in other sorrowful crises, two roads opened before him; the one tempting, the other terrible. Which should he take?

The one which terrified him was advised by the mysterious indicating finger which we all perceive whenever we fix our eyes upon the shadow.

Jean Valjean had, once again, the choice between the terrible haven and the smiling ambush.

The question which presented itself was this:

In what manner should Jean Valjean comport himself in regard to the happiness of Cosette and Marius? This happiness, it was he who had willed it, it was he who had made it; he had thrust it into his own heart, and at this hour, looking upon it, he might have the same satisfaction that an armourer would have, who should recognise his own mark upon a blade, on withdrawing it all reeking from his breast.

Cosette had Marius, Marius possessed Cosette. They had everything, even riches. And it was his work.

But this happiness, now that it existed, now that it was here, what was he to do with it, he, Jean Valjean? Should he impose himself upon this happiness? Should he treat it as belonging to him? Unquestionably, Cosette was another's; but should he, Jean Valjean, retain all of Cosette that he could retain? Should he remain the kind of father, scarcely seen, but respected, which he had been hitherto? Should he introduce himself quietly into Cosette's house? Should he bring, without saying a word, his past to this future? Should he present himself there as having a right, and should he come and take his seat, veiled, at that luminous hearth? Should he take, smiling upon them, the hands of those innocent beings into his two tragical hands?

We are never done with conscience. Choose your course by it, Brutus; choose your course by it, Cato. It is bottomless, being God. We cast into this pit the labour of our whole life, we cast in our fortune, we cast in our riches, we cast in our success, we cast in our liberty or our country, we cast in our well-being, we cast in our peace of mind, we cast in our happiness. More! more! more! Empty the vase! turn out the urn! We must at last cast in our heart.

At last Jean Valjean entered the calmness of despair.

He weighed, he thought, he considered the alternatives of the mysterious balance of light and shade.

To impose his galleys upon these two dazzling children, or to consummate by himself his irremediable engulfment. On the one side the sacrifice of Cosette, on the other of himself.

What resolution did he take? What was, within himself, his final answer to the incorruptible demand of fatality?

He remained there until dawn, in the same attitude, doubled over on the bed, prostrated under the enormity of fate, crushed perhaps, alas! his fists clenched, his arms extended at a right angle, like one taken from the cross and thrown down with his face to the ground. He remained twelve hours, the twelve hours of a long winter night, chilled, without lifting his head, and without uttering a word. He was as motionless as a corpse, while his thought writhed upon the ground and flew away, now like the hydra,* now like the eagle. To see him thus without motion, one would have said he was dead; suddenly he thrilled convulsively, and his mouth, fixed upon Cosette's garments, kissed them; then one saw that he was alive.

What one? since Jean Valjean was alone, and there was nobody there?

The One who is in the darkness.

---

*The hydra was a huge legendary serpent with seven heads; when you cut off one, several grew back. The image refers to Jean Valjean's temptation by angry, selfish thoughts.

BOOK SEVEN
THE LAST DROP IN THE CHALICE

1

THE SEVENTH CIRCLE
AND THE EIGHTH HEAVEN

THE DAY AFTER a wedding is solitary. The privacy of the happy is respected. And thus their slumber is a little belated. The tumult of visits and felicitations does not commence until later. On the morning of the 17th of February, it was a little after noon, when Basque, his napkin and duster under his arm, busy "doing his antechamber," heard a light rap at the door. There was no ring, which is considerate on such a day. Basque opened and saw M. Fauchelevent. He introduced him into the parlour, still littered and topsy-turvy, and which had the appearance of the battlefield of the evening's festivities.

"Faith, monsieur," observed Basque, "we are waking up late."

"Has your master risen?" inquired Jean Valjean.

"How is monsieur's arm?" answered Basque.

"Better. Has your master risen?"

"Which? the old or the new one?"

"Monsieur Pontmercy."

"Monsieur the Baron?" said Basque, drawing himself up.

One is baron to his domestics above all. Something of it is reflected upon them; they have what a philosopher would call the spattering of the title, and it flatters them. Marius, to speak of it in passing, a republican militant, and he had proved it, was now a baron in spite of himself. A slight revolution had taken place in the family in regard to this title. At present it was M. Gillenormand who clung to it and Marius who made light of it. But Colonel Pontmercy had written: *My son will bear my title*. Marius obeyed. And then Cosette, in whom the woman was beginning to dawn, was in raptures at being a baroness.

"Monsieur the Baron?" repeated Basque. "I will go and see. I will tell him that Monsieur Fauchelevent is here."

"No. Do not tell him that it is I. Tell him that somebody asks to speak with him in private, and do not give him any name."

"Ah!" said Basque.

"I wish to give him a surprise."

"Ah!" resumed Basque, giving himself his second ah! as an explanation of the first.

And he went out.

Jean Valjean remained alone.

A few minutes elapsed. Jean Valjean was motionless in the spot where Basque had left him. He was very pale. His eyes were hollow, and so sunken in their sockets from want of sleep that they could hardly be seen. His black coat had the weary folds of a garment which has passed the night. The elbows were whitened with that down which is left upon cloth by the chafing of linen. Jean Valjean was looking at the window marked out by the sun upon the floor at his feet.

There was a noise at the door, he raised his eyes.

Marius entered, his head erect, his mouth smiling, an indescribable light upon his face, his forehead radiant, his eye triumphant. He also had not slept.

"It is you, father!" exclaimed he on perceiving Jean Valjean, "that idiot of a Basque with his mysterious air! But you come too early. It is only half an hour after noon yet. Cosette is asleep."

That word: Father, said to M. Fauchelevent by Marius, signified: Supreme felicity. There had always been, as we know, barrier, coldness, and constraint between them; ice to break or to melt. Marius had reached that degree of intoxication where the barrier was falling, the ice was dissolving, and M. Fauchelevent was to him, as to Cosette, a father.

He continued; words overflowed from him, which is characteristic of these divine paroxysms of joy:

"How glad I am to see you! If you knew how we missed you yesterday! Good morning, father. How is your hand? Better, is it not?"

And, satisfied with the good answer which he made to himself, he went on: "We have both of us talked much about you. Cosette loves you so much! You will not forget that your room is here. We will have no more of the Rue de l'Homme Armé. We will have no more of it at all. How could you go to live in a street like that, which is sickly, which is scowling, which is ugly, which has a barrier at one end, where you are cold, and where you cannot get in? you will come and install yourself here. And that to-day. Or you will have a bone to pick with Cosette. She intends to lead us all by the nose, I warn you. You have seen your room, it is close by ours, it looks upon the gardens; the lock has been fixed, the bed is made, it is all ready; you have nothing to do but to come. Cosette has put a great old easy chair of Utrecht velvet beside your bed, to which she said: stretch out your arms for him. Every spring, in the clump of acacias which is in front of your windows, there comes a nightingale, you will have her in two months. You will have her nest at your left and ours at your right. By night she will sing, and by day Cosette will talk. Your room is full in the south. Cosette will arrange your books there for you, your voyage of Captain Cook, and the other, Vancouver's, all your things. There is, I believe, a little valise which you treasure, I have selected a place of honour for it. You have conquered my grandfather, you suit him. We will live together. Do you know whist? you will overjoy my grandfather, if you know whist. You will take Cosette to walk on my court-days, you will give her your arm, you know, as at the Luxembourg Gardens, formerly. We have absolutely decided to be very happy. And you are part of our happiness, do you understand, father? Come now, you breakfast with us to-day?"

"Monsieur," said Jean Valjean, "I have something to tell you. I am a former convict."

The limit of perceptible acute sounds may be passed quite as easily for the mind as for the ear. Those words: *I am a former convict,* coming from M. Fauchelevent's mouth and entering Marius' ear, went beyond the possible. Marius did not hear. It seemed to him that something had just been said to him; but he knew not what. He stood aghast.

He then perceived that the man who was talking to him was terrible. Excited as he was, he had not until this moment noticed that frightful pallor.

Jean Valjean untied the black cravat which sustained his right arm, took off the cloth wound about his head, laid his thumb bare, and showed it to Marius.

"There is nothing the matter with my hand," said he.

Marius looked at the thumb.

"There has never been anything the matter with it," continued Jean Valjean.

There was, in fact, no trace of a wound.

Jean Valjean pursued:

"It was best that I should be absent from your marriage. I absented myself as much as I could. I feigned this wound so as not to commit a forgery, not to introduce a nullity into the marriage acts, to be excused from signing."

Marius stammered out:

"What does this mean?"

"It means," answered Jean Valjean, "that I have been in the galleys."

"You drive me mad!" exclaimed Marius in dismay.

"Monsieur Pontmercy," said Jean Valjean, "I was nineteen years in the galleys. For robbery. Then I was sentenced for life. For robbery. For a second offence. If they knew I was alive, there'd be a warrant out for my arrest."

It was useless for Marius to recoil before the reality, to refuse the fact, to resist the evidence; he was compelled to yield. He began to comprehend, and as always happens in such a case, he comprehended beyond the truth. He felt the shiver of a horrible interior flash; an idea which made him shudder, crossed his mind. He caught a glimpse in the future of a hideous destiny for himself.

"Tell all, tell all!" cried he. "You are Cosette's father!"

And he took two steps backward with an expression of unspeakable horror.

Jean Valjean raised his head with such a majesty of attitude that he seemed to rise to the ceiling.

"It is necessary that you believe me in this, monsieur; although the oath of such as I be not received."

Here he made a pause; then, with a sort of sovereign and sepulchral authority, he added, articulating slowly and emphasising his syllables:

"——You will believe me. I, the father of Cosette! before God, no. Monsieur Baron Pontmercy, I am a peasant of Faverolles. I earned my living by pruning trees. My name is not Fauchelevent, my name is Jean Valjean. I am nothing to Cosette. Compose yourself."

Marius faltered:

"Who proves it to me——"

"I. Since I say so."

Marius looked at this man. He was mournful, yet self-possessed. No lie could come out of such a calmness. That which is frozen is sincere. We feel the truth in that sepulchral coldness.

"I believe you," said Marius.

Jean Valjean inclined his head as if taking oath, and continued:

"What am I to Cosette? a passer-by. Ten years ago, I did not know that she existed. I love her, it is true. A child whom one has seen when little, being himself already old, he loves. When a man is old, he feels like a grandfather towards all little children. You can, it seems to me, suppose that I have something which resembles a heart. She was an orphan. Without father or mother. She had need of me. That is why I began to love her. Children are so weak, that anybody, even a man like me, may be their protector. I performed that duty with regard to Cosette. I do not think that one could truly call so little a thing a good deed; but if it is a good deed; well, set it down that I have done it. Record that mitigating circumstance. Today Cosette leaves my life; our two roads separate. Henceforth I can do nothing more for her. She is Madame Pontmercy. Her protector is changed. And Cosette gains by the change. All is well. As for the six hundred thousand francs, you have not spoken of them to me, but I anticipate your thought; that is a trust. How did this trust come into my hands? What matters it? I make over the trust. Nothing more can be asked of me. I complete the restitution by telling my real name. This again concerns me. I desire, myself, that you should know who I am."

And Jean Valjean looked Marius in the face.

All that Marius felt was tumultuous and incoherent. Certain blasts of destiny make such waves in our soul.

We have all had such moments of trouble, in which everything within us is dispersed; we say the first things that come to mind, which are not always precisely those that we should say. There are sudden revelations which we cannot bear, and which intoxicate like a noxious wine. Marius was so stupefied at the new condition of affairs which opened before him that he spoke to this man almost as though he were angry with him for his avowal.

"But after all," exclaimed he, "why do you tell me all this? What compels you to do so? You could have kept the secret to yourself. You are neither denounced, nor pursued, nor hunted. You have some reason for voluntarily making such a revelation. Finish it. There is something else. In connection with what do you make this avowal? From what motive?"

"From what motive?" answered Jean Valjean, in a voice so low and so hollow that one would have said it was to himself he was speaking rather than to Marius. "From what motive, indeed, does this convict come and say: I am a convict? Well, yes! the motive is strange. It is from honour. Yes, my misfortune is a cord which I have here in my heart and which holds me fast. When one is old these cords are strong. The whole life wastes away about them; they hold fast. If I had been able to tear out this cord, to break it, to untie the knot, or to cut it, to go far away, I had been saved, I had only to depart; there are stagecoaches in the Rue du Bouloy; you are happy, I go away. I have tried to break this cord, I have pulled upon it, it held firmly, it did not snap, I was tearing my heart out with it. Then I said I cannot live away from here. I must stay. Well, yes; but you are right, I am a fool, why not just simply stay? You offer me a room in the house, Madame Pontmercy loves me well, she says to that arm-chair: Stretch out your arms for him, your grandfather asks nothing better than to have me, I suit him, we shall all live together, eat in common, I will give my arm to Cosette—to Madame Pontmercy, pardon me, it is from habit—we will have but one roof, but one table, but one fire, the same chimney corner in winter, the same promenade in summer, that is joy, that is happiness, that, it is every-thing. We will live as one family, one family!"

At this word Jean Valjean grew wild. He folded his arms, gazed at the floor at his feet as if he wished to hollow out an abyss in it, and his voice suddenly became piercing.

"One family! no. I am of no family. I am not of yours. I am not of the family of men. In houses where people are at home I am an incumbrance. There are families, but they are not for me. I am the unfortunate; I am out-side. Had I a father and a mother? I almost doubt it. The day that I mar-ried off that child it was all over, I saw that she was happy, and that she was with the man whom she loved, and that there was a good old man here, a household of two angels, all joys in this house, and that it was well, I said to myself: Enter thou not. I could have lied, it is true, have deceived you all, have remained Monsieur Fauchelevent. As long as it was for her, I could lie; but now it would be for myself, I must not do it. It was enough to remain silent, it is true, and everything would continue. You ask me what forces me to speak? a strange thing; my conscience. To remain silent was, however, very easy. I have passed the night in trying to persuade myself to do so; you are confessing me, and what I come to tell you is so strange that you have a right to do so; well, yes, I have passed the night in giving myself reasons, I have given myself very good reasons, I have done what I could, it was of no use. But there are two things in which I did not succeed; nei-ther in breaking the cord which holds me by the heart fixed, riveted, and sealed here, nor in silencing some one who speaks low to me when I am alone. That is why I have come to confess all to you this morning. All, or almost all. It is useless to tell what concerns only myself; I keep it for myself. The essential you know. So I have taken my mystery, and brought it to you. And I have ripped open my secret under your eyes. It was not an easy resolution to form. All night I have struggled with myself. Ah! you think I have not said to myself that this is not the Champmathieu affair, that in concealing my name I do no harm to anybody, that the name of Fauchelevent was given to me by Fauchelevent himself in gratitude for a service rendered, and I could very well keep it, and that I should be happy in this room which you offer me, that I should interfere with nothing, that I should be in my little corner, and that, while you would have Cosette, I should have the idea of being in the same house with her. Each one would have had his due share of happiness. To continue to be Monsieur Fauchelevent, smoothed the way for everything. Yes, except for my soul. There was joy everywhere about me, the depths of my soul were still black. It is not enough to be happy, we must be satisfied with ourselves. Thus I should have remained Monsieur Fauchelevent, thus I should have concealed my real face, thus, in presence of your cheerfulness, I should have borne an enigma, thus, in the midst of your broad day, I should have been darkness, thus, without openly crying beware, I should have introduced the galleys at your hearth, I should have sat down at your table with the thought that, if you knew who I was, you would drive me away, I should have let myself be served by domestics who, if they had known, would have said: How horrible! I should have touched you with my elbow which you have a right to shrink from, I should have stolen the clasp of your hand! There would have been in your house a division of respect between venerable white hairs and dishonoured white hairs; at your most intimate hours, when all hearts would have thought themselves open to each other to the bottom, when we should have been all four together, your grandfather, you two, and myself; there would have been a stranger there! I should have been side by side with you in your existence, having but one care, never to displace the covering of my terrible pit. Thus I, a dead man, should have imposed myself upon you, who are alive. Her I should have condemned to myself for ever. You, Cosette, and I, we should have been three heads in the lifer's green cap! Do you not shudder? I am only the most depressed of men, I should have been the most monstrous. And this crime I should have committed every day! And this lie I should have acted every day! And this face of night I should have worn every day! And of my disgrace, I should have given to you your share every day! every day! to You, my loved ones, you, my children, you, my innocents! To be quiet is nothing? to keep silence is simple? No, it is not simple. There is a silence which lies. And my lie, and my fraud, and my unworthiness, and my cowardice, and my treachery, and my crime, I should have drunk drop by drop, I should have spit it out, then drunk again, I should have finished at midnight and recommenced at noon, and my good-morning would have lied, and my good-night would have lied, and I should have slept upon it, and I should have eaten it with my bread, and I should have looked Cosette in the face, and I should have answered the smile of the angel with the smile of the damned, and I should have been a detestable impostor! What for? to be happy. To be happy, I! Have I the right to be happy? I am outside of life, monsieur."

Jean Valjean stopped. Marius listened. Such a chain of ideas and of pangs cannot be interrupted. Jean Valjean lowered his voice anew, but it was no longer a hollow voice, it was an ominous voice.

"You ask why I speak? I am neither informed against, nor pursued, nor hunted, say you. Yes! I am informed against! yes! I am pursued! yes! I am hunted? By whom? by myself. It is I myself who bar the way before myself, and I drag myself, and I urge myself, and I check myself, and I exert myself, and when one holds himself he is well held."

And seizing his own coat in his clenched hand and drawing it towards Marius:

"Look at this hand, now," continued he. "Don't you think that it holds this collar in such a way as not to let go? Well! conscience has quite another grasp! If we wish to be happy, monsieur, we must never comprehend duty; for, as soon as we comprehend it, it is implacable. One would say that it punishes you for comprehending it; but no, it rewards you for it; for it puts you into a hell where you feel God at your side. Your heart is not so soon lacerated when you are at peace with yourself."

And, with a bitter emphasis, he added:

"Monsieur Pontmercy, this is not common sense, but I am an honest man. It is by degrading myself in your eyes that I elevate myself in my own. This has already happened to me once, but it was less grievous then; it was nothing. Yes, an honest man. I should not be one if you had, by my fault, continued to esteem me; now that you despise me, I am one. I have this fatality upon me that, being forever unable to have any but stolen consideration, that consideration humiliates me and depresses me inwardly, and in order that I may respect myself, I must be despised. Then I hold myself erect. I am a galley slave who obeys his conscience. I know well that is improbable. But what would you have me do? it is so. I have assumed engagements towards myself; I keep them. There are accidents which bind us, there are chances which drag us into duties. You see, Monsieur Pontmercy, some things have happened to me in my life?"

Jean Valjean paused again, swallowing his saliva with effort, as if his words had a bitter after-taste, and resumed:

"When one has such a horror over him, he has no right to make others share it without their knowledge, he has no right to communicate his pestilence to them, he has no right to make them slip down his precipice without warning of it, he has no right to let his convict's cap be placed upon them, he has no right craftily to encumber the happiness of others with his own misery. To approach those who are well, and to touch them in the shadow with his invisible ulcer, that is horrible. Fauchelevent lent me his name in vain. I had no right to make use of it; he could give it to me, I could not take it. A name is a Me. You see, monsieur, I have thought a little, I have read a little, although I am a peasant; and you see that I express myself tolerably. I form my own idea of things. I have given myself an education of my own. Well, yes, to purloin a name, and to put yourself under it, is dishonest. The letters of the alphabet may be stolen as well as a purse or a watch. To be a false signature in flesh and blood, to be a living false key, to enter the houses of honest people by picking their locks, never to look again, always to squint, to be infamous within myself, no! no! no! no! It is better to suffer, to bleed, to weep, to tear the skin from the flesh with the nails, to pass the nights in writhing, in anguish, to gnaw away body and soul. That is why I come to tell you all this. Voluntarily, as you say."

He breathed with difficulty, and forced out these final words:

"To live, once I stole a loaf of bread; to-day, to live, I will not steal a name."

"To live!" interrupted Marius. "You have no need of that name to live!"

"Ah! I understand," answered Jean Valjean, raising and lowering his head several times in succession.

There was a pause. Both were silent, each sunk in an abyss of thought. Marius had seated himself beside a table, and was resting the corner of his mouth on one of his bent fingers. Jean Valjean was walking back and forth. He stopped before a glass and stood motionless. Then, as if answering some inward reasoning, he said, looking at that glass in which he did not see himself:

"While at present, I am relieved!"

He resumed his walk and went to the other end of the parlour. Just as he began to turn, he perceived that Marius was noticing his walk. He said to him with an inexpressible accent:

"I drag one leg a little. You understand why now."

Then he turned quite round towards Marius:

"And now, monsieur, picture this to yourself: I have said nothing, I have remained Monsieur Fauchelevent, I have taken my place in your house, I am one of you, I am in my room, I come to breakfast in the morning in slippers, at night we all three go to the theatre, I accompany Madame Pontmercy to the Tuileries and to the Place Royale, we are together, you suppose me your equal; some fine day I am there, you are there, we are chatting, we are laughing, suddenly you hear a voice shout this name: Jean Valjean! and you see that appalling hand, the police, spring out of the shadow and abruptly tear off my mask!"

He ceased again; Marius had risen with a shudder. Jean Valjean resumed:

"What say you?"

Marius' silence answered.

Jean Valjean continued:

"You see very well that I am right in not keeping quiet. Go on, be happy, be in heaven, be an angel of an angel, be in the sunshine, and be contented with it, and do not trouble yourself about the way which a poor condemned man takes to open his heart and do his duty; you have a wretched man before you, monsieur."

Marius crossed the parlour slowly, and, when he was near Jean Valjean, extended him his hand.

But Marius had to take that hand which did not offer itself, Jean Valjean was passive, and it seemed to Marius that he was grasping a hand of marble.

"My grandfather has friends," said Marius. "I will procure your pardon."

"It is useless," answered Jean Valjean. "They think me dead, that is enough. The dead are not subjected to surveillance. They are supposed to moulder tranquilly. Death is the same thing as pardon."

And, disengaging his hand, which Marius held, he added with a sort of inexorable dignity:

"Besides, to do my duty, that is the friend to which I have recourse; and I need pardon of but one, that is my conscience."

Just then, at the other end of the parlour, the door was softly opened a little way, and Cosette's head made its appearance. They saw only her sweet face, her hair was in charming disorder, her eyelids were still swollen with sleep. She made the movement of a bird passing its head out of its nest, looked first at her husband, then at Jean Valjean, and called to them with a laugh, you would have thought you saw a smile at the bottom of a rose:

"I'll wager that you're talking politics. How stupid that is, instead of being with me!"

Jean Valjean shuddered.

"Cosette," faltered Marius—and he stopped. One would have said that they were two culprits.

Cosette, radiant, continued to look at them both. The frolic of paradise was in her eyes.

"I catch you in the very act," said Cosette. "I just heard my father Fauchelevent say, through the door: 'Conscience—Do his duty.'—It is politics, that is. I will not have it. You ought not to talk politics the very next day. It is not right."

"You are mistaken, Cosette," answered Marius. "We were talking business. We are talking of the best investment for your six hundred thousand francs——"

"That's not all there is to talk about," interrupted Cosette. "I am coming. Do you want me here?"

And, passing resolutely through the door, she came into the parlour. She was dressed in a full white morning gown, with a thousand folds and with wide sleeves which, starting from the neck, fell to her feet. There are in the golden skies of old Gothic pictures such charming robes for angels to wear.

She viewed herself from head to foot in a large glass, then exclaimed with an explosion of ineffable ecstasy:

"Once there was a king and a queen. Oh! how happy I am!"

So saying, she made a reverence to Marius and to Jean Valjean.

"There," said she, "I am going to install myself by you in an arm-chair; we breakfast in half an hour, you shall say all you wish to; I know very well that men must talk, I shall be very good."

Marius took her arm, and said to her lovingly:

"We are talking business."

"By the way," answered Cosette, "I have opened my window, a flock of *pierrots* [sparrows or masks] have just arrived in the garden. Birds, not masks. It is Ash Wednesday to-day; but not for the birds."

"I tell you that we are talking business; go, my darling Cosette, leave us a moment. We are talking figures. It will tire you."

"You have put on a charming cravat this morning, Marius. You are very coquettish, monsieur. It will not tire me."

"I assure you that it will tire you."

"No. Because it is you. I shall not understand you, but I will listen to you. When we hear voices that we love, we need not understand the words they say. To be here together is all that I want. I shall stay with you; pshaw!"

"You are my darling Cosette! Impossible."

"Impossible!"

"Yes."

"Very well," replied Cosette. "I would have told you the news. I would have told you that grandfather is still asleep, that your aunt is at mass, that the chimney in my father Fauchelevent's room smokes, that Nicolette has sent for the sweep, that Toussaint and Nicolette have had a quarrel already, that Nicolette makes fun of Toussaint's stuttering. Well, you shall know nothing. Ah! it is impossible! I too, in my turn, you shall see, monsieur, I will say: it is impossible. Then who will be caught? I pray you, my darling Marius, let me stay here with you two."

"I swear to you that we must be alone."

"Well, am I anybody?"

Jean Valjean did not utter a word. Cosette turned towards him. "In the first place, father, I want you to come and kiss me. What are you doing there, saying nothing, instead of taking my part? who gave me such a father as that? You see plainly that I am very unfortunate in my domestic affairs. My husband beats me. Come, kiss me this instant."

Jean Valjean approached.

Cosette turned towards Marius.

"You, sir, I make faces at you."

Then she offered her forehead to Jean Valjean.

Jean Valjean took a step towards her.

Cosette drew back.

"Father, you are pale. Does your arm hurt you?"

"It is well," said Jean Valjean.

"Have you slept badly?"

"No."

"Are you sad?"

"No."

"Kiss me. If you are well, if you sleep well, if you are happy, I will not scold you."

And again she offered him her forehead.

Jean Valjean kissed that forehead, upon which there was a celestial reflection.

"Smile."

Jean Valjean obeyed. It was the smile of a spectre.

"Now defend me against my husband."

"Cosette!—" said Marius.

"Get angry, father. Tell him that I must stay. You can surely talk before me. So you think me very silly. It is very astonishing then what you are saying! business, putting money in a bank, that is a great affair. Men play the mysterious for nothing. I want to stay. I am very pretty this morning. Look at me, Marius."

And with an adorable shrug of the shoulders and an inexpressibly exquisite pout, she looked at Marius. It was like a flash between these two beings. That somebody was there mattered little.

"I love you!" said Marius.

"I adore you!" said Cosette.

And they fell irresistibly into each other's arms.

"Now," resumed Cosette, readjusting a fold of her gown with a little triumphant pout, "I shall stay."

"What, no," answered Marius, in a tone of entreaty, "we have something to finish."

"No, still?"

Marius assumed a grave tone of voice:

"I assure you, Cosette, that it is impossible."

"Ah! you put on your man's voice, monsieur. Very well, I'll go. You, father, you have not supported me. Monsieur my husband, monsieur my papa, you are tyrants. I am going to tell grandfather on you. If you think that I shall come back and talk nonsense to you, you are mistaken. I am proud. I wait for you now, you will see that it is you who will get bored without me. I am going away, very well."

And she went out.

Two seconds later, the door opened again, her fresh rosy face passed once more between the two folding doors, and she cried to them:

"I am very angry."

The door closed again and the darkness returned.

It was like a stray sunbeam which, without suspecting it, should have suddenly traversed the night.

Marius made sure that the door was well closed.

"Poor Cosette!" murmured he, "when she knows——"

At these words, Jean Valjean trembled in every limb. He fixed upon Marius a bewildered eye.

"Cosette! Oh, yes, it is true, you will tell this to Cosette. That is right. Stop, I had not thought of that. People have the strength for some things, but not for others. Monsieur, I beseech you, I entreat you, Monsieur, give me your most sacred word, do not tell her. Is it not enough that you know it yourself? I could have told it by myself without being forced to it, I would have told it to the universe, to all the world, that would be nothing to me. But she, she doesn't know what it is, it would appall her. A convict, why! you would have to explain it to her, to tell her: It is a man who has been in the galleys. She saw the chain pass by one day. Oh, my God!"

He sank into an arm-chair and hid his face in both hands. He could not be heard, but by the shaking of his shoulders it could be seen that he was weeping. Silent tears, terrible tears.

There is a stifling in the sob. A sort of convulsion seized him, he bent over upon the back of the arm-chair as if to breathe, letting his arms hang down and allowing Marius to see his face bathed in tears, and Marius heard him murmur so low that his voice seemed to come from a bottomless depth: "Oh! would that I could die!"

"Don't worry," said Marius, "I will keep your secret for myself alone."

And, less softened perhaps than he should have been, but obliged for an hour past to familiarise himself with a fearful surprise, seeing by degrees a convict superimposed before his eyes upon M. Fauchelevent, possessed little by little of this dismal reality, and led by the natural tendency of the position to determine the distance which had just been put between this man and himself, Marius added:

"It is impossible that I should not say a word to you of the trust which you have so faithfully and so honestly restored. That is an act of probity. It is just that a recompense should be given you. Fix the sum yourself, it shall be counted out to you. Do not be afraid to fix it very high."

"I thank you, monsieur," answered Jean Valjean gently.

He remained thoughtful a moment, passing the end of his forefinger over his thumb-nail mechanically, then he raised his voice:

"It is all nearly finished. There is one thing left——"

"What?"

Jean Valjean had as it were a supreme hesitation, and, voiceless, almost breathless, he faltered out rather than said:

"Now that you know, do you think, monsieur, you who are the master, that I ought not to see Cosette again?"

"I think that would be best," answered Marius coldly.

"I shall not see her again," murmured Jean Valjean.

And he walked towards the door.

He placed his hand upon the knob, the latch yielded, the door started, Jean Valjean opened it wide enough to enable him to pass out, stopped a second motionless, then shut the door, and turned towards Marius.

He was no longer pale, he was livid. There were no longer tears in his eyes, but a sort of tragical flame. His voice had again become strangely calm.

"But, monsieur," said he, "if you are willing, I will come and see her. I assure you that I desire it very much. If I had not clung to seeing Cosette, I should not have made the avowal which I have made, I should have gone away; but wishing to stay in the place where Cosette is and to continue to see her, I was compelled in honour to tell you all. You follow my reasoning, do you not? that is a thing which explains itself. You see, for nine years past, I have had her near me. We lived first in that ruin on the boulevard, then in the convent, then near the Luxembourg Gardens. It was there that you saw her for the first time. You remember her blue plush hat. We were afterwards in the neighborhood of the Invalides where there was a grating and a garden. Rue Plumet. I lived in a little back-yard where I heard her piano. That was my life. We never left each other. That lasted nine years and some months. I was like her father, and she was my child. I don't know whether you understand me, Monsieur Pontmercy, but from the present time, to see her no more, to speak to her no more, to have nothing more, that would be hard. If you do not think it wrong, I will come from time to time to see Cosette. I should not come often. I would not stay long. You might say I should be received in the little low room. On the ground floor. I would willingly come in by the back door, which is for the servants, but that would excite wonder, perhaps. It is better, I suppose, that I should enter by the usual door. Monsieur, indeed, I would really like to see Cosette a little still. As rarely as you please. Put yourself in my place, it is all that I have. And then, we must take care. If I should not come at all, it would have a bad effect, it would be thought singular. For instance, what I can do, is to come in the evening, at nightfall."

"You will come every evening," said Marius, "and Cosette will expect you."

"You are kind, monsieur," said Jean Valjean.

Marius bowed to Jean Valjean, happiness conducted despair to the door, and these two men separated.

2

THE OBSCURITIES WHICH A REVELATION MAY CONTAIN

MARIUS was completely unhinged.

The kind of repulsion which he had always felt for the man with whom he saw Cosette was now explained. There was something strangely enigmatic in this person, of which his instinct had warned him. This enigma was the most hideous of disgraces, the galleys. This M. Fauchelevent was the convict Jean Valjean.

To suddenly find such a secret in the midst of one's happiness is like the discovery of a scorpion in a nest of turtle-doves.

Was the happiness of Marius and Cosette condemned henceforth to this fellowship? Was that a foregone conclusion? Did the acceptance of this man form a part of the marriage which had been consummated? Was there nothing more to be done?

Had Marius espoused the convict also?

As always happens in changes of view of this kind, Marius questioned himself whether he had not some fault to find with himself? Had he been wanting in perception? Had he been wanting in prudence? Had he been involuntarily stupefied? A little, perhaps. Had he entered, without enough precaution in clearing up its surroundings, upon this love adventure which had ended in his marriage with Cosette? He determined—it is thus, by a succession of determinations by ourselves in regard to ourselves, that life improves us little by little—he determined the chimerical and visionary side of his nature, a sort of interior cloud peculiar to many organisations, and which, in paroxysms of passion and grief, dilates, the temperature of the soul changing, and pervades the entire man, to such an extent as to make him nothing more than a consciousness steeped in a fog. We have more than once indicated this characteristic element of Marius' individuality. He recollected that, in the infatuation of his love, in the Rue Plumet, during those six or seven ecstatic weeks, he had not even spoken to Cosette of that drama of the Gorbeau den in which the victim had taken the very strange course of silence during the struggle, and of escape after it. How had he managed not to speak of it to Cosette? Yet it was so near and so frightful. How had he managed not even to name the Thénardiers to her, and, particularly, the day that he met Eponine? He had great difficulty now in explaining to himself his former silence. He did account for it, however. He recalled his stupor, his intoxication for Cosette, love absorbing everything, that uplifting of one by the other into the ideal, and perhaps also, as the imperceptible quantity of reason mingled with this violent and charming state of the soul, a vague and dull instinct to hide and to abolish in his memory that terrible affair with which he dreaded contact, in which he wished to play no part, which he shunned, and in regard to which he could be neither narrator nor witness without being accuser. Besides, those few weeks had been but a flash; they had had time for nothing, except to love. Finally, everything being weighed, turned over, and examined, if he had told the story of the Gorbeau ambush to Cosette, if he had named the Thénardiers to her, what would have been the consequences, if he had even discovered Jean Valjean was a convict, would that have changed him, Marius? Would that have changed her, Cosette? Would he have shrunk back? Would he have adored her less? Would he the less have married her? No. Would it have changed anything in what had taken place? No. Nothing then to regret, nothing to reproach himself with. All was well. There is a God for these drunkards who are called lovers. Blind, Marius had followed the route which he would have chosen had he seen clearly. Love had bandaged his eyes, to lead him where? To Paradise.

But this paradise was henceforth complicated with an infernal accompaniment.

The former repulsion of Marius towards this man, towards this Fauchelevent become Jean Valjean, was now mingled with horror.

In this horror, we must say, there was some pity, and also a certain astonishment.

This robber, this twice-convicted robber, had restored a trust. And what a trust? Six hundred thousand francs. He was alone in the secret of the trust. He might have kept all, he had given up all.

Moreover, he had revealed his condition of his own accord. Nothing obliged him to do so. If it were known who he was, it was through himself. There was more in that avowal than the acceptance of humiliation, there was the acceptance of peril. To a condemned man a mask is not a mask, but a shelter. He had renounced that shelter. A false name is security; he had thrown away this false name. He could, he, a galley-slave, have hidden himself for ever in an honourable family; he had resisted this temptation. And from what motive? from conscientious scruples. He had explained it himself with the irresistible accent of reality. In short, whatever this Jean Valjean might be, he had incontestably an awakened conscience. There was in him some mysterious regeneration begun; and, according to all appearance, for a long time already the scruple had been master of the man. Such paroxysms of justice and goodness do not belong to vulgar natures. An awakening of conscience is greatness of soul.

Jean Valjean was sincere. This sincerity, visible, palpable, unquestionable, evident even by the grief which it caused him, rendered investigation useless and gave authority to all that this man said. Here, for Marius, a strange inversion of situations. What came from M. Fauchelevent? distrust. What flowed from Jean Valjean? confidence.

The trust honestly surrendered, the probity of the avowal, that was good. It was like a break in the cloud, but the cloud again became black.

Confused as Marius' recollections were, some shadow of them returned to him.

What was the exact nature of that affair in the Jondrette garret? Why, on the arrival of the police, did this man, instead of making his complaint, make his escape? Here Marius found the answer. Because this man was a fugitive from justice in breach of ban.

Another question: Why had this man come into the barricade? For now Marius saw that reminiscence again distinctly, reappearing in these emotions like sympathetic ink before the fire. This man was in the barricade. He did not fight there. What did he come there for? Before this question a spectre arose, and made response. Javert. Marius recalled perfectly to mind at this hour the fatal sight of Jean Valjean dragging Javert bound outside the barricade, and he again heard the frightful pistol-shot behind the corner of the little Rue Mondétour.* There was, probably, hatred between the spy and this galley-slave. The one cramped the other. Jean Valjean had gone to the barricade to avenge himself. He had arrived late. He knew probably that Javert was a prisoner there. The Corsican vendetta has penetrated into certain lower depths and is their law; it is so natural that it does not astonish souls half turned back towards the good; and these hearts are so constituted that a criminal, in the path of repentance, may be scrupulous in regard to robbery and not be so in regard to vengeance. Jean Valjean had killed Javert. At least, that seemed evident.

Finally, a last question: but to this no answer. This question Marius felt like a sting. How did it happen that Jean Valjean's existence had touched Cosette's so long? What was this gloomy game of providence which had placed this child in contact with this man? Are coupling chains then forged on high also, and does it please God to pair the angel with the demon? Can then a crime and an innocence be room-mates in the mysterious galleys of misery? Who had been able to bind the lamb to the wolf, and, a thing still more incomprehensible, attach the wolf to the lamb? For the wolf loved the lamb, for the savage being adored the frail being, for, during nine years, the angel had had the monster for a support. Cosette's childhood and youth, her coming to the day, her maidenly growth towards life and light, had been protected

---

*For the remainder of this paragraph and the next, and intermittently throughout the rest of the chapter, Hugo renders Marius' inner questioning with free indirect discourse, to make him more vividly, intimately present to us.

by this monstrous devotion. Here, the questions exfoliated, so to speak, into innumerable enigmas, abyss opened at the bottom of abyss, and Marius could no longer contemplate Jean Valjean without dizziness. What then was this man-precipice?*

God was as visible in this as Jean Valjean. God has his instruments. He uses what tool He pleases. He is not responsible to man. Do we know the ways of God? Jean Valjean had laboured upon Cosette. He had, to some extent, formed that soul. That was incontestable. Well, what then? The workman was horrible; but the work admirable. God performs His miracles as seems good to Himself. He had constructed this enchanting Cosette, and he had employed Jean Valjean on the work. It had pleased Him to choose this strange co-worker. What reckoning have we to ask of Him? Is it the first time that the dunghill has aided the spring to make the rose?

Marius made these answers to himself, and declared that they were good. On all the points which we have just indicated, he had not dared to press Jean Valjean, without avowing to himself that he dared not. He adored Cosette, he possessed Cosette. Cosette was resplendently pure. That was enough for him. What explanation did he need? Cosette was a light. Does light need to be explained? He had all; what could he desire? All, is not that enough? The personal affairs of Jean Valjean did not concern him. In bending over the fatal shade of this man, he clung to this solemn declaration of the miserable being: *"I am nothing to Cosette. Ten years ago, I did not know of her existence."*

Jean Valjean was a passer-by. He had said so, himself. Well, he was passing away. Whatever he might be, his part was finished. Henceforth Marius was to perform the functions of Providence for Cosette. Cosette had come forth to find in the azure her mate, her lover, her husband, her celestial male. In taking flight, Cosette winged and transfigured, left behind her on the ground, empty and hideous, her chrysalis, Jean Valjean.

In whatever circle of ideas Marius turned, he always came back from it to a certain horror of Jean Valjean. A sacred horror, perhaps, for, as we have just indicated, he felt a *quid divinum* in this man. But, whatever he did, and whatever mitigation he sought, he was always obliged to fall back upon this: he was a convict; that is, the creature who, on the social ladder, has no place, being below the lowest round. After the lowest of men, comes the convict.

Marius, upon penal questions, although a democrat, still adhered to the inexorable system, and he had, in regard to those whom the law smites, all the ideas of the law. He had not yet, let us say, adopted all the ideas of progress. He had not yet come to distinguish between what is written by man and what is written by God, between law and right. He had not examined and weighed the right which man assumes to dispose of the irrevocable and

---

*The *métaphore maxima* conveys the supernatural mysteries that underlie Jean Valjean's extraordinary behavior.

the irreparable. He had not revolted from the word *vengeance*. He thought it natural that certain infractions of the written law should be followed by eternal penalties, and he accepted social damnation as growing out of civilisation. He was still at that point, infallibly to advance in time, his nature being good, and in reality entirely composed of latent progress.*

Through the medium of these ideas, Jean Valjean appeared to him deformed and repulsive. He was the outcast. He was the convict. This word was for him like a sound of the last trumpet; and, after having considered Jean Valjean long, his final action was to turn away his head. *Vade retro.*†

Marius, we must remember, and even insist upon it, though he had questioned Jean Valjean to such an extent, that Jean Valjean had said to him: *You are confessing me,* had not, however, put to him two or three decisive questions. Not that they had not presented themselves to his mind, but he was afraid of them. The Jondrette garret? The barricade? Javert? Who knows where the revelations would have stopped? Jean Valjean did not seem the man to shrink, and who knows whether Marius, after having urged him on, would not have desired to restrain him? In certain supreme conjunctures, has it not happened to all of us, after having put a question, to stop our ears that we might not hear the response? We have this cowardice especially when we love. It is not prudent to question untoward situations to the last degree, especially when the indissoluble portion of our own life is fatally interwoven with them. From Jean Valjean's despairing explanations, some appalling light might have sprung, and who knows but that hideous brilliancy might have been thrown even upon Cosette? Wrongly or rightly Marius had been afraid. He knew too much already. He sought rather to blind than to enlighten himself. In desperation, he carried off Cosette in his arms, closing his eyes upon Jean Valjean.

What should be done now? Jean Valjean's visits were very repugnant to him. Of what use was this man in his house? What should he do? Here he shook off his thoughts; he was unwilling to probe, he was unwilling to go deeper; he was unwilling to fathom himself. He had promised, he had allowed himself to be led into a promise; Jean Valjean had his promise; even to a convict, especially to a convict, a man should keep his word. Still, his first duty was towards Cosette. In short, a repulsion, which predominated over all else, possessed him.

He put without apparent object, some questions to Cosette, who, as candid as a dove is white, suspected nothing; he talked with her of her childhood and her youth, and he convinced himself more and more that all a man can be that is good, paternal, and venerable, this convict had been to Cosette. All that Marius had dimly seen and conjectured was real. This darkly mysterious nettle had loved and protected this lily.

---

*Marius is at the beginning of his moral progress, and Jean Valjean at the end of his.
†"Begone, Satan"—Christ's final reply to the Devil's three temptations in the Bible, Matthew 4:10.

BOOK EIGHT
THE FINAL TWILIGHT

1

THE BASEMENT ROOM

THE NEXT DAY, at nightfall, Jean Valjean knocked at the M. Gillenormand porte-cochère. Basque received him. Basque happened to be in the court-yard very conveniently, and as if he had had orders. It sometimes happens that one says to a servant: "You will be on the watch for Monsieur So-and-so, when he comes."

Basque, without waiting for Jean Valjean to come up to him, addressed him as follows:

"Monsieur the Baron told me to ask monsieur whether he desires to go upstairs or to remain below?"

"To remain below," answered Jean Valjean.

Basque, who was moreover absolutely respectful, opened the door of the basement room and said: "I will inform madame."

The room which Jean Valjean entered was an arched and damp base-ment, used as a cellar when necessary, looking upon the street paved with red tiles, and dimly lighted by a window with an iron grating.

The room was not of those which are harassed by the brush, the duster, and the broom. In it the dust was tranquil. There the persecution of the spi-ders had not been organised. A fine web, broadly spread out, very black, adorned with dead flies, ornamented one of the window-panes. The room, small and low, was furnished with a pile of empty bottles heaped up in one corner. The wall had been washed with a wash of yellow ochre, which was scaling off in large flakes. At the end was a wooden mantel, painted black, with a narrow shelf. A fire was kindled, which indicated that somebody had anticipated Jean Valjean's answer: *To remain below*.

Two arm-chairs were placed at the corners of the fireplace. Between the chairs was spread, in guise of a carpet, an old bed-side rug, showing more warp than wool.

Suddenly he started up. Cosette was behind him.

He had not seen her come in, but he had felt that she was coming.

He turned. He gazed at her. She was adorably beautiful. But what he looked upon with that deep look, was not her beauty but her soul.

"Ah, well!" exclaimed Cosette, "father, I knew that you were singular, but I should never have thought this. What an idea! Marius tells me that it is you who wish me to receive you here."

"Yes, it is I."

"I expected the answer. Well, I warn you that I am going to make a scene. Let us begin at the beginning. Father, kiss me."

And she offered her cheek.

Jean Valjean remained motionless.

"You do not stir. I see it. You act guilty. But it is all the same, I forgive you. Jesus Christ said: 'Offer the other cheek.' Here it is."

And she offered the other cheek.

Jean Valjean did not move. It seemed as if his feet were nailed to the floor.

"This is getting serious," said Cosette. "What have I done to you? I declare I am confounded. You owe me amends. You will dine with us."

"I have dined."

"That is not true. I will have Monsieur Gillenormand scold you. Grand-fathers are made to scold fathers. Come. Go up to the parlour with me. Immediately."

"Impossible."

Cosette here lost ground a little. She ceased to order and passed to questions.

"But why not? and you choose the ugliest room in the house to see me in. It is horrible here."

"You know, madame, I am peculiar, I have my whims."

Cosette clapped her little hands together.

"Madame! Still again! What does this mean?"

Jean Valjean fixed upon her that distressing smile to which he some-times had recourse:

"You have wished to be madame. You are so."

"Not to you, father."

"Don't call me father any more."

"What."

"Call me Monsieur Jean. Jean, if you will."

"You are no longer father? I am no longer Cosette? Monsieur Jean? What does this mean? but these are revolutions, these are! what then has happened? look me in the face now. And you will not live with us! And you will not have my room! What have I done to you? what have I done to you? Is there anything the matter?"

"Nothing."

"Well then?"

"All is as usual."

"Why do you change your name?"

"You have certainly changed yours."

He smiled again with that same smile and added:

"Since you are Madame Pontmercy I can surely be Monsieur Jean."

"I don't understand anything about it. It is all nonsense; I shall ask my husband's permission for you to be Monsieur Jean. I hope that he will not consent to it. You make me a great deal of trouble. You may have whims, but you must not grieve your darling Cosette. It is wrong. You have no right to be naughty, you are too good."

He made no answer.

She seized both his hands hastily and, with an irresistible impulse, rais-ing them towards her face, she pressed them against her neck under her chin, which is a deep token of affection.

"Oh!" said she to him, "be good!"

And she continued:

"This is what I call being good: being nice, coming to stay here, there are birds here as well as in the Rue Plumet, living with us, leaving that hole in the Rue de l'Homme Armé, not giving us riddles to guess, being like other people, dining with us, breakfasting with us, being my father."

He disengaged his hands.

"You have no more need of a father, you have a husband."

Cosette could not contain herself.

"I no more need of a father! To things like that which have no common sense, one really doesn't know what to say!"

"If Toussaint was here," replied Jean Valjean, like one who is in search of authorities and who catches at every straw, "she would be the first to acknowledge that it is true that I always had my peculiar ways. There is nothing new in this. I have always liked my dark corner."

"But it is cold here. We can't see clearly. It is horrid, too, to want to be Monsieur Jean. I don't want you to talk so to me."

"Just now, on my way here," answered Jean Valjean, "I saw a piece of furniture in the Rue Saint Louis. At a cabinet maker's. If I were a pretty woman, I should make myself a present of that piece of furniture. A very fine toilet table; in the present style. What you call rosewood, I think. It is inlaid. A pretty large glass. There are drawers in it. It is handsome."

"Oh! the ugly bear!" replied Cosette.

And with a bewitching sauciness, pressing her teeth together and separating her lips, she blew upon Jean Valjean. It was a Grace copying a kitten.

"I am furious," she said. "Since yesterday, you all make me rage. Everybody spites me. I don't understand. You don't defend me against Marius. Marius doesn't uphold me against you, I am all alone. I arrange a room handsomely. If I could have put the good God into it, I would have done it. You leave me my room upon my hands. My tenant bankrupts me. I order Nicolette to have a nice little dinner. Nobody wants your dinner, madame. And my father Fauchelevent, wishes me to call him Monsieur Jean, and to receive him in a hideous, old, ugly, mouldy cellar, where the walls have a beard, and where there are empty bottles for vases, and spiders' webs for curtains. You are singular, I admit, that is your way, but a truce is granted to people who get married. You should not have gone back to being singular immediately. So you are going to be well satisfied with your horrid Rue de l'Homme Armé. I was very forlorn there, myself! What have you against me? You give me a great deal of trouble. Fie!"

And, growing suddenly serious, she looked fixedly at Jean Valjean, and added:

"So you don't like it that I am happy?"

Artlessness, unconsciously, sometimes penetrates very deep. This question, simple to Cosette, was severe to Jean Valjean. Cosette wished to scratch; she tore.

Jean Valjean grew pale. For a moment he did not answer, then, with an indescribable accent and talking to himself, he murmured:

"Her happiness was the aim of my life. Now, God may beckon me away. Cosette, you are happy; my time is full."

"Ah, you have called me Cosette!" exclaimed she.

And she sprang upon his neck.

Jean Valjean, in desperation, clasped her to his breast wildly. It seemed to him almost as if he were taking her back.

"Thank you, father!" said Cosette to him.

The transport was becoming poignant to Jean Valjean. He gently put away Cosette's arms, and took his hat.

"Well?" said Cosette.

Jean Valjean answered:

"I will leave you, madame; they are waiting for you."

And, from the door, he added:

"I called you Cosette. Tell your husband that that shall not happen again. Pardon me."

Jean Valjean went out, leaving Cosette astounded at that enigmatic farewell.

2

OTHER STEPS BACKWARD

THE FOLLOWING DAY, at the same hour, Jean Valjean came.

Cosette put no questions to him, was no longer astonished, no longer exclaimed that she was cold, no longer talked of the parlour, she avoided saying either father or Monsieur Jean. She let him speak as he would. She allowed herself to be called madame. Only she betrayed a certain diminution of joy. She would have been sad, if sadness had been possible for her.

It is probable that she had had one of those conversations with Marius, in which the beloved man says what he pleases, explains nothing, and satisfies the beloved woman. The curiosity of lovers does not go very far beyond their love.

The basement room had been cleaned up a little. Basque had suppressed the bottles, and Nicolette the spiders.

Every succeeding morrow brought Jean Valjean at the same hour. He came every day, not having the strength to take Marius' words otherwise than literally. Marius made his arrangements, so as to be absent at the hours when Jean Valjean came. The house became accustomed to M. Fauchelevent's new mode of life. Toussaint aided: *"Monsieur always was just so,"* she repeated. The grandfather issued this decree: "He is an original!" and all was said. Besides, at ninety, no further tie is possible; all is juxtaposition; a new-comer is an annoyance. There is no more room; all the habits are formed.

Nobody caught a glimpse of the nether gloom. Who could have guessed such a thing, moreover? There are such marshes in India; the water seems strange, inexplicable, quivering when there is no wind; agitated where it should be calm. You see upon the surface this causeless boiling; you do not perceive the Hydra crawling at the bottom.

Certain strange habits, coming at the time when others are gone, shrinking away while others make a display, wearing on all occasions what might be called a wall-coloured cloak, seeking the solitary path, preferring the deserted street, not mingling in conversations, avoiding gatherings and festivals, seeming well-off but living like a pauper, coming in by the side door, going up the back stairs, all these insignificant peculiarities, wrinkles, air bubbles, fugitive folds on the surface, often come from a formidable deep.

Several weeks passed thus. A new life gradually took possession of Cosette; the relations which marriage creates, the visits, the care of the house, the pleasures, those grand affairs. Cosette's pleasures were not costly; they consisted in a single one: being with Marius. Going out with him, staying at home with him, this was the great occupation of her life. It was a joy to them for ever new, to go out arm in arm, in the face of the sun, in the open street, without hiding, in sight of everybody, all alone with each other. Cosette had one vexation. Toussaint could not agree with Nicolette, the wedding of two old maids being impossible, and went away. The grandfather was in good health; Marius argued a few cases now and then; Aunt Gillenormand peacefully led by the side of the new household, that lateral life which was enough for her. Jean Valjean came every day.

The disappearance of familiarity, the madame, the Monsieur Jean, all this made him different to Cosette. The care which he had taken to detach her from him, succeeded with her. She became more and more cheerful, and less and less affectionate. However, she still loved him very much, and he felt it. One day she suddenly said to him, "You were my father, you are no longer my father, you were my uncle, you are no longer my uncle, you were Monsieur Fauchelevent, you are Jean. Who are you then? I don't like all that. If I did not know you were so good, I should be afraid of you."

He still lived in the Rue de l'Homme Armé, unable to resolve to move further from the neighborhood in which Cosette dwelt.

At first he stayed with Cosette only a few minutes, then went away.

Little by little he got into the habit of making his visits longer. One would have said that he took advantage of the example of the days which were growing longer: he came earlier and went away later.

One day Cosette inadvertently said to him: "Father." A flash of joy illuminated Jean Valjean's gloomy old face. He replied to her: "Say Jean." "Ah! true," she answered with a burst of laughter, "Monsieur Jean." "That is right," said he, and he turned away that she might not see him wipe his eyes.

3

THEY REMEMBER THE GARDEN
IN THE RUE PLUMET

THAT WAS the last time. From that last gleam onward, there was complete extinction. No more familiarity, no more good-day with a kiss, never again that word so intensely sweet: Father! he was, upon his own demand and through his own complicity, driven in succession from every happiness; and he had this misery, that after having lost Cosette wholly in one day, he had been obliged afterwards to lose her again little by little.

The eye at last becomes accustomed to the light of a cellar. In short, to have a vision of Cosette every day sufficed him. His whole life was concentrated in that hour. He sat by her side, he looked at her in silence, or rather he talked to her of the years long gone, of her childhood, of the convent, of her friends of those days.

One afternoon—it was one of the early days of April, already warm, still fresh, the season of the great cheerfulness of the sunshine, the gardens which lay about Marius' and Cosette's windows felt the emotion of awakening, the hawthorn was beginning to peep, a jewelled array of gilliflowers displayed themselves upon the old walls, the rosy wolf-mouths gaped in the cracks of the stones, there was a charming beginning of daisies and buttercups in the grass, the white butterflies of the year made their first appearance, the wind, that minstrel of the eternal wedding, essayed in the trees the first notes of that grand auroral symphony which the old poets called the *renouveau*—Marius said to Cosette: "We have said that we would go to see our garden in the Rue Plumet again. Let us go. We must not be ungrateful." And they flew away like two swallows towards the spring. This garden in the Rue Plumet had the effect of the dawn upon them. They had behind them in life already something which was like the spring time of their love. The house in the Rue Plumet being taken on a lease, still belonged to Cosette. They went to this garden and this house. In it they found themselves again; they forgot themselves. At night, at the usual hour, Jean Valjean came to the Rue des Filles du Calvaire. "Madame has gone out with monsieur, and has not returned yet," said Basque to him. He sat down in silence, and waited an hour. Cosette did not return. He bowed his head and went away.

Cosette was so intoxicated with her walk to "the garden," and so happy over having "lived a whole day in her past," that she did not speak of anything else the next day. It did not occur to her that she had not seen Jean Valjean.

"How did you go there?" Jean Valjean asked her.

"We walked."

"And how did you return?"

"In a fiacre."

For some time Jean Valjean had noticed the frugal life which the young couple led. He was annoyed at it. Marius' economy was severe, and the word to Jean Valjean had its absolute sense. He ventured a question:

"Why have you no carriage of your own? A pretty brougham would cost you only five hundred francs a month. You are rich."

"I don't know," answered Cosette.

"So with Toussaint," continued Jean Valjean. "She has gone away. You have not replaced her. Why not?"

"Nicolette is enough."

"But you must have a waiting maid."

"Have not I Marius?"

"You ought to have a house of your own, servants of your own, a carriage, a box at the theatre. There is nothing too good for you. Why not have the advantages of being rich? Riches add to happiness."

Cosette made no answer.

Jean Valjean's visits did not grow shorter. Far from it. When the heart is slipping we do not stop on the descent.

When Jean Valjean desired to prolong his visit, and to make the hours pass unnoticed, he eulogised Marius; he thought him beautiful, noble, courageous, intellectual, eloquent, good. Cosette surpassed him. Jean Valjean began again. They were never silent. Marius, this word was inexhaustible; there were volumes in these six letters. In this way Jean Valjean succeeded in staying a long time. To see Cosette, to forget at her side, it was so sweet to him. It was the staunching of his wound. It happened several times that Basque came down twice to say: "Monsieur Gillenormand sends me to remind Madame the Baroness that dinner is served."

On those days, Jean Valjean returned home very thoughtful.

Was there, then, some truth in that comparison of the chrysalis which had presented itself to Marius' mind? Was Jean Valjean indeed a chrysalis who was obstinate, and who came to make visits to his butterfly?

One day he stayed longer than usual. The next day, he noticed that there was no fire in the fireplace. "What!" thought he. "No fire." And he made the explanation to himself: "It is a matter of course. We are in April. The cold weather is over."

"Goodness! how cold it is here!" exclaimed Cosette as she came in.

"Why no," said Jean Valjean.

"So it is you who told Basque not to make a fire?"

"Yes. We are close upon May."

"But we have fire until the month of June. In this cellar, it is needed the year round."

"I thought that the fire was unnecessary."

"That is just one of your ideas!" replied Cosette.

The next day there was a fire. But the two arm-chairs were placed at the other end of the room, near the door. "What does that mean?" thought Jean Valjean.

He went for the arm-chairs, and put them back in their usual place near the chimney.

This fire being kindled again encouraged him, however. He continued the conversation still longer than usual. As he was getting up to go away, Cosette said to him:

"My husband said a funny thing to me yesterday."

"What was it?"

"He said: 'Cosette, we have an income of thirty thousand francs. Twenty-seven that you have, three that my grandfather allows me.' I answered: 'That makes thirty.' 'Would you have the courage to live on three thousand?' I answered: 'Yes, on nothing. Provided it be with you.' And then I asked: 'Why do you say this?' He answered: 'To know.'"

Jean Valjean did not say a word. Cosette probably expected some explanation from him; he listened to her in a mournful silence. He went back to the Rue de l'Homme Armé; he was so deeply absorbed that he mistook the door, and instead of entering his own house, he entered the next one. Not until he had gone up almost to the second story did he perceive his mistake, and go down again.

His mind was racked with conjectures. It was evident that Marius had doubts in regard to the origin of these six hundred thousand francs, that he feared some impure source, who knows? that he had perhaps discovered that this money came from him, Jean Valjean, that he hesitated before this suspicious fortune, and disliked to take it as his own, preferring to remain poor, himself and Cosette, than to be rich with a doubtful wealth.

Besides, vaguely, Jean Valjean began to feel that the door was shown him.

The next day, he received, on entering the basement room, something like a shock. The arm-chairs had disappeared. There was not even a chair of any kind.

"Ah now," exclaimed Cosette as she came in, "no chairs! Where are the arm-chairs, then?"

"They are gone," answered Jean Valjean.

"That is a pretty business!"

Jean Valjean stammered:

"I told Basque to take them away."

"And what for?"

"I shall stay only a few minutes to-day."

"Staying a little while is no reason for standing while you do stay."

"I believe that Basque needed some arm-chairs for the parlour."

"What for?"

"You doubtless have company this evening."

"We have nobody."

Jean Valjean could not say a word more.

Cosette shrugged her shoulders.

"To have the chairs carried away! The other day you had the fire put out. How singular you are!"

"Good-bye," murmured Jean Valjean.

He did not say: "Good-bye, Cosette." But he had not the strength to say: "Good-bye, madame."

He went away overwhelmed.

This time he had understood.

The next day he did not come. Cosette did not notice it until night.

"Why," said she, "Monsieur Jean has not come to-day."

She felt something like a slight oppression of the heart, but she hardly perceived it, being immediately diverted by a kiss from Marius.

The next day he did not come.

Cosette paid no attention to it, passed the evening and slept as usual, and thought of it only on awaking. She was so happy! She sent Nicolette very quickly to Monsieur Jean's to know if he were sick, and why he had not come the day before. Nicolette brought back Monsieur Jean's answer. He was not sick. He was busy. He would come very soon. As soon as he could. However, he was going to make a little journey. Madame must remember that he was in the habit of making journeys from time to time. Let there be no anxiety. Let them not be troubled about him.

Nicolette, on entering Monsieur Jean's house, had repeated to him the very words of her mistress. That madame sent to know "why Monsieur Jean had not come the day before." "It is two days that I have not been there," said Jean Valjean mildly.

But the remark escaped the notice of Nicolette, who reported nothing of it to Cosette.

4

ATTRACTION AND EXTINCTION

DURING the last months of the spring and the first months of the summer of 1833, the scattered wayfarers in the Marais, the storekeepers, the idlers upon the doorsteps, noticed an old man neatly dressed in black, every day, about the same hour, at nightfall, come out of the Rue de l'Homme Armé, in the direction of the Rue Sainte Croix de la Bretonnerie, pass by the Blancs Manteaux, to the Rue Culture Sainte Catherine, and, reaching the Rue de l'Echarpe, turn to the left, and enter the Rue Saint Louis.

There he walked with slow steps, his head bent forward, seeing nothing, hearing nothing, his eye immovably fixed upon one point, always the same, which seemed studded with stars to him, and which was nothing more nor less than the corner of the Rue des Filles du Calvaire. As he approached the corner of that street, his face lighted up; a kind of joy illuminated his eye like an interior halo, he had a fascinated and softened expression, his lips moved vaguely, as if he were speaking to some one whom he did not see, he smiled faintly, and he advanced as slowly as he could. You would have said that even while wishing to reach some destination, he dreaded the moment when he should be near it. When there were but a few houses left between him and that street which appeared to attract him, his pace became so slow, that at times you might have supposed he had ceased to move. The vacillation of his head and the fixedness of his eye reminded you of the needle seeking the pole. However long he succeeded in deferring it, he must arrive at last; he reached the Rue des Filles du Calvaire; then he stopped, he trembled, he put his head with a kind of gloomy timidity beyond the corner of the last house, and he looked into that street, and there was in that tragical look something which resembled the bewilderment of the impossible, and the reflection of a forbidden paradise. Then a tear, which had gradually gathered in the corner of his eye, grown large enough to fall, glided over his cheek, and sometimes stopped at his mouth. The old man tasted its bitterness. He remained thus a few minutes, as if he had been stone; then he returned by the same route and at the same pace; and, in proportion as he receded, that look was extinguished.

Little by little, this old man ceased to go as far as the corner of the Rue des Filles du Calvaire; he stopped half way down the Rue Saint Louis; sometimes a little further, sometimes a little nearer. One day, he stopped at the corner of the Rue Culture Sainte Catherine, and looked at the Rue des Filles du Calvaire from the distance. Then he silently moved his head from right to left as if he were refusing himself something, and retraced his steps.

Very soon he no longer came even as far as the Rue Saint Louis. He reached the Rue Pavée, shook his head, and went back; then he no longer went beyond the Rue des Trois Pavillons; then he no longer passed the Blancs Manteaux. You would have said a pendulum which has not been wound up, and the oscillations of which are growing shorter ere they stop.

Every day, he came out of his house at the same hour, he commenced the same walk, but he did not finish it, and, perhaps unconsciously, he continually shortened it. His whole countenance expressed this single idea; What is the use? The eye was dull; no more radiance. The tear also was gone; it no longer gathered at the corner of the lids; that thoughtful eye was dry. The old man's head was still bent forward; his chin quivered at times; the wrinkles of his thin neck were painful to behold. Sometimes, when the weather was bad, he carried an umbrella under his arm, which he never opened. The good women of the neighbourhood said: "He is a natural." The children followed him laughing.

BOOK NINE
THE LAST NIGHT YIELDS
TO THE LAST DAWN

1

PITY FOR THE UNHAPPY, BUT INDULGENCE FOR THE HAPPY

IT IS a fearsome thing to be happy! How pleased we are with it! How all-sufficient we think it! How, being in possession of the false aim of life, happiness, we forget the true aim, duty!

We must say, however, that it would be unjust to blame Marius.

Marius as we have explained, before his marriage, had put no questions to M. Fauchelevent, and, since, he had feared to put any to Jean Valjean. He had regretted the promise into which he had allowed himself to be led. He had reiterated to himself many times that he had done wrong in making that concession to despair. He did nothing more than gradually to banish Jean Valjean from his house, and to obliterate him as much as possible from Cosette's mind. He had in some sort constantly placed himself between Cosette and Jean Valjean, sure that in that way she would not notice him, and would never think of him. It was more than obliteration, it was eclipse.

Marius did what he deemed necessary and just. He supposed he had, for discarding Jean Valjean, without harshness, but without weakness, serious reasons, which we have already seen, and still others which we shall see further on. Having chanced to meet, in a cause in which he was engaged, an old clerk of the house of Laffitte, he had obtained, without seeking it, some mysterious information which he could not, in truth, probe to the bottom, from respect for the secret which he had promised to keep, and from care for Jean Valjean's perilous situation. He believed, at that very time, that he had a solemn duty to perform, the restitution of the six hundred thousand francs to somebody whom he was seeking as cautiously as possible. In the meantime, he abstained from using that money.

As for Cosette, she was in none of these secrets; but it would be hard to condemn her also.

There was an all-powerful magnetism flowing from Marius to her, which compelled her to do, instinctively and almost mechanically, what Marius wished. She felt, in regard to "Monsieur Jean," a will from Marius; she conformed to it. Her husband had had nothing to say to her; she experienced the vague, but clear pressure of his unspoken wishes, and obeyed blindly. Her obedience in this consisted in not remembering what Marius forgot. She had to make no effort for that. Without knowing why herself, and without affording any grounds for censure, her soul had so thoroughly become her husband's soul, that whatever was covered with shadow in Marius' thought, was obscured in hers.

We must not go too far, however; in what concerns Jean Valjean, this forgetfulness and this obliteration were only superficial. She was rather thoughtless than forgetful. At heart, she really loved him whom she had so long called father. But she loved her husband still more. It was that which had somewhat swayed the balance of this heart, inclined in a single direction.

It sometimes happened that Cosette spoke of Jean Valjean, and wondered. Then Marius calmed her: "He is absent, I think. Didn't he say that he was going away on a journey?" "That is true," thought Cosette. "He was in the habit of disappearing in this way. But not for so long." Two or three times she sent Nicolette to inquire in the Rue de l'Homme Armé if Monsieur Jean had returned from his journey. Jean Valjean had the answer returned that he had not.

Cosette did not inquire further, having but one need on earth, Marius.

We must also say that, on their part, Marius and Cosette had been absent. They had been to Vernon. Marius had taken Cosette to his father's grave.

Marius had little by little withdrawn Cosette from Jean Valjean. Cosette was passive.

Moreover, what is called much too harshly, in certain cases, the ingratitude of children, is not always as blameworthy a thing as is supposed. It is the ingratitude of nature. Nature, as we have said elsewhere, "looks forward." Nature divides living beings into the coming and the going. The going are turned towards the shadow, the coming towards the light. Hence a separation, which, on the part of the old, is a fatality, and, on the part of the young, involuntary. This separation, at first insensible, gradually increases, like every separation of branches. The limbs, without parting from the trunk, recede from it. It is not their fault. Youth goes where joy is, to festivals, to brilliant lights, to loves. Old age goes to its end. They do not lose sight of each other, but the ties are loosened. The affection of the young is chilled by life; that of the old by the grave. We must not blame these poor children.

2

THE LAST FLICKERINGS OF
THE EXHAUSTED LAMP

ONE DAY Jean Valjean went down stairs, took three steps into the street, sat down upon a stone block, upon that same block where Gavroche, on the night of the 5th of June, had found him musing; he remained there a few minutes, then went upstairs again. This was the last oscillation of the pendulum. The next day, he did not leave his room. The day after he did not leave his bed.

His portress, who prepared his frugal meal, some cabbage, a few potatoes with a little pork, looked into the brown earthen plate, and exclaimed:

"Why, you didn't eat anything yesterday, poor dear man!"

"Yes, I did," answered Jean Valjean.

"The plate is all full."

"Look at the water-pitcher. That is empty."

"That shows that you have drunk; it don't show that you have eaten."

"Well," said Jean Valjean, "suppose I have only been hungry for water?"

"That is called thirst, and, when people don't eat at the same time, it is called fever."

"I will eat to-morrow."

"Or at Christmas. Why not eat to-day? Do people say: I will eat tomorrow! To leave me my whole plateful without touching it! My cole slaw, which was so good!"

Jean Valjean took the old woman's hand:

"I promise to eat it," said he to her in his benevolent voice.

"I am not satisfied with you," answered the portress.

Jean Valjean scarcely ever saw any other human being than this good woman. There are streets in Paris in which nobody walks, and houses into which nobody comes. He was in one of those streets, and in one of those houses.

While he still went out, he had bought of a brazier for a few sous a little copper crucifix, which he had hung upon a nail before his bed. The cross is always good to look upon.

A week elapsed, and Jean Valjean had not taken a step in his room. He was still in bed. The portress said to her husband: "The goodman upstairs does not get up any more, he does not eat any more, he won't last long. He has trouble, he has. Nobody can get it out of my head that his daughter has made a bad match."

The porter replied, with the accent of the marital sovereignty:

"If he is rich, let him have a doctor. If he is not rich, let him not have any. If he doesn't have a doctor, he will die."

"And if he does have one?"

"He will die," said the porter.

The portress began to dig up with an old knife some grass which was sprouting in what she called her pavement, and, while she was pulling up the grass, she muttered:

"It is a pity. An old man who is so nice! He is white as a chicken."

She saw a physician of the neighbourhood passing at the end of the street; she took it upon herself to beg him to go up.

"It is on the third floor," said she to him. "You will have nothing to do but go in. As the goodman does not stir from his bed now, the key is in the door all the time."

The physician saw Jean Valjean, and spoke with him.

When he came down, the portress questioned him:

"Well, doctor?"

"Your sick man is very sick."

"What is the matter with him?"

"Everything and nothing. He is a man who, to all appearance, has lost some dear friend. People die of that."

"What did he tell you?"

"He told me that he was well."

"Will you come again, doctor?"

"Yes," answered the physician. "But another than I must come again."

3

A PEN IS HEAVY TO HIM WHO LIFTED FAUCHELEVENT'S CART

ONE EVENING Jean Valjean had difficulty in raising himself upon his elbow; he felt his wrist and found no pulse; his breathing was shallow, and stopped at intervals; he realised that he was weaker than he had been before. Then, undoubtedly under the pressure of some supreme desire, he made an effort, sat up in bed, and dressed himself. He put on his old working-man's garb. As he went out no longer, he had returned to it, and he preferred it. He was obliged to stop several times while dressing; the mere effort of putting on his waistcoat, made the sweat roll down his forehead.

Since he had been alone, he had made his bed in the ante-room, so as to occupy this desolate tenement as little as possible.

He opened the valise and took out Cosette's outfit.

He spread it out upon his bed.

The bishop's candlesticks were in their place, on the mantel. He took two wax tapers from a drawer, and put them into the candlesticks. Then, although it was still broad daylight, it was in summer, he lighted them. We sometimes see torches lighted thus in broad day, in rooms where the dead lie.

Each step that he took in going from one piece of furniture to another exhausted him, and he was obliged to sit down. One of the chairs upon which he sank was standing before that mirror, so fatal for him, so providential for Marius, in which he had read Cosette's note, reversed on the blotter. He saw himself in this mirror, and did not recognise himself. He was eighty years old; before Marius' marriage, one would hardly have thought him fifty; this year had counted thirty. What was now upon his forehead was not the wrinkle of age, it was the mysterious mark of death.

Night had come. With much labour he drew a table and an old arm-chair near the fireplace, and put upon the table pen, ink, and paper.

Then he fainted. When he regained consciousness he was thirsty. Being unable to lift the water-pitcher, with great effort he tipped it towards his mouth, and drank a swallow.

Then he turned to the bed, and, still sitting, for he could stand but a moment, he looked at the little black dress, and all those dear objects.

Such contemplations last for hours which seem minutes. Suddenly he shivered, he felt that the chill was coming, he leaned upon the table which was lighted by the bishop's candlesticks, and took the pen.

As neither the pen nor the ink had been used for a long time, the tip of the pen was bent back, the ink was dried, he was obliged to get up and put a few drops of water into the ink, which he could not do without stopping and sitting down two or three times, and he was compelled to write with the back of the pen. He wiped his forehead from time to time.

His hand trembled. He slowly wrote the few lines which follow:

"Cosette, I bless you. I am going to make an explanation to you. Your husband was quite right in giving me to understand that I ought to leave; there is some mistake in what he believed, but he was right. He is very good. Always love him well when I am dead. Monsieur Pontmercy, always love my darling child. Cosette, this paper will be found, this is what I want to tell you, you shall see the figures, if I have the strength to recall them, listen well, this money is really your own.

Here he stopped, the pen fell from his fingers, he gave way to one of those despairing sobs which rose at times from the depths of his being, the poor man clasped his head with both hands, and reflected.

"Oh!" exclaimed he within himself (pitiful cries, heard by God alone), "it is all over. I shall never see her more. She is a smile which has passed over me. I am going to enter into the night without even seeing her again. Oh! a minute, an instant, to hear her voice, to touch her dress, to look at her, the angel! and then to die! It is nothing to die, but it is dreadful to die without seeing her. She would smile upon me, she would say a word to me. Would that harm anybody? No, it is over, forever. Here I am, all alone. My God! my God! I shall never see her again."

At this moment there was a rap at his door.

4

A BOTTLE OF INK WHICH SERVES
ONLY TO WHITEN

THAT VERY DAY, or rather that very evening, just as Marius had left the table and retired into his office, having a dossier to study, Basque had handed him a letter, saying: "the person who wrote the letter is in the antechamber."

Cosette had taken grandfather's arm, and was walking in the garden.

A letter, as well as a man, may have a forbidding appearance. Coarse paper, clumsy fold, the mere sight of certain missives displeases. The letter which Basque brought was of this kind.

Marius took it. It smelt of tobacco. Nothing awakens a reminiscence like an odour. Marius recognised this tobacco. He looked at the address: *To Monsieur, Monsieur the Baron Pommerci. In his hôtel*. The recognition of the tobacco made him recognise the handwriting. We might say that astonishment has its flashes. Marius was, as it were, illuminated by one of those flashes.

The scent, the mysterious aid-memory, revived a whole world within him. Here was the very paper, the manner of folding, the paleness of the ink; here was, indeed, the well-known handwriting; above all, here was the tobacco. The Jondrette garret appeared before him.

Thus, strange freak of chance! one of the two traces which he had sought so long, the one which he had again recently made so many efforts to find, and which he believed forever lost, came of itself to him.

He broke the seal eagerly, and read:——

"Monsieur Baron,—If the Supreme Being had given me the talents for it, I could have been Baron Thénard, member of the Institute (Academy of Ciences), but I am not so. I merely bear the same name that he does, happy if this remembrance commends me to the excellence of your bounties. The benefit with which you honour me will be reciprocal. I am in possession of a secret conserning an individual. This individual conserns you. I hold the secret at your disposition, desiring to have the honour of being yuseful to you. I will give you the simple means of drivving from your honourable family this individual who has no right in it, Madame the Baroness being of high birth. The sanctuary of virtue could not coabit longer with crime without abdicating.

"I attend in the entichamber the orders of Monsieur the Baron. With respect."

The letter was signed "THÉNARD."

This signature was not a false one. It was only a little abridged.

Besides the rigmarole and the orthography completed the revelation. The certificate of origin was perfect. There was no doubt possible.

The emotion of Marius was deep. After the feeling of surprise, he had a feeling of happiness. Let him now find the other man whom he sought, the man who had saved him, Marius, and he would have nothing more to wish.

He opened one of his secretary drawers, took out some bank-notes, put them in his pockets, closed the secretary, and rang. Basque appeared.

"Show him in," said Marius.

Basque announced:

"Monsieur Thénard."

A man entered.

A new surprise for Marius. The man who came in was perfectly unknown to him.

This man, old withal, had a large nose, his chin in his cravat, green spectacles, with double shade of green silk over his eyes, his hair polished and smoothed down, his forehead close to the eyebrows, like the wigs of English coachmen in high life. His hair was grey. He was dressed in black from head to foot, in a well worn but tidy black; a bunch of trinkets, hanging from his fob, suggested a watch. He held an old hat in his hand. He walked with a stoop, and the crook of his back increased the lowliness of his bow.

Hugo describes "an ingenious Jew" known as The Changer, who rents an elaborate selection of disguises and uniforms that can give a criminal the appearance of an honest and even distinguished person.

Marius' disappointment, on seeing another man enter than the one he was expecting, turned into dislike towards the new-comer. He examined him from head to foot, while the personage bowed without measure, and asked him in a sharp tone:

"What do you want?"

The man answered with an amiable grin of which the caressing smile of a crocodile would give some idea:

"It seems to me impossible that I have not already had the honour of seeing Monsieur the Baron in society. I really think that I met him privately some years ago, at Madame the Princess Bagration's and in the salons of his lordship the Viscount Dambray, peer of France."

It is always good tactics in rascality to pretend to recognise one whom you do not know.

Marius listened attentively to the voice of this man. He watched for the tone and gesture eagerly, but his disappointment increased; it was a whining pronunciation, entirely different from the sharp and dry sound of the voice which he expected. He was completely bewildered.

"I don't know," said he, "either Madame Bagration or M. Dambray. I have never in my life set foot in the house of either the one or the other."

The answer was testy. The person, gracious notwithstanding, persisted:

"Then it must be at Chateaubriand's that I have seen monsieur? I know Chateaubriand well. He is very affable. He says to me sometimes: 'Thénard, my friend, won't you drink a glass of wine with me?'"

Marius' brow grew more and more severe:

"I have never had the honour of being received at Monsieur de Chateaubriand's. Come to the point. What is it you wish?"

The man, in view of the harsher voice, made a lower bow.

"Monsieur Baron, deign to listen to me. There is in America, in a region which is near Panama, a village called La Joya. This village is composed of a single house. A large, square, three-story adobe house, each side of the square five hundred feet long, each story set back twelve feet from the story below, so as to leave in front a terrace which runs round the building, in the centre an interior court in which are provisions and ammunition, no windows, loopholes, no door, ladders, ladders to mount from the ground to the first terrace, and from the first to the second, and from the second to the third, ladders to descend into the interior court, no doors to the rooms, hatchways, no stairs to the rooms, ladders; at night the hatchways are closed, the ladders drawn in: swivels and carbines are aimed through the port-holes; no means of entering; a house by day, a citadel by night, eight hundred inhabitants, such is this village. Why so much precaution? because the country is dangerous; it is full of anthropophagi. Then why do people go there? because that country is wonderful; gold is found there."

"What are you coming to?" Marius interrupted, who from disappointment was passing to impatience.

"To this, Monsieur Baron. I am an old weary diplomatist. The old civilisation has used me up. I wish to try the savages."

"What then?"

"Monsieur Baron, selfishness is the law of the world. The proletarian country-woman who works by the day, turns round when the stagecoach passes, the proprietary country-woman who works in her own field, does not turn round. The poor man's dog barks at the rich man, the rich man's dog barks at the poor man. Every one for himself. Interest is the motive of men. Gold is the magnet."

"What then? Conclude."

"I would like to go and establish myself at La Joya. There are three of us. I have my spouse and my young lady; a girl who is very beautiful. The voyage is long and dear. I must have a little money."

"How does that concern me?" inquired Marius.

The stranger stretched his neck out of his cravat, a movement characteristic of the vulture, and replied, with redoubled smiles:

"Then Monsieur the Baron has not read my letter?"

That was not far from true. The fact is, that the contents of the epistle had glanced off from Marius. He had seen the handwriting rather than read the letter. He scarcely remembered it. Within a moment a new clue had been given him. He had noticed this remark: My spouse and my young lady. He fixed a searching eye upon the stranger. An examining judge could not have done better. He seemed to be lying in ambush for him. He answered:

"Explain."

The stranger thrust his hands into his fobs, raised his head without straightening his backbone, but scrutinising Marius in his turn with the green gaze of his spectacles.

"Certainly, Monsieur the Baron. I will explain. I have a secret to sell you."

"A secret?"

"A secret."

"Which concerns me?"

"Somewhat."

"What is this secret?"

Marius examined the man more and more closely, while listening to him.

"I commence gratis," said the stranger. "You will see that I am interesting."

"Go on."

"Monsieur Baron, you have in your house a robber and an assassin."

Marius shuddered.

"In my house? no," said he.

The stranger, imperturbable, brushed his hat with his sleeve, and continued:

"Assassin and robber. Observe, Monsieur Baron, that I do not speak here of acts, old, by-gone, and withered, which may be cancelled by prescription in the eye of the law, and by repentance in the eye of God. I speak of recent acts, present acts, acts yet unknown to justice at this hour. I will proceed. This man has glided into your confidence, and almost into your family, under a false name. I am going to tell you his true name. And to tell it to you for nothing."

"I am listening."

"His name is Jean Valjean."

"I know it."

"I am going to tell you, also for nothing, who he is."

"Say on."

"He is a former convict."

"I know it."

"You know it since I have had the honour of telling you."

"No. I knew it before."

Marius' cool tone, that double reply, *I know it*, his laconic method of speech, embarrassing to conversation, excited some suppressed anger in the stranger. He shot furtively at Marius a furious look, which was immediately extinguished. Quick as it was, this look was one of those which are recognised after they have once been seen; it did not escape Marius. Certain flames can only come from certain souls; the eye, that window of the thought, blazes with it; spectacles hide nothing; you might as well put a glass over hell.

The stranger resumed with a smile:

"I do not permit myself to contradict Monsieur the Baron. At all events, you must see that I am informed. Now, what I have to acquaint you with, is known to myself alone. It concerns the fortune of Madame the Baroness. It is an extraordinary secret. It is for sale. I offer it to you first. Cheap. Twenty thousand francs."

"I know that secret as well as the others," said Marius.

The person felt the necessity of lowering his price a little.

"Monsieur Baron, say ten thousand francs, and I will go on."

"I repeat, that you have nothing to acquaint me with. I know what you wish to tell me."

There was a new flash in the man's eye. He exclaimed:

"Still I must dine to-day. It is an extraordinary secret, I tell you. Monsieur the Baron, I am going to speak. I will speak. Give me twenty francs."

Marius looked at him steadily:

"I know your extraordinary secret; just as I knew Jean Valjean's name; just as I know your name."

"My name?"

"Yes."

"That is not difficult, Monsieur Baron. I have had the honour of writing it to you and telling it to you. Thénard."

"Dier."

"Eh?"

"Thénardier."

"Who is that?"

In danger the porcupine bristles, the beetle feigns death, the Old Guard forms a square; this man began to laugh.

Then, with a fillip, he brushed a speck of dust from his coat-sleeve.

Marius continued:

"You are also the working-man Jondrette, the comedian Fabantou, the poet Genflot, the Spaniard Don Alvarès, and the woman Balizard."

"The woman what?"

"And you have kept a tavern at Montfermeil."

"A tavern! never."

"And I tell you that you are Thénardier."

"I deny it."

"And that you are a scoundrel. Here."

And Marius, taking a bank-note from his pocket, threw it in his face.

"Thanks! pardon! five hundred francs! Monsieur Baron!"

And the man, bewildered, bowing, catching the note, examined it.

"Five hundred francs!" he repeated in astonishment. And he stammered out in an undertone: "A serious *fafiot* [bundle]!"

Then bluntly:

"Well, so be it," exclaimed he. "Let us make ourselves comfortable."

And, with the agility of a monkey, throwing his hair off backwards, pulling off his spectacles, taking out of his nose and pocketing the two quill tubes of which we have just spoken, and which we have already seen elsewhere on another page of this book, he took off his countenance as one takes off his hat.

His eye kindled; his forehead, uneven, ravined, humped in spots, hideously wrinkled at the top, emerged; his nose became as sharp as a beak; the fierce and cunning profile of the man of prey appeared again.

"Monsieur the Baron is infallible," said he in a clear voice from which all nasality has disappeared, "I am Thénardier."

And he straightened his bent back.

Thénardier, for it was indeed he, was strangely surprised; he would have been disconcerted if he could have been. He had come to bring astonishment, and he himself received it. This humiliation had been compensated by five hundred francs, and, all things considered, he accepted it; but he was none the less astounded.

He saw this Baron Pontmercy for the first time, and in spite of his disguise, this Baron Pontmercy recognised him and recognised him thoroughly. And not only was this baron fully informed, in regard to Thénardier, but he seemed fully informed in regard to Jean Valjean. Who was this almost beardless young man, so icy and so generous, who knew people's names, who knew all their names, and who opened his purse to them, who abused rogues like a judge and who paid them like a dupe?

Thénardier, it will be remembered, although he had been a neighbour of Marius, had never seen him, which is frequent in Paris; he had once heard some talk of his daughters about a very poor young man named Marius who lived in the house. He had written to him, without knowing him, the letter which we have seen. No connection was possible in his mind between that Marius and M. the Baron Pontmercy.

Through his daughter Azelma, however, whom he had put upon the track of the couple married on the 16th of February, and through his own researches, he had succeeded in finding out many things and, from the depth of his darkness, he had been able to seize more than one mysterious clue. He had, by dint of industry, discovered, or, at least, by dint of induction, guessed who the man was whom he had met on a certain day in the Grand Sewer. From the man, he had easily arrived at the name. He knew that Madame the Baroness Pontmercy was Cosette. But, in that respect, he intended to be prudent. Who was Cosette? He did not know exactly himself. He suspected indeed some illegitimacy. Fantine's story had always seemed to him ambiguous; but why speak of it? to get paid for his silence? He had, or thought he had, something better to sell than that. And to all appearances, to come and make, without any proof, this revelation to Baron Pontmercy: *Your wife is a bastard,* would only have attracted the husband's boot towards the revelator's back.

In Thénardier's opinion, the conversation with Marius had not yet commenced. He had been obliged to retreat, to modify his strategy, to abandon a position, to change his base; but nothing essential was yet lost, and he had five hundred francs in his pocket. Moreover, he had something decisive to say, and even against this Baron Pontmercy, so well informed and so well armed, he felt himself strong. To men of Thénardier's nature, every dialogue is a battle. In that which was about to be commenced what was his situation? He did not know to whom he was speaking, but he knew about what he was speaking. He rapidly made this interior review of his forces, and after saying: *"I am Thénardier,"* he waited.

Marius remained absorbed in thought. At last, then, he had caught Thénardier; this man, whom he had so much desired to find again, was before him: so he would be able to do honour to Colonel Pontmercy's injunction. He was humiliated that that hero should owe anything to this bandit, and that the bill of exchange drawn by his father from the depth of the grave upon him, Marius, should have remained unpaid until this day. It appeared to him, also, in the complex position of his mind with regard to Thénardier, that here was an opportunity to avenge the colonel for the misfortune of having been saved by such a rascal. However that might be, he was pleased. He was about to deliver the colonel's shade at last from his unworthy creditor, and it seemed to him that he was about to release his father's memory from imprisonment for debt.

Besides this duty, he had another, to clear up, if he could, the source of Cosette's fortune. The opportunity seemed to present itself. Thénardier knew something, perhaps. It might be useful to probe this man to the bottom. He began with that.

Thénardier had slipped the "serious *fafiot*" into his fob, and was looking at Marius with an almost affectionate humility.

Marius interrupted the silence.

"Thénardier, I have told you your name. Now your secret, what you came to make known to me, do you want me to tell you that? I too have my means of information. You shall see that I know more about it than you do. Jean Valjean, as you have said, is an assassin and a robber. A robber, because he robbed a rich manufacturer, M. Madeleine, whose ruin he caused. An assassin, because he assassinated the police-officer, Javert."

"I don't understand, Monsieur Baron," said Thénardier.

"I will make myself understood. Listen. There was, in an arrondissement of the Pas-de-Calais, about 1822, a man who had had some old difficulty with justice, and who, under the name of M. Madeleine, had reformed and re-established himself. He had become in the full force of the term an upright man. By means of a manufacture, that of black glass trinkets, he had made the fortune of an entire city. As for his own personal fortune, he had made it also, but secondarily, and, in some sort, incidentally. He was the foster-father of the poor. He founded hospitals, opened schools, visited the sick, endowed daughters, supported widows, adopted orphans; he was, as it were, the guardian of the country. He had refused the Cross, he had been appointed mayor. A liberated convict knew the secret of a penalty once incurred by this man; he informed against him and had him arrested, and took advantage of the arrest to come to Paris and draw from the banker, Laffitte—I have the fact from the cashier himself—by means of a false signature, a sum of more than half a million which belonged to M. Madeleine. This convict who robbed M. Madeleine is Jean Valjean. As to the other act, you have just as little to tell me. Jean Valjean killed the officer Javert; he killed him with a pistol. I, who am now speaking to you, I was present."

Thénardier cast upon Marius the sovereign glance of a beaten man, who lays hold on victory again, and who has just recovered in one minute all the ground which he had lost. But the smile returned immediately; the inferior before the superior can only have a skulking triumph, and Thénardier merely said to Marius:

"Monsieur Baron, we are on the wrong track."

And he emphasised this phrase by giving his bunch of trinkets an expressive twirl.

"What!" replied Marius, "do you deny that? These are facts."

"They are chimeras. The confidence with which Monsieur the Baron honours me makes it my duty to tell him so. Before all things, truth and justice. I do not like to see people accused unjustly. Monsieur Baron, Jean Valjean never robbed Monsieur Madeleine, and Jean Valjean never killed Javert."

"You speak strongly! how is that?"

"For two reasons."

"What are they? tell me."

"The first is this: he did not rob Monsieur Madeleine, since it is Jean Valjean himself who was Monsieur Madeleine."

"What is that you are telling me?"

"And the second is this: he did not assassinate Javert, since Javert himself killed Javert."

"What do you mean?"

"That Javert committed suicide."

"Prove it! prove it!" cried Marius, beside himself.

Thénardier resumed, scanning his phrase in the fashion of an ancient Alexandrine:

"The—police—of—ficer—Ja—vert—was—found—drowned—under—a—boat—by—the—Pont—au—Change."

"But prove it now!"

Thénardier took from his pocket a large envelope of grey paper, which seemed to contain folded sheets of different sizes.

"I have my documents," said he, with calmness.

And he added:

"Monsieur Baron, in your interest, I wished to find out Jean Valjean to the bottom. I say that Jean Valjean and Madeleine are the same man; and I say that Javert had no other assassin than Javert; and when I speak I have the proofs. Not manuscript proofs; writing is suspicious; writing is complaisant, but proofs in print."

While speaking, Thénardier took out of the envelope two newspapers, yellow, faded, and strongly saturated with tobacco. One of these two newspapers, broken at all the folds, and falling in square pieces, seemed much older than the other.

"Two facts, two proofs," said Thénardier. And unfolding the two papers, he handed them to Marius.

With these two newspapers the reader is acquainted. One, the oldest, a copy of the *Drapeau Blanc,* of the 25th of July, 1823, established the identity of M. Madeleine and Jean Valjean. The other, a *Moniteur* of the 15th of June, 1832, verified the suicide of Javert, adding that it appeared from a verbal report made by Javert to the prefect that, taken prisoner in the barricade of the Rue de la Chanvrerie, he had owed his life to the magnanimity of an insurgent who, though he had him at the muzzle of his pistol, instead of blowing out his brains, had fired into the air.

Marius read. There was evidence, certain date, unquestionable proof; these two newspapers had not been printed expressly to support Thénardier's words. The note published in the *Moniteur* was an official communication from the prefecture of police. Marius could not doubt. The information derived from the cashier was false, and he himself was mistaken. Jean Valjean, suddenly growing grand, arose from the cloud. Marius could not restrain a cry of joy:

"Well, then, this unhappy man is a wonderful man! all that fortune was really his own! he is Madeleine, the providence of a whole region! he is Jean Valjean, the saviour of Javert! he is a hero! he is a saint!"

"He is not a saint, and he is not a hero," said Thénardier. "He is an assassin and a robber."

And he added with the tone of a man who begins to feel some authority in himself: "Let us be calm."

Robber, assassin; these words, which Marius supposed were gone, yet which came back, fell upon him like a shower of ice.

"Let's start again," said he.

"Still," said Thénardier. "Jean Valjean did not rob Madeleine, but he is a robber. He did not kill Javert, but he is a murderer."

"Are you referring," resumed Marius, "to that petty theft of forty years ago, expiated, as appears from your newspapers themselves, by a whole life of repentance, abnegation, and virtue?"

"I said assassination and robbery, Monsieur Baron. And I repeat that I speak of recent facts. What I have to reveal to you is absolutely unknown. It belongs to the unpublished. And perhaps you will find in it the source of the fortune adroitly presented by Jean Valjean to Madame the Baroness. I say adroitly, for, by a donation of this kind, to glide into an honourable house, the comforts of which he will share, and, by the same stroke, to conceal his crime to enjoy his robbery, to bury his name, and to create himself a family, that would not be very unskilful."

"I might interrupt you here," observed Marius; "but continue."

"Monsieur Baron, I will tell you all, leaving the recompense to your generosity. This secret is worth a pile of gold. You will say to me: why have you not gone to Jean Valjean? For a very simple reason: I know that he has dispossessed himself, and dispossessed in your favour, and I think the contrivance ingenious; but he has not a sou left, he would show me his empty hands, and, since I need some money for my voyage to La Joya, I prefer you, who have all, to him who has nothing. I am somewhat fatigued; allow me to take a chair."

Marius sat down, and made sign to him to sit down.

Thénardier installed himself in an upholstered chair, took up the two newspapers, thrust them back into the envelope, and muttered, striking the *Drapeau Blanc* with his nail: "It cost me some hard work to get this one." This done, he crossed his legs and lay back in his chair, an attitude characteristic of people who are sure of what they are saying, then entered into the subject seriously, and emphasising his words:

"Monsieur Baron, on the 6th of June, 1832, about a year ago, the day of the émeute, a man was in the Grand Sewer of Paris, near where the sewer empties into the Seine, between the Pont des Invalides and the Pont d'Iéna."

Marius suddenly drew his chair near Thénardier's. Thénardier noticed this movement, and continued with the deliberation of a speaker who holds his interlocutor fast, and who feels the palpitation of his adversary beneath his words:

"This man, compelled to conceal himself, for reasons foreign to politics, however, had taken the sewer for his dwelling, and had a key to it. It was, I repeat it, the 6th of June; it might have been eight o'clock in the evening. The man heard a noise in the sewer. Very much surprised, he hid himself, and watched. It was a sound of steps, somebody was walking in the darkness; somebody was coming in his direction. Strange to say, there was another man in the sewer beside him. The grating of the outlet of the sewer was not far off. A little light which came from it enabled him to recognise the new-comer, and to see that this man was carrying something on his back. He walked bent over. The man who was walking bent over was a former convict, and what he was carrying upon his shoulders was a corpse. Assassination *in flagrante delicto,* if ever there was such a thing. As for the robbery, it follows of course; nobody kills a man for nothing. This convict was going to throw his corpse into the river. It is a noteworthy fact, that before reaching the grating of the outlet, this convict, who came from a distance in the sewer, had been compelled to pass through a horrible quagmire in which it would seem that he might have left the corpse; but, the sewermen working upon the quagmire might, the very next day, have found the assassinated man, and that was not the assassin's game. He preferred to go through the quagmire with his load, and his efforts must have been terrible; it is impossible to put one's life in greater peril; I do not understand how he came out of it alive."

Marius' chair drew still nearer. Thénardier took advantage of it to draw a long breath. He continued:

"Monsieur Baron, a sewer is not the Champ de Mars. One lacks everything there, even room. When two men are in a sewer, they must meet each other. That is what happened. The resident and the traveller were compelled to say good-day to each other, to their mutual regret. The traveller said to the resident: *"You see what I have on my back, I must get out, you have the key, give it to me."* This convict was a man of terrible strength. There was no refusing him. Still he who had the key parleyed, merely to gain time. He examined the dead man, but he could see nothing, except that he was young, well dressed, apparently a rich man, and all disfigured with blood. While he was talking, he found means to cut and tear off from behind, without the assassin perceiving it, a piece of the assassinated man's coat. A piece of evidence, you understand; means of getting trace of the affair, and proving the crime upon the criminal. He put this piece of evidence in his pocket. After which he opened the grating, let the man out with his incumbrance on his back, shut the grating again and escaped, little caring to be mixed up with the remainder of the adventure, and especially desiring not to be present when the assassin should throw the assassinated man into the river. You understand now. He who was carrying the corpse was Jean Valjean; he who had the key is now speaking to you, and the piece of the coat——"

Thénardier finished the phrase by drawing from his pocket and holding up, on a level with his eyes, between his thumbs and his forefingers, a strip of ragged black cloth, covered with dark stains.

Marius had risen, pale, hardly breathing, his eye fixed upon the scrap of black cloth, and, without uttering a word, without losing sight of this rag, he retreated to the wall, and, with his right hand stretched behind him, groped about for a key which was in the lock of a closet near the chimney. He found this key, opened the closet, and thrust his arm into it without looking, and without removing his startled eyes from the fragment that Thénardier held up.

Meanwhile Thénardier continued:

"Monsieur Baron, I have the strongest reasons to believe that the assassinated young man was an opulent stranger drawn into a snare by Jean Valjean, and the bearer of an enormous sum."

"The young man was myself, and there is the coat!" cried Marius, and he threw an old black coat covered with blood upon the carpet.

Then, snatching the fragment from Thénardier's hands, he bent down over the coat, and applied the piece to the cut skirt. The edges fitted exactly, and the strip completed the coat.

Thénardier was petrified. He thought this: "I am floored."

Marius rose up, quivering, desperate, flashing.

He felt in his pocket, and walked, furious, towards Thénardier, offering him and almost pushing into his face his fist full of five hundred and a thousand franc notes.

"You are a wretch! you are a liar, a slanderer, a scoundrel. You came to accuse this man, you have justified him; you wanted to destroy him, you have succeeded only in glorifying him. And it is you who are a robber! and it is you who are an assassin. I saw you, Thénardier, Jondrette, in that den on the Boulevard de l'Hôpital. I know enough about you to send you to the galleys, and further even, if I wished. Here, there are a thousand francs, bandit that you are!"

And he threw a bill for a thousand francs to Thénardier.

"Ah! Jondrette, Thénardier, vile knave! let this be a lesson to you, pedlar of secrets, trader in mysteries, fumbler in the dark, wretch! Take these five hundred francs, and leave this place! Waterloo protects you."

"Waterloo!" muttered Thénardier, pocketing the five hundred francs with the thousand francs.

"Yes, assassin! you saved the life of a colonel there——"

"Of a general," said Thénardier, raising his head.

"Of a colonel!" replied Marius with a burst of passion. "I would not

give a farthing for a general. And you came here to act out your infamy! I
tell you that you have committed every crime. Go! out of my sight! Be
happy only, that is all that I desire. Ah! monster! there are three thousand
francs more. Take them. You will start to-morrow for America, with your
daughter, for your wife is dead, abominable liar. I will see to your departure, bandit, and I will count out to you then twenty thousand francs. Go
and get hung elsewhere!"

"Monsieur Baron," answered Thénardier, bowing to the ground, "eternal gratitude."

And Thénardier went out, comprehending nothing, astounded and
transported with this sweet crushing under sacks of gold and with this
thunderbolt bursting upon his head in bank-notes.

Thunderstruck he was, but happy also; and he would have been very
sorry to have had a lightning rod against that thunderbolt.

Let us finish with this man at once. Two days after the events which we
are now relating, he left, through Marius' care, for America, under a false
name, with his daughter Azelma, provided with a draft upon New York for
twenty thousand francs. Thénardier, the moral misery of Thénardier, the
brokendown bourgeois, was irremediable; he was in America what he had
been in Europe. The touch of a wicked man is often enough to corrupt a
good deed and to make an evil result spring from it. With Marius' money,
Thénardier became a slaver.

As soon as Thénardier was out of doors, Marius ran to the garden
where Cosette was still walking:

"Cosette! Cosette!" cried he. "Come! come quick! Let us go. Basque, a
fiacre! Cosette, come. Oh! my God! It was he who saved my life! Let us
not lose a minute! Put on your shawl."

Cosette thought him mad, and obeyed.

He did not breathe, he put his hand upon his heart to repress its beating. He walked to and fro with rapid strides, he embraced Cosette: "Oh!
Cosette! I am an unhappy man!" said he.

Marius was amazed. He began to see in this Jean Valjean a strangely
lofty and saddened form. An unparalleled virtue appeared before him,
supreme and mild, humble in its immensity. The convict was transfigured
into Christ. Marius was bewildered by this marvel. He did not know exactly
what he saw, but it was grand.

In a moment, a fiacre was at the door.

Marius helped Cosette in and sprang in himself.

"Driver," said he, "Rue de l'Homme Armé, Number 7."

The fiacre started.

"Oh! what happiness!" said Cosette. "Rue de l'Homme Armé! I dared
not speak to you of it again. We are going to see Monsieur Jean."

"Your father! Cosette, your father more than ever. Cosette, I see it. You
told me that you never received the letter which I sent you by Gavroche.
It must have fallen into his hands. Cosette, he went to the barricade to save
me. As it is a necessity for him to be an angel, on the way, he saved others;
he saved Javert. He snatched me out of that gulf to give me to you. He car-

ried me on his back in that frightful sewer. Oh! I am an unnatural ingrate.
Cosette, after having been your providence, he was mine. Only think that
there was a horrible quagmire, enough to drown him a hundred times, to
drown him in the mire, Cosette! he carried me through that. I had fainted;
I saw nothing, I heard nothing, I could know nothing of my own fate. We
are going to bring him back, take him with us, whether he will or no, he
shall never leave us again. If he is only at home! If we only find him! I will
pass the rest of my life in venerating him. Yes, that must be it, do you see,
Cosette? Gavroche must have handed my letter to him. It is all explained.
You understand."

Cosette did not understand a word.

"You are right," said she to him.

Meanwhile the fiacre rolled on.

5

NIGHT BEHIND WHICH IS DAWN

At the knock which he heard at his door, Jean Valjean turned his head.

"Come in," said he feebly.

The door opened. Cosette and Marius appeared.

Cosette rushed into the room.

Marius remained upon the threshold, leaning against the casing of the
door.

"Cosette!" said Jean Valjean, and he rose in his chair, his arms stretched
out and trembling, haggard, livid, terrible, with immense joy in his eyes.

Cosette stifled with emotion, fell upon Jean Valjean's breast.

"Father!" said she.

Jean Valjean, beside himself, stammered:

"Cosette! she? you, madame? it is you, Cosette? Oh, my God!" And,
clasped in Cosette's arms, he exclaimed:

"It is you, Cosette? you are here? You forgive me then!"

Marius, dropping his eyelids that the tears might not fall, stepped forward and murmured between his lips which were contracted convulsively
to check the sobs:

"Father!"

"And you too, you forgive me!" said Jean Valjean.

Marius could not utter a word, and Jean Valjean added: "Thanks."

Cosette took off her shawl and threw her hat upon the bed.

"They are in my way," said she.

And, seating herself upon the old man's knees, she stroked away his white hair with an adorable grace, and kissed his forehead.

Jean Valjean, bewildered, offered no resistance.

Cosette, who had but a very confused understanding of all this, redoubled her caresses, as if she would pay Marius' debt.

Jean Valjean faltered:

"How foolish we are! I thought I should never see her again. Only think, Monsieur Pontmercy, that at the moment you came in, I was saying to myself: It is over. There is her little dress, I am a miserable man, I shall never see Cosette again, I was saying that at the very moment you were coming up the stairs. Was I not silly? I was as silly as that! But we reckon without God. God said: You think that you are going to be abandoned, dolt? No. No, it shall not come to pass like that. Come, here is a poor goodman who has need of an angel. And the angel comes; and I see my Cosette again! and I see my darling Cosette again! Oh! I was very miserable!"

For a moment he could not speak, then he continued:

"I really needed to see Cosette a little while from time to time. A heart does want a bone to gnaw. Still I felt plainly that I was in the way. I gave myself reasons: they have no need of you, stay in your corner, you have no right to continue for ever. Oh! bless God, I see her again! Do you know, Cosette, that your husband is very handsome? Ah, you have a pretty embroidered collar, yes, yes. I like that pattern. Your husband chose it, did he not? And then, Cosette, you must have cashmeres. Monsieur Pontmercy, let me call her Cosette. It will not be very long."

And Cosette continued again:

"How naughty to have left us in this way! Where have you been? why were you away so long? Your journeys did not used to last more than three or four days. I sent Nicolette, the answer always was: He is absent. How long since you returned? Why did not you let us know? Do you know that you are very much changed. Oh! the naughty father! he has been sick, and we did not know it! Here, Marius, feel his hand, how cold it is!"

"So you are here, Monsieur Pontmercy, you forgive me!" repeated Jean Valjean.

At these words, which Jean Valjean now said for the second time, all that was swelling in Marius' heart found an outlet, he broke forth:

"Cosette, do you hear? that is the way with him! he begs my pardon, and do you know what he has done for me, Cosette? he has saved my life. He has done more. He has given you to me. And, after having saved me, and after having given you to me, Cosette, what did he do with himself? he sacrificed himself. There is the man. And, to me the ungrateful, to me the forgetful, to me the pitiless, to me the guilty, he says: Thanks! Cosette, my whole life passed at the feet of this man would be too little. That barricade, that sewer, that furnace, that cloaca, he went through everything for me, for you, Cosette! He bore me through death in every form which he put aside from me, and which he accepted for himself. All courage, all virtue, all heroism, all sanctity, he has it all, Cosette, that man is an angel!"

"Hush! hush!" said Jean Valjean in a whisper. "Why tell all that?"

"But you!" exclaimed Marius, with a passion in which veneration was mingled, "why have not you told it? It is your fault, too. You save people's lives, and you hide it from them! You do more, under pretence of unmasking yourself, you calumniate yourself. It is frightful."

"I told the truth," answered Jean Valjean.

"No," replied Marius, "the truth is the whole truth; and you did not tell it. You were Monsieur Madeleine, why not have said so? You had saved Javert, why not have said so? I owe my life to you, why not have said so?"

"Because I thought as you did. I felt that you were right. It was necessary that I should go away. If you had known that affair of the sewer, you would have made me stay with you. I should then have had to keep silent. If I had spoken, it would have embarrassed all."

"Embarrassed what? embarrassed whom?" replied Marius. "Do you suppose you are going to stay here? We are going to carry you back. Oh! my God! when I think it was by accident that I learned it all! We are going to carry you back. You are a part of us. You are her father and mine. You shall not spend another day in this horrid house. Do not imagine that you will be here to-morrow."

"To-morrow," said Jean Valjean, "I shall not be here, but I shall not be at your house."

"What do you mean?" replied Marius. "Ah now, we shall allow no more journeys. You shall never leave us again. You belong to us. We will not let you go."

"This time, it is for good," added Cosette. "We have a carriage below. I am going to carry you off. If necessary, I shall use force."

And laughing, she made as if she would lift the old man in her arms.

"Your room is still in our house," she continued. "If you knew how pretty the garden is now. The azalias are growing finely. The paths are sanded with river sand: there are some little violet shells. You shall eat some of my strawberries. I water them myself. And no more madame, and no more Monsieur Jean, we are a republic, are we not, Marius? The programme is changed. If you knew, father, I have had some trouble, there was a red-breast which had made her nest in a hole in the wall, a horrid cat ate her up for me. My poor pretty little red-breast who put her head out at her window and looked at me! I cried over it. I would have killed the cat! But now, nobody cries any more. Everybody laughs, everybody is happy. You are coming with us. How glad grandfather will be! You shall have your bed in the garden, you shall tend it, and we will see if your strawberries are as fine as mine. And then, I will do what ever you wish, and then, you will obey me."

Jean Valjean listened to her without hearing her. He heard the music of her voice rather than the meaning of her words; one of those big tears which are the gloomy pearls of the soul, gathered slowly in his eye. He murmured:

"The proof that God is good is that she is here."

"Father!" cried Cosette.

Jean Valjean continued:

"It is very true that it would be charming to live together. They have their trees full of birds. I would walk with Cosette. To be with people who live, who bid each other good morning, who call each other into the garden, would be sweet. We would see each other as soon as it was morning. We would each cultivate our little corner. She would have me eat her strawberries. I would have her pick my roses. It would be charming. Only——"

He paused and said mildly:

"It is a pity."

The tear did not fall, it went back, and Jean Valjean replaced it with a smile.

Cosette took both the old man's hands in her own.

"My God!" said she, "your hands are colder yet. Are you sick? Are you suffering?"

"No," answered Jean Valjean. "I am very well. Only——"

He stopped.

"Only what?"

"I shall die in a few minutes."

Cosette and Marius shuddered.

"Die!" exclaimed Marius.

"Yes, but that is nothing," said Jean Valjean.

He breathed, smiled, and continued.

"Cosette, you are speaking to me, go on, speak again, your little red-breast is dead then, speak, let me hear your voice!"

Marius, petrified, gazed upon the old man.

Cosette uttered a piercing cry:

"Father! my father! you shall live. You are going to live. I will have you live, do you hear!"

Jean Valjean raised his head towards her with adoration.

"Oh yes, forbid me to die. Who knows? I shall obey perhaps. I was just dying when you came. That stopped me, it seemed to me that I was born again."

"You are full of strength and life," exclaimed Marius. "Do you think people die like that? You have had trouble, you shall have no more. I ask your pardon now, and that on my knees! You shall live, and live with us, and live long. We will take you back. Both of us here will have but one thought henceforth, your happiness!"

"You see," added Cosette in tears, "that Marius says you will not die."

Jean Valjean continued to smile.

"If you should take me back, Monsieur Pontmercy, would that make me different from what I am? No; God thought as you and I did, and he has not changed his mind; it is best that I should go away. Death is a good arrangement. God knows better than we do what we need. That you are happy, that Monsieur Pontmercy has Cosette, that youth espouses morning, that there are about you, my children, lilacs and nightingales, that your life is a beautiful lawn in the sunshine, that all the enchantments of heaven fill your souls, and now, that I who am good for nothing, that I die; surely all this is well. Look you, be reasonable, there is nothing else possible now, I am sure that it is all over. An hour ago I had a fainting fit. And then, last night, I drank that pitcher full of water. How good your husband is, Cosette! You are much better off than with me."

There was a noise at the door. It was the physician coming in.

"Good day and good-by, doctor," said Jean Valjean. "Here are my poor children."

Marius approached the physician. He addressed this single word to him: "Monsieur?" but in the manner of pronouncing it, there was a complete question.

The physician answered the question by an expressive glance.

"Because things are unpleasant," said Jean Valjean, "that is no reason for being unjust towards God."

There was a silence. All hearts were oppressed.

Jean Valjean turned towards Cosette. He began to gaze at her as if he would take a look which should endure through eternity. At the depth of shadow to which he had already descended, ecstasy was still possible to him while beholding Cosette. The reflection of that sweet countenance illumined his pale face. The sepulchre may have its enchantments.

The physician felt his pulse.

"Ah! it was you he needed!" murmured he, looking at Cosette and Marius.

And, bending towards Marius' ear he added very low:

"Too late."

Jean Valjean, almost without ceasing to gaze upon Cosette, turned upon Marius and the physician a look of serenity. They heard these almost inarticulate words come from his lips:

"It is nothing to die; it is frightful not to live."

Suddenly he arose. These returns of strength are sometimes a sign of the death-struggle. He walked with a firm step to the wall, put aside Marius and the physician, who offered to assist him, took down from the wall the little copper crucifix which hung there, came back, and sat down with all the freedom of motion of perfect health, and said in a loud voice, laying the crucifix on the table:

"Behold the great martyr."

Then his breast sank in, his head wavered, as if the dizziness of the tomb seized him, and his hands resting upon his knees, began to clutch at his trousers.

Cosette supported his shoulders, and sobbed, and attempted to speak to him, but could not. There could be distinguished, among the words mingled with that mournful saliva which accompanies tears, sentences like this: "Father! do not leave us. Is it possible that we have found you again only to lose you?"

The agony of death may be said to meander. It goes, comes, advances towards the grave, and returns towards life. There is some groping in the act of dying.

Jean Valjean, after this half-faint, gathered strength, shook his forehead as if to throw off the darkness, and became almost completely lucid once more. He took a fold of Cosette's sleeve, and kissed it.

"He is reviving! doctor, he is reviving!" cried Marius.

"You are both kind," said Jean Valjean. "I will tell you what has given me pain. What has given me pain, Monsieur Pontmercy, was that you have been unwilling to touch that money. That money really belongs to your wife. I will explain it to you, my children, on that account I am glad to see you. The black jet comes from England, the white jet comes from Norway. All this is in the paper you see there, which you will read. For bracelets, I invented the substitution of clasps made by bending the metal, for clasps made by soldering the metal. They are handsomer, better, and cheaper. You understand how much money can be made. So Cosette's fortune is really her own. I give you these particulars so that your minds may be at rest."

The portress had come up, and was looking through the half-open door. The physician motioned her away, but he could not prevent that good, zealous woman from crying to the dying man before she went:

"Do you want a priest?"

"I have one," answered Jean Valjean.

And, with his finger, he seemed to designate a point above his head, where, you would have said, he saw some one.

It is probable that the Bishop was indeed a witness of this death-agony.

Cosette slipped a pillow under his back gently.

Jean Valjean resumed:

"Monsieur Pontmercy, have no fear, I conjure you. The six hundred thousand francs are really Cosette's. I shall have lost my life if you do not enjoy it! We succeeded very well in making glasswork. We rivalled what is called Berlin jewellery. Indeed, the German black glass cannot be compared with it. A gross, which contains twelve hundred grains very well cut, costs only three francs."

When a being who is dear to us is about to die, we look at him with a look which clings to him, and which would hold him back. Both, dumb with anguish, knowing not what to say to death, despairing and trembling, they stood before him, Marius holding Cosette's hand.

From moment to moment, Jean Valjean grew weaker. He was sinking; he was approaching the dark horizon. His breath had become intermittent; it was interrupted by a slight rattle. He had difficulty in moving his wrist, his feet had lost all motion, and, at the same time that the distress of the limbs and the exhaustion of the body increased, all the majesty of the soul rose and displayed itself upon his forehead. The light of the unknown world was already visible in his eye.

His face grew pale, and at the same time smiled. Life was no longer present, there was something else. His breath died away, his look grew grand. It was a corpse on which you felt wings.

He motioned to Cosette to approach, then to Marius; it was evidently the last minute of the last hour, and he began to speak to them in a voice so faint it seemed to come from afar, and you would have said that there was already a wall between them and him.

"Come closer, come closer, both of you. I love you dearly. Oh! it is good to die so! You too, you love me, my Cosette. I knew very well that you still had some affection for your old goodman. How kind you are to put this cushion under my back! You will weep for me a little, will you not? Not too much. I do not wish you to have any deep grief. You must amuse yourselves a great deal, my children. I forgot to tell you that on buckles without tongues still more is made than on anything else. A gross, twelve dozen, costs ten francs, and sells for sixty. That is really a good business. So you need not be astonished at the six hundred thousand francs, Monsieur Pontmercy. It is honest money. You can be rich without concern. You must have a carriage, from time to time a box at the theatres, beautiful ball dresses, my Cosette, and then give good dinners to your friends, be very happy. I was writing just now to Cosette. She will find my letter. To her I bequeath the two candlesticks which are on the mantel. They are silver; but to me they are gold, they are diamond; they change the candles which are put into them, into consecrated tapers. I do not know whether he who gave them to me is satisfied with me in heaven. I have done what I could. My children, you will not forget that I am a poor man, you will have me buried in the most convenient piece of ground under a stone to mark the spot. That is my wish. No name on the stone. If Cosette will come for a little while sometimes, it will give me a pleasure. You too, Monsieur Pontmercy. I must confess to you that I have not always loved you; I ask your pardon. Now, she and you are but one to me. I am very grateful to you. I feel that you make Cosette happy. If you knew, Monsieur Pontmercy, her beautiful rosy cheeks were my joy; when I saw her a little pale, I was sad. There is a five hundred franc bill in the bureau. I have not touched it. It is for the poor. Cosette, do you see your little dress, there on the bed? do you recognise it? Yet it was only ten years ago. How time passes! We have been very happy. It is over. My children, do not weep, I am not going very far, I shall see you from there. You will only have to look when it is night, you will see me smile. Cosette, do you remember Montfermeil? You were in the wood, you were very much frightened; do you remember when I took the handle of the water-bucket? That was the first time I touched your poor little hand. It was so cold! Ah! you had red hands in those days, mademoiselle, your hands are very white now. And the great doll! do you remember? you called her Catharine. You regretted that you did not carry her to the convent. How you made me laugh sometimes, my sweet angel! When it had rained you launched spears of straw in the gutters, and you watched them. One day, I gave you a willow battledore, and a shuttlecock with yellow, blue, and green feathers. You have forgotten it. You were so cunning when you were little! You played. You put cherries in your ears. Those are things of the past. The forests through which we have passed with our child, the trees under which we have walked, the convents in which we have hidden, the games, the free laughter of childhood, all is in shadow. I imagined that all that belonged to me. There was my folly. Those Thénardiers were wicked. We must forgive them. Cosette, the time has come to tell you the name of your mother. Her name was Fantine. Remember that name: Fantine. Fall on your knees whenever you pronounce it. She suffered much. And loved you much. Her measure of unhappiness was as full as yours of happiness. Such are the distributions of God. He is on high, he sees us all, and he knows what he does in the midst of his great stars. So I am going away, my children. Love each other dearly always. There is scarcely anything else in the world but that: to love one another. You will think sometimes of the poor old man who died here. O my Cosette! it is not my fault, indeed, if I have not seen you all this time, it broke my heart; I went as far as the corner of the street, I must have seemed strange to the people who saw me pass, I looked like a crazy man, once I went out with no hat. My children, I do not see very clearly now, I had some more things to say, but it makes no difference. Think of me a little. You are blessed creatures. I do not know what is the matter with me, I see a light. Come nearer. I die happy. Let me put my hands upon your dear beloved heads."

Cosette and Marius fell on their knees, overwhelmed, choked with tears, each grasping one of Jean Valjean's hands. Those august hands moved no more.

He had fallen backwards, the light from the candlesticks fell upon him; his white face looked up towards heaven, he let Cosette and Marius cover his hands with kisses; he was dead.

The night was starless and very dark. Without doubt, in the gloom some mighty angel was standing, with outstretched wings, awaiting the soul.

ENDNOTES

Part I: Fantine

Book One: An Upright Man

1. (p. 14) *a senator of the empire . . . wrote to M. Bigot de Préameneu:* The Senator who complains of Myriel's asking 3,000 francs annually for "carriage expenses" had been rewarded with a rich estate for supporting Napoléon's quasi-legal coup d'état of the dix-huit Brumaire (May 18, 1804), by means of which he became Emperor. The name of the Minister of Public Worship, Bigot, means a narrow-mindedly, excessively religious person.

2. (p. 21) *Some admire it, like Le Maistre; others execrate it, like Beccaria:* Joseph de Maistre (1753–1821), a far-right Ultramontanist, advocated for restoring supreme authority in all church matters to the Pope. He was the leading polemicist against the French Revolution, characterizing its disorders as Evil being forced by God to cleanse itself with its own hands (through the deaths of rival revolutionary leaders during the Reign of Terror in 1793). He believed that constitutions and all human institutions derive from God. The English writer Edmund Burke was his Anglo-Saxon counterpart. Cesare de Beccaria (1738–1794), an economist and criminologist, wrote the influential *Traité des délits et des peines* (A Treatise on Felonies and Their Punishment), which had great influence on eliminating the death penalty in certain places, and in securing a more humane treatment for prisoners. Hugo greatly admired his work.

3. (p. 26) *This man . . . had been a member of the National Convention:* The Convention Nationale, a revolutionary legislative body, ruled France from September 21, 1792, till October 6, 1795. It proclaimed the First French Republic, defended France against royalist insurrections in the Vendée (the Loire valley and Brittany) and the South, forced the coalition of European monarchs to sign a peace treaty, and condemned the King to death for treason after he tried to flee France secretly to join these Allied Powers. The old conventionist whom Myriel goes to visit had served in this assembly. He did not vote for the death of the king, but royalists considered every member of the Convention to be a bloodthirsty regicide.

4. (p. 32) *"What do you think of Bossuet chanting the Te Deum over the dragonnades?":* Jacques-Bénigne Bossuet (1627–1704), Bishop of

Meaux and the most influential French cleric during the Classical Age, supported and blessed the *Dragonnades,* the systematic persecution of Protestants (then called Huguenots or Réformés) by royal troops, in several regions of France before and after the revocation of the Edict of Nantes, which had guaranteed religious tolerance (1681–1685). Most of the Protestants fled abroad. Today we would call these Catholic actions "ethnic cleansing."

Book Two: The Fall

5. (pp. 37–38) *the stone bench which General Drouot mounted on the fourth of March, to read . . . the proclamation of the* Golfe Juan: General Antoine Drouot (1774–1847), one of Napoléon's most loyal supporters, followed him into exile on the island of Elba. When the Emperor escaped to France, he landed at the Mediterranean beach resort le Golfe-Juan, near Vallauris, and proclaimed his return to power. The statement was read aloud in various towns along his route north.

Book Three: In the Year 1817

6. (p. 76) *Paris has no longer the same environs. . . . a city which has France for its suburbs:* Fécamp is an Atlantic beach resort near Le Havre, about 170 miles from Paris; Saint-Cloud is a park on the Seine near Versailles, about 14 miles from Paris. Hugo means that mechanized rapid transport—steamboats and railways—shrinks space by a factor of 12, and that Paris becomes an ever-more-dominant center as a result.

7. (p. 78) *Love is a fault; be it so. Fantine was innocence floating upon the surface of this fault:* Despite his frequent use of the symbolism of light and darkness to connote good and evil, respectively, Hugo's moral portraits are always complex and subtle. Until near the end of his life, the virtuous Jean Valjean must struggle against impulses to resentment and selfishness; the vile Thénardier in other circumstances might have become a decent if not a virtuous man rather than a monster; and Fantine, the "fallen woman" condemned by her hypocritical society, becomes an unwed mother through innocent devotion. Later she prostitutes herself only to save her child.

Book Five: The Descent

8. (p. 112) *It is a mournful task to break the sombre attachments of the past:* The word "sombre" has special meanings in Hugo's cosmology. It refers not to a dark (evil) but to a provisionally darkened state, to the human condition in which moral insight has been obscured by what the Cabalists called "occultation." In order to preserve human free will and the resulting opportunities for meritorious and redemptive choices, God "withdraws" the fullness of His essence from the material world. If God revealed Himself fully, we would have no choice but to do His will. The stars are the masks of God. Once reincarnated as animals, plants, or inanimate objects, however, souls see God clearly and suffer redemptively from their distance from Him. See the poems "Pleurs dans la nuit" and "Spes" in Hugo's poetry collection *Les Contemplations* (VI, 6 and 21).

Book Seven: The Champmathieu Case

9. (p. 155) *Forms Assumed by Suffering during Sleep:* Like other romantics, but more richly than most, Hugo depicts "second states" of consciousness—supernatural visions, dreams, madness, and hallucinations caused by insomnia, terror, starvation, or illness—to represent his characters' intuitions of a spiritual super-reality.

10. (p. 156) *Obstacles:* The repeated breakdowns of Jean Valjean's carriage, and the delays occasioned by various obstacles on the road tempt him to abandon his plan to exonerate the innocent Champmathieu and to condemn himself to life in prison instead. These delays exemplify the *tentatio probationis* (temptation as an ordeal) that tests and refines one's faith—as opposed to the *tentatio subversionis* (temptation to submit to evil). For an example of the latter, on an outwardly similar, difficult journey, see Jacques Cazotte's *Le Diable amoureux* (1772), with Satan as a luscious, amorous woman seeking sex before marriage to the hero.

11. (p. 172) *When he was tried, God was not there:* During Jean Valjean's original trial, "God was not there" both literally (the image was gone) and spiritually (mercy and forgiveness were unavailable to the prisoner). Compare the last paragraph of "Fantine": "Happily, God knows where to find the soul."

Book Eight: Counter-stroke

12. (p. 193) *Without a wrinkle in his duty or his uniform:* This phrase is an example of the daring rhetorical figure called hendiadys ("one from two"). When criticized by classicists for using this device in his poetry (for example, *vêtu de candeur et de lin blanc*—"clothed in candor and in white linen"), Hugo triumphantly produced many examples from classical Greek and Roman literature, which he knew far better than did his detractors.

13. (p. 197) *she distinctly saw an ineffable smile beam on those pale lips ... full of the wonder of the tomb:* Suggested strongly here by the dead Fantine's smile, Hugo's faith in the Afterlife will be expressly articulated by Eponine as she dies at the end of chapter 4 (6), book fourteen, part IV ("We do meet again, don't we? ... Promise to kiss me on the forehead when I am dead. I shall feel it."), and once again by the author, when Jean Valjean dies: "Without doubt, in the gloom some mighty angel was standing, with outstretched wings, awaiting the soul."

Part II: Cosette

Book Two: The Convict Ship *Orion*

1. (p. 214) *Some of the newspapers . . . held up this commutation as a tri-umph of the clerical party:* Moved by blind partisanship, some left-wing commentators inaccurately see the commutation of Jean Valjean's death sentence as undue interference by the Church in sec-ular affairs. "The clerical party" refers to the *Congrégation,* which throughout the 1820s was feared to be a Catholic secret society con-trolled by the Pope, seeking to end the "Gallican liberties" that allowed French rulers rather than the Pope to make many decisions regarding the French Catholic Church, and to dominate European politics. For a fully developed dramatization of this supposed inter-national Jesuit conspiracy, see Stendhal's *Le Rouge et le Noir* (1830).

Book Three: Keeping the Promise to the Dead Woman

2. (p. 252) *"Monsieur owes twenty-six sous":* After preparing a padded bill for Jean Valjean's room and supper, for twenty times the proper amount (which he can implicitly blame on his wife, because Jean Val-jean did not see who drew up the bill), Thénardier suddenly reverses his strategy. He realizes that Jean Valjean badly wants to take Cosette with him. He quickly adjusts. By now telling his guest what he truly owes, Thénardier lays the groundwork for portraying him-self as a scrupulous person, who could not possibly hand over a child in his care to a stranger . . . without receiving a substantial bribe.

Book Four: The Old Gorbeau House

3. (p. 268) *as he was fifty-five:* Ten years later, at the conclusion, Jean Valjean is described as being eighty. To salvage chronological coher-ence, we must assume that Hugo means his emotional sufferings had suddenly aged him so that he looked like eighty.

There are autobiographical elements in Hugo's characterization of Jean Valjean's relationship with Cosette. The author loved his grand-children deeply, and devoted a volume of poetry to them, called *L'Art d'être grand-père* (1877).

Book Five: A Sinister Hunt Requires a Silent Pack

4. (p. 277) *The sufferings of the first six years of her life had introduced something of the passive into her nature:* The critic Nicole Savy severely criticized Cosette as a nonentity (see "For Further Reading"). She is correct, but at this juncture, Hugo clearly explains why this is so. To be sure, Hugo's female characters often lack substance—but the master-ful depiction of the monstrous Mme Thénardier, for example, proves him capable of imagining a woman with a forceful personality.

Part III: Marius

Book Three: The Grandfather and the Grandson

1. (p. 359) *the God-man:* Commonplace in English, but usually unidiomatic in French, this combination of two nouns modifying each other is Hugo's *métaphore maxima,* which is typically associated with moments of religious revelation; he used it frequently in his visionary poetry from *Les Contemplations* (1856) on. It blurs two familiar categories into a new, unprecedented one.

2. (p. 367) *the first of these two places of rendezvous was near the working-men, the second near the students:* Left-wing alliances of workers with students, usually no more than a distant dream in the United States, have been much more common in France, in part because nearly free access to higher education in France narrows the financial gap between the two groups, while militantly Socialist or Communist labor unions narrow the ideological gap with some intellectuals. "Les Événements" of 1968 provide a prime example.

3. (p. 370) *You cannot pick the mark out of a nation as you can out of a handkerchief:* Feuilly's respect for national sovereignty means that he, like all the other members of "Les Amis de l'ABC," opposes Napoléon's politics of conquest. One can readily predict a confrontation with Marius, who has come to idealize his Napoleonic father. This evolution, and Marius's later move toward democratic ideals, echoes Hugo's own political trajectory in his youth, as Marius's passionate love for Cosette echoes Hugo's love for Adèle Foucher before her betrayal.

Book Seven: Patron-Minette

4. (p. 415) *the descending ladder: L'échelle des êtres* renders the English "the Great Chain of Being," the concept that all created things are arranged in an infinite hierarchy of relative perfection, each rung separated by the least possible degree of distance, but with an infinite distance between the highest of the angels, and God. Hugo believes in successive reincarnations: we rise or fall according to our merits in each life. At the end of time, all beings, even Satan, will be redeemed by suffering and taken up into the bosom of God. To begin the paragraph, Hugo half-playfully and half-seriously ranks a series of theologians and philosophers according to the relative spirituality of their doctrines.

Book Eight: The Criminal Poor

5. (p. 433) *"Sometimes I go away at night. . . . When one has not eaten, it is very queer":* Hugo, who was relatively insensitive to women, had difficulty portraying them in interesting ways. This paragraph is an exception. Eponine describes an altered state of consciousness, brought about by starvation, in which her hallucinations show her haunted by guilt, and fearing death on the gallows. The stars seem accusing spotlights

focusing on her; but they seem to be guttering out like candles (as did the stars around Satan when he fell into the Pit in *La Fin de Satan*). For God to be absent would be even worse than His accusing presence. The horses would be those of the mounted police pursuing her.

6. (p. 464) *Nos amours . . . devrait durer toujours:* Our love lasted for an entire week; / How briefly the moments of joy descend! / A love that short was not worthwhile to seek! / The time of our love should have known no end! / Should have known no end! Should have known no end!

7. (p. 474) *"No more than before":* Hugo can dramatize the combination of an emotional reaction and of perfect self-control only with an absurdity. With the next remark, "Marius did not hear this answer," Hugo drops the pretense of seeing everything through the young man's eyes, in order to dramatize the intensity of Marius's reaction to the revelation of Thénardier's identity. "Could anyone have seen him . . . in that darkness" introduces an episodic observer who is incapable of observation, because Hugo wants to intensify "the reality effect" of the events by multiplying the numbers and the viewpoints of the spectators.

8. (p. 477) *David desired to immortalise that feat of arms:* Jacques Louis David (1748–1825) dominated French painting for the last forty years of his life. He was Napoléon's official painter, working in the "Neoclassic Stoic" style that evoked heroic feats under the ancient Roman Empire and the Roman Republic. He never would have bothered to immortalize the deeds of an obscure person such as Thénardier, even if the latter had been a soldier rather than a scavenger. To exalt his importance, Thénardier promotes Pontmercy by at least one grade in rank (from Colonel to General), and by two grades of nobility (counts outranked viscounts, who outranked barons).

9. (p. 481) *all this . . . was awkward for Marius, and painfully astonished him:* This detail prepares for the final chapters. Until just before the very end, Marius feels uncomfortable with Jean Valjean, and will suspect him of having stolen the 600,000 francs he offers Cosette, and of having murdered Javert at the barricade to exact revenge. Thus, having married Cosette, Marius will progressively discourage Valjean from seeing her.

Part IV: The Epic on the Rue Saint-Denis and the Idyll of the Rue Plumet

Book One: A Few Pages of History

1. (p. 499) *A capital error which led that family to lay its hand upon the guarantees "granted" in 1814. . . . our rights:* As early as 1830, Hugo had bluntly warned the French monarchs at least to accept gracefully the compromise of constitutional monarchy, comparing the People, on the march, to a rising tide:

Rois, hâtez-vous! Rentrez dans le siècle où nous sommes,
Quittez l'ancien rivage!—À cette mer des hommes
Faites place, ou voyez si vous voulez périr
Sur le siècle passé que son flot doit couvrir !

[Kings, hasten to reenter our age, / Leave ancient shores!—To
human seas in ráge / Give way, or realize you'll soon have died /
On outmoded strands covered by that tide!]

Book Eight: Enchantment and Despair

2. (p. 581) *"Why does life continue afterwards?"* Hugo thinks sadly of
his passionate devotion to his childhood playmate Adèle Foucher,
whom he married at twenty. They had four children in eight years.
Exhausted by her pregnancies, she refused to have sex with him any
longer, and soon betrayed him with his best friend, Sainte-Beuve.
The Hugos stayed together but were never any more than friends
thenceforth, whereas Adèle's affair with Sainte-Beuve continued
secretly, on and off, for decades.

Part V: Jean Valjean

Book One: War between Four Walls

1. (p. 686) *On est laid à Nanterre... C'est la faute de Rousseau:* These
lines and the ones that follow translate as: "They're ugly in Nanterre /
It's the fault of Voltaire, / And dumb in Palaiseau, / It's the fault of
Rousseau. // I'm not a notary, / . . . / I am a little bird, / . . . // Joyous
my character, / . . . / Poverty my trousseau, / . . . // I have fallen down,
/ . . . / My nose in the gutter, / . . . //

INSPIRED BY *LES MISÉRABLES*

Musical

"I thought it would last two or three years," Cameron Mackintosh, producer of the record-breaking musical adaptation of *Les Misérables*, told the *New York Times*. So much for theatrical fortune-telling. The Broadway production of *"Les Miz"* was one of the most successful musicals of all time. The show originally opened on September 17, 1980, in Paris and in 1985 premiered in London, directed by Trevor Nunn and John Caird of the Royal Shakespeare Company. On March 12, 1987, the London production came to Broadway. Like Hugo's novel, the musical was initially greeted with mixed reviews, but it was soon embraced by the theatergoing public. The New York production ran for sixteen years, until March 15, 2003. *Les Misérables* is the second longest running musical in Broadway history, second only to the T. S. Eliot-inspired *Cats*.

The musical *Les Misérables* was created by Claude-Michel Schönberg (music) and Alain Boublil (original French lyrics), who together wrote the songbook; Herbert Kretzmer wrote the lyrics for the American version. The three-hour spectacle features fluid costumes that are simultaneously ragged and glamorous, revolving sets, sweeping lights, and a showcase of memorable numbers. The production is passionate, ecstatically energetic, and ultimately uplifting.

Les Misérables has been produced in thirty-eight countries and twenty-one languages, and has received numerous awards the world over. In the United States, it won eight Tony Awards—Best Book, Best Score, Best Set Design, Best Lighting, Best Actor (Michael Maguire), Best Actress (Frances Ruffelle), Best Director (Trevor Nunn), and Best Musical. *Les Misérables* also won two Grammys: one for a 1988 cast recording and another for a 1991 symphonic recording, one of a total of thirty-one recordings that have been made.

Film

The first feature film based on the novel was Charles Pathé's version of 1909, the same year J. Stuart Blackton filmed *Les Misérables* in England. Indeed, France's first film to find a wide international audience was Albert Capellani's faithful screen version of 1912. Fredric March played Jean Valjean and Charles Laughton was Inspector Javert in Richard Boleslawski's superbly staged version of 1935. *Les Misérables* has been filmed more than twenty times, including musical productions.

In the mid-1990s a suite of film adaptations appeared, perhaps prompted by the hugely popular musical. Writer and director Claude Lelouch's brilliant 1995 retelling of the novel is a layered epic that takes Hugo's novel as its central reference point, much in the same way that Michael Cunningham's novel *The Hours* draws on Virginia Woolf's *Mrs. Dalloway*. Set during the Nazi occupation of France, Lelouch's *Les Misérables* focuses on Henri Fortin, an illiterate boxer turned furniture mover who comes to see parallels between himself and Jean Valjean. The film moves between Fortin's tale, the story of his father, and scenes from Hugo's novel. Fortin is played by legendary French actor Jean-Paul Belmondo, now aged and creased, and convincingly miserable; he also plays Fortin's father and Jean Valjean. Belmondo's exemplary performances and Lelouch's skillfully woven cinematic tapestry unify all three stories, rendering them incarnations of one story: the common man's struggle against the implacable powers that be.

Director Bille August (*Pelle the Conqueror* and *Smilla's Sense of Snow*) remains strictly faithful to Hugo's text and sets his 1998 film of *Les Misérables* in early-nineteenth-century France. This sweeping costume drama, which stars Liam Neeson as Valjean, avoids political overtones and concentrates instead on the adversarial relationship between the persevering Valjean and Geoffrey Rush's icy Javert, characters who are more similar than different. The all-star cast includes Uma Thurman as a pallid Fantine, Claire Danes as Cosette, and Hans Matheson as Marius.

In 2000 director Josée Dayan, screenwriter Didier Decoin, and actor Gérard Depardieu collaborated in a faithful, made-for-television adaptation. The three talents, who had collaborated on *The Count of Monte Cristo* and a bio-pic of Balzac, convey the grit, grimness, and grime of pre-Revolution street life. The film stars Depardieu as Jean Valjean and John Malkovich as his nemesis Javert.

COMMENTS & QUESTIONS

In this section, we aim to provide the reader with an array of perspectives on the text, as well as questions that challenge those perspectives. The commentary has been culled from sources as diverse as reviews contemporaneous with the work, letters written by the author, literary criticism of later generations, and appreciations written throughout the work's history. Following the commentary, a series of questions seeks to filter Victor Hugo's Les Misérables *through a variety of voices and bring about a richer understanding of this enduring work.*

Comments

EDWIN PERCY WHIPPLE

Fantine, the first of five novels under the general title of *Les Misérables,* has produced an impression all over Europe, and we already hear of nine translations. It has evidently been "engineered" with immense energy by the French publisher. Translations have appeared in numerous languages almost simultaneously with its publication in Paris. Every resource of bookselling ingenuity has been exhausted in order to make every human being who can read think that the salvation of his body and soul depends on his reading *Les Misérables.* The glory and the obloquy of the author have both been forced into aids to a system of puffing at which Barnum himself would stare amazed, and confess that he had never conceived of a "dodge" in which literary genius and philanthropy could be allied with the grossest bookselling humbug. But we trust that, after our American showman has recovered from his first shock of surprise, he will vindicate the claim of America to be considered the "first nation on the face of the earth," by immediately offering Dickens a hundred thousand dollars to superintend his exhibition of dogs, and Florence Nightingale a half a million to appear at his exhibition of babies.

The French bookseller also piqued the curiosity of the universal public by a story that Victor Hugo wrote *Les Misérables* twenty-five years ago, but, being bound to give a certain French publisher all his works after his first celebrated novel, he would not delight the world with this product of his genius until he had forced the said publisher into a compliance with his terms. The publisher shrank aghast from the sum which the author demanded, and this sum was yearly increased in amount, as years rolled away and as Victor Hugo's reputation grew more splendid. At last the publisher died, probably from vexation, and Victor Hugo was free. Then he condescended to allow the present publisher to issue *Les Misérables* on the payment of eighty thousand dollars. It is not surprising, that, to get his money back, this publisher has been compelled to resort to tricks which exceed everything known in the whole history of literature. . . .

From the bare abstract, the story does not seem to promise much pleasure to novel-readers, yet it is all alive with the fiery genius of Victor Hugo, and the whole representation is so intense and vivid that it is impossible to escape from the fascination it exerts over the mind. Few who take the book up will leave it until they have read it through. It is morbid to a degree that no eminent English author, not even Lord Byron, ever approached; but its morbid elements are so combined with sentiments abstractly Christian that it is calculated to wield a more pernicious influence than Byron ever exerted. Its tendency is to weaken that abhorrence of crime which is the great shield of most of the virtue which society possesses, and it does this by attempting to prove that society itself is responsible for crimes it cannot prevent, but can only punish. To legislators, to Magdalen societies, to prison-reformers, it may suggest many useful hints; but, considered as a passionate romance, appealing to the sympathies of the ordinary readers of novels, it will do infinitely more harm than good. The bigotries of virtue are better than the charities of vice. On the whole, therefore, we think that Victor Hugo, when he stood out twenty-five years for his price, did a service to the human race. The great value of his new gospel consisted in its not being published. We wish that another quarter of a century had elapsed before it found a bookseller capable of venturing on so reckless a speculation.

—from *The Atlantic Monthly* (July 1862)

ROBERT LOUIS STEVENSON
In *Les Misérables* . . . there is perhaps the nearest approach to literary restraint that Hugo has ever made: there is here certainly the ripest and most easy development of his powers. It is the moral intention of this great novel to awaken us a little, if it may be—for such awakenings are unpleasant—to the great cost of this society that we enjoy and profit by, to the labor and sweat of those who support the litter, civilization, in which we ourselves are so smoothly carried forward. People are all glad to shut their eyes; and it gives them a very simple pleasure when they can forget that our laws commit a million individual injustices, to be once roughly just in the general; that the bread that we eat, and the quiet of the family, and all that embellishes life and makes it worth having, have to be purchased by death—by the deaths of animals, and the deaths of men wearied out with labor, and the deaths of those criminals called tyrants and revolutionaries, and the deaths of those revolutionaries called criminals. It is to something of all this that Victor Hugo wishes to open men's eyes in *Les Misérables;* and this moral lesson is worked out in masterly coincidence with the artistic effect. The deadly weight of civilization to those who are below presses

sensibly on our shoulders as we read. A sort of mocking indignation grows upon us as we find Society rejecting, again and again, the services of the most serviceable; setting Jean Valjean to pick oakum, casting Galileo into prison, even crucifying Christ. There is a haunting and horrible sense of insecurity about the book. The terror we thus feel is a terror for the machinery of law, that we can hear tearing, in the dark, good and bad between its formidable wheels with the iron stolidity of all machinery, human or divine. This terror incarnates itself sometimes and leaps horribly out upon us; as when the crouching mendicant looks up, and Jean Valjean, in the light of the street lamp, recognizes the face of the detective; as when the lantern of the patrol flashes suddenly through the darkness of the sewer; or as when the fugitive comes forth at last at evening, by the quiet riverside, and finds the police there also, waiting stolidly for vice and stolidly satisfied to take virtue instead. The whole book is full of oppression, and full of prejudice, which is the great cause of oppression. We have the prejudices of M. Gillenormand, the prejudices of Marius, the prejudices in revolt that defend the barricade, and the throned prejudices that carry it by storm. And then we have the admirable but ill-written character of Javert, the man who had made a religion of the police, and would not survive the moment when he learned that there was another truth outside the truth of laws; a just creation, over which the reader will do well to ponder.

With so gloomy a design this great work is still full of life and light and love. The portrait of the good Bishop is one of the most agreeable things in modern literature. The whole scene at Montfermeil is full of the charm that Hugo knows so well how to throw about children. Who can forget the passage where Cosette, sent out at night to draw water, stands in admiration before the illuminated booth and the huckster behind "lui faisait un peu l'effet d'être le Père éternal?" The pathos of the forlorn sabot laid trustingly by the chimney in expectation of the Santa Claus that was not, takes us fairly by the throat; there is nothing in Shakespeare that touches the heart more nearly. The loves of Cosette and Marius are very pure and pleasant, and we cannot refuse our affection to Gavroche, although we may make a mental reservation of our profound disbelief in his existence. Take it for all in all, there are few books in the world that can be compared with it.

—from *Cornhill Magazine* (August 1874)

NEWELL DWIGHT HILLIS

Victor Hugo's "Les Misérables" represents the first attempt in fiction to show that if sin dims the divine image, conscience disturbs the soul with sore discontent, while Christ never despairs of making bad men good, but toils ever on until publican and outcast alike stand forth, clothed in every courage, every heroism, and every virtue, being of goodness all compact.

—from *Great Books as Life-Teachers: Studies of Character Real and Ideal* (1898)

GEORGE McLEAN HARPER

It has always been impossible for [Hugo's] English and American critics to find common ground. Matthew Arnold, for example, could say of him, in that apparently casual and parenthetical manner which veils some of his most audacious assumptions, that if the French were more at home in the higher regions of poetry "they would perceive with us that M. Victor Hugo, for instance, or Sir Walter Scott, may be a great romance-writer, and may yet be by no means a great poet." In the eyes of Mr. Swinburne, Hugo was "the greatest Frenchman of all time," "the greatest poet of the century," "the spiritual sovereign of the nineteenth century,"—no less! Mr. Dowden, in an eloquent and sympathetic essay, considers chiefly Victor Hugo's public aspect,—his relation to politics, his patriotism, his character as a representative Frenchman. Throughout at least the early half of Hugo's career a large part of our public knew him as a dramatist and romancer almost exclusively. And yet, of the eminent French writers who, in this hundredth year from his birth, are estimating his place and importance in their literature, it is unlikely that many will take his romances into very serious account, or treat his dramas as if they possessed much vital and intrinsic excellence. Already, too, as in the case of Coleridge, it is being said of Victor Hugo that his value lies in the innovations which he made and the impulse he gave to other writers as much as in the power or the beauty of his works.

—from *The Atlantic Monthly* (February 1902)

Questions

1. *Les Misérables* has many coincidental encounters among the characters, all of which have large and dramatic consequences. Do these coincidences shake our faith in Hugo's aesthetic integrity, or do they work in a way that redeems it?

2. Realism is a method; it creates the illusion of a fidelity of word to thing, of a direct relation between the novel's words and observable reality. But realism is not the only way of getting at the truth—think, for example, of Franz Kafka's metaphorical writing. Is Hugo a realist, an occasional realist, or something else?

3. Does Hugo strive to represent observable reality or to present fictional events that illustrate a system of religious belief?

4. Would the novel have been more satisfying if Hugo had allowed Jean Valjean to live?

5. What is the source of evil in Hugo's world? Human nature? Bad social arrangements and laws? Accident? Some supernatural agent?

FOR FURTHER READING

Works by Victor Hugo

The Hunchback of Notre-Dame. New York: Random House, 1995.
The Last Day of a Condemned Man. New York: Oxford University Press, 1992.
Napoleon the Little. New York: H. Fertig, 1992.
Ninety-Three. Mattituck, NY: Amereon, 1976.
Notre-Dame de Paris. New York: Oxford University Press, 1993; New York: Penguin (film and TV tie-in edition), 1996.
Œuvres complètes de Victor Hugo. Edited by Jacques Seebacher and Guy Rosa. 16 vols. Paris: Laffont, 1985–1990.

Works about Hugo and Les Misérables

Affron, Charles. *A Stage for Poets: Studies in the Theatre of Hugo and Musset.* Princeton, NJ: Princeton University Press, 1971.
Barrielle, Jean-François. *Le Grand Imagier Victor Hugo.* Paris: Flammarion, 1985.
Brombert, Victor. *Victor Hugo and the Visionary Novel.* Cambridge, MA: Harvard University Press, 1984.
Grant, Richard B. *The Perilous Quest: Image, Myth, and Prophecy in the Narratives of Victor Hugo.* Durham, NC: Duke University Press, 1968.
Grossman, Kathryn M. *Figuring Transcendence in "Les Misérables": Hugo's Romantic Sublime.* Carbondale: Southern Illinois University Press, 1994.
———. *"Les Misérables": Conversion, Revolution, Redemption.* New York: Twayne Publishers, 1996.
Hiddleston, J. A., ed. *Victor Hugo: Romancier de l'abîme.* Oxford: Legenda, 2002. Half the chapters are in English, including an introduction by L. M. Porter.
Petrey, Sandy. *History in the Text: "Quatrevingt-treize" and the French Revolution.* Lafayette, IN: Purdue University Monographs in Romance Languages, 1980.
Porter, Laurence M. *The Renaissance of the Lyric in French Romanticism.* Lexington, KY: French Forum Monographs, 1978.
———. *Victor Hugo.* New York: Twayne Publishers/Macmillan, 1999.

Poulet, Georges. *The Interior Distance*. Translated by Elliott Coleman. Baltimore, MD: Johns Hopkins University Press, 1959, pp. 153–181.

Robb, Graham. *Victor Hugo*. New York: W. W. Norton, 1997.

Savy, Nicole. "Cosette: Un personnage qui n'existe pas." In *Lire "Les Misérables,"* edited by Anne Ubersfeld and Guy Rosa. Paris: Corti, 1985.

Swinburne, Algernon Charles. *A Study of Victor Hugo*. Port Washington, NY: Kennikat Press, 1970.

Background

Bernheimer, Charles. *Figures of Ill Repute: Representing Prostitution in Nineteenth-Century France*. Cambridge, MA: Harvard University Press, 1989.

Briggs, Asa, ed. *The Nineteenth Century: The Contradictions of Progress*. New York: McGraw-Hill, 1970.

Chevalier, Louis. *Laboring Classes and Dangerous Classes in Paris during the First Half of the Nineteenth Century*. Translated from the French by Frank Jellinek. New York: H. Fertig, 1973.

Driskel, Michael Paul. *Representing Belief: Religion, Art, and Society in Nineteenth-Century France*. University Park: Pennsylvania State University Press, 1992.

Ferguson, Priscilla Parkhurst. *Paris as Revolution: Writing the Nineteenth-century City*. Berkeley: University of California Press, 1994.

Geyl, Pieter. *Napoleon: For and Against*. Translated from the Dutch by Olive Renier. New Haven, CT: Yale University Press, 1949.

Hemmings, F. W. J. *Culture and Society in France, 1789–1848*. Leicester, England: Leicester University Press, 1987.

Kselman, Thomas A. *Death and the Afterlife in Modern France*. Princeton, NJ: Princeton University Press, 1993.

The New Oxford Companion to Literature in French. Edited by Peter France. Oxford and New York: Clarendon Press, 1995.

Schama, Simon. *Citizens: A Chronicle of the French Revolution*. New York: Alfred A. Knopf, 1989.

Willms, Johannes. *Paris: Capital of Europe: From the Revolution to the Belle Époque*. Translated by Eveline L. Kanes. New York: Holmes and Meier, 1997.

Wright, Gordon. *France in Modern Times: From the Enlightenment to the Present*. Fifth edition. New York: W. W. Norton, 1995.

Wright, Lawrence. *Clean and Decent: The Fascinating History of the Bathroom and the Water Closet, and of Sundry Habits, Fashions, and Accessories of the Toilet, Principally in Great Britain, France, and America*. New York: Viking, 1960.

Look for the following titles, available now from
BARNES & NOBLE CLASSICS

Visit your local bookstore for these and more fine titles.
Or to order online go to: WWW.BN.COM/CLASSICS

Adventures of Huckleberry Finn	Mark Twain	1-59308-112-X	$5.95
The Adventures of Tom Sawyer	Mark Twain	1-59308-139-1	$5.95
The Aeneid	Vergil	1-59308-237-1	$7.95
Aesop's Fables		1-59308-062-X	$5.95
The Age of Innocence	Edith Wharton	1-59308-143-X	$5.95
Agnes Grey	Anne Brontë	1-59308-323-8	$5.95
Alice's Adventures in Wonderland and Through the Looking-Glass	Lewis Carroll	1-59308-015-8	$5.95
The Ambassadors	Henry James	1-59308-378-5	$7.95
Anna Karenina	Leo Tolstoy	1-59308-027-1	$8.95
The Arabian Nights	Anonymous	1-59308-281-9	$9.95
The Art of War	Sun Tzu	1-59308-017-4	$7.95
The Autobiography of an Ex-Colored Man and Other Writings	James Weldon Johnson	1-59308-289-4	$5.95
The Awakening and Selected Short Fiction	Kate Chopin	1-59308-113-8	$6.95
Babbitt	Sinclair Lewis	1-59308-267-3	$7.95
The Beautiful and Damned	F. Scott Fitzgerald	1-59308-245-2	$7.95
Beowulf	Anonymous	1-59308-266-5	$4.95
Billy Budd and The Piazza Tales	Herman Melville	1-59308-253-3	$6.95
Bleak House	Charles Dickens	1-59308-311-4	$9.95
The Bostonians	Henry James	1-59308-297-5	$7.95
The Brothers Karamazov	Fyodor Dostoevsky	1-59308-045-X	$9.95
Bulfinch's Mythology	Thomas Bulfinch	1-59308-273-8	$12.95
The Call of the Wild and White Fang	Jack London	1-59308-200-2	$5.95
Candide	Voltaire	1-59308-028-X	$4.95
The Canterbury Tales	Geoffrey Chaucer	1-59308-080-8	$9.95
A Christmas Carol, The Chimes and The Cricket on the Hearth	Charles Dickens	1-59308-033-6	$5.95
The Collected Oscar Wilde		1-59308-310-6	$9.95
The Collected Poems of Emily Dickinson		1-59308-050-6	$5.95
Common Sense and Other Writings	Thomas Paine	1-59308-209-6	$6.95
The Communist Manifesto and Other Writings	Karl Marx and Friedrich Engels	1-59308-100-6	$5.95
The Complete Sherlock Holmes, Vol. I	Sir Arthur Conan Doyle	1-59308-034-4	$7.95
The Complete Sherlock Holmes, Vol. II	Sir Arthur Conan Doyle	1-59308-040-9	$7.95
Confessions	Saint Augustine	1-59308-259-2	$6.95
A Connecticut Yankee in King Arthur's Court	Mark Twain	1-59308-210-X	$7.95
The Count of Monte Cristo	Alexandre Dumas	1-59308-151-0	$7.95
The Country of the Pointed Firs and Selected Short Fiction	Sarah Orne Jewett	1-59308-262-2	$7.95
Crime and Punishment	Fyodor Dostoevsky	1-59308-081-6	$8.95
Cyrano de Bergerac	Edmond Rostand	1-59308-387-4	$6.95
Daisy Miller and Washington Square	Henry James	1-59308-105-7	$4.95
Daniel Deronda	George Eliot	1-59308-290-8	$8.95
Dead Souls	Nikolai Gogol	1-59308-092-1	$7.95

(continued)

The Deerslayer	James Fenimore Cooper	1-59308-211-8	$7.95
Don Quixote	Miguel de Cervantes	1-59308-046-8	$9.95
Dracula	Bram Stoker	1-59308-114-6	$6.95
Emma	Jane Austen	1-59308-152-9	$6.95
Essays and Poems by Ralph Waldo Emerson		1-59308-076-X	$6.95
Essential Dialogues of Plato		1-59308-269-X	$9.95
The Essential Tales and Poems of Edgar Allan Poe		1-59308-064-6	$7.95
Ethan Frome and Selected Stories	Edith Wharton	1-59308-090-5	$5.95
Fairy Tales	Hans Christian Andersen	1-59308-260-6	$9.95
Far from the Madding Crowd	Thomas Hardy	1-59308-223-1	$7.95
The Federalist	Hamilton, Madison, Jay	1-59308-282-7	$7.95
Founding America: Documents from the Revolution to the Bill of Rights	Jefferson, et al.	1-59308-230-4	$9.95
Frankenstein	Mary Shelley	1-59308-115-4	$4.95
The Good Soldier	Ford Madox Ford	1-59308-268-1	$6.95
Great American Short Stories: From Hawthorne to Hemingway	Various	1-59308-086-7	$7.95
The Great Escapes: Four Slave Narratives	Various	1-59308-294-0	$6.95
Great Expectations	Charles Dickens	1-59308-116-2	$6.95
Grimm's Fairy Tales	Jacob and Wilhelm Grimm	1-59308-056-5	$7.95
Gulliver's Travels	Jonathan Swift	1-59308-132-4	$5.95
Hard Times	Charles Dickens	1-59308-156-1	$5.95
Heart of Darkness and Selected Short Fiction	Joseph Conrad	1-59308-123-5	$5.95
The History of the Peloponnesian War	Thucydides	1-59308-091-3	$9.95
The House of Mirth	Edith Wharton	1-59308-153-7	$6.95
The House of the Dead and Poor Folk	Fyodor Dostoevsky	1-59308-194-4	$7.95
The House of the Seven Gables	Nathaniel Hawthorne	1-59308-231-2	$6.95
The Hunchback of Notre Dame	Victor Hugo	1-59308-140-5	$7.95
The Idiot	Fyodor Dostoevsky	1-59308-058-1	$7.95
The Iliad	Homer	1-59308-232-0	$7.95
The Importance of Being Earnest and Four Other Plays	Oscar Wilde	1-59308-059-X	$6.95
Incidents in the Life of a Slave Girl	Harriet Jacobs	1-59308-283-5	$5.95
The Inferno	Dante Alighieri	1-59308-051-4	$6.95
The Interpretation of Dreams	Sigmund Freud	1-59308-298-3	$8.95
Ivanhoe	Sir Walter Scott	1-59308-246-0	$8.95
Jane Eyre	Charlotte Brontë	1-59308-117-0	$7.95
Journey to the Center of the Earth	Jules Verne	1-59308-252-5	$4.95
Jude the Obscure	Thomas Hardy	1-59308-035-2	$6.95
The Jungle Books	Rudyard Kipling	1-59308-109-X	$5.95
The Jungle	Upton Sinclair	1-59308-118-9	$6.95
King Solomon's Mines	H. Rider Haggard	1-59308-275-4	$5.95
Lady Chatterley's Lover	D. H. Lawrence	1-59308-239-8	$6.95
The Last of the Mohicans	James Fenimore Cooper	1-59308-137-5	$5.95
Leaves of Grass: First and "Death-bed" Editions	Walt Whitman	1-59308-083-2	$9.95
The Legend of Sleepy Hollow and Other Writings	Washington Irving	1-59308-225-8	$6.95
Les Misérables	Victor Hugo	1-59308-066-2	$9.95
Les Liaisons Dangereuses	Pierre Choderlos de Laclos	1-59308-240-1	$7.95
Little Women	Louisa May Alcott	1-59308-108-1	$6.95
Lost Illusions	Honoré de Balzac	1-59308-315-7	$9.95

(continued)

Madame Bovary	Gustave Flaubert	1-59308-052-2	$6.95
Maggie: A Girl of the Streets and Other Writings about New York	Stephen Crane	1-59308-248-7	$6.95
The Magnificent Ambersons	Booth Tarkington	1-59308-263-0	$7.95
Main Street	Sinclair Lewis	1-59308-386-6	$8.95
Man and Superman and Three Other Plays	George Bernard Shaw	1-59308-067-0	$7.95
The Man in the Iron Mask	Alexandre Dumas	1-59308-233-9	$9.95
Mansfield Park	Jane Austen	1-59308-154-5	$5.95
The Mayor of Casterbridge	Thomas Hardy	1-59308-309-2	$5.95
The Metamorphoses	Ovid	1-59308-276-2	$7.95
The Metamorphosis and Other Stories	Franz Kafka	1-59308-029-8	$6.95
Moby-Dick	Herman Melville	1-59308-018-2	$9.95
Moll Flanders	Daniel Defoe	1-59308-216-9	$5.95
My Ántonia	Willa Cather	1-59308-202-9	$5.95
My Bondage and My Freedom	Frederick Douglass	1-59308-301-7	$6.95
Narrative of Sojourner Truth		1-59308-293-2	$6.95
Narrative of the Life of Frederick Douglass, an American Slave		1-59308-041-7	$4.95
Nicholas Nickleby	Charles Dickens	1-59308-300-9	$8.95
Night and Day	Virginia Woolf	1-59308-212-6	$7.95
Nostromo	Joseph Conrad	1-59308-193-6	$7.95
Notes from Underground, The Double and Other Stories	Fyodor Dostoevsky	1-59308-124-3	$7.95
O Pioneers!	Willa Cather	1-59308-205-3	$5.95
The Odyssey	Homer	1-59308-009-3	$5.95
Of Human Bondage	W. Somerset Maugham	1-59308-238-X	$9.95
Oliver Twist	Charles Dickens	1-59308-206-1	$6.95
The Origin of Species	Charles Darwin	1-59308-077-8	$7.95
Paradise Lost	John Milton	1-59308-095-6	$7.95
The Paradiso	Dante Alighieri	1-59308-317-3	$7.95
Père Goriot	Honoré de Balzac	1-59308-285-1	$8.95
Persuasion	Jane Austen	1-59308-130-8	$5.95
Peter Pan	J. M. Barrie	1-59308-213-4	$4.95
The Phantom of the Opera	Gaston Leroux	1-59308-249-5	$6.95
The Picture of Dorian Gray	Oscar Wilde	1-59308-025-5	$4.95
The Pilgrim's Progress	John Bunyan	1-59308-254-1	$7.95
A Portrait of the Artist as a Young Man and Dubliners	James Joyce	1-59308-031-X	$6.95
The Possessed	Fyodor Dostoevsky	1-59308-250-9	$9.95
Pride and Prejudice	Jane Austen	1-59308-201-0	$6.95
The Prince and Other Writings	Niccolò Machiavelli	1-59308-060-3	$5.95
The Prince and the Pauper	Mark Twain	1-59308-218-5	$4.95
Pudd'nhead Wilson and Those Extraordinary Twins	Mark Twain	1-59308-255-X	$6.95
The Purgatorio	Dante Alighieri	1-59308-219-3	$8.95
Pygmalion and Three Other Plays	George Bernard Shaw	1-59308-078-6	$7.95
The Red Badge of Courage and Selected Short Fiction	Stephen Crane	1-59308-119-7	$4.95
Republic	Plato	1-59308-097-2	$6.95
The Return of the Native	Thomas Hardy	1-59308-220-7	$7.95
Robinson Crusoe	Daniel Defoe	1-59308-360-2	$5.95
A Room with a View	E. M. Forster	1-59308-288-6	$5.95
Scaramouche	Rafael Sabatini	1-59308-242-8	$7.95
The Scarlet Letter	Nathaniel Hawthorne	1-59308-207-X	$5.95

(continued)

The Scarlet Pimpernel	Baroness Orczy	1-59308-234-7	$5.95
The Secret Agent	Joseph Conrad	1-59308-305-X	$6.95
The Secret Garden	Frances Hodgson Burnett	1-59308-277-0	$5.95
Selected Stories of O. Henry		1-59308-042-5	$5.95
Sense and Sensibility	Jane Austen	1-59308-125-1	$5.95
Siddhartha	Hermann Hesse	1-59308-379-3	$5.95
Silas Marner and Two Short Stories	George Eliot	1-59308-251-7	$6.95
Sister Carrie	Theodore Dreiser	1-59308-226-6	$8.95
The Souls of Black Folk	W. E. B. Du Bois	1-59308-014-X	$5.95
The Strange Case of Dr. Jekyll and Mr. Hyde and Other Stories	Robert Louis Stevenson	1-59308-131-6	$4.95
Swann's Way	Marcel Proust	1-59308-295-9	$8.95
A Tale of Two Cities	Charles Dickens	1-59308-138-3	$5.95
Tarzan of the Apes	Edgar Rice Burroughs	1-59308-227-4	$6.95
Tess of the d'Urbervilles	Thomas Hardy	1-59308-228-2	$7.95
This Side of Paradise	F. Scott Fitzgerald	1-59308-243-6	$6.95
Three Theban Plays	Sophocles	1-59308-235-5	$6.95
Thus Spoke Zarathustra	Friedrich Nietzsche	1-59308-278-9	$7.95
The Time Machine and The Invisible Man	H. G. Wells	1-59308-388-2	$6.95
Tom Jones	Henry Fielding	1-59308-070-0	$8.95
Treasure Island	Robert Louis Stevenson	1-59308-247-9	$4.95
The Turn of the Screw, The Aspern Papers and Two Stories	Henry James	1-59308-043-3	$5.95
Twenty Thousand Leagues Under the Sea	Jules Verne	1-59308-302-5	$5.95
Uncle Tom's Cabin	Harriet Beecher Stowe	1-59308-121-9	$7.95
Vanity Fair	William Makepeace Thackeray	1-59308-071-9	$7.95
The Varieties of Religious Experience	William James	1-59308-072-7	$7.95
Villette	Charlotte Brontë	1-59308-316-5	$7.95
The Virginian	Owen Wister	1-59308-236-3	$7.95
Walden and Civil Disobedience	Henry David Thoreau	1-59308-208-8	$5.95
War and Peace	Leo Tolstoy	1-59308-073-5	$12.95
The War of the Worlds	H. G. Wells	1-59308-362-9	$5.95
Ward No. 6 and Other Stories	Anton Chekhov	1-59308-003-4	$7.95
The Waste Land and Other Poems	T. S. Eliot	1-59308-279-7	$4.95
The Way We Live Now	Anthony Trollope	1-59308-304-1	$10.95
The Wind in the Willows	Kenneth Grahame	1-59308-265-7	$4.95
The Wings of the Dove	Henry James	1-59308-296-7	$7.95
Wives and Daughters	Elizabeth Gaskell	1-59308-257-6	$7.95
The Woman in White	Wilkie Collins	1-59308-280-0	$7.95
Women in Love	D. H. Lawrence	1-59308-258-4	$8.95
The Wonderful Wizard of Oz	L. Frank Baum	1-59308-221-5	$6.95
Wuthering Heights	Emily Brontë	1-59308-128-6	$5.95

ℬ
BARNES & NOBLE CLASSICS

If you are an educator and would like to receive an
Examination or Desk Copy of a Barnes & Noble Classics edition,
please refer to Academic Resources on our website at
WWW.BN.COM/CLASSICS
or contact us at
BNCLASSICS@BN.COM

All prices are subject to change.